# CRUEL
## A FLAWED SERIES
### BOOK 4

## AURYN HADLEY

## KITTY COX

SPOTTED HORSE PRODUCTIONS

*Cruel* is a work of fiction. Names, characters, places, brands, media, and incidents are either the product of the author's imagination or are used fictitiously. Any resemblance to actual events, locales, or persons, living or dead, is entirely coincidental.

The author acknowledges the trademarked status and trademark owners of various products referenced in this work of fiction, which have been used without permission. The publication/ use of these trademarks is not authorized, associated with, or sponsored by the trademark owners.

Copyright © 2024 by Auryn Hadley / Kitty Cox

All Rights Reserved. In accordance with the U.S. Copyright Act of 1976, the scanning, uploading, and electronic sharing of any part of this book without the permission of the publisher and the copyright owner constitute unlawful piracy and theft of the author's intellectual property. Thank you for your support of the author's rights.

Cover Art by DAZED designs

Edited by Sarah Williams

## DEDICATION

*This book is for the ones who try. Life is hard. Triggers are real. Healing takes a while, and it should be celebrated as the challenge it definitely is.*

*You are not alone. Maybe our flaws are all different, but they do not make us lesser. Life is not black and white. It comes in so many vibrant colors. Don't miss the beauty because of the trauma.*

*Auryn Hadley*

*Kitty Cox*

# AUTHOR'S NOTE

Some events in *A Flawed Series* overlap those of *Gamer Girls* and *Shades of Trouble*. Many details mentioned within will allow the reader to understand what happened, but for those of you who want the in depth details, you will find them in the *Gamer Girls* and *Shades of Trouble* series.

For timeline purposes, this book falls after *Gamer Girls: Book 7: Game Over*. To have a full understanding of events referenced in this book, we highly recommend reading that series first. However, your enjoyment of *A Flawed Series* will be complete without it.

**Spoiler Alert** - each series has spoilers for the other.

# SENSITIVITY WARNING & LIFELINES

**TRIGGER WARNING:** Discussions of off-screen suicide, rape and assault, bullying, cyber harassment, violence, and more.

---

National Sexual Assault Hotline - RAINN (Rape, Abuse & Incest National Network) is the nation's largest anti-sexual violence organization.

*Anyone* affected by sexual assault, whether it happened to you or someone you care about, can find support on the National Sexual Assault Hotline. You can also visit **online.rainn.org** to receive support via confidential online chat.

**1-800-656-HOPE (4673)**

---

The 988 Suicide & Crisis Hotline is a national network of local crisis

## SENSITIVITY WARNING & LIFELINES

centers that provides free and confidential emotional support to people in suicidal crisis or emotional distress 24 hours a day, 7 days a week in the United States.
Dial - 988 or
Text **STRENGTH** to 741741
( 988lifeline.org )

---

National Suicide Prevention Lifeline - If you or someone you know is struggling with drug/alcohol addiction or having thoughts of suicide, please reach out to
**1-800-273-8255**
( suicidepreventionlifeline.org )

---

**Trevor Project** - If you are a young person in crisis, feeling suicidal, or in need of a safe and judgment-free place to talk, call the TrevorLifeline now at
**1-866-488-7386**
or over text message:
Text **START** to **678678**.

The **Trevor Project** ( thetrevorproject.org ) is an American non-profit organization focused on suicide prevention among lesbian, gay, bisexual, transgender, queer, and questioning youth.

---

**Trans Lifeline's Hotline** ( translifeline.org/hotline ) is a peer support phone service run by trans people for our trans and questioning peers. We believe that some of the best support that trans people can receive is from trans community members with shared lived experience.

# PROLOGUE

### JERICHO

The stream for the big F5 tournament was on a break. From the sounds of it, someone running it had messed something up, so my guys had decided to get the horses handled early. This way we could all watch our friends kick ass and take home the win when it finally came back on.

The whole week for our friends in Vegas had been one problem after another. Well, except for the weddings. Those had gone well. The rest? Their big plans to catch the leader of KoG? Not so much. I was a bit pissed that I wasn't able to be there with them, but Hottie had reminded me there were more ways to help people than online.

This time, it was assisting Kitty with the baby. Ok, and with their dog and horses. Running a draft horse farm took a few hands, and we had a few to offer. At least until college started next week. And maybe we'd put off moving until the last minute, but this? It was a *big* deal, and changing diapers really was helping - or so they said.

"How much shit can one baby make?" I asked as I tossed the dirty diaper into the trash and watched Zoe expertly re-wrap little Ryan.

Behind me, Kitty laughed. "A lot. Constantly. Then again, both of his parents are full of shit, so Ryan was doomed from the start."

I laughed and moved over so she could get to her son. "How's Murder liking all these horses?"

Because Kitty's boyfriend's name was Murder. Well, his game name, but it was what everyone called him, so I was going with it. He'd moved down here last March, and so far, things were working out.

Our whole summer had been like that. No, it hadn't been *easy*, but it had been easier than I was used to. The problems we'd been handed had been things like reviewing videos - *why* was it always videos? - and dropping files on computers. Easy stuff.

In truth, it was the sort of thing Ruin could do with our eyes closed. Hottie kept telling me it was because we were making a difference, but I wasn't convinced yet. Not until the bad guys were gone. But that should be this weekend. Just a few more hours. Days, at the longest. The whole thing was set and ready to go.

Kitty scooped the baby into her arms and tilted her head towards the stairs that led to their gamer basement. "Any updates on the stream?"

"Still on hold," Zoe said.

"I haven't heard anything eith-"

She didn't get to finish her sentence before my phone went off. I was swiping and pushing it to my ear on autopilot. "Yeah?"

It was Knock, and he didn't even bother saying hi. "Jer? All hands on deck, they have Riley and more. I need a trace on Kate Gaskill's watch." He sounded panicked.

My heart stopped. My skin went cold as I realized this had to be bad.

In the background, a man's voice added, "It sent an alert text to Adam's phone a little bit ago."

No, no, no, no. This could not be happening.

"Get that?" Knock asked.

"Adam?" I asked. "Like Adam Degrass?"

"Yep, Degrass with two S's," he clarified. "Promise he won't care."

"So you want me to hack his phone? Get the alert?" My mind was stalling out. *Fuck!*

"Yeah," Knock breathed. "Go crazy. Kitty should have the number if you need it. And Jeri? Life or fucking death. They have my sister, and I will do anything to get her back. Break it all down."

"Shit." I looked over at Kitty.

The expression on my face must've said too much, because she held Ryan closer. "What's wrong?"

"Jeri?" Zoe asked just as Kitty's phone began buzzing with notifications.

"Shit!" I said, this time with force. "Who do they have, Knock?"

"Riley, Dez, Kate, Rhaven, and Zara. They're missing. Kate has a smartwatch that sent out an alert. I need you to fucking *find* them, Jeri. KoG took them, and if we can't find them *now*, we may not find them alive."

"On it," I swore, my eyes jumping to Zoe. "Fire up all the computers. I need to get the guys."

Oh, it sounded good. Even my voice was nice and calm, but inside, my mind was whirling. My heart was hammering. Taken? How? *Where?!* Were they already dead?

It didn't matter. We were their only chance. Us, a group of misfit hackers. If anyone could track down where Kate Gaskill's watch was, it was us. I just needed a little backup.

So I ran. My feet thundered on the worn wooden floor of the old farmhouse. Quake scattered out of my way, leaping onto the sofa to cower from my intensity, but I didn't have time to reassure him. I needed help. I needed *all* the help!

Hitting the back door, I wrenched it open and was screaming before I was all the way outside. "Ruin! Help! Hottie! Jinxy! Ripper! *Help!*"

Hottie whipped around the edge of the barn to call back. "What's wrong?"

"They got the girls! I need Ruin. *Now!*"

Because it was happening again. Shit was hitting the fan, and just when we'd thought we were safe. This was supposed to have been our victory, yet everything was going wrong. People could die. Lives were on the line! Just when I thought we were safe, things always went wrong, and these were my friends. They were people I cared about, so I refused to just let this happen!

All three of them came running. It wasn't far to the barn, just across the driveway and backyard. Seeing they were moving, I spun and raced downstairs in time to see Kitty and Zoe powering on all the computers they had. More than even we could use.

"I need an update," Kitty demanded.

"Knock says they took the girls," I explained. "All the girls. Riley, Dez, Zara, Kate, and Rhaven."

"All the women involved in professional gaming," Kitty breathed, putting it together.

"I'm pulling up the toybox on each of these computers," Zoe said. "Jeri, tell me what to do."

"I need Adam Degrass's phone number," I said as I slid into my chair behind my own monitor.

Kitty read it off. "That's his personal phone," she explained.

I was already typing, even as the men came thundering downstairs. "Fill us in," Jinxy demanded.

"Smartwatch alert sent to a phone. All the women are missing. It's up to us to find them," I snapped.

"Zoe, pull up Google Maps," Hottie demanded. "When we get this geolocation, you're going to turn it into streets, ok?"

"On it," she said.

"I'm finding out how Las Vegas handles their traffic cams," Jinxy announced.

"I'm locating all the cell towers," Ripper said. "Soon as we have a place, we can track them down."

"I'm looking for Riley's phone," Hottie said.

"No," Kitty said. "Murder says they found their phones."

"Whose?" I demanded.

"The girls," Kitty said, sounding defeated.

"Fuck!" Hottie snapped. "But whoever has them has to have one. Ripper, I'm going to need the tower number closest to the location, because I'll check every damned phone there."

Kitty hurried over to the crib at the side and placed Ryan in it. "I'll pull the numbers on the tower next to the convention's hotel. We can compare and find who was at both!"

I merely nodded, because that actually made sense. It also proved these fuckers weren't as stupid as I'd hoped. Phones could be tracked, so they'd left them behind. But the smartwatch? It had sent a location, so we'd find them.

"Ask Murder if he knows what vehicle they're in?" I begged.

She typed, but it took too long. I found the alert message on the phone, copied the link for the location, and tossed that to Zoe. She began calling out street names and the companies around it. Keys were clicking. Computers were working.

My heart hadn't started back up yet.

This was my curse. I'd dared to get close to these people, and now they'd be ripped away from me! It always happened. Every single time. The moment I dared to care too much, life kicked my feet out from under me and we were left arranging another funeral.

Not. This. Time.

Maybe I was cursed. Maybe life just sucked this bad, but right now, we had a chance. One single chance to save the woman who'd accepted all my broken parts as easily as she did everyone else's. One fucking chance to cheat whatever evil destiny screwed over everyone around me.

I was done sitting back and simply letting it happen. No, I would no longer wait for fate to do its thing. This time, I was going to get ahead of the tragedy. I was going to prevent the grief. I was going to fucking *win*, because I refused to go to another goddamned funeral!

"Watch is still moving!" I announced when another update pinged off Adam Degrass's phone. "Link incoming."

I dropped that into our Discord chat so Zoe could copy it. She was sliding a map around, then yelled more street names. Jinxy said he had it and was locked on the watch.

"Zoe, update the guys," I demanded.

"This shit is so illegal," Jinxy muttered. "We're going to get so fucking busted."

"Don't care," I said.

"Me either," Jinxy promised. "But brace for it, Jeri. Brace hard."

Nodding, I kept going. I was already into Adam's phone, which made it easy to follow that back to Kate's watch. From there, I was chasing data. So much data, but it had been minutes. We were close. We had to be.

Then Zoe piped up, "Jeri, Knock wants you to call Cyn." And she pasted his number into Discord.

I clicked it and began typing it into my phone. "I need everything on this place!" I snapped at the guys. "Property records, internet access, blueprints. I want it all!"

"On city records," Ripper said.

"Kitty and I are finding their fucking phones!" Hottie snarled.

"Hotel to the north is close enough, it looks like their wifi might reach," Hottie said. "This place is dark. Completely fucking dark."

"Google Maps shows it's under construction," Zoe said.

Damn. I wanted to puke. I could feel my hands shaking, but I was ignoring it. We were doing this. We were all pulling out our best stuff, but would it be enough? Could it? Was the group of us enough to overcome my fucking curse?

Because I couldn't lose anyone else. I'd learned to love again. I'd let myself fall for all these guys - and Zoe, in my own way. I had people who mattered, and I should've known better. One by one, they'd all get picked off. That was what always happened. They were taken from me because life fucking sucked!

Time slowed. The clicks of keys were so loud. Ripper was calling out info. I was soaking it all up, cataloging it in my head as I lifted my phone, checking the number. We had one chance. One. If we failed, then five women would die.

Always women. Always ones too close to me. I was so fucking done with losing, so not this time. We were finally a step ahead. We would make this happen. I didn't care how fucking long they put me in jail, I would not back off, cut corners, or play it safe.

Never again. If it cost me everything, then it was my turn to pay.

# CHAPTER 1

JERICHO

The back seat of my car was filled with boxes. Along the street, every house seemed to have some super-expensive car parked out front. The lawns were all manicured and the bushes were trimmed to perfection. There were no wilting flowers or drooping trees. Nope, not in a neighborhood like this.

And there, halfway down the street, was my new home. The cream stucco outside was trimmed with Austin stone. A massive window was arched at the top, but tinted to reduce the heat of the Texas sun. The place was gorgeous, and the sort of house I would never have expected to live in.

It felt almost surreal to be doing this after what had happened over the weekend. Friday, our friends had almost died. Sunday, we'd all reunited. Today, we were moving. Too much. Too fast. This should've been amazing, but I felt like my mind was still trying to accept it was actually *real*.

But when I got to the drive, it was full. Chuckling, I moved my car to the curb and parked. I was barely out before Zoe came hurrying out of the house with the biggest grin on her face.

"Jeri, it's amazing! Ripper and I took the top floor."

I simply nodded, because I hadn't seen inside yet. "Ok? So you two have the second floor?" It sure looked like a two-story home.

"The attic," Ripper called from where he was unloading his truck in the garage. "So, more like the third floor. Knock and Cade claimed the first floor."

"Don't worry," Hottie called out. "You've got a nice room on the second floor."

I nodded again, then reached into the back seat to pull out a few boxes. Once my arms were full, I gestured for Zoe to lead the way. She was almost bouncing with excitement, so when she started walking, it was definitely "full speed ahead."

"Let me show you the fun stuff," she said. "So, there's a coat closet here." That was right inside the main door. "And the kitchen is absolutely massive. I guess Logan had them put in one of those supersized stoves or something." An arm showed me where that was, but we didn't slow.

I paused to look, though. I tended to do a lot of the cooking at home. Well, my old home. Mom's home? Whatever I was calling it, because as of today, this was my new home. I was an official college student now - all signed up and ready to start classes tomorrow - and this monstrosity of a mansion was our college crash pad.

Yep, it paid to have rich friends.

"So, has Logan decided on the rent yet?" I asked.

Zoe's response was an ear-splitting squeal of excitement. "Nothing! He says we have to mow the yard and do house maintenance, but he's paying the mortgage because it's an investment."

"Which means," Knock said, joining our conversation as he passed going the opposite direction, "he's trying to make sure we aren't working too hard and letting our grades suffer. Take it, Jeri."

All I could do was chuckle, because Zoe was dragging me towards the stairs. "Ok, so there's a den at the front over there, but it's kinda little. I figure that'll end up the study room. Let's drop your stuff in your room..."

She jogged up the stairs, so I followed. The second floor was just as fancy as the first. I couldn't even put my finger on why, though. Was it the rounded corners on the walls with the funny-looking pattern? Not popcorn ceilings like most places I'd lived, but more like plaster or something. Oh, the doors were nice too. They had something like arches over them. Molding? I didn't know what it was called.

Damn, this place looked like somewhere an Instagram model would want to pose. Over the stairs was the big window I'd seen from the front. The hallway came out in the middle and was doubled as it went around the stairway, making it extra-wide on both ends. Zoe just kept walking.

"And this is your room," she said, opening one of the doors on the left.

I walked into a gigantic space with another of those big windows. Setting my boxes down beside the wall, I headed over to look out - and gasped.

"There's a pool?" I asked.

Zoe's grin got even bigger, if it was possible. "Yep!"

"Holy shit," I breathed as I moved next to the glass to see our yard. "Ok, and a lawn out back. But what's that?" I pointed at a funny-looking roof.

"Outdoor kitchen," Zoe said. "Like a grill and a bar. Under the pergola, it's all concrete or something. There are little solar lights all around the pool area, and you can't see it from here, but there's a hot tub on the other side of the pool."

All I could do was stare. The pool wasn't one of those standard kidney bean-shaped things. Nope, it was all organically-shaped, like some kind of lagoon, with this natural-looking brown stone around it. Probably molded concrete, but I didn't care. The pergola area Zoe called a kitchen was to my right. That meant the hot tub was behind the garage, to my left.

"And Logan just up and bought this place?" I asked.

"Yeah," Zoe said, moving beside me. "Kitty told me it's because he's trying to take care of Knock and Cade, and taking care of us helps too. So we all get to win. She also said this was the only house they could find with seven bedrooms."

"There's four on this floor?" I asked, because it seemed like more doors than that.

"And two bathrooms." Zoe led me away from the window. "I think this door goes... Yep."

She opened one and showed me a very nice bathroom, but it had another door on the other side. That was ok, though. Only the sinks were accessible from both rooms. To get to the actual toilet and shower we had to go through another door. Unfortunately, there wasn't a bathtub.

"What's it like in the attic?" I asked.

"Come, come," she said, hauling me back out by my hand.

We headed for the stairs and went up again. On the third floor, we found three simple doors. One was on each side, and the last was at the end of a very short and boring hall. Zoe pulled me to the left. Throwing open that door, she waved proudly at a stack of boxes.

"So, I get to hear the rain on the roof," she bragged, gesturing to where the slope of the actual roof made one of her walls shorter. "And my room's about twice the size of yours. Ripper and I will share the bathroom at the end of the hall. It's kinda like yours, but no shared sink area."

"You're ok with that?" I asked.

She nodded. "Yep. I like it. I'm also on the top floor, so my parents like how no one can get up here without making it through all my roommates."

"And?" I pressed. "Zoe, how are they handling you living with a bunch of guys?"

She huffed out a laugh. "The same guys who busted my rapist? The same guys who stood up for me? The very same guys who have been patient and protective of me after all the bullshit last year?" She shook her head. "Jeri, my parents were going to make me live in the dorms until I said we'd all be living here. They didn't even care where 'here' was, but when they dropped off my stuff this morning? Yeah, they're so ok with this."

"Good."

"And your mom?" she asked.

I shook my head. "Mom's at work."

"Does she know you graduated high school?"

The best I could do was shrug. "No idea. Sometimes? I mean, when I talk to her on the phone, she seems like she remembers, but I'm never really sure. She knows I'm staying with Grayson at least."

"Hottie," Zoe corrected. "He's not a Grayson."

"He really is," I assured her. "He's more of a Hottie, though."

"Yeah, he is!" she agreed, gesturing for me to head back out. "And, on the upside, all these stairs? We will not gain the dreaded freshman fifteen."

She had a point there! I would only be hiking up and down one flight. She had two, but it wasn't really that bad. Yet when we made it down to the first floor, the chaos was back in full force. The arguing voices, however, seemed to be coming from the back of the house.

"Oh!" Zoe gasped. "The living room!" She turned, so I followed, and the voices were only getting louder.

"No," Hottie was saying. "I'm telling you, putting the couch there will be useless."

"But it's the only place to see the TV," Jinxy was insisting.

"And that's the south," Hottie said. "Bro, this is Texas. That glass wall's going to be hot!"

I didn't know what he was talking about for a few more steps, but as soon as I entered the room, it all made sense. This was more of a solarium or something, but a big one. There was a fireplace at one end, a glass wall beside it, and tile flooring. In the middle of all the windows were French doors that led outside to the pool.

"Wow," I said, killing their debate. "This is huge. So, what are we using this room for?"

"Movie nights," Jinxy said. "I figure the TV will go over the fireplace, and - "

"Put it on that wall," I suggested, pointing to the interior one. "Then you can see it from the pool too."

Hottie chuckled like he'd just won. "Two to one, Jinxy."

"Zoe? Help me out here?" he begged.

"I'm with Jeri on this," Zoe said. "Then you put the couch here, going sideways, and some chairs over by those windows. Then both the TV and the fireplace can be used."

"She's the designer," I reminded him. "Now where are the computers going?"

"Dining room," Hottie said.

Which made me pause. "Huh?"

"I'm showing!" Zoe assured them even as she towed me back out. "Ok, so we don't have a fancy dining room table, and there's a kitchen nook with a built-in table, plus a bar. Across from the living room is an office or something? No idea, but a separate room. And then here..." She waved with both arms at a very large, very fancy room.

I stepped in and looked up. The teardrop chandelier was impossible to miss. Soft grey walls had white wainscotting halfway up and more of those heavy crown molding-looking pieces around the large gaps that led to the kitchen on one side and the hall on the other.

"We're making this into the computer area?" I asked.

"Mood lighting," Zoe said as she flipped the switch and began dimming and brightening the chandelier to prove her point. "Plus, Knock pointed out that it's beside the coffee pot." She pointed to the kitchen. "And not far from the guest bathroom."

"Nice. Not what I expected, but nice. Now I need to set up."

"Desks in the middle," Zoe said.

But I was already headed for the front door. Our new house was huge. We were all still making trips to get loads of stuff. Thankfully, Sanger wasn't very far from Denton. Twenty minutes to my house with traffic, and my bedroom could wait.

"Hey!" Zoe asked, jogging after me. "Need help? Ripper and Knock were going to make a few more trips with the trucks, but..."

I didn't stop until I was at my car. "I just need my computer up and running. Please tell me the internet is already active? We can't be blind."

"Logan made sure of it," she promised. "Jericho, after last weekend..."

Which made me pause. "Yeah," I said, turning to lean my rump against my car. "But we saved them, Zoe."

"Right, which means we get to enjoy this part, Jeri. We get to be excited about our new house. We get to game tonight and have our first day of school tomorrow, and you? Blind? Jeri, they're ok. We saved them. Well, I mean Cynister did, but everything is fine now."

I bit my lips together, trying hard not to snap her head off. "Zoe, I need to make sure my machine is online."

"Why?" she pressed.

My next words came out soft. Too soft to carry. "Because what if it happens again?"

Zoe merely looked at me, her eyes searching my face. "Your curse?"
"Yeah."
"Ok," she said. "So this is what you need to feel better, right? Then hand me something. Let's get your computer hooked up. Mine's not here yet, but I'll make sure the guys know we need to get the computer room functional."

"War room," I corrected.

She reached over and clasped my hand. "Jeri, it's a game room. We're going to have fun this year. The bad stuff is over, remember? It's ok to actually relax for once. Soul Reaper is dead."

"But I love you, Zoe," I countered. "You are my best friend. Don't you get it? That means I can't relax. I have to make sure you're safe. And the guys. And - "

"Ok," she broke in. "Vigilant vigilantes. Got it. But maybe we can be *happy* vigilant vigilantes?"

That was enough to finally let me crack a smile. "With hats?"

"Oh!" she gasped. "Cade got me a hat in Vegas! It's red! Now hand me your monitor!"

I passed one over, then reached for my computer case. We had internet. We had a war room. We had one hell of a nice house. That meant this would be ok. By the time I was moved in tonight, I'd have my system up and running, and my curse could kiss my ass.

# CHAPTER 2

JERICHO

A day of moving. That was all it really took, since most of us were only moving a bedroom. Hottie and Jinxy were the ones with real, adult furniture. Although, since we had two living areas, that kinda worked out. Hottie's stuff went in the "den" – which Zoe had renamed the "study" - and Jinxy's went in the "living room." The guys said the colors worked better that way.

The tiny little table Hottie owned went into a small office-type room in the back that was now a private dining area. For dates, the guys decided. They meant in-house dates - which I thought was cute. Beds went in rooms, with the guys working together to carry those up all the stairs. Mine was the third to be put in place.

But one of our rooms was still empty. Supposedly it was Cade's, and it would've been across the hall from Hottie. Instead, Cade and Knock had decided to share the master bedroom down on the first floor. Since Knock's brother had bought the place - and was paying for it - we all agreed he got the best bedroom. Since he and Cade were used to sharing a room, well, it actually made sense.

Hottie and Jinxy were on the second floor with me, which worked. I'd known them the longest. I'd been living with Hottie, and he was the one who shared the bathroom with me. Jinxy basically had his own, so he was pretty happy. The weird thing, though, was hearing footsteps above me. That was Zoe.

I finally got my bed together and the mattress in place, then simply flopped down on top of it. Sheets could wait. My arms were killing me, and I knew my back would be screaming in the morning, but this was so worth it. I was finally all grown up. Maybe my mom's mental health wouldn't let her realize that, but it had still happened. I'd somehow managed to survive adolescence.

So many others hadn't.

Letting out a sigh, I stretched my arms out and lay spread like a star. The sunset was barely visible through my kickass window. It was sideways, but I liked it. Like this, I could see the pinks to the right and the purples of night to the left. I liked the transition.

I was watching it for a while, letting my body rest when a soft tap sounded at my door. "Come in!" I yelled, not wanting to get up.

My door cracked open, and Ripper poked his head in. "You decent?"

"Nope, but I'm dressed," I assured him. "Come in."

He did, then closed the door behind him, looking around. "I like it," he said before making his way over to my bed. "Now move over."

I did, and he flopped down beside me. Without waiting, I moved in to use his shoulder as a pillow. When his arm wrapped around my back, I felt myself sigh again, and this time it felt like a little of my tension went with it. Not all, but enough.

"Hey," he breathed, reaching up to push the fine hairs away from my face before toying with my pink dreadlocks. "Zoe said you're kinda triggered by last weekend."

"So she sent you?" I rolled a little more so I could see his face better.

"Not exactly," he admitted. "She was more asking for advice. I offered to check on you because I wanted to."

"Mm." I snuggled deeper into his chest. "You know they almost died?"

"Riley and her friends?" he asked.

I nodded. "Dez. She's the co-owner of Deviant Games. She helped us with the toybox, Ripper. Rhaven? She's a developer for the company. I've never done more than said hi to Kate, but Zara is Cynister's new wife."

"And Riley." He leaned in to kiss my brow. "Your actual friend. Yeah. I was scared too."

"But..." I grunted.

He waited, giving me the chance to finish that thought. When I didn't, he asked, "But what?"

"Ripper, we broke the law to save them." I sighed one more time, then rolled onto my back so I could look up at the ceiling. "I don't mean kinda. I mean, we hacked shit that the people in charge won't like that we hacked, and we didn't really hide our footprints."

"Cynister will handle it," he assured me. "We're his confidential informants, remember?"

"I'm not sure," I said softly. "Traffic cams? Cell towers? Hottie cracked that man's phone records, got his personal info, and ripped the data for the stream. I mean..."

"You mean we did it," he pointed out. "Jeri, our friends needed us, so we saved them. No one died. Well, none of ours died. Only the bad guys."

I laughed once. "Yeah, but isn't that just like putting it off?"

"What do you mean?"

Damn, even the ceiling of this room was cool. It was made of those fancy tiles. White, but they merged together to make a cool pattern. The ceiling fan was ultra-modern, which I didn't think fit with all the ornate woodwork, but oh well. It worked well, and that was pretty much all that mattered to me.

"Jeri?" Ripper pressed.

"I love you," I said, daring to roll my head so I could see him. "And I love them. Fuck, I love Zoe and Jinxy too. I mean, different, but you know."

"Friends," he said, proving he did. "Maybe even like family?"

Which made me grimace. "But see, family dies."

"And there it is," he said, lifting his hand so he could smooth my hair some more. "You're waiting for the other shoe to drop, huh?"

"DeathAdder goes to the University of North Texas," I reminded him.

"Mhm, but the FBI is supposedly going through the Kings of Gaming website and tracking down all the idiots who were on there. All of them, Jeri."

"Yeah, and how long is that going to take? I mean, if we're already in shit for hacking Las Vegas, maybe we should - "

"No," he said gently. "You should go to your first day of college tomorrow. You should focus on getting a degree. You should dress cute, take lots of notes, and do whatever else we're supposed to do now that we're out of high school."

Which made me giggle. "Are you going to dress cute?"

"Yep. I'm wearing a Deviant Games shirt and some jeans. Mostly because I haven't found anything else yet. I have so many boxes in my room, and no clue where I'm supposed to put anything."

I gestured at my own stack of boxes. "Yep. Know how that is. I did get a parking permit, though."

"We all did, thanks to Hottie's insistence," Ripper admitted. "And we get to stare at our phones like idiots, trying to figure out which buildings we're supposed to be in. Kinda like tourists."

"More like freshmen," I teased. "But I know my schedule isn't too heavy. The guys from Death Over Dishonor said to keep my first semester light, because I'll need to get used to doing college-y things."

"I just didn't get any good options," he admitted. "Core courses.

Zoe's got some cool classes, but Knock and Cade were basically as screwed as me."

"Same."

"So maybe we'll do a big raid in Flawed as a celebration of being real college kids?" he asked.

Yeah, but I could hear something in his voice. It was worry, and the kind that was always so gentle and reassuring from him. It was still there, which meant he was trying to lead me to something.

Then again, that was what I loved most about Ripper. Maybe Cade was more muscular, and Knock was better connected. Hottie was the stunningly handsome one of the guys, but Ripper? He'd somehow managed to become the perfect one.

He was a little overweight. He wore black-framed glasses. For that, he'd been bullied in high school. But he also had some amazing green eyes, adorable dimples, and the most important thing, a heart of gold. This man had slipped inside all my defenses and figured out how to make me feel safe when only Hottie had managed before. He loved me in a way I'd never thought anyone could: completely.

"I want to find DeathAdder," I mumbled. "Ripper, we need to."

"No, we don't," he assured me. "Cynister's doing that. Our job is done, Jeri. The Kings of Gaming are done. The entire nightmare is over."

"But it's not." I sat up and turned so I could face him. "Look, maybe you haven't thought about this yet, but DeathAdder? That message we found? He helped Dylan. That means he helped all of Alpha Team. Those guys raped twenty-three girls!" I pulled in a breath to keep my voice from rising. "One of them was Zoe."

"Yeah, but - "

"He helped Dylan get away with hurting our best friend, Ripper."

Which made his mouth snap shut.

"That fucker was part of it," I insisted. "She doesn't know that, but I do. He helped them. He made it easy for them to hide it, which let them get away with it, and you know what? I'm going to make *damned* sure he pays. No one gets to hurt my friends!"

Ripper grabbed my hand quickly enough to stop my rant. "Jeri, it's over. Let it be over, ok?"

"But I can't."

"The fucking FBI is on it now," he insisted.

"And?" I leaned my head back and groaned. "Look at the cops in Sanger! No, law enforcement won't get it right. DeathAdder's just some minor nobody. They'll let him plead out, for all we know. He'll get a slap on the wrist, like the assholes who bullied Nina to death."

"Hottie's fiancée?"

I nodded. "Yeah. Probation. That is not enough for hurting Zoe. No. I'm done with being nice. Those fuckers online think they can come after women and we'll just ignore it? We'll let the feds handle it? We'll turn it over to the cops? Well, *screw that!*"

"But that's how we get justice," he told me.

"No, it's how this shit gets ignored. I mean, Cyn doesn't count. He's kinda like one of us, you know? He's a gamer. He's a hacker. He gets it, but everyone else? They're going to be more worried about clocking out at the end of the day, not catching these fuckers. To them, this is a job. To us, it's vengeance. To us, it's protecting our own. Fuck, it's the only way - " And again, I stopped myself.

"Your curse," Ripper guessed.

I dropped my head and let out a groan. "I know. It's stupid. It just feels like..." And I made a gesture towards my chest. "I don't even know. Like we're not done?"

"Ok, but what is your big plan, Jeri?"

"Um..." Yeah, he kinda had me there. "Find DeathAdder?"

"And then?"

"I don't know!" I hissed. "I just know I have to stay ahead of them. I have to make sure I'm ready. I need to - "

He sat up and wrapped his arms around my shoulders in a hard hug. "You need to stop the curse, right? But you can't. It doesn't really exist. It's simply the world being a shitty place. The FBI is handling the Kings of Gaming. The guys from school are going to jail. They all pled guilty - eventually. Even Jinxy's family is ok. You've won, Jeri. You did it. You beat the curse."

"So why doesn't it feel like it?" I asked.

"Because you care." He leaned back to cup the side of my face and meet my eyes. "You finally admitted you care, and now you're scared to death. I get it. Shit, I think we all do, but fear isn't the best way to accurately guess what will come next."

"But there's always more bad guys," I reminded him. "And we're Ruin. We're a hacktivist group. Aren't we supposed to, I dunno, hack?"

"Not every day." A soft smile found his lips, causing one of his dimples to appear. "Baby, even hackers get to celebrate a big win. You saved the damsels. I mean, they weren't the kind I'd call in distress, but you still saved them."

"Cyn kinda did that," I grumbled.

"And you helped," he assured me. "And we helped you. Now we're here, living the seriously good life. I mean, we have a fucking pool!"

"And a hot tub," I pointed out.

His smile grew enough to show both dimples. "Yeah. So don't we get to enjoy all of this for at least a few days?"

I could only shrug. "But what if shit hits the fan?"

"Then we'll hit back," he swore. "Jeri, you're not alone anymore. Maybe you don't trust law enforcement, but you trust us, right?"

"Yeah," I breathed.

"Then *trust us*," he begged. "Enjoy this. We've just moved into our first place on our own. Well, the without-parents type. We have some kickass roommates. We have one hell of an internet connection. We have a house that's fucking massive, and a zero-turn mower in the garage for the yard, and a benefactor who says we don't even have to pay rent."

"That's just because Logan's awesome."

"Yep," he agreed. "So let it be awesome. One week, ok? And after that, if you still want to chase DeathAdder, I'll help."

Letting my eyes slip closed, I leaned in, throwing my arms around his neck. "Thank you. Fuck. Thank you, Ripper. That's what I needed. Shit, that's exactly why I love you."

"I love you too, Jeri," he whispered against my shoulder. "That means I don't want to lose you. Not even to yourself."

# CHAPTER 3

### SPECIAL AGENT JASON RAIGE

I barely made it back home from F5 before I had to climb on a plane again. I'd been promised a week. Not that I really needed it to make my decision, but I needed the time with Zara. Seeing my new wife with a gun to her head for the second time had rocked me hard. Thankfully, Crysis, my loyal service dog, made it better.

I also owed my wife a honeymoon. Vegas had been our excuse to catch the man running the Kings of Gaming. To me, it did *not* count as a honeymoon. To Zara, it was just part of the fucked-up way things worked out for us. Damn, I loved that woman. Knowing she was going to make me a dad already? Yeah. Happy endings, right?

But when I arrived in Washington, D.C., my former partner was standing there, waiting for me. "Heard you might need a ride," he joked. My dog's tail immediately began to wag.

"Did you also hear why we got called in *today*?"

"Sadly, no," he admitted. "But I do know one thing. Our little save in Vegas? Yeah, Alex Watts got a promotion. That's why we're in D.C. instead of New York."

"Uh huh." I grunted at that and kept walking.

My dog, behaving perfectly, stayed right at my side. His orange vest marked him as an official service animal. My FBI badge made sure no one doubted it. The gun on my belt tended to be a bigger problem. But since this was a day trip, I'd packed light. My carry-on had everything I needed, so I headed for the well-marked exit.

"Jason," Bradley grumbled. "Just tell me you aren't pissed?"

"Not pissed," I promised. "I want to get home, but I'm not pissed."

"I'd say trying to start a family, but sounds like that's already going well." He jogged two steps to catch up with me. "How's the baby?"

"Haven't heard anything new since Vegas," I assured him. "Zara says she's fine, so..." I shrugged. "I think that means she's fine."

"This is me being a worried Uncle Bradley," he explained. "I'm also worried about you, Jason."

"I'm ok."

"Jason..."

I laughed once, then paused to face him. "Bradley, I am ok. Look at Crysis if you don't believe me."

We both turned to look at my dog. Confused, he sat, his eyes bouncing between us as he waited for a command. What he wasn't doing was pressing against me, ignoring my commands, or climbing into my lap. If there was any way for me to prove I was doing fine, his calm demeanor was it.

"Even after what happened to Zara?" Bradley asked.

Ducking my head, I reached up to push a hand through my dark brown hair. "She pulled out the band holding her hair in a ponytail. When that dipshit put a gun in her face, she didn't have a panic attack. She let her hair down."

"Ok?"

"Because I once told her I'd used her hair to judge the wind, Bradley. It meant she knew I was there. She trusted that I would save her, because I swore to her that I would, and you know what? I did. I was willing to let Braden die so she could live. Didn't want to, but if I have to choose, I choose her. I will always choose her, and she knows it."

"Can't wait until junior gets here," Bradley laughed, slapping me on the back and turning me towards the door. "And our ride's waiting out here."

"Which means you just got here too," I realized, because he was supposed to be in New York.

Sure enough, our ride was an Uber. The trip from the airport to the FBI headquarters was supposed to be a short one. By miles, it was. Traffic, on the other hand, meant it took a while. Crysis didn't care. He was happy to sit in the back and pant at the window as we drove over the Potomac.

The driver dropped us off at the main entrance. When I got out of the back with my dog, we got a few looks, but no one tried to stop us. Not until we made it inside. There, our badges were checked, our names were verified. Then and only then were we directed up a few floors and down a hall. The woman leading us clearly knew where she was going.

"Deputy Director?" she asked as she peeked her head into an open door.

That made me exchange a look with Bradley. The Deputy Director of the FBI was the second in charge of this place. This was one of the people who talked to the President on a regular basis. If we'd been summoned to talk to him, then either this was very good or very, very bad.

"I'm so fired," I breathed.

"Not yet, you aren't," Bradley swore.

Then the woman who'd been escorting us waved for us to go in. "She'll see you now."

Wait, she? Confused, I rounded the corner to see the barest office I'd ever experienced in this building. My feet stalled out. Beside me, Bradley was looking around in obvious confusion, doing nothing to hide it.

"In here!" And that was a voice I recognized: Alex's.

"Ma'am," I said as I rounded the corner, expecting her to be waiting beside the Deputy Director.

Instead, she was alone. Crysis whined softly, but instead of leaning into to me, he pushed against Bradley. It was enough to make Alex chuckle.

"Sit," she told us. "The chairs are one thing this office still has." Then she walked around us to close the door to the more private half of the dual-room office.

"Ma'am?" This time it was a question.

"Sit," she ordered, because neither of us had moved.

She made her way around to the large leather chair on the opposite side of the desk and claimed it. Then she pulled open a drawer, lifting out something long, metallic, and narrow. With a half-smile playing on her lips, she flipped it around and set it on the edge of the desk closest to us.

"And now," she said, "you can both sit."

Because the thing was a nameplate, and it said "Alexandra Watts, Deputy Director."

"Yeah, I'm confused," I admitted, but I did finally sit.

So did Bradley, yet before I could command Crysis to lie beside me, Alex leaned around the edge and made kissy noises at him. My dog checked with me, but a release command let him know it was ok to get some attention. He bounded around the desk and all but crawled up in Alex's lap, proving she was one of the good ones.

Because if my dog liked someone, they couldn't be too bad. He was almost as picky as me. More intuitive, though. I had to warm up to new people, but Crysis? I was pretty sure he could smell it.

"Oh, you're the bestest boy ever, aren't you?" Alex cooed. "Yes, a real hero, so far as I care. I'm so happy to see you with your person. Yeah, you're doing the hard stuff." Then she gently guided him down, leaned back, and sighed.

"Crysis, come. Down," I commanded.

Immediately, my dog was lying at my side, but I still had no fucking clue what was happening. Three days ago, Alex had been the Deputy Assistant Director of my division. Now she was sitting in a bigger office in a more important town, with a nameplate that called her the second in charge of the United States' federal domestic law enforcement division.

"What's going on?" Bradley asked.

"Well," Alex said, "it seems the pair of you got me the promotion I wanted. I barely made it back to New York before the Director called me here. I'd applied months ago, but the former Deputy Director had a few things to close out before he could retire. During that time, I managed to go from the third choice for his replacement to the first."

"Congratulations," I said. And while my voice was calm and cold, I honestly meant it.

"That's wonderful," Bradley told her.

"It is, isn't it?" She grinned, proving her arrogance was mostly excitement. "But it seems catching the uncatchable, and doing it the way we did, using Jason's confidential informants, targeted cyber-tracking, and having no hostages harmed in the process? Especially when it's on the national news? The President likes that."

"And that means the Director likes it too," I realized.

"Yes, it does," she agreed. "He likes it enough that he offered to let me start a pet project, Jason. One I think you'll be interested in."

"You promised me a week to make my decision," I reminded her.

"I did. I'm not going back on that. I made sure you no longer have a leash, but think of this as me offering a little bacon in exchange for you to come closer."

I laughed once because her dog analogies were a little too apt. "Ok? So you're sweetening the pot?"

"More than you can imagine," she said. "This weekend, we took down Soul Reaper. Rhaven Moore made it a national story with her press conference. You made it a happy ending. Me? I made it proof that one virtual terrorist is a good sign there are more. Virtual sexism, racism, and every other sort of discrimination is all but untouchable online. Well, the Director agrees."

"Ok?" I asked, not quite sure where she was going with this.

"So he's allowing me to start a new branch of the Cybersecurity division. You, Jason, are getting the first offer to handle the consultants I want to hire."

My eyes narrowed. "I don't work well with others."

"Bullshit," she said, leaning over her desk. "Because these consultants I want to hire? They learned it all from you."

"Ruin," Bradley breathed.

Alex just nodded. "My plan is to have one agent assigned as a handler to each hacker group we can contract. As consultants, they will not have to pass the typical FBI requirements. This means no drug testing, no age limits, no degrees, and so on. The director has said I can run a test case, but there will be stipulations on it."

"Like what?" I asked, braced for the worst.

"The consultants must be FBI-certified to carry weapons. In the event of another situation like we had in Vegas, he wants his people armed. Otherwise, he believes it would be a national embarrassment."

"I can see that," I admitted. "Ruin doesn't know how to use guns, though."

"You can teach them," Bradley assured me.

Alex gestured to him like he'd made her point. "They also need to pass the basic legal certifications for law enforcement. To have an understanding of what is and is not actionable."

"Easy," I assured her.

"Plus background checks and a psychological evaluation."

A groan fell out and there was no way I could've stopped it. "Harder. Alex, one of their members is a rape victim. Another has a sealed juvenile record."

"Like yours?" she asked.

I shook my head. "No, nothing that serious. He hacked a phone to stop a bully. They should be willing to ignore it since he was rehabilitated."

She lifted a brow. "And still hacking, so very rehabilitated, hm?"

"Pretty much," I agreed. "But they work, you know they work, and with a little training, they will be unstoppable."

"Good." Then she tipped her head at me. "So does this mean you've decided yet? Or do you still need the rest of the week? What does your wife think?"

Leaning back, I let my arm drop so I could pet my dog. "Zara says she married an agent. She says I'm a hero, and that the world needs a few." My fingers trailed over the short hair on Crysis's head. "I just don't want to shoot anymore."

"Not unless you have to," she assured me. "Keep the sniper certification, Jason. That way, if someone else tries to grab one of your friends, you can pull one more miracle out of your ass. I will make sure you are *not* on the rotation for call-ins, but I want to make sure you *are* allowed to be as deadly as you need to be."

"When is this program going to start?" I asked.

"I'd like to fly to Dallas at the end of the week and see if your hackers are even interested," she said. "To make sure they are, I'd really like to have you with me."

"And between now and then?" I asked.

"I expect you to spend every single second with your new wife." She paused to make a little humming sound like she'd had a thought. "Oh, and if this works? Well, then it would mean a reassignment."

"Zara doesn't want to move again," I countered.

"I think she might consider this one," Alex assured me. "You would be stationed at the Dallas FBI office, working virtually. I'd suggest buying a house somewhere around Sanger or Denton. I mean, since both of you have family there now."

That felt like a punch in my chest. My throat closed up. My stupid fucking eyes began to burn. Crysis immediately hopped up and crawled in my lap, licking at my face with a speed only a bully breed could manage. Wrapping my arms around him, I buried my face in his neck and pulled in one slow breath after another.

"Jason?" Alex asked, sounding worried.

A moment later, Bradley's hand began to rub my back soothingly. "This is happiness, Alex. He hasn't had much. I think you just blindsided him, and for a man like Jason Raige, that's not an easy thing to do."

Sucking in a deep breath, I managed to lift my face, not even ashamed of the moisture welling in my eyes. "And I don't have to hide our association? I'm allowed to care about these people?"

"You are," Alex promised. "I'd like to make sure the Andrews' household are still your CIs, just in case you ever need help. But the group who calls themselves Ruin? They will be your team. Yours, Agent Raige, and you will report to Bradley, who will report to me. No more middlemen to worry about, because if we're going to do this, we're going to do this right."

Pushing my dog off my lap, I stood and held out my hand. "Then I accept your offer, Deputy Director Watts. This?" I had to pause to clear my throat. "This is what the world really needs."

# CHAPTER 4

### JERICHO

My alarm went off at nine the next morning. Grumbling, I twisted in my bed so I could swipe for a snooze. That should've given me ten minutes, but my mind started going. Today was my first day of college. A big day.

Dammit.

I didn't want to be excited about this, but since I clearly wasn't going back to sleep, I decided to give up. Crawling out of bed, I headed across my room for clothes. Ripper had a point. I wanted to look cute, but not too cute. This was college, after all.

My goal was to dress like I wasn't trying too hard. A pair of jeans and a tee made that work. My hair went back in a ponytail, held with a very well-worn, extra-large band. Makeup consisted of mascara, some Chapstick, and a couple dots of concealer under my eyes. I finished just as my snooze announced it was time to get out of bed.

But since I was early, I had time to get my things together. My backpack had a space for my new laptop. This one was a graduation present from Hottie, and it kicked ass. The purpose was to take notes online. Combined with the unlimited hotspot on my phone, I could upload them directly to the cloud. I also had some notebooks, a few pens, a pencil - just to be safe - and a battery pack to charge anything that might go dead.

With all of my crap together, I headed downstairs. Our place was still a wreck, but it sorta had that homey type of chaos going on now. The war room had seven different desks backed up to each other. Our desktop computers were glowing brightly, since we no longer needed to shut them down at night. The soft hum they gave off almost made me miss the sound of coffee brewing in the kitchen.

I came around the corner to see Hottie filling a cup. Not a little one, either. This matched the size and style Riley always offered us at her place. Oddly, the cup he was filling was pink. Mine.

"What are you doing?" I asked, making him look up.

That earned me a smile. "My baby girl is now all grown up," he said, heading towards the fridge to pull out cream. "And unlike high school, you can sip this in your classes now. I have twenty bucks for you too."

"Why?" Yeah, I wasn't all the way awake yet.

"Because you need to eat between classes," he explained. "Do homework or whatnot while you're at it, but on your first day, you will not find the cheap places."

"Uh huh." I moved to lean against the counter. "And when's your first class?"

"Noon."

I groaned. "I couldn't get mine in the afternoon like I wanted. All mornings. I mean, ten for Feminism, and then an hour break, and Calculus is at noon."

"With Knock," he said, proving he knew that much.

I just shrugged. "I mean, it works, right?"

"Enjoy it while you can, Jeri. And you already declared your major?" He stirred the coffee, slapped a lid on it and passed it over.

I nodded even as I took the travel mug. "Cybersecurity. It's one of the Computer Science majors, and it kinda called to me."

"No shit," he agreed. "But no coding classes?"

I groaned. "No. They were all filled before I could even start picking. I heard that's the shit part about being a first-semester freshman."

"Well, you'll also want time to find a parking spot, the right building, and your classroom. So, get out of here, baby girl."

"Going!" But instead of leaving, I caught his pants and tugged him in for a quick kiss.

He almost let me get away with the quick part, but when I pulled back, he leaned in for a second. Then a third. When a giggle slipped from my lips, he turned me towards the front door and gave me a nudge.

"Tonight, we make an agreement for where all these cars go," he warned.

Like that was a bad thing! We had a three-car garage here. Not just two like most people. Nope, three. Then there was the extra-wide driveway. And on top of that, we had enough curb space in front of the house to park three more cars.

Man, this place was nice. And yet, as I walked across the lawn towards my car, I noticed the woman watering her flowerbed - and staring at me. She looked like some trophy wife. Thirty? Maybe? Young, at any rate, but the glare on her face was clearly upper-class.

Maybe it was because my car was a bit of a beater? The thing was older, not so shiny anymore, but it ran great. Hottie, Jinxy, and Knock had the nice cars. Cade's was a classic. Zoe's was kinda like mine. Ripper's truck? Well, it screamed redneck, but I loved that thing.

Yet as I pulled away from the house, I realized our place was the only one packed with vehicles. Most had the cars stored safely behind closed garage doors. Then again, these weren't college places. This neighborhood? It was one of the nicest in Denton. That it was close to the University of North Texas was just a bonus.

Leaving the neighborhood, I hit the main road, and eventually turned up one of the many one-way streets heading to campus. The cars got thicker the closer I got, and when they all started turning, I was pretty sure I should follow. Sure enough, that was my street.

I found the designated commuter parking lot. From there, I opened the campus map on my phone and started walking. Feminism. That was my first class. Technically, it was a philosophy course, which satisfied one of my core requirements. It also sounded a hell of a lot better than the other options I'd been given!

But no matter how many times I'd been to the UNT campus to fill out papers, sign forms, get my ID, or any of the other necessary steps to actually being a student here, today was different. Today, I wasn't aiming for one place and then going home. Today, I didn't have an easy set of directions for where I was supposed to be. The course listing said the Environmental Sciences building. From my map, that was way the fuck over there!

So I walked. Then I walked some more. I passed big buildings and small ones. Around me, quite a few people were doing the same. It was funny because the freshmen like me were all staring at our phones. Others, clearly students who'd been here a few semesters, were just wandering to wherever they were supposed to be.

Finally, I reached the right building - or so I hoped. This one said it was the Environmental Sciences building on a sign out front. I had no clue why a philosophy class would be in this building. Still, I made it inside and damned near stopped when the overactive air conditioning hit me. It was like walking into a wall of cold.

Ok, that was nice, since September in Texas was rather molten. And if the room numbers here made any sense at all, my class was on the second floor. I needed to find some stairs.

After wandering for a bit, I found the right room and headed in. Clearly Hottie had been onto something with leaving so early, because there were only four minutes until my class started. I found a seat, aware the other students around me looked older, and then pulled out my notebook and a pen. Mostly because that was what everyone else had.

There was no bell to announce the start of class like there had been in high school. In the distance, I could hear the campus clock tower chime the hour, but it was faint. Almost a minute after that, a young woman hurried in with an armload of papers.

"Philosophy 4130?" she asked. When someone in the front row agreed, she started handing out those papers. "This is your course syllabus. My name is Chanda, and I will be your instructor for this class." She passed out another clump of papers. "While this is a senior- and graduate-level class, some of you may notice the many younger students. That's because this course is a core for many degrees."

I couldn't help myself. I looked around the same way everyone else was. Not surprisingly, the vast majority of students were women. Probably about three-quarters of the class. Still that meant twenty-five percent were men, which was kinda nice.

"In this course," Chanda continued, "we will study feminism, what makes feminism, the different types of feminism, such as radical and liberal feminism, as well as the evolution of feminism over time. Now, your syllabus has a list of reading requirements. Your textbook is listed on the first page. I do not care if you use an ebook or a physical one. We will never require the book in class, so there's no need to carry it. Your test schedule is clearly marked. My office hours are on the last page, and if you have any problems, I encourage you to speak with me."

Someone's hand shot up. "I heard we're going to have an essay for the final grade."

"No, not an essay," Chanda said. "A full paper. You will pick a portion of feminism you're most interested in and write a complete paper on it. Twenty pages, with citations. This class, no matter what you think, is not an easy grade. We are studying the philosophy of feminism in all its peculiarities. But, if you have no further questions..." She looked around, pausing long enough to give someone time to raise their hand. "Then you may go. Hopefully, you will go buy your textbook. I will see all of you on Thursday."

Immediately, the class began putting away their things and filing out. I simply looked down at my blank page and the packet of papers that had been passed back to me. This? It was not at all what I'd expected from college - especially not a senior-level course!

Everyone had always said university was harder than high school. They'd never really said *how* it was supposed to be harder. I was starting to realize that in many ways, it might actually be easier. Our teachers wouldn't nag us, wouldn't constantly be looking over our shoulders, and didn't really care if we passed or failed.

Yep, I could deal with that. So after putting my stuff away, I pulled out my phone and texted Knock.

**Jericho:**
Hey, let me know when you're out of class. I'm heading over towards the calculus class.

I didn't get an answer, but I wasn't expecting one. Instead, I retraced my steps, walking back the way I'd come, but taking a slightly different route. Instead of going on that side of a building, I tried the other.

Holy crap, this way was easier! Ok, I was starting to realize the campus map didn't have sidewalks or trails on it for a reason. Most of these buildings were set in the middle of nothing, with no road beside them. Statues and gardens were placed everywhere, making some smaller gaps end up bigger when I had to go around them. All of this was stuff I'd figure out with time, but it was part of the whole experience Hottie had been trying to explain to me.

I made it halfway back when my phone vibrated. Checking, I found a message from Knock.

**Knock:**
I'm outside this GAB building. Back side.

**Jericho:**
Which side is the back? I'm looking at a map!

**Knock:**
West.

**Jericho:**
Almost there!

I rounded another building and saw a circular area with benches. Sitting on one of those was a guy with bright blue hair. I couldn't see his lip ring from here, but I knew he had it. So, stretching my legs a little more, I headed towards him.

"Hey, sexy!" I called out.

His head snapped up and a smile found his face. "Hey! Aren't you supposed to be in class right now?"

I just blew out a breath and shrugged. "Got a syllabus. Now I have an extra-long wait."

"And I happen to know where there's a pizza place," he said, pushing to his feet just as I reached him. "I'll buy lunch if you tell me all about your first day on campus. I'll share my own horror stories."

"Deal," I agreed.

So he reached down and took my hand. Confused, I looked down. His fingers laced between mine - and then held on. Knock wasn't a hand holder. He wasn't the overly cutesy type. Shit, I'd take it, though.

"Lead on," I told him.

# CHAPTER 5

### KNOCK

J eri seemed confused when I took her hand, but she didn't pull away. Yeah, I knew it was a dumbass thing to do, but I was doing it anyway. It also made it easier to guide her across the street to a little pizza place that was supposed to be amazing.

The pair of us got in line, ordered a slice and a drink, then went to find tables. The slices they served were thick and massive. The sodas - er, cokes here - were ice cold. The tables were rickety, the decor was cheap, and the space was packed. In other words, it was exactly what I expected for a college campus hot spot.

"So," I said, pausing to take a bite of my pizza. "Mm. Good." Then a sip of my coke. "So you got the whole brush-off for your first class?"

"Pretty much," she admitted. "The instructor passed out papers then turned us loose. It's crazy."

"Yeah, because half the class doesn't have books yet," I explained. "Some will drop. No sense wasting time when no one really wants to learn today. We're all kinda transitioning, you know?"

"I guess that makes sense," she admitted. "But it's just weird. I mean, everyone has been telling me how much harder college is, and how I would have to get serious, and all that shit. And now? It's like I'm half-assing this."

"It's just different," I promised. "Riley, Logan, and Kitty have all given me the blow-by-blow of what to expect, and I've been in Denton enough to know my way around."

She chuckled. "So do you think Calculus will be the same?"

"Probably," I admitted. "My first class was. I mean, we got a little more than just a packet and kicked out, but it was mostly a very detailed description of grading."

"Ah..." She paused to take a bite. "So does this mean we'll have time to do some snooping?"

She said that casually, but I knew exactly what she was talking about. Ripper had warned me she was on the warpath, and the truth was I didn't blame her. Maybe the crew at home hadn't been as afraid? Maybe standing at the FBI command center when they put my friend in a bulletproof vest and sent him off to die changed something?

I wasn't sure, but I knew there was this tension humming inside me. Last weekend was still a little too close. Could I play it off? Sure. But with Jeri, I didn't have to. Of all the people in the world, she would understand. Hell, she was giving me the chance to do exactly what I wanted, even if it wasn't a good idea.

"We're supposed to give them time to clean up," I said, reaching across to palm her wrist. "I kinda don't want to."

"Was it bad?" Her pretty blue eyes looked up into mine.

"Fuck," I breathed. "I've never been so scared in my life. Braden was going in for a suicide mission. Cyn was doing his thing, and being pissy about it. Adam and Chance were losing their minds, Psyc was frantic, Void was on the verge of tears..." I shrugged. "I think bad's an understatement."

"And they're still out there," she reminded me.

I nodded slowly. "Trust me, I know. We cut the head off, but the minions are scurrying right now. Thousands of them, Jeri. There's no way they'll all get caught."

"Yeah," she breathed. "And we know DeathAdder goes to school here."

I nodded slowly. "He's also big enough he might get caught. I mean, Cynister's dealt with him personally, so there's that."

She just slammed her hand down on the table. "Not good enough!"

So I shifted my hand over to that one, hoping to keep her from doing it again. "No, it's not. For a few minutes, I got to experience the horror you've had to live with over and over again. For me, it was minutes and then everyone was ok. Here's the thing. I'm not."

"You held my hand."

"Yeah," I mumbled. "Jer..."

"And you've shortened my name even more," she pointed out.

That earned her a weak little laugh. "I was standing there, on the street, thinking my big sister was about to die. I was sure this couldn't end well, right? And the one thing that kept me calm was thinking about you. I knew you'd help me plan a funeral. I knew you'd know how to help Logan. I knew you'd hold me and Cade if we lost it." I smiled and forced myself to look up again.

God, she was beautiful. With those soft pink dreads, her big blue eyes, and the honesty written all over her face, she was the kind of beautiful so many people overlooked. She was rough around the edges, raw in all the right places, and real. Just completely real, in a take-it-or-leave-it sort of way.

She was the strength I'd held onto. Maybe my hands had clung to Cade in that moment, but Jeri had been my security, even though she'd been states away. Just knowing she was helping, that her hands were on a keyboard and her eyes were on a monitor, had given me hope.

And it had worked out.

Everything had ended perfectly. We all got to go home and be happy. The problem was that after something like that, happy was easier said than done. So, for the last few days, I'd been going through the motions. From the sounds of it, so was she.

"We have to wait a bit," I told her. "Cyn needs the time, Jeri. But once he's back online, I'm going to tell him we're going for it."

"Yeah?" She sounded hopeful.

"Yeah," I promised. "Me and you, if nothing else. Jeri, I..." The words failed me.

She simply turned her hand and curled her fingers with mine. "I like it when you hold my hand. Or when you throw your arm around my shoulders. All those guy things, you know? It's cute. It makes me feel like you're real, and like you're still here. Like my curse failed."

"We're going to make sure of it."

"But can we?" she asked. "Knock, we didn't cover our tracks. We were in too big of a hurry."

"And we're all working with CI contracts that give us some freedom," I countered.

"Not *that* much." She took another bite, then washed it down. "Look, we got immunity for some pretty minor stuff. This was major. Jinxy made sure we knew the risks. None of us cared. We had to pick, so we picked our friends. We hacked into so much shit that will piss people off. I mean, Hottie was comparing the cell phones from two towers. If that's not an invasion of privacy..."

"And Logan's a damned good attorney," I reminded her. "We'll make it work."

"Yeah, but if we do, then what does that do to catching the rest?"

And now I could see how her mind was spiraling. "You want to catch the KoG fuckers, you're worried you're going to get arrested for hacking, and that in the process of getting out of it, they'll get away?" I asked.

"Or that I won't be allowed to keep doing this because the need for a confidential informant is over, or that we'll be so busy in court, or being detained, or whatever the fuck happens when we get busted that we won't have time. I dunno, Knock, but it's not good! We're working on a clock here!"

"And that clock goes both ways," I reminded her. "Pushing in now when there's a million data analysts all over the Kings of Gaming website? When there are cybersecurity agents chasing anyone who connected to that stream? Yeah, that's kinda like waving a flag and saying 'I'm right here.' So how about we don't do that?"

She groaned. "Ok, valid point."

"And here's another. We were hacking before we had those CI contracts. I have a feeling we'll be hacking after they're taken back. This gig is done, but there's always another."

"It. Is. Not. Done!" she hissed.

I patted the air, calming her down. "Technically, it's done. We're now in the aftermath. Soul Reaper got caught."

"Shot," she corrected.

"Dead," I agreed. "Along with quite a few of his accomplices. I'd also like to say that Cyn is a scary motherfucker, Jeri. They took his wife and kid, so - "

"Kid?" she asked.

"Zara's pregnant," I explained. "So, kid. Riley's his best friend. Dez is his spirit animal or something. I don't even know. He loves those women, and Soul Reaper had no fucking clue the monster he'd woken up."

"Did you?"

I shook my head. "I knew Cyn was FBI. I knew he was creepy. I knew he's a Jedi Master, not a Sith Lord."

"I don't even know what that means," she said around a little laugh.

"Sith are bad guys," I explained. "Jedi are the good ones, but in Star Wars, the good guys wear black."

"Ah."

"Yeah, but here's the thing. Cyn's a good guy, but he's also kinda not. He's the sort of person who'd agree with you. He'd say we need to chase down these fuckers because no one else would get it right."

"That's my point!" she broke in.

"But he'd also remind us not to stick our necks into a trap and get caught."

The excitement on her face fell. "Oh."

"So we wait," I told her. "We play this smart. We make plans and get ready for it. Then, once the FBI is out of our way, we pick a wall, get some markers, and start making a game plan."

"The house is kinda nice to be writing on the walls," she countered.

"Logan won't care."

"Or maybe we should just get a whiteboard?"

Ok, she had a pretty good point with that. "I'll call him after calculus and see what he thinks, but you're not wrong."

She trailed her fingers across my palm. "And you're going to help me?"

"Always," I swore. "I love you, Jericho Williams. I also think I can finally understand you. So yeah. Maybe we can burn down the world together?"

"That," she said, "might be the sweetest thing a man has ever asked me. I think you're trying to give Ripper a run for his money."

"Nah, just Hottie," I joked. "But in exchange I want something from you, ok?"

Her eyes narrowed as she searched my face, trying to find the loophole. "What?"

"Help me help Cade? He's so sure he's going to flunk out of college."

"Cade?" She shook her head in confusion. "But he's smart."

"He doesn't know it," I explained. "Jeri, his dad said he was a useless piece of shit. His grades in high school weren't great. He barely got the scores to make it into UNT, and he feels like he only understands half the hacking shit we're doing."

"So teach him all of it?" she asked.

"Nope," I said. "Help him with his classes. When it comes to hacking, I want to redirect him."

"To what?"

I squeezed her hand, then leaned back in my chair with a pleased little smile. "We need a social hacking specialist, Jeri. We need a do-er. We need a hardware guy. Look at what he's good at, and help me find ways to make him useful."

"Or," she said, "we teach him both, because he's not an idiot, Knock. Cade's brilliant. It's why I like him, and he's vicious in player vs. player gaming. That means he's tactical. He knows how to stay a step ahead, and right now, I think we're going to need that more than we want to admit."

"And he's all-in," I assured her. "The both of us, Jeri. DeathAdder isn't getting away."

"He helped Dylan cover up Zoe's rape. Probably Evan too."

"Just one more reason for him to fry," I agreed.

She murmured almost like this conversation had been too easy. "So that's it? We wait until the feds are out of our way and then we go as crazy as we want?"

"How about we agree on testing the waters?" I suggested. "See if Cyn has anything he wants to add. You know, use the connections we have. I know he's out of pocket for a little while, but he's the one with the inside scoop." Then I checked my watch. "And we have college to worry about, right? Buying books and all that shit?"

"Fuck," she groaned. "Yeah, I'm trying to find the discount options."

"We'll go over that when we get home," I promised. "Trust me, Riley gave me all the links for cheap books. Now eat. We have half an hour until calculus."

"Almost feels like a waste of a day," she said, but she also took another bite.

"Welcome to college, Jericho. Today, you get to be the cute little clueless one. Tomorrow will be a bit better. The day after, even better, until you're handling all of this on autopilot while we're burning the world."

"One KoG member at a time," she said, lifting her cup of soda and tipping it like a toast. "I can get behind that."

# CHAPTER 6

## ZOE

Logan had said we could do anything to the house we wanted. To make it feel like our home. I was hoping that included putting holes in the walls, because Ripper had hung a set of shelves for me this morning while I'd been in my eight o'clock class.

Now, I was filling them full. Music went on one side of the window. Books went on the other. Ok, so most of those were fashion and sewing books, but I wasn't ready to let them go. Maybe it was insane, but I wanted to do a major in Computer Sciences and a minor in Fashion Design. To me, that sounded like the best of both worlds.

I'd just emptied a box and was breaking it down when a soft tap rapped on my open door. I glanced back to see Jeri standing there with a printed piece of paper. For some reason, my guts twisted in worry.

"Everything ok?" I asked.

"Discount bookstores," she said, flapping the page to show what she meant. "Riley gave this to Knock, and he printed it for everyone. I figured you might want a copy, because these textbooks? Zoe, they're like three hundred bucks each!"

"I know," I admitted. "I mean, my student loans have enough to cover them, but..."

"No shit," she agreed. "I'm trying to decide how bad homework will be so I can apply for a part-time job."

"Or full-time," I said, since she at least had her mom helping her financially.

My parents couldn't afford it. Oh, they'd make it happen if I asked, but I knew they didn't have any spare money. They'd scrimped and saved just to get me the little bit of therapy I'd had, and that had affected the grocery budget. Living paycheck to paycheck sucked.

"So, how discount are these sites?" I asked, taking the paper she was offering.

"I just got two books for fifty bucks," Jeri said, moving to sit on the edge of my bed. "So very."

"Nice!"

"Ebooks," she cautioned.

"And I have a laptop now," I said. "Compliments of Kitty, as a graduation present."

Jericho laughed. "Hottie got me one. Logan got Cade one. Knock already had one."

"Jinxy already had his too," I agreed. "Sounds to me like that crew made sure we were all ready. And yes, Riley got Ripper one."

"Speaking of Jinxy..." She patted the bed beside her. "Talk, girl."

So I pointed at a box. "Help put books on the shelves and I'll spill."

"Deal," she agreed, hopping up to crack open another one of my boxes. "So how are you handling living with him?"

I felt the smile taking over my lips. "Um, it's nice, and he's kinda amazing."

"And cute?" Jeri asked.

I huffed at her. "Fuck cute! That man is hot! I mean, he has tattoos!

Full sleeves on both sides! He also has glasses. How much hotter could he get?"

She passed me a set of books. "He's just always been dorky Jinxy to me. But I'm kinda more worried about, you know, the touching."

Yeah, and the truth was that I kinda was too. I'd gotten better about it. My friends in Ruin helped more than I'd expected, but with Jinxy it was different. More personal? I wasn't even sure, but I could feel it.

"I'm mostly ok," I assured her. "I can hug him. I can hold his hand, and he always lets me initiate. He says he gets it."

"But?" she asked.

I let out a heavy sigh. "No kissing. No lying under him. Um, I mean, it's just certain things that make me remember."

"No, makes sense," she agreed.

Which let me relax a bit. I really did like Jinxy. Fuck, the guy was perfect. Sadly, perfect didn't seem to matter when my brain decided to go into some post-traumatic episode. I still had nightmares. I still had moments when I tensed up and pulled into myself. I still wasn't over being drugged and raped, and it fucking sucked!

But I was going to get there. Step-by-step, I'd been doing my best to tackle my own issues. My friends kept telling me they understood, I could take it at my own pace, and all of that. I just wanted my pace to be a hell of a lot faster than it currently was. Too bad life didn't work like that.

"I like him, though," I offered. "Not just as a friend, and not just as some guy online. I honestly like him, and I've liked hanging out with him since he's been here."

That made her face light up. "Yeah?"

So I nodded. "Yeah, I mean he feels safe. I'd say that's stupid, but I'm pretty sure you get it."

She passed me even more books. "Zoe, safe is the thing that outranks everything else."

"No shit," I agreed, pointing to another box when hers was empty.

"And he makes me feel like my ideas are good ones, and that it's not insane to still kinda want to do fashion."

"Is that your major?"

I scoffed. "No. I'm completely on the geek train with everyone else. I'm just minoring in fashion."

"Nice!"

That made me pause and look back. "Really?" Because I hadn't expected such enthusiasm.

"Well, sure," Jeri said. "I mean, if you think about it, we should all be studying what we have a passion for. You're a good gamer, but you've always loved fashion. Sounds to me like you're mixing them both, and I can see a million ways that would work out."

"Like?" I asked, because in all honesty, I didn't have a clue how they fit together.

"Videogame clothing," she said, ticking things off on her fingers. "Disguises for any personas we have to make and get photos of. Virtual animation, so you know how fabric moves. I mean, there's so many ways you could spin that."

"I just kinda wanted to take some fashion classes," I admitted.

"So take them," she said. "Zoe, stop trying to be what anyone else expects. Not me, not Jinxy, and certainly not the rest of Ruin. People we don't know? Fuck 'em. Their opinions don't count. If this is what you want to do, then go all-in."

"It is," I admitted. "And I really want to get better at hacking so I can make a difference. I mean, that comes first, but fashion is still a close second. Besides, it kinda helps that Jinxy thinks my style is sexy."

"Oh?" She caught my shoulders and spun me to face her. "So there's been sexy talk?"

"And feelings talk, and what are we doing talk, yeah," I admitted. "Lots of talk. I just keep thinking he's going to get bored of me."

"Jinxy?" Jericho laughed. "Not likely. Trust me, the man doesn't jump from girl to girl. I mean, he's a nerd, so he's not exactly high on most women's pickup list. I happen to think they're idiots, but he knows it, and he's convinced he's just a tall, skinny, ugly guy."

"But he's not ugly!" I insisted.

"Nope," she agreed.

"And it's not fair, you know?" I asked. "He's being so good to me, and I want to make sure he's just as good to himself, so I keep thinking about your little arrangement with the guys."

"An open relationship?"

I shrugged. "Maybe? I mean, if I'm not going to be throwing myself at him, then shouldn't he be allowed to play the field? After all, this is college! This is supposed to be the time of our lives, when we get to live it up, and all that."

"Who's to say he isn't?" she countered.

Which made me pause with my mouth hanging open. "What?"

"Zoe, just because I like fucking a bunch of different guys doesn't mean everyone feels the same! I mean, Knock and Cade have their little romance, and that works. I'm cool with it. Hottie, on the other hand, doesn't want to date anyone else. We've talked about it, and he's only interested in me - and supposedly he's cool with me having other boyfriends. Everyone is different!"

"Well, yeah," I agreed.

"And some people like monogamy," she said gently. "Zoe, there is nothing wrong with that. There's no reason to push away a guy you like because you aren't ready to jump on his dick, ok? I mean, from the sounds of it, Jinxy's the monogamous type too. One girl for him at a time, you know? He says he gets insecure if she's seeing other people, and he'd feel like he's going to be replaced, and all the normal things most people say."

"When?" I asked.

She just waved that off. "Long ago. Uh, before I moved to Sanger. Like, gods, I think I was in like ninth or tenth grade?"

"Which means he could've changed his mind," I pointed out. "You did, Jeri. When you met the guys, you didn't want to date at all. Hookups only. Now you're in love with them."

"Thanks to you." She sighed and moved over to flop back on my bed. "And the truth is, being in love with them scares the shit out of me. Zoe, it's a big thing. It feels like I'm putting them in the crosshairs, or something."

I moved to stand over her legs. "So give them up. Dump them, move into the dorms, and never look back."

She looked up at me with a weak smile. "I don't wanna."

"Yeah, I know," I agreed. "Just like I don't wanna lose Jinxy. I still feel this thing. It's different from your thing, but it keeps trying to convince me to sabotage us. It's almost like my subconscious thinks I'll be safer if I'm all alone, but Ripper said something to me the other night and it kinda stuck."

"What's that?"

I moved to lie down beside her, both of our legs hanging off the side and resting on the floor. "If I ditch Jinxy to be safe on my own, the only thing I'll really get? I'll be lonely. I won't be safer. In fact, I'll be less safe, because he won't be around to look out for me. Not that I expect him to, but he still does, you know? And it'll cause a rift in Ruin, which means we could all fall apart, and the more I think about it, the more I realize this little voice in my head is what my therapist called self-sabotage."

She breathed out a dry laugh. "Oh, I'm familiar with that one."

"But it's easy," I said.

She nodded even as she looked over. "So easy."

"It's also a liar," I told her. "It's our fears trying to prove they're right. I kinda think of that voice as sounding like Dylan when he taunted us at school. He would lie and pull out all this asshole shit to look cool, but he was wrong. Over and over again, he was wrong, and I'm not going to let the Dylan part of my brain win."

"I like that," she breathed.

"Maybe he's also your evil voice?"

It took a little too long before she answered. "No, mine sounds more like my dad. He keeps promising it's all going to be ok and we'll get through this, and then he's just splattered everywhere."

I cringed, hating how bluntly she'd phrased that, but this was Jeri. To her, it was some coping mechanism. Gallows humor? I wasn't even sure. But the more she hit her traumas head on and spoke about them without trying to clean up the horror of it, the easier it was for her to admit she even had them.

I couldn't blame her. We were all fucked up in our own ways. The amazing thing was that somehow, once we'd all found each other, we'd figured out ways to numb the pain. All of our pain, in one way or another. Then we'd turned our magic powers of "making it better" towards the internet to help others.

It had started with Cade, then me, and eventually ended up as a whole ordeal when we found out the popular guys at school were serial rapists. In the course of chasing them down, the seven of us had completely forgotten to put up barriers between each other. We'd stopped trying to be tough or cool, and we'd gone all-in.

And now, I was pretty sure none of us knew how to untangle from the mess we'd made. While I couldn't speak for anyone else, I knew *I* didn't want to. For me, this mess of our friendship-polycule thing was a lifeline.

We all had bonds. Different bonds between different people, but those bonds weren't better or worse than anyone else's. Didn't matter if that was just friends, sleeping together, or anything else. We all had bonds, and those bonds meant we weren't alone.

So reaching over, I found Jeri's hand and clasped it gently. "No splattering, Jeri. We are Ruin. We splatter others. We keep them from splattering us."

"Yeah, but - " she tried.

"No," I broke in. "The bad shit happened when we were alone. We're not alone anymore."

She rolled into me and wrapped her arms around my shoulders. "Never again, Zoe. I swear."

"Me too," I breathed into her shoulder as I hugged her back. "That's what best friends are for. To get your back, no matter what."

# CHAPTER 7

## HOTSHOT

For the undergrads, Wednesday was all but a repeat of their first day, but with different classes. That wasn't the case for either me or Jinxy. Nope, our master's-level courses wanted to dive in immediately. By the time Thursday rolled around, I felt like I was back in the swing of things again.

So I walked into my Intro to Computer Security course and made my way over to the professor. "Excuse me," I said. "Do you mind if I set this on your desk?"

"What is it?" he asked.

"Bluetooth microphone. I have a dictation program so I can transcribe your lectures word for word - or pretty darned close. I figured I'd make them available to the class in a Google doc for studying."

The man held out his hand. "So if I clip it on, does that make it better?"

"Yes, sir," I said with a smile. "Thank you."

I made my way back to sit just as Jinxy sauntered into the class.

"Bro!" he said, claiming the chair in front of me. "Hey, did you get the mic set up?"

I flicked a finger to the front of the class where the professor was wearing it on his collar. "Looks like we got a winner this time."

"Sweet," Jinxy said before pulling out his own laptop.

He wasn't the only one. Everyone in our classes seemed to use them. Lectures were typically punctuated with the comfortable sound of keystrokes. Still, I had a feeling my little trick would make me one of the popular people in here. To me, that meant a good chance to get notes if I ever missed class. To everyone else in here? Well, a transcription of every lecture was all but a cheat sheet.

So when the professor started talking, I watched the words appear on my screen. I cleaned up the mistakes that would've confused me later, but didn't worry about the grammar or punctuation. And for anything I wanted to focus on, I wrote that out by hand.

This was my system. Jinxy's was a little different. He had a digital recorder on his desk and typed fast enough to keep up. Combined, I was pretty sure we'd end up making A's in this class. It was one we seriously needed.

Computer security was merely a fancy way of talking about keeping people like us out. I had a feeling half this class would call themselves hackers if asked. It was part of what drew people to computer degrees. But the reality was that most wanted to grow up and become game developers, network engineers, or information techs. Secure jobs. Stable jobs.

Safe jobs.

Me? I wanted skills. I wanted to make sure I knew every single thing I needed to ensure Jericho was never taken from me the way my fiancée had been. I knew there was shit out there online, and with each passing year, our society shifted more and more into the virtual world. Knowing how to protect the ones I cared about was my real goal.

My notebook began to fill up. My screen was scrolling with the information we were being given. A lot of it was pretty basic, but some? Yeah, I wanted to do my own research on a few things he said. But when the class was finally over, the professor dismissed us.

"And you?" he called out, jerking his chin at me while he pulled off the mic. "What's your name?"

"Grayson," I told him.

He tossed over my mic. "I'll wear it if that worked."

"Looking good so far," I assured him. "Thanks."

Then the girl sitting beside me leaned in. "Grayson?"

"Yeah?"

She smiled in a way that was a whole lot more than polite. "Um, is there any way I can get a link to that?"

"Not yet," I admitted. "But I'll set up the drive tonight. If you'd like to give me your email, I'll send it over."

"Oh! Sure!" And she listed it off.

I added it at the bottom of the notes. "You'll have it before tomorrow morning," I promised.

"If you include a phone number with it..." she offered.

"Grayson!" Jinxy gasped, spinning to glare at me. "I know you are not flirting with some girl!" And his mannerisms had suddenly become the most feminine thing ever.

I sighed. "No, I'm not," I promised.

"I know how you are," Jinxy huffed even as he put his stuff away. "So buy me a coffee to make up for it?"

"Yes, dear," I agreed, aware he was chasing this girl off in what was probably the most effective manner.

"Sorry," the girl said. "I just meant, you know, for studying." Then she scooted out of her chair and hurried from the room.

I turned to Jinxy and gave him a weary look. "Happy?"

"Yep," he agreed. "So are you." Then he stood and offered his hand. "Hold my hand, baby?"

Yep, that was a dare I couldn't resist. Slinging my bag over my shoulder, I not only grabbed his hand but shoved my fingers between his and held on tight enough he wouldn't be able to pull free. Then I pushed up close behind him as I guided him through the row of chairs and towards the door.

"Since you're now my bitch..." I whispered in his ear.

"Careful," he warned. "I'm not afraid of the gay, bro."

"Me either," I said, finally letting him go when he made it to the hall. "Just figured the last thing we need is for Zoe to see you walking across campus while holding my hand."

"Shit..." he drawled. "She'd laugh."

"Or think you were over her?" I asked.

Which earned me a grunt. "Yeah, that's a good point too. Sounds like she's already worried I'm going to get sick of her. And that's from Cade, not Ripper."

I rolled my eyes. "Like that would happen."

"So how are things with you and Jeri now that you're not always sharing a bed?"

I scrubbed at my face. "Yeah, um..."

"Bad?" he pressed.

But something caught my eye. Turning, I tried to figure out what. It took a moment, but then I saw it. A girl walking the other way had on a black shirt, and I was sure the logo was one I'd hoped to never see again.

"Hot!" Jinxy snapped, using the shortest version of my game name.

"Her shirt!" I hissed back.

So Jinxy, being the kind of guy he was, called out, "Hey girl! Yo! You in the black shirt!"

At least three women stopped and turned to face us. Jinxy pointed at the right one, but my heart was clenched up in my chest. On the front, in the center. Was that a skull? Was it wearing a crooked crown?

I took a step forward almost in a daze, but my eyes were working hard, dissecting the image from what I'd expected to what it really was. The face was white, but it was a woman. Yes, that was a crown, but it said "Notorious" across it. Fuck! The face? It was Ruth Bader

Ginsberg, the late Supreme Court justice. The shirt was a Notorious RBG shirt, not one for the Kings of Gaming.

I sucked in a breath as the girl decided we were insane and hurried away. Beside me, Jinxy looked confused. His attention was jumping back and forth between her and me.

"Hot?" he asked, sounding pretty worried.

"I thought it was a KoG shirt," I groaned. "Fuck! The white, the crooked crown. Even the black background. I fucking thought that girl was wearing - "

"And it's not," he assured me, turning me back the way we'd been going. "Breathe, bro. We're good. We got this. KoG is gone."

"Not gone," I reminded him. "Just broken. And Jeri's been on this rampage, you know? She's so sure they're going to get away and she wants to go chasing them."

"Bad idea," Jinxy said.

"I know that and you know that," I agreed, "but she's worried about it happening again."

"It?" He pulled me to a stop, then moved in front of me. "Which 'it,' Hot?"

"That's the problem. I don't know."

Slowly, he nodded. "And you're not calling us all to deep-dive because why again? You trying to teach her a lesson, or are you just sick of her shit?"

"Fuck off," I growled, pushing past him and making sure our shoulders hit hard enough to force him out of my way.

"Yo, jock bro!" Jinxy called after me. "Engage the damned brain and answer the question."

"I'm not fucking sick of her!" I snapped, spinning back to turn my fear and fury on him.

Lifting both hands, Jinxy simply made his way closer. "Hot, she's got you on edge. You're cracking because she is. How long are you going to do this to yourself, hm?"

"How long are you going to spend with your hand because Zoe isn't ready to even kiss you yet?" I asked back.

He canted his head as if it was a fair question. "I dunno, but I haven't gotten there yet. But you? Hot, you've been chasing that girl since she was a fumbling idiot. At some point, it's going to be too much, isn't it?"

"No."

"You sure about that? Everyone has a limit."

I licked my lips, wanting to look anywhere but at his face. "I don't with her, Shawn. I'm fucking serious here. Jericho? She's my everything. She's..."

"Completely neurotic, hyperfocused, with no sense of self-preservation, and always ready to rush in before even pausing to think about things. Sound about right?"

Finally, I looked over and met his eyes. "Yeah, it's also called perfect, so fuck off."

I watched as his lids narrowed and he judged my answer. Absentmindedly, he reached up to adjust his glasses, then finally smiled. Between one second and the next, Jinxy's entire demeanor changed. My friend moved to my side, slapped me on the shoulder, and got me walking again.

"She's right, you know."

That was not at all what I'd expected him to say. Confused, I looked over to find him smirking at me. This fucker was even crazier in person than he was online, and online he was kinda nutso.

"About KoG?" I asked.

"Mhm," he agreed. "You're right too. We do need to wait. We need to let the feds get the fuck out of our way, but the stragglers? The KoG fuckers who are too little for the government to worry about? They still hurt people. They abused women. They ruined careers. They broke up relationships, terrorized people, and who knows what else. They are not innocent."

"Not by a long shot," I agreed.

"And what is Ruin if not the group who should clean it all up?" Jinxy asked.

"Not worried about your record anymore?"

"Nope," he said. "After last weekend, I'm either busted or I'm not. I figure if I'm going down, then I don't want to be remembered as the dumb shit who couldn't even hack a phone. I want to be the guy who puts the Pentagon's budget out there or something. You know, something big."

"Something like being the bounty hunters of the internet?" I asked.

He murmured thoughtfully. "Bigger, Hottie."

I tossed up my hands. "What is the deal with everyone calling me Hottie lately?"

"Uh, the girls do?" Jinxy replied, sounding a little confused.

"Yeah, but you're doing it now, and so's Ripper. I mean, Knock thinks it's funny, but even Cade has shifted from Hot to Hottie."

"Just accept you're a hottie, bro," Jinxy said with a shrug. "Dude, I seriously don't know. I think it started over the summer, when we all got together. I mean, hearing Jeri say it so much, it just started to slip out. Now you're stuck with it."

"Could be worse," I admitted. "I'm still going to be HotShot online, though. I mean, hunting KoG members? Yeah, Hottie is not a name that strikes fear in the hearts of incel fuckheads."

"So we're gonna do it?" he asked.

I nodded. "I think we have to. Jeri wants to fuck them up. That means I'll help her. I will *always* help her."

"I want to be their Ruin," Jinxy said. "I want to destroy anyone who thinks they can use *our* internet to hurt little girls, to brag about their conquests, or to send any more dick pics."

"Get a lot of dick pics?" I teased.

He shrugged. "Nope, but I've already pulled three out of Zoe's forum inbox. Jeri handles her own, but your girl is a mean bitch."

"Yeah," I said, dropping my eyes to watch the sidewalk passing under my feet. "She is, Shawn. She's exactly what she needs to be, but it kinda feels like..." I sighed. "I dunno."

"What?" he pressed.

I pulled in a breath, then decided to simply drop it out there. "It feels like she's cracking. Like she learned how to be hard, but she never learned how to bend. Man, she fell in love with these guys - "

"And you," he broke in.

I waved that off. "We've kinda been in love for a while. We just didn't use that word. But these guys of hers? They changed something."

"A good change or a bad one?"

All I could do was shrug. "I don't know. What I do know is she's scared. The girl who always ran off half-cocked, so sure she could handle everything, is scared. It's like she's realized she has something she can lose, you know?"

"Which means she really doesn't want to lose it," he pointed out. "So, Grayson, let's make sure she never has to. I mean, if you're down with this insanity of a polycule thing we're doing."

I nodded, because I was. Shit, I hadn't expected to be, but I actually was ok with her having these other boyfriends. For Jeri, it just worked. For me, it meant a little space without always being so worried she was going to disappear.

No. That was me lying to myself. Space to breathe without worrying she would kill herself. My girlfriend was still a teenager, and while she was one of the strongest, smartest, and most driven people I knew, she wasn't impervious.

Her entire life had been a storm of shit, just one fucked-up thing after another. Stronger people than her had been broken by such things. So yes, I was terrified she'd leave me. I was scared to death that the last person I loved would give up on me when I needed her most. I also knew her guys helped make sure it didn't happen.

"You just got quiet," Jinxy said.

"Jeri is too much for one man," I finally said. "She needs all of us, and you know what? I think I need those guys just as much. I mean, look at us, Jinxy! Ruin is a work of art. Knock's idea to make this a polycule? It's actually fucking working, and I don't just mean for her."

"Kinda works for me too," Jinxy admitted. "And, since we're partners and all, it means I wasn't even lying when I chased off that girl in class."

Which was enough to finally let me laugh. "Yeah, but now we'll have to spend the rest of the semester holding hands or something."

"I'm so down for it," he swore. "But only on one condition?"

I was almost too scared to ask. "What's that?"

"Maybe you can chase girls away from me too? I mean, so Zoe never has to worry?"

So I tossed my arm around his waist and pulled him up against my side. "Baby, we're going to be the cutest couple on campus. Promise. Besides, we're totally cute enough to pull off the gay thing, right?"

"You know it," he lisped back. But what he didn't do was pull away.

Because it didn't matter. It wasn't weird. This? It was what made us stronger, and I fucking liked it. When Jinxy dropped his arm over my shoulders, I was pretty sure he even agreed.

# CHAPTER 8

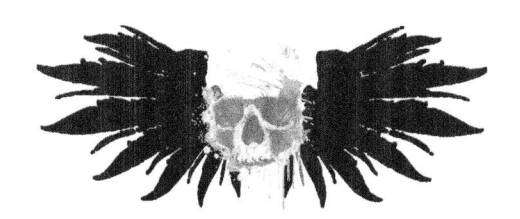

**SPECIAL AGENT JASON RAIGE**

Crysis had a new vest. This one wasn't orange. No, it was dark blue and had the FBI's crest on both sides. It marked him as a federal service animal. Alex had made sure my new "partner" would never need to be away from my side again, thanks to Bradley's nagging.

So when we arrived in Dallas and stepped off the plane, my dog got all the funny looks. He was thrilled with it. To him, any attention was good attention. To me, the press of people in this place had me hyper-aware, my eyes jumping around following movement.

I barely made it out of the arrival area before a dark-skinned woman in a suit fell in beside me. She didn't try to make some friendly greeting. She simply pointed to the exit she was aiming for. I nodded, aware we'd likely get stopped at least once before leaving this place. The bulges under our suits tended to have that effect.

"You look good in a suit," Alex said as she flashed her badge at a pair of TSA agents.

I grunted. "My wife thinks I look better in jeans."

"And how is Zara?"

That earned her a hum as we moved to get our luggage from the carousel. Her bag came around first. Mine was almost a full revolution behind it. Once we had those, she gestured again, and I followed her lead, keeping her at my right side. Crysis trotted along on my left.

"She's good," I said when we left the building and stepped into the oppressive Texas heat.

Damn, but this place liked to hold onto summer as long as possible. At least it was the dry kind, not filled with humidity. In many ways, it reminded me of the Middle East.

"Good doesn't tell me much," Alex taunted, but her eyes had already moved to a pair of dark SUVs parked against the curb.

"Deputy Director," a man said, stepping forward with his hand out. "Welcome to Dallas. If the field office can help you in any way..."

"We'll just need the use of the vehicle for the weekend," she assured him. "Thank you for making this easy for us."

"Yes, ma'am," the agent said, but his eyes drifted to my dog.

"He's certified," I grumbled.

"And makes you recognizable," Alex explained. "Jason, between the shooting in Sanger, the takedown of KoG, and your other shots? I'm guessing 'the sniper with the service dog' is not going to fit anyone else."

"Not a sniper anymore," I reminded her.

"Sure you are," she said. "Just not one for hire." Then she gestured to the closest SUV. "Thank you, gentlemen. I'll let you know when we're done with it. Try not to work too hard this week, ok? I really don't want to be dragged away from my pet project."

"Yes, ma'am!" the agent said crisply, making me think he'd done a few years in the military.

But I opened the back door and let my dog in. Crysis was already starting to pant in this heat. Luckily, the SUV had been left running, so it was cool inside. Groaning in satisfaction, the spoiled mutt flopped down on the expensive leather and let the air blow right on his belly.

Chuckling at his antics, I took my place in the passenger seat. I wasn't really surprised Alex wanted to drive. She seemed the kind who liked to be in control. I was the kind who preferred to have time to think, so this worked for me. At least it did until she made it out of the crazy airport spiral roads and onto the main highway.

"So," she said, "what does your wife really think of your assignment, Jason?"

My eyes were on the buildings we were passing, but a little smile touched my lips. "Well, she asked me what the fuck my bosses were doing this time, and when I told her you'd sweetened the offer, she was ready to play the devil's advocate."

"I like her already," Alex teased.

"Me too," I agreed. "Yet when I said you wanted me to work with Ruin? I got beat with a pillow, chased around the house, and ultimately thrown in bed because it's not fair that she can't tell them until we do."

That was enough to make Alex actually laugh out loud, and it was a nice sound. Calm, like she was used to it. I glanced over to see the woman's eyes sparkling and nothing but honest mirth on her face.

"The two of you work," she said. "You know, quite a few of your superiors were convinced this was some complication. Either she was blackmailing you, the pair of you were involved in something illegal, or some other reason for it to be a fake marriage."

"Because it was fast." I shrugged that off. "It was. It also worked for us."

"I made it very clear that after seeing the pair of you together, I have no doubts about the marriage, your happiness, or that this is the sort of pairing which will last through the hard stuff."

"Because we already have," I admitted.

"And you will again," she assured me. "Jason, sometimes the hard things are getting the wrong anniversary present. Maybe it's fighting over how to discipline the kid. Not all 'hard things' have to be seen through a scope, you know."

"But the worst ones are." I reached back just as Crysis began to whine.

"And that is why I'm taking you off the rotation," she said. "You are one lethal motherfucker, Jason, and you have skills the Bureau desperately needs, but you are not ok."

"No, I'm not." I shifted my hand so I could rub my dog's head. "But I'm getting better."

"And I think this group will make you even better," she said. "My gut tells me that pulling you away from all of this would do more harm than good. You actually want to help people. You just don't necessarily like the rules you have to follow with this job. Am I close?"

"Close enough," I admitted.

She hummed at that. "So, very close. Well, my hope is you can teach these hackers how to fake it well enough to make a case that will stick. I won't poke too hard if your team doesn't make the issues too obvious. Deal?"

"I think I can agree to that."

"Good." She put on her blinker and shifted over a lane. "So, the basic background checks have all of them attending the University of North Texas. Do we want to have them meet in a central location, or do you want to do this individually?"

"It's a house," I told her. "A very big, very nice house."

"A house?" she asked, clearly not following.

"Logan bought them a house," I explained. "He can afford it, and they need to stay together, so he made sure of it. All seven of them, Alex. Roommates." I chuckled. "It's a pretty nice neighborhood too."

"Your hacktivist group lives in a house, together, and don't think they'll get tracked?"

"Because they won't," I promised. "They're good, Alex. That's why you want them. They know not to shit where they eat, so they will never track their work back to their home. Their place is also locked down better than the government. I can't find it unless I'm invited in."

"Which says a lot," she breathed. "Ok. Give me the address." I typed it into the dash GPS while she kept talking. "So how many of them did I meet at F5?"

"Just two." Once I had the location right, I clicked to activate the GPS. "Bradley met more at the Dallas convention, so they know him."

"And you think that will matter?"

The SUV's speakers began explaining how much longer we'd be on this road, so I leaned back, reclining my chair a bit. When the synthetic voice finally stopped, I decided to just lay it all out there.

"I think Ruin is not what you're going to expect. I think they range from openly hostile to so sweet you'd never know they aren't giving you everything. I think their mess works for them, it makes them stronger, and these kids have the sort of talent the Bureau will never be able to draw in on its own. See, once they get their degrees, you won't be able to afford them."

"Better than you?" she asked.

"They will be," I promised. "Considering they're between eighteen and twenty-two? Yeah. They'll be a shit-ton better than me." Then I looked over to see her profile. "They're also serious. They aren't fucking around for the lulz."

"The what?"

I grunted. "Internet slang for laughs. Alex, these kids are on a mission. They're all fucked up in some way, so they want to make sure they help others. Knock's parents kicked him out. He landed with Logan and Riley, came out as bisexual, and was in the right place to find himself. He did, and now he's a powerhouse with a computer. Cade? His dad kicked him out, tried to kill him in the process, and the kid was taken in by Logan and Riley. Yes, Knock and Cade are a thing."

"And a cute thing," she assured me. "Saw that last weekend."

"Well, but they're with Jericho. That girl?" I sighed. "She's a fucking dumpster fire. Her brother died when she was in middle school. Her mom lost it and went for treatment. Her dad stuck around until mom got out, then offed himself." I grimaced. "I mean died by suicide."

"Shit," Alex breathed.

"And a guy in her game took her in under his wing. He was her big brother's best friend, so he mentored her. Well, he got engaged. KoG bullied his fiancée until she also died by suicide. The pair of them leaned on each other, and another guy they gamed with helped. That guy? He was busted for hacking as a kid - and wasn't good at it. He entered a teen rehabilitation program that obeys the rules about as well as I do. So by the time he got out, he was a good hacker. Also a gaming addict."

"I see a theme here," she teased.

Which actually made me smile. "Games, the bastion for the unwanted. But that hacker? He's dating the girl who was raped. We busted her rapist for distributing child porn."

"Funny how that worked out so well," Alex pointed out.

"Sure is," I agreed. "And then there's Ripper. He was bullied at school, so probably the most stable of the group."

"Just bullied," she grumbled. "Fuck, Jason. I mean, I'm not surprised. Hackers all tend to have some pretty tragic pasts, don't they?"

"Some reason to seek out the internet for solace," I admitted. "So yeah, loneliness is pretty common. Desperation, wanting to prove themselves. All of that."

"But you think they can do this?"

I nodded, never taking my eyes off the road before us, even as she moved over to take an exit. "I do. I think that if you'd offered me anyone else, I would've refused. Alex, I think this group can actually make a difference, and they actually *want* to."

"Good," she said. "Because this isn't going to be easy."

But she didn't bother explaining. Instead, she got caught up with merging and following the directions through a rather large and bustling college town. I found myself scanning the landmarks we passed, trying to familiarize myself. I'd be coming back this way often if they accepted the offer.

Who was I kidding? Of course they would. They'd pushed to be confidential informants because they wanted to *help*. Not be heroes. Not get recognition. These kids wanted to stop the bad guys, just like I did. They wanted to save the victims.

Yet when Alex turned down a quiet road, I found myself checking the GPS to make sure we were going the right way. For a while, there was nothing but empty land, and then the neighborhood began to appear. Massive houses. Fancy cars. This was the high-end section of town, evidently.

"And I'm going to guess that's it," Alex said, tipping her head at the house with all the cars in front of it.

"The beater truck is Ripper's, so yeah," I agreed.

She pulled up at the curb, and the pair of us got out. I hadn't been allowed to tell them we were coming. Alex didn't want any information about this program to be shared, and hackers? They were known to record things. That meant this was definitely going to be a surprise. I just hoped it was a good one.

Crysis hopped out and moved to my side. I didn't bother with his leash, though. Yet as we walked across the lawn, I could feel eyes on me. Curious, I turned around to see the neighbor across the street peeking through their window. To the right, someone stepped outside to look over. Down a few houses, more curtains were moving.

It seemed our big black SUV had been noticed. I couldn't be sure if that was the government plates or simply the stereotype. Either way, I realized Logan had given these kids one more line of defense. Nosy neighbors meant witnesses. Witnesses meant convictions. So if anyone ever came at these kids the way they'd come at Riley, the cops would be here before shots could be fired.

It seemed my friends learned quickly.

# CHAPTER 9

## ZOE

I liked the study. Hottie's brown leather sofa was amazingly comfortable. The coffee table was massive, which meant I had room for my books. The best part, though, was that the room was small enough it felt quiet without being eerily silent.

It was Friday, so I'd made it through my first week of college, and now I wanted to get ahead of the game. So, sitting on the floor with the sofa as my backrest, I had my legs stuck through the bottom of the coffee table, and I was currently color-coding my notes. Anything I couldn't read, I rewrote while I still remembered it. Before my first test, I'd copy all of this again, making it pretty, and memorizing it in the process.

I'd just pulled out the highlighters when someone rapped at the front door. Confused, I looked out the window, but couldn't see anything. Then again, the drive was filled with our cars. Maybe it was one of the neighbors?

Climbing to my feet, I headed for the door. It was a heavy wooden thing, and the only windows were at the top. No peephole. So, unlocking the deadbolt, I carefully pulled it open and peeked through the gap left by the chain.

"Can I help you?" I asked, seeing a pair of people in suits.

Probably religious recruiters or something. This was Texas, so we didn't get all kinds, but the Church of Christ and the Baptist churches often sent people around. I half expected to be handed a pamphlet and offered a prayer. Instead, the Black woman smiled kindly and lifted up a slim little wallet.

The bottom flopped down and three letters were easily visible, even through the tiny gap: FBI. My heart dropped. My mind immediately went back to Jinxy saying we were going to get busted. So, before she could even speak, I simply shook my head at her.

"No thank you." I closed the door and flipped the deadbolt, feeling my fingers tremble.

Then I took off running. My socks slid on the expensive tiles, but I didn't care. That was the FBI. One person would know how to deal with this. When I reached the war room, I caught the door frame and pulled myself in without slowing.

"Knock, call Logan!" I gasped. "The cops are here!"

"What?" Jeri hissed.

"Where?" Cade asked.

"Two of them," I said, pointing back at the front door. "They just knocked. I, uh, closed the door."

"Which is the right call, Zoe," Knock promised even as he pulled out his phone and dialed.

"Shut it down," Jeri snapped. "Everything, Cade. Even the damned router!"

"Got the router!" I said, heading for the back, because that was where we kept the router.

Evidently, Ripper had heard the commotion, because he'd paused his show. "Zoe?" he asked.

"Cops," I said. "I'm killing the router."

"I'll get the guys," he promised before taking off and heading upstairs.

Seconds. That was all it had taken, but the house was now quiet in a weird sort of way. I could hear people moving. Fuck, all of us were, but the music, the games, and everything else we used for entertainment all came with our internet connection.

But shutting down the router would take a little more than simply turning off the power. Once the thing was down, I began unplugging all the cords, moved this one to the side, then pulled out the nice and safe backup that came with our ISP. The one that had a clean history in its memory.

Then I hit the stairs, not stopping until I made it up to my room. If they had a warrant, we were so fucked. Then again, if we took a while, that would give Logan time to get here. Damn, I really didn't want to destroy this thing, but Jinxy had said it would give proof of every MAC address we owned. Anything we used would be stored here, which was why we had the super-locked-down secured version.

Yeah, and I was pretty sure they'd done something to it, but that was pretty par for the course. So when I reached my room, I moved a few books, tucked the router behind it, and then pushed a stuffed animal over all of it. Not perfect, but good enough.

But on my way back downstairs, I met Ripper, Hottie, and Jinxy on the balcony on the second floor. They were huddled close, their voices down, and all three of them looked worried.

"I'm sure Logan's being called," Ripper was assuring them.

"He is," I promised. "Router's in my room. Dummy's hooked up. I guess we should put on some music or something to look normal?"

"Have they tried knocking again?" Jinxy asked.

I shook my head. "I don't really know. I kinda bolted."

"Which means we might be ignoring them."

Snarling out a string of curses, Jinxy headed into the guest room, leaving the door open behind him. He also wasn't in there long. Only a few seconds later, he came back.

"There's one dark SUV out front. What exactly did you see, Zoe?"

"Black woman, FBI badge," I explained. "I politely declined as if talking to a solicitor and shut the door before she could say anything."

"Nice," Hottie purred. "I think you trained her well, Jinxy."

"You know it," Jinxy agreed. "But that's good. First, it's not the cops, it's the feds. It also means they're either going to start hitting the doorbell or will come back later. They might call for backup, but since our hacking didn't start here, I doubt it."

"So what do we do?" I asked.

"We talk to Knock," Hottie said. "Logan will give him a game plan, so let's stick to that."

Together, the three of us headed back downstairs. There, Knock was still on the phone. Jeri and Cade had all the computers powered down. The power strip that ran them was now missing. Considering it was an extension cord that ran from the wall, its absence was noticeable.

"Plan?" Jinxy asked.

"Logan's on his way," Knock said before gesturing to Jeri.

So she took over. "Computers are still being set up," she explained. "Extension cord is in the dining room now. We just moved in, haven't done anything, and will not be answering any questions."

"Pretty sure it's not a good idea to keep the feds waiting, though," Jinxy pointed out.

"No, but talking to my attorney first is," Knock said.

"And we look guilty as fuck," Cade said. "Hottie, put on some music. Someone make the TV go. I don't even care what. We need to look confused, not like accessories to whatever."

"Got it," Hottie said, heading for the back.

Then a dog barked.

That made Hottie stop. Knock turned towards the front door with a surprised look on his face. I was confused, because I didn't think our closest neighbors had a dog that sounded so big. The one to the left had a little yappy thing.

"Oh, shit," Knock laughed, heading for the front door. "Zoe, who did you see?"

"Uh..." I trailed behind him. "A Black woman."

"Alone?"

"No, there was a man too."

Now Knock was chuckling. Without explaining, he flipped the deadbolt, pulled off the chain, and opened the door to show the woman, looking completely confused. Behind her, the man was bent over, laughing so hard he could barely breathe. Beside him, a brindle-and-white spotted dog was doing his best to lick the guy's face and hands.

"Hello, Alex," Knock said. Then he looked back into the house. "Guys, it's cool. Just Cyn!"

"What?" I asked.

And the man finally pushed himself up straight, but there was dampness in his eyes. His strange, silvery-green eyes. Dancing ones which sparkled deviously.

"No thank you!" he tittered. "Oh my god." Another laugh slipped out. "Zoe, that was perfect."

"Uh..." I was so fucking confused.

So he offered his hand. "Special Agent Jason Raige. You know me best as Cyn or Cynister." I took his hand and gripped politely, but I felt like someone was playing a joke on me. "And this," he went on, "is the Deputy Director of the FBI, Alex Watts."

"Jeff," she greeted him.

"Knock," he corrected. "I really go by that to my friends."

"Fits him better," I agreed.

The woman turned her attention on me. "So, may we come in now?"

"You have to do the whole thing, Alex," Jason teased.

Sighing, the woman showed her badge again. "I'm Deputy Director Alex Watts, with the FBI, and I'd like to come in and speak to you about an opportunity."

I laughed once, because that was *not* what I'd expected her to say.

Knock merely looked over at the man. "And you were going to let her try *that?*"

"Bro, she's my boss. I didn't ask what her plan was. I just agreed to come and share my opinions."

"Because that sucks," Knock told her. "Seriously. Not the best way to approach a hacker's house, Alex, but come in."

"Really?" I asked.

"She was there," he explained. "Zoe, she put my friend in a vest. She trusted us."

"I also kept the brass from stopping them," the woman explained. "And now I'm here to beg a bit."

"Sounds like a house meeting." Knock gestured down the hall. "I think we need the living room, because the others are too small."

"Small?" Jason asked.

"Small," Knock repeated. "Logan's coming and Riley's driving, so yeah. Small."

As Knock led our new guests through the house, he pointed out the rooms. I followed behind, feeling like I was stuck in a dream. Not necessarily a bad one, but one of those confusing types where two things were true at the same time.

This was Cynister? He was the crazy hacker freak who'd helped us catch Evan? The man was nothing at all like I'd expected, and yet everything. He was kinda short. Definitely under six feet. His build wasn't all buff like Hottie, but he wasn't lean like Jinxy either. He was more like Knock, I realized. A bit lighter than Cade.

The woman, on the other hand, was definitely the professional type. Her boots were stylish, the heel just tall enough to count as dressy, but wide enough she'd be able to run in them. Her suit was cut and tailored, the fabric was definitely expensive, and yet her hair was pulled back into a boring low ponytail. She was a mix of executive and pure functionality that actually worked well. I was impressed.

When we made it to the back of the house, Knock gestured for them both to sit. Cade lifted a hand in greeting, clearly recognizing them. The rest of us didn't. So, Knock began introductions. He listed off each of our real names and our game handles. When he was done, he once again named Alex and Jason, offering both their FBI ranks and Jason's more common name, Cynister.

But Jinxy decided to face this head on. "So are we in shit for last weekend?" he asked.

"Nope," Jason said.

Alex lifted a hand, begging for the chance to speak. "The report I filed with the Bureau makes it clear I authorized Jason's use of his confidential informants to rescue the hostages before any harm could come to them. The group known as Ruin did exactly that, finding not only the location, but also other necessary information which allowed our sniper to close the case."

"Kill Soul Reaper," Jason clarified.

"And save Braden," Cade added.

"Mm, that too," Jason agreed. "Plus the girls."

"Yeah, but you were going to do that anyway," Knock said.

"True," Jason admitted, a little smile touching one side of his mouth.

But his eyes had just changed. The sparkle I'd seen earlier had frozen in them, turning cold. Like this, I could believe he was a killer, but it seemed he was a lot more than that. This was the man who'd saved me. He was the guy who'd made sure my rapist not only went to jail, but would stay there.

So, not caring about the thousand-mile stare he had, I moved closer so I was standing right before him. "Cyn?" I grunted. "I mean, Agent Raige?"

"Jason works," he assured me.

I nodded to show I'd heard. "Um, thank you. I mean, really. Thank you. You... Evan..."

He pushed to his feet and wrapped his arms around my shoulders, hugging me the way I really wanted to hug him. "You did that, Zoe," he said softly. "You made sure he can't hurt you - or anyone else. I just called someone to pick him up."

"But you were there when everyone else was trying to tell me it didn't matter," I explained. "Not my friends, I mean, but like the cops."

Standing before me like this, I could see it when he swallowed hard. "Zoe..."

"You made a difference, Jason," I insisted. "You helped me, so thank you."

"Fuck," he grumbled before pulling me back in for another hug. "You're welcome, Zoe. Thank you for reminding me why I do this."

And beside him, Alex leaned back. "Cade, can I have a beer? I'm pretty sure you have some in the fridge."

"Yep," Cade said. "Jason?"

"Coffee," Knock said. "He'll want coffee. Crysis probably wants a bowl of water."

"On it!" Cade promised.

"How long until Logan gets here?" Alex asked as Jason sat back down.

"Fifteen minutes," Knock said. "Maybe less. I mean, Riley's driving."

"So sit down and tell me about your classes," Alex said, "because I'm not dumb enough to think any of you will say a damned thing without your attorney present. Kinda why I'm here."

# CHAPTER 10

### KNOCK

Ten minutes. That was how long it took for Riley to get from her place to ours. I didn't even want to think about how fast she'd been going on the backroads, but when Logan's car pulled up with my crazy-ass big sister behind the wheel, I had a feeling the proper word was "very."

I'd texted them to make sure they knew it wasn't an emergency anymore. That didn't matter. Riley probably enjoyed the excuse to put Logan's sports car to the test. But when they walked in without knocking, I realized my chosen family was still a little worried.

"Everything good, Knock?" Logan asked.

"Alex and Cyn. Zoe didn't recognize them so we pulled out lockdown procedures."

"Which includes calling us," Riley realized.

I nodded in agreement. "Exactly. And now, Alex says we'll want our attorney for the rest of this conversation, so..." I led them towards the back.

"Love what you did to the place," Riley said, gawking as she passed.

But when she reached the formal dining room, a true laugh slipped out. "Ok, that's perfect."

"War room," I explained, and then pointed to the little study. "Private dining room."

"Date room," Cade corrected from where he was sitting on the couch by Jeri.

But I paused, because they weren't alone. Pushed between Jeri's knees was Crysis, Jason's PTSD dog. He kept pushing and scooting, begging for more petting. It wasn't too bad, but it was the same way he reacted when Zara got nervous, or when anyone was stressing out around him.

Confused, I glanced over to Jason, but he shook his head subtly. Yeah, he'd noticed too. Well, ok then.

"Alex!" Logan said as he headed over to offer his hand.

"Logan," she greeted him. "And Riley. Nice to see both of you again. Sit. I have something to bring up with your clients."

They sat. I sat. Jinxy and Hottie sat on the hearth of the fireplace, and all the furniture was packed, but we had just enough room for this crowd. The real question was why she and Jason had come all this way without even a heads-up.

"You're probably wondering why we didn't arrange a meeting," Alex said, echoing my thoughts. "It's because this offer doesn't officially exist yet. The program doesn't either."

Beside her, Jason said nothing. The man merely picked at his thumbnail, making me think he knew all of this.

"So you want non-disclosure agreements before we talk?" Logan asked.

Alex waved him down. "I wanted to make sure there's no proof that could be used against me later. No recordings, no copies of emails, or anything like that."

"Valid," I muttered.

Which made her chuckle. "I also know an NDA wouldn't stop any of you from sharing this if you really wanted to, so I'm cutting to the chase. Due to the events last weekend, I received a promotion. I am now the Deputy Director of the FBI."

"How high is that?" Riley asked.

"Second in charge," Jason explained. "Director is the only one above her now."

"Damn," Jinxy muttered.

"This promotion happened because I closed a case which was making national news," she explained. "It seems a group of gamers and game developers have a lot more reach than the politicians in D.C. expected. Things were just starting to get uncomfortable for them when the members of Ruin helped my agent fix everything."

"Kill Soul Reaper," Jason muttered. "Don't sanitize it."

"That's not how the Bureau sees it," Alex corrected. "Nor the President. This was a problem that is now fixed. So, because of that, I get a nice little boon. They want me to make a stamp on the Bureau to show how differently I'd do things. To show the Bureau is progressing with the times. I asked for a dedicated internet task force. One made of cybersecurity specialists with unconventional skills, headed by a coordinating agent. My example was based off the early operations of departments like the BAU."

"Serial killer hunters," Zoe said. "I watched Criminal Minds."

"Which isn't completely accurate," Alex assured her. "But it's close enough. Still, the idea is that while we can't hire the computer specialists we need - because of governmental restrictions, low pay, and other problems - we can contract people to assist. These people are consultants. They are required to pass specific requirements, are given access to FBI buildings, and have some law enforcement credentials for things such as filing cases."

Logan lifted a hand. "Lay it out, Alex. Their eyes are glazing over."

"I want to hire hackers to work with a handler. These hackers will hunt down the assholes online who are currently getting away with shit because our laws haven't caught up to our technology."

"The Wild West," Jason said softly.

But Jeri's head snapped up. "What? You want to turn us loose?"

"I do," Alex said. "I want to make you Jason's partners. I want you to become his team. I'd like for the..." She paused to count. "Seven of you to become the test team to prove to the congressional committee that this can work."

"Which means," Riley broke in, "it's not greenlit yet."

Yeah, and that was going to be a problem. No wonder she'd come here in person. If this was still controversial in her circles, then any proof of her recruiting us could blow up in her face.

"Not completely," Alex admitted. "There are concerns about national security, governmental budgets, and more. The biggest thing holding us back is the concern that what I want to do isn't possible."

"And what do *you* want to do?" Jeri asked.

"Make sure fuckers like Soul Reaper never hurt anyone else," Alex almost growled. "The next time someone is stalked online, kidnapped, and tortured, I want to make sure we can find them before they're killed. The next time a woman's nudes are leaked, I want the one who took them to be sitting behind bars for theft - among other things. I want to use the laws we have now, but with a team who can actually put together a case, get me proof of it, and move without being seen."

"Us?" Ripper asked.

Alex nodded slowly. "I looked through the dozens of reports after F5. A group of women - " She paused to look over at Riley and nod in acknowledgement. " - were kidnapped from a secure hotel room, on a secure floor, and removed from the building in a way that left no video evidence."

"And they knew what they were doing," Riley growled.

"Yes, they did," Alex agreed. "That's the type of situation where we typically end up recovering bodies. Instead, one smartwatch and five hackers were enough to change the outcome. A group of professional gamers secured enough evidence for us to prosecute the surviving perpetrators. A heads-up prevented the swatting distraction from causing casualties." Alex leaned forward. "Geeks. A group of geeks that

I know all of you still have access to and will use if you need to. That's how I got a promotion to the second in charge of the FBI, and now I want to make sure we can *do* something about the crimes that are being committed online."

Holy shit. This? It was the chance of a lifetime, so why was I braced? And yet, when I looked across the room at my friends, they were just as stoic-looking as I felt. None of us were happy, even though this would be amazing. We all knew there had to be a catch, I supposed.

"We focus on crimes against women," Hottie said. "We're not going to be your jack-of-all-trades type of hackers."

I grunted at that, because he had a point. "It's our specialty, Alex. That's why we were tracking KoG."

"And a large percentage of the crimes online are against women," she countered. "Human trafficking, harassment, assault, stalking. C'mon, we all know our digital footprint is one of the many ways women are targeted. Doesn't matter if it starts on a dating app or at a library. From facial recognition to hacking phones, people aren't safe because no one knows what to *do* with these crimes."

She was right. I knew she was right. We'd all said something similar at some point when trying to deal with the assholes at school. Because things were online, they were dismissed much too easily. It wasn't harassment if it wasn't in person. It wasn't stalking if it wasn't in person. I called bullshit on all of it.

"Thoughts?" I asked the group. "Questions?"

"Limitations," Jinxy said.

And while that wasn't exactly a question, it was definitely a good point. If Alex wanted us to do this, we wouldn't get very far if our hands were tied.

"The members of Ruin will need to pass certain qualifications for the FBI," Alex said. "Gun certifications, law enforcement basic knowledge testing, and a psychological evaluation. That will need to happen in order for this program to be approved."

"And then?" Jinxy pressed. "You're asking us to bust our asses, and for what? If we get these certifications, what will that allow us to do?"

"To start with," she explained, "you will pick your own cases."

"No, no, no," I said, breaking in. "Alex, Jinxy has a point. You want us to do all of this without even a program to go into? How does that work? What happens if this gets canceled before we can start?"

"It gets canceled if you don't do this," Jason said. "Look, she has to deal with the suits in D.C. Don't worry about that. If you want to have unlimited access to do what you're going to be doing anyway, then you need this." He turned his strange eyes on each of us in turn. "This is how we help people. This is what I've been needing since Soul Reaper first attacked Dez. *This* is how we prevent another version of him from getting as powerful!"

"Even if it's not guaranteed?" Cade asked.

Jason laughed once, the sound dry. "Has any of this been guaranteed?"

"Good point," Cade relented.

"Ok," Jinxy said. "So what cases will we be used for?"

"At this time," Alex said, "the Bureau doesn't even know what to do with a team like you, so I'll trust you to create good examples of what crimes can be stopped and how cases can be made. The truth is you're going to see more than we will. You're the ones on the inside, so I'm going to follow your lead, and I'm including Jason in that."

"She saw the file for Alpha Team," Jason told us. "I made sure she knew you did it while I was 'unavailable.'"

"Pulled," Riley grumbled.

"Working on another case," Jason reminded her. Then, under his breath, he added, "Fucking credit card readers."

"But what are the limits?" Jericho pressed. "You're talking all around it, but it's the thing that will get us to open up."

Alex just sighed. "Right now, I simply want all of you to get certified. If we can prove you're competent enough to pass the restrictions, then we can move to the next step."

"And why would we do that?" I asked, seeing the one thing my friends were missing. "Why are we going to show our hand - to the feds, of all people - and then just shrug it off if it doesn't work?"

"Knock, you've already shown your hand," she countered. "Your confidential informant agreements make it clear that all of you are hackers."

"Minor cyber vandalism," Cade countered. "Rookie stuff, Alex. Not like what they did last weekend. Nothing compared to what we can do when we try."

Which made Alex look over at Jason. He simply nodded. "They are that good - and they're only getting better. Pretty sure all of them are getting degrees in fucking up the world."

"Or hacking," I said. "I mean, the University of North Texas calls it things like Cybersecurity and Computer Sciences. We call it useful information."

"So spill," Zoe said.

"The Senate oversight committee hasn't agreed to this yet," Alex told us. "They keep trying to add on more criteria, shorter timeframes for certifications, and so on. They're playing politics, and I'm trying to save lives, so I need a group I can trust to ignore their bullshit and push through. I need someone who wants to *fix shit*."

"What kind of bullshit?" Riley asked.

Alex sighed. "Typical politics. The problem is this team I'm designing? Hell, this entire division? It's going to shake things up. This will not be easy. From the agents in the Bureau to the police you'll work with to the politicians trying to get re-elected, people will resist it, because change is terrifying."

"And," Jason said calmly, "from the sounds of it, this change is going to skip most of the common chain of command. It breaks rules. Consultants are supposed to be lesser than agents, but Alex is setting this up so you have a direct line to her. That means being the chosen ones. The special little snowflakes who got the easy break, or so they'll say."

"Don't fucking care," Cade grumbled.

Jeri hummed in agreement. "Fuck what others think."

"But that's going to make this hard," Hottie pointed out. "If the FBI is against us, the politicians are against us, and from the sounds of it, no one wants this but Alex? That's going to make this all but impossible."

Alex slapped her hand down on the arm of the loveseat. "Fuck impossible! Now is the time for impossible. As for limitations? The ones you'll be given and the ones I'll hold you to are not the same. Ask Jason if you don't believe me. He will be the agent you report to. He will report to Bradley, his former partner. Bradley will report to me, with no one else between us, so yes, skipping the normal chain of command. This is *my* pet project, people. I'm going to make this happen, one way or another, and I think Ruin is that way. This is something I've wanted to do for so long, but it's never been possible."

"Until now," Logan finished for her.

"Until them," Alex corrected. "Seven kids with no ties to anything to cause complications - like a triple-A gaming company. Seven intelligent and nearly spotless citizens who have the exact skills we need to shine a light into the dark web. Seven hackers with the skills to go toe-to-toe with anyone out there, or close."

"Close enough," Jeri grumbled.

"But right now," Alex continued, "this is a clusterfuck. I need to get this started. I need to reassign your chain-of-command. I need to make this even possible, which means getting all of you certified before they can stop us. I also need to make sure my proposal isn't rejected."

"And if it is?" Logan asked.

"Well, that's why the contract I brought has a complete immunity clause." She smiled. "Complete, Logan. No restriction on the classification of the crime. It's a get out of jail free card for all of them, and it will cover last weekend, in case their CI agreements don't."

"Because that wasn't minor cybercrimes," Jinxy said.

"Exactly," Alex agreed. "But I'm not holding this over your head. If you pass on my offer, I will find a way to wipe that away, because you got me promoted. I'm in your debt, Ruin. I know it. I think all of you know it too."

"But this is our chance," Jeri said softly.

With a whine, Crysis pushed into her lap.

"Pet his ears," Jason told her. "He likes that, and he's a spoiled mutt."

She did, and I watched as a tiny little smile began to appear on her face. Slowly, Jeri's shoulders relaxed. Then again, that was the dog's job. His entire purpose was to break the cycle of post-traumatic stress, to help people relax so they could deal with the anxiety and fear.

Yet she was right. Jeri might have her own personal reasons for wanting to do this, but she wasn't wrong. No, this wouldn't thwart her curse, but it was needed. It was also what we were good at. For me, the part about reporting to Jason sealed the deal. This man had been there when we needed him most. Now it was time to return the favor.

"I want to do it," I told the rest.

"What about school?" Zoe asked.

"Weekends to start," Alex said. "Jason will be flying down to handle your training, so this is part-time. Sadly, your pay will reflect that."

"Pay?" Ripper asked.

"What kind of pay?" Cade wanted to know.

"I'm authorized to offer each of you fifty thousand a year for this stage. Technically, it's compensation for being an informant. At least on paper."

Which made all of us share a look. Yeah, I made more than that from my gaming sponsorships, but adding on fifty more? That put me over the six-figure mark. For the rest, that was a pretty decent income!

"Cyn?" I asked. "Things to consider?"

"Busting your asses to make this work," he said. "Shooting guns, memorizing the rules for what you can and can't do as a consultant, and getting your shit together so you all pass the evals, knowing you'll be graded harder than most. It's work. It won't be easy."

"And then?" Hottie asked.

Jason turned his cold gaze on the man. "Then we get turned loose and show the world exactly what's going on right under their noses."

Logan sighed and leaned forward. "Ok. Let me see the contracts. Sounds like you won, Alex."

"Yes, it does, doesn't it?" she asked. "I also like the idea that this group? They'll help me put these idiot politicians in their place. They don't think we can do this. I think they're scared they might be wrong."

"So wrong," I said.

"Then prove it," Alex taunted.

# CHAPTER 11

### JERICHO

While Logan read over the contract Alex had for us, I got up and headed into the other room. I paused at the war room, but didn't stay. No, it was too close. I needed space to think. I needed a little distance. That meant the study would work.

Stepping into there let me see Zoe's books and notes still spread out. Her laptop was open, so I closed it. Taking a deep breath, I moved over to look out the window. Our driveway - and all the cars in it - was on one side. The front lawn took up most of the view, and the SUV Jason and Alex had come in was to the far right, parked in front of Ripper's truck.

"You ok?" Hottie asked, coming into the room behind me.

I glanced back to see Jinxy, Zoe, and Ripper behind him. The moment I nodded, the group made their way into the room. Knock and Cade came last, proving they'd been just around the corner. Clearly, I hadn't been the only one to need a moment.

"This feels like a trick," I admitted.

"It's not," Knock promised. "Jeri, Alex was there all last week. Well, most of it. She had Jason's back. He took the shots without permission because he needed to, so she claimed she'd authorized it. What you don't get is that he never should've been behind the scope."

"Why?" Zoe asked.

"Personal ties," Cade said. "His wife was one of the hostages. The others are his friends. That's going to skew his objectivity."

"But he's already not objective," Knock explained. "Alex knows that and doesn't care. Also, Crysis? He's here. Before, Jason wasn't allowed to have his dog with him as much because the dog stands out. Now, that dog is wearing an FBI vest. I'm willing to bet Alex had something to do with it."

"Shit, I didn't even notice that," Cade admitted. "Crysis had an orange vest in Vegas."

"Yep," Knock said.

I just waved them down. "So we can trust her?"

"As much as we do Bradley," Knock said. "Which is pretty far. Jason? He's one of us. The others are just trustworthy."

"Makes sense," Ripper said. "There's a difference between being one of us and one of our friends."

"Exactly!" Zoe agreed. "But friends still help. We also can't do everything alone - and maybe I'm missing something, but isn't that what we're being offered? The chance to actually do this, get paid to do this, and not get arrested for what we're going to do anyway?"

"So what's the 'but?'" I asked. "There's always one. The string attached to the deal, the downside, or whatever it is, there's always a catch."

"It's easy." The voice came from behind us, making us all turn.

There, Riley leaned against the archway which led into the room. Her synthetic dreads were vivid at the ends but black at the top. Her shirt had her game outfit's logo on it. Her shoes were the working kind, which meant she'd probably been in the barn when Knock had called.

"Ok?" I asked. "What's easy?"

"May I?" Riley asked. "I figure this is a private conversation, but while those three work out details and debate semantics, I thought I'd see what Ruin's thinking."

"Yeah, come in," I told her.

"So," she said, moving over to a bare spot on the wall and leaning against it. "For years, Jason couldn't close the case against the Kings of Gaming because he didn't have help. He couldn't admit to knowing us, couldn't use us, but still did. We had to bend ourselves in knots to keep it all looking official."

"Like when Jason was at my house and took a bullet in his vest so Riley wouldn't get hit in her head," Knock said. "Then she had to pretend she didn't recognize him."

"Yeah, like that," Riley said. "And killing him in tournaments, pretending to believe he delivered pizza, and more. But here's the thing. His hands were tied. Ours aren't, and yours? The group of you has no limits. Sometimes, having the answer gives us the path to finding it legally, and you're the means to find the answer."

"There's that," I agreed.

"Alex knows this," Riley went on. "She's now the second in charge of the FBI. That means she has some power. Ruin works well with Jason. There's an official chain of command, or custody, or whatever they call it. With your help, the FBI can close virtual cases, which have previously been ignored. It will make them look good."

"And?" I pressed. "What's the catch for *us*?"

"It's proving this program can work," Riley said. "Why do you think all these crimes get ignored? Because there's no sense wasting time and money on them, since they will never get convictions. It's always 'he said, she said' shit. Law enforcement has to follow rules. A hacktivist group does not."

"Still not sure of the catch," Zoe said.

Riley just chuckled. "Because you're looking at this from the wrong side. You're all so sure of your abilities that it's obvious to you. The people in power? They think it's impossible. Hackers are just out-of-control kids, right? That means you need to prove them wrong, and Alex wants you to be the test case. The prototype. The first ones. She picked you because she knows you work. And if you work, then the oversight committee she's talking about will be stupid to refuse this chance. It'll end up biting them in the asses, because it'd be ignoring national security or some shit."

"Wait," I begged. "You're saying the 'catch' is that we're blazing the trail for more hackers like us to get hired?"

"Ding, ding, ding, we have a winner," Riley teased. "Yeah, that's exactly what I'm saying. Blazing a trail through people who really like things to stay the same. People who are terrified of the implications this offer comes with. So this means all of you will have to work harder, will probably have more hoops to jump through, and will get more pushback than the next group. I also think you can do it."

"And if we do," Hottie said, leaning over his knees to clasp his hands before him, "it means we'll be able to make a difference, Jeri. We can stop them before they target the next Nina."

Nina was gone and KoG was in the process of being torn down, but I knew what he meant. There would be another group. There would be another victim. There would be someone else out there getting bullied, harassed, and stalked until they believed death was the only escape.

Yet we could change that. Us, a group of fuckups who'd stumbled into each other by chance. A group of hackers who worked together like a well-oiled machine. Friends, lovers, and everything else we were. It made us stronger. Hell, it made us unstoppable most days.

"The question," Riley went on, "is whether or not you're willing to deal with the bullshit to make this possible. And that bullshit could be anything from dragging up your pasts to trying to tear you down."

"Bullying?" I asked. "Really?"

"The adult and professional version," Riley clarified. "You know, things like how you don't have certifications for coding languages, or that you're just an overly emotional kid who feels unloved because her brother and father died. Things like getting kicked out, raped, surfing the foster system, and all the shit you'd rather not have dissected. Ways for them to show you aren't 'credible' enough."

"Fuck that," Zoe grumbled. "Let them talk about my rape. Everyone at school already did."

"And we made it through that," Ripper pointed out.

"It's not like I'm hiding my sexuality anymore," Cade said.

Knock just grunted. "Me either, but it'll still suck. When they hit us and keep hitting us, it's going to suck."

"And we aren't perfect," Jinxy said. "Not a single one of us."

"Shit," I muttered. "Jinxy, we're so far from perfect it's not even funny. We're basically the definitions of fuckups."

"Which is exactly why they'll come after you," Riley said. "The first time is always the hardest, Jeri, and this will be the first time for a program like this. It's when we figure out the pitfalls and find the mistakes to avoid. The first time is where the rules are made, and you'll be watched."

"We all will," Jinxy said. "So what happens if this is shut down? Does that mean our hacking days are over?"

Ripper scoffed. "We'd change the logo, get a new name, and use more layers of encryption. That's the whole point, Jinxy. They can't catch *us* - and they *know* we exist - so how the fuck can they catch the bad guys?"

"And I want to do this," Zoe said. "C'mon, y'all. You know you do too. You're just scared this is too good, so you're ready to back away from it. You're convinced it's a trap, and I'm sure it is, but the trap is getting us on their side."

"Whose?" Cade asked.

"The FBI's!" Zoe insisted. "It's like all those shows where the cops try to convince the criminals to help them. Cops don't know how to think like us, so they get stuck. Criminals don't know how to think any other way. So yeah. Of *course* they want our help. We know how to survive the internet. We know how to move, where to look, and can blend in. We're naturals at this, and the cops?"

"Feds," Knock corrected. "We're talking about the FBI, Zoe, not local cops."

"Whatever!" she huffed. "In order for them to be feds, they had to learn how to be feds, right? Years and years and years of being taught right from wrong. Legal from illegal. Police from civilian. Us? We wanna, so we do. We think about vulnerabilities in code and network security. We think about MAC addresses, IP addresses, and password difficulty. It's like we're not even speaking the same language, you know?"

"Shit," I breathed. "That's a good point."

Zoe sat up a little straighter. "It is?"

"No, I mean you're right," I told her. "But Riley's right too. I was coming at this from my perspective, not theirs. Cynister's the only person in law enforcement I've ever met who wasn't all about the rules. He's literally one of us, so I keep thinking of this as being too easy, but if he's the only person like us the entire FBI has?"

"And he is," Riley said. "Special Agent Jason Raige was a hacker as a teen. He got busted, lost computer privileges, and so joined the military. There, he worked up to special forces, ended up having to pick up tech on a mission when things went bad, and kept going because he was good at it. And no one tells the country's top unit that a member can't use a radio or laptop to complete their missions."

"He was special forces?" Hottie asked.

Riley nodded slowly. "Yep. Delta Force. The same people from Black Hawk Down, that movie. No, I don't think he was a part of that, but he was in the same level of badass. That's where he became a sniper. A good one."

"A fucked-up one," Jason said as he walked into view. "You telling my stories, Riley?"

"Mhm," she agreed. "Figured they need to know."

He nodded, then patted his leg. Immediately, Crysis was at his side, pushing his head under Jason's hand. For a little too long, Jason just stood there. Then he glanced over, found an empty spot on the floor, and sat. His dog was right there, pushing into his lap.

"I started cracking with the kills," he explained. "I was fine with hitting the bad guys. Their wives? Kids?" He shook his head. "Even if they were carrying bombs, it was still hard. So I pushed it down. I was sure I had it under control, until we hit an IED. Saw my friends torn apart. Watched my girlfriend at the time die." He looked down and hugged his dog. "She was a journalist. I was pinned. Got a few scars from it. And when I finally got free, my battle buddy was still trying to survive, but he didn't have half his body, so I put a bullet in him to make it stop."

"Shit," I breathed.

Jason just nodded. "Fucked me up enough that I got a dog out of it. I also tried to pull a gun on an officer, got taken down, and pretty much kicked out. Because of my skill set, the government didn't want to turn me loose - especially not with me being a little crazy. So, they informed me I would help the FBI. My options were a court martial or a contract. I took the contract and just got released from it last weekend."

"Bro, that's rough," Jinxy said.

"Yep," Jason agreed. "But Alex is the one who got me out. Bradley covered for me all those years. This team we've been given? It doesn't get any better."

"So what's the catch?" I asked. "C'mon, Cyn. You know that's why we're balking. There has to be a catch. There *always* is."

"This time, it's obvious," he assured me. "They want to see us fail, so they're gonna fuck with us."

"Who's 'they'?" Cade asked.

"The United States Congress. That's the senators and representatives who oversee the Bureau. I believe this committee is in the Senate, though. Still, for them, this is all a game to get elected again. For us, it's about catching the bad guys. Our goals are not the same, but *they* are the catch."

"And?" I asked. "I mean, you're talking about politics, and it kinda doesn't really matter, does it?"

"When they sign the budget checks, it does," he explained. "Congress makes these programs. They approve them or shut them down. They're going to want to brag about whatever they think will get them elected again. To us? It's a red light or a green light. Dealing with their bullshit is Alex's problem. But that's the catch. Because this program doesn't exist yet - and can't until it's approved - we're working in the shadows."

"Like always," Hottie joked.

Which made Jason laugh. "Yeah, pretty much. Yet Alex needs us to get all of you qualified so she can do this. You need to pass the certifications before they can prevent you from taking them with some stupid new rule. She needs to assign positions within the Bureau so this can work. She has to start this program before it can legally start so we can prove it works the moment they ask for an example. We have to be a step ahead of them, without leaking what we're doing, and *that*, Jericho, is the catch you're worried about."

Which made me smile. "Well, that's easy."

"Yeah, it kinda is," he agreed.

So I looked at the rest of Ruin. "We do this on the sly, make sure they have nothing to complain about, all while being ordinary college kids. Kinda sounds right up our alley, hm?"

"I'm so in," Knock said.

"Will my record be a problem?" Jinxy asked.

Jason shook his head. "Already handled. Alex knows, and your arrest proved you weren't a bad kid. You're fine."

"Then I'm in," Jinxy said.

"Same," Hottie agreed.

"All-in," Zoe announced.

"I'll bust my ass to make it happen," Cade said.

So we looked at Ripper, who was sitting there with a little smile on his face. "What?" I asked him.

"I'm gonna be a badass," he said. "Fuck yeah, I'm in. I mean, I get one of those badges, right?"

"And a gun - eventually," Jason told him.

I just had one more question. "But we don't have to be the good guys, right?"

Jason turned his grey-green eyes on me and smiled coldly. "Fuck being good. Alex is doing everything in her power to make sure we can be cruel if we have to."

"Then I'm all fucking in," I swore.

# CHAPTER 12

### CADE

Our discussion in the study led to another in the living room, pushing Alex a little more. Jeri was taking point on this, it seemed. Jinxy was right there with her. Knock seemed to want to do this, but he didn't try to call them off, and I loved him a little more for it.

I knew he had some history with Cynister - er, Special Agent Jason Raige. Yeah, that was going to take a bit for me to get used to. It made sense, though. Calling him Jason wouldn't give away his gamer name. It also looked a bit more "professional," and if we were going to be working around other FBI agents, we needed to get used to it.

But our trust in Jason wasn't the same as trusting an entire department of federal law enforcement, so I agreed with Jeri on this. We needed to ask questions before we signed anything - even if we wanted to. That Alex was willing to answer made it nice. And yet, at some point, we ran out of things to ask.

So, after assuring us she knew we'd come up with more, Alex announced she was going to find a hotel. Riley offered Jason a room, and when he tried to refuse, Alex ordered him to take it. For me, that was one more point in her favor. However, it brought up something else.

"Guess we're going to need to set up the guest room, huh?" I joked as our company was making their way out.

Riley glanced back. "What guest room?"

"Cade's sharing with me," Knock said, "so we have an extra on the second floor."

Riley just caught my eye and smiled. "You. Me. Tomorrow. I'm gonna use your muscles, deal?"

"Yeah, sure," I agreed.

Thankfully, Riley's definition of "tomorrow" didn't start early, yet the woman still showed up right at the crack of noon. Her big truck was blocking the driveway since it wouldn't fit anywhere else. She also didn't bother to knock.

"Morning, Ruin!" she yelled out as she wandered through our place like she lived here.

"I don't have on pants," I grumbled from where I stood in the kitchen, watching this all play out.

She shrugged and moved to lean over the island counter. "Stores close early. Also, I figured everyone else would want to know that Cyn wants to meet the horses. He said no riding, so I need some devious assistants to coax him into it while I'm not there."

"Wait!" Zoe squealed, zooming into the room on her sock-covered feet. "How'd Crysis and Quake do?"

"They played, then played, and then played some more," Riley admitted. "And Jason got to be a good guy because he brought a dog with him. I guess that's better than pets to the big chickenshit. And yes, they both slept with him."

"Aw," Zoe murmured.

Riley just looked back at me. "Pants, Cade. And tell Knock he's driving the crew home for the weekend."

"On it," I agreed as I headed across the hall and towards our bedroom.

Knock was still in bed, but he was awake. As I crossed the room, his eyes slid down my body, making me have a few bad thoughts. Sadly, knowing Riley was in the other room killed them. That woman *would* come in to hurry us up, and I was so tired of being interrupted.

"Riley's here. She wants to take me shopping for something, and you're supposed to haul everyone else back home," I told him. "I guess Jason's meeting the horses."

"Well, there goes my naked morning," he grumbled as he threw off the blanket. "But worth it. What are you shopping for?"

"No idea," I admitted. "I was simply drafted. She said she wants my muscles."

Knock murmured at that, but didn't question it. Then again, it was such a Riley thing to do, and trying to get out of it would never work. When that woman made up her mind, it was easier to agree.

So we got dressed. He promised he'd handle transport back to Sanger since he now had a shiny new SUV of his own. I was hauled out of the house and towards the full-size truck this woman liked so much. Climbing up into the passenger seat, I couldn't help but smile as she got behind the wheel. Riley wasn't a tiny woman, but somehow this thing still managed to make her look delicate.

"What?" she demanded.

"Little girl, big truck," I teased.

"Gamer freak likes horses," she shot back. "I know, I know. I'm just one big contradiction." Then she started the thing and pulled away from the house.

"So, where are we going?" I asked.

"You said guest room," she explained as she navigated the streets like she'd been here a few times too many. "Since we all know this deal is going to happen, well, it means your new handler's going to need a crash pad, right?"

"Cyn?" I grunted. "I mean Jason?"

"Jason," she agreed. "Cynister is still a gamer with no ties to law enforcement. I mean, just in case we need him again. So he's Jason. Get used to it."

"Working on it," I promised.

"And I figured you'd let Jason crash there so you don't lose time with him going back and forth to a hotel. Also, it'll give Crysis a yard."

"Yeah, there's that," I agreed. "Poor dog doesn't need to live in hotels. We're going to need another desk too, you know."

She glanced over. "Huh?"

"For the war room," I explained. "He can set up a desktop here and game with us. I'm pretty sure he has at least one laptop he'll carry back and forth. But if he has a rig here, he doesn't have to admit he owns it."

"Oh, nice," Riley breathed. "I'll tell Murder to handle that."

I just nodded, because Murder was hooked up. His sponsors basically got him any computer parts he wanted, and for free. Never mind that the man made more money than Riley and Logan combined!

"So, we're getting stuff for the extra bedroom?" Because I wanted to make sure I was actually keeping up.

"Yep," she said, nodding as she drove. "Bed, nightstands, and maybe even a dresser. I'd say a dog bed, but Crysis sleeps on the real one. Jason won't need much, but this way, if one of you has company, you'll have a place to put them."

I scoffed at that. "Riley, we don't do company. I mean, except you."

"Relatives?" she said. "Maybe Zoe has a cousin out of state or something. You never know, Cade, and this is the nice part about being a grownup, you know? Besides, back before we built the basement, I never had a spare room, so I know how nice it is to be able to make space."

"You still don't really have one," I countered.

"Your old room," she reminded me. "I mean, we put a bed in there, but we need to get the rest. Besides, if you and Knock ever have a fight, we want one of you to be able to come home to sleep it off instead of hitting a bar."

Which made me chuckle to myself. Yeah, because she was family, and I was still getting used to this. The Andrews clan, regardless of where they started, were the kind of support most people imagined when they thought of blood relatives. No questions were asked, all mistakes were forgiven, and home was always a welcoming place.

I hadn't gotten to live there long, but that hadn't mattered. From the moment I'd moved in, I'd been accepted without hesitation. Logan had become the sort of brother I'd always wanted and had never thought was possible. The rules to stay in this woman's good graces were simple: don't drink and drive. That was how she'd lost her parents. Anything else she could work with.

Literally anything else.

So I decided to just ask her what I really wanted to know. "Do you think we should do this thing with the FBI?"

"Without a doubt," she said. "I think Jason's in on it, so you know he'll have your back. I also think we need this. Like, the whole world needs this." She paused to move into a turn lane and stop at a red light. Then she looked over. "It doesn't matter how messy it gets, Cade. I think Jeri really needs this."

"Yeah, she's kinda been struggling since F5."

"She has?"

I nodded. "Her life has been shit, right? Everyone she cares about dies. Well, she came out and said she loves us. All of us, Riley, even Zoe and Jinxy. And no, she's not sleeping with them. But she cares, and caring is dangerous. You and the other gamer girls almost died, so that's proof it can still happen, and now she's kinda..."

"Triggered," Riley finished for me.

"Yeah," I agreed.

The light turned green and the truck started moving, but Riley was making little thoughtful noises. When she pulled into a parking lot and killed the engine, she was still doing it. Popping off her seatbelt, the woman climbed out and gestured for me to join her. I did, but when I met her around the front of the truck, she kept going like there hadn't been a pause.

"Do you love her, Cade?"

"Oh yeah," I admitted. "Like, head over heels. And yes, I love Knock too."

That made Riley smile. "Good. But here's the thing. Being in love isn't always easy. It isn't even always good. If anything can bring out those inner fears and insecurities in a person, love will do it, because in order to love fully, we have to strip ourselves bare. If we hold back at all, thinking we're protecting ourselves, then we're just hiding who we really are."

"I don't think I'm doing that," I admitted.

"No, but is she?"

Yeah, and I didn't have a good answer for that. "I dunno, Riley. I know she's trying, though. I know this is a huge step for her, but the polycule helps. I know she hides things, but I think it's because she's mostly hiding it from herself. Like this - I mean how scared she is of losing y'all."

"And how does that make you feel?" Riley asked as she reached the door and held it open for me to go through first.

I stepped inside a very nice furniture store and paused to look around. Riley moved around me, then waved for me to follow. She acted like she didn't care about my answer, but I knew she was casually giving me time to process. It was kinda what she did.

"Can I help you with anything?" a young man asked.

"Nope, we're just looking," Riley said.

The guy nodded as if he hadn't expected anything else and wandered off the other way. Riley made a straight line for the bedroom sets. Damn, there were a lot of them, and they ranged from simple to seriously fancy.

"Well?" she asked as she moved to look at one of the beds.

"I think all of this makes me feel like I want to protect her," I admitted. "Not in a hold her back and hide her away sort of way. I mean protect her the way you did when Dad kicked me out. Protect her the way Logan did me by being an attorney. Not by pushing me aside, but by standing there and helping me face it. I think all the shit Jeri's been through has been hard, and I can't even fathom what it was like."

"I think she's kinda fucked up," Riley said.

I murmured because she wasn't wrong. "Aren't we all?"

"Yep," Riley agreed. "It's why we work so well. But that's the thing, Cade. She *is* fucked up, and you love her anyway. That won't make it easier, though. It'll make it messy, it means you'll break the rules, and none of that will matter. Love is love is love is love! Add a few more for the rest of those people in your house." She flashed me a grin. "But you know what will really help her?"

"What?" I asked.

She smiled. "Fighting back. That's what Jason's offering y'all. This is a chance to fight back. It's a chance to turn her loose - and all the rest of you. Sure, you'll probably take a few hits in the process, but it's a sort of vengeance against all the shit in the world, and I think every one of you needs that. So take it. Run with it. Make something of this, and do what all the rest of us have always dreamed of."

"By working with the FBI?" I asked.

"By policing the darkest places of the web," she clarified. "By being Ruin. By making that word - ruin - into a threat the bad guys will learn to fear. Give yourselves power by letting the FBI have your back. That power? It will cure a lot of trauma."

I ducked my head and pushed away the stupid lock of hair that never stayed in my ponytail. "So was this talk even about her?"

"No," Riley promised. "It was about you, because you deserve to get some vengeance too, Cade. You deserve to protect the ones you love. You are one hell of an amazing young man, and one I'm proud to call family. I also know that if I say that, you'll try to push it off because you think you have to, so if I turn this around and direct you at helping someone else..."

"Which is kinda what the FBI wants us to do, right?"

She winked. "Now you're getting it. I knew I liked you for some reason."

So I pointed behind us. "I think the black set fits best."

"Not too boring?" she asked.

I just thrust out my lower lip and shrugged. "I mean, it has slats that would be perfect for handcuffs."

The laugh that burst from her mouth was louder than expected. "And now I know what to get you for Christmas!" she warned. Then she moved closer and wrapped her arm around my waist. "And Cade? We're all proud of you, you know. For Knock to do this? It's almost expected. But you? You had to work for it, and you worked hard. Don't think we missed it."

I had to glance away. "Fuck, Riley." My damned eyes were stinging.

"You didn't think you lost your family just because you went to college, did you?" she asked. "Sorry, bro. That's not how it works in the Andrews clan."

"Fuck it," I breathed before turning to wrap her up in a hug. "Thanks, big sis."

She just pressed her head into my chest. "Damn it, Cade! I have on mascara! No sensitive shit!"

Which was enough to make both of us laugh. Now we just had to manage to buy a bed.

## CHAPTER 13

### JINXY

Four years in Colorado meant a lot of stuff. Having it shipped down here with a moving company meant all that stuff was no longer in the order I'd originally had it. Even worse, some dumbass - me - hadn't labeled the boxes very well.

So when Knock had carted off everyone else to Riley's place for a little relaxation, I'd stayed behind. My goal? Figure out where the fuck I'd packed my damned socks! At least I'd been smart enough to bring my computers in the car with me.

But bit by bit, my room was starting to look like I lived here. It was amazing how much shit I'd acquired over the years after leaving Southwind. For a guy who'd started out with nothing but the clothes he was wearing, I was doing pretty good now. My Gran had made that possible.

I missed her. Every single day, I missed her, but I'd had the luxury of getting to say goodbye, and most didn't get that. I also knew I'd made her proud. She'd taken a complete fuckup, had nurtured my ability to get in trouble, and had guided me towards using it for good. Well, a type of good, at least.

When I'd told her Zoe was also a hacker? Yeah, she'd been so happy for me. She said the good ones were worth waiting for, even if it felt impossible, and she'd know. She and Bea had never been able to admit they were more than business partners. We'd known. Once we earned our color, we'd been treated more like family than a project, and those women had stopped hiding their relationship from us. Not from everyone, but definitely from the family.

I chuckled. It sounded so mafia-like when phrased that way, and in truth, our mess was a lot like the mafia. We had a godmother of sorts in Violet. Granted, most of the family weren't criminals. They didn't mind bending the rules more than they should, but they tended to land on the side of the law.

This deal meant I could do the same.

Opening another box, I found all my bed linens. Well, I'd need those, but we had a closet down the hall for them. So, grabbing the box, I headed that way, thinking about how Gran would've had a million questions about me working for the FBI. She definitely would've told me to be careful, but we kinda were, weren't we?

As I was stacking my sheets and blankets on the shelves, I heard something clank. I paused, thinking I was home alone, but then there was banging. Soft, like someone tapping a nail into a wall, maybe? Even more confusing, it was coming from the guest room.

So once my box was empty, I left it by the closet and gently eased open the door to the unused bedroom. The first thing I saw was a board. It was dark, maybe even black lacquer? As the door opened a little wider, I saw a leg.

"Cade?" I asked, stepping into the room.

He looked up from the instructions on his lap. "Hey, Jinxy."

"What the fuck are you doing?"

He laughed once. "Well, Riley bought us a guest bed. I'm trying to put it together." Then his brow creased. "Why aren't you in Sanger with everyone else?"

"Unpacking," I explained. "Besides, I thought horses were big when they were the normal kind. Knock's monsters? Yeah, my feet get panic attacks around them."

"Your feet, huh?" He grinned, but looked back down at his instructions.

"Uh..." I moved a little closer. "Need help?"

"I'm so fucking lost," he admitted. "Part A and bolt Q? Like, none of this shit is labeled, so I'm just supposed to guess which one matches the picture?"

"Pretty much," I agreed, "but I've done this a few times. Lemme see?"

He passed over the instructions gleefully. "I thought I'd have this all worked out before everyone got home, but Jesus."

"Yeah," I breathed after looking at the mess he'd been trying to read. "Ok. So we need to do the headboard first."

Cade simply waved at the mess on the ground. "Just tell me what parts I need."

For a bit, we worked through it. With me checking the instructions, and him moving the parts into piles, we got it organized enough to actually make some progress. Then, the pair of us began holding things together and screwing those bolts into the pre-drilled holes.

"So is everyone excited about this FBI thing?" I asked, holding a board in place.

"I think so," he said. The small drill whirred as it worked. "I know Riley's been friends with Jason for a while. She told me Alex is trustworthy too, which is nice. I mean, I didn't have a problem with her, and she didn't freak out about us drinking at F5, but it's always nice to get another opinion."

"Kinda what I'm doing right now," I admitted. "If I get busted again, I'm screwed, and Zoe? She's got her entire future ahead of her. After everything that's happened, she needs a bit of good, not more crap to wade through."

"And Jeri," Cade said. "Yeah, I kinda think she needs this."

We moved to the next set of boards. "Jeri's always been a bit out of control," I told him.

"Figured."

"But," I went on, "she knows what this means."

He paused just before inserting the screw. "What does it mean, Jinxy?"

I waited for the drill to fall silent again. "It means we won't have to rely on anyone else. It means that when we stumble on shit like a bunch of assholes raping girls, then we can bust them ourselves. It means, Cade, that this is a hacker's dream come true."

"So why are none of you acting like it?" he asked.

"Because how often do dreams come true?" I shot back.

"Uh, a lot." He leaned back, holding himself up with his arms so he could look at me. "That place you grew up, uh, South something?"

"Southwind."

He nodded slowly. "There's one dream. Riley Andrews, she's another. I mean, she took in both me and Knock. Logan Weiss? Isn't he a dream? And I don't just mean sexy."

Which made me laugh. "I'm only into girls, bro."

"Well, he is," Cade went on. "He's an amazing attorney, and one who has our backs. Jason is another, because who'd ever imagine an FBI agent has been helping us hack shit? Hell, so far as I care, Jeri's another dream. She's the reason we're all even together like this."

I had to hand it to him - he had a point. That was a lot of amazing things, but most of them were people. Still, those people had made miracles happen, and those miracles had gotten us here. Now, we were being offered the chance at another, and it sounded too good to be true.

But that was my problem. Deals this sweet were supposed to have a downside. This one really didn't. What Alex and Jason were offering us was going to be a bit of work, but it was the type of work we'd do anyway. So where was the part that made it feel like we deserved it?

"Why us?" I finally asked. "I mean, is it just because Jason knows us?"

"Partly," Cade admitted. "It's also because Alex saw us working. See, what most of you don't understand is she was there. Alex was in that hotel room in Vegas with us. She was wandering around, looking at the notes we were making, noticing how much info came in from the ones we'd left at home, and how we were *all* putting it together. From Dez to you, Jinxy. She saw the teamwork, and like Knock always says..."

"Teamwork is overpowered," I repeated, having heard it a few times in the last couple of months. "Ok, that actually makes sense. Hackers aren't really known to be team players."

"But they need a team," Cade pointed out. "One agent babysitting a group of hackers. That's what Alex said. So if those hackers are helping each other, it's much nicer than them trying to one-up, shut down, or even compete with each other."

"There's that," I relented. "But what about the bigger groups? I mean, Anonymous? Lulzsec?"

"Black hat," Cade muttered, dismissing them.

I just lifted my brows. "Look who's been doing his homework!"

What made his hands pause. "Huh?"

"Tell me, do you think the guy who gamed with the Reapers a few years ago would've known the difference between black hat and white hat hackers?" I asked.

"Yeah, but I've kinda been living with gamers for a few months," he said.

"And learned," I countered. "Cade, all I'm saying is that while you used to be a damned good PvPer, you're now getting to be one hell of a hacker too."

He looked up, and I swore there was a tint of pink on his face. "Yeah?"

"Definitely," I said. "Now, what color hat would you give us?"

"Grey," he said without hesitation. "Black hat hackers are the bad guys. They want to fuck shit up and don't care about anything else. White hat hackers are the good guys who just want to help. We kinda do both, so we're grey hats."

"Exactly," I agreed. "But now think about that. We're grey, Cade. We aren't the good guys. We're the chaos. In D&D terms, we'd be chaotic neutral, right?"

He pondered that for a moment. "Probably. We might be chaotic good. We're definitely not lawful anything."

"I'm leaning to chaotic neutral," I told him. "Because we don't always do shit for good. Sometimes we do shit for ourselves, like taking down Jason's pics when he was in that shooting."

"Which is kinda good," he pointed out. "It helped him stay on the case."

"Which helped us," I reminded him. "We fucked with Dylan and his friends just to piss them off. Before we knew about anyone but Zoe, I mean. We do good, but our goal? It's to fuck shit up and not let the bad guys get away with it."

"Which is good," he said, smirking at me a bit. "I think we're right on that line between good and neutral. We wobble, but we tend to lean more towards good, even if we're going about it in ways most wouldn't agree with."

"And that," I said, "is why this deal is a dream come true. They aren't asking us to change, Cade. Oh, they will try to smear us and chase us off, but if we can actually do this? They'll turn us loose and wipe away our crimes. They're offering us the chance to go all-out, with no holding back so we don't get caught, and do you know what we'll be able to do?"

"But what do we have *left* to do?" he asked. "C'mon, Jinxy. That's the part I'm stuck on. Everyone keeps saying the feds are already cleaning up KoG, so what's left?"

"Kiwi Farms," I offered. "That's just off the top of my head. What about revenge porn? Doxxing women? Especially gamer girls? I mean, that's not just KoG, my man. That's pretty common shit. Stalkers. There's about a million things going on all the time. Social media is a cesspool of shit for a lot of women. Or what about that child porn shit we handled over the summer?"

Cade made gagging noises. "That's just gross. Yeah, I can get behind taking out fuckers like that." Then he huffed. "But do you think I can?"

"I think you're a vital part of the team," I assured him. "Cade, you came into this knowing nothing - "

"So did Zoe!" he shot back. "Shit, she's blown me away. Ripper knew a bit, and now he's some kind of data genius! Me? I'm still reminding myself to check my damned VPN."

I leaned in to grab his shoulder. "Zoe's got a mind like a steel trap, and thinking about coding meant she didn't have to think about what Evan did to her. Do not judge yourself against her. Ripper had a head start. You?" I ducked my head to make sure he was listening. "You were in the process of coming out, dealing with a shit home life, and trying to juggle not just one, but *two* relationships, while hiding all of it. I think you're doing pretty damned good, all things considered."

A tiny little smile flickered in the corner of his mouth. "I just..."

"What?" I pressed when he didn't finish the thought.

"Jinxy, my dad always said I'd amount to nothing, and I kinda believed him."

"Yeah?" I asked, shifting so I was sitting across from him. "Mine always said I was gay. He told me I'd never get a girl unless I buffed up. He said to get my ass off those computers because he wouldn't have me living with him when I was thirty. When I got arrested, he told me I was a dumbass and deserved it. He said he never wanted to see me again, and you know what?"

"Hm?"

"He didn't." I shrugged. "Gran picked me up, my parents wanted nothing to do with me, and I don't even know if they're alive or dead. I also don't give a shit. That's not my family, Cade. This, right here, is my family. Fuck the ones who don't believe in us."

For a little too long, Cade held my eyes, and when he dropped them, he began playing with the board in front of him. I knew that feeling, though. I knew exactly what this poor guy was going through, but when I'd done it, I'd had someone to lean on. I'd had an entire herd of big brothers to remind me I'd be ok on my own, and in doing so, to make me feel a lot less alone.

Shit. Maybe I'd been one of the youngest to go through Southwind, and I hadn't had anyone there to mentor, but I did here. I had Cade. He was sitting right in front of me, with a story so close to my own, and I had the experience. I'd watched as Hot took care of Jeri, helping her become whatever the fuck she was now. I could do that for this guy.

"Besides," I said gently, "I'm here now. I'll make sure you can hack as good as me. It's what big brothers do."

Cade just leaned his head back and groaned. "What the fuck is with all you people trying to hit me in the emotions today! Damn it, Jinxy."

"You can call me Shawn, you know," I reminded him.

"Nope, it's Jinxy," he said. "And I'm going to hold you to that whole training thing."

"Good," I said. "Now show me how we're going to make this mess into a bed."

"That," he assured me, "I think I can do. Maybe not a good bed, but it will be *a* bed. And when Cyn falls on the floor, I'm telling him my big brother built it."

But the smile on his face? Yeah, it made my mouth match. Evidently Cade was right when he'd said dreams did come true. I'd just never stopped to think about how they came from people. *These* people, and they were all worth taking a risk for.

## CHAPTER 14

### JERICHO

We talked. Everyone in Ruin, over the course of the weekend, talked about the deal we were being offered. Sometimes all of us, but mostly it was in smaller groups. Zoe pulled me aside at Riley's with a list of questions. Jinxy had more when I got home. Ripper and Knock wanted to know my concerns.

Over and over, we all checked on each other, making sure we were on the same page. Saturday night, there was an entire debate about it over dinner. Ok, so we'd eaten in the living room while streaming replays of the PLG tournaments, but that was beside the point.

And in the end, we couldn't come up with a single good reason to say no.

Sure, this could go sideways. No, people wouldn't like it. Yeah, maybe we'd get embarrassed about a few things. Giving authority to a group of criminals? That wouldn't go over well, but was the risk worth it? Definitely!

That was why, when Alex and Jason returned on Sunday, we not only signed our contracts and filled out paperwork for our paychecks, but also made plans to have Jason come back next weekend and actually get started. This was happening. It was real. Holy shit, we were going to be able to do everything we'd wanted!

So why was I lying in bed Sunday night, staring at the ceiling and unable to make my mind shut up? I had class tomorrow morning. I needed to get some sleep, but I just couldn't stop thinking. Every time I tried, some other stupid thought popped up.

I tossed. I turned. When the bathroom door opened, I sighed and sat up, not surprised at all to see Hottie slipping into my room. His chest was bare. His pants looked like pajamas. When I moved over to make room for him, he realized I was awake, so there was no point in sneaking.

"You're supposed to be out," he said.

I just grunted. "Right. Kinda know that. It's still not happening."

"Me either." Then he lifted the blankets and crawled in beside me. "You thinking about our deal?"

"Is that what we're calling it?"

"Jobs?" he tried next.

I sighed and rolled into him, not surprised at all when he moved his arm to let me curl up against his chest. So many nights, we'd slept like this. His fears weren't the same as mine, but they matched. Just like our bodies did as we held each other. A bump here filled the hollow there. Almost like we were made to be together.

"Hottie?" I asked softly. "Do you know what this means?"

"If it works," he said, "yeah. We'll be able to change the whole world, Jeri."

"The problem is what happens if it doesn't," I said, proving I was on the same page.

The arm behind my back curled, holding me tighter. "Jeri, we don't have families to back us up. Not me, not Jinxy, Cade, Knock, or even you. Sure, Melissa would try to help, but there's no way of knowing if she'd be able to remember you were in trouble."

"I know."

"And while we have some connections, that's not the same as parents who won't let it go, you know? An attorney won't get the same respect from the public as a weeping mother. And while Ripper and Zoe have good families, that's not enough."

"Ok?" Because I wasn't sure what families had to do with this.

"It means we're the leftovers, Jeri. We're nice, tidy little opportunities with no strings attached. If we screw up, the blame *will* land on us. If we don't get this right, it won't matter if Alex and Jason have our backs. The fucking President could be the one turning us into the next criminal masterminds caught and finally behind bars. We're vulnerable, and I don't fucking like it."

Oh. Well that was one thing I hadn't thought about. "But you still signed?" I asked.

"Yeah, because this is the chance we've been waiting for," he admitted. "This is everything. It's worth the risk, and I believe in Ruin. I think we can prove ourselves, get some fancy FBI badges - although Jason says they're a little different for consultants - and we'll be able to do a whole hell of a lot more than kick our friends offline."

"Maybe we can track down DeathAdder?" I asked.

He leaned in and kissed the top of my head. "If he isn't put away by the guys currently chasing the baddies, sure. Hell, we'll be able to clean up all the rest of KoG if we want to. But not until we have those consultant cards, ok?"

"What?!" I hissed, not only pulling away, but also sitting up to look at him. "Damn it, Hottie. You knew I wanted to bust that fucker. Now you're saying I can't?"

So he sat up to match me. "I'm saying this is bigger than even him."

"But he *raped* Zoe!"

"No, he helped hide her rape," Hottie corrected. "And when we have those consultant badges, we'll be able to build a case that puts him in fucking *jail* for it. If we tag him now, then what? You've got a single message on a single forum. He could say he was 'just joking around' and it'd be dismissed because of lack of evidence."

"But he was in on it," I insisted. "He probably wasn't the only one. I mean, we have Dylan's login information, but if we got the others? Who knows what they were talking about in private messages, Hottie. There could be others. And anyone who touched her? I'm going to make sure they fucking pay!"

"Shh..." he breathed, reaching over to smooth the hair over my ear. "Jeri, we will. But stop and think about it. If DeathAdder is picked up, we can still make a case against him. If he's not, we can make sure he is. But we need to be FBI consultants to make it happen. That means we need to focus on this first. Just like we focused on training Ruin before we went after the Alpha Team. Just like we check our VPN and encryption before we dive into someone's network. There are steps to this, baby girl."

I flopped forward with a groan, stopping only when my arms were wrapped around his shoulders. "I just want it all to happen faster!"

"Oh, to be young again," he teased. "Jeri, it's happening. Shit, this thing we're doing? It's every hacker's dream. We've just been given permission to do what we'd do anyway, and have the entire FBI behind us. Not chasing us. Not trying to stop us. They're handling the shit work for us."

"Yeah?" I asked, looking up at his face.

"Yeah," he breathed. "And there's something else you need to think about."

"What's that?"

"Working for the FBI means that if shit happens, you have people to call, and you will get a response quickly."

My brow furrowed. "Huh?"

"If Zoe gets hurt. Jeri, do you know how fast the ambulance comes when an agent is down? Real fast. If someone is chasing you, do you know how willing cops are to help someone with one of those little blue-and-white badges? Super willing." His hand moved to cup my cheek. "It means that even if they do get hurt, you can do something about it."

"My curse," I realized.

He nodded slowly. "Bad things happen to good people, but just look at F5. The worst thing happened to Riley and those other girls, but they're ok. They're all ok because they had someone with power looking out for them. Well, if we do this, then we'll be the ones with power."

That made me lean back, because I needed enough space to actually focus on him. "But it wouldn't have stopped Nina, Hottie. Nor Dad."

"Are you sure?" he asked. "Because if I'd been able to stop those fuckers from sending her those emails, she never would've gotten depressed."

"And Dad?" I pressed.

He sighed. "Yeah, not as easy, but if you'd been working for the FBI back then, I'm sure things would've been different. Your brother would've gotten an ambulance sooner, or maybe have never been able to take those drugs. I dunno. But if he'd been ok, then your dad would've too, and..." He let his words trail off. "Fuck. I don't know if that's true. I'm just trying here."

But his trying was actually helping. I was pretty sure he was wrong about Drake and Dad, but he still had a point. Nina would've been ok. So maybe that would've meant he'd be happily married to her now and none of this would've happened, but I would've still been happy. We all would've.

As for my dad and brother? Well, one was an accident and the other was grief. That whole shit-show was a mess, and it had destroyed my childhood, but at the same time, therapy had helped Mom. No, it hadn't fixed her, and she was a complete mental wreck, but it had helped her handle the grief so she didn't want to die.

"We can stop it from happening to anyone else," I realized, the words falling from my mouth.

"Huh?" Hottie asked. "I think you switched gears, Jeri, and forgot to bring me along with your mind."

"Dad died because he couldn't stop grieving," I explained. "Drake was an accident. A stupid one, but still. Somewhere out there, someone else is getting ready to make a stupid mistake. Doesn't matter if that's a girl who's about to send her nudes to her boyfriend or some boy who's going to take drugs that are laced with bad shit. People fuck up, and those fuckups are normal. They shouldn't destroy everything."

"And we'll be able to do something about it now," he said softly. "That's the thing. We could've found the guy who laced Drake's drugs and made sure he rotted in jail. We could've stopped the distribution so no one else took them. We could've done something, if we had this kind of power. Jeri, if we can do this, we're no longer helpless."

"We can make a difference," I breathed.

He nodded. "A big one. Baby girl, we are going to be part of an elite FBI takedown team. We're going to be the internet cops. I mean, you remember back when we were trying to bust Dylan and his friends, when you saw the news story about the dead girl?"

"The one they killed?" I asked.

"Yeah, but before you knew it was them," he said. "That day, you said something that's kinda stuck with me. You asked if our work was ever going to be done. You said there will always be another and another, and you meant women who are victims. You were so pissed off because men would never stop hurting women, but you know what? Now we can finally do something about it."

"Well, not *now*," I reminded him.

"Soon," he assured me. "Once we're official consultants, we will become their ruin, Jeri."

"I will take revenge," I quoted. "I will pay them back. In due time, their feet will slip. Their day of disaster will arrive, and their destiny will overtake them. We *will* be their ruin."

"In due time," he said gently. "But we will make them pay. We will get revenge for the wrongs they have done. We will bring about their day of disaster, because we *are* Ruin. This is just one step in making sure we have all the power we need to become the scariest motherfuckers on the internet."

So I pushed him down and then curled up against him again. "In other words, I have to be patient, huh?"

"One step at a time," he told me. "And so you know, for most people? They have to graduate college with at least a bachelor's degree, be twenty-three, and then apply to do what we're being offered. They can't have records, have to be three years free of drugs, and basically miss out on all the excitement of college in order to get in."

"But not us."

"Nope, not us," he said. "We're jumping to the front of the line, and we won't be held back by their rules. We're getting everything we've ever wanted, so how about we don't fuck this up, hm?"

"But Jason basically said it's not going to be easy. Politicians are going to do politics, and we'll have hoops to jump through. They'll try to smear us, chase us off, and make qualifying nearly impossible."

"So we jump through the hoops," he said. "You know we can. Shit, if we can make all of this work so far, I'm convinced we can do anything."

I knew I should simply agree. He wanted me to. This was supposed to be Hottie's way of comforting me so I could finally relax and get some sleep, but there was one thing I had to get out there. One little secret that could only be shared in the darkness with his arms around me.

"We saved them, you know," I said. "Riley and her friends? We broke all the rules and we made sure they wouldn't be taken from us."

"Trust me," he breathed, "I know. It's what made me sign the paper."

"Because this might break my curse?" I asked.

"No," he admitted. "Jeri, there is no curse. The world just sucks, and this means we can make it suck a whole lot less."

"Yeah," I whispered. "I like your way better."

"Then close your eyes and let me stay the night?"

I wrapped my arm across his chest. "Always," I promised. "I sleep better when you're here anyway."

"That's my girl," he said softly. Then I felt his lips on my head again. Like a miracle, my thoughts finally stopped spinning.

# CHAPTER 15

## CADE

There was a strange excitement to knowing we were actually doing this thing. It stuck with me as I headed to school on Monday with Knock in the passenger seat. While our schedules on Tuesdays and Thursdays might not match up nicely, we could ride together three days of the week.

After finding a parking space, we got out and headed towards our first class. They were in the same direction, but my building was closer. Yet when Knock slid his hand into mine, I tensed a bit, glancing over at him in confusion.

"It's ok, Cade. I can keep my hands to myself," he assured me.

"Nope," I said, lacing my fingers with his. "I just didn't expect it." Then I lifted our joined hands to my mouth and kissed the back of his knuckles.

That made him glance down and the edges of his ears brightened. Damn, but he was cute. I simply couldn't get over how amazing this man was - or that he was into me. I kept waiting to hit the point where being with him was boring and mundane, but it still hadn't happened.

"You know," I said, changing the subject while relaxing our arms so they could sway between us, "I now have confirmation that Jinxy is definitely straight."

"And how exactly did that happen?" Knock asked.

"We were putting together the guest bed. He offered up that he's only into women." I shrugged. "And he said he's going to help me learn more of this hacking shit."

"Oh, I see how it is," Knock teased. "Replacing me for a taller man?"

I scoffed. "I prefer your muscles to his height. Besides, that would be weird. The man's like seven feet tall."

"Not quite," Knock said. "I think he's six-four. I approve of his tattoos, though."

I gaped at him playfully. "So *you* were checking him out?"

"No." He gave me a wary look. "I was checking out his tattoos. C'mon, they're cool. But he's also the one we know the least."

"He's kinda been around a while," I countered.

"And only talks about gaming or hacking," Knock pointed out. "I have no clue what his favorite color is, or what food he hates, or all the things I've figured out about the rest of you."

"I'm guessing teal is his favorite color," I teased, bumping my shoulder against his. "That's the one he got in his teen program. Zoe says it's a big deal to them."

"Yeah." He moved closer, letting go of my hand to slip his arm around my waist. "Hey, maybe we can try out the private date room sometime?"

"Just us, or with Jeri?" I asked.

He shrugged against my side. "Either way. I'd just like to make a habit of spoiling you both, and I think we deserve it."

"Because of the contracts?" I asked.

"Nope, because we're still happy together." Then he glanced over. "I think that's yours."

He meant the building, and it was. Yet instead of letting me pull away to walk to my class, Knock paused, his arm around my waist, holding me to him. I shifted to face him, and he reached up to guide a piece of hair back.

"I don't want you to ever think I'm tired of this," he said softly.

Then he leaned in and kissed me. Here, in the middle of campus! For a moment, my entire body tensed. Years of thinking I had to hide this meant holding his hand in public was a lot. This? What the hell?

But I liked it. Fuck that, I loved it, so I pushed away the shock and leaned in. When my mouth parted, he was right there, tangling his tongue with mine. I grabbed at his arm to hold him close. He gripped the back of my neck, kissing me so wonderfully hard. For a moment, everything else became unimportant, and it was just us.

The feel of his lips. The brush of his nose on my cheek. The feather-light touch of his hair, drifting in the breeze. Even the subtle moan trapped in the back of his throat. I noticed it all, loving it, and refused to let myself care about whether anyone else would approve of us.

I loved this man. I'd gone through hell to make sure I could love him, and he'd done the same for me. The people who mattered didn't care about us being bisexual. They didn't make it weird, so fuck it if random strangers had a problem, because I didn't. I refused to let those thoughts hold me back any more.

Finally, he pulled away. We were both breathing just a little harder. "Class," Knock managed to whisper.

"Yeah," I agreed. "You too." I trailed a finger down the edge of his face, right beside that brilliantly blue hair of his. "I love you."

The most amazing smile appeared on his lips. "I love you too." Then he pushed at my chest. "Now go, before we skip."

"Going!" I lifted my hands and took a step back. "Try to be a good boy for a bit."

"Never." But he was smiling as wide as I was.

I now had this giddy feeling in my chest. I also found myself glancing around to check for people staring at us. Nothing. Not a single glare from any of the dozens of people making their way to their own classes. Something about that put a little spring in my step.

But when I walked into the building for my first class, a woman moved to catch my attention. "Hey..." she said, turning to walk with me.

I had no clue who she was. I'd never seen this girl before, so I couldn't figure out why she was walking with me. "Uh, hi," I muttered.

"So, cute boyfriend," she said, gesturing back to the door. "I like his hair. But, um..." She passed me a piece of paper. "I figured I could invite the two of you to our Pride club? We're always looking for more members. Allies too. We just want to make sure there's a support network available to all the LGBTQ students on campus."

I accepted the flier and nodded. "I'll see what I can do. Thanks."

"Hope to see you there!" Then she turned and headed back the other way.

I breathed out a laugh, because that was not at all what I'd expected. Oh, I should've. The University of North Texas was not only a good science school, but it was one of the best art colleges in the state. Not that I was ever on that side of campus, but everyone knew the art department was very friendly to queer students of all kinds.

I made it up to my class and sat through my lecture thinking about that. UNT was gay-friendly. No one thought me kissing my boyfriend was weird. Well, at least no one had said anything about it. I was pretty sure someone would hate it, but they'd be in the minority. Still, all of this meant it was ok.

Me and him. We were fine. We didn't have to hide anything. I could kiss him the same way I could kiss Jeri. Even back at Sanger High, us doing anything had drawn attention. Sure, a lot of it had been girls saying we were cute, but it still felt weird. This? It was so very normal.

My father wasn't around to threaten my life for being into guys. My former "friends" weren't around to blackmail me for being bisexual. Pissed-off dudes weren't waiting to beat the shit out of us or anything else. I'd walked all the way to my first class, with my boyfriend, and it had been completely and totally...

Normal.

When class let out, I meandered back outside still in some kind of daze. I couldn't even describe the feeling. Relieved was the best I had, but that wasn't right. I'd never asked for anyone to approve who I was into. This was more like realizing the monster under the bed was just a shadow. That one of the bad things I'd been ready to fight didn't even exist. I was simply allowed to be me - finally.

Pulling out my phone, I was typing up a cute message to my boyfriend when movement caught my eye. Looking up, I saw a girl pressed up against the arm of the bench she was on, almost like she was trying to crawl off the thing. Her arms were close to her body and some guy was leaning over her. Clearly, she didn't want to be talking to him, but he had her pinned.

Letting out a sigh, I sent the text, put my phone away, and angled my steps over there. One good thing and one bad, right? But a few more steps allowed me to see the girl's face - and it was one I knew.

"Tiffany?" I asked, lifting my voice to cross the distance.

Her head snapped over and relief consumed her. "Cade!"

"Hey, fuckhead!" I snapped. "Back off my girlfriend!"

Ok, ex-girlfriend, but I knew most guys were more likely to listen to a boyfriend than the girl trying her hardest to be left alone. I was also willing to throw down. I'd expected it to be over kissing Knock, but this? Yeah, same shit, different bigots.

"I was just trying to be nice," the guy smarted off.

So I squared my shoulders and walked a little faster. "Yeah? Trying to be real nice, huh? So nice she's all curled up trying to get away from you?" Then I reached out my arm. "C'mere, babe." But my eyes stayed on the guy, daring him to block her.

Tiffany hurried towards me, her bag dangling from her hand. When she reached my side, I pulled her up against me, then jerked my chin at the asshole.

"Time to go, bud."

"Oh, fuck off," he grumbled.

"Problem?" And a broad-shouldered man moved in from the side.

It took me a second to recognize him. Hottie's shirt was looser than normal. He had on a baseball cap and sunglasses. With his backpack over his shoulders, he looked like some football jock, not the geek I knew him to be. He was also marching right up in this guy's face.

"Hey, my bro says to go, then it's time to go," he told the man.

"Fuck!" The guy huffed, tossing his hands up. "Was just being nice. Don't get your panties in a wad."

And Hottie smiled. "But I like the way they tickle my ass."

"Fuck off," the guy muttered, but he was leaving.

I immediately turned my focus on Tiffany. "Are you ok?"

She let out a relieved sigh and dropped her head against my shoulder. "Your timing, Cade? Fucking amazing. He wanted my number and wasn't taking no for an answer."

"Give him a fake," Hottie said, coming over to join us.

She shook her head. "Doesn't work. They text it to make sure it rings."

"Get a Google number," I suggested. "It'll forward to you when you want, and not when you don't. Also makes blocking easier and isn't tied to your GPS."

Tiffany laughed. "And there's the gamer boy I know so well. It's good to see you again, Cade."

"Same," I agreed. "I had no idea you were going here, though. I thought you'd be at Harvard or something."

"Can't afford it," she admitted. "Doing the local thing for lower tuition. You?"

"Got a sweet house on the other side of town, and I'm with the entire crew. We all go here." I tipped my head at Hottie. "You know Hottie, right?"

"Never met her before," Hottie admitted, offering his hand.

"Grayson Harlan, although my supposed friends have dubbed me Hottie it seems."

Tiffany's brows went up. "Hottie?"

"Short for HotShot," I explained. "That's his game name."

"Well, Hottie, I'm Tiffany Bowen," she said, taking his hand. "No game name, but my friends call me Tiff."

"The bitch," Hottie said, nodding to show he'd heard of her. "Yeah, Jeri has opinions."

"Good ones now," I promised.

Tiffany just shrugged. "She and I met on bad terms. You know, the kind influenced by asshole guys trying to pit us against each other because they knew that if we'd joined up back then, shit would've gotten ugly."

"Shit did get ugly," Hottie said.

Tiffany flashed him a smile. "Yep. Jericho is a badass. I'm a bitch. Combined? Well, we're a whole lot of people's nightmares, huh?"

I chuckled, but Hottie looked up at me. "Got time before your next class?"

"An hour," Tiffany said. "And it's right over there."

I gave her a confused look, surprised she knew where my class was. "How do you know that?"

"Cade, I'm in the back. We're in the same class."

Now my mouth was hanging open. "How did I not know this?"

"Because you," she said, "are always looking at your phone when you come in, and I'm not yelling across the room at you."

Hottie just chuckled. "Well, sounds like I get to buy you both a coffee at the Student Union and hear all about this, hm? My treat, Tiff."

"Lead on," I told him.

# CHAPTER 16

## HOTSHOT

The girl was cute. Like knockout sort of cute. The kind of cute that got boyfriends in trouble with their girlfriends, and Cade had his arm wrapped around Tiffany's shoulders. Needless to say, I wanted to know a lot more about this relationship, and a coffee seemed like an easy way to do it.

Together, the three of us hit the Student Union. I got their requests and told them to find a table, then went to order us coffees from the Starbucks in here. Thankfully, it didn't take long, but when I made my way back, the pair were sitting across from each other and leaning in, talking animatedly.

"...Both going to UCLA. And Yvette is in Boston, I think. I dunno, but I'm the only one who stayed local."

"Damn, that sucks," Cade said, looking up as I sat down. "Thanks, man." And he passed Tiffany's drink to her before taking his own. "Hottie's another one of Jeri's boyfriends. The first, I think."

"And you weren't supposed to know that part," I told him. "She was testing the waters."

"We found out after the fact," Cade said. "She sorta 'fessed up." He shrugged. "But it's what she needed. She's known you forever, and it all worked out in the end."

"I just have to say that y'all are adorable," Tiffany told us. "I have no clue how Jericho managed to make this thing with all of you work, but it's cute as fuck."

Ok, I liked the girl a little more than I expected. She also didn't seem to be flirting, so that was a plus. Still, she was Cade's ex, and one he'd dumped to hook up with Jeri, so I had no clue how all of this fit together now.

"So, boyfriends for you?" I asked. "Girlfriends?"

Tiffany laughed. "Nope. I'm currently working on grades. My major is accounting, so I'm about to be drowning in math homework soon. Never mind that I don't exactly have the best track record with guys." And she stuck her tongue out at Cade.

"And you weren't into me," Cade said.

Tiff just groaned and dropped her head. "I wasn't *not* into you." Then she grimaced. "Ok, I was kinda dating you to keep Dylan away, and it seemed like a good idea back then."

"Trust me, I could tell," Cade assured her. "I mean, I assumed you were trying to piss off an ex or something, because you'd hang all over me in public, then ignore me the moment we were alone."

"I'm sorry," Tiffany muttered. "Cade, I really am. You're a good guy, and I'm glad I got to know that, but..."

"Yeah," he agreed. "It was a bad idea."

"Dylan's idea," Tiffany clarified. "Which, by definition, means a bad one. And no offense, but you're so much happier with Jeri than you ever were with me."

"What about you?" I asked. "Happier being single?"

She paused to turn her cup before her a few times. "Um, actually, yeah." Then she licked her lips, moistening them. "When those guys were arrested? All my friends wanted to date again. I just wanted to enjoy not having to look over my shoulder. This summer? I got to hang out with the girls at the lake, laugh about stupid shit, and binge-watch Netflix to my heart's content. So, yeah. Maybe it's avoidance or something, but I'm honestly good with it."

Trauma, probably. What those girls had gone through last year would mess anyone up. Still, I liked that she respected how Jeri was dating us. I liked that she seemed to be smart and obviously opinionated. I just wasn't sure about how easily she'd moved to curl up against Cade's side.

Yeah, I was being protective. This time, it wasn't just of Jeri. It was also Knock. Ruin was the only family I had, and that meant I'd do anything to keep us together. I liked these kids, even if they were no longer feeling quite as young as they had last year. I was going to keep calling them that until they made me stop, though.

"So all of Ruin lives together?" Tiffany asked Cade.

And that made me tense. "What do you know about Ruin?"

"Everything," Cade said. "Hot, she's the one Knock told. The one who got drugged with Jeri."

Ok, now I was putting her into place. She'd been the ringleader of the mean girls. The one Jeri had hated, then worked with, and eventually came to respect. They'd also let her in much too deep, trusting that she wouldn't say shit.

Oddly, she hadn't.

"Why didn't you tell your friends about us after Alpha Team got arrested?" I asked.

She looked over and smiled. "Illegal. Zoe told me that, and I knew Jeri had swiped Evan's phone. Days later, Evan got arrested for distributing child porn - from his *phone*? Yeah, that was easy to put together, and the last thing I wanted to do was mess it up. But see, it also meant Jericho was helping Zoe. When I asked her to help me - even after I'd been a total bitch about Cade here? She did."

"And you were a bitch," Cade told her. "Seriously, slut-shaming?"

"It was all I had!" Tiffany huffed. "I mean, she'd been in Sanger a matter of days, Cade. I couldn't call her stupid, because she'd end up as an honors student or something. Plus, I didn't think slut would hurt too bad, because who really cares about that shit anyway? But I wanted the yelling to make her notice me."

"She did," I promised. "She also has a very bad history with bullying."

"And I got lectured," Tiffany admitted. "With an arm over my throat and a few threats added in. Yeah, Jeri and I've talked about it since. It's just that my friends and I knew we needed to keep girls away from Dylan and his buddies. I knew that if I lost Cade, Dylan would make me suffer. So, um, yeah."

"A complete clusterfuck," Cade clarified for me.

I grunted, but Tiffany kept going. "My friends and I had been backed into a corner, and we're not proud of what we did. They left it all behind when they went away to college. Me? I'm still here, trying to avoid most of the people I went to school with."

"So this means I shouldn't sit with you in class?" Cade asked.

She laughed. "No, you're cool. I'll also tell Jeri if you get creepy and make her deal with you."

Which made Cade roar out a laugh, but now I was finally smiling. "You should come over sometime," I said. "Well, if you have a car? We're on the east side of town."

"Over by the high school?" she asked.

"Closer to the mall," I admitted. "Between the two."

"And we have a pool," Cade added. "You, Zoe, and Jeri could hang out and catch up."

The smile she gave him? Thankful was the best word I had for it. It took me a second to realize why: because Cade hadn't included himself in that. He was pointing out that she could hang out with a few girls, just the way she'd said she wanted to earlier.

"So are all of you still hacking?" she asked. "And if so, what does a hacktivist group do when the bad guy gets busted?"

"Turn him over to the feds," I explained. "Although, it was a bit messier than that."

"Dylan's login to that group's website?" Cade said. "It got the FBI closer to catching the leader. The leader figured it out and went after Knock's big sister."

Tiffany sucked in a breath. "Riley?"

"Mhm," Cade agreed. "And a few others. They were held hostage, there was a shootout, a gamer friend of ours broke a rib, I think? But the good guys survived, the bad guys were killed, and now all the rest are being rounded up, so the FBI wants us to help."

"Cade!" I snapped.

He huffed at me. "Seriously, Hottie? She already knows most of this."

"And Alex said she didn't need news of our thing getting out."

"Thing?" Tiff asked. Then she waved that away. "Nope. Do not want to know. More fighting bad guy stuff?"

"Possibly legally fighting bad guy stuff," Cade explained. "And Hot, if she's coming over, she'll hear enough. Besides, we know she's not going to tell anyone."

"Who would I tell?" she asked. "My parents? Fuck no. They were pissed about the whole Dylan thing. Said I should've known better than to hang out with the wrong crowd. Never mind that they spent all year telling me he was such a nice boy. Fuckers."

"I'm sorry," Cade said gently, reaching across to rub her arm.

But high, like near her elbow. It was the sort of gesture he used with me or Jinxy. Kind, compassionate, but not too soft or sensual. Yeah, and come to think of it, I was being a fucking ass for worrying like this. Cade swung both ways. Would I be acting like this if he was talking to some guy from his high school? Probably not.

I just knew Jeri was fragile right now. She was trying to be strong, but my baby girl needed to learn how to roll with things a little more. She needed to accept that not everything was her fault. Then again, I also knew exactly how huge it was for her to actually admit she was in love - with all of us.

Which meant I needed to shift this talk a bit. "So you know Zoe too?"

"Knew her first," Tiff said. "I mean, we all went to the same school growing up. Sanger only has one of each. So I knew her and Elliot - Ripper - by name. When she started dating Evan, I actually got to know her, and she's cool. A little shy, but that made sense."

"Why?" I pressed.

"Because she was nothing until she started dating him," Tiff explained. "Those guys were the football team. The hottest players making all the girls chase them, and all that typical high school bullshit we think is important. Well, Zoe was doing her best to walk that line, you know? To be both the good girl and a jock's girlfriend. I didn't realize it at the time, but the whole thing is just a no-win situation for us girls."

"You seemed to do ok," I countered.

"Fuck..." She laughed. "I dated a guy because I didn't want to date another who was with one of my closest friends. Yeah, very ok, Hottie. I was so busy trying to be popular and accepted by my friends that it took me a while to realize they were being blackmailed by their boyfriends. Real fucking ok. But that's my point."

"What is?" Cade asked.

"We girls were trying so hard to be what the boys wanted in high school," she explained. "We made some dumb mistakes because of it. I'm sure I'll make more, but now that I'm here? Being in college means I don't have the entire school talking about what I'm wearing, who I'm talking to at my locker, and all that other shit. I get to just go to class, go back to my dorm, and get my homework done."

"Just don't forget to enjoy it while you're in the middle of it," I warned her. "I know what happened last year was hard, but you are still allowed to have the full college experience. The one *you* want, Tiffany."

"Sounds like something you've told Jeri," Cade teased.

I tilted my head in acknowledgement. "Kinda is. A slightly

different version, but yeah. I know when I got to college, I was so worried about losing my scholarship that I refused to do anything but study. Then I burned out. Jinxy's the one who told me to go out, get drunk, and do something dumb."

"No offense," Tiff said, "but getting drunk around strangers is no longer high on my to-do list."

I looked over at her and smiled. "So make sure you aren't alone. I have six roommates who would be willing to watch your back. Well, plus me."

So the girl thrust her arm out at me. "Friends, Hottie?"

I accepted her hand and shook once. "Sure. Just friends. I'm kinda taken."

Which made Tiff laugh. "The whole house is. It's one big polycule, I hear. And I'm hoping it's still just as good as it was when it started."

"Better," Cade said. "Somewhere in there, my girlfriend fell in love with us, and my boyfriend?" His eyes dropped to the table. "Being with him is normal. I no longer have to hide it."

"I'm so, so, so happy for you," Tiffany said, clasping his arm. "Oh, Cade, you definitely deserve this. Yeah, I'll come hang sometime, just because I want to see all that cuteness in person. Ok, and maybe because I want to meet Zoe's boyfriend. I've only heard about him."

Which was when my watch began to beep with an alarm. "Time to get to class," I warned them. "See you at home, Cade?"

"Yep," he agreed. "I got Knock with me." He and Tiff stood, grabbed their cups, then waved.

I sat there for a moment longer, watching the pair walk away. This time, Cade wasn't hanging on her. She wasn't pressed up against him. They looked like nothing more than two people who happened to know each other. Even Zoe walked closer to Cade than this girl.

Which made me feel a little sorry for her. Now that I knew who she was in the whole scheme of things, I couldn't hate her. No, she was the one Jeri had said was strong. The one who'd been willing to fight back. The bitch my girlfriend had learned a few things from, and for Jeri, that said a lot.

And now she was here, at college, alone? Granted, she'd eventually make friends. Some girl in her dorms, or maybe a pal from class. It wouldn't matter, but it would happen. That was how it always went. But if she was still a bit twitchy from the shitshow that had been her senior year of high school?

Then yeah, I had no problem with Cade draping his arm around her. We were Ruin. We helped the women who needed it most, and I was starting to wonder if this girl might be in that category still, because trauma was a bitch to wade through. Jeri was proof enough of that.

So was I.

# CHAPTER 17

**KNOCK**

I met up with Cade after my last class. He'd been waiting, but the smile on his face when he saw me? Yeah, I could get used to that. I was also trying my hardest to get used to holding hands. It was such a simple little gesture, and felt nice when I did it. Yet for so long, girls had pulled away from me when I'd tried, so I'd learned to stop trying.

Well, this wasn't high school, Cade and Jeri weren't some random girls I had a crush on, and Riley had told me relationships only worked if everyone put in an effort. So, here I was, efforting my little heart out. With our fingers laced together, we walked back across campus to find his car.

Along the way, he told me about Tiffany. It seemed she was in his political science class. She'd seen him last week, but he'd been a little oblivious. Sadly, it sounded just like him. Kinda like how he'd missed me trying to flirt with him back when I'd been coming out.

But it seemed Hottie had invited her over. Hottie, of all people! He and Jinxy were the only ones who'd never met her, so I supposed it made sense. I didn't have a problem with it, though. She was trustworthy. Considering how I'd been the one to spill the beans to the girl, yet she'd kept it all to herself? Even when the Alpha Team had been arrested, Tiff had kept our secret, not even telling her best friends.

And we were all starting to fall into a comfortable routine. Studying was common. We were all figuring out where and how we preferred to focus. Dinner was a group effort, usually with a few of us cooking and the rest cleaning or serving. For me, a movie was my way of winding down, and then I had to get ready to start it all over again the next day.

That night, I headed into the bedroom to have a shower and pass out. The water was running, which meant Cade had beat me. I managed to pull off my clothes, then flopped down on the bed, ass up. While I waited, I grabbed my phone and started scrolling, checking to see what was going on with my gamer friends.

Riley was doing TikToks now with little Void. Murder was falling in the rankings of the PLG, but only a bit. The hours with his son meant less time to game. Our little virtual world was still recovering from the shock of what had happened at F5, but people on the internet had a very short attention span. That meant they were more worried about the game balance of a new gun in Eternal Combat than anything else.

Then a kiss caressed the back of my thigh. I dimmed my phone and glanced back to see Cade crawling onto the bed behind me. A white towel was wrapped around his waist, his amazing abs were visible as he moved, and my blood was quickly running downwards.

"Tease," I said playfully.

With a laugh, he flopped down beside me. "I just wanted to see if I could distract you."

"Consider me distracted," I promised as I leaned to put my phone away. "I was waiting for the shower."

"Could've joined me," he pointed out, rolling onto his side.

So I did the same, putting us face to face. "I wanted to wash my hair, and this blue shit leaves a bit of a mess."

"Don't care," he promised, grabbing my hip and scooting even closer. Then he sucked in a breath like he'd just had a thought. "Oh, I forgot to tell you."

"Mm?"

"A girl asked me if we wanted to join the school's Pride group."

"Us?" I was a little confused.

"She saw you kiss me before my first class, said you were cute, and then gave me a flier." He reached between us to trail a finger over my chest. "It was kinda nice."

"I mean, we can join a Pride group if you want," I decided.

He just shook his head. "It's not really that, Knock. It's..." He paused, biting his lips together as he thought. "It was so casual. I kissed you in the middle of campus and no one had a problem. No one tried to crack a joke about wanting to watch. Some girl asked if we wanted to join Pride, and that was it. No threats, no one wanting to beat me up or hurt you because we're not like them."

"Because we are like them," I countered. "We're young, horny, and proud of our partner."

"Two guys," he pointed out.

"So?"

Cade opened his mouth to reply, but merely paused. "I have no comeback for that."

"Exactly," I whispered. "Because nothing about us is weird, babe."

"Yeah, but after listening to my dad, and trying to hide it, and Dylan holding it over my head, I just feel like it's second nature to pretend to be straight."

"Which makes sense," I promised. "I'm also not offended."

"But I don't want to," he said. "I really liked how that felt. The way that girl called you my boyfriend without any hesitation? How she called you cute like a compliment to me? I mean, isn't that basically what Zoe and Jeri do to each other? Hype up the other's partners for the ego boost or something?"

"Kinda," I agreed. "I'm not really sure how it works, but it's not a jealousy thing."

"That!" Cade said. "It's an 'excited for them' thing. Like telling someone they have a nice car, you know? It doesn't mean you want to steal their car. Shit, it doesn't even mean you want to drive it. You can simply say it's nice and mean nothing else. Still feels kinda good when it happens, and that's what they do. It's what the girl today did."

"Saying I was cute?" I asked, making sure I was keeping up.

"That *my boyfriend* was cute," he corrected. "Mine. The guy I was almost tongue-fucking."

"It was not that good of a kiss," I joked, moving a bit closer.

He sighed and his face slipped a bit. "Never mind. It was just kinda cool."

"Hey," I breathed, palming the side of his face so he'd look at me again. "Cade, we're coming at this from two different places. You spent years hiding this and being told it was something to hate. Me?" I scoffed. "I figured it out when I was checking out Kitty's boyfriend! I didn't have a clue I was into guys. I was just confused about everything. You? You knew. You kissed a boy. You lived with this as a dirty secret, and me coming out to Riley because there was a picture? Not even the same." I leaned in a little more. "So tell me, babe?"

He glanced up, his caramel eyes holding mine intensely enough to make my pulse pick up. "It was so normal," he said. "You held my hand, then we had our arms around each other, kissed, and it was just like when I'm with Jeri. No one looked. No one cared. No one got in our faces or tried to hurt us, and for the first time..." His gaze shifted from one of my eyes to the other. "I could just love you. Nothing more. Nothing less."

"Yeah," I breathed. "I like that."

And I leaned in to kiss him. Immediately, his hand came up to cup the back of my neck. Mine was already on his face, but this kiss wasn't frantic. It was soft, slow, and passionate. It was loving, and these were the kind I liked the most.

"I want to be on bottom tonight," Cade whispered against my lips.

My eyes jumped open. His face was right there, and now my dick was so damned hard. "I definitely like this idea," I agreed.

So he jerked his chin at the nightstand. "Lube. Condoms."

"Yes, dear." I rolled on my back, aware my dick was now sticking straight up.

Cade looked. He also shifted onto his stomach, which made another rush of blood head downwards hard enough I could now feel the throbbing. His towel had come off, his bare ass was begging me to look, and all those muscles in his back were there for me to kiss, caress, and enjoy.

"Killing me," I groaned even as I found a condom and managed to roll it on.

"That," he said, "is the point." Then the jerk hiked his ass up, making it clear exactly what he wanted.

Yep, I fumbled. The condom was good. The lube was a little too cooperative, but a heavy handful of it would work. Half of that went on my dick. The other half? I closed my fist and pushed myself up to get into place behind him. Then I wiped my hand from his ass all the way down and under until I felt his hard dick against my palm.

"Shit, cold!" he hissed.

Chuckling, I leaned in over him until my mouth was by his ear. "You're the one who's skipping the foreplay." Then I nipped at his lobe and dragged my dick down his crack.

"Fuck, Knock." He pressed back towards me. "Babe, please?"

"God, I love you," I mumbled even as I lined myself up and began pressing in.

Hot. Tight. He felt so good and looked even better under me like this. In the months we'd lived together, we'd learned each other's bodies, but this man could still get me going so easily. As I gently, carefully pushed my way into his body, I let my lips slide down the back of his neck.

Then I bit.

My teeth closed on the space just above his shoulder, and for a second his body reacted. He flinched, his ass relaxed, and I pushed in all the way to my balls. The moan of approval, however, was the best part.

"Cheater," he panted.

"You love it," I reminded him as I started to move.

Slowly at first, I let myself feel him. Damn, it was good. The pressure of his body around me was so much better than jacking off. The dip of his back turned me on even more. The way he pressed his head into the pillow to hide his face - and mostly failed? Sexy as fuck.

When I'd first imagined dating a guy, I'd assumed it would be some ugly dorky nerd. Instead, I'd met Cade. Everything about him was beautiful, from the way his hair refused to obey to the full lips that were parted in pleasure as I rocked into him.

He was my dream man. Jericho was all I'd ever wanted in a girl. That we were all together felt like some dream I was going to wake up from, and I never wanted it to end. I wanted to enjoy each and every second of this. I wanted to love him like this was as normal as he'd just realized.

Like he was one of my everythings.

"I'm never giving you up," I breathed against his ear. "Not if people have problems with it, and certainly not if they don't. This?" I pumped into him as deep as I could. "This is us, Cade, and I don't care who knows."

"Knock," he gasped, pulling a hand out and dropping it on the pillow he was trying so hard not to bite.

I moved my hand to grab it, holding him as tightly as I could while still thrusting. "My first crush, Cade. *My* boyfriend. My lover." Each phrase came with another push into his body. "And when you hold my hand?" I began to move a little faster.

He pressed back, his shoulders pushing into my chest as his ass bucked, driving me even deeper. That made me groan in approval. Fuck, he was sensual. Like this, it was hard to remember how much shit he'd been through to accept this, but he had.

And he'd done it all for me.

"When you hold my hand," I tried again, my words coming out hard with my breath, "it makes me the proudest man in the world."

"Oh fuck," he muttered, turning his face to cry out into the pillow.

So I shifted my hips and rode him the way I knew he liked most. His body moved with mine. I didn't bother reaching around. Hell, I couldn't while holding myself off him, but it didn't matter. Again, then again, then again, I buried myself in his ass, until he threw his head back and sucked in a deep breath before pushing it out in a growl.

His ass tightened around me. I tried to keep going. I wanted to make this last as long as possible, but that? Seeing him completely lose control? I was a goner, and not just my body. My heart and mind lost control as well, nothing but euphoria taking over as I collapsed against his back and let myself just feel it. All of it.

For a moment, the pair of us struggled to breathe. The sound was loud in the room, but I didn't care. Let our roommates hear. It wasn't like we had anything to hide.

Then Cade reached back and stroked my bicep. "Ok, you're crushing me," he admitted.

So I pushed off and slid from his body. "Damn," I huffed before flopping down beside him. "I think being with you will never get old."

"Same," he agreed, turning so he could see me. "Knock, this?" A wistful smile claimed his lips. "I feel like I might finally be getting it right."

"You are," I assured him. "Babe, you're getting it so right, and I'm such a complete mush right now."

"Then make that shower cold," he said, nudging me. "I'll also warm up the bed and let you use my shoulder tonight."

"And that," I told him, "is just one more thing that makes you perfect."

# CHAPTER 18

### JINXY

My stomach growled. I had a nice long break between classes, and Google said there was a McDonald's up here. I'd skipped food this morning because I'd hit snooze too many times, and now I was paying for it. I knew better. I also knew I couldn't afford to miss a class.

But something red caught my eye. Pushing my glasses higher, I did a double take, and sure enough, it was exactly who I thought it was. Her little pink shirt clashed with her hair, her sunglasses were the big type, and her bag looked heavy.

"Zoe!" I called out, lifting my arm in an attempt to get her to see me.

She paused, looking around in confusion. When her eyes finally landed on me, the biggest smile took over her face. She didn't bother to walk towards me, though. Nope, my girlfriend ran, squealing with delight, until she slammed into my chest, throwing her arms around my waist.

"Jinxy!" she said with so much excitement. "What are you doing here?"

"Starving," I admitted. "I have an hour and a half break between classes, so I was going to hit up some food. You?"

"Only an hour," she said, giving me a cute little pout.

"Well, I bet I can buy you lunch in that time. There's supposed to be a place right over here."

She wrapped her arm around my waist and let me guide her. I knew touching like this was a big deal for her, just like I knew she'd been pushing through her own fears so she could be "normal." I tried to make sure she knew it wasn't necessary, but she insisted she was doing it for herself, not me.

"So, do you always have this break?" I asked as we reached the road. The restaurant was just on the other side of the street.

"Mondays, Wednesdays, and Fridays," she said.

"I have Mondays and Wednesdays." The light changed, so we started walking. "Maybe I can make a little lunch date with you? Twice a week, my treat?"

"You don't have to," she assured me.

I hated how she always acted like I was supposed to find her annoying or something. High-maintenance, maybe? I wasn't sure, but Zoe was probably one of the easiest people to be around I'd ever met. She didn't ask for a lot, and just being near her was amazing.

In truth, she made me smile. No matter how bad things got, even thinking about her could make it better. Spending time with her? It was like a drug without any downsides.

"Kinda want to," I promised. "C'mon, Zoe. I like seeing my girl. I like talking to you. So for me, this would be a very nice habit to make."

"A date?" she asked.

"Your call," I assured her.

"Well..." She let go of me to hurry ahead and open the door. "Call it a date and agree to meet me in the Student Union, and I'm good with it."

"Why the union?" I asked.

She gasped in mock-astonishment. "They have a Starbucks!"

"Addict," I joked, guiding her into the line.

We got our food for "here," waited while the tray was filled and our coffees were made, then found a table to sit at. It was small, but I was fine with that. It gave me the chance to stare without seeming creepy.

Most nights, we still sent texts. That was easier for her, and I was trying my damnedest not to press. And while we flirted, it was a little less intense than it had been before I moved to Texas. Granted, knowing I was a few states away had made me a lot safer than being down a floor.

"So how are you liking college?" I asked, knowing it was a lame question, but still needing something to break the ice.

She rocked her head back and forth, thinking hard. "It's a love-hate relationship. I like the setup. I really like the way things are taught. I absolutely hate half my classes. Fucking core courses!"

I chuckled, knowing that feeling. "It does get better. Next semester, you'll probably get one class you want, then more the one after. By the time you're a senior, it'll be nothing but the cool shit."

"Like yours?" she asked.

I nodded slowly. "Yeah. I mean, I have a massive project I have to do at the end of the year, and that's going to suck, but I'm good with it."

"And your thesis," she said.

"That's when I'm done. So next year or the one after, depending on how I do with my classes."

"I don't even understand all that stuff yet," she admitted. "In high school, we level up with each fall. Here? It's all about how many credit hours of classes I have to shift from a freshman to a sophomore. Like, the structure is completely gone."

"Which is what fucks up a lot of people," I admitted. "I was lucky, though. Southwind didn't really have grades the way you did. We had schedules for what we needed to learn, and it was more like a one-room schoolhouse."

"Cool," she said.

I made a face and shrugged. "Small," I countered. "Closer to homeschooling, but state testing. Mostly we excelled because of the extra classes we got. Gran and Bea made sure we all had something to keep us invested in our futures, not just passing time."

"How are you doing without her?" she asked, looking up at me.

Her lashes were so thick. Her eyeshadow made her eyes pop. The hazel kaleidoscope of them took my breath away and turned me stupid. Everything about this girl was so soft, gentle, and amazing, but so was her strength. I'd seen dozens of people struggling with issues that were nothing compared to hers, and they'd shattered. Zoe? She just kept going - with a smile.

"You're amazing, you know?" I asked.

Confusion swept across her face, then she shook her head. "Why do you say that?"

"Just... all of this," I admitted. "The way you're always so happy, I guess? I don't even know, but I always find myself shocked by how strong you are. From starting college to the feds to your trauma? I dunno. You make it all look easy."

"Me?" she asked.

I nodded, pausing to take a bite. "Yeah. I think that's the thing that drew me in. You should've been like Jeri, hating everyone and everything. Instead, you're just..." I huffed a weak laugh. "Ok, this is going to sound lame, but you're a pleasure to be around, even when you should be completely melting down. And just to put it out there, you don't have to be happy for me - or anyone else."

"It's for me," she admitted. "If I focus on all the bad shit, then I start thinking about it, and that's just like this black spiral which sucks me in, you know? But when I focus on the good stuff? Like you being so understanding with me, or how Cade and Ripper are besties now, and all the little things? I mean, our house!"

"Our house is fucking amazing," I agreed.

"And a pool," she reminded me.

"A hot tub," I pointed out.

Which made her grin. "I need a new swimsuit, though."

My eyes narrowed. "Do I want to ask why?"

"Because I don't like my old one." Her eyes jumped to the side. "I kinda picked it to impress guys."

"Then you definitely need a new one," I agreed. "One that fits your style, because I like this whole bohemian pinup-girl vibe you've got going on."

"Yeah?"

I nodded. "It's like you took the 1950s and made them cool and punk."

"Yes!" she breathed. "That's what I was going for. I mean, I don't like the pastels and flowery patterns, but I love the shapes of those clothes. And I want to include some modern twists, like cats!" She gestured to her shirt.

"You should get a cat," I suggested.

The words just fell out, and yet I found I meant them. Yep, I was officially stupid for this girl. I wanted to give her anything and everything she could dream of. I wanted to spoil her and impress her, and yet I knew she wasn't materialistic like that. She'd never had the chance to be.

It was mostly that I wanted to show her I was worth something. I wanted her to pick me back. Now that I was living in the middle of this mess with Jericho and her polycule, I wasn't completely sure where I fit in.

Hottie was cool with his girlfriend sleeping with other guys. I was pretty sure I couldn't do it. I'd spend all my time waiting for her to find someone better, replace me, or get sick of my shit. I'd be so insanely jealous, I'd probably turn into some kind of asshole.

And yet I was also a part of this mess. I preferred to think of my "bond" to Jeri as a brotherly one. There was no way I'd stick my dick in my bro's girl - or my little bro-sis. Not interested. What I wanted was a relationship with the girl sitting across from me, and I was pretty sure I was about to crash and burn if I didn't turn my brain on.

She paused with a fry almost to her lips. "Huh?"

"You should get a cat," I said again. "You know, like a real one. I'm getting the impression you like them."

Her bright red lips fell open for a second, and then she shoved the fry in to hide it. "I've never been able to have a cat, and we're renting, Jinxy. That means pets aren't going to happen."

"And it's Logan," I reminded her. "I bet he'd be ok with it. But why no cats?"

"Mom's allergic," she said. "I'm not, but she gets hives. We had a little kitten when I was in sixth grade, but we had to give her away because Mom reacted so badly. I've wanted another cat ever since."

"What kind?" I asked. "I mean, are you into those hairless ones? Black ones? Calico, long hair, or what?"

She shrugged. "I'd be happy with pretty much any cat. I just like how chill they are, and how they hang out without needing so much work, like Quake. Don't get me wrong, I love dogs too, but I think I'd get a cat for myself."

"I'm totally a cat guy," I told her. "Had a roommate with this big orange tabby. He'd lie in the window of our apartment - well, dorm apartment - and purr so loud. When I moved, I was bummed to lose the cat. The roommate, however, was an idiot."

"I kinda see you as the loner type," she admitted.

I shook my head. "I'm really not. I grew up in a herd almost as crazy as this. I simply figured out friendships can be just as real when they're virtual."

"And us?" Her question was soft, almost like she was scared to ask.

My heart slammed to a halt. Crap! This was one of those bad questions. Was this when she told me she wanted to have her own polycule like Jeri? Was it when I was supposed to profess my undying love? Yeah, um, I didn't move that fast. Shit. Ok, so I'd just be honest with her.

"We're figuring it out," I said. "I'm also not in a rush, Zoe. I *like* that we're figuring it out. I enjoy learning more about you - like the cat thing! I know you don't believe me, and I promise Hottie has told me how you're worried about us, but I'm actually enjoying having the chance to get to know you. The real you."

"Jeri said you're ok with this," she said, but the words were almost a mumble. "It's just that I don't know what's in it for you, except that we're not the single ones in the house."

"You're what's in it for me," I admitted. "I know, sounds cheesy as fuck, but it's true. I like how you're all into being girly. I think it's cool as fuck, ok? I mean, guys? Our fashion consists of jeans and t-shirts, so I like seeing what you do." I laughed once. "And in full disclosure, I have fashion people in the family, so I'm not an idiot about it. Just *mostly* ignorant."

"Yeah?"

I nodded, deciding to lay it all out there. "And I like this. I like having someone who doesn't expect me to be cool, or tough, or care about normal shit. I like being able to say fashion is cool. I like being able to go off on the new armor I got in Flawed. I really like how you don't just smile and nod at me when I do it. Zoe, I like that we click. I like that we never run out of things to talk about."

"But like, um, kissing?"

I lifted my drink and sucked back a gulp through the straw. Fuck. I didn't want to lie to her, but I definitely didn't want to come across as clingy. Granted, I kinda wanted to be clingy, but that would only chase her off.

"I like kissing," I said. "It's also been a while. Believe it or not, I'm not a virgin. I don't have the sort of body count Jericho does, but I'm also kinda shy when it comes to talking to real people."

"Real?" she asked. "As opposed to?"

"Gamers," I explained. "People online who I can't see who will judge me for my stats, not my face, or my lack of biceps. I dunno. It's easier to be funny or cool when no one's looking, I guess?"

"Yeah, it is," she agreed. "But I kinda like your biceps."

I laughed, thinking that was a joke.

"I'm serious!" she insisted. "Jinxy, I like goth guys. I like the lean ones. I've always been into the thin guys with nice faces, and that's you. I mean, when you sent me that first picture? I was so sure you were punking me with some celebrity off the internet."

"Me?"

No way. She was just being nice, right? That was what she did, but it was still sweet. It also made my stomach feel like it was spinning. Damn it. I hadn't been this stupid over a girl since... Well, in my entire life.

Zoe nodded emphatically. "Yeah. I mean, I was so fucked up about guys, and you're so cute. I just don't understand why a guy who could get a million normal girls would want to put up with my issues."

Fuck. My face was getting warmer. I felt like I had to be floating a bit. No wonder they called it cloud nine. Clearing my throat, I pushed my glasses up, trying to convince my skin it would not turn red. I was pretty sure it wasn't working, though.

"Uh, yeah. I kinda thought the same. I mean, this amazingly hot girl, and she was talking to me? I figured I had to be, like, the 'safely across the country' guy or something. And now I'm not, so I get it if you're not into this."

"But I am!"

"Me too," I said softly, aware my face was now burning. "So, yeah. If I'm patient, I have a chance to kiss a perfect ten? Why wouldn't I be patient, Zoe?"

"Me?"

"You."

She quickly shoved a bit of food into her mouth, then chewed. "But I'm not a perfect ten."

"I think you are." And I leaned back, crossing my arms, because I clearly wasn't doing as bad as I'd feared. "I mean, look at us. We're bickering about each other being cute. Doesn't that mean this is kinda working?"

"Yeah," she agreed, a little smile taking over. "And I think more dates will help."

"All the dates," I swore before she could back out. "All you have to do, Zoe, is let me know your limits."

"I'm kinda trying to find them," she told me.

So I nodded. "Makes sense. Just promise you'll tell me to back off if I cross a line?"

For a long moment she thought about that. It was the sort of thing I'd expected her to simply agree to, but instead she was pondering it just a little too hard. Thankfully, she answered before I lost all the giddy feelings she'd given me a moment before.

"No," she decided. "I mean, I will if it's a big thing, but I need to get over this, Jinxy."

I swore I heard a record scratch in my brain. What? *Needed* to *get over* this? Never mind what she was considering as "this." The needing part and the getting over part were bad enough!

"No, baby, you don't," I said. "Zoe, you *need* to be comfortable. With me, with Ruin, and with everything else. You *need* to find your boundaries, fortify them, and trust that we will not think less of you for having them. If anything, we'll be even more impressed, ok?"

"Yeah?"

"Swear to god," I promised. "And baby? I'm already more impressed than you can imagine. And no, I'm not talking about your recovery. I'm talking about you. All of you, because you are so much more than what happened to you."

"That," she said. "That's why I want to try harder. I want to be the girl you think I am."

"I promise you already are." I looked up, finding her eyes again. "Kinda why I get so nervous around you. I sorta feel like I was cooler online, and I'm trying so hard not to let all of my nerdy idiot side show."

"Let it show," she said softly. "It's my favorite part."

Fuck. I was gonna fall for this girl so hard. I could already feel myself tipping.

# CHAPTER 19

## HOTSHOT

I was still trying to decide what I thought of Jason. He'd arrived Friday evening with his dog, but nothing about the man seemed to make sense. He was an FBI agent. He was a hacker. He had a PTSD service dog, but always seemed chill. Supposedly, he was one hell of a sniper and just as deadly with any gun.

I had all the facts, but putting those things together with the man meant to train us? I didn't quite know how to make it all work. Oh, I got along with him, and I certainly respected his skills, but I couldn't decide if I actually liked him or not. The best way I had to describe the guy was "weird," and yet that fit all of us in one way or another.

But he made our training easy. Friday, we all got the basics of gun handling. Hooking his laptop up to the TV, Jason showed us schematics of the weapon we'd be using. He explained the parts, their names, and how they worked. Mostly, it was the basic things like "this will get hot" and "that part will pinch."

In other words, he knew he was teaching complete dumbasses, and yet he didn't treat us like such. But when he lifted his shirt and pulled out an actual gun? Yeah, my mouth dropped open. The guy had been hanging out with us, and I hadn't even *guessed* he'd been armed.

He also emptied the weapon, did something with the top bit, and then showed us how the concept worked with a real weapon. Over and over, he said the same thing: do not point it at anything you don't want to kill. Empty, loaded, or any other way. If we weren't willing to make the thing dead, then the end of the gun would not go near it.

When that was done, we all got to hold the weapon, feel its weight, and "dry fire" it at the ground - not pointing it near another person. The trigger was a little weird, but it was enough to prepare us for using it, because first thing Saturday morning, we had an appointment to shoot the real thing.

My alarm went off much too early. Thankfully, when I made it downstairs, a line of travel mugs was already being filled. I paused when I saw who was doing the filling, though.

"Jason?" I asked, making my way into the kitchen.

He chuckled once. "Morning, Hottie. Why am I not surprised you're the first downstairs?"

"Because the girls need makeup, Knock and Cade aren't functional before noon, Ripper's going to check on Zoe about eight hundred times, and Jinxy is habitually late." I turned for the fridge and pulled out the cream. "I'm guessing you know those cups are color-coded?"

"I've spent enough time with Riley," he assured me. "And while it seems like a cute habit of hers, it's actually a useful memory device. Correlate the color with the preferred coffee mixture."

"And her way of showing she cares," I pointed out. "For Riley, making coffee is the same as a hug."

He paused. "Yeah. She gets that not everyone wants to be touched." Then he turned the black cup at the end. "But I'm being all official."

There was an FBI logo on the side of his mug. Seal? I wasn't sure what the thing was called, but his had it, proving he was as much an addict as the rest of us. That he'd brought a cup?

"So, you're leaving that one here, right?" I asked.

"Could."

"Should," I said. "I mean, since you'll spend a bit of time here. Kinda makes you feel more like a member of the crew."

He didn't get the chance to reply because Ripper and Zoe were making their way downstairs. That seemed to trigger the rest. We were all dressed about the same, in some version of jeans and t-shirts. Hair was pulled back into ponytails - and not just the girls'. Knock and Cade had theirs out of the way as well.

Coffees were handed out. Shoes were put on, and then we all piled into Knock's SUV. The thing could fit eight, barely. We were crammed in there shoulder to shoulder, and Crysis got to ride in the very back, but it worked for the drive to Dallas.

When we pulled into an unmarked parking lot, I was sure we were in the wrong place. The building was the pale grey color of concrete. There weren't many windows. Enough cars were here to prove this place wasn't abandoned, but there wasn't any signage visible. Still, at Jason's urging, we all got out and followed him in.

"Good morning, I'm going to need to see some ID," a guy said from a counter at the front.

Jason headed straight for him. "Special Agent Jason Raige. You should have a reservation for my group? Eight stalls, six hours?"

The clerk's eyes narrowed. "I'm going to need their IDs too."

He waved us forward, and we all pulled out our driver's licenses. The man looked at those, then back to Jason, and finally at his computer screen, which was turned away from us.

"Law enforcement IDs are preferred," he finally said.

"They don't have them," Jason explained. "I do. The Deputy Director of the FBI should've cleared this."

"We're only contracted for law enforcement," the clerk said coldly.

"Mhm," Jason muttered. "Which is why the FBI's request to use your facility for training would count." He sighed and pulled an envelope from his pocket. "Documentation for their authorization.

Agent in charge: me. I'm going to need seven guns. Glock 19s. I have eight stalls."

"And the dog?" the man asked.

"Service dog," Jeri said, butting in. "You can't keep him out."

"Maybe not, but the gunfire isn't good for his hearing either." The man gave Jeri a scathing look.

"Handled," Jason assured him. "He's my dog. He's certified. He's used to this. Now, about the guns?"

The clerk gave all of us a disgusted look, sighed heavily, and then gave in. One by one, we were each handed a small case with a gun and bullets inside. He opened each to check that everything was included, assigned it to one of us, and recorded our driver's license numbers on his computer.

While he was doing that, Jason bent to the bag he'd brought with him, and pulled something out. Headphones? No, sound protection! But when he put the bright orange ear protectors on Crysis? I tried to bite back my laugh, and mostly failed.

"What?" Jason asked. "You'll be wearing your own."

Then he made a gesture and Crysis lay down, perfectly happy with the hard plastic sound protectors strapped to his head. When Jason pulled out another set and put them around his own neck, I realized they were basically the same thing, just with fewer straps.

Then the clerk began passing out the same hearing protection headsets to all of us. "You will want to put those on before entering the shooting range," he warned, gesturing to a door.

"I got it," Jason promised. "Which stalls?"

"The first eight," the man said. "They're the only ones still empty and marked as reserved."

"Good," Jason purred.

Then, pulling on his own headset-looking thing, he gestured for us to do the same and follow him. Crysis was immediately at his side. I was lost, just doing my best to follow along. Yet when we walked through the door the man had indicated, it all started falling into place.

This was an indoor shooting range. Back here, there were lanes like in a bowling alley, with shields between them like in the movies. Dozens of people were stationed at the ones further down, and the sound? There was a lot of it. Even with the hard-shell earmuffs on, I could still hear it, but it wasn't too bad.

"Pick a spot," Jason ordered. "No sharing. Put your gun case on the counter before you. Do not open it. Do not start playing with the buttons or switches. I will come to each of you and make sure you know what we're doing." He gestured to the empty spots we got to choose from. "We have all day, so you'll have plenty of time."

Then he moved to the first stall himself, set his bag on top, and opened it. Inside was ammunition, and a lot of it. Beside him, Crysis found a spot and simply lay down. The dog looked relaxed and comfortable with all of this, which made sense if he was used to it.

I decided to take the spot at the end. That put me next to some guy firing off rounds as fast as he could. From the ordeal when we'd come in, I could only guess this guy had to be either a cop or fed, but he was completely ignoring us. Granted, he had a gun in his hands, so it made sense.

Jeri moved beside me. Knock was beside her, then Cade, Jinxy, Ripper, and Zoe beside Jason. Setting my things down, I looked at the little area I'd be using. There was a red and a green button on the left side. I had a counter in front of me. Beyond that was a very long room with a heavy wall at the end. Everyone else had paper targets with silhouettes of men on them. Those were attached to a track above, which I could only assume was controlled by the buttons.

"Hey." That came from the man beside me, so I looked over. "Which department?"

"Excuse me?"

He grinned. "Which police department are you with?"

"I'm not."

"So FBI or Homeland?"

"Working on FBI weapons qualifications," I said, because that sounded safest. It was also true in the most vague way.

The guy set his gun down, then offered me his hand. "Keith. I'm with missing persons, but I don't think I've seen you around."

"Grayson," I said. "I'm not officially at the Dallas office."

"Ah, trying to get into Quantico? You already have the look of an agent."

"Something like that," I said.

Which made the man give me a suspicious look. "Is your group undercover or something? I mean, they look pretty young."

"Useful, huh?"

"Very. And the hair? Definitely not standard dress code."

I chuckled. "No, they certainly aren't. Good at what they do, though."

"Which means you're not going to tell me," he said, thrusting out his lower lip and nodding. "I can respect that. I just didn't think we were running any training courses in Dallas."

"What makes you think it's a training course?" I asked.

Keith flicked a finger behind me. "Because the agent in charge is teaching that girl how to hold a gun. Not shoot, just hold and aim. Wait..."

I turned to see what he was talking about. Sure enough, Jason was adjusting Zoe's hands around her gun, then making her move her legs. Setting her stance, I realized. Although that didn't seem to be what this guy was looking at.

"What?" I asked him.

"Is that the sniper?"

"What sniper?" I was so far out of my depth.

"The agent who took the shots in Vegas," he said. "Heard he has a service dog. I didn't even know that was allowed."

"It's a cool dog," I said, hoping to shift this conversation slightly.

"And most field agents don't tend to have them," Keith countered.

"I heard the guy was part of an operation in Sanger too. Part of some tech terrorism thing." Then he paused. "Wait."

I smiled. "What?"

Keith looked me over, then shifted his gaze to my friends. "You don't look like the rest of them. What the fuck are they trying to push on us now?"

"I have no clue what you're talking about," I assured him. "I'm just here to learn enough to pass the qualifications."

"Well, let your boss know we're already overloaded, and the last thing we need are more cases dropped on us. If they want us to take on a whole new division, we're going to need more agents, not just new ones either."

"I'll make sure my boss knows that," I promised. "Not sure it applies, but I will make sure they know."

"Good," the man said before picking up his gun, slapping another magazine into it, and then doing his best to empty the whole thing.

Yep, he was pissed. Evidently Alex's idea was not going to be popular. No wonder she didn't want us talking about it yet. Still, if they wanted us armed, then these people would have to get used to seeing us, because we weren't going to fail.

# CHAPTER 20

## JERICHO

Jason got all of us set up, gave us a target, then told us to hit the bullseye marked on the chest. Yeah, easier said than done. I looked down the iron sights - that's what they were called on a real gun, right? - and tried to aim the way I did in game.

It wasn't working.

This thing kicked. In Flawed, my guns would stay centered for the most part. They always returned to the same place after the recoil of a shot. In reality, my arms didn't work like that. Nope, I was putting little holes in my target, but they were not at all where I was aiming.

I'd just used up my first fifteen bullets when Jason dropped a new magazine on the counter. "Need help changing that?" he asked.

"Fuck," I grumbled. "I need help with all of this. I mean..." I set the gun down and waved at the target. "Look at that!"

"Which isn't bad for your first time firing a gun," he assured me.

"But how am I going to pass qualifications like this?" I demanded. "I thought it would be easier. I mean, I've got hours in game, and isn't that kinda like a shooting simulator?"

The look he gave me was some strangled smile like he was struggling not to laugh his ass off. "No." Then he reached around me to pick up my gun. "Move over, Jeri."

I did, so the man showed me how to expel the clip - er, magazine - and replace it with a new one. Then he lifted it with both hands, pointing it downrange.

"In games, the animation is stable. In the real world, it's all about your arms," he explained. "You have to keep your weight balanced so your arms are comfortable out here like this."

"Uh-huh..." I crossed my arms and glared at him. "So can you hit the bullseye?"

He glanced over. "Yeah."

"Do it."

Letting out a sigh, he dropped the muzzle a bit and gave me a dirty look. "You know I can."

"Do it anyway," I pressed. "I want to see what you're doing."

"Fine."

The gun came up, his finger tensed, and the man fired off shot after shot. Five of them in a row. What he didn't do was tense up. He didn't strain to make the gun stay in place. Instead, he just let it all happen. Where the rest of us were struggling with our weapons and trying too hard, Jason shot the gun like it was no different than scratching his ass. Just an unconscious habit that was little more than human nature.

"How do I learn to do it like that?" I asked.

He dropped the magazine and grabbed another from his belt. "You shoot more." And he offered me the weapon, keeping the end pointed away.

"Fine." I took the gun and lifted it, trying to keep my arms soft.

"Legs," he said, guiding me away from the counter a bit. "Stand balanced, Jericho. Relaxed. Don't brace your arms. You just want the gun in front of you."

I shifted a bit. "Like this?"

"Mhm," he agreed. "And don't worry about it jumping. One shot, then reset."

"But you - "

"Have put a million bullets downrange," he broke in. "I reset faster because I'm used to it. Just like you aim for the head faster than Zoe. Experience requires practice. So practice." He gestured for me to shoot.

I took my time about it. I aimed to the best of my ability. When I thought I was ready, I pulled the trigger - only to see a hole appear right around the silhouette's balls. Well, if such things had them, that's where it would've been. Crotch level.

A little snort-like laugh slipped out of Jason. "That would definitely stop someone. Wouldn't pass, though."

"Fuck it," I grumbled, pulling off three more shots and not caring where they went.

Wild, that was where. Bullets hit the paper, for the most part. They weren't close to center, and they weren't really aimed. I didn't fucking care, because this wasn't as easy as he made it look. It was hard, and it was going to take time, and we didn't fucking have that!

"Enough!" he snapped, palming the top of my gun to pull it from my hands. "Either you take this seriously, or you're cut, Jeri."

I let him have the gun then turned on him. "And how the fuck do you plan to make us all sharpshooters in the time we have, huh?"

"Jeri?" Hottie asked, leaning around the stall to look at me.

"I got her," Jason assured him. Then he grabbed my arm and pulled me back. "We're going to talk. You're going to listen." Without letting me go, he headed for the exit. "Cade, you're in charge for a minute."

"Can do!" Cade agreed.

"What?!" I asked. "Why him?"

When he hit the door, Crysis hopped up and moved to his side. Jason didn't bother answering. Instead, he pulled off his ear muffs and kept going, aiming for the door that led outside. The dog kept pace.

With a groan of frustration, I pulled off my own ear protection just as we reached the door. And nope, he didn't stop until we were a few paces away from the entrance - then he was the one spinning on me.

"Now have your fit," he said, gesturing for me to get on with it.

"Excuse me?"

"Tantrum," he ordered. "Now. Get it out. Have your little rant, get it all out of your system, and then get your head back in the game."

"Fuck you!"

Crysis whined.

"Go ahead," Jason told his dog.

Immediately, Crysis pushed himself against my leg and started licking at my hand. Without thinking, I petted him, but I had no idea what Jason was trying to do here.

"You're supposed to be teaching me how to shoot," I told him.

He looked at me for a little too long before answering. "I am."

"This is not shooting!"

"Neither was that." His eyes dropped to where I was petting his dog. "You want to skip to the end. You want to go right to being the master of this skill, skipping over the work to learn how to do it."

"No, I want to get this out of the way so we can start doing things that matter," I shot back.

He leaned in. "This matters."

With a groan, I threw up my arms. "I know, I know. We're going to be able to do so much, and - "

"No," he said, cutting me off. "Jeri, this changes the rules. This is going to piss people off. This is the right way to fix a serious hole in law enforcement, but it's not going to be liked. This? Making sure you - all of you - are not only good enough, but fucking amazing at the skills they're going to say you need?"

"*Say* we need?" I asked, catching that part.

"Mhm," he said. "I mean, unless you're planning on shooting someone?"

My mind immediately jumped back to Dylan. When he'd come

into my kitchen, if I'd had a gun, I would've. Shit, I would've put a bullet in Wade too. To know they were no longer a problem? It would've been worth it.

"I could," I said, lifting my chin defiantly.

His cold eyes looked me over, weighing me. "Yeah, figured that out when you put a knife in that boy."

"I also made him nod to show he liked it," I grumbled.

Jason's response wasn't at all what I expected. The man actually chuckled. "So you don't need me to teach you to be cruel. You need me to teach you to be consistent."

"Fuck consistent!" I huffed.

But his arm snapped out, catching my bicep gently. "No," he said. "No, that's where you're wrong. Consistency is the best weapon, Jeri. Just like PvP in a game. If your aim is second nature, then your mind can worry about tactics. If you lift the gun enough times, it will feel natural. If you make yourself always hit exactly where you want, then you never really aim. It becomes a reflex. Once you know in your bones that the bullet will land where you intend, then the fear leaves. The calm takes over. The weapon is no longer an item, but just an effect of your decision to put them down."

"In-game?" I asked, not sure how I felt about his phrasing.

"And when some asshole is holding a gun to my wife's head, or my friend's, or a dozen Middle Eastern students at their university, or a woman's on a loading dock. If I have a gun in my hand, they're already dead, Jeri. I know it. I don't think or hope. I *know* it. And you? If Dylan had a gun to Zoe's head, you'd be more likely to hit her instead of him."

"Oh."

He rubbed my arm, then let go. Again, his eyes dropped to his dog, then a little curl touched his lips. "I know what it feels like to be pissed, you know. I've felt that push to do more, do it faster, and just get it over with. There's so much shit, and no one's doing a damned thing about it, so you feel like it's all on you, right?"

Ok, so my mouth was hanging open a bit. I hadn't expected this guy, of all people, to understand. He was a damned fed, after all. And yet, he kinda wasn't. Well, not like most of them, at least.

"There's this guy," I said. "He helped Dylan hide all those videos, and he was with KoG. He's still out there, and it sounds like he goes to UNT, so he's walking around on campus, but I have no fucking clue what he looks like."

"DeathAdder?"

I nodded.

"Watch QQ's first demo for Deviant Games."

My brow creased and I shook my head, trying to make that make sense. "Huh?"

"It's archived," he assured me. "The fucker stuck his hand up her dress. She went head-to-head with him. He lost." He tilted his head slightly. "And his face is on that stream."

"You fucking know about him?"

"Oh yeah," he said. "I know all about him. He touched my best friend without consent."

"So why aren't we doing something about it?" I demanded.

Jason just flicked a finger at the entrance to the shooting range. "We are."

"Putting him away!"

"We are."

"But he's still out there, and who knows what the fuck - "

"*We are!*" Jason roared. "We, Jericho. All of us. There's no I in team, or whatever bullshit thing I'm supposed to say. 'We' are more than you and me. One person cannot chase down every asshole in the world. Trying to do that means most of them will get away. Sometimes, we have to delegate. Sometimes, we have to learn a few skills before we can finish what we've started. Sometimes, Jericho, we have to be fucking patient!"

"I don't want to!" I yelled back.

"And there it is," he said proudly. "There's the anger."

"I've been fucking pissed since this started, don't you get that?" I asked. "Since I heard Cade was being blackmailed, and Zoe had been hurt, and women are being targeted, and bullies are killing people, and..."

"And bad shit happens to good people," he finished for me. "Yeah, it fucking sucks, huh? Makes you want to scream at the top of your lungs, but that doesn't do any good. Makes you want to hit something, break something, or kill something, but there's nothing you can hit, break, or kill?"

"Yeah," I breathed.

"So focus it." He jerked his chin at the doors again. "Go in there, take all of that rage, and condense it into the tightest, narrowest band you can. Like a laser, Jeri. Hone it. Know that you need this skill, because one day, an inch might be the difference between you screaming at the top of your lungs or saving someone's life. Stop reacting, and start preparing to fuck them up."

"Oh," I said, because that?

Yeah, I could get behind that. Preparing to fuck someone up sounded a whole lot better to me than wasting time with some bullshit qualifications I'd never use. Preparing to fuck someone up was basically the thing I wanted to do right now. There was just one little problem with all of this.

"But what about the KoG members who are still out there?" I asked.

"If the data analysts can catch them, it means they weren't worth your time," Jason said. "If they can't, it means you'll have the authorization to take their freedom away, lock them up, and not just throw away the key, but melt that fucker down so there's no way out."

"But only if this program gets approved," I countered.

"So do not be the reason it's shut down," he told me. "Stop acting like some flighty little girl - because that's what they'll try to call you - and make it clear you are a goddamned weapon."

"With a computer, maybe," I said, trying to make a joke of how bad I'd been shooting.

"With all of it," he corrected. "Because if Soul Reaper had taken you, I'm pretty sure you wouldn't have used a computer to kill him."

"I'd use my bare fucking hands if I had to."

He nodded once. "And I'm trying to give you a gun. All you have to do is stop fighting me and start fighting them."

"Learn," I said, rephrasing that.

"Exactly," he agreed. "Believe it or not, we're on the same side. I really do have your back. You know what? The rest of Ruin does too. So let them, Jeri. Stop trying to do this on your own and let them shine too."

# CHAPTER 21

### SPECIAL AGENT JASON RAIGE

Well, our first gun lesson hadn't gone as badly as I'd feared. Unfortunately, it hadn't gone as well as I'd hoped. Still, a lot of progress had been made. After the first hour, I'd taught each member of Ruin how to load bullets into a magazine, then made them handle their own. After the second hour, I'd ordered them to take a break and look over their targets to see if they'd improved or gotten worse over time.

By the end of the day, each one of them had a stack of paper silhouettes and an empty box of bullets. While that would allow them to see how they were improving, it showed me who was going to need more help than others. The results surprised me a bit.

Cade had experience with guns. He'd actually fired a very similar handgun to what they would eventually be assigned. His groupings weren't as close as I'd like, but he could probably qualify without any more training.

Knock disliked the guns. That made sense when I stopped to think about it. Too often, weapons had been used against people he cared about. However, he pushed through it and had done rather decently. He would need a few more lessons, but he was definitely adequate.

Grayson was good. The man had little experience, but he paid attention. Each time I gave him a correction, he listened, practiced, and the groupings on his targets proved he was a natural. With a few more lessons, he'd shoot as well as most agents.

Jinxy, on the other hand, kept jerking his gun. He knew the recoil was coming, and either he pushed against it or tried to move with it. That resulted in his first few shots being too low and the later ones being too high. A common problem, though. I could work with it.

Surprisingly, Jericho learned well once she stopped fighting her lack of experience. Her issue was focus. She needed a reason to give a damn, but once she had it, nothing could distract her from her goal.

Zoe? She'd shocked the hell out of me. The girl had never held a gun before, and she accepted that. When I'd explained the concept to her, she'd asked intelligent questions. When I'd helped to set her stance, she'd memorized it. Each time she fired, she tried to learn from the last mistake she'd made and adjust for it. I had a feeling she'd be impressive with only a few more days of this.

Then there was Ripper. He was scared of the gun. Pulling the trigger made him flinch. The bang made him flinch. The flinch made his aim atrocious. Still, the guy was trying, and I refused to make him feel bad for it, but getting him good enough to qualify? That was going to be a challenge.

I was trying to come up with a plan for how to help get Ripper used to the weapons while I took Crysis out back for a chance to relieve himself. Yeah, the yard was fenced, but there was a pool, and I didn't like the idea of him falling in it with no one to pull him out.

It also meant a little silence, because Ruin's house was almost as chaotic as Riley's. It was a good chaos, though. The kind that felt productive and comfortable. The type that was alluring enough to distract me from what we still had to do and convince me I could rest for a moment - but I needed to think first. I needed a few minutes to get my thoughts organized.

I was in the middle of making a game plan - which involved pacing the grassy area of the yard - when my phone rang. The number on the screen was Bradley's, which meant he was checking in on me.

"Yeah?" I answered.

There was a chuckle on the other end. "Not even a 'Special Agent Jason Raige' for me?" Bradley teased.

"Nope. Was in the middle of thinking."

"Mm, so shooting didn't go well, huh?"

Which made me push out a heavy breath. "In all honesty, it wasn't as bad as I'd feared. Ripper's going to be a problem, though. He's scared of the weapon."

"So make him shoot more," Bradley suggested. "And the rest?"

"Jinxy shoves at the gun," I said. "Cade's done this a few times. Hottie and Zoe are good." Then I murmured under my breath. "Then there's Jericho."

"Yeah, that one's a hothead," Bradley agreed.

"Pissed," I corrected. "A live wire."

"Sounds like your favorite then."

I chuckled, because he wasn't exactly wrong. "She needs a mentor, Bradley. This girl has been on her own for most of her life. Well, since she was a teen. She's struggling with the concept of a timeline. She wants it all, and she wants it right now."

"Mm..." He didn't sound surprised at all. "Let me guess. She's highly reactive, with too many skills, and nothing to hold her back? She's damned good, knows how to get around the rules, and is willing to lie to your face if that's what it takes? Gonna guess she's more than willing to take shortcuts, even if they're bad ideas, and only cares about the end results?"

"Yep, pretty much," I agreed.

"Then she sounds just like you, back when you were assigned as my partner."

I paused, even my feet forgetting I was supposed to be pacing the backyard. "What?" I asked.

"A young punk, thinks they know it all, has the skills to prove it, and just wants to fight the entire world. Angry, too. Just completely pissed, but pushes it down and puts on the perfect little smile for the bosses. Sound familiar?" he asked.

"I wasn't that pissed," I mumbled.

"Yeah, Jason, you were," he countered. "The difference is she yells. You killed. You shoved it all down deep inside, trying to disconnect yourself from it. That girl? She uses it as fuel."

"She's not like Dez," I said, but that was mostly to myself.

"Because you think Dez is like you?" he asked. "She's not. Jason, I promise your problems are a scratch compared to Dez's wounds."

That made me sigh. "I know. But this girl?" I looked back at the house to make sure no one was listening to me. "Bradley, she's dangerous."

"Your kind?" he asked.

"Yeah," I admitted. "Tell me, is this call official?"

"Not at all," he assured me. "Personal cell phone. Not the work line."

"Good, because I'm pretty sure there was no self-defense. In the heat of the moment, she got her revenge, made it look plausible, and got away with it."

"Kinda like sending in a gamer for negotiations?"

"Yeah," I agreed. "Just like that."

"Then sounds like you know how to help her," he said. "Also sounds like you might be the only one she'll actually listen to, although I thought one of those guys was her big brother or something?"

Another sigh fell out. Yeah, this entire situation was making me good at it. The problem was that explaining their mess made it sound like a pile of shit. In person, they worked. The fucking insanity of this entire group just worked, and I had no clue how to make anyone get that part.

"So, she's fucking most of these guys," I told him. "Not Jinxy or Zoe."

"Zoe's not a guy," he countered.

"You know what I mean," I grumbled.

Which made him laugh. "I do. I also know you made it work with Zara, and right under my nose. I know Riley made it work. I know that if you tell me it's not a problem, then it's not a problem. It also doesn't need to be on any of their official paperwork, Jason."

"Yeah, but regulations," I countered.

"Which is why Alex wants them to be consultants," he said. "You can't date an agent without reporting it. Them? They're not agents. But, speaking of that, I didn't just call to check-in."

"Shit," I breathed. "What now? Problems with the KoG case?"

"No, that's handled," he assured me. "This? It came down from Alex."

Which meant my team. Pinching the bridge of my nose, I gave in and sighed again. At this rate, I was going to have one hell of a headache.

"Crysis!" I said, calling my dog over.

"Well, that's one thing I don't have to ask," Bradley said. "Are you sitting down?"

"I'm in the backyard, so no. Just lay it on me."

"Because there isn't an official listing in the governmental database for the position these consultants will be filling, three members of the voting committee have added a requirement that the applicants need to pass an extensive background check. The same kind they'd have to pass to become an agent, Jason."

"Shit, they're going to pull up everything in their pasts."

"Yeah," Bradley agreed. "Alex thinks they're hoping to run off criminals, and since hackers are typically criminals, well, this is effectively shutting her down."

"Fuck that," I snapped. "Jinxy's the only one with a record."

"And that's sealed and handled," Bradley assured me. "It'll come up as a minor juvenile infraction, nothing more. The bigger concern is going to be their mental state, because that will be considered in this."

"But if they pass, they get their security clearance," I countered.

"Same level as us," Bradley agreed. "Alex is pretty sure they didn't think that far ahead, so she isn't pushing back."

I murmured under my breath. "Which says a lot. It just means I need to prepare these kids to have their lives picked through. Teachers, parents, family, and so on."

"And Jericho's mother," Bradley said.

"Fuck," I groaned. "Yeah, but they won't hold that against her. It's trauma, not genetic."

"They'll still ask her about it in the interviews. Just make sure she's ready," he said. "But Jason? They've already started giving Alex heat for this. The Director was asked if he was convinced she was truly qualified for the position. When I was in her office going over the latest changes to Ruin's requirements, I saw a few things."

"What kind of things?"

"Her email was open and someone is sending her threats. Comments about her race were what caught my eye, because the N-word is not something I'm used to seeing in the Deputy Director's office."

That was when I gave up and sank down to sit in the grass. Immediately, Crysis moved to lie beside me, but he wasn't pushing in yet. He was just leaning, letting me pet him to calm myself down.

"She hasn't been in the position more than a week," I pointed out.

"And some people have a problem with the color of her skin," Bradley said. "I don't know if this was internal or external. I asked her if everything was ok with her promotion, and she assured me that while there have been a few hiccups, she's handling it. But Jason, she's worried. No, she won't say it, but she's lost the enthusiasm she had at our last meeting."

"Which means they're pushing her hard," I realized. "The question is who is doing the pushing."

"Exactly," he agreed. "She has an entire staff, but I'm not sure she trusts them yet."

"Does she trust you?" I asked.

He chuckled. "Yes, and you. She made a comment about how there's a difference between being bound by the rules and guided by them. She also says she's not giving this up."

"Find out why," I told him. "If she's fighting this hard, then it's personal."

"Like it is for you?"

"Exactly," I told him. "Same for Ruin. We need to know what she's hiding, because that's the only way we can shield it."

"I'm not sure you need to pass this on to your team yet," he countered.

"Not them," I said. "Us, Bradley. Me and you. That woman pulled us up with her, so we're going to make sure she stays there. Get me some background, and do it subtly."

"Can do," he promised. "Figure I need to head to Ohio and do a closing interview for that cyber case, right? Is there a password I should use or something?"

He meant to speak to the owners of Deviant Games. They were the ones who'd opened the case that had led to the Kings of Gaming being tracked down. Destiny Pierce was both Soul Reaper's first and last victim. Her partner, Chance Hunter, was now rich enough to be able to push even the FBI to kiss his ass. That they were part of the gamers who'd helped me for so long meant he'd be able to get everything on Alex without alerting the Bureau at all.

"Please," I said. "That's the word that makes information appear with her. And tell her it's for someone who had my back when I needed it most."

Bradley chuckled. "And I'll stop by to check on Zara when I'm done there. You should be home by then. Now go give your team the bad news."

"Yep," I agreed. "Thanks for the heads-up, bro."

I ended the call and pushed to my feet. Inside, I could see the group of them lounging around the living room, laughing at whatever was on the television. Jericho was leaning against Ripper. Knock was curled up with Cade. Hottie had his hand on Jeri's knee. Zoe and Jinxy had their legs tangled on the love seat.

Standing on the outside looking in, all I could see was a group of happy college kids doing their thing. Like this, they looked completely normal, but I knew better. Each and every one of them was broken in some way, but they'd figured out how to use that to make themselves stronger - and happier.

No, they weren't healed, but most people would never know. This group was a complete clusterfuck of issues, with minds that could tear down the internet without trying. They were what would save so many kids like the one I'd been. They'd stop the shit before the shit hit, if we could just make this happen.

So I sighed one last time, then headed in to give them the bad news. I had a funny feeling they'd simply roll with it, though. It was part of what made them so unstoppable.

# CHAPTER 22

## JERICHO

Jason came in the backdoor with Crysis. Without saying a word, he walked over to the remote and paused the series we were currently watching. That made everyone fall silent and turn to look at him.

"I have bad news," he said.

"Fuck," I groaned, braced for the worst.

"We weren't that bad at the range, were we?" Knock asked.

Jason waved him down. "Has nothing to do with the range. Bradley just called. He's my boss now, which means your boss too."

"Ok?" Hottie asked, sounding confused.

"It appears the committee added an amendment to the bill that is still being worked on. The one that will allow us to start this program."

"Which means some stupid bullshit is going to make this harder for us," Cade explained. "It's like political football. Politicians add on something for their side, then the other side does the same until a clean bill turns into a convoluted mess that suddenly sends a million bucks to a Nigerian prince or something."

I ducked my head and giggled because that was actually a pretty good way of explaining it. Considering I didn't follow politics, thought both sides were lying assholes, and hadn't actually had a chance to vote yet, the whole Congress thing was confusing as fuck for me.

"What's this one?" Jinxy asked.

"Your background checks."

Which made all of us look at each other. Ok, we knew they'd dig into our pasts, but background checks? That sounded very official. It made sense, but I had no clue what the hell they expected to find besides the obvious shit.

"Um, Jason?" I asked, sitting up so I could turn to face him. "I kinda don't know what that means."

He looked at me for a little too long. Oddly, while everything else about this guy was pretty average, his gaze had a way of pinning me in place. It was hollow in a way I hadn't expected, like he had no empathy. I knew better, but having him stare at me was the sort of thing that made me want to shiver.

"Ok," he said, walking across the room so he could sit down on the hearth. "For some reason, I thought hackers would be twitchy about their history."

"We are," Ripper assured him. "We're also eighteen, so it's not like we have a whole lot of history to worry about."

"Speak for yourself," Jinxy said.

Jason just lifted a hand. "Typically, consultants have a pretty standard background check. We look to make sure you aren't a wanted criminal, aren't part of a known terrorist group, and don't owe a lot of money to anyone, because that could make you susceptible to bribes. Basic stuff."

"And?" I pressed.

"This?" He clasped his hands before him. "They're going to do the type of check they do on every agent. The sort of background check that proves you have never, ever done anything wrong."

"And we won't pass," Knock said.

Jason made a noise like he wasn't so sure he agreed. "You might. My concern is how this will drag up everything. They'll know Zoe's a victim. They'll know Jericho's family history, including her mother's mental health problems. They'll know all about you hacking your school in Michigan, Knock. Cade? All your speeding tickets will come up. Hottie, they'll have a list of every foster home you've lived in."

"And me," Jinxy said. "They'll have everything from Southwind."

"I'm more concerned about everything from Colorado," Jason told him.

"What about me?" Ripper asked.

Jason actually chuckled at that. "You're clean. Your history consists of failing your first driving test, getting a CI agreement with me, your SAT scores, acceptance here, and a credit card you pay off monthly. I'm not worried about you at all."

"Least there's that," I said. "One of us passes."

"Jericho, your histories don't mean you'll fail," he assured me. "It just means they'll know, and then they'll try to use it against you."

"Is that all?" Zoe asked. "Jesus, Jason. In case you missed it, we survived high school. I mean, what can these big shots do to us that Dylan and his friends didn't?"

The man blinked. "What?" he asked.

Which made me realize we had the upper hand here. "We already knew they'd bully us, Jason. We had that talk before we signed, and we all agreed we can take it. Our concern is if we're going to fail because of the shit that's hit us in our lives."

"The problem is more how you'll react to them knowing this stuff about you," he admitted.

"But everyone knows it," Zoe said. "I mean, have you ever lived in a small town? There are no secrets."

"Which is why I kept asking about my record," Jinxy said. "That brings up Southwind, and I'm not completely convinced Southwind can pass."

"The place looks clean on the outside," Jason promised. "You also have success stories that make sure it's seen as something to be proud of, like that guy in the Texas Senate."

"Cobalt," Jinxy said. "Ok. That helps."

"But even if they find nothing," Jason warned us, "they will ask you about it. They will try to make you crack and admit to anything illegal you may have done. The goal of this process is to convince you that being honest will make it acceptable, and then refuse you because you weren't good enough."

"Good how?" I asked.

"Silver-spoon type of good," Hottie realized. "The feds aren't looking for sob stories. They want nepo babies, right?"

"Nepo what?" Zoe asked.

So I explained. "The kids of people with power, prestige, or money. Basically being born into it, like celebrity kids."

"Ah, ok." She nodded. "But I'm going to guess most agents aren't like that, right?"

"Right," Jason agreed. "Most agents aren't hackers either."

"Fuck," I groaned. "They're going to use our confidential informant agreements against us, aren't they?"

"Probably," he admitted. "That's the catch-22 here. You're all hackers who are good enough for the FBI to need your help. Being a hacker means you've likely broken the law."

"Coders," Knock said. "We're coders who know the vulnerabilities of specific software in order to maintain our own network security. That it gives us the same skills as groups like Anonymous is irrelevant. We use our knowledge for good. Initially to help bug-test games, and ultimately to help law enforcement."

"Nice," I said, nodding to show I liked his answer. "Think it'll fly, Cyn?"

"Jason," he corrected. "Cynister needs to disappear for a while. I'm your handler, which means you can call me Jason or Agent Raige. As civilians, the more casual use of my first name would be expected."

"He's grooming us," Zoe said.

Jason's head snapped over towards her and he gave her a disgusted look. "What?!"

"Not like that!" she insisted. "I mean you're training us how to handle interviews with the uppity-ups. How to twist our shit to sound like a good thing, not a problem."

"I prefer mentoring," he told her. "I promise I'm not interested in women more than ten years younger than me."

"His wife's Hottie's age," Knock fake-whispered.

Which made me giggle. "Robbing the cradle? How old are you anyway, Jason?"

"Thirty-three," he said. "And Zara's twenty-three. She also picked me up, although I still don't know why."

"Your charming personality," Cade said with a devious grin.

"Funny," Jason said dryly. "But here's my concern about the background check. It will include not only the Bureau looking through all of your history, but it will also include an interview. This will be done with a polygraph. There is no lying. You need to answer the questions honestly, believe what you are saying, and be calm while doing it."

"Fuck," I breathed.

He looked at me and nodded. "There's no bullshitting this."

"Not exactly," Jinxy said. "Studies show polygraphs are incredibly unreliable. There's plenty of bullshitting it, Jason. We just have to be good enough to get away with it."

"Can we buy a polygraph?" Ripper asked.

I grabbed my phone and began searching. "Looks like there are a few on Amazon."

"And it won't work," Jason said. "If you don't know how to read one, having one does nothing for you. It's better to stick to the truth, but the simplest version you can manage. Like if they ask you if you've ever committed a crime, admit to something like a speeding ticket. Although most of these questions will be yes or no type."

"Makes it harder," Cade said. "But what do we really have that would prevent us from doing this? That I'm bi? That Jeri's brother and father died? That we had shitty parents? How is any of that our fault? We all ended up in college. We got high school diplomas. Like, aren't we good enough?"

"They'll want to find a reason to say you aren't," Jason told us. "That's the issue. It's not about you. It's about them being willing to drag each of you through shit to win a few seconds on the news."

"Who is they?" I finally asked. "We keep talking about them and they. The powers that be, the ones in charge, and all that shit - but who the fuck are they?"

"Politicians," he said. "Senators, Jeri. Representatives. Rich fuckers who think the rest of us are here to serve them. Trust me, they don't give a shit about any of this. All they care about is getting re-elected."

"And killing this program will do that?" Zoe asked.

"Depends," Cade answered. "My dad was real big into all this politics shit. He used to hate the government spending money on anything. At the same time, he was all about supporting law enforcement. So it just depends on how they play it."

"And we get caught in the middle," I mumbled. "It's not fucking fair!"

"No, it's not," Jason agreed. "Doesn't change anything."

I groaned and shoved my dreads back. "But that's the thing, isn't it? None of this is fair. That's how we *all* ended up here. We got fucked over, we figured out that no one else is going to help, so we decided to do something about it. And now these fucking assholes in Washington are trying to pile on?"

"We'll make it work, baby girl," Hottie assured me.

And while I loved him for that, it didn't really change anything. "But we shouldn't have to!" I snapped. "Don't you get it? That's the whole problem here. That's the entire reason I'm fucking doing this - because it's *not* fucking fair! Some people get shit on, and then they never get a good chance again. Well, if no one else is going to do a damned thing about it, then I will, and I don't fucking care if the FBI approves or not!"

"Which doesn't help right now," Knock said.

I jerked my head over to look at where he was lying so comfortably against Cade's chest. "What?"

"Be pissed," he said. "I get it. Scream if it helps. I mean, our neighbors will probably think we're either having an orgy or killing you, but who cares? Be pissed, Jeri, but just know it won't change a damned thing. Jason's right. The politicians are trying to fuck us, so we need to make sure we're a step ahead of them."

"And what the hell can we do?" Ripper asked.

"Clean up our backgrounds," I realized.

"No," Jason said. "That is the last thing you need to do." He patted the air, begging all of us to calm down a bit. "And if you're going to stress out my dog, Jericho, then at least pet him."

Which was when I realized Crysis was sitting right in front of me, looking up at me as if he wasn't sure if he was about to get yelled at or attention.

"I'm so sorry, buddy," I cooed, bending to hug him. "You're a good boy."

"There is an upside to this," Jason finally said. "Since they are doing an extensive background check on each of you, that means you'll get Top-Secret Sensitive Compartmented Information Clearance if you pass. We call it SCI."

"Which means?" Ripper asked.

"You'll be able to look at all the case files the FBI has," he said. "Once this program is going, they won't be able to lock you out, say you can't help, or limit your usefulness. By trying to fuck you over now, not knowing who the hell any of you are, they're simply making it easier for us later."

"Well, shit," I breathed. "So if we can pass this, we'll be kinda equivalent to you?"

"Clearance-wise, yes," he agreed.

So I nodded. "We'll figure it out, Jason. I'm not sure what they'll find, but we will figure it out."

"And this is the part you can't really do much about," he assured me. "You just have to be ready to explain when they blindside you with the things you thought were private."

"Nothing's private anymore," Zoe said. "The internet exists. Trust me, our generation knows exactly what that means."

"And theirs doesn't," Jason said. "So use that." Then he stood and headed back for the remote control. "By the way, what are we watching?"

"The one about whether or not it's cake," Jinxy said. "If it's cake, you have to drink."

Jason paused and looked at each of us. The confusion on his face was obvious, so I lifted my coffee cup. "First one sleeping is the winner. Means you've reached peak caffeine tolerance."

The man laughed so hard he snorted. "Yeah, I'm down for this. Let me grab a coffee."

# CHAPTER 23

**RIPPER**

I was pretty embarrassed about how I'd done at the range. I couldn't help it, though! I fucking hated guns, and I didn't even know why. They just freaked me out. Maybe it was how everyone talked about a lack of gun safety, or how my parents refused to have a gun in the house because so many kids died by accidents.

There were a million reasons, but I was pretty sure it was the sound. Even with those stupid, dorky-looking earmuff things on, it had been loud. It also didn't sound like the movies. These guns made a pop. When people talked about mass shootings, they called it a pop. Ok, and then there was the really big part of it: guns made people get dead.

As I sat through my data analysis class, I kept going back to the way I'd jumped every time I'd pulled the trigger. I could tell Jason was getting frustrated with me, but he was used to the damned things. Still, he'd been pretty cool, so I couldn't complain. I just had to work harder.

I also really needed to pay attention, but my mind was spacing out.

When class was over, I barely had any notes taken, so I let out a heavy sigh and gave up. I'd have to read the chapter, it seemed. Then again, I'd have to do that anyway.

"Hey, um, Elliot?" a girl asked.

I looked back to see the girl across and behind me. She was smiling and leaning my way. She was also really cute. The smart-looking type, with her act together. I couldn't decide if her hair was dark blonde or light brown, but she had freckles across her nose, round glasses, and lipstick that Zoe would've loved. It was caught perfectly between red and pink.

"Yeah?" I asked, trying not to stutter or blush. Girls didn't usually *talk* to me.

"Um, I kinda noticed you weren't taking notes. I have a copy if you want it? I mean, I just saved it to a spare USB drive, and you can give it back to me later, ok?"

"Yeah, no, uh..." Fuck. There was the stuttering and stupid. "How'd you know I wasn't taking notes?"

Immediately, her cheeks turned pink. That only made those freckles more obvious. "Um, I..." She flashed a quick and nervous smile my way. "Because you type so fast, you know?"

Nope. I had no clue, but right about now, I'd take it. "Thanks, I owe you one. I also don't know your name."

"Piper," she supplied. "Hopefully whatever's distracting you isn't bad, like a breakup or something?"

"No!" I assured her. "No, nothing like that. I'm just bombing another class. At this rate, I'll start racking them up. And seriously, thanks."

"Welcome," she said chipperly before standing. "Means you have to sit next to me on Wednesday to give that back." Then she winked and made her way out.

Wait. Was she flirting with me? No. That girl was *cute*! Like, seriously cute, and cute girls didn't go for me. Well, except Jeri, and she was insane. The perfect kind of insane, so far as I cared, but she didn't really follow the rules.

Yet the ordeal left me with a stupid smile on my face. I was pretty sure she'd been *flirting* with me, and I couldn't figure out why. Granted, I didn't have all the assholes in school around to remind people I was a loser. This was college, so the rules were all different. Maybe I wasn't as ugly as I thought, though?

It was a nice thought, and yet I really didn't care if the girl in my class approved. I did, however, like the idea of not being Jeri's pity boyfriend. Not that she'd ever think of me that way, but I kinda did. Yet the hit of pride I got from that one little encounter had me stepping just a bit lighter and worrying a whole lot less about how things had gone last weekend - until I saw Cade.

He was sitting inside the Student Union, on the other side of a big glass window, and shoving his hand through his hair. I knew his first class was earlier than mine, and his break was longer, so he clearly needed a distraction. Turning my feet that way, I found his table and sat down across from him.

"Hey," I said.

He looked up, smiled, dropped his eyes back to his laptop, then jerked his entire head up. "Why the fuck are you smirking?" he demanded.

The little moment of excitement vanished. "Sorry. It's just, see, there was a girl in my last class, and I think she may have been flirting with me."

"Probably," Cade said.

Which made me do a double take. "Huh?"

"Ripper, you're cute," he said. Then his own stupid smile appeared. "And I can say that and not worry about who's going to overhear. I'm just curious why you care what some rando chick in class thinks."

"Because no one has ever thought I'm worth flirting with before," I reminded him.

He huffed a single laugh. "Jericho. Your argument is invalid. I mean, I'd flirt more if I thought it might go somewhere."

"That's Knock's line," I grumbled.

Cade thrust a hand out at me like I'd made his point. "And what, we don't count because we have dicks? I mean, we can flirt more if you want." He chuckled. "But seriously, you into this chick or something?"

"What?!" I gasped. "No! Fuck no. I mean, she's just cute and flirted, so it kinda felt nice." Then I sighed. "Never mind. You probably get that all the time so don't understand."

"Totally understand," he assured me. "It's like a rush, right? Like this intense hit of joy and ego, all at once. And even if you're not going to go there, there's still something about having someone tell you you're hot, right? Even if they don't exactly say it. You still feel like you're on top of the world, the biggest man in the room, and all that shit, right?"

"Yes!" I agreed. "That!"

"Because girls don't really say when we're attractive," he explained. "They hint and giggle and do other things, but they never say they like our hair or we have a nice ass. Well, not to *us*. They tell their friends."

"You have a nice ass," I told him. "And amazing arms, a sexy chest, and uh..." I grunted, trying to think. "Hair. That little piece? The girls love it. Zoe and Jeri are always giggling about it."

"This shit?" he asked, tugging at the piece which never seemed to grow all the way. "Huh. Who knew?"

"I did," I admitted. "Because they can hit some pretty high octaves when talking about it. And it's sexy when you push it back. They like your hands."

His face softened and his smile turned wistful. "Thanks, man. That's cool. And yeah, their opinion is pretty much the only ones that matter to me, but I completely get what you mean about having someone flirt. Guess this means you're having a good day, huh?"

I dropped my bag down by my feet and sighed. "No. I've been stuck on how bad I screwed up this weekend."

"What?" Cade asked. "How?"

"The shooting," I said, because it should've been obvious.

"But you've never shot before," he reminded me.

"And Zoe didn't flinch," I countered. "Or Hottie, Jeri, Jinxy - "

"Jinxy definitely flinched," he broke in. "Either that or he thinks he's some kind of gangster. But seriously, Ripper, this weekend was all about learning how the guns feel and getting used to them. That's what Jason said."

"Says the guy who shot like a pro," I mumbled.

Ok, so maybe I was sulking a bit about this, but it was because I didn't want to let my team down. I felt like everyone else had done better. They'd all made progress, and I'd almost shit myself each time I pulled the trigger. Feeling the gun buck in my hands? Nope. I was not a fan.

"My dad had a few hundred guns," Cade explained. "Well, not really, but it felt like it. We had handguns for self-defense, rifles for hunting, and two automatic rifles for ripping up cans. Dad said we needed them for the hogs, but seriously? I've never seen a feral hog out there. He just wanted to shoot across the neighbor's field."

I murmured at that, because what else could I do? "I think I've heard too many horror stories," I admitted. "The whole time, I kept thinking about how gun accidents are the leading cause of death for our age group. Shit like that."

"Then let me counter it," he offered. "If Dylan had gone after Jeri, a gun would've stopped him."

"A knife worked pretty good," I reminded him.

"Your gun," he clarified.

"I wasn't there."

Cade just leaned his head back and groaned. "I'm talking about a made-up situation, Ripper! Like, just think about if you'd caught those guys drugging Zoe? If you'd had a gun?"

"I'd be in jail and they'd still be free."

"You are not making this easy," he muttered.

"Cade, that's my point!" I lifted a hand to scrub at my face. "We fix shit with computers, not guns. And..." I let the words trail off, realizing I was about to make myself look even more stupid.

"What?" Cade pressed.

"And I'm kinda scared of hurting the people I care about," I said, the words nearly under my breath.

"You just have to qualify," Cade assured me. "That's it, Ripper. Think of it like gaming, maybe? You shoot at a paper target, so you never take the gun out of the 'game' - which is the range. Hell, it could even be the booth you stand in. So long as you're there, you can't hurt anyone unless you're trying to."

"Yeah?"

He nodded. "Yep, those walls between us are meant to prevent an accidental discharge from hurting anyone. It's safe. Safe enough for Jason to give us all live ammo, right? So try to think of it like a game, and you only have to get leveled up enough to qualify, then never have to touch one again."

"Ok, I can try that," I agreed. "And maybe I can even pretend like I'm backing up Jeri or something? I dunno. Probably lame, right?"

"Shit," Cade breathed. "No, it's probably more accurate than you know. I mean, she kinda lost it on Cyn."

"Jason," I corrected.

He sighed. "Yeah, him. I don't know what they talked about outside, but she came back and was burning through the rounds."

"Yeah," I agreed. "It's like something's changed with her."

"It's F5," he said. "Knock told me she's having a hard time with what happened."

"But everyone's ok," I pointed out.

"Yeah, and it's Jeri," he said.

Which actually made complete sense. I could still remember when I'd heard her call for us to come help. The complete terror in her voice had chilled me to the bones. She hadn't been yelling orders. She'd been wailing for help, and we'd all come running. Rakes had been dropped; stalls had been ignored. None of it had mattered the moment we heard her.

Because she'd been scared.

Not pissed. Not determined. Jericho had been completely horrified when she'd heard some of the people she cared about were in danger. Too many times in her life, that had ended badly, and she'd been convinced it was going to happen again.

"But we stopped it," I said, rephrasing my thoughts. "We stopped it, and now she's got a whole new reason to try hard, right?"

"I dunno," Cade admitted. "I just know she's doing her fucking homework."

"And she's been super-serious," I agreed. "I mean about everything. Zoe was telling me how she said we had to have the internet, and that the computer room was the 'war room.'"

"That's why we call it that?" Cade asked.

I nodded. "Because for Jeri, it's the planning area."

"Mm." He nodded. "Well, Riley said something about ordering whiteboards for the walls. I guess Knock asked Logan, and Logan asked her, and she has Kitty looking for some that will take up the entire walls, but they're kinda hard to find."

"Nice," I said. "No more sharpies on walls."

"Yeah, but if Jeri's treating these qualifications like she did the videos?" Cade asked.

I looked up and met his eyes. "Fuck."

"Mhm," Cade agreed. "Hope you're all-in, bro, because she doesn't know any other way."

"She's on a mission," I realized. "But Cade, how long can she keep this up?"

"No fucking idea. I just know that eventually she's going to snap, and I hope like hell Hottie'll be there to patch her back up."

"Yeah, he knows how to handle her," I agreed. "Any ideas on how we can help her?"

"We make this FBI shit happen," he said. "You have to learn how to shoot. I have to learn all the rest of it. So..." He smiled. "Wanna tutor the dumbass?"

"Wanna tutor the loser?" I countered.

"Yep," he agreed. "I mean, you really do have a nice ass. It's the green eyes that get me, though. Be still my beating heart."

I just leaned my head back and laughed. "You're good for my ego too, Cade. I also care more about your opinion than some cute girl in my class."

"So I do have a chance?" he teased.

I laughed and shook my head. "No way. I'm Jeri's guy. Taken. Completely taken and so perfectly ok with that."

"And it's working for you," he promised. "For all of us, really."

"So long as we can keep up with her, it is," I agreed.

# CHAPTER 24

### SPECIAL AGENT JASON RAIGE

I got home late Sunday night. Zara had cleaned while I was gone, which meant she'd been bored. I managed to make it up to her, though. For the next two days, I walked her to her classes and showed up before she got out so I could walk her home. Each time, she smiled like she had back when we'd first met.

Damn, I couldn't get enough of this woman. I was the luckiest man in the world. But when I came back from picking up groceries on Wednesday, there was a big, black SUV parked in my normal spot. Evidently, it was time to go back to work.

Crysis and I made our way to the apartment, but when I opened the door, the first thing I heard was laughter, and not my wife's. Bradley was cackling like a little boy. Confused, I quietly moved deeper into the house just to find the pair in the kitchen. The wash of pale-yellow powder all over the floor explained everything.

"So..." I said, setting my bag down on the counter. "Who - "

"Crysis, no!" Zara snapped. "Go lie down!"

The dog actually huffed at her, but he obeyed. That only made Bradley laugh harder. "He never listens to me!"

"You're not his person," I explained before pointing at the floor. "So, anyone wanna explain?"

"You like your curry spicy, right?" Zara asked.

"How spicy?"

She gave me one of those cute looks I couldn't resist. "Well, the top came off the ginger..."

Fuck, but my heart melted. The way her nearly green eyes sparkled, the pout on her lips, and the curl at the corners of her mouth? I wanted to pick her up, tell her I loved ginger, and swear it'd be the best meal ever.

Instead I said, "I trust you."

"Whipped," Bradley said. "So whipped. I also need to steal him for a bit, Zara."

"Office if it's private, or the living room if it's not," she said. "You are staying for dinner, right, Bradley?"

"I happen to like ginger," he said around another laugh. "Just not sure you can save that."

"Watch me," she said.

And now I was chuckling, because I had a feeling she could. Ok, so I would never let her cook me eggs any way but scrambled. Middle Eastern food, though? She'd grown up on all varieties, and I was an addict. Mostly I was just addicted to her.

"It's not salvageable," Bradley whispered when we reached the living room. "The whole bottle went in there."

"And you will eat it and like it," I told him.

"Yes, I will," he promised. "Trust me, I had a few bad meals back in the early years. I know exactly how to pretend it's amazing." He grinned to show he was joking. "But this is likely going to be open knowledge in your world soon."

"You found out about Alex?" I guessed.

He nodded. "Dez did. Took her all of five minutes to find exactly what we needed."

"And?" I sat down beside the corner table.

Bradley claimed the middle of the other sofa. "About seven years ago, she was working with Child Crimes. They had an abduction of a ten-year-old boy in the middle of nowhere Mississippi. Kid met another boy online in a video game, they wanted to meet up, and turns out the 'friend' was a forty-something pedophile with a long rap sheet."

"Fuck," I grumbled.

He nodded in agreement. "Yeah, but it gets worse. Alex and her partner worked the case by the book, Jason. They did everything right. Unfortunately, when the Amber alert went out, the pedo lost it, the kid disappeared - presumed dead - and the asshole tried to head for Mexico."

"Which is why no one stays in Child Crimes for long," I mumbled.

"Oh, it gets worse," Bradley said. "According to Dez, Alex has a daughter right around the same age. Played the same game. Records show her account went inactive less than a week after the case was closed."

"Which means Alex felt a tie between the kids," I realized. "Having a victim the same age as your own child? Or *any* child you know?"

"In a situation so similar," Bradley added. "Yeah. Like a kick in the balls. On top of that, Alex's daughter is not overly online anymore, almost like her mother is paranoid about it." He waved it off. "But the kicker is, the report shows it was Alex's call to issue the Amber alert. She spooked the guy, causing him to panic and run. And all of the setup? It was online. The guy had fake information on his account, was pretending to be a middle school boy, and he used the internet to lure this child away from his parents. A boy just wanted a friend, and he hasn't been seen since. No body. No closure."

"And it happened on the internet," I said softly. "That's why she wants Ruin."

"I think so," Bradley agreed.

"And she's probably had her own fair share of harassment," Zara added.

I turned to see her leaning against the edge of the kitchen, right where it changed into the dining room. My eyes immediately dropped to her belly, but there was nothing there yet. I couldn't help it. I was excited. I also heard what she'd said, though.

"Would that be enough to make her take career risks to get this program started, Zara?"

"Could," she said, coming closer. "Most of us get dick pics at some point. There's always the person who tries to say we're sleeping our way to the top. Doesn't matter if the 'top' is a better grade, better promotion, or anything else. And dating?" She laughed sardonically.

"Alex is single, right?" I asked, looking back at Bradley.

"Could be a rape victim herself," Zara pointed out. "I mean, most women are."

"Don't want to know," Bradley said.

"But it's reality," Zara told him. "Every woman I've ever known has been at least sexually harassed. In a bar, in a class, in a job - doesn't matter. Some guy thinks he can slap our ass, tell us to shut up, or be a complete pervert. He also won't get in shit for it. Maybe a warning, at best."

I pushed out a heavy sigh. "I fucking hate men."

"Same," Bradley agreed. "What I don't understand is why women keep dating us."

"Because we're horny," Zara told him. "Yeah, and we're taught this is all normal. We're supposed to make it work, right? But when we find the right guy..." She smiled at me.

"Baby, we fucked it all up."

"Exactly," she agreed, turning back to the kitchen. "But you were real, Jason. Broken, adorable, and completely real. Oh, and a little sensitive too. I like that part best."

Bradley just chuckled. "She has your number, you know that, right?"

"Wrapped around her little finger," I agreed.

And yet, I felt a chill down my spine. I'd come so close to losing her so many times. The first had been before I'd even met her. All I'd known was that she'd been defiant. I'd respected her need to die with a little pride, even if she'd been terrified at the time.

She hadn't backed down since. Fear didn't stop Zara. Yes, it changed her. What had happened at F5 had definitely changed her, and while I wouldn't say it was for the better, there was a new confidence to her. I liked it. I hated why she had it, but I loved that she was so sure I'd always save her that she'd managed to recover so much faster than I'd expected.

"Earth to Jason!" Bradley said, snapping his fingers in my direction.

"Sorry," I told him, turning back around to face him. "Newlywed syndrome."

"And it looks damned good on you," Bradley agreed. "But now that we know what is driving Alex, what can we do with it?"

"Nothing." I shrugged one shoulder. "It was an FBI case. She didn't break the rules. The victim was lost and it'll become a statistic. The oversight committee can't use it against her, so we don't need to hide it."

"I did all of this for nothing?" he asked.

"No, you got to spend the weekend with Deviant," I said. "I'm sure they spoiled you. I have a feeling your son has a few new games to try out. Our case is closed, and all is good."

Bradley kept looking at me. "So what are you planning to do with this information?"

"He's going to use it to his advantage!" Zara called from the kitchen.

I chuckled. "That."

"Lay it out for me?" Bradley begged.

"This is what the pro gamers do, Bradley. They learn their

opponents. They spend more time learning their allies. Why? Because I need to know when she's going to go right instead of left. Right now, we know Alex is on our side. We know she's made a lot of questionable calls which helped us out, but we had no reason to think she was doing more than covering her ass, right?"

"Right," he agreed.

"And now I fucking know why," I explained. "She feels like she killed that kid. She followed the rules and lost one. I broke the rules and saved all of them. If she'd bent the rules back then, would that kid still be alive? If she'd played outside the box, would she have been able to bring that boy home? That's probably spinning around in her head, because it's how mine works."

"All the ones you've shot," he said, nodding to show he understood.

"Yeah," I grumbled. "And the first is the hardest. The first sticks with you. The first one is what shapes everything. One dead, but that one is a game changer. So now I know why Alex is so willing to let me do my thing. It's because she honestly thinks it's the right thing to do. It means I can push a little further with Ruin. I can hack the system. I can manipulate the mechanics of the game to my advantage, because she isn't going to try to rein me in."

"And what good will that do?" he asked.

"I'm training a group of hackers, Bradley. They don't like playing by the rules. I've already talked to them about these background checks, and you know how they reacted?"

"Pissed someone's poking around in their shit?" he guessed.

"Nope." I kicked my legs out in front of me and smiled. "They said it's not as bad as high school. They made it clear they've survived bullying, so who cares what's brought up. They didn't ask for it, so they have no reason to be ashamed of it."

"Shit," Bradley breathed. "They also aren't wrong."

"And Ripper said it best. They don't have histories to worry about. Most of them are barely eighteen. Juvenile shit can't be used against them. Well, not the kind of shit they have, which is just being dumb kids with assholes for parents."

"Thought a few were cool?" Zara called to us.

"Ripper and Zoe's families," I replied. "The rest are shit. Jericho's mother tries, but she's mentally unstable in a big way."

"That's the one with the crap, right?" Zara asked, peeking her head around the corner. "Knock's girl?"

"Yep." Because she knew Knock best, so that was how she remembered his lovers. "And I convinced them to keep their relationship to themselves for now."

"Relationships," Bradley corrected.

I just shook my head. "It's only one. The mess has branches which make sense to them, but they are Ruin. One group. One relationship. They're all tied in a way that doesn't make sense to most people, but it means they have a place to lean."

"It's from that game," Zara said. "They are all flawed, so they are not alone. They found their fellow Flawed. Oh, and Knock's been playing that one more than Eternal Combat."

"Baby, being a gamer is working for you."

She grinned. "Murder says I still suck."

"He'll always say that, until you get a kill streak on him."

She giggled. "I'll work on that next weekend. Oh, and can you put the video software on my machine for me? That way I can show you when you get home?"

"Can do," I promised. "Just tell me you made the ginger work?"

She fanned the air in my direction. "Smell it. Nice and spicy. It's going to be so good."

"And I'm definitely staying for dinner," Bradley decided after sniffing the scents coming from the kitchen. "Means we can talk about getting your kids a normal social life. Won't look good if they're isolationists."

"They have friends," I assured him.

"They have online friends," he countered. "They need some in real life."

I scoffed at that. "They're hackers, Bradley. They're supposed to be losers. They aren't, but if Congress thinks they're merely overachieving students? It'll probably work out for the best."

"Just don't let them get arrested at some party?" he begged. "That would be a fuckup we might not be able to unfuck."

My mind jumped back to their "drinking game" with coffee. "I think we're safe. I also think it's better if they don't tell anyone else what we're doing. Alex wants this off the books until she can make it official."

"And they're college students," he reminded me. "Partying and bad decisions are par for the course. They're finally free from all the rules. They will fuck up. Just try to keep it to minor things?"

"We've got this," I promised. "Besides, they're used to keeping secrets. We'll be fine."

# CHAPTER 25

### TIFFANY

My roommate was out with her boyfriend again. Nadia had been with this guy a while. I thought he was a dick, but she insisted he respected her. Whatever. The more time she spent with him, the more I had our dorm room to myself, which meant it was easier to study.

I was in the middle of my statistics homework when my phone dinged with a message. No one texted me anymore. My friends from high school had all moved out of state, trying to put their pasts behind them. My roommate only did to let me know when she was busy in our room. Since she was gone, I couldn't imagine who it was.

> **Cade:**
> I will bribe you with unlimited coffee, a kick ass internet connection, and home cooked dinner if you will help me with poly sci.

I ducked my head and chuckled. Yeah, he hadn't changed. Cade had a tendency to get himself so anxious about what he thought he couldn't do that he convinced himself he was already failing. I blamed his asshole of a father for it. The prick had done nothing but tell Cade how stupid and useless he was, but his new situation? It seemed to be helping.

**Tiffany:**
When?

**Cade:**
Now? We have a quiz tomorrow!

Shit, he was right. The professor had said it would be ten questions, written in short answer, and there was no curve. I should probably study for it as well, and since my math wasn't due until next week, it could wait.

**Tiffany:**
Gonna tell me where you live?

**Cade:**
Need a ride?

**Tiffany:**
Have a car. Need address, will make you get an A.

**Cade:**
This is why you're amazing!

His address followed. I saved that in Google Maps, then packed up my shit. I'd need the book, my laptop, and probably a notebook. It didn't take long, and it was still pretty early, so I might even have time to finish my math before I passed out. Then again, it was their place, and it had been a while since I'd hung out with anyone. I deserved a little relaxation.

**Tiffany:**
OMW. Be there in fifteen.

Then I headed out. It was a short walk to my car. Turning on the directions, I listened to my phone as I made my way across town. Surprisingly, Cade was right. It was an easy trip. But when I turned off the main road and into the subdivision, I was sure I'd taken a wrong turn somewhere.

"Your destination is on your right," my phone said.

I slowed, gaping at the mansions around me. Huge, all of them. And yet, one house had a driveway filled with cars. I recognized Cade's Impala, so I pulled in behind it, hoping I wasn't blocking anyone. The drive was extra-wide, and the garage was huge, so hopefully not.

Then I climbed out. They'd said it was a nice place, but damn. This was a few levels above "nice." It was fancy enough that as I made my way to the front door, I half expected to have someone say I was in the wrong place.

My fingers rapped on the door, and I waited. Why was I nervous about this? Cade and I were just friends. He knew that, so it wasn't like I was doing anything wrong. I certainly wasn't trying to get back with him! No, he and Jericho worked. So did he and Knock. Still, I felt like I should be sending Jeri a text to make sure she knew this was all on the up and up.

Finally, the deadbolt thunked and the door cracked open. Through the gap, I caught a glimpse of red hair, and then, "Tiffany?"

"Zoe?" I gasped. "Hey! I'm supposed to help Cade study."

"Nice!" Then she shut the door again. I could hear the chain rattling before she opened it back up. "Come in!"

"Holy hell," I breathed as I stepped into Wonderland. "This is nice!"

"Who's here?" someone yelled from one of the other rooms.

"It's Tiffany!" Zoe called back.

"Tiff!" That was Jeri. Then, "Cover me. I'm going to say hi."

What I didn't expect was for her to come out of a room beside the kitchen. Still, she was smiling, so I lifted my hand in a little wave. "Hey, Jeri."

"How the hell did you end up at UNT?" she asked. "I would've expected you to go away for college."

"Paying for it myself," I explained, "so I went cheap. Besides, I need a bachelor's in accounting before the school really matters. I figured I could get my master's at one of the big schools."

"Nice," she said. "Cade had mentioned you were in one of his classes, so yeah, um, make yourself at home."

"This is nothing like my home," I pointed out.

Which made Zoe laugh. "I know, it's pretty amazing, right?"

"How the hell do you afford a place like this? I didn't even think they went up for lease."

"Knock's big brother bought it," Jeri explained. "We've got seven bedrooms, a pool, a hot tub, and like a zillion living areas."

"It's kinda perfect for us," Zoe added. "But hey, let me show you to the dining room. I think that's where Cade's at."

"He is," Jeri agreed. "Studying for a quiz."

"Which is why I'm here," I admitted. "He asked for help, and I don't really mind having someone to study with."

Zoe waved for me to follow, so I trailed behind her. Jeri followed me. As we passed the kitchen, I gawked. On my other side was a small room with a couch in it. I couldn't see what else, but it looked like a pretty typical living room. A little further, Zoe pointed at the door for the bathroom, but on the other side of the hall was a massive arch which showed a bank of computers.

I honestly didn't know if that was the right term for it, but it was the one that sprang to mind. I paused, recognizing Knock and Hottie in there. Jeri made her way around me and took her place at one of the many computers, pulling on a headset.

They each had their own desk. All the computers were different, and the type I'd never owned. The stationary ones. And yet I was pretty sure that room was supposed to be a dining room. It had the fancy chandelier like one would, but this seemed somehow more appropriate.

"I like it," I said as Zoe kept going.

"This is the living room," she said, gesturing to the wall with a very large television on it. Then she knocked on a door across from it. "Cade?"

"Come in!" he yelled from the other side.

Zoe opened the door to reveal him sitting at a small, round table. There were books open around him, music playing softly, and pens scattered everywhere. Combined with the rumpled look of his longer hair, I could tell he was in the process of melting down.

"Hey," I said, peeking around Zoe. "You requested help."

"Tiff!" he sighed in relief. "Thank fuck. Yeah, I'm so confused."

"Kitchen's at the other end," Zoe told me. "Everything is a free-for-all. Seriously, act like you live here. No one will notice." Then she clasped my shoulder and left.

So I stepped into the small room. From what I'd seen, this was probably the tiniest space this house had. It was cozy, though. Against the back wall was a window which looked out over the pool. There was a grassy yard behind that. Up above was a ceiling fan with a comfortably warm shade of light spilling down on us.

I found a chair and dropped my bag on the table between us. "Nice place."

"No shit," he agreed. "You should see our room. Knock and I share the master, and - " He paused, looking up quickly as if he'd just realized what he'd said.

"Oh, so you're not only living with him, you're sharing a bed?" I teased. "That's awesome, Cade. I'm kinda curious what Jeri thinks of it, though."

He grunted. "She has her own room. I think Hottie spends most of his nights with her. No, it's just that after Dad kicked me out, I ended up sharing with Knock, and I mean, we're used to it."

"And it's nice to curl up with someone," I said, showing I understood. "Cade, I'm not judging."

A little smile flickered over his lips. "I'm kinda still getting used to it."

"Being bi?"

"Being *allowed to be* bi," he corrected. "Tiff, I've liked guys since I was about thirteen. I mean, that's what Dylan had on me. It's how he kept me around, you know? He'd threaten to tell my dad."

"Yeah," I grumbled. "He was a fucking waste of flesh. And fuck your dad. Seriously, this whole thing you're doing? I'm not kidding when I say it's working for you."

"Kinda is, yeah," he agreed. "But what about you? How's college working for you?"

I could only shrug. "I'm still in the 'getting used to it' phase."

"With dicks hitting on you outside class," he reminded me. "But seriously, I mean, you've got to have a million guys hitting on you."

I quickly shifted my focus to my bag, rummaging in there to find my political science book. "Yeah, um, those kind of guys don't really do it for me."

"Remind you of Dylan?" he asked gently.

I opened my mouth to say yes. I nearly did, just because it was easier, but something about the openness of Cade's expression changed my mind. He wasn't looking at me as if he expected anything. He was listening. Truly listening, and something inside me felt like it released a bit.

"Guys look at me and want to fuck." I pushed a smile to my lips and shrugged. "Not get to know me. Not hang out and do things. They want to fuck me, Cade, and that doesn't really do it for me."

"So hang here," he offered.

"Kinda what I'm doing."

He grunted. "I mean more often, Tiff. I promise none of my roommates want to fuck you. If any, it'd be Jeri, simply because she's the horny one. Jinxy's into Zoe. Hottie's only got eyes for Jeri. Ripper's busy hanging with Zoe and trying to set the bar for being Jeri's perfect boyfriend. Knock and me?"

"Are fucking each other," I chimed in. "Least I'm pretty sure you are."

"We are," he admitted. "And Jeri. Yeah, so we kinda have a full plate. We also have a pool. I think Jinxy has every streaming subscription in existence. Um, I'd say there's gaming, but you're not into that."

"Because Dylan was," I admitted. "I mean, I've seen Flawed, but yeah. He'd bitch at me about how girls always sucked and shit."

"Jeri kicks my ass on the regular," Cade told me. "Zoe's pretty damned good too. Knock's big sisters? They are literally some of the best professional gamers in the world. So that 'girls suck' line? Nothing but bullshit. I mean, if you ever want to learn, we have enough hardware around here."

"Yeah?" I asked. "And what's it gonna take to convince you to help me with that?"

He tapped his poli sci book. "Help me with this? Seriously, Tiff. Between my classes and this FBI shit..." His eyes closed. "Fuck."

"What FBI shit?" I asked.

"It's a thing," he admitted. "Um, Zoe's case? Yeah, we kinda, um, had an inside guy."

"With the FBI?"

He glanced at the door, then nodded. "He said distributing child porn would stick. Rape gets ignored, but that would stick, and it was federal, not local."

"Which is why Jeri took Evan's phone," I realized. "Not just to set him up, but to make sure your guy could bust him."

"And our guy kinda set it up so he'd be arrested during the pep rally."

My mouth fell open. "No shit?"

"No shit," he agreed. "His boss also helped with arresting the rest. Um, yeah, it probably wouldn't have happened as fast if we didn't have feds supporting us. I mean, we set up the whole case and everything, but yeah. Like, turning that in would've been illegal. The way we got it, I mean."

"So when you say you have a guy, you mean you really have a guy, huh?" I asked.

He looked at me for a little too long. "Um, Tiff? If I say something, can you promise to keep it - "

Which was when the door opened. "Hey, Cade?" Jeri asked, leaning into the room. But she paused. "What promise?" she asked.

"About Ruin," he said. "And, um, our guy."

"Oh, Jason?" Jeri nodded. "Yeah, I was going to ask if you still had those gun diagrams. Ripper needs help with the safety and the clip release."

"Magazine," Cade corrected, "and the safety's on the trigger. The diagram's on my desktop. Glock parts, Jeri. Easy to find."

My head was whipping back and forth between them. "Guns?"

"For our FBI shooting qualifications," Jeri said. "Tell her, Cade. I mean, she'll find out anyway, if she's coming over. Oh, and we're supposed to get the test booklets next week, but Hottie said he found practice tests online."

Then she was gone, but I was looking at Cade with my mouth hanging there, completely stunned. "You're trying to get into the FBI? Don't you need a degree first or something?"

"And to be like twenty-three," he admitted. "To be an agent, at least. But, um..." He breathed out a little chuckle. "Yeah, so all of that? The FBI wants Ruin to do contract work. Legal hacking, Tiff, but we have to pass these tests, and combined with my classes..."

"Which is why you're melting down," I realized. "And let me guess, they're all the 'see it once and have it memorized' types, huh?"

"Kinda," he agreed. "Not all of them, but yeah. At least I have the shooting part down, though."

"With guns," I said, because that bit still didn't make sense.

"With FBI guns," he assured me. "Tiff, if this happens - if we can do this? We'll get the little cards and a gun and authorization to hack anything we want. Guys like Dylan? It won't take us months and months to stop them. We'd just slam into their networks, rip out what we want, and leave a .gif to prove they're fucked. This? It's fucking important, but if I fail these classes, I'll lose my grants, and I can't afford this without them."

I reached over and clasped his arm. "And we got this, Cade," I assured him. "You get to be Batman and I'll be Alfred, ok? Besides, if I can help at all, well, I kinda owe you. All of you."

"I just..." He sighed. "Tiff, you always make studying easy, so I was hoping you'd do your thing."

So I shifted over to the chair beside him. "Well, let's look at what this quiz is over. In an hour, you'll be able to make an A. Promise."

He met my eyes and smiled. "Thanks. You know, you really do make a better friend than girlfriend. No offense or anything, but I missed this part. The friend part."

"I kinda did too," I admitted. "Besides, you have a pool."

Which made him laugh, but it was true. I had missed this. I'd really missed how easy it was to be around him - and his friends. I missed the way they treated me like I was just a person, not some hot girl to conquer, so I would *definitely* be taking him up on his offer.

# CHAPTER 26

### JINXY

The weeks passed. Cade's ex was becoming a regular around the house. Her name was Tiffany, and she was actually really nice. In my opinion, she was too good for Cade, but in the mismatched personalities kind of way. Tiffany was definitely one of the "it" girls. Cade was so far from that type it wasn't funny.

Even better, the girls liked her. The three of them could get laughing in a way we men never managed, and I loved the sound of it. Zoe had evidently known this chick for years, so her coming over was just comfortable - even if they'd already told her all about our FBI shit.

And every weekend, Jason came to the house. Usually, we spent Friday evenings with a lesson on something. Saturdays were spent at the range, learning how to shoot. My friends were getting better, but me? I was clearly not meant to hold a gun.

Still, I'd progressed to actually hitting the target with every shot. Jason said I was jerking the gun, trying to shoot it like actors did in movies. It wasn't intentional! On the upside, Zoe was doing amazing.

When she showed me her targets, it was with the biggest smile on her face.

Cade was also good at it. Jericho was getting better, but she hated not being good to start with. Hottie made this all look easy, and Knock was focused, challenging himself to improve with each fucking shot. Yeah, of course he was.

At least Ripper sucked as bad as I did. That made it nicer. We joked about how much guns sucked. We commiserated over seeing our friends kicking our asses. At one point, the guy even said he might have to give up violence and become our squad's healer. It was a game joke, and I may have laughed harder than I should have, but only because I understood.

We'd also been given the study guides for the FBI's Phase I exam. This was the test about law enforcement rules, but it was so much more than that. The damned thing covered everything from what was legal for us to do, all the way through determining when a suspect was withholding information. Like, how the fuck was I supposed to know that shit?

Granted, learning it was easier than shooting. We now had manuals. Jason had gotten us access to a few of the books they used in Quantico. That helped, and I was pretty good at cramming for an exam, but this shit was dry as fuck. The Fundamentals of Law? Basics of Investigations? Really?

I felt like I was simultaneously doing two different college courses. The most obvious was my master's here at UNT. The secondary one was the degree I should be getting in the FBI. Worse, the hours we were all putting into this meant I saw Zoe less and less.

She liked to study alone. She said she got distracted too easily, so she'd been hiding up in her room a lot lately. Granted, we were now far enough into the semester that most of us had suffered through at least one exam in our classes. Typically more.

But on our fourth week at the range, I started to figure out how to handle my gun. Finally, I was finding the balance everyone else talked about. The recoil happened, and I could let it. Aiming was easy. I'd done that in a million games over my lifetime. There were little marks on the gun I just had to line up, but the whole angle of things was different.

In games, the weapon was depicted to the side. The aiming point was the center of the screen. That was to allow us a full field of view in the game. The reality, however, was nothing like that. I had to look down my gun with both eyes. I had to relax into the weapon. I had to follow all the safety rules. Then, on top of all of that, I needed to hit the center of the target!

I felt like I'd finally figured something out, but my paper targets didn't agree. The groupings were wild - if I could even call the random holes in the thing a "grouping." It was as if learning how to stop pushing the gun had made me actually worse, and I felt like I was failing.

But Zoe had finally gotten a grouping close enough together to make a large hole in her paper. Six bullets, she said, had hit the perfect center. The whole drive home, she was telling me about it, nearly bouncing in her excitement. It made me smile, even if I really wanted to curse and throw things because I wasn't able to fucking keep up.

By the time we finally got back to the house, we were all ready to uncramp ourselves. Knock's SUV was nice and all, but we were a bit of a herd. I helped Zoe out, then was guiding her to the door when Jason called my name.

"Hey, Jinxy?" I turned to see him jerk his chin at me. "Got a second?"

"Yep," I replied, pretty sure I was about to get my ass chewed.

"Cool. Brew us both a coffee?" he asked. "Crysis needs some time out back."

Fuck. That meant this was going to be a long talk. Nodding, I steered Zoe inside, telling her she should put this target on the wall of her room. Maybe even the ceiling, so she could see what a badass she was before falling asleep. But at the kitchen, I broke off. She squeezed my hand before letting it go, and then headed up the stairs.

Yeah, this was getting to be our normal. I got a few minutes with her on our lunch dates. I got a few more when we had lessons with Jason. Other than that, it was like she was so busy she didn't have time for anything else. Not even me.

Everyone else came in. They broke off to change clothes or have a shower. I finished brewing the coffees and headed out back, not really surprised to see Jason was already there. He was sitting under the pergola, in the outdoor kitchen, and had a cigarette between his lips.

"You smoke?" I asked when I made it outside.

"Quitting," he explained. "Zara said she doesn't care, but it's not good for the baby." Then he chuckled. "I also don't want to be grumpy, so thought I'd rule out one reason."

I passed over his coffee cup. "Because my shooting sucks, huh?"

"It was better today," he said, gesturing for me to take a seat across from him.

This space had built-in benches around the edges. It was like a circle, but broken up. Each bench was big enough for two, but more comfortable for one. I sat down, then kicked my overly-long legs out before me.

"My score would've been worse by the holes in the targets," I said.

"Yep," he agreed. "But fuck that. I think you've figured out how to shoot. Now we can teach you how to aim."

"Which means doing it more," I grumbled.

"Always," he agreed. "That's how we get good. It's how we level up, man."

I huffed a dry laugh. "I always forget you're actually a gamer."

"Been doing it a lot longer than you," he assured me. "Also have no plan to stop. I love gaming. I love the relaxation of it. The way calming down makes it easier to spot movement."

"I tend to do more massively multiplayer games than shooters, though," I countered.

"And yet you PvP. In Flawed, it's almost the same. The skills are different, but the aim is the same. So is being a step ahead of your opponent."

"True."

He nodded like he'd made a point. "And you're a step behind right now."

I groaned. "So am I getting kicked out or something?"

His eyes narrowed, and for much too long, he watched me. "You don't feel like you're really in, do ya?"

Busted. Yep, this guy had just cut right through all the bullshit and hit my real problem. I was definitely a part of Death Over Dishonor. I was family with Jericho and HotShot. I knew where I stood with them, and sharing a floor with those two was nice and easy. The rest of this herd? I felt like I barely knew most of them.

"I was in Colorado last year," I explained. "And while helping bust those assholes pulled me in, it's not the same as what they have."

"No, it's not," he agreed. "You're also not fucking her."

For a moment, I wasn't sure which *her* he meant. "Jeri?" I finally asked.

He nodded. "You and Zoe are a thing, right?"

"That's a very good way to put it," I agreed.

"A couple?" he pressed.

Which made me sigh. "Yeah, sorta."

A boxy head immediately pressed under my hand. Across from me, Jason took a long drag on his smoke. A flick of his finger made it clear I should pet the dog.

"He's a trained emotional barometer dog," he said. "Crysis's only job is to make people happy. Well, he's also supposed to warn me before I snap, but it looks kinda the same."

"Do you snap a lot?"

He shrugged. "Yes and no. Killing people messes me up. Fucks me up bad, bro. The problem is I'm damned good at it. I don't miss. I'm also one of the top-rated snipers in the country, and the FBI owns - owned - my gun."

"Past tense," I noticed.

He smiled, but it was the empty kind. "Alex got me off the rotation. It's how I met my wife, though. The first time I saw her? She was about to be a victim. I made sure she lived. Didn't know it until later, though. First time I spoke to her, she was having a complete PTSD meltdown. Do it enough myself that I wanted to help. When she told me her name, I realized I was already in shit."

"But you married her anyway," I pointed out.

"Fuck yeah, I did," he said, and this time his smile was real. Relaxed even. "When the right woman comes around, nothing else matters. Not that my bosses said no, not that we were doing things all wrong, and not even that she was scared shitless of guns. We found a way to make it work. Kinda like you are with Zoe." He flicked the ash off his cigarette. "You're good with her too."

I grumbled under my breath. "I'm faking it. My brother's a shrink and he's given me a few pointers, which is probably the only reason I haven't completely crashed and burned."

"Dr. Cyan Marshall," Jason said. "Yeah, he was with the dad."

He meant at Southwind, because I'd asked for a favor. This guy had come through, and my friends had closed the deal. Jeri had just about lost her shit when she'd heard both "videos" and "child" in the same sentence. It had been enough to convince Ruin to fuck that shit up. Sadly, we couldn't fix everything.

"And it's still a shitshow over there," I said. "My sister's car was just trashed. The crew helped me go through the surveillance video to get screen grabs of who did it."

"Which is what Ruin's good at," he said. "Here's the thing you're missing. They jumped right in. They didn't hesitate. They don't think you're on the outside, Jinxy, but you do."

I leaned back and looked at this guy again. Visually, he was not at all what I expected. FBI agents were supposed to look like tough guys in suits. Jason Raige? He was a gamer, through and through. From his casual attitude, his give-no-fucks reactions, and even his clothing choices made him look more like one of us than our boss. And yet here he was, seeing things I would rather not have seen.

"Am I that obvious?" I asked.

He shook his head. "Nah. Mostly it's Zoe. You try so hard with her, and you look at her the same way I do my wife."

I laughed once. "Busted. I'm so into that girl."

"But you're just following her around," he countered. "You're not leading. You're not even walking beside her. You follow her like a needy puppy. Ever think that might be part of why you don't feel like you're really a part of Ruin?"

"Uh..." No, in all honesty, I hadn't thought about it.

But he had a point. A damned good one. I didn't want to push Zoe, and Cy said to let her lead. I'd thought that was what I'd been doing, but Jason clearly didn't agree. And the reason I felt like the addendum to this hacktivist group was because I hadn't gotten the chance to get to know everyone.

Lately, Ripper and I had been getting chummy. That was because we both sucked at shooting, though. We could commiserate. Hottie was basically my best friend, so things with him were good. Jericho was always invested in either her classes or her boyfriends. In truth, I had no clue how that girl balanced all of it.

Which meant, if I was being honest with myself, Knock and Cade were the only ones I didn't know well. I rarely found myself just hanging out with either one - or both - but I still knew them. I'd had moments with both of them, so it wasn't like we avoided each other or anything, but life had been kinda busy. Still, I wasn't doing as bad as I thought.

"You're too old to be one of the kids," Jason went on when it took too long for me to answer. "You're not fucking Jericho - like everyone else. Your girlfriend is more of a concept than an actuality, and that? That's setting the mood for everything else. You, Jinxy, are keeping to yourself because you don't want to be annoying and push in. You're trying to be considerate, but you're too damned good at it."

"So this isn't about my shooting," I realized.

He shook his head. "Nah. You'll get there. I'm actually impressed with how you're improving. My concern is how you interact with them. On the ride there and home, you focus on Zoe. You give her your entire attention. You never reach for her, never make a move, but you ignore the others because she might say something."

Yeah, he wasn't wrong. I was a little hung up on her. I also sucked at being the social butterfly. "So how do I change that?" I asked.

He smiled, but it was only one side of his mouth. "You do something different. You stop worrying about being accepted, realize you already are, and then you..." The other side curled as well. "Relax. Just like PvP, Jinxy. Sometimes you win. Sometimes you lose. Either way, you'll come back to try again. Ruin accepts you. Zoe seems to like you as much as you like her. Stop fucking overthinking it, and just let them see who you are."

"I'm kinda trying to figure that out," I admitted.

"You're the guy who hacked a phone to save someone else," he reminded me. "You're the guy who feels safest lost in code. You, Jinxy, are just like I used to be, back before I joined the military. You're a good man who tries too hard. So relax. Stop trying, and for once, just let it be. Maybe even break a few of those rules everyone keeps saying you need to follow. Things like not pushing, not being a dick, not getting pissed off and screaming. Just be you. See, that's when all the good things happen."

## CHAPTER 27

### ZOE

We were all getting overwhelmed. Jeri was handling it in her normal way. Of course she was. Her theory was that if she hit first, she'd win, so she was hitting everything just as hard as she could. The funny thing to me was how hard she was studying.

Jericho never studied. Hell, getting her to even do her homework last year had been challenging. We'd managed for a bit, but she'd skipped out of it just as soon as she could. But now that we were in college? Damn, that girl was ahead of the game and making me feel like I was slacking.

She said it was different when she was paying for it. Since she couldn't afford to do this twice, she wanted to get it right the first time. All of it. And somehow Jeri was making it happen. I was kinda jealous of how easy she made it look, though.

Jeri *did*. It didn't matter what she did. Once she set her mind to something, she did it. Hell, even her boyfriends got included in that, because somehow she was keeping things working with all of them!

I'd caught her, Knock, and Cade in the hot tub twice now. And yeah, I was pretty sure things under the water had been rated at least R. Hottie spent most nights in her bed. He always headed to his own room to pass out, but every time I'd caught him coming out of a room in the morning, it was hers.

Last night, she'd slipped into Ripper's room. It wasn't the first time, but I'd heard them. Sure, there had been some moaning and groaning, but mostly it was the giggles. Both of them! The moment Ripper's door closed, the pair had started giggling, and when she left to go cuddle with Hottie overnight, Ripper had still been giggling.

Yet I couldn't even kiss my own boyfriend.

Jericho was juggling four boyfriends easily, on top of her classes and this FBI shit, and the best I could manage with Jinxy was holding his hand! That had been spinning through my head all day. I didn't even want to look at my notes from my classes, because I knew I'd spaced out a few times, hating myself for not pushing through this shit.

I'd been raped. It had been a year ago. Yeah, it sucked, but Evan did not control me. What he'd done didn't change me! Except that it had. I fucking *hated* that it had, and I wanted to erase all of it. Every time I flinched, it was like he was controlling me again. What he'd done had left a permanent mark in my mind. And worse, the FBI was going to dive into our pasts, which meant this would come up!

They'd ask me if I was ok, and I wasn't. They'd want to know if I was in a stable relationship, and I felt like that was a lie too. Sure, things between me and Jinxy were *stable*. It was more like what I'd call stagnant, though. He was sweet, I did nothing, and we talked. Yeah, a lot of talking, and while I liked that part, I knew this would show up as a big red flag for me.

So I needed to get over it.

I had to push through.

I also *really fucking wanted to.*

I wanted to be able to kiss him and curl up against him, and lean my head on his shoulder. Thankfully, none of my friends were trying to pressure me. Everyone kept saying it was all ok - even Jinxy! The problem was *I* didn't think this was ok. I didn't want to let that fucker leave his mark in my mind. That he'd touched my body was bad enough, but I was not my body! I was me. I was a dork, an artist, a hacker, and a gamer.

Yet somehow that didn't really sound like very much, because the truth was, I still had nightmares. Not as often as I used to, but they did happen. I still flinched if Jinxy touched me when I didn't know he was there. I also really wanted to have all those things I was missing.

Like how I missed being held in someone's arms. Or how I missed the feel of closing my eyes and leaning back as my boyfriend kissed me. I missed giggling about all of it. I missed the tickle fights and shoulders as pillows. Most of all, I just missed the feeling of happiness that came when a guy as hot as my boyfriend touched me.

Little touches, like his fingers on my cheek. Stupid things, like falling asleep in his lap. Normal things, like kissing! I wanted all of it, but I was so scared I'd try and freak out. God, the last thing I needed to do was move in for a kiss and then have some kind of meltdown. Yeah, that would be a good way to convince Jinxy to give up on me and move on to safer and saner pastures.

Changing nothing was safe with us. He said he was ok with it, and he went out of his way to spoil me, so I'd kinda just let it happen. The problem was that nothing *else* had happened. Last year, I'd been so good at pushing through my own bullshit. Ok, I'd failed a few times, but I'd tried. And now? The thought of failing meant losing Jinxy.

I didn't want that. Fuck, I really liked the guy. He was so damned smart, and sensitive, and it was like he knew a little bit of everything. He had this insane family he adored, and it wasn't really that different from this mess we had with Ruin. He was a little shy, superhot, and amazing in every way I could imagine.

In other words, this guy was perfect, so fucking up meant risking that. Shit, I could still remember how bad I'd been triggered just by watching a piece of a video last spring. Thinking about a guy leaning over me? That made my heart start racing - even if I was alone. What if Jinxy tried and I did something stupid, like shove him off?

I pushed my textbook aside, aware I wasn't making any progress on my homework. What I needed to do was practice. This was no different than shooting the guns, right? I'd started out knowing nothing at all, and now I was doing pretty good. Not perfect, and I certainly couldn't shoot like Jason, but I was getting a lot closer to Cade's level. So maybe taking the next step was sort of the same thing?

I also knew one guy who'd help me out with this. So, since isolating myself in my room wasn't exactly doing anything but letting my thoughts spin more and more, I gave up. Heading across the hall, I found Ripper's bedroom wide open. Peeking my head in proved it was empty.

Well, damn. That would've made this so much easier. Still, I knew he was around here somewhere. Granted, that was the one downside to having a ginormous house. The chances of finding him hanging out with Jeri or someone else was high, and if I was looking for him, I'd have to have a reason. That was ok. I could just say I had a question about our shared Writing I class.

With a plan in place, I headed downstairs. First, I checked the living room. Jinxy was in there, on his computer, and the TV was off. He saw me, smiled, then went back to his laptop. Most likely, he was doing his own homework. The dining room door was open, and Cade was sitting in there with Knock. The pair of them had their books out.

So, I decided to try the other way. I knew Ripper could be upstairs with Jeri, but I was hoping he wasn't. Thankfully, when I passed the war room, she was there with Hottie. Both of them had their headsets on, which made me think they were gaming. I smiled when Hottie looked up, then kept going. One more place to check.

Sure enough, when I walked into the study, he was there. Ripper had three books spread out around him, his laptop on his lap, and notes took up every available space. There was a smudge on his glasses, and his hair was messed up like he'd run his hands through it at least once.

"Hey, you," I said as I walked in. "Stressed?"

"I have to read this chapter for history," he said, "but my data analysis class has a test next week, and pre-cal is kicking my ass." Pushing out a heavy breath, he closed his laptop and leaned back. "You?"

"I think you need a break."

Confusion took over his face. "And that usually means you want to talk about something. Zoe, what's going on?"

I grimaced. "Ripper, I think I'm overthinking things with Jinxy."

Immediately, he leaned forward to put his laptop on the coffee table. Gathering up his books, he put those aside as well, along with the notes he shoved between the pages. Then he turned on the couch to give me his full attention.

"What's wrong between you and Jinxy, Zoe?"

"Nothing," I admitted. "It's just that, well, after Evan..."

I saw his face fall. His shoulders slumped. "Zoe, I'm sorry..."

"No, no, no," I said, waving that off before this could go the wrong way. "I just mean that I overthink things, right? And Jinxy is amazing, so I was kinda thinking that if I test something on you, then maybe I can prove to myself it's ok? It's just, um, see..." I groaned, knowing I was fucking this up. "It's that he's bigger than me, and you're bigger than me, but I know you're safe, so will you be my test dummy?"

"Always," he swore. "What are we testing?"

So I moved into the center of the room and waved for him to come over. "Stand here, right in front of me?"

"Can do," he agreed, moving into place.

"And can you like, I dunno, maybe lean in?"

He did, and I realized just how much taller and broader he was now than when we'd been kids. Somewhere along the way, Ripper had grown. No, he wasn't as tall as Jinxy, but I was pretty sure he was at least as tall as Cade, but much, much broader.

And it wasn't all fluff anymore. He'd always been a little overweight, but now his shoulders were the strong kind. His arms were now kinda massive, and yet he somehow managed to give off the giant teddy bear vibe, not the hulking brute feeling.

"And lean a little more?" I asked. "I dunno, like, um... You know, like you're going to kiss me?"

"Zoe, are you scared of men looming over you?" he asked.

"I kinda wanna check," I mumbled. "I used to be, but you're you, so it's safe. I just don't know how I'll feel about someone blocking me, or holding me."

"Holding how?" he asked, those pretty green eyes searching mine.

"Anyhow," I replied. "But like, my face, my shoulder. You know, the way you do with Jeri."

"So, like this?" He slowly reached up to cup the back of my head.

I nodded. "Yeah, but more. Close. I just want to see if I can, you know? Because I want to, and I know you won't laugh at me or think I'm pissed at you."

His other hand palmed my cheek. "I will never laugh at you."

Then he leaned in. Slowly, and his eyes were searching mine the whole time, but there was no anger on his face. Ripper just moved closer and leaned over like he was my boyfriend. The same way he would with Jeri.

I felt my pulse speeding up, but this was ok. This was the guy who'd figured out sex with me. We'd been stupid about it together. We'd fumbled, we'd laughed, and we'd been so embarrassed, but we'd made it work. We'd lost our virginity, and I'd felt completely safe with him. Always safe with him. Secure, even.

So when his mouth was only a few inches from mine, I decided to just go for it. This was practice. I was simply making sure. Since I'd already had *sex* with him, it wasn't like we had lines, right? I had to take the next step, and I was always safe with Ripper.

So I stretched up and pressed my lips to his. My hand landed on his chest for balance, and he gasped. Deciding to just get it over, I pressed in a little more. My tongue found his mouth, his hands tightened on me, but I wasn't freaking out. This was ok. I was ok!

And then I heard Jeri laugh. It was close enough to be at the archway. Fuck! I was kissing her boyfriend!

The pair of us jerked apart instantly.

# CHAPTER 28

### JERICHO

I rounded the corner, intending to pull Ripper out of the study, but what I saw made my feet freeze. He had his hands on both sides of Zoe's face and they were kissing. Not just talking, but actually *kissing*!

Ripper was close to her, bent down so he could reach her mouth. His arms were pulled in, his fingers in her hair, and his shoulders pulled up like he was trying so hard to be gentle with her. Damn, he looked good like that. I hadn't realized he was so much bigger than us girls, but the guy was bulky in that perfect way. The big, strong, and protective type of size.

Against him, Zoe looked so little and delicate. Beautiful, even. Her entire body was relaxed, her lips were parted, and one hand was pressed on Ripper's chest. The guy had to curl a bit to reach down to her mouth, but he made it look, well, amazing.

Which made a little giggle slip out. Damn it! They both heard and jerked apart. Wide eyes snapped over to focus on me - all four of them. Both tensed like they'd just been busted, but that hadn't been my intention. I'd simply wanted to make sure Ripper knew he could come hang. I didn't want him to feel ignored, but *clearly* that wasn't a problem.

"Sorry," I said, taking a step back. "Wasn't trying to interrupt."

"No, Jeri!" Ripper begged, taking a half step towards me.

"It's my fault!" Zoe insisted.

I tried to wave them down. "Not my business, you two. Do your thing. I was just going to see if Ripper wanted to run a quest with me."

"It's not what it looked like," he immediately insisted, yet he was still hovering beside her protectively.

That was what I loved about him. This guy refused to give up Zoe just because we were together. He hadn't left her behind because he was getting laid. They were still close, and always would be. I'd always known that, so if things were moving to the next level, then good for them, right?

After all, I kinda had *four* boyfriends. There was no way in the world I could be everything to all of them. I also didn't want to. That was why our polycule worked. We all had bonds, and all of those bonds were important. They were allowed to be whatever they needed to be, and it only made us stronger.

Besides, Zoe was one of my best friends. I loved her as much as him. Different types of love, but I wanted her to be happy. I wanted him to be happy. We all fucking lived together, so where was the downside in this? The way I saw it, the only issue was guilt, and well, that was easy enough to fix.

"It's cool," I promised. "Honestly! No faults needed." I stepped back again, feeling like I needed to make an exit to salvage this before they broke apart. "I mean, this is kinda why we work, right? Carry on!"

Then I turned, intending to go giggle about this with Hottie. I made it two steps before Zoe caught my arm, pulling me back around.

"No, Jeri, I was just practicing!" she insisted.

I smiled at her. "Zoe, it's ok. Not mad. Figure it out, because that's kinda what I did, you know? And besides, there's nothing wrong with sleeping with your best friend. I am. And trust me, Ripper's so worth it."

"No - "

"And we can compare notes later," I said, lowering my voice. "Later being whenever that part happens."

"I was just trying to see if I could!" she blurted out.

"Could what?" Hottie asked.

"What's going on?" Jinxy wanted to know.

Evidently, our little discussion had gotten loud enough to make the guys come check on us. I turned to see, and sure enough, they were all in the hallway, looking at us. Knock and Cade were behind Jinxy, looking confused, but they were here too.

"Not a big deal," I told everyone. "I just need to learn to knock."

"I was trying to practice!" Zoe yelled at me. "It isn't what you seem to think!"

"What are you practicing?" Jinxy asked.

Oh, shit. Fuck, ok that was one thing I hadn't thought about. Jinxy wasn't necessarily ok with his girlfriend having another guy. Damn it! Ok, somehow I needed to smooth this over. Fuck. Maybe Hottie would help? He'd been cool with me wanting a few guys, and I knew he was close with Jinxy, so this could still be saved, right?

"Kissing!" Zoe snapped before I could think of something to say to lower the tension in here. "I wanted to practice to see if I could, ok? And I knew Ripper wouldn't hate me if I fucked it up, so I was testing it out because I want to be able to kiss someone again, Shawn! I wanted to make sure I could kiss you!"

"So you kissed..." He shook his head slightly. "Him?"

Fuck, fuck, fuck, fuck. Ok, I was an idiot! That was a given, but still. Zoe hadn't been kissing Ripper because things were progressing. She was doing it because he was safe in her mind. God! I was so used to thinking about how easily I made out with all of them that I'd completely missed the obvious.

Zoe hadn't touched anyone since she'd been raped.

Which meant I was now on damage control, and I had to stop this before it could implode. Thankfully, this was something I was good at. So, before anything could be yelled across the house that couldn't be taken back, I stormed towards Jinxy, grabbed his arm, and pulled.

"Come with me," I ordered, aiming for the stairs.

He twisted, trying to look back, but he did follow. At the edge of the war room, Hottie was watching me in complete confusion. Down the hall, Knock and Cade shared a look, almost like they were coming to their own conclusions. Hopefully not bad ones, because I could only stop so much at a time.

"She kissed him?" Jinxy asked when we hit the second floor.

"Yep," I said, but my feet didn't slow. We kept going until we hit his room, then I yanked him in there, following right after, and closed the door behind us. "And you are not going to freak out, right?"

It wasn't really a question. This was more of an order, and from the look on Jinxy's face, he knew it. I watched as he clenched his jaw, looked over at his window, then huffed in frustration.

"Listen to me," I insisted. "That's the first kiss she's even wanted since she woke up in a bathtub. Let her fucking have it, Jinxy."

"So she *was* kissing him?" he asked.

"Yeah, but it's not what you think."

"I think," he growled, pushing closer as he glared at me, "that you're making a whole lot of fucking assumptions, Jeri."

"I am helping my best friend!" I snapped back. "Right now, your ego doesn't get to matter. Those two are our friends. They are part of our polycule. They have known each other for most of their lives, and she knows he's safe. Safe, Jinxy! That's what matters, and it's what she needs, so you are going to sit down, shut up, and be happy she's even thinking about this!"

"No, I'm fucking not!" he insisted. "I don't have to handle things the way you do, Jericho. I don't have to wall off my fucking feelings, pretend like I don't have them, and use sex as a substitute."

"That is not what I'm doing!" I yelled back.

"No?" he asked.

"I fucking love my boyfriends!"

"Which doesn't change that you ignore your fears," he said. "You ignore them, Jeri, thinking you can just push it all aside like it doesn't matter. Like if you stick your damned head in the sand, then it will go away."

"I do not! I've been freaking the fuck out about KoG since we moved in!"

"And what have you done about it?" he asked. "You focused on learning to shoot, on memorizing those damned classes, on making better grades. When did you talk about being scared shitless? When did you have the balls to admit you're running yourself ragged trying to make sure each and every one of those guys gets an equal amount of time, because you're so terrified something will happen and you'll have regrets? *When*, Jeri, did you come fucking talk to me about it?"

"I..."

"Yeah, you ignore the fear part," he snapped. "You think you can fight it back, put it in a box, and it will fucking go away. Well, that's not how I work. That's not the type of relationship *I* want in this polycule. Not with you, not with Zoe, and not even with these guys, and I don't fucking care if you like it!"

"But you will not take it out on her!" I screamed.

He just leaned right into my face. "I. Am. Not. The. Bad guy."

Then he pushed past me, yanking the door open. His long legs gave him the lead, but I spun and raced to catch up, stopping him before he could reach the stairs. Once again, I grabbed his arm, making him stop.

"She needs this, Jinxy!"

He pulled, trying to break free, but my grip was too tight. "Zoe is not you. She will never be you. She doesn't have to do things your way, and you know what? Not all of us want to fuck everything, Jeri."

"If you make her feel bad..." I warned.

He turned to face me completely. "I love you like a little sister,

Jericho, but pull your fucking head out of your ass before you lose it. Not having jealousy makes people feel like they aren't loved."

"No, not having jealousy means they're my friends first, and I'm allowed to be happy for them." I lifted my chin. "Just because we do things differently doesn't mean one is right and the other is wrong. They can both be right. I just don't want your insecurities to fuck up a good thing."

"*My* insecurities?" he huffed.

"Yeah."

"And what about yours? You just assumed they were hooking up and that you needed to be ok with it. You were sitting there trying to say it's all good, and why? Maybe *your* insecurities make you think you aren't good enough to make them happy, huh? Maybe you react differently than I do to things, but don't try to pretend you're so self-confident. In case you missed it, we're all fucking flawed."

"But so is Zoe," I breathed. "Please, Jinxy? Don't make her feel bad."

"Give me some fucking credit," he grumbled.

And this time, when he pulled his arm, I let him go. Growling in the back of his throat, Jinxy marched down the stairs, leaving me to jog behind him. His long legs were moving, making it clear he was a man on a mission.

When we reached the first floor, Zoe had returned to the study. Hottie was back in the war room, but while he was sitting at a computer, he wasn't gaming. Instead, he was scrubbing at his face. Knock and Cade had moved into the kitchen, where they were watching us like they were trying not to be seen.

Jinxy stormed into the study. I rounded the corner right behind him to see Ripper and Zoe huddled close together. They both looked up as soon as we walked in, and both looked terrified.

"Zoe?" Jinxy asked. "Can we talk out back? I think that's the one place we can actually have some privacy."

"Shawn..." she breathed.

"Just talk," he said gently. "I'd kinda like to know what's going on without Jeri putting her spin on it, ok?"

"Yeah," she breathed.

But her shoulders slumped. Her head fell. She moved towards him almost timidly, but when she got close enough, Jinxy gently pressed a hand to her back, guiding her out of the study. I turned to follow them halfway down the hall.

He was being soft with her, so I didn't have a reason to stop him. And while I knew he wouldn't hurt her, this mess? Fuck. This had just imploded, and I wasn't sure I knew how to fix it. I wasn't even sure there was a way to fix it.

Damn it!

# CHAPTER 29

## JINXY

I could feel every single person in this house watching me as I guided Zoe towards the backyard. As we passed the war room, Hottie lifted his chin like he was asking if I needed help. I met his eyes, but didn't take him up on that. Nope, this was between me and Zoe.

We were barely into the living room when I heard Hottie call out, "Jeri? A second?"

Ok, so at least that was handled, because I seriously believed Jeri would push into the middle of my mess. Right now, I didn't want nor need her help. What I wanted was to have an honest talk with my girlfriend. I wanted to do it on our own, with no one making her feel like she had to answer any certain way, and to have the chance to be able to just listen.

Because she deserved to be heard.

Reaching around her, I opened the door that led outside, guided her through, then closed it behind us. That gave me the chance to steal a glance up the hall. Thankfully, it was empty. Everyone else had fucked off, which worked, because I felt like they should be staring at me.

But Zoe was still looking at the ground. So, as gently as I could, I clasped her shoulders and steered her over towards the pergola. I knew there was a place to sit there, and I had a feeling we'd both need it. This was not the type of talk to have standing over her.

"So, what happened?" I asked as I guided her down onto one of those benches.

"It wasn't what you think!" she whimpered.

So I lowered myself a little more, dropping my ass onto the concrete right in front of her. "That's why I'm asking, Zoe."

"I just..." She sighed, lifting those pretty hazel eyes up to meet mine.

They were glossy, shining with far too much moisture. They weren't brimming yet, and my goal was to make sure that didn't happen. I just needed her to open up and talk to me.

"I promise I can take it," I assured her.

She jiggled her head in a nervous and timid little nod, then started rambling. "Ripper and Jeri fucked in his room last night, and I could hear them. They giggled, you know? And I kept thinking about how happy they sounded, and the FBI is doing this background check, and they're going to figure out I'm a mess, so I need to make sure I'm not. But I can't even kiss you! I haven't kissed anyone since, you know. But I kinda did. I mean, Ripper, but like, that was a really stupid decision and it didn't mean what you think it means."

"Hey, hey, hey," I begged. "Baby, it's ok. You're tripping all over yourself, though. I just want to know what really happened. Not what Jericho thinks happened."

She licked her lips quickly, then bit the bottom one. Yep, my heart did a stupid little flip in my chest. The big eyes with that whole lip-bite thing? Damn, this girl knew how to push my buttons. She was fucking beautiful, had no damned clue, and made me want to turn stupid. I couldn't yet.

"I need to get better," she finally mumbled.

"Ok?" Hopefully that would keep her going.

"And, um..." She reached up to wipe at an eye. "Jeri's making it all look easy. She just does what she has to. It's like she always knows how to fix her shit, and I don't have a clue."

"She's a fucking dumpster fire," I countered.

Zoe shook her head. "She's doing something. Might not be the right thing, but she's not helpless. I am. I fucking *hate* that I am, Shawn! Evan screwed me up, and I can't get him out of my head. I can't make it all go away, but I won't let him own me! I won't let him change me, ok? I just have to put on my big girl panties and get over this shit!"

"Whoa, whoa, whoa," I begged. "Baby, this 'shit' isn't something anyone just 'gets over.' Life doesn't work like that. I mean, do you think I'm just 'over' my Gran dying? It's been long enough, so it no longer hurts?"

"You don't talk about it," she mumbled.

Ok, fuck. She had a point. "I'm sorry," I breathed. "You're right. I should, but I feel like talking about her makes me want to cry, and I'm so sick of that."

"You never cry."

"I do." Carefully, I reached out and rubbed her calf. It was the closest thing to me, and seemed safe enough. "I just tend to go into my room when I do it because I get embarrassed."

"Me too." She swallowed hard. "And I didn't want to mess us up, but I think I fucked up, huh?"

"How?" I asked, hoping she'd fill in the rest of the blanks.

"I kinda thought that Ripper's safe. He doesn't get offended when I do something stupid, and he never hates me, so I could practice."

"Practice what?"

"Kissing." That came out so soft I almost missed it.

"Zoe, why do you need to practice kissing?" I asked. I didn't want to influence her answer, but I couldn't think of another way to get her to explain that part.

She began twisting her hands. Not spinning them. No, she had her fingers laced together and was bending them to almost contortionist levels. I had to fight the urge to cover them so she wouldn't hurt herself.

"I'm tired of being in a rut, ok?" she whimpered. "I know I am, and last year I was making progress. I was getting better. I fucked up sometimes, and I triggered myself a bit, but I felt like I was in control. But I don't want to trigger myself with you and scare you off. I mean, I like you, Shawn."

"I like you too, Zoe," I promised.

"But if I act like you're the one who hurt me, you'll... I dunno, be hurt! I want to be your girlfriend, not just your girl who's a friend."

"Zoe, I'm not pushing you," I assured her. "I don't need you to do anything that makes you uncomfortable."

"*I* do!" she snapped. Immediately, her hands moved to cover her mouth. "Oh my god. I'm sorry."

But something inside my chest had just let go. It felt like a release. Like I could start to breathe again.

"I need to get over this, Jinxy. I need to stop being scared, because I won't let Evan have that anymore. I also *want* to! I miss being able to do all that shit."

"What shit?"

"Kiss, and cuddle, and tickle fights." She shrugged. "I miss the feel of a man. I mean, not like *that*. Like, um..."

"Like Knock and Cade curled up together on the couch," I offered. "Like Jeri and Hottie hanging on to each other even as they sleep. Like Ripper trailing a finger down Jeri's arm or wrapping her up against his chest, smothering her."

"Yes!" she gasped. "Those things. I want to do them, but I got triggered before, so I keep thinking I need to try again, and then I freak out because if you try and I hate it? Then what? I mean, you're being so patient, and I know you could have any girl you wanted, so why would you want to deal with my shit? So I don't want to fuck it up, and that ends up with me just not doing anything at all."

"Wait." I reached up for her hand. "Zoe, did you kiss Ripper?"

Her face fell. "Yeah."

"Like a real kiss, or just a peck?"

"I mean, I was kinda trying for a real one, but then Jeri giggled, and I didn't want to fuck things up for him, and I didn't even think about if you'd care, because it was just practice, and at the time it made so much sense, you know? I was just trying to fix things, and I really fucked it up."

"No," I swore. "You didn't, baby. I'm just trying to keep up." She nodded, so I kept going. "You kissed him, but didn't really get to see if it was ok? Or did you?"

"I did. I mean, he's bigger than me, and he was all..." She made a gesture of him over her, pushing downwards. "And it was ok because he's Elliot. He's the same guy he's always been, and I mean, that's why I suggested we sleep together to lose our virginity, because I've always trusted him, and - " Her eyes went wide and her mouth snapped shut.

I, however, was struggling not to laugh. "You've had sex with him?"

"In tenth grade!" she insisted. "Before I knew you, or Jeri, or anyone. We were nerds, Jinxy, and it kinda made sense. I mean, everyone else was doing it, and we wanted to know, but we weren't datable, so we kinda, and um, yeah. It happened."

I nodded slowly, but a smile was taking over my face. "Ok, I kinda respect the guy a bit more now."

Her brow furrowed. "Huh?"

"Ripper," I explained. "If he was the guy you asked for that? I mean, it's a big deal for a girl. I know that. For guys, it's more embarrassing, but for girls it's potentially dangerous. So it means he's even more trustworthy than I realized."

"But I kissed him!" she huffed.

"Yep," I agreed. "I'm starting to realize that happened."

"And so you're breaking up with me?" she asked.

I felt like time froze. "What?" I gasped. "Why would I do that?"

And her mouth flopped open. For a little too long, we both stared at the other in complete shock. I swore a million expressions crossed her face. Her eyes widened, then narrowed. Her brow pinched and then lifted. The only thing that didn't change were those amazing lips as they hung parted in a perfect little O.

"But I thought you were pissed!" she finally said.

I pushed my eyes closed and groaned. "Fuck! No, Zoe. God, no. Confused as fuck, yeah, and maybe feeling a bit like I was failing you somehow, but pissed? No, not at all. I mean, I kinda wanted to prove to you I was understanding enough that you could trust me like that, but I get it. You've known Ripper forever, and now that you said you lost your virginity with him? Shit, that makes so much sense. Of course you'd want to kiss him first, because he's already proven he's safe, and I'm still trying to, but I'm going to, ok? I'll figure out how to show you I will never hurt you, and that even if we mess it up, we can back up and try again, because I like - "

She leaned forward, grabbed both sides of my face, and shoved her mouth against mine. I froze. All the words I was about to say immediately left my brain, and my hands were both in the air, caught mid-motion as I'd been talking.

Then her hands shifted, pushing back into my hair. She leaned in a bit more, and my mind caught back up. Zoe was kissing me. I really didn't want to fuck this up, but *she was kissing me*!

Carefully, I leaned in. My lips parted, softening against hers, and the tip of her tongue flicked over the bottom one. I moaned in the back of my throat and finally dared to believe this was real.

Timidly, I explored, my tongue meeting hers halfway. When hers swirled, I matched it. Our lips moved, sliding against each other's mouth. Kiss by kiss, we both relaxed, stopped hesitating, and allowed ourselves to simply do this.

One hand found her waist, making sure she wouldn't fall

forward. The other palmed the side of her bicep, wanting her closer. I felt it when a smile flickered on her lips, and then she moved, sliding off the bench just to kneel before me without giving up my mouth.

And she kissed me. Oh, she kissed me the exact way I'd been dreaming of. She kissed me like she wanted to, with all of the new and wondrous things my mind had imagined. She kissed me gently, then harder, and with so much passion. Calm, contained passion that came out in soft pants and the sweetest little feminine sounds. She kissed me until I was completely convinced this had to be a dream, because I couldn't imagine anything so perfect.

But eventually she pulled back. When I cracked open my eyes, I found her still so close, and the little amber flecks in her eyes looked exactly like molten gold. All I could do was smile like a damned idiot, because I'd just been kissed by the most amazing woman I'd ever met in my life.

"Was that ok?" she asked.

"Uh-huh," I agreed, nodding to make sure my answer couldn't be misunderstood. "Yeah. I'm very ok with that."

Which made her glance away and giggle. "So maybe you can kiss me sometimes now?"

"Yeah?"

Her teeth found her lower lip again, and she lifted her eyes back to mine. "I like when a guy starts it."

"So should I try starting more than just kissing?" I asked. "Like cuddling too? Or maybe inviting you to spend the night with me?" I jerked as I realized how that sounded. "To sleep, Zoe. I mean just to curl up and sleep. Like, I get that we're not past that yet."

But she was smiling even bigger. "God, you are so fucking cute, Shawn. And perfect. Absolutely, completely, and so very perfect!"

"I'm really not," I admitted. "Baby, I was so worried that you kissing Ripper meant I was fucking this up. I'm not perfect, but I'm trying to be, because there's this girl, and I like her so much more than I'd ever imagined, and I am so scared I'm going to do the wrong thing and chase her off."

"Me?"

I nodded. "I kinda get insecure too."

"So..." She wrinkled up her nose. "Maybe we're both nervous, but we should try anyway? And like, it might even be ok if I say I do want to spend the night with you, but if I get nervous, I can bail?"

"Or kick me out, or anything," I swore. "I'm just over here trying my heart out, Zoe, because in case you missed it, it's already yours."

Her eyes widened a bit. "Yeah?"

"Yeah," I said. "I've never felt like this with anyone, so I'm trying really hard to get it right."

"You are," she swore. "I'm trying hard too."

I reached up to smooth her hair, letting my palm stop against her cheek. "Maybe we should stop trying? I dunno. Like, give ourselves permission to fuck up? Because I swear I'm not going anywhere, Zoe. You're not going to scare me off."

"Oh, Shawn," she breathed, throwing herself against me and wrapping her arms around my neck. "That's what I needed. I didn't even know it, but that's it. I don't want to fuck up because, yeah, that. I thought I'd scare you off."

"I'm a hacktivist, baby. Balls of steel," I whispered into her hair. "And yours. All yours."

She just hugged me a little harder, and it said everything words never could have.

# CHAPTER 30

### RIPPER

I stood there in shock as everyone left. Jinxy was taking Zoe out back. Jeri followed, so that was going to blow up. And while I really wanted to help, my feet were glued in place, stuck there by my own horror, because I'd just cheated on my girlfriend.

I hadn't meant for that to happen. I'd simply been helping Zoe, but it had all just kinda *happened,* and then she was kissing me, and of course Jeri had seen, and now I had no fucking clue how to unfuck this! But I was in love with Jericho! I was supposed to be the perfect boyfriend. I'd merely been trying to help Zoe and then, *boom*, it had all imploded.

I was still staring out the archway after the girls when Knock and Cade made their way in. I managed to blink, but my mind was stuck on a loop, trying to undo this somehow. Trying to find a way to make it all ok, go back to how it was, or something!

"Ripper?" Cade asked, moving closer to clasp my upper arm.

"I think I fucked up bad," I breathed, forcing my eyes to focus on him.

"You're fine," Knock promised, even as he dropped into one of the chocolate brown chairs in the room.

"But..." I thrust an arm out in the direction everyone had gone.

"Hey, it's ok," Cade breathed, pulling me in for a hug.

I resisted for a moment, and then just gave in. My arms went around his back. His closed around mine, which was all it took to make me drop my head down on his shoulder. My eyes were pressed into his shirt, just in case they started leaking, but mostly it was some attempt to find my own balance again.

"What am I going to do if she's done with me, Cade?" I blubbered against the fabric.

"She's not," he promised.

"But she hasn't been spending as much time with me as she used to," I countered. "And I mean, I'm ok with that. She's been worried about all of this, but now I've fucked it up, and what if she decides she's done with me? What if she realizes she doesn't *need* me?"

"You're fine," Cade said gently. "I don't even know what happened, but I know Jeri wasn't yelling about you. She said something about Jinxy and Zoe."

"Because I kissed Zoe!" I admitted, pulling back to look over at Knock. "That's what happened. I kissed Zoe, and Jeri walked in, and I think I fucked up bad!"

"Why the fuck did you kiss Zoe?" Cade asked.

But he didn't sound mad about it. He sounded confused, as if nothing about that sentence made sense to him. Yeah, the problem was it really didn't make sense to me either - and I'd been there! It had just been helping, then crashing and burning, and now things were so damned fucked up.

"Uh.." I stepped back a little more, forcing his arms off me. "Yeah..." And I headed for the couch where I'd been sitting when this all happened.

"Give him space, babe," Knock said.

"Just tell me you're ok, Ripper?" Cade asked, following me so he could take a seat on the other end of the couch.

I chuckled once, because this guy was a damned good best friend. Back in high school, he'd been one of those loner tough guys, or so I'd thought. Cade had mastered the ability to put on the right act at the right time. But the moment we'd all agreed to not worry about how manly we were, he'd turned into something else.

I didn't even know how to explain the guy he was now. Yeah, he was still one of those cool-guy types. He also hugged, talked about feelings, and when he didn't know how to say something, he kinda just word-vomited until he got the point across. Maybe that was what I should do?

So I tried. "Zoe asked me to help her check something to see if she'd be freaked out, and she wanted me to kinda stand over her, you know?" I looked between the guys. "And she said it's because I'm bigger than her, but I think everyone in the house is, but I get it. I'm a guy, and I'm safe, and so I just wanted to help, right?"

"How did that lead to kissing?" Knock asked.

"Um, so like, I bent over her," I explained. "And she wanted me to hold her like Jinxy might. I mean, that was the impression I got from what she asked. And then when I was close enough, she just kinda kissed me. It all just happened, and Jeri was there. I didn't even see her until she laughed, and I jumped back, but I didn't get the chance to explain, and now she's out there, and Jinxy and Zoe are out there, and..." I sighed, having run out of words.

"So Zoe kissed you?" Cade asked.

I groaned. "Fuck, not like that!"

"Like what?" Knock asked.

"Like making sure she'd be ok," I said. "Like, you know, she hasn't kissed a guy since..."

"Oh." The pair of them said that in tandem, like they were sharing a brain.

I simply leaned forward and shoved my hands into my hair. Fuck, this was not how today was supposed to have gone. I'd been worried enough about my tests. Never mind that I was shit at shooting a damned gun! Right now, I had so much crap I was trying to get right, and fucking it up with my girlfriend was nowhere on that list!

"Do you think Jeri's going to be pissed at me for cheating?" I asked, not daring to look up.

"Nope," Knock said.

"She'll be fine," Cade agreed.

"But I kissed another girl!"

Knock just chuckled. A moment later, I heard feet thump onto the coffee table, so I looked up to find it was him. He'd kicked back in his chair like he was completely relaxed.

"Let me tell you something about Jericho," he said. "Ripper, she doesn't care about that. Jeri is more likely to be proud of you for helping than anything else. She doesn't get jealous, and she feels like our relationships with each other keep this whole mess from coming down completely on her shoulders. She doesn't *want* to be solely responsible for keeping us happy, so knowing we take care of each other is a good thing in her mind."

"And she likes being happy for us," Cade added. "When Knock and I got together, I asked her. Ripper, she honestly sees all of us as a group. One big happy, you know? I mean, she doesn't want to get cut out, but she meant it when she said she wanted to be friends."

"I just..." I had to pause to keep my voice from tensing up. "Y'all, I don't want her to think I'm not into her anymore. Or bored, or who knows what she'll decide. She's got too much on her plate right now, and writing me off would make her whole life easier. I mean, she never comes up for air for anything, and now I'm just adding to her stress?"

"There's that," Cade agreed. "I was sure she'd write me off when I asked about Knock, but she didn't, so I think you're ok."

"You two are looking at this wrong," Knock said.

"I'm looking at this like I'm about to get dumped," I shot back. "C'mon, we all know she's fraying around the edges right now. And this? This is the sort of dumb fucking move she doesn't need right now!"

"Ripper, Jeri's values are different," Knock soothed. "She doesn't care what other people do, or what should be done, or what's expected. She wrote that shit off a long time ago. What Jeri wants is to be happy. To have people around her who are happy. For her, that's how she shows she cares, by helping *us* be happy in our own way."

"What do you mean?" I asked.

Knock gestured between him and Cade. "Like us. In Jeri's mind, I got to fall in love with a guy I had a crush on. She got to cheer me on, even while I was flirting with her. She doesn't think of it as an either-or type of thing. She doesn't see it as cheating, or doesn't care if it is. I'm not sure which, because no one taught her that, guys. She grew up being happy for Hottie because he fell in love with Nina, and we all know she was in love with him even back then."

"Oh," I mumbled, because I hadn't thought of it like that.

"And that's how she understood relationships," Knock continued. "Her brother died. Her mom went away. Mom came back and Dad died. Mom broke, so while she was there, she also wasn't. Jeri was alone, and everything was going to shit. The only people who loved her? The guys in DoD. The guys who were probably talking about girls they liked, and she was happy for them. The guys who joked about hooking up, getting laid, and having multiple women flirting with them. And the one man she thought about romantically was getting fucking married, yet she wanted the best for him."

"She learned to put everyone else first," Cade realized.

"And she doesn't care if it's harder for her," Knock said. "She cares if there's someone being happy. Any form of happy. So she's not going to hate you for kissing Zoe, Ripper. She might think she can worry about you less and end up pushing herself harder - which isn't good - but she won't be pissed at you."

I nodded, because that all made sense. "She braced for the worst, celebrated everyone else's happiness, and kept things shallow so it couldn't be taken from her. She also thinks she has to carry everything. I mean, she kinda had to, back before she moved here."

"Which means," Knock said, "that she will *not* be pissed at you for -"

"Who's pissed?" Jeri asked as she came into the room. Hottie was trailing behind her. "Zoe didn't seem pissed."

"You," I admitted. "I kinda kissed another girl."

Hottie snorted out a laugh and turned like he was about to leave, but Knock stopped him. "Nope, you get to sit in on this too," he ordered.

"Fuck," Hottie groaned. "I was gaming when all of this happened. I didn't do shit."

"Family talk time," Cade countered. "So sit, Hottie."

"And I'm sorry, Jeri," I said, holding out an arm so she'd come over by me. "I didn't know Zoe was going to do that."

"What did she do?" Jeri asked.

"Um, she was kinda checking to see if she'd be triggered."

"Sounds like she was wanting to kiss Jinxy," Cade explained.

Jeri just looked over at Hottie. "Will Jinxy be pissed?"

Hottie huffed. "Confused is more likely. Convinced he's about to be dumped. I doubt he'll be pissed. He doesn't really do that."

"He yelled at me!" she shot back.

"And that's about the only volume that works with you sometimes," Hottie countered.

"Oh." She shrugged. "Yeah, that's a good point."

So I reached over and rubbed her leg. "Jeri, can you please tell me if you're pissed at me or not?"

"Why would I be pissed?" she asked.

On her other side, Cade leaned closer. "Most girls don't like their boyfriends kissing someone else. If they see his mouth on anyone else, it's a full-on nuclear fit. Not just a breakup, but probably a slap, kicking him out, and the whole bit."

"It's not my house, though," she said, looking honestly confused. "And I still don't get why I'd be pissed at Ripper for kissing someone when you two are fucking!"

I damn near melted when she said that. My damned heart could start beating again. The band around my chest which made me feel like I couldn't breathe? Yeah, it vanished. In one sentence, Jeri had made it possible for me to stop panicking internally, so I flopped back against the couch and sighed in relief.

"Ripper?" she asked.

"Fuck me, I thought that was going to get me dumped," I admitted.

"No," she soothed, twisting to curl up against me. "You were just being a good guy. I mean, I thought that maybe things with you and Zoe had been brewing up on the third floor or something, and if they had, I'd be happy for you."

"See?" Knock asked.

I lifted my hand behind her back to flip him off. "Asshole."

"Yep," Cade agreed, "but a cute one."

Hottie simply groaned. "Yeah, great, but can someone *please* tell me what the hell just happened?"

So I shifted Jeri to be tucked in at my side, wrapped an arm around her back, and did my best. "Zoe has been trying to make progress. She feels like she should be over what happened to her, and she hates that what Evan did to her means he still has control over her, in a way. Like, she says that when she gets anxious about things, it's letting him force her all over again. So when she wanted to test something, I agreed without asking what, and the next thing I knew, I was bending over her."

"Bending?" Hottie asked.

"Like a guy does when he kisses a girl," Jeri explained. "You're taller, and you tend to hold us, which probably feels like being trapped to Zoe."

"Fuck," Cade breathed.

"Oh," Hottie muttered.

Knock murmured to himself, like that made sense to him, but I was replaying that whole moment in my mind. I was taller than her, and broader, and she'd asked me to hold her like that. I'd been gentle, but so would a good boyfriend - like Jinxy. It was still holding.

"And she thinks you're safe," Jeri reminded me. "Trustworthy, so don't go thinking it's a bad thing. It's a massive fucking compliment, ok? You guys don't get it, but being with a man? We know you can hurt us, and she's been hurt, so I can see her wanting to test the waters safely."

"Because you would?" Hottie asked.

She turned to stick her tongue out at him. "I know how to beat the shit out of him. Zoe's all nice and shit."

"Yeah, she is," I agreed. "But is Jinxy pissed?"

"They were kissing outside," Hottie said.

"Wait, what?" Jeri asked, leaning like she wanted to jump up.

So I grabbed her harder, holding her in place. "You will not fuck this up for her a second time in one day, Jeri."

She paused, and then a little giggle slipped out. "Oh. No, you're right."

Giving me a sweet smile, she turned a little more, pulling her feet up on the couch too, and then tucked herself in against my chest. I couldn't help but curl my arms around her a little more, not even caring if the other guys were watching.

No, fuck that. I liked that they were. It made me feel like a bigger or better man because I could do this. I wanted to puff up and strut, but at the same time, I wanted to look at my friends and make sure they noticed I'd been picked. I wanted to see them smiling for me, because I knew they would be.

And in that moment, I finally understood my girlfriend. We weren't competing. She wanted to let me prance around like an idiot too. She wanted to be able to brag, or laugh, or just celebrate the wins with us. That was what Knock meant when he said having multiple bonds worked for her. The same way I was both taking her from the guys right now, but also wanting my friends - those same guys - to be happy for me. That was all she was trying to make possible.

That was what she meant when she said friends first, because it really was possible to have it all. She'd made sure of it.

# CHAPTER 31

### JERICHO

The next day, I was sitting in calculus when I heard my phone vibrate in my bag. I glanced around, aware I'd forgotten to completely silence it, but no one seemed to care. Needless to say, as soon as I was out of class, I was swiping to see who'd messaged me.

**Zoe:**
I'm not sure when your math class is out, but lunch?

"Good news?" Knock asked, making me realize I was smiling.

"It's Zoe," I explained. "We kinda didn't get to talk about the whole kiss mess yet."

"Mm." He leaned in and kissed my temple. "Make sure you tell her you're not mad, ok? Most women would react like Tiffany did when Cade kept flirting with you."

"Yeah, but - "

He lifted a hand, halting me. "Most women would, Jeri. So just tell

Zoe. I know you're not mad, and you know you aren't, but everyone else keeps waiting for the cracks."

I sighed. "Don't we have enough cracks already? I mean, between classes and the stuff with Jason, and it taking so long to get all this done so we can actually *do* something?"

He chuckled as we passed through the door of the building, yet the moment we were outside, he pulled me around to face him. "Stop and count the wins, Jeri."

"What fucking *wins*?" I demanded.

"Zoe's safe because we got Evan put away. The girls at Sanger High are safe because we got Alpha Team put away. The little girl Jinxy's sister knows is safe because we busted that fucker. Whoever trashed the car is going to jail because we made sure there's video proof that can't be erased. The Kings of Gaming are done; the organization is being dismantled. Soul Reaper is dead. The fucker who drugged Destiny Pierce is behind bars. Do you really want me to keep going? Because I can."

My eyes were getting bigger and my mouth was hanging open a bit. "Shit, when you put it like that..."

"Yeah," he said. "So talk to your bestie. Make sure everything is ok, because it really is ok, Jeri. We got this. We're busting our asses to make sure of it, and maybe it's not happening as fast as you want, but none of that did either. We still won."

"Hey," I said, catching his hand. "This is why I love you, just so you know."

His eyes dropped to my lips, and he stepped closer. "Yeah?"

"Oh yeah," I promised, moving so I was pressed right up against him. "And Jason comes tomorrow evening."

"Mm, so I should make sure to sneak in my girl time tonight, huh?" he asked, reaching up to play with one of my dreads. "Remind you why you can't work yourself to death, and that there's more to life than the next crisis?"

"That is not making me want to invite you to spend the night in my room."

"Alone or with Hottie?" he teased.

"Either way."

He laughed, but shifted his hand to cup my cheek, and then bent to give me a quick and amazing kiss. His tongue swept through my mouth like he was claiming it. His hand held me like he would never let me go, but then he tipped his head, pressing our brows together.

"Alone," he said. "I deserve time alone with you." Then he stole another kiss that was just as fast. "Now call her, because I have to start walking or I'm going to have a stupid lump in the front of my pants."

Laughing, I stepped back. "Bye, Knock. Be a good boy."

"Never," he said, walking backwards. "Bye, Jericho. Be a very bad girl with your bestie!"

I was grinning, but I also pulled out my phone again to check why Zoe hadn't answered my text. She shouldn't be in class right now, but just as I pulled up her number, my phone rang in my hands. It was her calling.

"Zoe!" I answered.

"Hey, I'm down by Fry Street. Where are you?"

"Middle of campus, but around that side. Why?"

"I'm buying you lunch," she said. "There's a bunch of places on Avenue A, it looks like."

"I'm walking that way," I promised. "Want to meet me by the Language building? I think that's the one on the corner, right?"

"Yep, and I'm sitting here on the edge of the flowerbed, so see you in a minute!"

But when I finally made it over there, she wasn't alone. While Zoe was actually sitting on the edge of the tall brick flower beds that were next to the sidewalk, some woman was standing before her, gesturing as she talked. She was wearing a hoodie, and her hair was up in a messy bun, but I had to get six feet away before I actually realized who she was.

"Tiff?" I asked.

"Hey!" she called over to me with a smile. "Look who I found."

I laughed. "Yeah, and I was hunting for her. Hey, you want to do lunch with us?"

"You sure?" Zoe asked. "I mean, I'm cool with it, but I kinda figured with everything that happened yesterday..."

"What happened yesterday?" Tiffany asked.

"I kinda kissed her boyfriend," Zoe admitted.

"Oh." Tiffany lifted her hands and took a step back. "Yeah, I can butt right the fuck out. You two clearly have some talking to do."

"No, it's fine," I promised before looking over at Zoe. "You're fine. It's fine. Everything's fine and I'm not mad at all."

"Um, ok," Zoe said. "So wanna come get involved in our house-drama, Tiff?"

She kinda jerked her thumb over her shoulder. "This place is supposed to have good stuff. My roommate loves their vegan meals."

"You have a roommate?" I asked, gesturing for Zoe to get up.

"Dorms," she reminded me. "So yeah. Muslim girl from out of state. Like, she does the whole head scarf and everything. But don't let the stereotypes fool you. She's a lot of fun. Her boyfriend's a complete asshole, but I like her. I like her even more when she's not there, and since she's always with him, it works."

I laughed. "So you went from being an extrovert last year to an introvert this year?"

"Uh..." She glanced both ways, but since there wasn't any traffic, the three of us ran across the road. "Yeah, kinda. Although I'm not trying to be an introvert. I just keep meeting all the idiots, it seems. Except for Ruin."

"Because we happen to be cool," Zoe said as she reached the door. "This one?"

"Yep," Tiff agreed, waving for me to go first.

Together, we joined the line of other students waiting to get lunch. It took a bit, but that gave me time to look over the menu that hung above the counter. By the time it was our turn, we all ordered, Zoe insisted she was buying, since she had a paycheck now, and we went to sit down.

"Ok, so I have to get this out there," Zoe told me. "I didn't even think about how Ripper kissing me might upset you. I was just thinking I wanted to test it, you know? And he's not going to get pissed if I lose my shit, and I was so wrapped up in how much I wanted to get over this crap that I didn't even think, Jeri, and I'm sorry."

"Hey," I said, reaching over the table to press my hand on hers. "He's your best friend. We're all doing this thing. It's ok, and you don't need to feel bad about it."

"Yeah, she's not going to try to call you a slut or anything," Tiffany said, flashing me a smile. "And I am sorry about that."

"It's ok," I assured her. "Last year was a clusterfuck. This year is a mess. I mean, at this rate, we're all getting pretty good at talking things through, right?"

"Not so much," Zoe admitted. "Because when Jinxy was trying to talk to me, I sorta interrupted him with a kiss."

I sucked in a breath, but Tiffany squealed in excitement, leaning over to give Zoe a side hug. For a moment, the three of us just celebrated, but a server dropping our food in front of us made us bring it down a few levels.

"Sorry," I said as I took my plate. "And thank you."

"Trust me, it's normal," he said. "You ladies enjoy."

Tiff twisted to watch him walk away, then turned back. "Ok, for once, a guy wasn't a complete hornball."

"Gay," Zoe said. "I bet he's also an art student, but I saw him flirting with another guy in the back when we were ordering."

"Why are all the straight ones such pigs?" Tiffany asked.

"Or Jeri's," Zoe countered. "Because Ripper and Hottie are pretty amazing."

"Knock and Cade too," I reminded her.

"Not straight," Tiff countered. "But since we're confessing and all, is it really ok if I help Cade study like I've been, Jeri? I promise things between us are not at all romantic."

"No, it's fine," I swore. "Hell, even if it wasn't, that's Cade's decision. I mean, and Knock's."

"She's completely non-monogamous," Zoe said.

"New word," Tiffany teased.

Zoe giggled. "Jinxy and I were kinda talking about things last night, and I spent the whole night in his room, and it was pretty amazing."

"But no fucking yet?" I asked.

She shook her head. "I'm just happy with this, ok?"

"Because of last year?" Tiff asked.

"Yeah," Zoe said. "I just..." She looked over at me. "We're not supposed to talk about the thing, right?"

"It's Tiff," I said. "I mean, she knows about the phone, so it's not like we can really say worse."

"And I'm not about to say shit," Tiffany promised. "Y'all, that's what got him busted. I mean, I knew you were doing something, but I thought it would be embarrassing him. That's why I helped with the distraction, you know? But that? It's a million times better than anything I could imagine, and I will *not* say a thing to destroy the case."

"And she knows a bit about the FBI thing already," I told Zoe.

"A very small bit," Tiffany admitted.

So Zoe rounded on her. "Well, they have to do a background check on us. Like, big, top secret, make sure we've never screwed up type. But it's all adult stuff, because they don't know who we are."

"Who's they?" Tiff asked.

"The politicians writing the bill that will make this possible," I explained. "It's basically top-level FBI and government shit."

"Whoa," Tiffany breathed. "That's like, huge."

"But we'll be able to bust assholes like Dylan now," Zoe went on. "And so they have to do this background check, and part of it is how sane we are. Well, my child sexual abuse case is out there now, which means they'll know I'm a victim, so I want to make sure I'm technically ok mentally, right?"

"Ok how?" Tiff asked.

"Dating," I realized. "Relationships."

"Not traumatized, because while Jason might have a PTSD dog, I'm pretty sure they'd find a reason to nope me out if I'm nutso."

"Probably," I agreed.

"Who has a dog?" Tiffany asked.

"Our handler," Zoe said, waving that off. "But I was telling Jinxy how I want to try to get a little more, um, personal? Like, normal stuff. The kind of stuff that seems like 'good girl' stuff now, you know?"

"Like kissing," I realized.

She nodded emphatically. "So that's why I kissed Ripper, and I freaked when you walked in. But I told Jinxy I really want to be his girlfriend. Not his friend that's a girl. I want to kiss and cuddle, and he's ok with it. He said even if I freak out, it's fine. We'll work it out."

"Ugh, you two are so cute," Tiffany groaned.

"You have no idea," I assured her. "They're like straight sugar kind of sweet."

"Like you're one to talk," Tiffany said. "You have what, four boyfriends?"

"Yep."

"And I met Hottie. First off, good name. Secondly, he is so completely into you, it's not even funny. I think he was trying to chase me off, thinking I was hitting on Cade."

"I know better than that," I promised before looking at Zoe. "Just like I know you would never try to steal one of my guys. I mean, we don't poach, right?" I looked between them both. "That's how female friends should work. Not that I'm an expert on girl time, but it's how I always imagined it. We women stick together, and while I have no problem with sharing, we don't try to steal each other's guys away - or anyone else's."

"I can drink to that!" Tiffany agreed, lifting her cup of soda.

"Here, here!" Zoe chimed in.

I was smiling, but I lifted mine as well, and we thumped the plastic cups together before taking a long drink. And while it was fun, it also felt like more. It felt like some kind of promise - no, an oath. Like we were reaffirming our own bonds.

Because having girlfriends felt just as good as boyfriends. These two were my friends. Actual, real, trustworthy friends. Maybe we'd gotten here the long way around, but something about this oath made me think the three of us might actually have a chance of lasting.

"Here's to a whole new bitch squad," I said.

"Hoes before bros?" Zoe asked.

Tiffany laughed. "Friends. Let's just go with friends."

"Because friends should *always* come first," I agreed.

# CHAPTER 32

## JERICHO

Jason showed up on Friday with more bad news. Not that any of us were surprised, though. Evidently these politicians were going to keep increasing the difficulty level for anyone wanting to be a cybersecurity consultant for the FBI. That was what they were calling us, at any rate.

Initially, we'd been told we'd have to pass the Phase I test. This was what agents got months to learn in Quantico. Now, all of a sudden, we needed to know enough to pass the Phase II test. That meant more classes, *plus* an interview! Yeah, a second interview. It was almost like these assholes in Congress assumed putting us face-to-face with another person would scare us off or something.

But we could do it. No, it wouldn't be easy. We weren't used to easy, though. Everything that had come at us last year had been hard, so this almost felt like busywork. Hottie had even pointed out how it might be useful. If we knew enough to pass the real FBI testing requirements, then no one could say we weren't qualified to make busts.

I was hanging on to that thought like a lifeline. It was the silver lining to being told I needed to add more shit to this already heaping pile that felt like it was trying to suffocate me. Fuck, I wasn't the kind of person to sit down and study! And yet, I'd been making myself do it every day this semester.

I got two hours to play Flawed, three for my college classes, and the rest went towards this FBI shit. From memorizing the parts of the gun through taking the practice quizzes in our handy little FBI books, I pushed myself until I was sure I had it. The problem was making it all stick.

Regurgitating the crap a day after reading it? Easy. A week later? Not so much. What I had to do was actually *understand* all of this. If I wasn't completely sure of my knowledge, I read it again, tested myself again, then re-read it one more time.

Maybe it was a little manic. In truth, I simply didn't want to be the person holding us back. This whole thing? It was an opportunity too good to let slip past. If we could get these contracts, then we could clean up the entire fucking internet! Maybe that would be one case at a time, and no, there weren't enough of us to do it all, but we were the trailblazers, right?

If we could do this, then other groups could also be hired. More and more would be added, until the assholes who relied on their anonymity would no longer be safe. Being a hacker wouldn't be a bad thing anymore. It would be the start of a law enforcement career. Well, I kinda hoped it would end up that way, but that might be pushing things.

Lying in my room that night, I was staring at the tile pattern on the ceiling while Hottie slept peacefully. With each breath he took, my head rose and fell, but my brain simply refused to shut up. The Fundamentals of Law said that in order to search and seize evidence, we needed to have a pressing interest. That meant saving lives, but what counted as saving lives? Was preventing a suicide enough? Was stopping bullying enough? Yeah, this was what Jason meant when he said the internet was the Wild West.

These laws were made for physical locations and in-person crimes. The idea of an unknown stranger assaulting someone across the country hadn't even been in the minds of the ones writing our laws, let alone our constitution. Interpretations depended on judges and philosophical styles I couldn't give a shit about.

But as a consultant, we had so much more leeway, and I intended to use every inch, so why did they want to force me to think like an FBI agent? And worse, what if I already was because all these books had leaked into my head? Fuck!

Giving up on sleep, I carefully pulled myself away from Hottie and slipped off the side of the bed. I was sure I'd gotten away without waking him, but as I headed towards the bathroom, he murmured sleepily.

"Jeri?"

"It's ok, Hottie," I said softly. "Just have to pee."

"Mm. Miss you when you're gone," he murmured before rolling onto his side and falling back asleep.

Damn, I loved that man. The strangest thing was that it really had nothing to do with how gorgeous he was. It was him. The way he cared, the fact he wasn't ashamed to admit it, and how he always made me feel like I mattered. Hottie was so good to me, and even when we fought, he still listened. He also didn't back down when he thought he was right. We discussed things - often at the top of our lungs - without ever tearing the other down in the process.

That was why he was my rock. He made me grow. He challenged my beliefs and paranoias. He always made sure I never fell all the way down. If I tripped or stumbled in life, he was there to catch me, yet he did it without the blind part of loyalty. Somehow that made what we had feel even more important. He loved me because he knew me and all of my flaws.

But while I did go into the bathroom, it wasn't really my

destination. Closing the door behind me, I opened the one into his room, and then left through his door. Stepping softly, I made my way down the stairs, found my laptop, and carried it through the dark house and into the study.

While the machine booted up, I debated brewing a coffee. My mind was a little fuzzy - because I should be sleeping. I had to be up soon, but my brain needed me to check this rule so it could shut up. Finding the right ebook, I opened that, pulled up the test quiz, and then went to double-check my answer.

But one paragraph bled into the next. Why we could use evidence led me to how we should attain the evidence which turned into commentary on the ethics of evidence gathering. Not a single bit of this was about hacking, but it didn't matter. I had to pass this test. I needed to make sure I actually knew this shit!

The clink of a cup made me flinch. My eyes landed on the pink travel mug that was now beside my elbow - then jumped to the bearer of my coffee. There, standing in the middle of this dark room, was a silhouette that could only be Jason. From the angle of his arm, he was holding a cup of his own.

"Uh..." I glanced around, looking for his dog. "Why aren't you sleeping?"

"Could ask you the same," he said, easing himself down into one of the chairs across from me. "You do know we have to be up in a few hours, right?"

"Yeah, but I don't understand the search and seizure clause," I admitted. "I'm just re-reading it real fast."

"Mm." Jason paused, then chuckled as a set of very slow dog-nails dragged across the hallway. "Crysis," he said, letting the dog know where he was. Then he looked back at me. "The answer is a warrant or an immediate threat, Jeri. That's all you need to know."

"Yeah, but what's an immediate threat?" I asked. "I mean, suicide? How can we judge that? What about bullying? None of this shit is meant for us, so how do we use it?"

"You don't." He paused to sip his coffee, then gestured for me to set my laptop down. "You are Ruin. You are a hacker. You are not supposed to be a cop, think like a cop, or be restricted like a cop. The entire point of this is to have a resource who can see what's not meant to be seen, which makes it public access, and then I can then worry about evidence gathering."

"Yeah, but - "

"No," he said. "That's your answer. Now close that down and get some sleep while you can. I mean, unless you think you shoot better vibrating from caffeine."

Because we had another appointment to head to the range in the morning. My eyes dropped to the corner of my screen, where the clock showed it was almost three in the morning. Five hours of sleep would be enough. Well, probably four. Three if I didn't actually fall asleep right away.

"Let me just read this again, and then I'll go back to bed," I assured him. "Besides, aren't you supposed to be sleeping? Why do you get to be up if I can't?"

"I was talking to my wife," he explained. "She's not lying upstairs waiting for me to curl up next to her. Ok, she also just got a kill streak on Murder, and she wanted to brag, but bed is exactly where I was going before I saw you head this way."

"I just - "

"You need," he broke in again, "to sleep. Jericho, take this fucking seriously!"

"I am!" I hissed, struggling to keep my voice down because I knew Knock and Cade's room was too close. "Do you not get that, Jason? I'm sitting here fucking studying when I could be gaming. When I could be fucking. When I could be doing anything else! Me! I'm *studying*!"

"You aren't the one I'm worried about," he assured me.

"Well, you should be!" I snapped. "Zoe knows how to do this. Ripper's fucking smart, and he just gets it. Knock has a head start, and this bullshit actually makes sense to Cade. Jinxy and Hottie? They're used to studying and memorizing shit, but I'm not! I'm going to blank when they make us take this test, and I'll be the reason this doesn't happen. I'm going to fuck it all up just like I do everything, ok? So can't you please just let me read this again?!"

"Jeri..."

"No!" I snapped, slashing an arm through the air. "I'm not going to let it happen again. I'm not going to lose anyone else because I didn't try hard enough, or got distracted, or had too much to do. I can sleep later, after we have this contract. I can get an espresso machine or something. I mean, Alex got us paychecks, you know? And we got the first one, so I can afford that now, and if I add a little sugar, I'll be able to push through, but I can't take this for granted."

"I didn't - " he tried again.

But the words were coming out, and I couldn't stop them. "Drake, Dad, Nina, and then Zoe. It was almost Riley and the girls! Don't you see, Jason? It was too close, and this could fix all of it, so I have to make sure we can do this. DeathAdder is still out there. It's going to happen again, and the next time, I'll be ready. That's why Riley's still here. We were close enough to our computers, and we got you what you needed, so she didn't die. I stopped it that time, but it'll happen again, because it always happens again, and I need to make sure I don't get distracted, because the last time, Amber died, and I don't want anyone else to - "

Crysis shoved onto my lap and began licking at my face. He didn't ask, didn't slowly make his way up. The dog, who had been groggy a few seconds ago, had just exploded into my face, and his tongue was now going a million miles a minute. He licked at every inch of exposed skin he could find. My face, my neck, and even my hands were fair game.

"Just pet him," Jason soothed as he moved over to the couch. "Don't try to push him away. Just pet, Jeri - and breathe. You can do it. Big breath in while your hands move. C'mon, at least try?"

I sucked in a breath and did my best to rub at the back of Crysis's neck. That shifted his licking to my neck, which made it possible to hug him. My fingers moved to his back, sliding into his short, sleek fur, and I pulled in another breath.

"There you go," Jason said gently. "Breathing always comes first. Just focus on pulling the air in and pushing it out. Crysis is merely helping. He even smells like vanilla, right? Zara got shampoo so he smells good when you hug him like that."

I huffed out a little breath, but it was enough. Scooting even closer, Jason reached over to rub my back. Crysis just kept licking, and right now he was focused on my ear. It kinda tickled.

"You got this, Jeri," Jason swore. "I know you're fighting against your own demons, but you really do have this."

"But..." I looked over the dog's back. "What if I don't? What if I'm trying to make it all work and I fuck it up?"

"You won't," he promised. "That's why you have Hottie, and Knock, and Ripper, and Cade. It's why you brought in Jinxy and Zoe. You are Ruin. *All* of you. Not *just* you."

"It doesn't stop, though," I said, but the words came out like a whimper. "I saw the stream, Jason. He had a gun to their heads! I saw it when he hit Riley, and I just... I thought..."

"Shh," he breathed. "I know. Trust me, I know. She was on the far side, and I couldn't put a bullet in the bastard because Dez and Rhaven were in the way. I fucking *know*, Jericho."

So I tilted my head and pushed my entire face into Crysis's fur. He really did smell good. Sweet, and yeah, a bit like vanilla.

"But that's what you're forgetting," Jason continued. "You and me? We did that together. Ruin helped you. You helped me. I'm sure you're thinking that's obvious, but you're missing it, Jeri. You're fucking missing the forest for the trees. Those partners of yours? They fucking have your back. They will dig in just as hard as you will. They fucking well have been."

"I know."

His hand moved again, another gentle and reassuring caress. "And

I have you, too. I will fucking *carry* you through this if you need me to, and do you know why?"

I looked up, my eyes landing on his face. "No. Why?"

"Because you fucking carried me when I needed it most. Because I can't do it on my own, and you shouldn't have to either. Because..." His eyes searched my face, so pale in this darkness. "Because it's ok to need to be carried sometimes, and I think you'd do it for me."

My throat pinched up, all the stress and anxiety making me unable to talk. Instead, I nodded, showing I heard him. The problem was I felt those words. No one had ever offered me anything like that. Mom couldn't. Hottie had never had the chance, because what hit one of us tended to hit both. My friends tried, but it wasn't the same.

But Jason? He was different. He'd saved them. He'd bent the rules for Zoe. He'd been there for us, time and time again, and not always in nice ways. That was why his eyes were cold sometimes. It was why he felt distant. This man might be our handler, but his rules were the same as mine - which meant no rules at all.

"I can't sleep sometimes," I finally said.

He nodded slowly. "Me either."

"And I keep thinking it's going to happen again."

"It will."

My heart stumbled. That was not the response I'd expected. So many people had been trying to reassure me that my curse wasn't real, that we had this, and that people were safe. I'd gotten used to hearing it and ignoring it, but this? He wasn't bullshitting me. He was trusting me with a statement of simple truth.

"So what do we do?" I asked.

He tipped his head at his dog. "You pet him. Jeri, Crysis is a service dog. He recognizes anxiety from post-traumatic stress." His hand shifted to rub my shoulder. "I'm pretty sure you have it, so pet him a lot. It really does help."

"That's not what I meant." But my hands were still moving.

Jason murmured thoughtfully. "You breathe. You pet. And then you figure out how to lean on others, because you are not an island." He leaned in. "You need them. All six of them. You also need me, and you know what? I fucking need you back. *That* is why this works. That's what makes us a team, and if we want this to keep working? We need to stop trying to be what anyone else wants. You are Ruin. You are their destruction, so don't try to be a damned agent, Jericho. Be a hacker. Be pissed."

"Be cruel," I breathed, remembering him saying that before.

"As cruel as necessary to end up a hero. Yeah." His hand moved to caress his dog's back. "And then we push through our fears together."

# CHAPTER 33

## HOTSHOT

I woke up alone. The mattress beside me was cool, which meant Jeri had been gone for a while. Looking over, I realized the bathroom door was still closed, and my heart stopped hard in my chest. Panic hit. I was scrambling out of bed and headed that way before my brain was all the way awake.

Tapping lightly, I called out, "Jeri?"

Silence.

I couldn't hear water, or movement, or anything. It was too quiet. Dead quiet. Giving in, I opened the door and scanned the bathroom. The lights were all off, so I flipped them on and checked everything. The shower stall, the toilet, and even under the sink. I looked anywhere there could be a hint of her, but she was gone. Completely gone, and I was on the verge of melting down.

But if she wasn't in bed and wasn't in the bathroom, then she had to be in my room, right? Turning on the lights there, I found nothing - except the door open to the hall. Ok. That let me breathe again. Maybe she just needed a midnight snack or something?

Hoping not to wake anyone else up with my panic, I quietly headed downstairs to check for her. My heart was still thrumming too hard, but this would be ok. She'd promised me she wouldn't leave me like that. She was working hard for this FBI thing, and while it was a lot of pressure, she didn't seem depressed. Then again, neither had Nina.

The first floor of the house was dark, but the sound of voices led me on. It seemed like she was in the study? I was almost there when I heard Jason reply. I couldn't make out his words, not at first, but that was definitely his voice. I got a little closer.

"But that's what you're forgetting," Jason was saying. "You and me? We did that together. Ruin helped you. You helped me. I'm sure you're thinking that's obvious, but you're missing it, Jeri. You're fucking missing the forest for the trees. Those partners of yours? They fucking have your back. They will dig in just as hard as you will. They fucking well have been."

"I know." Her voice trembled.

Jason's response was so gentle. Paternal, even. "And I have you too. I will fucking *carry* you through this if you need me to..."

I didn't hear the rest, because I backed away slowly. She was cracking. I knew she had been, and this man was somehow talking her down. He was saying everything she needed to hear, but did he have any idea how she'd take that? Did he know how fragile she was right now?

Jeri had been pushing herself to her limit. That was why I was so worried about her. Well, never mind my own issues, but I could see her straining, and I refused to ignore it. I would not let her slip through the cracks the way Nina had. I would not allow her to feel worthless and unloved. I would never let her break alone. And if she did break, I would pick up every single piece and do my best to help her glue herself back together.

That was what it meant to love someone the way I loved her. I fucking needed this girl. If anything happened to her, it would tear me apart. My problem was, Jason seemed to have this. He was somehow soothing her in a way I'd never been able to, but did he realize what he was promising? Probably not.

So I made my way back upstairs, turning off all the lights I'd turned on in my hunt for her. I crawled back into her bed, closed my eyes, and pretended to sleep, but my mind was spinning. Why hadn't she talked to *me* about this? Why was she trying to power through? How the fuck was I supposed to make this better if she wouldn't even admit there was a problem?

Eventually, she came back. Jeri slipped into the bed and curled up against my back. I pretended to sleep through it, loving when she kissed my neck. Soon enough, her breathing slowed and she finally relaxed. I waited a little longer, then allowed myself to do the same, but I slept fitfully. My dreams were filled with red in the water, and I woke far too many times just to make sure she was still breathing.

When the morning light leaked through her window, I gave up. Kissing her head, I managed to get out from under her, then went hunting for clothes. Once dressed, I headed downstairs, knowing everyone else would start moving soon, so I might as well get the coffee pot going - but when I made it into the kitchen, someone else had gotten there first.

I came around the corner to see Jason lining up cups and the coffee maker trickling with a dark brew. From the tilt of his head, the man heard me, but I didn't care. Right now, the two of us were alone, and I was still stuck on what he'd told her last night.

"Do you sleep at all?" I grumbled.

Jason chuckled and grabbed the gold cup. "No, not much." He removed the glass carafe and put my cup under it. "I'm guessing you need a coffee?"

I decided to stop beating around the bush. "I heard you last night."

The man turned, pinning me with his icy gaze. "Good. Means I don't have to tell you that your girlfriend is straining."

"You fucking made her *promises*," I snapped. "You made it sound like you're going to make things all better, but did you stop and think about what happens when you can't? Huh?"

He grunted, pulled out my cup, and replaced the carafe. Adding in some cream and sugar, he passed the cup over, then moved away from the counter. Once I took the cup, he tapped his jaw, right beside his chin.

"I'd prefer you hit here. I mean, it'll screw up your aim, but probably make you feel a ton better. So go ahead. Let's just get this out of the way."

"What?" I asked.

"For when you punch me," he said. "It's what you wanna do, so I'm giving you the chance. Don't worry. I don't hit back."

"I'm not going to fucking hit you!" I gasped. "What the fuck?"

"It's what most men want when another is being nice to their girl. Just figured I'd let you run me off." Then the asshole turned back to the coffee maker like none of this was a big deal.

So I grabbed his arm and spun him back to face me. "I don't care if you fuck her. I don't care if you're into her - or not. I don't give a shit if you're cool, a badass hacker, or anything else. I just want you to fucking listen to me." Then I pointed back at the stairs. "She is not a game. She's real, she's hurting, and she is not ok. If you make her fucking promises and then let her down? If you give her one more reason to think this world is a piece of shit she doesn't want to be in?" Then I leaned in. "I will *kill* you."

I was growling in a way that should've made this man tense up. Spittle flew from my mouth with the intensity of my anger. Jason didn't even flinch. The man watched me, those grey-green eyes of his holding mine until I was done. Then he did the last thing I would've expected. He dipped his head in agreement.

"Good. That's what she needs." And he reached for another cup.

"Jason..." I warned.

"No, it's my turn," he said, but he didn't bother looking at me. "You don't fucking know me, Grayson, but I know you. I know each and every one of you, and do you know why? Because you got close to Knock. I knew Knock because he got close to Riley." Finally, he looked up. "I know Riley because I would not let her become a victim. Back then, I had no idea she didn't need my help, but that's why I know her. Now, I know you. All of you. I know more about you than you probably know about yourself." He blinked, nothing else. "And I know her."

"I heard you offer to 'carry' her," I said.

He went on as if I hadn't said a damned thing. "I *know* her, Grayson, because I used to *be* her. I know *her* because she's more than some fucking post-traumatic stress disorder. She's more than how fucked up she is. Under all that mess, that girl is amazing, and she needs someone to remind her of it. Someone who actually can, because I don't want in her fucking pants. I'm not trying to impress her. I'm just making sure she doesn't grow up and end up like *me*."

I had to take a step back, because while he didn't raise his voice, there was something so intense about it that it felt like a shove. His eyes. It had to be his eyes, because the look in them was fucking terrifying. There was no joke in anything he said. This man meant every word, and to a depth I couldn't even fathom.

"Why?" I asked. "Why do you give a shit about her?"

He shrugged. "When I was her, I fucking wished for someone to just reach out and offer me a hand. Just help up. It didn't even matter what kind of help or what kind of up. I was alone. I was cracking. I was desperate, and I had to pull my-fucking-self up because no one else gave a shit, so I swore I would. Know what? I do. I will carry her, and you, and everyone else in here, because I fucking-well can."

"You..." I shook my head, not sure what I was trying to say. "But..." None of this made sense.

"I'm on your side," he said, gentler this time. "I also meant what I told her. I don't give a shit how this mess with the FBI ends. I will not abandon Ruin. I will not leave you all to dig yourselves out. The part you don't understand is that it's not an empty offer. I am that good."

"We're getting there," I promised.

"Yeah, you are," he agreed. "But she's been triggered. Not a little trigger, Grayson. Jericho is trying to ignore her own trauma because she doesn't think she's worth feeling it. She thinks she needs to prove herself. She's convinced her value is only in what she can do for others, and you - not those other guys - are the only one who can prove otherwise."

"How?" I asked.

"I don't know," he admitted. "Maybe the same way you always have? Maybe like this? Maybe you should've hit me when I offered, to make it clear she's worth fighting for? I honestly don't know."

Which made me huff out a laugh. "So why me, then?"

"Because you're her rock. You are her stability. She needs you, but you need her. The two of you have been tied for a very long time. The pair of you grew up together and share that childhood bond. It's not something to ignore."

"But I was her mentor. I've been trying not to, you know, take advantage of that."

He scoffed. "Is that how you think she sees you?"

"Huh?"

"It's four years," Jason said. "I'm ten years older than my wife."

"Yeah, but I mean, she's - "

"A year older than you," Jason broke in. "So what, not a kid? Not impressionable? Not vulnerable? I fucking saved her life, so you think about the power dynamic there."

"How do you know about that?" I asked, because my fears about manipulating Jeri weren't something we'd talked about.

He chuckled once. "Riley. I heard all about your chat, and while I respect you for worrying, it's four years. You were a child. A slightly older one she could lean on. She was a child. A slightly wiser one you could cling to. That's what childhood is for, but do not think it doesn't matter. It does. Not the way you think it should. It matters because it means she's not *alone*."

"Oh."

"And now none of you are alone. Crack, Grayson. Let her break if she has to. Don't try to ignore the shit parts, because they fucking suck, and do you know what keeps us going?" He tapped his chest. "The fact that we never, *ever*, forget how to give a damn. It hurts more, but it keeps us human. Broken, fucked-up, desperate humans, but that's why it's called humanity. In order to have it, you have to feel it. Both of you."

"Does it ever stop?" I asked. "All this shit that keeps piling on, does it ever end?"

"No," he admitted. "But it does stop hurting. One day, you wake up and realize it was all worth it. You realize you're happy, and you don't know when that happened. It changes, and it's subtle. Maybe it still hurts sometimes, but somewhere along the way it feels more good than bad, and you figure out that you wouldn't change any of it, because you actually like where you ended up."

"You mean with her?" I asked.

"I mean all of it," he promised. "I mean life. I mean those fears you're trying to push down. One day, they will be distant enough that the ache will feel almost sweet, because it made you into a man you can honestly be proud of." He reached up and clasped my arm. "And I think you're close, otherwise you would've swung."

"Yeah," I mumbled. "Just..." I paused to pull in a breath. "Please don't let her down. She's... Jason, she's never had anyone like you in her life. Well, not since Drake, you know?"

"I'm not her big brother," he said.

"No," I agreed. "I think she thinks of you more like Russel." Her father.

The man's shoulders slumped and he reached out for the counter. "Fuck."

"So be careful what you promise," I said again before grabbing the carafe and the pink cup.

Because my girl deserved a coffee in bed this morning. I had a feeling she was going to need a little go-juice, and from the look on his face, Jason needed to realize Jericho wasn't like the rest of us.

She was fragile. The type that would explode if dropped, so *I'd* make sure she never hit rock bottom.

# CHAPTER 34

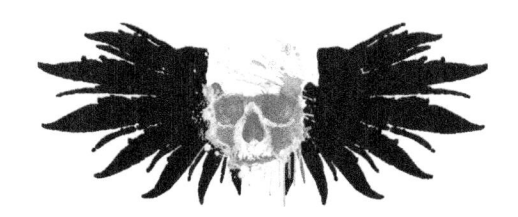

**SPECIAL AGENT JASON RAIGE**

A lack of sleep didn't help with shooting. Hottie's words, however, did keep me from snapping at the kids. They were trying hard - maybe too hard - and I needed to offer a little more praise. Surprisingly, that worked. Not on Jericho, but Ripper lifted his chin a bit and looked calmer. His groupings also improved dramatically.

They were starting to get proficient. No, fuck that, they were almost good. Not great, and they certainly weren't sharpshooters, but they were now comfortable with the weapons. On Sunday, I went over the latest testing requirements one more time, but this time I made sure they knew we'd find a way to hack it. They needed to pass. They didn't need to make perfect scores.

And Crysis was getting good at navigating the airport. Although when I flew out this time, I didn't get to head home. Our destination was Washington, D.C., for an official report. Alex needed one to keep Ruin's paychecks rolling, and I had a few questions of my own.

My dog and I spent Sunday night in a hotel, but first thing

Monday morning, we headed to FBI headquarters. Crysis was wearing his vest, looking very professional. I'd gone with jeans and a game shirt. As I headed towards the elevator, an agent in a suit stepped forward and lifted his hand, intending to stop me.

I pulled my badge from my back pocket. The man saw, nodded, and moved out of my way, meaning I didn't even have to slow down. So far, I'd only been here once, but I knew my way. When we reached the right floor, Crysis and I turned, ignoring the looks we were getting as we headed down the hall. At the far end, the door to Alex's office was wide open.

I walked in to find three people in the outer office. A young woman was sitting at the desk with the phone to her ear. A middle-aged man had a stack of papers in his hands, and he looked like he was waiting his turn. Then there was another woman. She was sitting in one of the chairs at the side.

"Agent Raige?" the girl on the phone asked, using her hand to get my attention. "You can go on in."

I nodded, having no clue what her name or position was. But when I opened the door to Alex's private space, there was yet another man in there. This one I recognized. Agent Dalton had been my boss once.

"Jason," the man greeted me.

"Isaiah," I replied, nodding at him. "Nice to see you again."

"Not so nice to see you," the man joked. "This secret project she has you on is turning everything on its head."

"And it's fine," Alex said. "I'll have Sarah write up a report for the committee. You'll have that by the end of the day, Agent Dalton. Agent Raige, please sit?"

I moved to take one of the chairs in front of her desk, and my former boss made his way out. When the door closed behind him, Alex sighed heavily, then dropped down into her chair. Immediately, Crysis pushed into her lap.

"Hey, big guy," she breathed. "I'm good. Tense, but good. I missed your big mushy head, though. Yeah, you're a good boy, hm?"

I chuckled. "I think you're a dog person, Alex."

"I'd love to be, but this job doesn't make it easy. Worse, my sister is a cat person." She waved that off. "Tell me how they're doing?"

And I smiled.

"Oh, that good?" she asked.

I just nodded. "They're shooting well enough to pass the qualifications. I explained to them about the additional testing, and while none of them are happy about it, they're taking it better than I would."

Alex's eyes narrowed. "So what are you leaving out, because it can't be this easy. Congress is pushing back just as hard as they can, so where are the cracks? We need to be ready for this to go sideways, you know."

"They're overworked, pushing themselves too hard, and each one thinks they're the weak link," I explained. "Right now, my team is running on caffeine and willpower, yet somehow still passing their college courses. I wouldn't expect them to come out with a 4.0 GPA or anything, but they are keeping up their grades enough to pass."

"What about the interviews?" she asked.

"Most are pushing nineteen. They have one year of admissible history, which means it was all while working as a confidential informant for the KoG case. Jeff Andrews - "

"Knock," she corrected, proving she knew their names as well as I did.

"Well, he made a good point. They shouldn't identify as hackers. They are simply computer security and computer science students who happen to know software and network vulnerabilities well enough to help with game development, which is how they all ended up in this mess. Hearing they could assist the FBI was enough to make them test their knowledge, since their contracts made it legal."

Alex chuckled. "And the illegal stuff?"

"I can't find it," I assured her. "That means no one else will either. The only issue we have is the data they found regarding the rapists at their school. Since that's covered under an immunity clause, we never asked how they got it, and they don't need to tell."

"If they're asked," she pressed, "what would they say?"

"That a dead girl sent it to them," I explained. "Amber Callahan sent Jericho her phone, a pregnancy test, and a USB drive. That makes all of it not only admissible, but also not criminal for these kids to have."

Which made a smile appear on Alex's lips. It seemed to be enough to convince Crysis he could finally slide off her lap. I noticed, because when my dog pressed that hard against someone, it proved there was more going on than a little work stress.

"How about you?" I asked her. "I hear things are getting tense."

"Who says?" she asked.

"Bradley."

Alex nodded at that. "He's not wrong. Apparently, my pet project could be in violation of the Fourth Amendment. We currently have legal analysts looking for reasons to refute that. No matter what, it's going to get ugly, though. Our current herd of politicians are gearing up for election season, and that's never good for anyone."

"But how are you?" I pressed, thinking about the insults and harassment Bradley had seen on her computer. "Alex, are they attacking you personally?"

She made a flipping gesture that looked good. It was casual and easy. If it wasn't for my dog, I never would have guessed this woman tensed up again at my question, but Crysis pushed in to drop his head on her lap.

So I pointed at him. "He says you're lying."

"You," Alex told my dog, "are betraying my trust. Guess I should give you some Pupperoni treats, hm?" And she pulled open a drawer to extract a small bag.

Crysis wagged with excitement, but he didn't lift his head. Alex still handed him three treats, one after the other, and then put the package away. But when Crysis still leaned on her, she finally gave in.

"There are certain members of the Senate who are not pleased with me being promoted to this position," she explained. "That I'm asking for this program only makes it worse."

"And the racial slurs?" I asked.

"It's not your problem, Jason."

"It is if it's in an email," I reminded her. "That's exactly why you want this team."

"No, I want this team to deal with cybercrimes. There are helpless victims out there unable to get anyone to listen because things that happen online are not a crime. I happen to be the Deputy Director of the FBI. I have skills, training, and an entire bureau of agents here to deal with any lawbreaking I stumble upon."

"Bradley saw the N-word," I countered.

"And I'm handling it," she assured me.

"On the Deputy Director's email," I continued. "An email address that should not be public knowledge, through a server that should be secure. I'm going to guess, since you aren't naming and shaming, that it came through spoofed or as anonymous, so you aren't quite sure who sent it. Now, explain to me again why this isn't something I should be worrying about?"

"Because I am not a weak and vulnerable person with nowhere to turn," she told me. "Yes, I've been getting some derogatory messages emailed to me. Yes, they are anonymous. No, our tech support cannot track them due to the use of a VPN. They also do not include any threats, are merely rants of opinion, and I've heard much worse on the nightly news about my promotion."

It was all true. I'd heard the late-night hosts cracking jokes about the newly assigned woman in the FBI. The whole thing had been a flash in the pan, so far as the news cycle cared, and now they were on to something else. But between Crysis's reaction and Alex's, I had a feeling this was a lot worse than she was letting on.

"At least let me take a look?" I asked.

"Jason," she chided, "it's fine. I asked you here to get an official update on Ruin and their progress. I'm pretty sure I can help with the Phase II interviews, but the extensive background checks will have an independent reviewer. That means you're going to need to hit them with everything, make sure they won't crack under pressure, and then prepare them for a full psychiatric evaluation."

Yeah, that was the part I was worried about. "How stable do they need to be?" I asked.

"Stable enough to hold a gun," she said. "They have to pass, Jason. All of it. Since they're already a team, I can argue for anyone who's a weak link, but they all have to *pass*."

"I'm spending three days a week with them, and pushing them hard," I promised. "I just don't know how long they can maintain this pace. Alex, they're kids."

"They're all over eighteen," she reminded me.

"They're kids," I said again. "They're finally in college, and not a one of them has gone to a party because this is all they do. They don't do drugs, they drink coffee - not alcohol - and they study. They study for their classes, for our classes, and for anything that might come up. I'm worried that if I keep pushing them this hard, they're going to crack, so how long is this going to take?"

"I don't know," she admitted. "Half want to push it back. Half want to rush it forward. Yes, the split is along party lines. Unfortunately, all the big stuff in the news is taking precedence. Some days, they make no progress. Others? Well, they give your team more hoops to jump through."

"And if this doesn't happen?" I asked. "What are we doing with Ruin?"

"I don't know," she breathed. "Jason, this has to work."

"What if it doesn't?" I asked again. "You need a fallback plan, Alex. You need a way to save this."

"Ideas?"

"Cybersecurity can't do what they do," I admitted.

"I know," she said. "Because if they could, you never would've taken so long to get KoG shut down. But that's the problem. I can't simply make them agents. I don't have that power. They'd have to apply, make it through Quantico, and then get assigned to Cybersecurity."

"And the rules we have now would still apply," I pointed out. "They'd have their hands tied, and this group? They don't do rules."

"Which means this has to work," she said.

I just smiled. "Or you keep those contracts you have with them and turn a blind eye."

Her head jerked up guiltily, and she met my eyes. "What do you mean?"

"Complete immunity," I said. "Off the books. No rules, no restrictions. I'm still an agent, so I can play nice. If I happen to get anonymous information? If a hacktivist group like, say, Anonymous, drops incriminating evidence on Wikileaks with enough sources for us to verify it? Well, it could work."

"I don't know if I could get them that much immunity," she admitted. "Not without us getting something back."

Yeah, but I could already see a way around that. "Would we hunt them?"

"I can't say what the next President or Director will do, Jason. Maybe?"

"Do you think we could catch them?"

"No," she admitted.

So I nodded. "There's our backup plan. Because Ruin can vanish. You just have to make sure you lose any record of their name. Do not tie my confidential informants to the hacktivist group known as Ruin. So long as you can forget that name, they will help."

She visibly relaxed. As the air rushed from her lungs, her shoulders loosened and she leaned back in her well-padded chair. Even Alex's eyes slipped closed for a moment, and that was not at all how I'd expected her to react.

"What happened, Alex?" I asked. "This is a hell of a lot more than losing a kidnapping victim. It's more than you thinking that boy reminded you of your daughter."

"How do you know that?" she asked.

"I do my homework too," I assured her. "And Bradley went to Deviant. Ruin doesn't know."

So she pulled in a deep breath. "My daughter got her first dick pic a month ago, or thereabouts. It's nothing. I had filters on her accounts so she never even saw it, but it still happened. It always happens, Jason. From the emails I'm getting to my sixteen-year-old daughter getting adult men's penises! It always happens, and no one gives a shit but us."

"But that's the thing," I reminded her. "We do. We give a very big shit."

"Which is why this has to work," she said, "because I'm scared to death of what else is hiding online. I'm terrified I won't know until it's too late. I'm a damned single mother, doing my best to stay a step ahead of this, and if that had been my child in Vegas?"

"I took the shot," I reminded her.

"And how much trauma are they all dealing with because of it?" Alex asked. "Jason, winning isn't enough. We need to stop it, because being a victim doesn't simply go away because we survived. It leaves scars." She gestured to my dog. "You know that."

"So do they," I promised.

"Which is why this has to work," Alex said. "Right now, Ruin is my Hail Mary."

# CHAPTER 35

**RIPPER**

Monday was almost relaxing. I managed to convince Jeri to watch a movie in my room with me. Since Zoe was spending quite a few nights with Jinxy now, I even made sure to tell Hottie about it, so no one would be surprised. Sure enough, Jeri passed out curled up against my side.

She was exhausted. I had a feeling this wasn't a new thing for her, though. All it had taken was for me to hold her close, kiss on her head and neck, and smooth down her hair a few times. The moment her eyes had closed for a second too long, she was out.

But when my alarm went off on Tuesday morning, it woke her up as well. I let her know she could go back to sleep, but since she'd left her phone in her room, she decided to do that in her own bed. Sadly, I had to get ready, because I had a nine o'clock class.

Cradling my cup - which was filled with vitamin water, not coffee - I ended up in my pre-calculus class. Somewhere over the last year, I'd learned to appreciate coffee, but I still liked mine with cream and sugar, which did no favors to my belly. If I wanted to lose that, I needed to cut out the extra calories. The downside was the yawning.

I was sucking back another massive gulp when Cade dropped down in the chair next to me. His eyes raked over me, then dropped to my cup. When I yawned again, he simply offered up his own coffee mug.

"You going decaf or something?" he asked.

"Water," I said, taking his cup and sucking back a decent drink. "Trying to slim down."

"Fuck, Ripper," he grumbled. "Why?"

I rolled my eyes and shook my head. "Because we have a pool *and* a hot tub. Means I'd kinda like to not be the only guy in the water with a shirt on."

"Or you could just go shirtless," he countered. "Seriously, bro. You're fine."

I waved that off. "Is this some part of the new super-supportive household we have going on or something? Because I didn't exactly get the memo."

Cade gave me a confused look. "Huh?"

"The whole vibe changed this weekend," I told him. "And now here you are telling me I look good again? I mean, was there some emotional support meeting I missed? Hell, even Jason was nice."

"Yeah, he kinda was," Cade realized. "But no one said shit to me. I was just being honest about the shirt thing."

"Ok, but what about Hottie?" I asked. "He was cool with me stealing Jeri last night."

"He's usually cool with that."

"And Jinxy was helping Knock with the investigation questions on Sunday," I added.

"Because Jinxy took some psychology class which covered that."

I grunted in frustration. "And something fucking changed, Cade. Don't tell me you can't feel it. It's like something happened that we don't know about, and now the pressure is letting up. Did we already fuck up or something?"

"Or maybe we're doing better than expected?" he countered. "C'mon. Look at your shooting. You finally got a half-decent grouping on the targets."

"I'm getting used to the bang," I admitted.

"Which is good," Cade assured me. "And Knock said there was a comment about how we didn't have to make A's on these tests. They aren't scored like that. We just need to pass, and since we're not going to be agents, barely passing is good enough."

"But barely passing means possibly failing," I pointed out.

"Or less stressing..." He paused. "Shit, it's Jeri."

"Huh?" Because he'd just lost me.

"It's Jeri," Cade said again. "She's been burning the candle at both ends, studying her ass off, and freaking the fuck out in her way, you know? I mean, I've never seen her this serious about anything but gaming."

"Gaming," I said just as the instructor walked in. "Cade, gaming is tactical. We're missing something."

But the class started, so we didn't exactly get the chance to say anything else. This instructor was the grumpy kind who had no problem telling us to take it outside and not come back. Since I really wanted to keep my grades up, I needed to make sure I learned all of this.

I took notes. I followed along with the practice problems. I wrote it all down, but in the back of my mind, I was still thinking about the vibe in the house. I was also remembering how easily Jeri had fallen asleep against me.

Damn, I liked that. Not that she was exhausted, but how she relaxed when she was with me. It was an ego boost of sorts. In truth, it was the type of connection I really wanted. I was so in love with that girl, and to know she trusted me? To see how much faith she had in me? I thought it was even better than sex.

And sure, she was beautiful naked. I definitely liked orgasms. I also hadn't exactly been one of the guys to get a piece of ass anytime I wanted, so I was a little more concerned about the whole emotional thing we had going on. Her mind fascinated me. Her determination was sexy as hell. Shit, I even liked that she was "crazy."

Not that she really was, but it was the term which got thrown at her so often. Jeri didn't play by the rules, and it was refreshing. She also put too much pressure on herself. She'd once told me she always had to do it herself because no one was left to do it for her.

That day, I'd decided I'd do as much as I could. Sadly, I felt like there wasn't much I *could* do to help, though. I couldn't do her FBI homework for her. I couldn't do her calculus homework, since I was only in pre-cal. She was a fucking genius and a half. She was miles ahead of the rest of us, but if I could lighten her load at all, I definitely would.

Wait. That was it.

For the rest of the class, I kept glancing at the clock, waiting for us to be released. I wanted to tell Cade what I'd realized. I was so sure I'd figured it all out, but I had to wait. Thankfully, the pair of us had a break after this. I was going to buy a very large coffee - and give up the water thing - then see if Cade thought I was right.

The instructor just kept going, though. The clock hit ten minutes till the hour, and he still didn't stop. Nope, the self-absorbed asshole had to finish the problem he was working on, even as the entire class started to fidget. The moment it was done, a student in the front row grabbed their book and stood, walking out without waiting for the class to officially end.

"And it looks like I kept you a whole minute too long," the instructor quipped. "We'll continue this next time."

"Hey," I said to Cade. "Starbucks?"

"I'm fucking buying," he told me. "I'm also going to convince you to give up the stupid dieting idea."

"Yeah, but..." I shoved my notebook into my bag, then stood. "Cade,

I think I know what changed this weekend."

He hurried to put his stuff away, then gestured for me to lead. I made my way up the aisle, having to turn so I could fit between the chairs. Yeah, this was why I'd gone with water. Everyone else could walk normally, but I felt like my ass was brushing the chairs on both sides. When I glanced back to see Cade walking without a problem, I grunted in annoyance.

"This," I said as we hit the door and turned into the hall, "is why I'm trying to get slimmer."

"Why?"

"Because I don't fit between the chairs, asshole."

Cade actually laughed, then hooked his hand on my shoulder so he could lean in. "Bro, you're twice as broad in the chest as me. I dunno how to break it to ya, but you're not fat. You're just a big guy."

"Which is the nice way of saying fat."

"I mean like a Viking," he corrected. "Hell, you could probably bench more than me. Pretty sure you're taller than me now too."

"Really?"

He nodded. "Ripper, got bad news, man. You turned into one of those linebacker types last summer."

"Is that... Um, is that bad?"

"Gets me going," he teased, reaching out to push open the door before it could close after the students ahead of us. "I mean, just look at our shoulders. Yours is taller."

I did. It was. Holy shit, how had I not noticed that? I knew my jeans had gotten "shorter" last year, and I'd had to get a different size. My shirts were tighter now, but I'd assumed I was just washing them wrong. Regardless, this wasn't what I was supposed to be talking about.

"I think I figured out the thing with Jeri," I told him as the two of us headed towards the Student Union.

"And?" he asked.

"She's always had to do it herself," I said. "When her brother died, her entire family fell apart. One after the other, bad things happened. She was thirteen when she had to grow up, right? Then her mom went to get mental help. Her dad died. Nina died. She moved. Always, Jeri has been the one doing all the adulting."

"Ok?" Cade clearly wasn't following along.

"Her *mother*," I told him, "couldn't take care of her. Jeri had to take care of her mom. Hottie lost it when Nina died. She took care of him. She took care of Death over Dishonor. She had to do more, do it better, and do it right so the good things in her life could continue to be good, right?"

"Yeah," he agreed. "And it sucks, but we knew that."

"But!" I said before he could distract me. "Everyone Jeri loves dies. That's why she didn't want to love us. It's her biggest fear. She blames her 'curse' for Zoe and all those girls last year. She takes it personally, Cade, and that's the part we've been missing. Jeri doesn't see this shit as just bullshit that sucks in life. She sees it as 'her curse.' That means *she* has to break it!"

"Oh fuck," he groaned. "No, that makes perfect sense."

"And it's not really a curse," I went on. "It's just her being so willing to help everyone else that she gets pulled in. It's her not ignoring it. This curse is nothing more than the sad truth that shit sucks all over, and yet because she sees it, she takes it all onto her shoulders and feels like she has to fix it, right?"

"Right," he agreed. "So how do we help?"

I held up a finger, making it clear I wasn't done yet. "But at F5, we - all of us - managed to work together and save the day. Riley didn't die. I mean, none of them did, but Riley's the one Jeri knows and cares about. Riley's the one who is a friend, and friends mean feelings, and feelings mean ripping her heart out."

"I'm keeping up so far," he promised.

So I stopped, turning to face him. "And Jeri took point on that. She was the one talking to Jason. She was the one organizing the hack. She was the one pushing us, rushing us, and deciding we would break any and all laws to make it happen."

"And it did happen," Cade agreed. "Jason took out that fucker."

"Jeri saved them." I lifted a brow. "She busted her ass, went all-in, and she broke the curse."

"Oh, fuck," Cade breathed as my words made sense. "What do you want to bet she doesn't even think of it like that?"

"She just feels it," I agreed. "The same way I feel her love when she trusts me, or how I get all embarrassed, but in a good way, when you compliment me. It doesn't make sense. There's no conscious thought to it. I just feel this thing is good, so I want more of this thing."

Cade's face immediately split into a grin. "So is this where I tell you you're hot?"

"Yes," I agreed, just to move on. "But think about it -"

"You're hot," he said. "So hot, Ripper. Like, I never knew I had a thing for bears. Wait, are you a bear? Does that count? Or is there a better term?"

"I don't fucking know," I huffed. "I'm not gay, Cade! But listen!"

"Ok, ok," he agreed.

"Jeri gets triggered by people being threatened. She gets a dopamine rush from saving them. That means, in her subconscious, she thinks she has to get this FBI thing perfect or she'll lose something. Maybe all of us, maybe something else. I don't know, and I'm willing to bet she's never stopped long enough to actually think about it. For her, it's just this vague feeling of dread. This pressure that she has to get this perfect 'or else.'"

"And she can't," he realized. "Fuck, she doesn't know any more about laws or investigations than the rest of us."

"Right," I agreed. "And she fell asleep against me last night while watching a movie. She's exhausted, she's at her limit, and I think Jason knows."

"Hottie probably does too," Cade pointed out.

"Which is why they dialed it back," I explained. "So we need to figure out how to help. We - you and me - need to lighten her load a bit."

"No," he murmured, clearly thinking. "Ripper, we need to help. We don't need to take it away or tell her it's ok. I mean, just look at you and the water. You thought you needed to lose weight because you don't see things we see. You know, like how you might be bigger, but in a grew-up-hot sort of way." He flashed me a smirk, but kept going. "So what we need to do is study *with* her. We need to make it more fun and less stress."

"Yeah," I agreed. "I like that."

"And I happen to know someone who might be able to help," he added. "I mean, we're good, but Tiffany? She took those prep classes about how to learn efficiently. I think I'm gonna ask for a little advice."

"I think we *all* could use it," I agreed. "And I really do need a coffee."

"If I pay, does that mean this is a date?" Cade joked.

"Sure," I agreed, "but I'm not kissing you."

"All good. We can trade spit through Jeri."

I just ducked my head and laughed. Yep, I liked this. I liked that he was my best friend, but most of all, I liked that he'd figured out how to be ok with himself. Hopefully, he'd teach me how to do the same, and then we'd both be able to show Jeri.

# CHAPTER 36

### JERICHO

I wasn't sure what had changed, but something had. After I'd had that talk with Jason, it was like the pressure had been dialed back to about a seven. Considering it had been a twelve before, I was going to call this a win. No, I couldn't slack off, but I felt like I now had room to breathe.

And it wasn't any specific thing. Our lesson at the gun range had been filled with more jokes and less competition. Our lesson on investigation techniques had been more about the cool stuff and less about memorizing. Even better, we now had fancy new whiteboards installed on the war room walls.

We didn't need them for anything, but they were there, ready and waiting. If shit went sideways, it was one less thing to worry about taking care of. And I knew it was stupid, but seeing them just made me feel like we were actually prepared.

Then, Monday evening, Tiffany came over to help Cade study, and offered to make flashcards for our FBI stuff. Ok, so that resulted in me giving her a pirated copy of the textbook so she could come up with a plan for us, but she'd offered. I just couldn't figure out why she cared. Not that I was complaining! I simply didn't get it. Tiffany wasn't in the middle of this. Her crap had been sorted out when the Alpha Team had been arrested, but this chick was still completely invested in helping us.

It kinda made me like her more. When Zoe asked her to come up with a way to memorize all the gun parts we were supposed to know? Tiffany busted out how she was sure her dad actually had that schematic. Hell, she thought he'd made her learn on one of these guns, but it could've been a slightly different version of a Glock.

That meant we had two people around with gun experience now. Three, when Jason was here on the weekends. One more person to ask technical questions. One more way to be sure we had the right information to make all of this happen. Then, when Tiffany showed up on Wednesday to do a group study session, I realized I wasn't as far behind the others as I'd feared.

The biggest change - to me - was how things had gone from feeling like an overwhelming weight on my shoulders to being fun. Yeah, the weight was still there, and I couldn't forget how important all of this was, but whatever had changed meant I no longer felt like I was drowning under all the pressure.

I wasn't fucking this up.

That stupid metaphorical "shoe" wasn't lurking out of sight, waiting to drop.

I had a team. My team had me. Oddly, I hadn't even thought of it in those terms until Jason had called us that. To me, Ruin had always been my crew, my friends, or my partners. But him saying we were a *team*? It changed something. Him saying he'd carry me if I needed it? Yeah, that was heavy.

It fell into the same category as "safe." I was pretty sure it was only because I knew he meant it. Something about that man felt just a little too real, like he could see behind the emotional walls I'd been relying on. Almost as if I was completely transparent to him, and still ended up being someone he approved of.

Which meant I could approve of me too. So, to celebrate how I was finally done with my homework for all my classes, I'd finished my mandatory studying for the FBI, and I was feeling a little more relaxed, I decided to spoil myself. That included a matching bra and panties set, then heading across the hall to flop down on Hottie's bed with my feet kicked up behind me. Just to be sure this worked, I sent him a text to ask if he could help me out and let him know I was in his room.

It didn't take long before he pushed through the door. "What are you looking for?" he asked.

Then he paused. A smile curled his lips as his eyes ran over me. Without looking back, Hottie closed his door, then flipped the dial that locked it. Shamelessly, he reached down to make an adjustment, smiling even more when my eyes followed.

"I was just looking for some attention," I said, trying my best to act innocent.

Yeah, I was failing. My little ploy was pretty pathetic, but the reaction I was getting was exactly the one I'd wanted. Hottie murmured in a way that made me think of a cat purring, then stepped closer. His eyes slid down my back, pausing on my ass, then moved to my legs.

"So, is this your idea of seducing me?" he asked.

I rolled over as he reached the edge of the bed. "Is it working?"

"Oh, fuck yeah," he breathed before pulling his shirt over his head. "I'm so ok with being summoned."

Which made me giggle. "I figured saying I need to get fucked might be a bit too blatant."

"Nope," he assured me. "That would be hot too."

Then he caught my ankle and pulled. My ass slipped around, my legs slid towards the side of the bed, and my body shifted on the covers. A little squeak of surprise broke free, but when Hottie had the parts he wanted pointed at him and my legs halfway over the edge of the bed, he finally leaned in.

"Does this mean my baby girl is stressed again, or finally relaxed?" he asked.

I leaned up, catching the back of his neck and pulling him closer. "It means I deserve a little reward." Then I kissed him.

But starting shit with Hottie was never the sort of thing that went the way I expected. I'd kissed him, thinking I was seducing this man, yet my lips barely met his before he took over. Leaning in even more, he pushed me back. The hand on my leg lifted it to his hip, and his other hand landed on the mattress by my head.

He was still standing, but bent to take control. I let him. Hooking my heel against the small of his back, I tugged, trying to encourage him to join me on the bed, but he resisted. The whole time, his mouth devoured mine. The way his tongue took over, sampling me like I was some kind of toy to play with, had my pulse rushing lower.

Then his hand began to slide higher up my leg. The touch was gentle but persistent, making me unable to think about anything else. He caressed my knee, my thigh, my hip, and kept moving higher. Tilting my head back, I sucked in a breath, a little moan wrapped up with it.

"Oh, now that's nice," he praised. "Almost like my baby girl needs a little stress relief, hm?"

"Oh yeah," I agreed as his mouth moved to my neck.

Then he kissed my shoulder, my collarbone, and down a bit more. When the heat of his breath landed on my bra, I could feel it. The fabric seemed both so thin and much too thick at the same time, but when I tried to lift up, his hand left my side to press between my breasts, holding me in place.

"For once in your life," he growled passionately, "stop fighting."

So I did, grabbing the back of his head instead. Hottie kissed again, dragging his tongue over my bra hard enough to taunt the nipple beneath. As his mouth moved to my sternum, his hand cupped my other breast, and his thumb teased me higher.

"Fuck, you look good like that," he breathed, making his way lower.

The feel of his beard on my belly was erotic. The heat of his tongue as it made circles on my skin had me squirming. I didn't resist, though. Instead, I closed my eyes and simply felt it all. Every touch, every caress, and all the desire fueling me.

When he hooked his fingers in my panties, I lifted up enough to let him pull those off. Hottie wasn't gentle about it, either. He didn't try to ease them off. No, he ripped, yanking the fabric down my legs so I had to shift to get my ankles free. The moment my panties were gone, his hands moved, spreading me open.

"Now that," he said, lowering himself down to his knees, "is the most beautiful thing I can imagine."

His thumb trailed over my folds, but he wasn't in a rush. Hottie parted me, caressed me, and then finally shifted his hand to tease my clit. Just a smooth rub, almost like he was enjoying the feel of my body. Only then did he lean in and suck at that sensitive little knot.

I gasped, letting my knees grip his sides. That earned me a murmur of approval, but this man was just getting started. He licked. He sucked. He toyed with me, flicking my clit with his tongue before pushing it into my opening. I wanted to buck into the contact. I wanted to stay completely still so I wouldn't move the wrong way. I just wanted to feel all of this, and he was doing a damned good job of making me forget about everything else.

When his hands slid up my sides to cup my breasts, I couldn't take it anymore. Screw being good. I wanted all of this, so I arched my back and unclasped my bra. He grabbed a cup and pulled, but I was pushing the straps off my arms at the same time. That went off the bed, out of our way, and I didn't even care where, because his mouth never slowed.

Only then did he use his hand. As his fingers pushed into my body, I could feel the slickness. When he pumped, I rocked my hips, taking his hand as deep as I could. My calves tightened on his waist. My ass was off the bed. His free hand teased my breast, and I couldn't imagine anything else in the world.

My mind could only focus on this. The next touch, lick, or thrust of his hand. The feel of his skin, the sounds he was making, and my own need to move. I rolled my hips. I grabbed at the sheets or him or even the pillows beside me. Fuck looking sexy. All I wanted was to feel. To lose myself in the moment. To be here, now, with him - and it felt so fucking good.

His tongue pressed harder and his hand moved faster. I felt like I could barely catch my breath, and I was groaning in a way that was far from quiet. I also didn't care, because I could feel it building. The euphoria was right there, and when he sucked at my clit one more time, it was all I could take.

I came - hard. A yell of pleasure was ripped from my mouth, and my entire body flexed with the intensity of it. Hottie kept sucking, his hand riding me through it until it suddenly felt like too much. I inhaled and jerked my eyes open as my back found the mattress again.

"Mm," he murmured before kissing the inside of my thigh. "Now that's a turn-on."

Before I could even form a coherent sentence, the man leaned back, grabbed my hip, and flipped me onto my stomach. It was as if tossing me around took almost no effort from him, and I loved it. But with my ass in the air, my legs were now sticking straight off the side.

"Knees," he ordered, and I heard a drawer open.

I glanced back to see his pants hanging open and him ripping open a condom packet. His eyes met mine and he tipped his head like a warning. Yep, I could get behind this. If he wanted to be in charge, then I would be a very good girl - for a moment, at least.

So I shifted so I was on my hands and knees, then crawled forward a pace. That was as far as I made it before his pants hit the ground. Hottie caught my hip, stopping me, and then crawled onto the bed behind me. One knee. The mattress tilted with his weight. The other knee balanced it back out, and then I felt him behind me.

"Am I being gentle with you, Jeri?" he asked, sliding the head of his dick down my slit.

"No fucking way," I decided.

"Good." And then he pushed in.

God, that felt amazing. From the way he filled me to the way his hand on my hip pulled me where he wanted, I loved all of it. But when he started thrusting into my body, I gave as good as I got. Maybe he was used to women who were sweet and submissive, but that wasn't me. I might not be fighting him, but this? I was taking what I wanted, demanding, and I was going to give him as much as he was giving me.

So I rocked, driving my body onto him as he rammed himself into me. The passion of our lovemaking had the bed creaking in protest, but I didn't care. I wanted to get fucked. I wanted to burn out this thing in my mind. I wanted to stop playing nice, being good, and obeying the rules.

I wanted to fucking *feel*! Every time our bodies collided, he grunted like he liked it. As the friction increased, I allowed myself to moan in pleasure. Wild, frantic, and out of control, that was how I loved him, and yes, this was love.

All of it was love. Him, them, and everything else. Me trying so hard was love. My raging when things went wrong was love. Maybe I burned hotter than everyone else, but I refused to be ashamed of it. I certainly wouldn't stop now, so I fucked back, shifting my hips so it felt just like I wanted, and I did my best to drive him absolutely crazy.

A hand landed in my hair, pulling me back. I went, lifting up a bit, and Hottie wrapped his other arm around my waist, but neither of us stopped. We thrust, meeting in the middle like equals, even if I had to reach back for balance. My hand found his hip, pulling him the way I wanted, and he obeyed.

Again, then again, we all but threw ourselves against each other until I heard him gasp. Inside me, I felt him growing thicker, or harder.

I couldn't tell, but I could feel it, and it was exactly what I needed. When he pushed his face into the back of my shoulder, it was the sexiest thing I could imagine. This man, who I loved more than I'd ever imagined, was losing control because of me.

Because he loved me, and that was enough to make me combust. My body locked up, the pleasure slamming into me. As the climax took over, I clung to him, knowing he wouldn't let go. He had me. I had him. Nothing else mattered, and pleasure became all I knew.

"Holy shit," he panted after a moment, angling his face to kiss my neck. "I think I've met my match." Then he slid back, extracting himself from my body.

Giggling, I flopped down on my side, then scooted up towards the pillows, making room for him to join me. "I just wanted to stop thinking for a second."

"Yeah..." He pulled off the condom, then headed for the bathroom, calling behind him, "So did it help?"

"I think so."

"Cuddling helps more." He returned, gesturing for me to get under the blankets. "So does talking about it, Jeri."

"There's nothing to talk about," I assured him.

He lifted the covers and slid in beside me. "Bullshit. Baby girl, no one fucks like that unless they have some frustration to work out, so what's the real problem?"

I shifted so I could curl up against his shoulder. "That's the thing. See, I don't really know."

He leaned in to kiss my head. "So we'll figure it out together."

# CHAPTER 37

### JERICHO

I lay against Hottie for a while, thinking about that. Yes, something was wrong, but what, exactly? The whole time, Hottie just rubbed my back and arm, not trying to push me for an answer. Eventually, I caught my breath, so I got up to use the bathroom, but I still didn't have an answer.

"I just feel like things got real this semester," I said as I crawled back onto the bed.

But instead of letting me curl up on his chest, he turned to face me. "What things?"

"Well, I don't want to fail my classes, because I have to pay to take them again."

"Have you ever failed anything?" he asked.

Which made me pause. "Well, no, but everyone says college is harder."

"Does it feel harder?"

Ok, I didn't like his questions. He also had a point. "No," I admitted.

"It kinda feels like it's easier, but I keep thinking I'm missing something, because *everyone* says it's supposed to be hard, Hottie."

"Fuck everyone," he shot back. "When has that ever mattered to you? Everyone does this, or everyone thinks that. You've never cared before."

And he had a point. A good one.

"I'm also running out of time," I said.

"So balance your time better," he suggested. "I mean, where's the problem? Because I'll help you figure it out."

"I have classes until about three-thirty. Well, Tuesdays and Thursdays, it's only one-thirty. Then it's half an hour home, giving me time to stop for food if I want. Um, I study until about six for my classes, and then I play Flawed for a couple of hours, and the FBI shit ends up taking from eight until about midnight - and that's it. That's a day."

"Four hours a day for the FBI shit?" he asked.

"It's kinda hard," I muttered.

"Jeri, that's more studying than you've ever done in your life. Why?"

Yeah, he had a point. I knew he did. The real problem was I couldn't explain it. I didn't really know the reason, I just felt like I had to. It was as if there was some pressure to make sure I didn't fuck this up, because if I did, then I'd screw it up for everyone, and they'd hate me, and none of it made sense.

"I don't really know," I admitted. "It's just this feeling, and it's dumb."

"So talk it out?" he begged.

"Hottie..." I tried.

"Jeri..." he mocked. "C'mon, baby girl. Something's going on. You aren't yourself lately, and it's been going on since school started, so this is me trying to get you to let me in, ok? Us against the world, right? But I can't do that if you're shutting me out."

"But I'm not!" I insisted. "I just don't know."

"So do like Cade and ramble it out."

I grunted, but he had a point. Ok. Pulling in a deep breath, I gave in and tried to let the words flow. "I know this thing with the FBI is a big deal, right? I mean, there are KoG guys still out there. Someone has to catch them, and the cops fucking suck at it. I'm including the FBI in that, because how long did it fucking take? And if they hadn't tried kidnapping the girls, they'd probably still be in the wind."

"We almost had them," he reminded me. "They panicked because we were so close."

"And it took years!" I snapped. "Fucking *years,* Hottie. I mean, ok, that was before we were involved, and we could've helped, but even with Dylan and his friends! It still took us months, and why? Because we're fucking hackers. Because hacking is illegal. Because we're not allowed to do this, but now we are. Or, well, we could be, if we get this shit right, so we *need* to get it right!"

"And we're stuck waiting on Congress to move at a snail's pace," he reminded me. "Jeri, we can't make this go faster."

"But what if I fuck it up?" I blurted.

For a moment, neither of us moved. I knew he'd heard me. Shit, I'd said that loud enough the group downstairs may have heard me. The difference was Hottie knew what I meant.

Finally he nodded. "Ok," he said, his tone gentle. "So you're scared of fucking up?"

"Yeah," I mumbled.

"Why?" he pressed. "Jeri, you don't fuck up."

"I *always* fuck up," I huffed. "C'mon, Hottie. You know I do. I mean, when Drake died? I kinda logged into his character and just dropped that shit on all of you. I didn't know how to tell you except to just say it. And that wasn't cool to anyone. I mean, hello blunt force trauma, right?"

"You were thirteen," he reminded me. "No one knows how to break that kind of news at that age."

"Yeah? Well, what about Dad? I tried to help him get past Drake's death, but I couldn't. I mean, I even did sports for him! He thought it was cute, and he told me I was doing good, but it wasn't the same. I get it, though. I'm not Drake, and he felt guilty. Yeah, I know. I've heard it all, but wasn't I enough of a reason to keep living?"

"That's not how depression works," he soothed. "Jeri, it's just not. When someone's that upset, they think they're doing you a favor by leaving. They aren't, but they're not well. Their mind is lying to them, and there's really nothing they can do. It takes someone outside to - "

"Exactly!" I broke in. "Me! I could see he wasn't ok, but I thought fucking sports would help. I tried to make him happy, not to get him help. I even lied to Mom and said everything was ok when she called, but it wasn't, and if I'd told her, then - I dunno - maybe he'd be ok?"

"You can't know that."

I shrugged, because he was right, but it still felt like a fuckup. "Ok, then look at us moving. I knew my friends were smoking pot, and Mom completely freaked. I could've stopped hanging with them, and - "

"She still would've gotten the promotion and moved," he said. "Jeri, you're not a fuckup. You've had a shit life, but it's not your fault nor your responsibility to always be perfect. Shit, I don't think you'd be happy like that. You are a bulldozer. You rush into things half-cocked, somehow make it work, and convince us all to love your passion. You are a force of fucking nature, and that's why we love you, not because you hack the bad guys, or are a squad lead in game, or make good grades. We love you because you're you."

"I know."

"Do you?" he pressed. "I'm being serious here, baby girl. Do you really believe you're amazing enough for four different men to have fallen in love with? For us to end up in this crazy arrangement and make it work?"

"You don't like our polycule?" I asked.

"Never said that," he assured me. "I'm saying it takes one hell of a woman to make a man like sharing his woman with others he hadn't met yet. I'm saying it takes something special for us dumbasses to put a girl before ourselves, because we tend to be selfish and greedy when it comes to women. I'm saying, Jeri, that Ruin is made up of people who are all fuckups by your definition, but we kick fucking ass, we're one hell of a family-thing, and I don't want you to lose sight of that because you're overwhelmed."

"No, I know," I promised. "Trust me, I know exactly how amazing this is. I mean, I love you, and them, and it's ok to say that, and I feel like the luckiest girl in the world..."

"Is it Tiffany?" he tried next. "She's been coming over a lot, and I know you weren't a fan of her initially."

"That's different."

"Care to explain?"

I rolled onto my back and groaned. "Ok, so this is going to sound like some feminazi shit, but it's really not. See, Tiffany hated me because she was scared of life without Cade. The reason? Dylan. So she called me names, and I hate bullying because of what happened to Nina, and I didn't know she was getting fucked around, you know?"

"But she was a bitch," he reminded me.

"Because of some guy!" I grunted. "Hottie, don't you see? Tiffany and I were being bitches to each other because of a guy. Cade flirted with me, which made it happen. Cade's a guy. Dylan was threatening her, so she felt like she had to have the right guy. Again, guys. And we were both trying to protect our friends, but we had different things getting rubbed in our faces - because of guys - so we went at each other because it was easier and more immediate. And the whole time, Dylan and his fucking idiot asshole friends were thrilled because girl fight, right? Because we women are supposed to compete with each other because we can't hit the men."

"But you did hit the men," he pointed out.

"Exactly!" I agreed. "And once we both realized it was Alpha Team, we became allies, and then kinda ended up friends because of it. I mean, she's cool. She's a bitch, but the right kind of bitch, and I'm not going to be all sweet with her and shit, but I respect that she won't be like that with me. You know, like mutual honesty and shit. Kinda how allies are supposed to be, not blowing sunshine, rainbows, and lies up each other's asses."

"And she's been at the house a lot," he said. "With Cade, Jeri. You're saying that doesn't stress you out at all?"

"No! I don't care if Cade fucks her, or Knock, or anyone else. That's not why I love him. I mean, he's really not into Tiff as anything more than a friend, and they were a *horrible* couple, but whatever. No, I actually like having Tiffany around. More girls, and being around girls is different than guys. A different energy, I guess?"

"Less sexual," he muttered, almost like he was agreeing. "Ok, I can see that. But if you get worried, let me know, ok?"

"I'm cool with Tiffany," I promised. "Without male bullshit between us, we get along great."

"The house is still filled with five men," Hottie said. "That's a lot of male bullshit to trip and end up between you."

"But you guys aren't like that." I shrugged. "It's different, Hottie. Ruin doesn't try to put us girls in a box. You don't think jealousy is hot, or stupid shit like that. Besides, Tiff, Zoe, and I have all realized fighting each other is pointless. We were doing that because we couldn't hit the guys. I didn't know the shit that was going on, and they didn't feel like they could change anything, so yeah."

"Yeah how?" he pressed.

"I dunno," I grumbled. "Look, it's just that girls are nasty to girls because we *can* hurt each other. We can't do the same with guys. They don't give a shit. And see, that's the thing! They really don't give a shit about us, and until we pulled our heads out of our asses and admitted it, we were bickering to get their attention. It's stupid, and Dylan didn't realize it, but his bullshit made Zoe, Tiffany, and Tiff's friends figure it out. Like, it shined a light on the problem, so we kinda regrouped, and Tiff even apologized. She was wrong, but I get what she was doing, so we're good."

"Ok, I can see that, but are you really good, Jeri? No grudges?"

"No grudges," I swore. "It's all good now. If guys cause problems, the three of us will go after that guy. Like, we're..." I felt my lips curling. "A girl team, maybe?"

But he wasn't going to let me off that easy. "So her coming over is why you're happier?"

Lifting both hands, I scrubbed at my face. "Kinda?"

"And?"

"I dunno!" Which was the whole problem we'd had in the first place. "I mean, Jason said we're a team, and I realized he's right, so that helps. Ruin has my back. We all have bonds, and Knock was right, those bonds do matter, but this is big."

"This?"

"The FBI shit," I clarified. "If we can get approval, then we can..." My words trailed off.

He waited while I was staring at the ceiling. Hottie rolled towards me, but I couldn't look over. The words were right there. My problem was *right there,* hanging on the end of that sentence. I hadn't even said them, but it still felt like someone had dumped a bucket of cold water on me.

"What, Jeri?" he asked, reaching up to take my hand.

"We can stop anyone else from getting hurt," I breathed, finally turning my head to look at him. "And that's what it is. That's the shoe. The one that's supposed to drop, you know? It's the pressure. That's why I feel like my hands are always shaking, and I'm scared shitless to not get my homework done, or to not know every word in those books. Because if we can do this, then..."

"It's not really a curse," he said softly. "Jeri, it's not."

"No, but it's still real," I shot back. "People around us die, Hottie. Drake, Dad, Nina, Amber, and almost Riley. But Riley didn't, because we did it. We stopped it, and this will make it easier to stop it, so I dunno. It just feels like I have a chance to fix things, you know? Like, maybe if I get this right, then no one else will have to go."

"Die," he supplied.

I nodded, the movement quick and jerky. "I won't lose you, or them, or my friends. I don't want to lose anyone else, and it's almost time for it to happen again, and..." My voice cracked.

"Oh, baby," he breathed, pulling me up against his chest and wrapping his arms around me.

"I'm scared," I whimpered. "I know it's not real, but it keeps happening, and maybe it's me? I don't know, but I'm so scared it'll be one of you next." One of my partners. One of the people I care about, because I care so *fucking* much!

"Jeri, we don't need the FBI clearance for that."

His voice was calm. The words were gentle, like a hug. It was enough to make me look up into his striking blue eyes.

"Huh?"

"We don't need to be working for the FBI to save each other," he said. "We are hackers. We saved Riley and the others because we broke the fucking law. We helped those girls because we ignored the rules. Jericho Grace Williams, we keep fucking winning because you say fuck it, run in half-cocked, and bulldoze your way through the entire fucking world. So do *that*. Keep doing that."

"Yeah?" I asked.

"That," he told me, "works for you. Not making perfect grades. Not being what others expect or want. Not even being responsible. Leave that shit for someone else, Jeri. Ruin works because you? You break rules, and someone needs to. So keep breaking them, baby girl. I swear your team will follow your lead."

And just like that, another hunk of weight fell from my shoulders.

# CHAPTER 38

**TIFFANY**

I was barely out of my last class on Monday before my phone began vibrating with a string of texts. I didn't even need to look to know it was Zoe. The weekend was over, so it was time to catch up with all the fun at their place.

I waited until I was outside and heading back to my dorm before reading what she'd sent. Sure enough, Zoe had an entire update about how their training had gone. She also said they had a new course to start. I chuckled to myself when I saw another notification from Cade that was a link to a pirated textbook. Yep, my friends were dorks.

My feet paused.

Shit. They really were my friends. Ok, that shouldn't feel so groundbreaking, since most of us had known each other last year, but that wasn't how I'd thought it. I'd meant that with the same tone I'd used for the girls I'd hung out with last year, but now they were gone and Ruin was here.

They were also really fucking cool.

No. Cool was definitely the wrong term for them. That implied bullshit they didn't care about, which was what actually made the term fit. Nope, I would not dive into that contradiction too deeply. I was going to blame it on the fact I'd just realized I spent more time with them than I did anyone else - and I kinda liked it.

So, after heading home and putting my shit away, I grabbed my keys. I almost made it to the door when my roommate came in, dragging her boyfriend, Matt, behind her. She was giggling, and he had his arms wrapped around her waist. His face was next to her head scarf, like he was whispering something, but I was right there, blocking their way.

"Oh!" Nadia gasped. "I didn't know you'd be here."

"Heading out," I assured her. "Probably be gone until like ten or so."

Matt looked me over in a way that annoyed the shit out of me. "Hope it's not a date," he joked.

"It's not," I assured him.

"Ever consider dressing up a bit?" He flashed a smile at his girlfriend. "Nadia could teach you how to look hot as fuck."

"Stop!" Nadia giggled.

"Yeah..." I said. "Means you two have a few hours to be all cute and shit. I'll text when I'm on my way back."

"Thanks, Tiff!" Nadia called after me.

I simply lifted my hand and headed out. Yeah, Nadia was all right, but Matt? I hated the way he looked at me. Granted, that could be all me. The guy never really said anything wrong. He just reminded me of the jocks, and those reminded me of Dylan. Guilt by association, and it wasn't even the guy's fault.

I didn't have that problem with Ruin, though. It wasn't even Jeri and Zoe. Those guys were just different. They weren't like most guys - which made me chuckle. It was such a stereotypical thing to say, but in this case it was true.

They hugged and hung out, and weren't scared of talking about feelings. Ok, so two were bi, two were best friends with girls, and Jinxy was sensitive or something. I didn't really know, but it worked for them. It made them feel like people I could talk to, which brought me right back to them being my friends.

Plus, I'd been hanging out at their place often enough I could almost drive there on autopilot. I now had my own parking spot in the driveway. Well, sorta. There was always a space behind Cade's impala, and my little car fit.

When I made it to the door and knocked, it opened faster than usual. On the other side was Knock, who smiled and stepped back, letting me in.

"You know you can just come in," he told me. "Zoe's the only one who locks the door during the day, so it's usually open."

"It's a habit!" Zoe groaned. "Mom always said it'd keep us from getting robbed."

"Yeah, I think you're in the wrong neighborhood for that," I assured her. "This is probably where the cops take their donut breaks. Besides, don't all these houses have like, security systems or something?"

"Not this one," Jinxy said, his voice coming from around the corner.

I followed it, peeking my head into the study. "Do I want to ask why?"

"Security systems track door openings," he explained. "Most are connected to the internet, which means a network vulnerability. Often, there are cameras pointing at doors to record who comes and goes, which isn't something we want a record of."

"Oh." I moved to one of the chairs, then dropped into it, setting my bag down beside me. "Yeah, um, that's actually kinda cool. I never even thought of the privacy violations."

He flicked both brows up and grinned. "We'll make you a geek yet."

I just groaned. "I will have you know I kick ass at spreadsheets, formulas, and online shopping, thank you very much." Then I looked over at Zoe. "Oh, I also got a copy of your latest book."

"I sent that!" Cade's voice came from the other side of the house.

"You're eavesdropping!" I yelled back.

"Gaming!" he replied.

I rolled my eyes and pulled out my phone to check the title. "It's Behavioral Science. Shouldn't you have gotten that before the interview crap?"

"Probably," Knock admitted. "So you gonna school us a little more?"

"Someone has to," I teased. "But no, I thought I could make up some outlines to break this down a bit, and we could go from there?"

"We need a healer!" Cade yelled. "Zoe! I'm dying!"

"Busy!" she yelled back.

"Go," I told her.

But Jinxy flicked a finger that way. "Wanna game? I mean, we got an extra computer in there now. We got Flawed on it. Could make you a character..."

"God, I'd suck so bad."

"So?" he asked. "You're supposed to at level one. Kinda the point."

"Yeah, but..."

"Tiff, if you don't want to, just say that," Knock told me. "It's allowed. We're simply making sure you know you can come play."

"Yeah?" I asked. "I mean..." I kinda wanted to, but I felt like everyone else here was so good at gaming, and I didn't have the first clue.

"Hottie, turn on the spare!" Jinxy yelled.

"Yes!" Zoe squealed, hopping up to run that way. "I'll load up Flawed. Jeri, message Tank? We need another account!"

"He's on sick leave," Knock called after them. "Try Dez."

"Wait, what?" Because Dez was a name I knew. It had come up a few times, and Dylan had been pissed about the woman who'd deleted his comments from their game. "Like, isn't she the owner?"

"Pretty much," Knock said, waving me up. "C'mon, Tiff. Come give us a reason to have some fun. I promise it doesn't hurt at all."

"Yeah, that's what guys always say," I teased.

"Doesn't hurt if you're doing it right," Jinxy agreed, following behind me as the pair herded me towards their formal dining room turned computer hall.

"Discord is installed and open," Zoe said, leaning over a computer at the end. "She just needs a name and we can get her into the chat. Flawed is loaded with the new character screen up."

"Whose account?" Knock asked.

Jeri chuckled. "Dez says hi, and the login is currently Tiffanyfriend, with a password of Ruinmate. Sounds like it can be changed once she picks something. Dez also said she's waiting to drop some shit as soon as the character is designed."

"What does that mean?" I asked as I sat down behind a gigantic monitor. "Oh, this is nice."

"I know, right?" Zoe asked. "That's Jason's computer on the weekends. Don't worry, it's not really his. More like our spare that he uses. And this is what you click to make a character. In this game, you get a randomly assigned flaw. What it does won't make sense for a bit, but it's cool."

"Ok, so what comes next?" I asked, faced with a screen and no idea how any of this worked.

"Design a character to look how you like," Hottie said. "She can look like you, not look like you, or even be a guy. You can pick hair color, eye color, skin color, and all that."

"Or you can hit random until you get something close, then tweak it," Jinxy suggested.

Zoe pointed at the random button, so I hit it. What came up was a very large man. Muscular, which was not at all like me. Nope, not what I wanted, but this didn't look as hard as I'd feared. There was a button for gender, one for sex, and sliders for a ton of other things.

So I clicked female and woman. That turned the buttons red. Clicking random now started giving me girl character options. I went through a few of those before one came up that I liked. She was tall, muscular, but not butch. Her boobs were small, her thighs could crush a man, and her hair was mint green.

"Ok, that's cool," I said.

"And you can tweak her out a bit here," Zoe told me.

It took a bit, but no one tried to rush me. Eventually, I ended up with this amazing punk character. She was the kind of woman I wished I had the courage to be. The kind who didn't give a shit about approval. I even got to add on a bicep tattoo.

"I like it," I decided.

"Ok, so pick a class," Zoe said, "then type in a name. It'll let you know if the name's taken."

"Don't use your real one," Hottie warned. "Guys in game will give you shit for being a faker, or for being a woman."

"It's just asking for harassment," Jeri explained. "I mean, I got away with it, but..."

"Your name is normally a guy's name," I pointed out. "So, yeah. Ok... What's the easiest class to play?"

"You can change later, so it's not set in stone," Knock assured me.

"Healer," I decided, because they'd just said they needed one. "And any suggestions for a name?"

"Something cool," Zoe said. "I'm Roux. Jinxy's, well, that's his game name. HotShot, Jericho, Knock, Qry -" She pronounced that like Cry. "- and Ripper."

"I heard my name!" Ripper yelled as his feet thundered on the stairs. "Raid time?"

"We're getting Tiff to play," Hottie explained.

"Fuck, I'm in," Ripper said as he hurried over to turn on one of the computers.

"I still need a name," I told them.

"Diva," Zoe suggested.

I typed that in and it turned red. Below the box were the words, "That name is taken."

"Fuck," I grumbled.

So they began calling out suggestions. RoseQuartz, BunnyFooFoo, Sphinx, and more. None of them worked. Knock pointed out that often the short and simple names went first, so a longer one might work.

On impulse, I typed in "HellOnHeels," and clicked away. The box - surprisingly enough - turned green.

"Click next!" Zoe said. "It's good, click next!"

So I did, and a loading cursor appeared. "Shit, that's my name now?"

"What is it?" Jeri asked.

"HellOnHeels," Zoe announced proudly. "It fits perfectly."

"Telling Dez," Jeri said as she began typing. "And a healer, right?"

"Yeah," I agreed.

Jeri grinned. "Dez says you're about to get the royalty treatment, whatever that means."

My character finally loaded into a very bright and happy-looking place, and then notices began flying off my head. I could barely read them, but all of them started with the same thing: You have acquired.

"What the hell?" I breathed just as a message appeared in my chat screen.

[Kohl] Any friend of Ruin is a friend of Deviant

[Kohl] Most of this is just for pretty.

[Kohl] And your personal flaw has been updated. I have been told you aren't the "Does not play well with others" type. I think I'll reassign that to "Unable to meet social expectations."

"Use a slash then R to reply," Cade called over.

"Huh?" I asked. "What?"

"Zoe's fangirling over there," Cade explained. "Means Dez is talking to you."

"It's someone named Kohl," I explained.

"Which is Dez!" Zoe squealed excitedly. "She's cool as shit too. So yeah, just..." She leaned over and hit the right keys for me. "And then type something. I dunno, like a thank you!"

[**HellOnHeels**] Thank you. I have never gamed before, so I'm completely lost, but I appreciate the help!
[**Kohl**] They saved my life. The real one. Game shit is nothing. Have fun noob, and remember, it's ok to be flawed. We are not alone, and that makes us stronger than the oppression can imagine.

Those words. I couldn't even explain them, but something about that phrase hit just right. I was flawed. Hell, everyone was, but she was right. Together, we all somehow became so much more. That was why I liked being here. It was why this group actually felt like friends, not merely people I knew.

It was because they didn't expect me to be perfect, or what *they* wanted. They accepted me as I was, flaws and all. They made me feel like I was cooler because of those flaws - which was why this was the one place I could finally relax.

[**HellOnHeels**] I kinda think game shit means more than you realize. My friends have been teaching me that. It's also what I need right now, so I won't take it for granted.
[**Kohl**] You're welcome, Hell. Enjoy the game.

I laughed once. "So, she just shortened my name to Hell."
"Then Hell it is," Zoe said, clasping my shoulder before heading over to her own computer.
"I think it's kinda fitting," Jeri said.
Knock just chuckled. "Considering we answer to 'God' and now have Hell on the team? Yep, I like it."
"Wait," Zoe said. "Who's God?"
He smiled slyly. "That's what Riley calls Jason when he's working. You know, from the rooftops, because he's looking down on us."
"And since we can't use his gamer name..." Jinxy said. "Yep, I think God fits nicely."

"I just bring the walls," Jericho said. "But I'm down with it. Now, everyone head to the newbie area. We need to get Tiff up and running to make sure she's having fun."

"Buying level one weapons for everyone," Knock announced.

"Brewing coffee!" Cade said as he pushed back his chair.

I was looking around, still lost, but this was fun. I hadn't even moved my character, had no clue what I'd been given by the developer, and I didn't care. It seemed they were right. There was something amazing about gaming, and that something was the people.

I could definitely get used to this.

# CHAPTER 39

### JERICHO

Time had flown. That was what happened when I lost myself in stressing about learning everything, but still. It felt like the events of F5 had been mere days ago. In reality, we were in the last week of October, while Riley had been held at gunpoint back at the end of August.

Nearly two months, gone. Then again, a lot had happened. I could now shoot a gun, I was making at least a B in most of my classes, and I was pretty good on the law enforcement part of our FBI lessons. I'd been busy, but it was the sort of busy that felt like nothing was happening while the clock just kept spinning.

But Sunday was my birthday. For the first time in my life, my mom wasn't going to be home for it. I hated that, but at the same time, there really was a lot going on. Most importantly, the whole FBI thing. Over the weekend, Jason had reminded us about the background checks and how our family members would likely get phone calls.

So as I walked back to my car after class, I decided to give my mom a call to warn her. It should be about lunchtime for her, but I was still prepared to leave a voicemail. Instead, on the third ring, she answered.

"Jericho?" she asked, sounding worried.

"Hey, Mom," I greeted her. "Nothing bad. Just checking in."

She sighed in relief. "Oh good. How's school, sweetie?"

"Good," I assured her. "I've had at least one test in all my classes, and my grades are pretty good. Hottie and Jinxy have been helping me figure out how to study the right way. The rest of us are appreciating their experience, you know?"

"Good!" she said. "And your brother?"

"Uh..."

"Grayson!" she laughed. "How are his grades?"

Yeah, ok. That was gross, and I couldn't think of Hottie as a brother, but whatever. Mom didn't need to know about my sex life. Hell, the fact she remembered I was in college and not still thirteen was kinda amazing. So, whatever, I'd roll with this.

"He seems to be doing good," I assured her. "He and Jinxy share a class, so there's that. Oh, and then there's the really cool thing that happened."

Because I was going to set this up as an opportunity. I did *not* want to explain to my mom about hacking and the mess last year. Instead, I was going to do a little bit of white lying, make this seem like a college thing, and see how she took it.

"What's that?" Mom asked.

"So, because we're all computer majors, right? Um, see, there's this thing. We got a chance to work as consultants for the FBI!"

"What?"

"Like, helping law enforcement with cybersecurity stuff," I explained. "It's a paying job, Mom."

"Jeri, I thought you were going to be a network person." She sounded completely confused.

"Right!" I agreed. "This is kinda like that. Things like checking for holes in other people's networks, and looking for signs bad guys have tried to get in. Stuff like that. It's what I'm doing for my major, and this is real-world experience that will look great on a resume, and get this! It's fifty grand a year for only part-time work!"

There was silence on the line for long enough I had to check to make sure I hadn't lost her.

"Mom?" I finally asked.

"That's a lot of money for a college job, Jeri," she finally said.

"I know!" I agreed. "But it's because Knock - the guy with the blue hair? Well, his big sister knows someone who knows someone. So it's not like just anyone could get this, but yeah. Um, there's just one catch."

"Of course there is," she grumbled.

"They have to do a background check on me," I explained. "That means they'll call you, and probably my teachers and stuff. They'll want to make sure I'm not a criminal or wrapped up with gangs and shit."

"You aren't, are you?"

"No!" I huffed. "Mom, there aren't any gangs here. I mean, this is serious suburbia. Our house is in the rich neighborhood, even! Like, the neighbor on the right? They have a BMW. Rich people."

She chuckled. "Ok, ok. So what do I need to tell them?"

"I don't actually know," I admitted. "I don't even know what they'll ask, but Jason - the guy who is training us so we can pass the tryouts? He said there's a chance they'll call. Like, just say good things? Like how I love computers, and how I play games all the time?"

"I can do that," she promised. "Honey, you have always been playing those games. When your brother got you started, I thought he was crazy. I told him the boys would pick on you, and yet it ended up being the best thing. I miss Drake, but..." She laughed sadly. "Maybe it's strange, but seeing you playing those games makes me feel like a piece of him is still around."

Her words hit me hard. Hard enough that I angled my feet towards one of the many benches scattered around the campus, because I had to sit down. For so long, Mom had been unable to realize I was growing up. She often forgot my brother had died. Sometimes, she even thought Hottie was Drake!

But this? Maybe it was being away from the house? The doctors had said her memory issues would be helped by distance, but having her finally accept I was no longer a child? Hearing her say something so... Did that count as sweet? Because it sure felt sweet to me.

"Oh, and I mailed you a present for your birthday," she said. "I know I'm not going to be home this weekend, and I figure you're too busy to want to hang out with your mom, so this way you'll still get it."

"Yeah?" I asked. "You know you didn't have to, right?"

"Oh, I had to," she assured me. "Jericho, you are the last of my family. I love you so much, sweetie, and the least I can do is make sure you get a good present, ok? Just tell me you have plans? You're going to do *something* fun, right?"

"Well, Knock's birthday is on the thirtieth," I said. "Mine's November first. So, we're doing a Halloween thing. Cake, handing out candy to the kids who knock on the door, and maybe hanging out in the hot tub."

"What hot tub?" she asked.

"Our house has a pool and a hot tub," I explained. "Mom, seriously, it's nice. Outdoor kitchen, three-car garage, and all the fancy stuff. But I think it's just going to be seven of us. My roommates, I mean."

"But that's still a party," she assured me. "You and seven friends? Just make sure someone else makes your cake, Jericho. No one should have to bake their own birthday cake."

"I think Grayson's handling that," I promised.

"He's such a good boy. I'm so glad you found him." She chuckled. "And I know I get confused a lot, but he never makes me feel bad for it. It's just nice to know he's there, taking care of you."

"Mom?" I groaned, because her words made me want to ask, but I also didn't.

"What, honey?"

Shit. Ok, maybe I should just put it out there? "You always said that once I went to college, you'd go back to the hospital. I'm in college now, so have you thought about it? Maybe see if you can, I dunno, get some help for the time lapses?"

"Jeri, it's a lot of money."

"And I'm going to be making enough to support myself," I reminded her. "Maybe if I get this gig, you'll think about it?"

"Well, I'm usually ok when I'm at work," she tried next.

"But Mom..." I paused, not wanting to whine. "I like this, Mom. I like you remembering I'm not a kid anymore. I like you caring about my birthday. I miss you, Mom, and when we lost everyone, I kinda lost you too, so maybe if you get help..."

"There's the chance it won't ever get better," she reminded me. "Jeri, this temporal amnesia I have is a problem with time and space relationships. Insurance won't cover all of my treatment, and if it doesn't work..."

"Then you'd at least have tried," I countered. "Mom, I want you to be able to come to my wedding one day. I want you to be at my college graduation and not think it's Drake's. I know it's selfish, but I dunno. I just want to see you in person and have you see *me*."

"Ok," she relented. "I'll look into it again, but with everything at work, I'm not sure. Taking time off might cause problems, and the company is going through some changes that might mean good things for us. So, let me think about it, ok?"

"Ok," I agreed. "But I miss you, Mom. I also worry about you when I'm not there to take care of you."

"I'm supposed to take care of you," she countered.

"Mhm," I agreed, because we both knew that was not how things worked.

She just chuckled. "Ok. I don't want sad things, Jericho. I mean, it's almost your birthday, and my little girl is growing up fast. So, um, tell me how you like college?"

I leaned back on the bench and looked at the students walking past. "I like it."

"Give me more," she teased.

Which made me chuckle. "Ok, um..." What was there to say? "Well, I have some of my roommates in a few classes. And while we live on the other side of town, the campus is easy to get to. I have gaps between all my classes, and there's a few coffee shops on campus, so I'm spending too much on caffeine, but it's ok. I also have some amazing roommates, and they all help me study. Mostly, it's been pretty boring."

"Because you aren't telling me about the parties, huh?"

I laughed. "No parties, Mom. Not enough time. Oh! I did learn how to shoot a gun, though. It was for that FBI thing I was talking about. And I'm studying law enforcement. Our trainer, Jason? He's in Cybersecurity for the FBI, and he says it pays almost two hundred grand a year. So, if I can't get a good job, this is setting me up for a fallback plan."

"You'd want to work for the FBI?" she asked.

"Yeah, maybe?" Not really. Not as an actual agent. "I mean, if nothing else, it gives me a good listing on my resume to get into those really high-paying computer jobs. And I declared my major as cybersecurity, which means it'd look really good."

"Look at my little girl, planning for her own future. Oh, honey, your father would've been so proud."

"And it's all because my brother made me play games so he could hang with his friends," I joked. "Letting the computer babysit me worked out, huh?"

"It sure did. But is there a boy in your life? Or a girl. I mean, you didn't really date in high school, so if it's a girl, that's perfectly fine too, sweetie."

"No girls!" I giggled. "Mom, I'm straight. And yeah, I'm kinda crushing on a guy, but I've been studying a lot, so nothing's really going to happen. Just me and my friends, mostly. Although one of my roommate's ex-girlfriends has been hanging out, so now there are three girls at the house most of the time."

"Who's this one?" she asked.

"Tiffany," I explained. "She went to school with us last year. Ok, and I hated her last year, but things are different in college."

"Different how?"

I had to pause, because that was a really good question. I could feel it, though. There was a change. It was like some kind of pressure that had been trying to smother all of us back in high school was gone. Wait. That was it!

"It's that the university is too big," I explained. "We don't know anyone. I don't even know the names of the people who sit beside me in most of my classes. No one cares about me, and it's nice."

"Jeri..." she tried, but I could hear her worry.

"No, it really is nice, Mom," I hurried to assure her. "No one knows about Drake and Dad. No one knows about all the crap. They don't feel bad for me, talk about rumors, or any of that stuff. It's a fresh start, you know? The people I meet want to know about *me*. They want to grab pizza or get notes. The pressure to be cool is gone, and it's just like... I dunno, like people."

"Like growing up," she clarified for me.

"Yeah, maybe?" I shrugged, even though she couldn't see it. "But I like it. I like feeling like I'll sink or swim based on who I am, not the crap we survived. My pink hair is also kinda normal here. I mean, there's a guy going into a building here with a rainbow mohawk. And I saw one wearing a feather boa with a bathrobe this morning."

"A guy?" she asked.

"Mhm," I agreed. "He was heading to the art building, which kinda explains that, but still. I'm not a freak, Mom. I'm nobody. I'm just me, doing my own thing and not having to explain it - and it's nice. It's..."

"A relief," she realized. "I'm so sorry, Jericho. I should've done more to make things easy on you."

"But you couldn't," I reminded her. "You were struggling too, and I get that. It sucked for all of us, but this? It kinda feels like we've turned the page or something. Like a second chance. I think that's why I was hoping you'd consider treatment for your mental health."

"A second chance," she repeated. "I like that. And I will check, ok? I promise."

"Maybe for a birthday present?" I begged.

"It will not happen that soon, but I'll shoot for Christmas or something. Deal?"

"I'll take it," I swore. "I just want you back, Mom. I love you, you know."

"I love you too," she said softly. "I might not show it, but I really do. More than you can imagine."

"Enough to make you keep trying," I said. "Mom, I know. I swear I know, because if nothing else, you didn't leave me."

She sniffed. "No, sweetie. I didn't. You deserved to have someone fight for you, so I've been trying. See, that's what real love is, and don't you ever accept anything else, ok? Not even from those really cute college boys I know you're checking out."

"Promise," I said.

Because while I wasn't ready to tell her about my love life, I knew my guys fit her definition. They were there for me in all ways. They'd stood behind me through thick and thin already. They were everything I could hope for, and then some.

I just hoped that if she got some help, then one day I might be able to tell her about us. All of us and this insane polycule that was actually working. Who knew, she might even be happy for me.

# CHAPTER 40

### RIPPER

The girls had decided to have a spa night. Zoe, Tiffany, and Jeri were out in the hot tub, since it was now a little too cool to be using the pool. Jinxy had supplied them with a six-pack of fruity drinks in bottles. Wine coolers, hard something, or one of those types of things.

But this was my chance.

Heading into the war room, I found Cade and Knock playing. I pointed at Cade. "I need you."

"Huh?" he asked.

Knock looked up. "Whatcha need, Ripper?"

"You stay," I told him. "Or go talk to the girls and keep them outside. Something."

"Why?" Cade asked.

I huffed. "Jeri's birthday? She doesn't have good ones, so I wanted to do something. And Knock, since it's yours too, you get to enjoy the fun. So, I dunno, help a guy out?"

Knock grinned and began tapping at his keyboard. "I'm recalling and logging out," he explained. "I'll get more drinks and go harass the girls. Just..." He looked between us. "Can we keep it kinda low-key?"

"No alcohol?" Cade asked.

"I wouldn't go that far," Knock said. "Just no trouble with the FBI type of low-key."

"Don't worry," I said. "I got this." And I waved for Cade to come with me.

Then I headed to the study. Both Jinxy and Hottie were in there with their laptops, working on a project for the class they shared. When Cade joined me, they both looked up suspiciously.

"No bad news," Jinxy informed me.

"Birthday planning," I assured him as I moved to take a chair. "Knock's got the girls outside, which means we can talk without one of them walking in. Zoe can't keep a secret to save her life, so yeah. Guys, I have a couple of ideas."

"Like?" Cade asked, stealing the other chair.

Hottie closed his laptop and turned to give me his full attention. Jinxy simply leaned back, a little smile on his face. Ok, I hadn't been shut down yet, so I was hoping they'd be on board for this.

"I know Jeri's birthday has always been shit," I explained. "Last year was pretty fucking boring, and she said it was one of the best she'd ever had."

"Because I showed up," Hottie explained. "Half the time, her mom gets drunk and cries about the ones she's lost. Jeri gets forgotten, gets to light her own candles, and all that shit."

"So let's make this a big deal?" I begged. "Not stupid or over the top. Just a real birthday party?"

"Like balloons and signs and shit?" Cade asked.

Jinxy chuckled. "Like the type a five-year-old would love?"

I almost said no, then actually thought about that. "Yeah, kinda?"

Jinxy was nodding like he understood my goal here. "Let's do it on Halloween, so there's an excuse to dress up. We'll have candy for the neighbors, we can have candy for everyone else, and we'll do those stupid balloons that look like animals and shit. Put up the banners that say 'Happy Birthday', we'll have streamers, party poppers, and just trash the hell out of the house."

"A cake," Cade said.

"Two," Hottie decided. "Blue and pink, so they each get one. And we're going to keep the childish theme. Like, I dunno, make Knock's dinosaurs and Jeri's unicorns or something. Or the other way around. Just childish and fun."

"What about friends?" I asked.

"Riley," Hottie suggested. "Jason too. Hell, Knock's whole house needs to be here. Even Kitty's boyfriend. What's his name?"

"Murder," Cade said.

"No, his real name," Hottie asked.

"Murder," Cade said again. "I mean, it's Samir, but no one calls him that. He's Murder."

"What about presents?" I asked.

Hottie scoffed at that. "Pretty sure there's nothing she wants. Maybe stupid shit?"

And yet, Jinxy was smiling in a way I really wanted to call a smirk. The guy looked like he finally had the upper hand. Smug. That was the best description I had.

"Stuffed animals," he said. "Board games. Card games. If you go with clothes, then the costume type. I'm talking tiaras, ballerina skirts, and just fun shit. Same for Knock. We're going with childish fun for the theme, right? Well, who doesn't like cool toys? I'm talking about the toy aisle type of crap. Barbies, and Transformers, and whatever seems like it'd be fun for at least ten minutes."

"Yeah, Knock would love that," Cade agreed. "Besides, how often do we guys get to do shit like that without getting laughed at for it? But if it's for Jeri? Then it's an excuse that'll let Knock actually enjoy it, and you know he will."

"We all will," I realized. "So, Cade? You get Knock to invite Jason. Tell him Saturday is a birthday party, not a work day. No debates. If he wants us at the range, he needs to do it another day. Someone needs to talk to Riley."

"That's also me," Cade said. "I mean, I did live there for a while."

"Ok, and who else?" I asked.

Cade laughed. "How about I just handle the guest list?"

"Then I'll handle presents," I decided.

"I got cakes," Hottie said.

Jinxy murmured in a very pleased way. "I get decorations. I have some ideas. This is going to be fun."

"God, I hope so," I breathed.

Which made Cade look over. "Why?"

"Because she's been ok lately," I said, knowing that sounded stupid. "I mean, I know I'm not the only one who's noticed it, right?"

"Nope," Hottie said, popping the P.

"But it's like something changed recently, and now she's kinda being, I dunno..." I couldn't quite quantify the change, because Jeri was still studying.

"She realized she's not carrying it all," Hottie said.

"Huh?" Cade asked.

Jinxy just groaned. "Seriously? How did she think she was going to make all of us able to do this?"

"She didn't think that far," Hottie explained. "Jeri just does. She bulldozes her way through shit because doing more, working harder, and fighting bigger is all she has ever been able to do."

"And she feels like she has to do it all," I added. "She said that with her mom's issues, she had to pay the bills and do all the shit like that, so she's never really had anyone to take care of her."

"So she's trying to take care of us," Cade agreed.

Again, Jinxy murmured. "And she's using the action of doing something to keep her from slowing down enough to face her own fears."

"Wait, what?" Hottie asked.

Jinxy just looked between the three of us. "Her insecurities."

"Which ones?" I pressed.

The man's mouth fell open. "Seriously?" he asked.

"Seriously," Cade agreed, gesturing for him to get going.

Jinxy huffed in what almost sounded like annoyance. "Ok, so this is Jeri we're talking about. Everyone she loved in her childhood died - except Hottie. That's a massive insecurity. It's right up there with abandonment issues, except she's putting the blame on herself somehow."

"Her curse," Hottie grumbled.

Jinxy just gestured to him like that was the point. "So she's scared of doing anything for herself. She's terrified of taking risks that might drag anyone down with her. Jeri's little bubble of safety is independence."

"Which is why the polycule works," I pointed out.

"Kinda," Jinxy said. "Because we're all tangled up, she feels safer in some ways, but also like a goddamned anchor. If she falls, she will end up pulling us all down with her, and then it'd all be her fault, and so she has to do more, do it better, and make sure she can cover for any of us if we have a problem, right?"

"Except - " Hottie tried.

But Jinxy held up a finger. "And Jeri knows how to seek and destroy. She knows how to make shit happen. Know what she doesn't know? How to let others take care of her. How to be pampered like a girlfriend, or a best friend, or just someone important. She *does not* think she deserves it. That's why I think this party is a great idea. It's also important to make it *fun*."

"But!" Hottie said, waving Jinxy back, "Jeri talked to Jason the other night. I overheard some of it, and she told me about the rest. He offered to carry her. He told her we're a team. To Jeri, those were big and important things. It's the first step in convincing her we're allowed to do some of the carrying."

"Because it all falls on her shoulders," I said, nodding to show I understood.

"Exactly," Hottie said. "I tried to take care of her, but - "

"No," Cade broke in. "You were a few states away, broke, in college, and all that shit. No one is blaming you, Hottie."

"He is," Jinxy muttered under his breath in a way meant to be heard.

Hottie just huffed at that. "Ok, fair point."

"But Nina broke you," Jinxy told him. "Jeri stepped in to help you. She felt more in control, and you needed her. You did the same for her, so don't go blaming yourself. All I'm saying is that's Jeri's thing. She jumps in, does what helps someone else, and never thinks about how she's tearing herself apart to make it happen, because she's never had the opportunity to even think about it."

"But she's been better this week," I reminded them. "I mean, she's seemed a lot less stressed to me, or am I missing something?"

"You're not," Hottie agreed. "Ripper, Jason offered to take care of her. May not have been what he intended, but it's what she heard. This man who is a better hacker, a better asshole, and who has the power to fix shit? He offered to help her if she needs it. Unlike me, he actually *can* do it."

"Fuck," Cade breathed. "And that man's seriously fucked up."

"So she can relate to him," Jinxy said. "Broken man, broken woman."

"No," I realized, dropping my eyes to the ground. "I don't think it's because he's broken."

"Ok?" Cade asked.

"I think it's because he gives a shit." Lifting my eyes, I looked at each of the guys in turn. "Just like Zoe did. Just like Hottie and Jinxy did, Cade. Someone stopped long enough to care about her."

"Like you guys did too," Hottie said. "And you didn't ask her to change."

"That!" I agreed, pointing at him. "And Jason is..."

"A fucking badass," Cade finished for me.

"Nuh uh," Jinxy said, shaking his head. "That's not what makes her willing to lean on him." He reached up to scrub at his mouth. "Fuck. She's screwed up."

"Why?" Hottie asked.

"It's because he's a killer," Jinxy said. "I mean, when she stabbed Dylan like that? She wanted to! She would've killed him too, if we hadn't been there."

"And Jason shot the gunmen who were going to hurt the girls at F5," I breathed. "He removed the threat. He *permanently* removed it, y'all."

"And he promised to carry her if she stumbled," Hottie breathed. "Shit. Is that something we need to worry about?"

"Nope," Cade said. "Believe it or not, Jason's a good guy. Weird as shit, but a good guy. He bends the rules, but always to help the victims. He's also damned good at what he does. Yeah, um, and from what Logan says, he's changed a lot since he met his wife."

"Changed how?" I asked.

Cade laughed once. "He's nicer now."

"Shit," Jinxy groaned. "The man busts my balls."

"Yeah, but he used to be like..." Cade grumbled under his breath, searching for words. "Like dead inside. Riley said he was always on the outside because of his job, until she refused to ignore the shit she saw. And then they started talking, got close, and he met his wife. He fell in love, y'all, and it made him live again."

"Which kinda makes him sound like the perfect mentor for Jeri," I pointed out. "He can convince her there really is a light at the end of the tunnel, right?"

"And," Cade said, "I think this party is a great idea. Let's keep shit light, make sure she can have fun, and not let her get too serious again. The kiddie concept? There's nothing at all serious about that."

"Get Zoe on costumes," Hottie told me. "Tell her the theme and she'll make sure Jeri doesn't pull a slutty-something costume."

"And maybe we can give her a moment to stop worrying about all of this?" I asked. "I mean, that was kinda my point, because she *has* been better, so if we bring in the fun, then maybe she'll keep relaxing more and more?"

"Dates," Cade said. "We have a dining room for a reason. No need to go out, but I think we all need to make time to just be with her and talk about anything but work and school."

"Oh, that's a good idea," I agreed. "And maybe we can help each other? Like, with cooking, or whatnot?"

"I'll help you, Ripper," Hottie promised.

"And me?" Cade asked.

"You have Knock," Jinxy teased. "I also think you need some solo time with that girl so she doesn't think she's an add-on."

"Can do," Cade promised. "And I'll relay all of this to Knock."

"Um..." I lifted a finger, showing I had a question left. "So, like, how are we going to afford a big party? Is this going to cost too much?"

"Nope," Hottie said. "We're going for cheap. Lots and lots and lots of cheap and childish fun. Lots of distractions and bright colors, and making a mess. Not expensive, just fun."

"Which means a few hundred bucks, split between all of us," Jinxy said. "Guys, seriously, we got this." Then he jerked his chin at me. "And Ripper? It's a damned good idea. We'll say it's Halloween, then bust out the surprise party."

"And Jeri will have fun," I agreed.

"Whether she likes it or not," Hottie added with a devious little smile. "Yeah, this is why this shit of ours works. Because we can gang up on our girlfriend."

Jinxy just sighed. "Yep. Girl-friend. Gotta put that pause in there, Hot. Otherwise, it gets kinda weird."

# CHAPTER 41

**KNOCK**

The plans had been made. Things were organized and delegated. I'd offered to help, but Cade had informed me this was my party too. I was supposed to simply enjoy it - and keep it all a secret from Jeri. But the best part was Jason. Once he'd been let in on the plan, he'd run with it.

We'd all received a very professional email about how this weekend included a holiday, Halloween, which meant he'd be unavailable for training. We were still expected to study and make advances in the subjects we'd been given. To do that, he'd listed off chapters we should read and be prepared to discuss next weekend.

Jeri had been a little bummed about that. Thankfully, Zoe had intervened, making it clear we would have kids come to get candy. We did kinda live in one of those safe neighborhoods, after all. The sort people drove to so their children got the good stuff. To make sure we didn't let them down, the girls headed out after class to buy as much candy as they could carry.

When I woke up on Saturday, it was to the perfect insanity. That was the only word I had for it. The moment I stepped out of my room, I was assaulted with colors. Balloons were everywhere! They floated up against the ceiling with long streamers that nearly reached the floor. It was a rainbow of colors, and the further I got into the house, the more balloons there seemed to be!

The kitchen and war room were mostly balloon-free. A few had drifted in there, but they were the runaways. The halls, the main rooms, and even the bathroom had them! Spread across the living room was a balloon banner that said "Happy 19," surrounded by even more balloons. All I could do was laugh.

Jeri loved it. She woke up giggling, and kept trying to ask who'd made this happen. No one would take credit, but Cade let me know Jinxy had been in charge of balloons. The guy had been up all night, turning our house into the happiest chaos I could imagine.

But as sunset neared, the girls headed upstairs to get ready. Hottie began passing out plastic-wrapped fabric, saying this was our costumes. I opened mine to find a blue cape with "Super Knock" printed on the back. It had clips to attach to my shoulders, was long enough to cover my ass, and the rest of the guys had something similar in their own color.

And that was when people started showing up. The doorbell rang, but Ripper answered it. I was half expecting the first batch of kids. Instead, Riley sauntered in wearing a little black onesie with a cat-ear hood.

"Happy birthday, Knock!" she said, hugging me hard. "Where are we putting the presents?"

"Uh..."

"Living room!" Zoe yelled as she and Jeri descended the stairs.

Zoe was in a bright red onesie with a demon tail. Jeri's was pink, and it took me a moment to realize the hood hanging against her back was supposed to be a pig. Oh, but it didn't stop there. Logan walked in with his own black cape - and an armful of presents. Murder followed, carrying little Ryan, and both of them had their own. Kitty trailed in last, wearing a purple unicorn onesie.

"So, it's a Halloween party?" I asked.

"And birthday!" Kitty squealed, making her way through the mass of streamers to give me a bone-crushing hug. "Happy old day, little brother."

"Wait, there's more," Ripper called, pulling the door open wider.

Wagging excitedly, Crysis rushed in wearing the most adorable bumble bee costume. When he saw the streamers, he paused, sniffed at a few, and then hurried down the hall like he lived here. Granted, he almost did, or so it felt.

Then Jason came in. His arm was around an incredibly beautiful woman in a pastel green onesie. It had spikes down the back and a little tail like a dragon or dinosaur. And Jason? Even he had gone with the superhero cape!

"Where's the alcohol?" his wife asked.

"Uh..." I kinda pointed towards the kitchen, but was confused.

"It's in here!" Jeri called out, coming out of the kitchen just to pause at the sight of the woman.

"Zara, meet Jericho," Jason introduced. "Jeri, this is my wife."

"We met in Dallas," Jeri said, turning to the woman. "But you probably don't remember. *Someone* was hunting down her man and ended up getting a proposal. I mean, keeping track of these boys is kinda distracting." Then she offered her hand. "Hi, Zara. Congratulations on all the things. And Jason, you seriously married up."

"No shit," he agreed. "But don't tell her that shit. The woman's blind or something, and I'm taking advantage of it."

Zara just laughed. "Oh, you'll earn it. And give me your keys. I can't drink, so you are."

"Can't." Jason said.

Zara simply turned, lifted a brow, and thrust out her hand. "If you give me some shit-ass reason like 'working' then I will remind you of the conventions. So give up already. Drink. Be stupid. Let me have some gamer girl time, ok?"

Sighing heavily, Jason thrust his hand into his pocket, passed over the keys, and then obediently headed into the kitchen. Jeri was pressing her lips together like she was struggling not to laugh, yet the moment Jason was out of sight, she guided the woman towards the back.

"Somehow, you are not at all who I imagined him marrying," she said.

I moved to trail behind them just as Zara replied, "Because I'm Middle Eastern?"

"Nope. I figured he'd end up with someone all sweet and gentle and domestic. From the little we interacted, you seem..."

"Not sweet, gentle, and only a tiny bit domestic?" Zara joked. "Basically. And he likes you guys, just so you know. He brags all of you up when he comes home and - "

"Do not!" Jason called after her. "Woman!"

"Drink!" Zara yelled back before bending closer to Jeri. "He is fascinated by your relationship. Says it's the craziest thing he's seen since he met Riley."

"Which is a huge compliment," I added.

"Oh yeah," Zara agreed. "And all of you have been put on the wall now. So I wanna get a picture of everyone together tonight, ok?"

"The wall?" Jeri asked.

Zara paused in the middle of the hall. "For so long, he had to keep his distance. He couldn't make real friends, has no family, and his life was the KoG case. Jason put pictures of everyone on his bedroom wall to remind him why he was doing this. Those people became his friends and, well, his family. Over the summer, he started adding all of Ruin." She laughed once, looking over at me. "And when you saved us?"

"Oh shit," Jeri breathed. "You were there too? Fuck, I'm sorry. I forgot about that. I mean, I knew, but it was kinda like a big jumble of panic."

"My third time to be held at gunpoint," Zara said with a grimace. "It's not something I planned to get good at. It's different with friends, though. Worse and better, you know?"

"I do," Jeri said. "Not about the gun thing, but the friends? Yeah. Speaking of that, come meet the rest of the team who couldn't make it to the convention."

They kept going, but I stayed, moving to lean against the wall. Was it weird that I liked how easily Jeri got along with these people? It shouldn't be, but something about her and Zara talking like old friends just made me happy. The balloons and streamers made me happy. Fuck, all of this did.

Naturally, that was when Murder made his way up the hall. "You good, Knock?" he asked.

"Just kinda being stupid over my girl," I admitted.

"Well, come help me bring in the fun. We've got more presents, more alcohol, and the women went nuts for this. I need some muscle."

That led to a few trips back and forth. When Riley bought alcohol, she didn't mess around. There was also food, far too many gifts, and an entire box of party poppers filled with confetti. Nope. When I read the label, I realized it was glitter. Fucking *glitter*.

"Riley!" I bellowed. "Do you hate me? No glitter."

"Sucks to be you," Logan laughed, plucking one out just to fire it over my head.

The sparkles rained down, making everyone laugh. It also led to a rush on the box. Zoe aimed one at Jeri. Jeri took off, running up the hall. Crysis barked and followed after, only to have Jason hit both of them over by the study. Ripper tagged Cade. Cade got Logan. Riley glittered Jason - and there was still most of a box left.

The group of us laughed. We paused the fun to answer the door and pass out heaping handfuls of candy to the kids who yelled, "Trick or treat!" We drank a bit, the outdoor kitchen was fired up and food was made by Logan and Murder, so we ate. And then, just as the trick-or-treaters tapered off, the cakes were brought out.

Happy birthday was sung for both of us. Candles were lit on two cakes. Photos were taken as we simultaneously blew them out. And while I was braced for a food fight, it didn't happen. We all just dug in to eat the cake instead of throwing it.

And then the real fun started. Presents were opened, and everything was a toy. Not some cool adult toy, but stupid, childish, and amazing things. There was an Etch A Sketch, a little robot dinosaur, a ton of stuffed animals and board games. Anything fun I could imagine, we now had it.

Somehow, the party spilled out into the backyard. A few balloons escaped, soaring off into the sky before anyone could catch them. I was starting to feel warm and fuzzy all over, and I felt like my cheeks couldn't stop smiling.

"There you are!" Jeri said, pulling me over to the side and away from the door. "Happy birthday, Knock."

I caught her by the waist. "Happy birthday, Jericho." Then I tugged her closer. "Where's my present?"

Her baby-blue eyes jumped up, hitting my face. For a moment, she didn't know what I was talking about, and then she remembered. Last year, I'd asked for one thing: a kiss. Since then, so much had changed, but that was really all I wanted from her this year too.

"Right here," she breathed, shifting closer - and taking her time about it. "I just needed the chance to slow down so I could get you alone."

"Mm, don't need to be alone," I swore, cupping the side of her face. "I just need you."

"And him, and them," she teased.

I canted my head, refusing to deny it. "Kinda why we all work. But I do need you, Jeri. Don't forget that part."

Her eyes shifted between mine, trying to judge if I was joking. I wasn't. I made sure she could see how I meant every word. This girl had changed my life in ways I'd never imagined. Considering my life had been pretty damned good before I met her? I thought that made her even more amazing.

"I need you too," she said softly. "I'm not used to this, but I need all of you."

"Hey," I whispered, guiding her hair back. "Believe it or not, it's ok to need people."

"Well, yeah, but..."

"Nope," I said, shaking my head. "No buts. It's ok, and we're all allowed to. And we're allowed to love each other, and give a shit, and be as crazy as we want. Jeri, we are allowed to do this. To be happy. To do whatever we want!"

She chuckled and leaned in, pressing her brow against my chest. "Is it stupid if I say this is the first good birthday I can remember?"

"No, kinda is for me too. I mean, last year was supposed to be amazing, but then someone fucked it up by trying to kill Logan and Riley."

She turned a bit, snuggling up to me. So, wrapping an arm around her, I leaned back. That let the wall hold us both up where we could see all of our friends out in the yard. Zara was throwing a ball for Crysis, who looked dumb as fuck running that hard with his costume on. Murder was trying to get his turn, and Logan was holding the baby while everyone else meandered and talked.

"I thought having Hottie visit last year was as good as it could get," she admitted before gesturing to the group. "But this? Knock, I have friends."

"A lot of them," I pointed out.

"Yeah, and that kinda freaks me out."

"So get over it," I said, glancing down to see her. "I don't mean 'just get over it.' I'm saying this is you. When you decide to do something, you do it. Nothing stops you. So convince yourself you deserve this or something. I don't even know."

"But what if being happier makes the next shit worse?" she asked.

Then she groaned. "Fuck, that sounds like crazy talk. I just mean by comparison, you know?"

"It will." I rubbed her arm with the one I had around her. "But see, here's the thing. My first real friend was Riley. I don't even fucking know why she picked me, but she did. That woman decided I was safe to befriend, pulled me out of obscurity, then made me a part of her family. And I love her. Oh, I had a crush on her when I first saw her, but that was being dumb. She's like a sister now, and closer than I ever was to my real family."

"Yeah," Jeri said softly.

"And every time she's been shot at? It has scared the *shit* out of me. Each time shit hit the fan, it freaked me out harder than anything has before. But you know what?"

"Hm?"

"It's worth it," I assured her. "The joy of having people around who honestly matter? Who give a fuck? It makes the bad moments easier to recover from. It makes the horror more intense, but that gets lost in all the good times. It fades, Jeri. When there are memories to replace it, the lingering anguish releases just a bit. No, it doesn't go away, but you at least have something else to hold on to. You know, kinda like those stuffed animals everyone gave you."

She looked up with a grin on her face. "So many! Like, what the fuck?"

"Fun birthday," I said as an explanation. "Childish, stupid, and silly fun. See, this? This is one of those moments you're supposed to remember. This is one of those times you think about when you miss someone, or are hurting, or if the worst happens. I'm not going to say it'll all be ok, because we're sticking our necks out pretty damned far with this FBI thing, right? So shit could go sideways. But this? If I'm sitting in jail for cyberterrorism or something, then this is what I'll think about as I fall asleep."

"I like that," she decided.

"So go play and make memories," I told her, giving her a nudge. "Be silly. Be stupid. Be girly, Jericho, because it looks so fucking good on you when you do."

"Ok," she agreed, peeling away from me to head towards the yard. "You too!"

"Piss and drinks," I said. "Then I'll be just as stupid. Promise."

"I'm going to hold you to that!" she laughed before skipping away.

But for a moment I just stood there, watching her. That pink fuzzy onesie was adorable, and it showed off her figure more than I'd expected. She looked good. All the types of good, from happy to sexy. And when she paused to hook her arm around Cade and hang off his side, I realized I was living my dream.

I was a guy in love - twice. I had it all. Tonight was everything I'd never known I'd wanted, and I had all these people to thank for it. Maybe I didn't fight the way Jeri did, but I understood her more than she knew. We'd been pulled up and out of the shit. We knew how important the good times were.

We also weren't alone, and that was the best part of tonight. Our friends and family had gone above and beyond to make sure we *knew* we would never be alone again. It didn't matter if we were flawed or not. We were still allowed to be happy.

# CHAPTER 42

### JERICHO

I'd forgotten to give Knock his kiss. It was the birthday present he wanted, and yet I'd ended up out in the backyard, giggling with everyone else. Worse, Riley had filled my cup over and over until half the night was just a happy blur.

But around two in the morning, people began making their way out. Cade was passed out on the couch, a bottle of vodka beside him. The label said it was "birthday cake" flavored. Jason was staggering, with his wife holding him up. That he kept telling her he loved her was adorable.

Riley looked sober, but she passed her keys to Murder before herding her crew out. He'd been on baby duty for most of the night, giving Kitty the chance to enjoy herself. Even better, little Ryan had only had one crying fit, and that had been due to a dirty diaper.

And the house was trashed.

There was glitter *everywhere*. The balloons were starting to sink a bit as their helium wore out. Bottles, paper plates, and empty cups littered every surface, but I didn't give a shit. I would've if Logan hadn't done his fair share of trashing the place, but since he was ok with it, then the rest could wait.

Zoe was so drunk, Jinxy had carried her up to his room about an hour ago. Ripper and Hottie were making a pass of the house, picking up anything that could spill. And while I felt nice and warm from what I'd been drinking, I wasn't even tipsy.

"Hey," I said, coming up behind Ripper to give him a hug. "Thanks for making this happen."

He turned, cupped my face, and kissed me softly. "Happy birthday, Jeri. This was fun."

"Won't be when we clean tomorrow, Ripper," Hottie countered. "Or when the hangovers hit."

"So late morning," I decided.

Hottie glanced over at Cade, bent to grab the bottle he'd clearly emptied, then chuckled. "I think we should leave him here."

Ripper just sighed. "The third floor is a long way away."

"I'll help you up there," I offered.

"Nope." He grabbed my shoulders and turned me up the hall. "It's your birthday, Jeri. It's his birthday. Go have birthday sex or something."

"Good call," Hottie agreed. "Also means you can crash in her room, Ripper."

"Might," Ripper said. "Probably not, but might. Just want to clean up a bit of this."

"I'll get a garbage bag," Hottie said. "Cups, plates, and bottles tonight, balloons and glitter tomorrow. Sound like a plan?"

"Works for me."

Then Hottie pointed. "Bed, Jericho. Knock's this time."

"Going!" I giggled, fighting my urge to help.

Because cleaning had always been my job. I'd been the only one in the house until Hottie moved in, and then we'd cleaned together. I was supposed to make sure the place didn't get trashed. I was supposed to be the responsible one. It was also my birthday, and it seemed that didn't end when the guests went home.

And since it was after midnight, it was really, actually, and truly my birthday now. Nineteen years old. Still a teenager, which meant being young and dumb was allowed. So what if that was my default position? Knock had said something about making memories, and I had this warm and fuzzy feeling in my chest that had nothing at all to do with alcohol.

So I turned the corner and slipped into Knock's room. The shower was going, which explained where he'd disappeared to. So, slipping out of my piggy onesie, I tossed that in the corner. Glitter drifted off it, which made me choke back a giggle. Oh, the house was going to be sparkling for months to come.

Oddly, I liked it. Yeah, glitter got everywhere, but that was kinda the best part. As I pulled off my shirt and pants, adding them to the pile, I realized it had even gotten down to my skin. The stuff was pervasive in a way that felt like the perfect metaphor. It slipped in and refused to go away. Wasn't that similar to this mess we all called a relationship?

When I was finally naked, I got under the covers and snuggled in to wait. If Cade woke up and came in, then the more the merrier. If he didn't, well, I still owed Knock a kiss. I had every intention of making it a memorable one.

The water eventually turned off and my boyfriend wandered out of his bathroom drying his hair. That left the rest of his body bare, just begging me to look. Like this, Knock's abs were defined. Those dips at his hips were fucking sexy. His thighs were strong from riding horses, and even his limp dick was kinda hot.

He lowered his towel to toss at the dirty clothes pile, and paused. A little smile began to claim his mouth. "You are not at all who I expected to end up in my bed."

"Mm, guess this means I've been ignoring you, huh?" I teased.

"Nope." He crawled up the mattress from the foot of the bed, not stopping until he was over me with the covers pinning me in place. "Where's Cade?"

"Drunk, passed out in the living room."

"He good?"

I nodded. "Not puking drunk, I don't think. Pretty sure he was just exhausted."

"Aren't we all." And Knock dropped down beside me, not even bothering to kiss me.

"Hey!" I huffed, rolling to face him. "Tease!"

He laughed. "Jer, you're leaving glitter in my bed. I literally just took a shower to get rid of it."

"I am?"

He pointed at the pillow. "You are a sparkly wonder."

Oh, but that kinda sounded like fun. "Which means I should share, huh?" I asked, shoving at the blankets so I could pin Knock down this time.

He gasped as I grabbed his arms, but didn't fight me. Instead, his eyes dropped, taking in my lack of clothes. When I tossed a leg over his lap, that smile turned sexy. Then, slowly, I leaned in, aware a few flakes of glitter drifted down from my hair.

"I owe you a present, remember?" I asked.

"God, you're fucking gorgeous," he breathed, lifting up to claim my mouth before I was all the way down.

And we kissed. There was something hot about the way he was always so into me. I loved how he had this calm and serene nature, without being stoic. The truth was that I just loved him in all ways. This man was an amazing friend and partner. He was kind, considerate, and hot as fuck. He made me feel like I mattered, even as he and Cade were building their own thing between them.

Knock was like a lifeline in so many ways, and it pulled at me. As my mouth dueled with his, our kisses getting hotter and deeper, I couldn't help but think about that red string myth. The whole story about an invisible thread which connected some people.

We had it - all seven of us. It made me feel grounded and secure. It made me fucking happy, and I wasn't used to that. My whole life, I'd had to push back against everything, struggling to survive the shit that kept getting dumped on us. But Knock? He helped. They all did, in their own way, but right now I only cared about this one.

My fingers moved to slide between his, pushing his hands over his head. My body lowered until my chest was right up against his. Skin to skin, our mouths moved, but our bodies didn't. It was a tease, and one that was turning me on more than I expected.

Then he tipped his head. "How drunk are you?" he asked.

I shook my head, sending more glitter floating down. "Not really. Stopped drinking a while ago. I was laughing with the girls instead."

"Good." Then he pushed rolling me onto my back without letting me go.

I gasped, using my legs to cling to him, and his hardness pressed into the pit of my belly. Knock's damp and messy blue hair hung down towards my face, framing his, and the man smiled softly. In one move, he'd completely changed the tone, and I kinda liked it.

"Hey..." he breathed. "Happy birthday."

Then he shifted his hips and pressed in. I let my eyes close and melted into the sensation. My body stretched around him. His hips pressed up against mine, and it all felt so fucking good. For a moment, he paused, allowing my body to adjust, and then he slid back.

My leg moved higher, hooking on his lower back. Pulling an arm free, I pushed his hair out of his face, and then stretched up to kiss him even as he pushed back in. Slow, sensual, and intense, this man loved me. Every rock of his hips was driving me higher, and it was the perfect way to end this amazing night.

I loved him. Maybe I didn't love him the way other girls loved their guys, but he was ok with that. All of my partners were. I could love them in my own way. I could let them make me feel good. I didn't have to feel bad about any of this, because they were my happy memory. They were my team. They were what I needed so fucking much.

And sometimes it was ok to just feel it. To feel the softness of his mouth and the way his touches had changed. To feel his body moving inside mine, driving me steadily higher. To fucking *feel* how much he treasured me.

I wasn't just a passing fancy to this man. I wasn't a girl he would fuck and forget. I wasn't some garbage to be thrown away because it was too complicated. I was here, with him, and the look in his eyes proved it. I couldn't explain how meaningful it felt, but each time his dark gaze caught mine, it made my pulse beat a little faster, even as our bodies rocked together in perfect harmony.

I loved him.

I *needed* him.

And all of that was ok.

So I just let go. From the little sparkle on his cheek to the deep rocking thrusts he was pumping into me, this was perfect. *We* were perfect. Maybe this crazy thing we were doing was messy and unconventional, but it worked, and tonight had been the kind of reminder I couldn't overlook. Love mattered. It could conquer all, right? It also felt really damned intense.

The gasping, moaning, bucking kind. The wild kisses and gripping fingers kind. The letting myself let go, not caring about being sexy, and just losing myself in my boyfriend kind of intense. The sort of thing that would've scared the shit out of me a year ago, and now felt as necessary as oxygen to keep me alive.

So I loved him back. With my body, with my mind, and with every piece of me I could. I drove him deeper into my body by rolling my hips. I grabbed the back of his head, holding his mouth to mine. And when his hand moved to tease my breast, I couldn't handle anymore.

I cried out, not sure who was still on the first floor and not caring. Knock just kissed the sound away and pumped a little harder. Not faster. Oh, no. He made me feel every inch as it worked my body. He took his time about loving me, almost like it was some challenge to be met. He gave in, making me feel like every movement was some kind of triumph I should celebrate, even as I was losing all of my control.

And it hit. My climax took over, making me call out even louder this time as pleasure slammed into me like a tsunami. Wave after wave of it, and Knock kept going, kept moving, and kept kissing me, making his way down my neck even as I writhed in the most intense pleasure I could imagine.

Until his eyes clamped tightly closed and he groaned. Just as I was coming down, he pressed his face into my neck and gave in, finding his own release. My arms wrapped around his back, holding him tightly. No, fuck that. Clinging to him desperately, because that was how intense these emotions felt.

And for a moment, we just paused, both gulping back air as we recovered. I felt his lips curl as a smile washed over them, then he lifted, looking down at me so sweetly.

"Jeri?" He slid out of my body. "You gotta let me go, baby."

"Mm, don't wanna." I still did.

He chuckled. "Yeah, but, um..." He moved to lie beside me, reaching over to trace circles on my bare stomach. "I kinda forgot the condom."

"Fuck," I groaned.

His hand paused. "Bad?"

"No, I'm still on birth control," I assured him. "I just have to make it to the bathroom now."

"Yeah, hence the letting go." But he shifted closer. "Kinda sorry, but also kinda not. I've, um... Never, you know."

"Bareback?"

He nodded. "Not even with Cade."

I turned to find worry on his face. "It's ok, Knock. I mean, it's not like we're all fucking around, right? It's just us, and I'm good with it. I mean, if this relationship of ours isn't serious, then I don't know what would be."

"Very serious," he swore. "The kind of serious that makes me not even care that you covered my bed in glitter." Then he leaned in and kissed me. "To make up for it, maybe I should run a long, hot shower for you, and help wash that out, huh?"

"Ready for round two already?" I teased.

His eyes slid over my face, and the smile on his lips was wistful. "Ready for all night with the woman I love. Yeah. How about we make it a very happy birthday, hm?"

"I love you," I blurted out. "I don't say it enough, but I really do."

"Trust me, I know," he promised. "You don't say it, Jeri. You prove it, and I'm actually ok with that."

"Then shower sex it is," I decided. "Because I'm going to prove it all night long."

# CHAPTER 43

## HOTSHOT

It started out soft. Just a little tinkling sound. The problem was it kept getting louder and louder until it pulled me all the way awake. It also wasn't quitting. Rubbing at my face, I realized that was Jeri's alarm tone, and since she wasn't in her room, it wasn't going to get turned off unless I got up and did it.

Grumbling at the way my head was throbbing, I tossed off my blankets and headed through the bathroom to her room. There, the sound was even louder. Fuck, how long had this thing been playing?

When I reached her phone, I swiped to shut the damned thing off for good, not simply snooze it. Immediately, her phone changed to show the lock screen. I was just about to turn away when something caught my eye.

**Unknown:**
You crossed a line when you helped the FBI

That was it, just the sender and subject of an email waiting for her to read it, but it said too much. My hangover was instantly forgotten, and I was now completely awake. Unplugging her phone, I unlocked it and tapped to read the email.

I know who you are, Jericho Williams. I know all about your plan to become a consultant for the FBI. Who do you think has been dragging this shit through Congress? Me.

I will never let this program happen, and yes, I do have the power to stop it. That's what happens when you're born with a dick you stupid sniveling bitch. Stay the fuck out of my world, you half-ass hacker cunt.

Vyrus

Fuck. I had no clue who this Vyrus guy was, but seeing that? My heart hung, remembering the last time Jeri's name had been called out. This wasn't good. No one should know we were involved with the FBI. Not then and not now. That meant this had to be real enough to take seriously.

So I stormed out of the room, pushing aside the barely floating balloons, and pounded on Jinxy's door. "Wake up! We have a situation!"

A feminine yelp proved he wasn't alone in there. I almost felt sorry for scaring Zoe, but right now, I was on the verge of losing my shit. Someone was threatening Jeri? No. This was an all-hands-on-deck sort of thing.

I was headed for the stairs when Zoe peeked her head of Jinxy's room. "What's going on? Is everyone ok?"

"We have a problem," I told her. "A virtual one. I need everyone up and thinking as soon as possible."

"I'll get Ripper," she promised, hurrying towards me.

But while she went up, I went down. On the first floor, I waded through more balloons and celebratory destruction to the war room so I could turn on the computers. I was in the middle of that when I heard a clank from the kitchen. Heading that way, I found Cade leaning over the counter with his head in his hands while a cup of coffee brewed.

"You'll need to make one for everyone," I told him. "Someone's after Jeri."

He immediately jerked straight up. "Who?"

"No fucking clue, but he calls himself Vyrus and knows about the FBI. He named her, Cade. We gotta figure out who this is and how he found her."

"Which means calling Jason," Cade said, pulling his phone from his pocket. "Fuck, I didn't charge it, but I've got enough. Pretty sure Jeri's in my room with Knock." And he made a gesture like he was shooing me that way.

Damn it. I was still in my underwear, but fuck this shit. Heading for the master bedroom, I pounded on the door, but the only reply I got sounded something like, "fuck off." Since this couldn't wait, I turned the knob, somewhat surprised to find it unlocked, and stormed in.

"Up!" I demanded. "We have a problem, and I think it's a big one."

Jeri grumbled and rolled towards me, so I tossed her phone beside her. On the far side, Knock sat up, scrubbing at his face. Both of their hair was a mess. Something sparkled on Knock's cheek. The bed was past rumpled, but not completely trashed. All of it proved the pair had fucked each other's brains out last night - and yet that made me feel a little better.

"What am I looking for?" Jeri asked as she picked up her phone.

"Email. The one from unknown."

She tapped and swiped, then tilted the screen so Knock could read over her shoulder. For a moment, both of them were still, but I knew when they were done. Jeri's eyes slipped closed and she sighed in frustration, but Knock?

He threw off the blankets and headed for the closest dresser, not giving a shit that he was butt-ass naked. "We need Jason, and yesterday," he snapped.

"Cade's on it," I assured him.

"Computers on?" Jeri asked.

"Yep," I agreed. "Looks like you need some clothes, baby girl."

"I got some," Knock promised, tossing a pair of sweats and a t-shirt towards her.

"Bra and panties are in the pile, Hottie," she told me, pointing where she meant. "Gonna need those too."

I found them, feeling a little smile tease my lips at the reflective sparkles on them. Evidently, Jeri had gotten more glitter on her last night than I'd expected. And while I hated ruining her morning like this, I was not about to fuck around with any threats directed at her.

"Happy birthday, baby girl," I said as I carried them over. "I'm sorry to fuck up your birthday, but this can't wait."

"It's ok," she assured me, taking the lingerie. "I already had a good birthday."

"Good," I breathed, cupping her face so I could kiss her softly. "I just want to know why this fucker sent you a message this morning."

"Last night," Knock corrected. "The time on it was eleven p.m. Maybe someone fucking around on Halloween?"

"Or it auto-sent on her birthday," I countered. "That's midnight on the east coast, and I do not like the implications of them knowing this much about her."

"Soul Reaper posted my name," Jeri reminded me. "I mean, everyone else's too, it feels like, but I might not be the only one. Knock, see if Riley got anything?"

"Yep," he agreed.

Then Jeri looked at me. "Pants, Hottie. Pretty sure Knock's won't fit you. If this dumbass sent me an email, we'll find him."

"Sure it's a him?" Knock asked.

"Yeah, he types like a dude," Jeri said. "Short, lots of bitches and cunts. Not a full-on rant like a girl would have. Probably one of those leftover KoG fuckers."

"Who knows about our deal with the FBI?" I broke in. "Don't fucking think so. This isn't some low-level idiot, Jeri. This person knows shit they shouldn't know."

"Shit," she breathed. "I need a damned coffee."

Then she got out of bed and started pulling on clothes. I took the chance to run back upstairs to get some for myself. The damned balloons that had been so fun yesterday were now an obstruction, slowing me down when every fiber in my body was telling me to hurry. This couldn't wait. That it had been sent last night was bad enough, but if this fucker knew her name?

I couldn't do this. I couldn't lose Jeri the way I'd lost Nina. Getting bullied online was the sort of thing that seemed like nothing when it started, but it built up. It never quit. It would push her down, over and over, until she eventually broke. And considering we'd only just got her to relax again? No. I would not take any fucking chances.

When I finally made it back downstairs, the entire group was waiting. Jeri was reading the email to them, along with all the other important information, like how it was anonymous, the time it had been sent, and the perfect punctuation. I'd just dropped down behind my own computer when the front door opened.

"I'm here!" Jason called out.

"War room!" Jeri yelled back.

The sound of his dog's nails on the floor proved Crysis was on his way. A soft murmur of voices convinced me Jason wasn't alone, so when Zara followed him around the corner, I wasn't surprised. The woman looked us over, nodded, then turned for the kitchen.

"Garbage bags?" she asked.

"I'll show you," Zoe offered, heading that way from the other side of the computers.

But Zara clasped Jason's shoulder. "I'll get the party out of the way. You focus on work, ok?"

"Fuck, I love you," he said softly, leaning in to kiss her. "Thanks, babe." Then he turned to us. "I need to see it."

"Over here," Jeri said.

"I'm getting redirects all over," Jinxy said. "This fucker definitely used a VPN. Pretty sure the email server is Russian, too."

"Why Russian?" Jason asked.

"Because I'm bouncing all over Belarus, Ukraine, and Georgia. I'm not deep enough to see more yet, but pretty sure it's supposed to be dark."

"Russian botnet?" Knock asked.

"Can't rule it out," Jason said. "The comment about the FBI means this could be a governmental attack. What I want to know is why they sent it to you, Jeri."

"Happy birthday to me?" she asked with a shrug. "Or maybe it's because Soul Reaper called me out the same time he shit on Zara?"

"Over the summer!" Zara called from what sounded like the study.

"Did you get one, Zara?" I yelled.

"Nope!"

Well, that screwed up the theory about someone hitting all the women on Soul Reaper's list. "So this fucker might not be full of shit," I grumbled.

"Wait!" Zoe said, sliding back into the room through the archway from the kitchen. "Look at what he said, y'all!"

"So sure it's a man?" Jason asked.

Jeri groaned, but Zoe was nodding. "Types like a guy. Definitely a man." Then she gestured to Jeri. "Read it again?"

"I know who you are, Jericho Williams. I know all about your plan to become a consultant for the FBI. Who do you think has been dragging this shit through Congress? Me. I will never let this program happen, and yes, I do have the power to stop it. That's what happens when you're born with a dick you stupid sniveling bitch. Stay the fuck out of my world, you half-ass hacker cunt. From Vyrus," Jeri read.

"FBI consultant," Zoe said, ticking that off on her first finger.

"Congress." That was another finger. "Program, power to stop it, sniveling bitch. His world." She lifted a brow and looked around. "Y'all, this is someone with power. Like maybe in Congress, or working for someone there. Maybe FBI themselves?"

Jason went completely still. I noticed it, but Zoe had just made a lot of really good points. She'd called out all the words that didn't fit with the typical gamer slang. Whoever this person was, they used the *right* terms for what we were doing. They used words that weren't common, like sniveling. No one said that sort of shit.

"It's someone on the inside," I breathed.

"Shut it down," Jason said, his words cold as ice.

"Don't fucking think so," Cade told him. "No one comes at us and gets away with it."

"Shut. It. Down!" Jason demanded, storming over to close something on Jeri's computer. "This just became higher than your pay grade."

"Well, good thing we're hackers who don't give a shit," Jinxy told him.

"And right now, you all need to give a shit," Jason growled. "This? If Zoe's right, then this just became a real big fucking problem. Someone knows what team we're training up. They know *Ruin*, people. They know who all of you are, what we're doing, and will shut the entire program down, just like they threatened, so back the fuck off!"

"Wait, what?" Zara asked, coming around the corner to glare at her husband. "You're going to ignore someone going after Jericho?"

"No." He pushed his hand over his mouth. "I'm going to chase them. *I* have authorization. I came down for a little birthday party for some friends, and this is restricted information. *I'm* completely authorized to look into it, but they aren't."

"When have we ever given a shit about that?" I demanded. "They know her *fucking name,* Jason!"

"Yeah, sounds like they know a hell of a lot more than that. Jeri, what email address was it sent to?"

"My main," she admitted.

"Who has it?"

She opened her mouth, paused, then grabbed her phone. "Um, Amazon, most of my subscriptions, school, my friends, and my bills."

"And your name is unique enough to find it," he said. "Someone hacked something - one of those companies - and found Jericho. It's not exactly hard, but hiding their trail in Russian servers? That has me worried. For all we know, this is a test. This is someone looking for a reason to shut down the program before we can even get it started, so let me fucking handle it."

"Don't like it," I said, crossing my arms and leaning back. "That's my girlfriend you're talking about. I'm supposed to just pretend no one's fucking with her?"

"Shit," Jinxy said. "Bro, you good?"

"I'm not Nina," Jeri assured me. "And I'll even remove the email from my phone. You can check it, Hottie. I'll stay out of it, ok?"

"Because," Ripper said, leaning forward to push his face into his hands, "Jason's right. I fucking hate to admit it, but he is."

"I don't fucking care!" I snapped.

"But you should!" Ripper shot back, dropping his arms. "Did you hear what Zoe just said? The person who wrote that isn't a punk. That's not how hackers talk, Hot. That's CIA shit. That's Homeland. That's a hired professional, testing to see if our confidential informant contracts with Jason mean we're involved with this. Someone's trying to figure out *who* is being recruited so they can find an obstacle we can't get around. They're trying to shut us down, so we need to let Jason handle this."

"What if they're not?" Zoe asked.

"Then I'll still find them," Jason swore. "And when I do, I'll let you have them."

Jeri moved her mouse, clicked, and leaned closer to her monitor. "Guys, there's no threat to me. This prick goes on about the program. He never threatened to hurt me at all."

"Because," Ripper said, "that's a crime. Pretty sure a fed couldn't do that, right?"

"Mostly," Jason agreed. "There are times, but yeah. If this is on their own time, or as a favor, then no, they couldn't."

"Which means," Jeri said, standing up and making her way over to me, "we need to back off. Yeah, I fucking hate it, but you know what? Sometimes, doing nothing is the best way to fight back. They're taunting us to fuck up, so we don't fuck up."

"Jeri..." I tried.

"I'm fine, Hottie," she swore. "There is no threat of harming me. I don't know why they picked me, but whatever. Jason will figure it out, ok?"

"And I will," Jason swore.

Yet a little nudge against my elbow made me look down. Crysis was sitting beside me, waiting. He was just starting to fidget, though. Pushing back my chair, I made room for him, then called the dog into my lap.

"I'm ok, buddy," I told the dog, petting him enthusiastically. "Only a little triggered."

Zara just leaned in to bump her shoulder against Jason's. "He's babysitting them too, huh?"

"He likes them," Jason admitted. "Kinda why I won't let anyone fuck with them."

"Ok." She turned to us. "There's a lot of balloons that need to be popped, since they're all tied. That's called stress relief. I'm going to take Jason back to Riley's where he can chase this down without drawing attention, ok? But we don't leave until tonight."

"And stay the fuck out of this," Jason said yet again. "Eat some fucking cake and play Flawed or something."

"Because," Jeri said, "it's officially my birthday now. I'm not letting this fucker screw it up."

But I caught when she looked over and met Jason's eyes. He dipped his head slightly, and something passed between them. I wasn't sure what it was, but I could guess.

That man had made her a promise. She was holding him to it.

# CHAPTER 44

## CADE

Sunday sucked. From waking up in a panic to the hangover that just would not give up. Hearing about how Knock had spent the night loving Jeri, however, was amazing. The way he smiled so brightly as he told me about it? The little touches when he explained his feelings for her? It was enough to convince me passing out on the couch had been a good thing.

Not that I'd mind being in the middle of that, but they needed time together too. Sometimes I felt like I was stealing all of Knock's attention, since we shared a room. Jeri always said it wasn't a big deal, but still. Then again, Hottie snuck into her room to sleep most nights, so their situation was almost the same.

I just felt bad for Ripper. Living up on the third floor, it was like he got less alone time with Jeri, but he always said it was ok. He got to talk to her. She had no problem throwing him into bed and having her way with him. Ripper swore it was all good, and I actually believed him. The guy just wasn't quite as horny as the rest of us, it seemed. He liked the sweet shit with her, and she definitely gave him that.

But when my alarm went off Monday morning, I stretched just enough to shut that shit off. Knock's went off a moment later, and he sat up. I didn't. Nope, I knew exactly what day today was.

"Skipping class?" he asked.

"Mhm," I mumbled into my pillow. "Gotta take care of Jeri."

Which made Knock's head twitch. "Huh?"

"It's the day after her birthday, babe," I reminded him. "The anniversary of her dad, you know? She once said today sucked, so I thought I'd distract her, and I'm pretty sure she's not going to make it to class."

"Yeah, good plan," he said. "Need help?"

"I think too much will freak her out." So I shifted to put my foot against his ass, and pushed. "So get out of bed."

"Fucker," he grumbled, but he did stand up.

Then he ran a hand through his hair, sending those blue locks out in every direction. Damn, he was sexy when he was half asleep. I could also see the red lines behind his shoulders where Jeri had clearly been a bit too enthusiastic. She hadn't broken skin, but she'd still left her mark. It kinda made me think things had been pretty wild in here that night.

Pulling the covers up over my shoulders, I snuggled back into bed and watched my boyfriend get ready for class. It was the little things like this which made me so happy. Him, her, them. It didn't even matter. From the game we'd made of cleaning up the house - although I was pretty sure there was still glitter in the carpets - to the lazy moments we could share, I found myself truly, completely, and totally happy.

And that happiness was about to come crashing down. My plan for today was to distract Jeri, but that was not the same as making her happy. I just wanted to make sure she knew she wasn't alone. That she didn't have to constantly think about the bad shit. That the past might suck, but the present was actually pretty damned good, all things considered.

Except this Vyrus fucker had thrown a wrench in my plans. All seven of us had agreed to stay away from that email. We'd promised we wouldn't hunt down the asshole until Jason said something - or it got worse. None of us liked it, though.

But for this to happen now? When she would be at her most vulnerable? It made me wonder if this dick knew more than he'd let on. Granted, her father's death was public record. I'd found his obituary online, so anyone could. And if Ripper was right and the sender was CIA? He'd definitely know that shit about her.

Which meant she'd been picked because she was the one who might crack.

If Jeri got pissed and went after Vyrus, it would prove we were the hackers he assumed. If he was waiting, he could catch her, get proof of her committing cybercrimes which would disqualify us, and then the whole thing with the FBI would be fucked. There was no way a politician would greenlight a project with hackers who hit the United States government, or whatever spin they'd put on it.

Somewhere in there, I fell back asleep. Knock didn't even wake me up for a kiss before sneaking out. While I appreciated that, the sound of Zoe leaving was enough to remind me I had plans. So, dragging my lazy ass out of bed, I got dressed, then headed into the kitchen to get myself some go-juice.

Full coffee in hand, I then went to log into Flawed. Seeing some rainbow sparkles shining in the morning sunlight made me chuckle. Those assholes. I wasn't sure whose idea it had been to glitter-bomb our house with the poppers, but that shit was never going to go away now.

But Flawed was dead at this time of day. Most people were either at work or school. I decided that meant I should do the most popular quests and get a little extra experience built up for our next raid. I hadn't been playing this character long enough to have the buffer I did on my old one, but I preferred my new guild.

I was in the middle of killing some supermodels when Hottie

looked in from the kitchen side. "Cade?" he asked, sounding confused. "Aren't you supposed to be in class?"

"Skipping," I explained.

His eyes narrowed. "Why?"

"For Jeri."

He nodded. "Same. Jinxy's getting notes for me."

"And Jeri?" I asked.

He vanished for a moment, then returned with a coffee cup of his own. "She's still sleeping. I canceled her alarm last night, will say I must've disabled it when I saw the email from Vyrus, and take the blame. If no one disturbs her, she should sleep until well after noon."

"Nice."

"So how are we distracting her?" he asked.

"PvP," I said. "It's been a while since she and I have gone head-to-head, so..."

"Good plan." He moved closer. "And what about this Vyrus guy?"

I hit a button to send my character back to a safe place, then turned my chair so I was facing him. "I think they targeted Jeri because she's the reactive one."

"How would they know?"

Lucky for me, I'd been thinking about it this morning, so I actually had an answer. "Her dad's death is public. Her trauma is out there, Hottie. She's got enough online presence to make it clear she's got an attitude. I mean, just look at the Flawed forums!"

"Ok, good point," he agreed.

"And I'm going to bet you, Jinxy, and even Knock are all chill when it comes to that shit, right?"

"Fuck," Hottie grumbled. "And the stream. I used to do Twitch stuff. She was in the chat, and she can rant when we're losing."

"Hot-headed," I pointed out. "So it wouldn't take a lot of research to figure that out. If it's someone from CIA or such, they'd be able to check all of us. Knock and I got kicked out. You and Jinxy are foster kids, basically. You both have degrees, though. Ripper? He's a ghost.

The guy has nothing out there to implicate him. Zoe? She's a victim, and that might be a line too far, you know?"

"But Jeri's not?" Hottie asked.

"She's loud, she's reactive, and it's a memorable day where she'll be vulnerable. The email didn't say shit about her dad, but the timing? She'll already be stressed, so it's more likely she'll lash out. If they had to pick one of us, it makes sense to hit her and get her to go off, proving their theory."

Hottie just murmured. I couldn't tell if he agreed or was mulling it over, but the attack made sense to me. No personal threat, no violence mentioned, and right on Jeri's birthday. If we were any other hacker group, it would be a time she'd be alone, likely drunk or high, and able to pull some stupid shit.

"It just bothers me that someone with so much power is poking us," Hottie finally said.

"Huh?"

"If the theory is right, and this person does have that high of clearance, then why are they testing us? They aren't supposed to *know* about us, Cade. And worse, testing Jeri? Something about this isn't sitting right with me."

"Politicians pull strings," I countered. "Fuck, Hottie, that's how they do all their shit. And getting 'proof' they can use to shut us down, then bragging about saving government money? Like, that's a pretty standard play."

He simply murmured again, but this time it sounded more annoyed. "I won't let them screw up her life. That's the only reason I'm not hunting that fucker down. I will not let her lose anything else."

I nodded. "Yeah. Trust me, I want to hack the fuck out of them, but I know I'd drag it back here. Not my area of expertise, but I still feel it."

"You're better than you know," he assured me. "And if you happen to head upstairs and give her someone to cuddle with, I'll make myself scarce."

I jerked my chin at him. "What happened to not waking her up?"

"Just realized you're right. She *is* vulnerable, and maybe waking up nicely will be a distraction." He pulled in a big breath, then let it all out in a rush. "And I can't. I'm too worried about this, too triggered by how close it is to Nina. Cade, that's why we all work, because when I'm about to fuck shit up, someone else can make it better, so I dunno. Go make it better?"

I stood and clasped his shoulder. "You're a good man, Hottie. I'll take care of her."

"Yeah, I know," he replied. "And that's the craziest thing. I honestly know that."

I headed for the stairs, but his words? They made me feel better. More manly? No, that wasn't it. They made me feel like I was a good man, though. Like I'd turned out to be something I should be proud of. I wasn't completely convinced I'd made it that far, but hearing Hottie say that? It was a lot nicer than I'd expected.

But when I entered Jeri's room, she was still sleeping. As quietly as I could, I made my way around the bed, then slipped in behind her. The moment my arm moved around her waist, she stirred, shifting back to press into me.

Then she sucked in a breath and looked back. "Cade?"

"We're skipping school together today," I told her. "And I've got big plans for some PvP, ok?"

Rubbing at her eyes, she rolled to face me, then pressed in close enough to bury her head in my chest. "Are you spoiling me?"

"I'm sure as shit trying," I admitted.

"It's working," she breathed, sliding her hands down, under my shirt, and then up and around my back. "I'm supposed to pretend like today is no big deal, though."

Immediately, all of my big plans shattered. Gently, I eased her hair back so I could see her face. Jeri's eyes were still closed, and she was only barely awake, but this beautiful woman was vulnerable right now. It was a state I'd never seen on her before and I fucking hated it.

"Jeri, you don't have to lie about it to make me feel better. I can't imagine how shitty this is, but I'm here because I didn't want you to be alone, ok?"

Her lashes flickered, and then her eyes opened. "Yeah?"

"Yell, cry, or anything else," I said softly. "Ignore it, talk about it, or have a fucking meltdown. I don't care, but you do *not* have to put on a fake smile so my fucking male feelings will be fine."

Her brow pinched, and I watched as her eyes jumped between both of mine, trying to settle. "Oh."

"Oh?" I asked.

"You made your point with the male feelings." Then she scooted up just a bit more, putting our faces even. "You know, I knew you were a good guy, Cade. Even when you were being an asshole, there was something about you that kept me from writing you off."

"What thing?"

She shrugged. "I dunno, but it's the same thing that made you skip class for me. I also really like the PvP idea. I don't want to think about it, ok? Fuck Dad for doing that to me. Fuck him for thinking the day after my birthday would make it ok. This is my time to be happy, and I'm done with keeping everyone at arm's length. I'm fucking done with, I dunno, this bullshit."

"Feelings aren't bullshit, baby," I countered. "They're what make me love you."

She paused so intensely her entire body stilled. Her eyes were locked on something I couldn't see, but it convinced me her mind was working. Slowly, one corner of her mouth began to lift a bit higher. It wasn't a smile, but it was getting there.

"Cade, I'm kinda a mess."

"Same," I agreed.

"And that's the thing." Her hands moved against my back. "You make me feel like it's ok. Hottie makes me feel safe. Knock makes me feel grounded, in a way - "

"Because he's so calm about the bad shit," I broke in. "Yeah, I get that. He never cracks under pressure."

"I know!" she huffed, clearly more awake now. "And Ripper's the nicest, kindest, most considerate guy ever. But you? You are a fuckup. I don't mean that in a bad way. I mean you don't give a shit, make it look good, and you kinda have this little swagger like you're hot shit, and I adore it. You fuck it up, don't give a damn, and it's different when I see you do it than when I try."

"But those things are why I dumped Tiffany so I could ask you out," I admitted. "Jeri, from the moment I saw you in the hall at school, it was like the air had been stolen from my lungs. There was something about you, and that give-no-fucks attitude? The bitching me out? All of it made me want to try more, because you might be a fuckup, or a mess, or whatever else we call ourselves, but it just makes you more amazing. Laughing, screaming, and even crying - although I've never seen that. It makes me feel like..."

"Like it's ok to not be ok?" she offered.

"Yeah," I breathed. "Just like that."

"Good," she said, stretching a bit more to find my mouth. "Because I know a very good way to forget today's supposed to be shit."

When she kissed me again, she also pulled, lifting my shirt higher. Well, I'd decided to make today all about her, so I'd follow her lead. If we cuddled, then we did. If we fucked, then I was ok with that. And if we fell back asleep, then that was allowed as well.

Because for once, Jericho didn't have to pretend for anyone else. I was going to spoil her in the only way I knew how, by being here for her. Completely here. All for her.

# CHAPTER 45

### JERICHO

Strangely enough, skipping class was good for me. I didn't realize it until I went back on Tuesday, though. Yet there was some freedom in slacking off and not getting in shit that removed a bit of the pressure I'd been heaping on myself. Spending time with my guys? That made it even better.

Tiffany showed up Monday afternoon, or so I was told. I was in my bedroom, being a sulky bitch, so I missed her. But on Tuesday, she brought me flowers. They were in a little glass vase with two stick balloons that said "Happy Birthday" and "Get Well." Evidently they didn't have "Give no fucks" as an option, she said.

For Knock, she got a t-shirt that said "Over The Hill" on it. The thing was black, perfectly his size - as in it fit instead of hung on him - and I approved. Tiffany said she was sorry, but somehow *no one* had told her it was our birthday weekend. Evidently, in the chaos, we'd completely forgotten, and since we did training on the weekends, she'd just assumed everything was normal.

But realizing I didn't have to constantly bust my ass? That was nice. Yes, I still had to study, and a few of my classes had some insane amounts of homework, but I really did have this. I was currently making A's in all but one of my classes, and that was a high B.

The FBI shit was a different story. Wednesday, Jason sent us all two more books, plus a list of what we'd need to know or prove proficiency in before we'd get approved. Apparently Congress was at it again, trying to up the difficulty level. And while he only said he was working on the email, I had a feeling the timing of this new heap of shit was a little too coincidental.

Thankfully, Tiffany was all-in. By Thursday, she had a new set of flashcards for us. Each subject was in a different color, and she had everything covered. Then, she turned it into a competition between us. Tiffany would shuffle all the flashcards together, hold one up, and whoever answered first - correctly - got a point. The person with the most points didn't have to cook dinner.

It was a stupid game, and the reward was nothing, but it gave us just enough of a reason to actually try. Even better, since we went through the cards more than once, screwing up an answer meant it would most likely stick the next time. In other words, Tiff was a damned genius.

That was why we were cramming Friday evening. Jason had dumped *two* new subjects on us and basically doubled our homework for the week, and none of us wanted to let him down. Tiffany was sitting on the couch, lifting the cards, and all seven of us tried to call out an answer first.

"Firing pin!" I yelled.

"Clip release!" Cade said at the same time.

"Shit," Zoe grumbled. "I was going to say that."

Tiffany just pointed at Cade. "That's the clip release, Jeri. The firing pin is on the inside. It strikes the bullet."

"Fuck," I groaned. "Why do we need to know the parts of the gun? I mean, it's not like - "

"You will be expected to clean your weapons," Jason said as he rounded the corner. "Once you are..." His words trailed off as his eyes landed on Tiffany. "Who are you?"

"Where's Crysis?" I asked, since his dog typically announced Jason's arrival.

"Out back. He needed to potty." Then he crossed his arms. "Who is she, Jericho?"

"Hi," Tiffany said. "Um, I'm Tiffany."

"And why the fuck is she here?" Jason growled, his eyes locked right on me.

"That's my fault," Cade said. "I asked her if she'd help me study."

"*No one* is supposed to know about this shit!" Jason snapped.

"I'm sorry," Tiffany said, gathering up the flashcards and trying to put them in a pile. "I didn't mean to get anyone in trouble."

"How much do you know, girl?" Jason demanded, turning his cold grey-green eyes on her.

"Uh..."

"Back the fuck off!" I yelled, shoving to my feet. "She's here to help us, and she doesn't have to."

"And no one is supposed to know!" he said again.

Which was when Crysis woofed at the back door. Snarling in frustration, Jason stormed that way to let the dog in. Immediately, Crysis jumped up, licking at Jason's hands and trying to reach higher. Over and over, he made a production of wanting attention, refusing to quit until Jason bent down and ruffled the dog's fur.

"I'm ok, buddy."

"You are losing your fucking shit," I countered.

Which made him turn and glare at me. "Because I was clear. This is top-secret, Jericho. This is the sort of thing we don't brag about at school. This is not something you're doing to be cool, and now you've been - "

"Fuck off!" I yelled, interrupting him. "She knows, ok? Tiffany knows all of it, and she's fucking smart. She knows how to cram, and she's gone out of her way to help us. She. Didn't. Have. To."

"Because it sounds cool, huh?" he asked. "Oh, look. I'm hanging out with people who can do shit. I can just brag about these fucking hackers I know. I can tell everyone their real names, what they go by online, and make sure *you are not fucking safe at home anymore*!"

"No, I wouldn't," Tiffany breathed.

"Hey, hey, it's ok," Cade said, moving to sit between her and Jason.

Ripper claimed the spot on her other side. Zoe stood up, crossing her arms and glaring at Jason, while Hottie and Jinxy merely moved the flashcards and study materials out of everyone's way. When Ripper wrapped his arms around Tiff's shoulders, I felt something burning inside me that was a little too hot: rage.

"You do *not* come into our house and bitch at the ones on our side," I growled, storming towards him. "You do not lash out at her for doing a nice thing. You sure as shit do not *yell* at a woman under this roof because you have no fucking idea what she's been through! Do you fucking hear me, Jason?"

His brows went up. "Ok..."

So I stabbed a finger at the ground. "This is Ruin. This is how we work. Yeah, we trust her, and you know why? Because Tiff has proven herself, but if you want to act like a fucking titty-baby, then fine. Have your fit, but you fucking yell at *me*, because I'm the one who said she was fine."

"Well..." Zoe said.

"In your car," I reminded her. "I said we'd help. I never took it back, and she kept her word."

"With. What?" Jason asked, moving closer.

Crysis whined, pushing himself between us. We were now standing face to face, one ninety-pound-dog width between us, and both refusing to back down. And while Jason might not be a tall man, or a broad one, there was something so alien about him that I felt a chill run down my spine.

I still wouldn't back down.

"With Evan," I said. "With Dylan. Oh, and when the Alpha Team caught me alone at my car last year, you know what kept them from beating the shit out of me, raping me, or even killing me?" I thrust an arm back to point at the couch. "That girl."

"The bitch squad," Hottie clarified.

"There's more than one?" Jason asked, fury rippling across his words.

"Not anymore," Zoe said. "Well, no, but kinda? Like, they knew about the rapes."

Which made me lift my chin. "You aren't the only damned hero in the world. Some of us are just normal fuckers trying to figure it out as we go, and she did a damned good job."

"I haven't cleared her," he said, finally lowering his volume.

"Then clear her." I lifted my chin. "She's not leaving."

"How long has she known?"

"Since she helped me steal Evan's phone."

Jason just sighed, dropped his head, and pressed a hand over his face. "Fuck."

"Oh, don't give me that shit."

"This is a goddamn mess, Jeri."

"And?" I flopped my arms out. "Of course it fucking is. We're hackers, Jason. We fucking break the rules. Now, tell me. What part of that sounds like I'm going to ask your fucking permission before doing shit, huh? Oh, should I suddenly become a little bitch, unable to make any decisions on my own without you here to spoon-feed them to me? Is that what you want? Because if so, you have a whole fucking bureau of them back at the FBI. I think that's the Cybersecurity division, hm?"

"And Counterterrorism," Tiffany mumbled. "They do online stuff too."

"Fuck!" Jason yelled, turning to storm out of the room.

"Sorry!" Tiffany whimpered.

"You're fine," I assured her, even as I followed Jason. "Guys, make sure she's good?"

Jason made it all the way to the war room, then turned in, but that was it - because I almost ran into him when I rounded the corner. The man was there, clearly waiting for me. His hand caught my arm, holding me in place.

"No one is supposed to know, Jeri," he hissed. "Congress wants to shut this shit down. That email? Yeah, I fucking got blocked when I hit a Pentagon-level firewall! That means it came from us, Jeri. From the fucking U.S. government!"

"So find the vulnerability in the firewall, get past it, and get me a fucking name!" I shot back.

"I can't."

I huffed in astonishment. "You fucking taught us how!"

"No." He paused for a moment, then exhaled, pushing his breath out in a rush. "I could, but I'd likely be traced, and that would tip our hand. Instead, I asked Alex to get an email address to go with the data I have. She has the authority to request it through proper channels without fucking this up. It's going to take a little longer, but it won't expose you."

"Because you think this is a test to see if Ruin is your team?" I asked.

He nodded. "Looks that way. I can't be sure, but all signs are supporting Ripper's theory. There are only three places that have this level of a security lock on them: the White House, Congress, and the Pentagon. Basically, the top tiers of our federal government."

"Fuck."

"Yeah," he agreed. "Someone's playing games. They think you're all so fucking stupid, you'll walk into the mousetrap because of the hunk of cheese." Then he gestured back towards the living room. "And that? That's a fucking leak waiting to happen."

"No," I said calmly. "That is Tiffany Bowen, freshman at the University of North Texas. Jason, she helped me get Evan's phone. She didn't have a fucking clue what we were doing, but she accidentally interrupted, then went out of her way to distract him. She knew I stole his phone, but she didn't say shit because Zoe deserved the justice. It's also why she told me about the other girls."

"The blackmail?" he asked.

I nodded. "She asked us to help because we helped Zoe. She was trying to cover for her friends. Now here's the big thing. Tiffany wasn't dating them. Yeah, Dylan told her he could get to her, but she wasn't being directly blackmailed. She was just helping her friends. You know, kinda like Riley helping you last year."

"Low blow," he said, but his anger was pretty much gone. "Riley was vetted, and she was a victim."

"Shit," I laughed. "Riley is never a victim. A target, maybe, but she's not a victim. Neither is Tiff. She's a fucking bitch, she's brilliant, and you know what? She's *loyal*."

"And she knows your secrets," he pointed out.

"Yep," I agreed. "She also fucked Cade. All the rules say I should hate her. She's supposed to be my competition, right? Well, we tried that and realized it's dumb shit, so we joined forces. Wanna know how that's going?" I jerked my chin at him. "Ask me a question about the shit you just gave us. Go ahead."

"When does law enforcement use fingerprint evidence?" he tossed out.

I smiled. "In cases where there's limited chance of a witness or video. Fingerprint evidence is not only unreliable, but often discarded as circumstantial. DNA is the preferred form of evidence, if possible."

He chuckled once. "Two days, huh? She's that much help?"

"Yeah," I said, "she really is. Jason, she already knows about Ruin. She's already in up to her eyeballs. All her friends went away to other schools, and she's fucking good at this. She knows how to make this shit actually stick in our heads instead of turning into a jumble of too much, too fast."

"Well, I can't make her forget, and I can't kill her..." One corner of his mouth flicked up, proving that was mostly a joke.

"No shooting my friends, Jason."

He just sighed. "Ok, but I want to at least talk to her. Is that allowed?"

"Can I stop you?"

"Not really, no," he admitted before reaching out to rub my arm. "But I'm proud of you for pushing back."

And I felt like the air rushed from my lungs. That was not at all what I'd expected him to say! I'd been braced for a lecture about the dangers or something, but proud? Jason was proud of me?

"Really?" I asked.

He nodded slowly. "I don't want you to be my 'little bitch,' unable to make decisions for yourself. I picked you, Jericho, because you fight. I like that you fight, and yeah, I'm fucking proud of the fact you never back down when you know you're right." Those cold eyes of his softened a bit. "Because here's the thing. I'm starting to realize you usually are. So yes, I'm damned fucking proud of you."

"So maybe you'll even be nice to her?" I tried.

He actually laughed. "Don't push it, kid."

# CHAPTER 46

## CADE

From the moment Jason walked into the room, the tension shot through the roof. Tiff could tell something was wrong, but we didn't get the chance to explain who this man was before he started yelling about her being here. I wanted to shield her a bit, so I moved to sit on the couch between her and Jason. Ripper moved to the other side, and then Zoe placed her body between us.

But it was Jeri who was willing to throw down about this. The way she stormed into Jason's face, I wasn't sure if they were going to start slinging punches at each other, but the words were bad enough. Hell, the simple fact Crysis was trying to make them stop said more than I wanted to admit.

Then Jason left. Jeri followed. Immediately, I turned to Tiff, checking to make sure she was ok. Ripper had his arm around her shoulders and she was leaning into him a bit. Her eyes were wide, but she didn't look scared. Not exactly. Shocked was probably a better word.

"They'll sort it out," I assured her, "but I'm sure you really want to get out of here now, huh?"

"I do not want to walk past that!" she said, gesturing to where Jeri and Cyn could be heard in the other room.

"Take her upstairs," Jinxy offered.

"Or how about around the house?" I suggested, standing and then offering Tiff a hand up. "Zoe, when they come back, let them know I snuck her out?"

"Can do," Zoe promised before reaching over to clasp Tiff's arm. "It's ok. His bark is worse than his bite."

"It's really not," Knock said almost regretfully. "He's just a little single-minded."

"It's ok," Tiff said. "I mean, I get it. This shit is a big deal, I'm not on the approved list, and y'all just got busted. I hope I didn't get you in too much trouble."

"You're fine," I assured her, finding her hand to tow her towards the back door.

Tiff followed, but I could feel the tension in her. So, once we were on the other side of the pool, I turned to face her. She'd glanced back again, looking through the massive windows that made up the living room wall.

"How bad is this going to be for you?" she asked.

"Jeri will put him in his place," I assured her. "And you've been so much help. Fuck it if Jason doesn't like it."

"But he's, like, an agent, right? Actually with the FBI?"

"Uh, yeah..." Which was when I realized we hadn't exactly explained who this guy was. "Tiff, um, he's a special agent, and technically our handler. See, when we were doing that shit to bust Dylan? Jason got us confidential informant agreements. They came a bit late for busting Dylan, but there was some other shit over the summer too, and we were all kinda wrapped up in it."

"What kind of shit?" she asked.

"Knock's sister almost got killed."

She started to nod, paused, blinked, and then tried to finish the gesture. "Um, ok." Then she huffed, clearly at a loss for word. "Fuck, Cade. That's..."

"Intense?" I offered. "Trust me, we know. Jeri and the guys basically saved them. One of those guys was Jason. See, he kinda took the shot that killed the guy holding the gun."

"Holy shit," she breathed.

"He's a hacker and a sniper, and he's damned good at both. That's why he was assigned to the Kings of Gaming case. And Dylan kinda dragged all of us in. Well, plus Riley and her mess, which - ok, this is not getting easier to follow, is it?"

"Riley was targeted by those fuckers too," Tiffany said. "Knock was helping his family, Ruin was helping us girls at school, and there was some crossover, right? Kinda like all the incel bullshit? One leader and a fucking million and one followers all wanting to fuck with any girl he can?"

Laughing, I ducked my head. "And this is why we didn't work as a couple."

"Why?" she asked. Then she lifted her hand, holding me off. "Don't get me wrong, I agree we were bad, but I'm curious why you think so."

"Because you're too damned smart to be with a guy like me," I explained. "Tiff, you're the professional. You're the one who should be wearing the suit here. I'm the one who gets his hands dirty, cusses like a sailor, and does the grunt work."

She stepped closer, her hand moving to press against my chest. "Cade, that's... Ok, I mean, you're wrong. You're also kinda right."

"See?" I teased.

"You're wrong because you don't see what you do with these people as being a big deal, but it is. The shit y'all pulled off last year? Fucking amazing. The way you played Dylan and Evan, and put yourself out there to get hit how many times? I mean, you're the meat, right? Or, um... what do you call it in your game?"

"Tank," I corrected. "And I'd really rather not be, but yeah. I'd rather they hit me than Ripper."

"What about Jeri?" she asked.

I rocked my head from side to side. "Ok, maybe? I mean, I'd rather no one hit her, but at least with Jeri, I know she'd do some damage back. Ripper's just sweet, and Zoe's too gentle. Hottie could throw down, Knock would if he had to, and I'm not sure about Jinxy. Jeri? She'd make them bleed."

"That," she said, patting my chest. "See, I've been trying to figure out why I always want to come over and hang out. Why I actually enjoy helping all of you study for something I have no business sticking my nose in. But I do, and when you said the thing about the suit?"

"That you're the one who belongs in a suit?" I asked.

She nodded slowly. "You say it like it's no big deal. You didn't say I'm wearing the pants, or taking your balls, or the real man here. You didn't try to make me feel like shit for having goals, Cade. You make it sound like a good thing. I dunno, like you respect me for chasing down the shit I want, even if that's just a damned accounting degree."

"Because I do," I admitted. "Tiff, that's why I even considered dating you to begin with. Don't get me wrong. You're beautiful, but not my kind of beautiful, if you know what I mean."

"You seem to have a thing for neon hair and bad attitudes," she teased.

"And your attitude is just a little too polished to get me going," I admitted. "That's not a bad thing, and I didn't even realize it back then. It's just..."

"You like the punks." She chuckled. "Cade, that's fine. I mean, isn't that what dating in high school is for? It's how we figure out what we like and don't like. But the thing I realized? I like friends who don't expect me to be the pretty little princess all the time. I like showing up without makeup and no one cares. I like baggy pants and comfortable clothes." She made a little noise, then shrugged. "I also like dressing up sometimes, but I fucking hate being treated like I'm just something to fuck, and none of you do that to me."

"Because you're so much more than that," I assured her. "Jesus, Tiff. Look at the flashcards! You figured out how to manipulate the seven of us into speed-memorizing this shit. You've been a godsend, ok? And I don't care if Jason likes it or not. If you still want to come hang out, then I'm sure the entire house is down for it."

"So I'm not banished because we got busted?"

"Nope," I promised. "I mean, you already know everything."

"Not everything," she admitted. "I'm also trying really hard not to push, but it kinda feels like there's a reason y'all are trying to do all of this, and I'm thinking a paycheck isn't it."

"Busted."

"What part am I not supposed to know?" she asked. "The motivations or the people you want to chase down?"

"Um, kinda both?"

She just smiled. "Then I don't know a damned thing. And thanks."

That made me pause. "For?"

She gestured back at the house. "For shielding me from the crazy guy I've never met before. For not being weird when Ripper was being nice. I dunno, Cade. For being a friend and not a shitty ex? For being a fucking amazing man who I actually respect?"

I could feel this warmth trying to take over my face, so I had to deflect. "I'll have you know I'm a taken man, Tiff. Your overly polite compliments will not make me succumb."

"And what do you think you're succumbing to?" she teased.

Oh yeah, I was full on blushing now. I could feel it. "And I've failed," I admitted, reaching up to rub the redness away.

She just laughed and jerked her thumb towards the side of the house. "Is this the way out?"

"Yeah." I turned, placing my hand between her shoulders to guide her that way. "And you should turn some of those compliments on Ripper. Did you know he thinks he's fat?"

"Ripper?" She gaped at me. "I mean, he's cuddly, but I would not call him fat. Maybe pudgy last year, but I think he's like two inches taller."

"At least." We reached the side, so I stepped ahead to get the gate. "But he was trying a diet thing, and he just sees himself as the dork Dylan tormented."

"Because that's what bullying does," Tiff said. "Damn it. That's why Jeri was so pissed about it. Ok, I'll make sure he figures it out, but can you make sure Jeri's cool with it? She told me she doesn't care, and Zoe says she doesn't have any jealousy, but I do not want her to think I'm hitting on her boyfriends. We kinda have a girl pact."

"Do I even want to know?"

She paused to avoid a pothole in the side yard as we made our way around to the front. "Hoes before bros?" She laughed. "I mean, that's basically it, but in the worst way possible. No poaching boyfriends, no screwing each other over, and no letting men mess up our friendship."

"Kinda think that should apply to all of Ruin," I said, liking the concept. "I mean, and you, but it's just a good... Fuck. I'm being a dork again."

"You're cute when you're a dork," she assured me, pausing on the driveway to clasp my arm. "Cade, be cute. Be a dork. Stop trying to fit into a mold made by your dad and the asshole boys at school. They were fucking rapists, and your dad's a piece of shit. These guys? They're the kind of men women really want."

"Like Hottie?"

Because I knew he was hot. He was ripped, gorgeous, smart, and had this attitude that just dripped sex appeal at times. I'd also heard enough people comment about him to know he was the man in the house most likely to be called the hot one.

"Like Ripper," Tiffany corrected. "Cade, beauty is in the eye of the beholder. Women like dad bods, chunky bods, skinny bods, and so much more - when it comes with kindness. We like honesty and gentleness. We like men who aren't fucking evil, ok? We like men who don't look at us and see something to put their dicks in, but rather guys who realize we have thoughts, feelings, opinions, and even personal goals. We like men who see us as people first and beautiful second."

"Which explains the suit comment," I realized. "Ok. That makes sense."

"And your entire house is like that," she said. "It's why I want to be here, not talking to the fucking assholes on campus. The dicks from the parties and shit. They look at me and hand me a drink, thinking I'll get tipsy and then horny. Or whatever they think. But they don't give a shit about *me*. They don't want to know me."

"Which is why you're helping us?"

"Yeah," she breathed, ducking her head. "It's stupid."

"Not to me."

"I don't miss having a boyfriend," she explained. "Cade, you were the last guy I dated. It's been a fucking year, and I don't feel like I'm missing out. I don't want to just fuck someone because it's expected. I don't want to giggle the right way to make him notice me, or bat my lashes, or do any of that shit. I don't want to worry about if I'm going to be good enough for him. I want to fucking worry about if I'm good enough for *me*, and it's like..." She flopped her arms. "Everyone in this house treats me like me. Not like the pretty girl, or the cool girl, or the smart girl, or the way to pass their classes. I know I'm helping with that, but it's because y'all don't act like it's all I'm good for!"

"That's called friendship, Tiff."

"Yeah," she agreed. "And most people are doing it fucking wrong. Kinda why - "

The front door opened, and Jason came storming out. "Tiffany?"

"Shit," I grumbled. "She's leaving, Jason."

"No," he said, "she's not." He reached up and pushed back his hair, almost like he was trying not to look intimidating. "I mean, she doesn't have to." Then his strange eyes shifted over to her. "I'd just like to talk to you for a moment, if that's ok?"

"Uh..." She turned to look at me as if seeking a hint.

But Jason spoke up before I could. "Jeri made it clear you're welcome here. I just want to talk about what needs to stay secret."

"And you can walk if he's a dick," I assured her. "Promise, Tiff. He's legally bound and shit."

"Kinda am," Jason agreed, lifting a hand towards the front door. "I also don't bite."

Tiff huffed at that, but headed towards the house. "No, you just growl, right?" Then she lifted her head, straightened her spine, and pushed past him like the serious bitch I'd come to respect so damned much.

"Don't fuck with her, Jason," I warned. "She can hold her own."

"Kinda what Jeri said," he agreed, turning to follow her. "But you need to get me a complete profile on her. Like yesterday."

Fuck.

# CHAPTER 47

## TIFFANY

Jason caught up to me by the time I reached the front door, then gestured for me to head into the study. I could feel my guts clenching with nerves, but I ignored it. Instead, I gave him the same sweet smile that had worked on all my teachers and claimed one of the chairs. He took a corner of the sofa.

Then he looked me over. Something about this guy was off a bit. His gaze was creepy, but not in a perverted way. This was more like what I imagined a psychopomp would look like when weighing a soul. Death, Charon, or whichever version of the guide to the afterlife one picked, they'd have eyes like this man.

Like he was deciding my fate.

"You wanted to talk?" I asked, deciding to give him a little nudge.

A little smile touched his mouth. "Yeah. I wanna know why you're helping them study."

"Because they're my friends."

"Mm." He leaned back, but those eyes were even more intense. "So tell me what you know, because they weren't supposed to say shit."

Great. He'd just put me in a position to rat out my friends or piss him off. And yet, the way his eyes narrowed made me think this was some sort of test. Well, too bad for him, I knew how to deal with creepy older men.

I shifted to the side, bracing my forearm on the arm of the chair. Then I crossed my legs, glad I was wearing jeans today instead of sweats. For a little too long, I held his eyes, then smiled and looked away.

"I know you're with the FBI. I know they have to learn some stuff from books, and they're all worried they won't remember it. I also know how to organize a group study, because a few of my friends last year needed help. They kinda had other things to worry about."

The man didn't even blink. His eyes never dropped down my body. He checked my hands, he watched my face, but he didn't ogle me like I'd expected.

"You're holding back," he said calmly.

Which made me huff out a laugh. "Duh. See, that's what happens when you try to catch me in the middle. I can piss you off, or them, right? Well, hate to break it to you, hot stuff, but you're the least important one in this house."

"Crysis!" Jason snapped.

A clattering of claws made it clear the dog was hurrying. I could only imagine Crysis was his name. He was huge, looked like some kind of brindle-and-white spotted pit bull thing, and acted like he knew his way around the house as well as I did.

But when the dog loped into the room, he headed straight for Jason. The man's brow creased for a moment, but then he actually smiled. Bending to pet the dog, he looked at me again, but this time it didn't feel like a threat.

"You're not scared of me," he said.

"The dog tell you that?"

"Yep."

Ok, and now I was fucking lost. "How?"

"PTSD service dog," he explained. "His name is Crysis. I'm Special Agent Jason Raige, with the FBI. I'm currently assigned to the Cybersecurity division, formerly working domestic terrorism." He looked down at the dog again, but didn't slow down. "You are Tiffany Bowen, Cade's former girlfriend, Zoe's acquaintance, and Jericho thinks you're a bitch." He paused. "Which is a compliment from her."

"Would be from me too," I assured him. "Kinda why she and I get along."

"I just want to know if the name Ruin rings a bell?"

I shrugged, doing my best innocent-but-sexy girl routine. "Should it?"

"My wife is the hottest woman I've ever met," Jason suddenly said. "So the little flirting? It's transparent, won't work, and is actually pretty good."

My fucking mouth dropped open. "Excuse me?"

"I've spent a decade watching people, Tiffany. I know how to read you. I also know you're not trying to hit on me. You want to distract me because you know about Ruin. Knock told you."

"Uh..."

"And Jeri gave me a quick overview before I tried to find you," he went on. "You're not in shit, but it seems I am."

"I thought you were the handler?" I asked.

And he relaxed. "So you know quite a bit. Fill in the gaps for me, Tiffany."

Thankfully, that was when Cade sauntered into the room carrying a few pages of paper. "Top page is public. Under that is applicable. I'm not ripping her world open for you, though."

"I told you I wanted a fucking profile," Jason said, a hint of annoyance in his voice.

Cade simply shrugged. "You got what you need. If you wanna stalk her Instagram, do that on your own time."

Jason just murmured, but his eyes were already scanning the pages.

"Don't worry about getting us in shit, Tiff," Cade told me. "Knock's sister Riley? Yeah, she's his best friend. He kinda works best at full volume and without a filter."

"Go. Away," Jason ordered.

Cade chuckled. "See? We threw him off his game and now he's pissy. Oh, and she knows about Ruin, our polycule, and pretty much the basics. We also got her playing Flawed, and Dez loaded her out."

"Name?" Jason asked.

"HellOnHeels," Cade answered for me. "Dez calls her Hell."

"Nice," Jason almost purred, and everything about his attitude changed. "But really, go away, Cade. Pretty sure you all were doing something before I got here."

"Studying," Cade said. "Don't let him push you around, Tiff."

"Promise," I assured him, but I didn't really mean it.

This guy was a fucking FBI agent, after all. That was a step up from a cop, wasn't it? And yet, the way my friends talked to him was the way they talked to each other. Kinda. A little louder and blunter. That meant they weren't scared of him or the repercussions of this, so I'd be ok, right?

"Now," Jason said, setting the papers aside, "let's try this again. What do you know about Ruin?"

So I explained to him about last year. I started with the fucking new girl trying to steal my boyfriend, why that mattered, and ended with hearing Dylan and his friends had been arrested. So what if I skipped over the bits that were a little less than legal?

But Jason didn't have that problem. "Jeri says you helped her steal Evan's phone."

My heart stopped dead in my chest. "He dropped it. It wasn't a big deal."

"I told her to steal it," he said. "I told Knock the only way to get justice for Zoe was to bust that fucker for distributing child porn, which meant he had to distribute it. I walked them through that shit. I also testified that Dylan hated Jericho enough that I believed he would try to kill her, so Jeri stabbing him was self-defense. It wasn't a lie, but I think we both know he was pinned when she buried that knife in him."

"She what?" I gasped. "I mean, I'd heard he'd been hurt, but I thought Hottie and Jinxy beat the shit out of him."

"So you don't know everything," he realized. "Interesting. Well, she did. From the sounds of it, she also made him nod to show he liked it."

My lips curled into a smile, and nothing I could do would stop it. "Good. And I don't care if I'm supposed to say that or not. I know what he did, Jason. I heard the stories from all those girls they raped. I'm the one who made the support group to help them out, because no one else was."

"And now you're helping my team study," he said, leaning forward to rest his arms on his knees. "So, let's cut the bullshit. I'm a shitty fucking agent. I never wanted to work for the FBI, but I wasn't given a choice because I fucked up that bad. Thing is, I'm also damned good at it. I'm a top-rated sniper, an unstoppable hacker, and a loyal friend. Seems you are too."

"Not quite a sniper," I said, but the joke fell flat.

"I meant the loyal part," he assured me. "I just want to know why you're putting in so much effort to help them with something that no longer matters to you."

"What do you mean?"

"Them getting this deal. It doesn't do a damned thing for you. It doesn't protect your friends. It doesn't stop a boy from harassing you. It doesn't make your life easier at all, and that's a whole lot of time you're investing into people you started out hating last year."

"I didn't hate them," I countered. "Well, Jeri, but she's easy to hate. Easier to like, too."

"Yeah, she kinda is," he agreed. "But avoiding the question isn't the same as answering it. Why are you helping them?"

"Because they helped me."

"Mm..." He shook his head. "No. That's why you make cookies, it's not - "

"Oh, you think that because I'm a girl, I'm going to bake to pay my debts?" I scoffed. "Fucking typical."

"I think you took a cooking class with a girl named Stephanie," he countered. "I think you are feminine, and that isn't inherently a bad thing. I also think you're avoiding the answer."

"Or maybe," I shot back, "I don't fucking know the answer. They helped me. Cade asked if I could help, so I'm helping back. Like, this is what friends do, Jason. Maybe not your friends, but you know what? Most friends are shit compared to these people. Most friends want to get fucked, or get popular, or get something. They don't help the girl they fucking hate because it's the right thing to do, ok?"

"Guilt?" he asked. "You feel guilty that you were a bitch to Jeri, yet she still helped? Is that your answer?"

"No!" I groaned in annoyance. "Look, this is what I'm good at, and you know what? Those people helped me, so I'm not going to say shit that will screw them over. If that's what this little interrogation is about, you're fine. You're safe. I didn't even tell my friends last year, because I knew how big of a deal this is. I also know already. I've known about their hacking since Evan got arrested, but they're hacking for us. They're doing something to help everyone else. They didn't ask for payback, or try to use shit against me. They fucking dropped everything to track down some damned videos so my friends would stop getting sexually harassed, ok? And you probably don't understand, but there aren't a lot of people in the world with the *power* to do that."

"The hacking?"

"To stop the harassment!"

"And there it is," he said proudly. "That's the real reason you're here, isn't it?"

"Huh?"

He patted the cushion, calling his dog up on the couch beside him.

"You're a pretty girl. Pretty girls get it the worst. You're probably sick and fucking tired of being treated like a piece of ass to be used, right? You're so over the shallow pickup lines and fuck-boys."

"Yeah..."

"And Ruin is stopping them," he pointed out.

But he was wrong. Well, partially. "No, Jason. Ruin isn't *like* them. It's not that they're stopping that shit, because nothing will. Boys will be boys, right? Guys are going to grab my ass at a party, try to get me drunk so I'll go home with them, and stare at my tits in class. They're just being boys, after all." I rolled my eyes to show what I thought of that. "But this? It's the one place that doesn't happen."

Jason leaned back again, his hand going to his dog's back almost automatically. "Huh."

"What does that mean?"

"It means that wasn't the answer I expected." He canted his head in a weak shrug. "It also sounds honest as fuck."

"Yeah."

"So why are you helping them?" he asked again. "Don't think about it. Just answer, because I'm getting the impression you don't really know."

"It's..." I curled my legs up under me, trying to find the words. "There's this feeling. I mean, I've had friends. Oh, I've had some good ones, and we checked off all the boxes, but it's different with these people. Like..."

"I'm not rushing you," he promised.

So I bit my lips together and really thought about it. All this time, I'd had this feeling, but I'd never slowed down long enough to analyze it before. It was just this pull towards this. This feeling of safety when I was around them. A sort of normalcy I couldn't even explain, but that word wasn't nearly strong enough.

"They make me feel like it's ok to be me," I said softly. "And I've seen what they can do. I know how big of a difference it can make. So if I can put together some fucking flashcards for them? Then why not?

It's like doing my little part, you know? All Rosie the Riveter and girl power and shit."

"Ruin consists of five men and two women," he reminded me.

"And those guys would agree it's girl power," I said. "See, that's the thing. They don't see anything wrong with a woman being the one who belongs in the suit." I waved that off, because it wouldn't make sense to him. "They make miracles, Jason. They fix the bad shit. I can help, so why wouldn't I?"

He just murmured under his breath. "So, basically what you're saying is you're here because teamwork is overpowered?"

"Huh?"

"It's a gamer thing," he clarified. "Together, we become more than we are apart, and we can feel it. Someone else's strengths complement your weaknesses, and vice versa. It's like becoming god for a moment, in a small way. When you feel it, you know you have to do your part, so here you are."

"Yeah," I agreed. "I mean, that's pretty much it."

"Ok." And he pushed to his feet. "Oh, and thank you for helping them get ahead. This program is classified, so please keep any and all information about it to yourself. It is not something to brag about. It is not the sort of thing you want to tell your friends. All of this could fall apart if you so much as breathe a word of it to anyone outside this house or Knock's family."

"So a big fucking deal, huh?" I asked.

And the man actually smiled at me. "Yeah. And yet they're hackers. They're supposed to break the rules. I'm just trying to make sure they're breaking the right ones."

He turned to leave, but I had to ask, "Are they?"

He paused at the archway. "Yeah," he said, glancing back. "I think they are. That's why they're going to be the best."

# CHAPTER 48

**SPECIAL AGENT JASON RAIGE**

The girl hadn't been what I'd expected. Even talking to her, she had an air of authority that was impressive. That she didn't try to hide the way she and Jeri had initially butted heads? Surprising. Then, the moment I got back home after training my crew for the weekend, I did a deep dive into her history.

Tiffany Bowen, nineteen years old, enrolled as a freshman at the University of North Texas and declared as an accounting major. Her SAT scores were through the roof; her GPA was good enough, with her scores dipping at the end of her senior year. Her application had a short essay about the power of womanhood in modern society.

Her family was solidly middle class; she had both a younger brother and sister. It looked like her brother had just started high school and her sister was now in middle school. So the kids had been spread out. Tiffany's credit was tolerable, but not the best. She had a small personal loan, cosigned by her father, for a car. That led me to her driving record, which was clean. She'd even passed her driving test on the first try.

In other words, there was nothing at all about her to worry me - but I knew how involved she'd been in the ordeal with Alpha Team. I knew this girl had been sleeping with Cade, which meant she was a frayed thread in Ruin's relationship. If someone pulled at it too hard, the whole thing might unravel, and Cade was a teen boy. That meant horny.

But my gut said this would work. The team trusted her. She was putting in the work to make herself valuable. Ok, and she'd already made a difference. I'd dropped shit on them, and thanks to this girl, they'd actually learned it. Hell, it made me wonder how long she'd been helping, because her method could be why Ruin seemed to be acing everything I was throwing at them.

However I did keep one thing in mind. Before I went to stalk her Instagram, I told Zara about her, then we looked through it together. My wife wasn't stupid, though. The moment Tiffany's first picture appeared, Zara began laughing her ass off, because it was the girls at the lake last summer.

"Oh, Jason," she tittered. "Is she even eighteen?"

"Nineteen."

Zara just shook her head, stood, and grabbed both of our coffee cups. "And I'm not worried. You married me, not her. I also know you're looking into her for Ruin. I'm not jealous." Then she kissed my brow. "I'll get you a coffee."

God, I loved that woman. I also didn't deserve her, but I wasn't about to bitch. She knew me too well, and it was nice. Granted, that was probably the same reason Tiffany had latched onto Ruin. She was clearly not the kind of girl who'd been in their social circles back in high school. She'd evidently realized college was not the same, and Ruin was special.

Special enough that I was putting everything I had into getting them ready. Last Saturday, even Ripper had shot well enough to pass the gun qualifications. Barely, but I was willing to take it. Next week, I intended to make sure it wasn't a fluke. They knew the subjects for all their tests, they had all of the material now, and unless Congress dropped something else on us, the only thing I had left to worry about would be their psych evals and background interviews.

So I spent the week trying to find holes which might cause problems. I dove so deep into their lives I ended up with a copy of Jericho's elementary school report cards. She'd been a "bright and happy" kid back then. Now she was a walking terror. Trauma had a way of doing that to a person, though.

I was up to my eyes in potential issues when my doorbell rang on Thursday. Zara was in class, so I almost ignored it. Probably a package being delivered, but Crysis began whuffing softly at the door. Confused, I headed that way and glanced through the peephole. All I could see was an FBI badge, clearly pressed up against the lens on the other side.

Chuckling, I opened the door to see exactly who I expected. "What are you doing out this way, Bradley?" I asked, moving back so he could come in.

"Hey, Crysis," he said to my dog, petting the mutt as he entered the apartment. "Where's Zara?"

"School."

He nodded, but there was something off about it. A little too tense. "Jason, we need to talk."

Letting out a sigh, I waved at the couch. "What did they find?"

Bradley didn't respond until he was sitting. Then and only then did he loosen his tie and lean back. The man was still in his suit, which made me think he'd driven here straight from the office. Since it was mid-afternoon and a few hours drive, that meant his news was bad. The in-person kind of bad.

"I just had a lunch meeting with, well, politicians."

"In New York?"

"Mhm." He looked at me pointedly. "Two senators, three representatives, four lobbyists, and the fucking president's son."

"In... New York?" Because that was not the sort of thing that happened by accident.

"About the program."

Fuck. There was no way this could be good. If they were hitting up my boss, then they already knew too much. They knew we were structuring a chain of command. That meant they were too close to figuring out who, which would make it easier to put up roadblocks.

"So they know about Ruin?" I asked.

"They know about you. They know you've been assigned as the liaison with whoever will be hired. They know this program is ground-breaking, could be controversial, and are worried about the potential ramifications of privacy laws." He lifted a hand when I opened my mouth to break in. "They also made it clear they think it can work."

"So they're on board with the plan?" Because I'd met plenty of politicians from all the available parties. Not a damned one did something without thinking it would be good for his or her career.

"They offered me a promotion."

"To block the program?"

Letting out a heavy sigh, he reached up to pinch the bridge of his nose. "I'm a company man, Jason. I've made sure of it. I play by the rules, do not cause problems, and keep shit clean. I'm financially stable enough to mingle with the right crowd, white enough to make certain groups happy, and male enough to fit the status quo."

"Ok?" And now I was getting worried.

"So they offered to make me the Deputy Director of the FBI."

I sat up. "Alex's job?"

"And that's why I'm here, not calling you," Bradley explained. "It seems I've been a little *too* good at playing my part. You're the rogue agent, I'm the guy who's by the book. My wife's job is respectable enough that - on paper - we look like the perfectly safe bet. Thanks to you, there's nothing out there to show my political affiliation, my involvement with gamers, hackers, or other 'unsavory' types. Basically, I'm the stiff suit guys like this approve of."

"Guys," I repeated, catching that word.

Bradley snapped and pointed at me. "Their casual and slick discussion basically came down to Alex's Blackness and femaleness being a concern. They want her and this program gone, Jason. I countered with the rise in virtual crimes, pointing to a few of the hacking events in the news lately. From identity theft on a mass scale to the power grid one a while back."

"I remember that," I assured him. "Ransomware that almost shut down an electric company."

"And that's what I pushed," Bradley explained. "They liked the idea. They weren't thrilled with the concept of chasing virtual terrorists, though. One of the senators kept saying we should be focusing on China. Another pointed out the Russian interference in, well, everything."

"Because Russian hackers are governmentally supported," I said. "Almost like a whole fucking military branch."

"And a national security threat," Bradley agreed. "So they offered me Alex's job." He paused. "Jason, I don't fucking *want* her job. I don't think I'm qualified. I'm also fucking *pissed* that they're trying to remove her because she's an intersectional minority!"

I had to chuckle at that. "Hope you didn't phrase it like that to them."

"No, but I have to my wife," he said. "They simply assumed I'd be pissed she got promoted over me. They have no idea I actually liked being your partner, that I was completely invested in busting Soul Reaper, or that I come across like a hard-ass because it makes your fucking job easier. They just see white, male, and a potential puppet, but it means this just got bad."

"Real bad," I agreed. "They're going behind Alex's back, trying to get her pulled from her spot because she's inconvenient. Granted, that means she's doing her damned job."

"Exactly."

"Think this is related to the email Jericho got?" I asked.

"The timing makes me suspicious," he said.

I pushed out a breath, then bent to pet my dog. Shit. This was bad. All kinds of bad. "I need names, Bradley. I need everything, because if they know it's Ruin, we're fucked."

"I think I convinced them we hadn't picked a team yet." Bradley pushed to his feet, pulled off his suit coat, then sat back down. "I listed off a few of the other groups I've been researching, made it clear the program doesn't have approval yet, so it's all in the exploratory phase, and explained away the paychecks as part of the confidential informant agreements we had out there, casually, blending Ruin's with a few others we have on the books."

"Nice," I breathed.

"Alex made sure nothing would stand out when we started this," he promised. "While there are a few additional lines in Ruin's contracts, it's mostly the standard ones used with other high-profile assets. The story is we want to make sure they will testify, so they're being retained for that reason because of concerns about the legality of the Vegas situation."

"Which all makes sense," I agreed.

"The problem is the president's son," Bradley said. "He made it clear his father is not pleased with the attention Alex is drawing to cybercrimes at this time. He has an election coming up, and he doesn't need virtual fears keeping his voters from the polls."

"And his son told you all of this?"

"Mhm," Bradley murmured. "His son isn't an official channel. That means this was a threat, Jason. They're making a move on Alex, and I've been picked as the replacement."

"But why you?" I asked.

"Because you're a fucking mess," he said. "Seriously. I think that's why. They mentioned the news coverage of the 'Vegas incident' a few times. They pointed out how your little quip to the press got noticed, and my control of you was impressive. They made it clear my face and name are known well enough to make me an easy shoe-in for the job."

"Because Soul Reaper got noticed."

"Holding a group of women hostage, at gunpoint, in an abandoned casino? Yeah, that's memorable. Having a sniper handle the situation so fast? Before the news helicopters could even get into place? More so. That it was all streamed live, and is now viral?" He lifted a brow.

"Fuck," I grumbled.

"They want this to go away. They want to discuss abortion and tax laws. They want the election season to focus on the economy and gas prices. This shit? It scares people, Jason, and politicians don't like it when *their* voters are that kind of scared. They want to make sure they're only scared of the other side winning."

"We need a plan," I realized.

"I need to tell Alex."

I looked up, meeting his eyes. "And I have to tell Ruin."

"No, you need to keep them out of this," he countered. "We need those kids to be the most home-grown American bullshit we can make them. A group of college kids, all studying computer shit to become the good guys. It'll play well, so make sure they stay that."

"But they aren't that!" I snapped.

"So fucking make them *into* it."

All I could do was shake my head. "They're after Alex, Bradley. The president's son made that clear, and if the president doesn't want her in that office, she won't stay there. We *need* her there, because she's the only one who can make this happen. Shit, she *is* making this happen, and this shit? This is why it took us fucking years to catch Soul Reaper. We *need this!*"

"And we're playing politics," he countered.

"Fuck politics!" I snapped. "I don't give a shit about parties and affiliations. I care about lives. I care about the people being told it's not a crime because it's just online. The ones being tortured and harassed, and we're this close..." I held up my fingers, pinched close together.

"...to changing the world. I can't do that if they don't trust me, and they won't trust me if I don't tell them."

"Just keep them in line," he warned.

I laughed once. "They're hackers, Bradley. There is no line. After all, it's *their* internet."

# CHAPTER 49

**SPECIAL AGENT JASON RAIGE**

Bradley stayed into the evening. Zara was thrilled to have him visit, so she forced him to join us for dinner, which I cooked. We also came up with a plan. He sent me the names of all the people who'd been at his lunch. I saved those to have Ruin check them out. It'd be a good way to get them started on writing reports. But while I was waiting to board my plane to Texas on Friday, Alex called.

"We have appointments for their psych evals," she said as soon as I answered.

"When?"

"Next Friday."

I grumbled, because that wasn't enough time. One week. Then again, it also wouldn't change anything. Sadly, psychological evaluations weren't exactly the sort of test they could study for.

"When?"

"Bright and early at eight a.m.," she said. "Because of the size of your team, we had to book the contractor for the entire day. It'll be one after the other."

"I'll make it happen," I promised. "Means I'll have to fly back a day early, though. That way I can take them down to Dallas."

"Which is why I made it Friday, not Wednesday," she assured me.

"We'll manage," I promised. "But, Alex? Did Bradley talk to you?"

She murmured, the sound not giving me enough to work with. "He did."

"And?" I pressed.

"This is not your problem, Jason," she warned. "I promised to take you off the leash. I have no intention of putting you back on it, so let me handle this. You focus on the team."

"I am," I assured her. "In case you missed it, you're the head of this team."

She chuckled softly. "I'm your boss, Jason. It's my job to deal with the messy parts."

"And you don't think losing you will affect my team?" I countered. "Alex, what's the plan?"

"To get Congress to approve this fucking program," she said. "You should also know there's one big problem. These psych evals? Yeah, they were authorized this morning. In order for them to be completed, I have to send over a list of the people being tested. They want to know who, Jason, and to make this happen, we have to show our hand."

"Fuck."

"So focus on the team," she said. "Make sure they're clean, because passing these will start the entire process. Background checks will begin. References will get checked. This means things are happening, but I dislike that we still don't have full authorization."

"Because they're fucking dragging their feet," I shot back. "They want to know *who* so they can make sure it doesn't happen."

"Then make those kids perfect!" she growled. "Jason, if you could pull off friendships with the entire high table in the PLG tournaments without raising a brow, then you can do this. Make miracles, dammit."

"Yes, ma'am," I promised.

But how? The shit with the gamers hadn't really been my doing. Riley was the one who'd made that possible. She'd suspected me of something, had decided to trust me anyway, and then had covered for me once she figured it out. I hadn't done shit, but I was the one getting credit for it.

Which might explain how I needed to handle this. Ruin were the bastard children of Riley's army, in a way. She'd set the stage and built the mess they now called a family. Knock was passing that on to his hacktivist polycule thing. None of these kids were stupid, so maybe we could figure out how the fuck to make all of this work?

So I had to trust them. I had to let them know everything - whether my bosses liked it or not. Fuck their security clearance, because they knew better than to tell anyone. Didn't mean they'd listen, though. Just look at the girl last weekend.

The whole flight, Crysis kept leaning on me. That meant I was too tense, too worried. I tried to convince myself we'd make it work, but this? It was my dream. I could be working at Deviant Games right now, making a shit-ton more money, but this would make a difference. This was why I'd busted my ass for years to track down the leader of KoG. *This* was the one thing I was good at.

And they were too.

When I made it to the house, I found the front door locked. That didn't matter, because they'd given me a key. I debated knocking for a moment, then gave in and let myself in. This house was starting to feel like my second home, and while I hated the time away from my wife, she not only understood, but encouraged me to actually enjoy myself.

The locks clicked. I eased the door open, and Crysis barreled in. Shutting that behind me, I paused for a moment to simply listen to the house. Laughter leaked out of their "war room." The TV was on in the living room. A soft conversation was barely audible from the study.

It sounded like a home. Seven college students, crowded close together under one roof, and they'd figured out how to make it into a good thing. From the shared cooking plans to the room jumping I was sure they did at night, this mess actually worked. And it worked fucking well.

Then, "Crysis!" Jeri said, greeting my dog. "Hey, boy!"

Yeah, that mutt adored her. The only other person he liked as much was Zara, so I knew he had good taste. It also meant they all knew I was here, so I left the doorway and looked into the study. There, Zoe and Jinxy were sitting in the middle of their books.

"I have news everyone needs to hear," I said, not waiting long enough for a response before I kept going.

"Jason's here!" Cade bellowed from the war room.

That brought Ripper and Hottie in from the living room, the pair smiling at me as we converged on the computer area from two different directions. When I rounded the corner, I saw Jeri, Knock, and Cade all sitting at their desks, headphones on, and my dog making his rounds. I moved to the back of the room and leaned against the wall, making it clear I had something to say.

One by one, the entire team came in and sat down. Mismatched chairs swiveled to face me. Headphones were pulled off and set on desks, and seven sets of eyes locked on me.

"We have a problem," I told them.

They didn't interrupt. They didn't start calling out questions. The entire group waited patiently, nothing more. There was no panic, no annoyance, or any of the reactions I would've expected from most people.

"Alex's job is being threatened," I explained. "Weeks ago, Bradley saw what he thought were threats on her computer. A glimpse of an email, so not enough to run with. Alex said she was handling it. Yesterday, Bradley was invited to a meeting with multiple high-level politicians and lobbyists, and offered Alex's job as second in charge of the entire FBI. He's not qualified, but it appears the Soul Reaper takedown made an impression on the public that can't be ignored."

"Least there's that," Knock grumbled.

I hummed in agreement. "This morning, Alex was told to set up your psychological evaluations. They will take place at the Dallas FBI office. The person - or persons - doing the evaluations are not employees of the FBI, but are contracted by the government. This is a third-party organization with the intent of a fair review. However, doing this means they will know exactly who each of you are. They will have your names, address, and even date of birth. Anonymity is now off the table - unless you back out."

"When?" Jeri asked.

"Friday," I said.

She ran her tongue over her teeth inside her mouth. "What kind of threats?"

"Huh?" She'd lost me.

Jeri huffed. "Against Alex, Jason! You said she's being threatened, and maybe I'm wrong, but look at what you just said."

"Yep, saw it too," Knock agreed. "Alex gets threats. She doesn't bend, so Jeri gets one. Makes sense, because we had confidential informant contracts with Jason. Since Alex shuffled around his and Bradley's place in the FBI, they'll be overly obvious, and ties to them would look suspicious."

"But why Jeri?" Ripper asked. "Why not all of us, or like Hottie?"

"No fucking clue," Knock admitted. "Maybe because she was named by Soul Reaper? The rest of us weren't, which makes me think someone did a little research. Getting called out by the bad guy would make Jeri look more important."

"Makes sense," Ripper relented.

"Still," Knock went on, "after all of that, this person gets nothing, so they threaten Alex's job, trying to find a weaker link - because Bradley comes across like a fucking yes-man. When that doesn't pan out the way they wanted..." He paused to smile. "Because I'm assuming he didn't jump at the chance? Well, the next move is to figure out if we're the group she's trying to hire, and getting our names will do that."

"Because we aren't the only hackers in the world," Jinxy agreed.

"Just the most obvious, because we have a tie. Since Jeri didn't respond, it probably has that fucker confused as fuck."

"So we need to stop this before it can start," Jeri said.

"Wait," Zoe begged. "So we shouldn't do the psych evals?"

Jinxy laughed once. "Not what she's saying."

"We have until Friday," Jeri told everyone.

Hottie leaned forward and turned his computer on. "What's the plan?"

Jeri simply turned her chair so she was facing the group. "They're fucking with Alex. Alex is *ours*."

"Technically..." I tried.

But the girl lifted a hand, thrusting it my way to silence me and kept going. "We need to find what threats they're using, how serious they are, and the possible repercussions. We need to track the email they sent me, and see if shit matches. Is this one rogue fucker, or a group?"

"Party," Cade corrected. "Jeri, this shit usually falls along political party lines."

"I don't fucking care!" Jeri screamed, her calm facade shattering. "They can't have her! They can't fucking take anyone else from me, ok? I knew something was going to go wrong. It always fucking does, but I will not let them fuck over one of the few people who have stood up for us! If they want a fucking fight, then *fine!* They can have one! But what they can't do is fucking destroy one of ours!"

"Jeri..." I tried, looking to the side at my dog.

But Crysis was lying quietly in the corner. Jeri's rant hadn't bothered him at all. He knew better than to listen to the tone of voice, though. As a service dog, he'd been trained to react to fear, tension, and panic. This? Jeri's reaction was pure rage, and the controlled kind.

"Don't 'Jeri' me," she snapped. "We need to know what threats were made." And the girl lifted her chin at me like a dare.

"Alex is good at her job," I reminded her. "She's been working for the Bureau for years. She's not worried about it, so you shouldn't be either."

"Bullshit," Knock grumbled.

My head whipped over to him. "Don't help her."

"Or maybe you're wrong, Jason," he returned. "Has that fucking crossed your mind? Because this is the same shit they did to you. They tied your hands, and my sister almost died because of it. No."

Which was when Crysis pushed to his feet and moved in. But it wasn't Jeri he headed to. It was Knock. Squeezing in beside his chair, my dog wiggled his head under the armrest and onto the guy's lap. Without thinking about it, Knock began petting.

"What threats?" Jeri asked again.

"Might as well tell her," Cade said almost lazily, making a gesture at me.

"I'm going to check the router," Zoe said. "If we're deep-diving, we need to cover our tracks, right?"

"Thanks, Zoe," Hottie said even as he leaned back and looked up at me. "They tried to take a Black woman's job and offered it to Bradley?"

"Which one's Bradley?" Jinxy asked.

"White," Jeri replied, "male, perfect little Agent Smith type."

"He's really not," I added.

"Looks it," Knock said. "And he's a fucking prick about it too. For the right reasons, but Riley hated him for a *while*. He's a little too good at being 'by the book,' if you know what I mean."

"He's really not that either," I clarified. "Bradley is the good cop to my bad cop."

Zoe giggled as she came back in the room. "And your bad cop is pretty good, which means Bradley's good one probably is too. Ok. So we have some sexist fuckers targeting the one woman helping us. That means they're going after the whole program, right?" She made her way over to the longer wall behind Jericho and started looking around. "Where are the markers?"

"Upstairs," Ripper said. "We haven't had a reason to use the whiteboards yet."

Zoe just pointed. "I think we do now. Can you grab them?"

The look Ripper gave her was weary. "Fuck. I hate living on the third floor. Jinxy, wanna trade?"

"Tempting!" Jinxy said.

But Jericho was still sitting there, her eyes on the floor, and looking much too calm. I could almost see the wheels turning in her mind, and I was caught between the desire to encourage her and to call her off.

So I decided to hedge my bets. "Play this out for me?" I begged. "What's the risk level we're looking at?"

A cruel smile touched her mouth as she raised her head. "The risk? Really, Jason? Don't you see? They just took away our reason to play nice-nice. These people have more than made it clear they don't want this program. Hitting Alex didn't work, so they came at me. Now they're poking Bradley. Friday, they will be sure it's us. Once that happens, there's no going back. Once they know who we are, they will know how to stop us, so we will *not* let them take Alex down in the process."

"Fuck," Zoe breathed, moving to her side. "She's right."

Ripper paused at the hall. "The risk? It's that we'll get caught. It's always been that we'll get caught, but fuck that, Jason. We know how to cover our tracks. We know how to work as a team. We know..." He gestured at the whole group. "...what happens when something is someone else's problem."

"Nothing," Hottie clarified. "Not a single damned thing, because when people stay in their lanes, the victims are isolated, alone, and made vulnerable by others obeying the rules. You know, like Alex is now."

"And they're doing it again," Knock growled. "It always starts with one, right? First it was Dez, then it was every woman in a video game. This time, it's Alex. She's in their way, so they think they can erase her because she's 'just' a woman. They can get her out of the way because she's Black. No one will care. No one will notice. But *we fucking care!*"

Crysis whined, shifting even more in an attempt to get to Knock's lap. One leg made it up, but the guy's desk was in the way. Thankfully, Knock leaned forward and petted a little more, not fighting my dog's need for attention. But shit, I hadn't expected him to react so intensely to this news. It was enough to make my eyes jump over to Cade, hoping for a little backup here.

"We can still walk this line," I said, even though I didn't honestly believe it myself. "Alex isn't a helpless woman. She's a professional, and a damned good one. We need to respect that she can take care of herself."

"So could Riley!" Knock roared, shoving to his feet.

Crysis whined.

"And it only *starts* with calling someone names," Zoe said. "It ends in a bathtub, or a fucking dead girl at the park. But Alex says she has it, right? You know why? Because she has to 'have it.' If she doesn't, she's weak, she's a failure, and she's not good enough. But she also has us, and we're not just going to ignore it when someone decides to attack another woman." She looked around, checking her friends' faces. "This is what Ruin does!"

"And if this was aboveboard," Cade said, "they wouldn't be sending anonymous emails and threats. If this was legit, it would be shut down in Congress, not trying to scare us off - or replace the Deputy Director. That means something real hinky is going on."

Jeri reached over for Knock's hand, but her eyes landed on me. "We have until Friday, Jason. That's the risk. Between now and Friday, we need to figure out what the fuck is really going on." Her voice was much too calm. "They didn't stop to think this through, though. They're so sure they have us backed into a corner where they can just walk all over us, but fuck that. Someone is trying to hide something, and Alex is not disposable. No one is, and I'm fucking sick and tired of this shit." She pulled in a long, deep breath. "I will not lose anyone else."

Her eyes - they were the coldest shade of blue I'd ever seen. Pale, like a glacier. Icy, like she'd just locked her emotions away. Vivid, making it clear this girl was far from passive.

"It's not our fight," I tried. "Alex wants us to present as qualified but respectable computer specialists. This is just Congress playing politics, and she can handle it. We need to let Alex do her job."

Jeri kept staring. "Not our fight?"

"You do not work for the FBI yet, and you might not if you do this," I warned.

She merely scoffed. "You wanted hackers. You got us. You picked the group who knows how shitty the world can be, especially when it's hidden in code. This, Jason, is what we do, and Alex should know that."

"This," I shot back, "is going to destroy the program we're trying to get approved!"

"They're already doing that!" she screamed. "Don't you get it? If they could shut down the program, they would've already. This? They're trying to fuck over Alex. They're trying to destroy us. They're not playing within the rules, so why the fuck should we? If they're trying to replace her, then shit has already hit the fan, and we need to fucking know what's going on!"

"Or you're jumping the gun," I countered. "Jeri, we need to be smart about this.

"Smart?" she asked. "I *knew* it would happen again. It always fucking does! But this time? No. This time, Jason, we're ahead of it. Alex stuck her neck out for us, and do you know what that means? It means we're supposed to have her back. Well, guess what? We do! If Bradley noticed the harassment, that means it was bad enough she couldn't hide it all. See, that's how this shit works. That's what happens to a woman who dares to step out of line, and Alex? She's risen above her place, right? Shot straight to the top, because how fucking *dare* a woman have that much ambition?"

"Probably," I agreed.

"And I want to know what those threats are," she went on. "I want to know exactly what Alex is hiding, because she won't complain. She's too fucking strong for that, but guess what?" She paused to lick her lips. "We are too."

"And you'll risk the entire program for this?" I asked, trying to remind her of the risks here.

"That's what you don't get," she shot back. "They wanted our names. They're about to get them. We have until Friday, because that's when they'll learn who we are. See, that's where they fucked up, because they're the ones taking away any reason for us to keep our heads down anymore. We were supposed to be good, pretend like we're no big deal, and learn faster than they expected, right?"

"That was the hope," I agreed, still holding her gaze.

"But someone wants this program stopped. They want it bad enough they *will* stop it - one way or another - so why are we trying to slam our heads against an immovable wall? They're going to get our names. They're going to put up enough roadblocks that this program is already dead, Jason. They're going to fuck over the one good thing that could've come out of my fucking friends being held at gunpoint!"

"And that's how the law works," I reminded her. "It's not all sunshine and roses, Jericho. There are laws, and rules, and hoops to jump through. Otherwise, you're just a fucking vigilante."

"And *they're* the ones making us vigilantes!" she screeched. "This shit? This is to stop us. Fuck that. We do not stop! They want to see why the world needs people like us? Well, I'm more than willing to show them. They came after the wrong bitch this time. Maybe they thought Alex was all alone, but they were wrong. She stood for us when we needed it most. All of us - even you! So you know what?"

It was Hottie who replied. "Ruin 32:35, Jason. I will take revenge; I will pay them back. In due time, their feet will slip. Their day of disaster will arrive, and their destiny will overtake them."

"We will be their ruin," Jeri agreed. "I'm fucking tired of being cursed, so we will ruin them before they can ruin us - and Alex is one of us."

All I could do was tip my head in agreement, because she wasn't wrong. This girl couldn't be more right, and I was starting to realize the leash they'd put on me had worked better than I'd realized. This was my team. These were my partners now, and maybe it was time to stop worrying so much about getting it right.

Instead, we should *make* it right.

## CHAPTER 50

**KNOCK**

Once Jeri and Jason stopped yelling at each other, Ripper hurried upstairs to get those dry-erase markers for us. Cade and Jinxy headed into the kitchen to start brewing coffee. Hottie was running a check on our network, making sure the entire house - and all the tech devices in it - were locked down tightly enough no one could slip in.

I sat in my chair, petting Crysis. The dog would not fucking leave me alone, and I knew why. In the pit of my stomach, acid was rolling like crazy, which made no sense. I didn't know Alex well. Sure, she'd helped us a few times, and yes, I liked her so far, but she wasn't a friend.

And yet, when I'd heard she was being threatened, it was as if someone had rewound time.

Visions of my sisters being harassed flashed in the back of my mind. Memories of Kitty having her nudes and sex tape leaked. That moment in the club when the gunshot had gone off, and Riley hadn't been in the same place as the last time I'd seen her. Time after time, shit had hit the fan, and it had always started the same way.

A woman had been harassed.

Such an easy thing to do. Fuck, for some men, it was almost socially acceptable. Call her a bitch, say she's angry, blame everything on her being emotional. Women weren't cut out for this, right? Whatever excuse they came up with, they latched onto so they could justify their actions, making it easier to escalate just a little more, then a little more after that.

Until people were being hurt.

"Well," Ripper said as he came back into the room with the markers, "at least he didn't say there was a video of it."

Jeri's head snapped over to Jason. "Is there?"

"There is not," Jason promised. "Politicians tend to be careful about such things. They don't like soundbites they didn't intentionally release."

"And we're secure," Hottie announced.

"Coffee's coming!" Jinxy yelled. "We need a plan before we dive in."

"What we need," Jeri said, "is to find out what threats were made, who made them, and why."

"Where were they seen?" I asked Jason.

"In her office," he said. "Bradley's pretty sure it was her official email."

"So the FBI server," I realized, turning to catch Jeri's eye. "That's why he wants us to leave it alone."

"But he doesn't," Jeri said, glancing at Jason quickly before her eyes returned to mine. "He's not stopping us."

"This a test?" Ripper asked.

"Nope," Jason said.

Which was when Jinxy and Cade came back in carrying travel mugs for everyone. Jinxy made his way down our side, matching the color of the cup to the user. Cade hit the other, but he ended with Jason, passing the man his FBI logo-marked cup.

"So where do you stand on this, Jason?" Cade demanded.

Jason accepted the cup, but didn't immediately drink. "I'm not sure," he admitted.

"Lay it out?" I begged.

Pushing out a breath, he finally left the wall he'd been leaning on and moved to the chair in front of "his" computer. Pressing a button powered the thing up, and I knew his rig was nice. It was Murder's gift to us for helping out. A gift his sponsors had been thrilled to donate parts for, but still.

"I do believe Alex is not only qualified, but also capable of taking care of herself," Jason said. "I also think Zoe's right. Women can't complain, especially not the Deputy Director in her first year at the job. I think politics is being played, which is so fucking far above my pay grade it's not funny."

"Doesn't tell me shit," Jeri said.

"Yet you're still ready to charge in head first," he countered. "I brought this to all of you because I wanted a discussion. You immediately call in the cavalry and start *doing*. Jinxy's right, we need a plan, and I'm in on this."

"Have your tools?" I asked.

His eyes jumped over to me. "Always. Laptop's in my luggage."

I nodded, accepting that. "And we all know Dez is in play if we ask."

"Busy," Jason countered. "They're working on a new game, she's finally happy, and I do not want to drag her back into the bullshit that fucked her up."

"I mean with toys," I clarified. "If we get stuck, she'll have a script to unfuck it."

"Ok, there's that," he relented. "But I'm willing to bet most of you can write your own now."

"Don't push it," Cade joked.

"You can too," Jason assured him. "But something about this doesn't sit right with me. I wanted to mention it when Bradley saw the harassment." He paused to look at each of us. "They used the N-word. They sent a slur like that to her official FBI email, anonymized, and no one could trace it to a sender."

"They clearly didn't try hard," Zoe mumbled.

"No, they didn't," Jason agreed. Then he paused, his eyes losing focus. "There probably wasn't a personal threat. Just a complaint. Nothing actionable."

"Just like the email to Jeri," Hottie pointed out.

Which pulled Jason's attention right back. "I have a list of the politicians who 'requested' Bradley's presence at a luncheon. I'm counting the lobbyists in that group, because they're all the same shit. None of them are tech-savvy, though."

"Staff? Aids?" Cade asked.

"Contractors?" Jinxy suggested.

"No way to even guess until we know what threats were made," Jeri pointed out. "So what we need is to get into Alex's email. Jason, will she give us access to that?"

"It's better if she doesn't," he admitted. "Then she can deny anything we do."

"Wait, wait, wait," I begged. "Jason, what do *you* think we should do?"

He leaned his elbows onto the desk and scrubbed at his face with both hands. "I think the women have made a very good point. The committee is taking away the only protection we really have at this point: your anonymity. Friday, they will know the test group for this project will be Ruin. They will be able to access information on all of you - although only the public stuff, thankfully. Jinxy's juvenile record will stay locked and adjudicated."

"Expunged too," he added. "To most people, it doesn't exist. To the feds? Yeah, I know you can see that shit still."

"The problem we have is that most of your complications are all public," Jason told us. "Zoe's a victim of child pornography. Jericho had multiple family tragedies. Knock and Cade were both kicked out of their homes, changed addresses to Riley's place, and cut family contact. Hot and Jinxy? Foster kids, basically, because that's what Southwind looks like on the outside, Jinxy."

"Yeah, Gran was good like that," Jinxy agreed.

"And none of that makes us criminals," Zoe said.

"The question will be if you can be flipped," Jason said. "That's what the politicians will try to use against you. All of those things are weaknesses, but none of them are your fault. Any of yours. That makes you very nice candidates to the bureau. But this? Hacking into the FBI, and who knows what else? Slipping past encryptions, passwords, and other cybersecurity protections to reveal Alex's harasser?"

"Criminal," Jinxy said. "And the higher we go, the more criminal it gets."

"And fucking with secure devices is something they really don't like," Jason said. "Trust me on that."

For a moment, the room was quiet, all of us thinking this over. Crysis bumped my leg again, reminding me I wasn't petting him enough. Yeah, I was tense. I didn't think I was *that* tense, but clearly, he disagreed.

"I'm fine, buddy," I promised.

"You're triggered," Zoe said. "That means you're going to be experiencing mild anxiety, likely some fucked-up hormones, right? See, studies show victims of sexual trauma have the same rate of PTSD as soldiers. I'm going to guess the shit at F5 was just as bad as getting raped, right?"

"I don't..." I tried.

She just smiled softly at me. "Knock, it's ok. You lived. You have mental scars. You suffered intense fear, not knowing what was going to happen, and feeling powerless against it. I mean, that's basically what fucks us up about rape."

"And the whole use of your body thing!" I shot back.

She waved that off. "I mean, that's obvious. My point is you're triggered, you have a right to be triggered, and there's nothing to be ashamed of. Trust me, we *all* get it. I think everyone in this room has something that triggers us."

"Uh..." Ripper lifted his hand halfway. "Not so sure."

"Bullying," Cade told him. "Pretty sure that shit would trigger you."

Ripper's hand dropped. "Not really on the same level at all."

"But it's a trigger!" Zoe insisted, slapping her thin desk. "Y'all! Fucking listen to me! In my gender studies class, we've been talking about this, and triggers are real, ok? Men can't admit them because that makes you a pussy. Women can't admit them because we're already weak and emotional. Doesn't make it any better, so fuck that. We're a goddamn family, right?" She looked up and down the table. "That means we need to make it ok to talk about it!"

"Always," Hottie assured her.

"But if I'm triggered," I said, "then Jeri must be too. This is her button."

I watched as Jericho licked her lips, then paused to bite the lower one. "But I'm not. Well, kinda, but..." She groaned.

"We're ahead of it," Hottie said. "Alex hasn't been hurt. Alex is still safe. The risk is ours, but right now, we can stop this, so she hasn't been triggered yet."

"Yes!" Jeri agreed, pointing at him. "All of that! But why do we have to always be behind the curve? Why do we have to wait until there *is* a video of it? I think we need to get this shit, figure out who it is, why they're doing it, and what their real goals are. We can slip in, slip out, and leave no trace. If it's a test, then fuck 'em. They'll never be able to catch us. If it's not, and they're fucking with our boss?"

"Not your boss yet," Jason pointed out.

"The woman who took a risk for us," Jeri growled at him. "Better?"

"If you do this, Jeri," Jason said, "you could be putting the entire program at risk. Not just Ruin. Every hacktivist and hacker group we want to contract in the future. Every cyber-specialist on the FBI's payrolls could be cut. The repercussions of this could be long-lasting, and then what?"

"I don't fucking care!" she shouted. "What part of that is hard to understand? There is right, Jason, and there is wrong. This is wrong. This is what we can stop. This is the entire reason Ripper made a real pretty logo for us. It's why Zoe picked a name. It's why the seven of us threw in together, because we can make a real change, and so we are."

Tossing herself back, she made her chair rock hard as it protested the force of her movement. "I wanted to chase the KoG members who haven't been caught yet, but everyone said no. You all said to wait. Everything has been wait, be good, and don't fuck up the chance. But you know what? I'm not a fucking agent, Jason! I'm not a cop. I don't give a shit about what is and is not allowed because of the details of the law. I know what is right and wrong, and this shit? Trying to tear down one of the few women in power? Going after her because of her race? *Threatening* her? That shit's not ok! That's exactly what Ruin is supposed to stop! So why aren't we stopping it?"

"She's right," I said softly.

"Yeah," Ripper agreed. "She is."

"This is definitely an attack on a woman," Zoe said, "which makes it our job to handle."

"Well, I'm in on principle," Cade assured us.

Jinxy chuckled softly. "I mean, she's got a point about the risk. Once they know who we are, they'll find some way to disqualify us no matter what we do, so I say we go for it."

Which made Hottie murmur. "If they want proof of what we do and why we do it?" He flicked a finger at his screen. "This would do it. Someone attacked a senior FBI agent. Threats are threats, Jason, regardless of how explicit they are. The N-word makes this a hate crime, right?"

"Potentially," he agreed. "Depending upon what else was said. Could be freedom of expression, though."

"But we all know it's not," I said. "They offered Bradley her job.

Fucking *Bradley?*" I scoffed. "That's a threat, and maybe it's all quid pro quo, subtle and shit. Don't care. The ones in power are making a move. Alex is the target - "

"And Ruin," Jinxy added. "Knock, don't forget the real target."

"The program," Jason said.

"But we're not fucking victims," Jeri said, pushing to her feet. "So we're going to do this."

She held out her hand, and Ripper passed her a dry-erase marker. It was black, and she tossed that over to Jason. When she pushed her hand at Ripper again, he gave her the blue and red ones. The blue was sent towards me, and Jeri pulled the lid off the red one.

"Ok, here's the plan. Jason, you take the short wall. Make a list of all those people you have. Jinxy? I want you to see what info you can *easily* get on them. Office locations, IP addresses, and such. Cade? You're on politics. Let me know who has a racial or gender bias. Zoe, I want you to search the entire internet for Alex. We need to know what is out there."

"I'm on the FBI firewall," Hottie told her.

"Yep," she agreed. "And I'm going to let you open that up for me, so I can get into her email. Knock, I need that password cracker, and we need to set up storage for our case. Ripper, you're going to need to get us one hell of a spreadsheet for all of this, because I have a feeling there will be links. Someone threatened our boss, people, and we aren't going to let them get away with it!"

Jason leaned back in his chair and smiled. "What else do you want me doing, boss?"

"What can you do?" Jeri asked.

His smile grew a little more. "Everything."

For a moment, Jeri looked at him, and then her lips curled to match. "You're going to find out who sent me that fucking email, Jason. I don't give a shit about proper channels. Get in, get out, and do not leave a trail, but I want to know where that shit came from."

"Yes, ma'am," he said, reaching for his keyboard.

# CHAPTER 51

### JERICHO

With my red marker, I began making titles on the bigger of the two whiteboards. This was the long wall, right behind my desk. Starting in the left corner, I wrote "Alex:" then put a line under it. A few feet over, I put "Threats:" with a line under that. Next came "Identifiers:" and then "Verified:".

"Here's what I want," I explained. "Under Alex, we're putting the times and dates of the emails, so we can find them again. Under threats, I want the main concept. Racial, female, death, or whatever. Identifiers are anything we can use to figure out who fucking sent it, and verified is the end result, like IP addresses, email hosts, or anything else."

Jason was already at the other wall, making a list of names. "These are the ones Bradley had lunch with," he said. "For now, that's useless."

I laughed once. "Sure, until Jinxy gets us some basics. Then we can start looking in on those fuckers and see what email host they use and such. We'll rule them out or rule them in." Then I tipped my head at Knock. "As we verify possibilities, you get to take lead on those, ok?"

"Can do," he agreed. "I'm guessing in blue, huh?"

"Black is unverified targets. Red is the problem. Blue will be the suspects," I explained.

"Got it," he said, those dark eyes of his finding mine.

There was something in the way he looked at me. It wasn't sexy. It also wasn't *not* sexy, but this had nothing to do with being horny. No, this looked more like relief. Pride too. He looked like he needed me, if I was honest, and the strange thing was how I liked it.

So I headed to his desk first, and leaned over to kiss him. "We're going to stop this," I promised.

"Yeah, we are," he agreed. "No more curse, Jeri. Even if we fuck up this FBI gig, we're going to find a way to make a difference."

Yeah, and that was the problem: the FBI deal. That shit was a dream. It was the sort of offer that was a damned golden ticket to Wonka-land, or whatever Willy Wonka's factory was called. The kind of shit that was too good to be true, so throwing it away really didn't hurt as bad as I'd expected.

But I felt its loss anyway. It was hard to explain the death of a dream, but I was pretty sure we'd all known this wasn't going to happen. Sure, we'd tried. At least that way we'd all know it wasn't our fault when it got fucked up. But politics, government, and hackers? Yeah, not a good mix.

The sound of keyboards clicking was loud. Around the room, people made little grunts or murmurs as they found - or didn't find - something. The concentration was intense, and it was starting to feel too real. Too much like when we'd been watching the videos.

"Music!" I blurted out.

"Yes!" Zoe breathed. "Oh my god, I'm about to lose my shit. Um, Jason? Preference?"

The man looked over all of us, his eyes cold and serious, then he lifted his phone. "Is there a sound system in here?"

Cade pointed down. "Soundbar's between the desks. Bass and

surround are tucked underneath. It's called Bam-bam on the network."

"Because boom-boom sounded like bad porn," Jinxy clarified.

"Got it," Jason said before tapping his phone.

And hypnotic, entrancing tones began to fill the room. This was some kind of fucked-up cross between epic soundtrack music, electronic dance music, and something else. Something with haunting vocals and a damned good remix, if I was honest.

"What is this?" I asked.

Jason just chuckled, but it was Knock who answered. "Pretty sure it's the Renegade soundtrack. Zara made it."

"Holy shit," Zoe breathed. "No way!"

"She puts feelings into sounds," Jason said. "She's good, and she works full-time for Deviant Games now. It's a win-win for us."

"And it sounds nothing like trauma," I said before diving back into my work.

Because Zoe was right about the triggers. We were all too close. This shit was verging on a very bad nightmare, and the sounds had been just a little too similar. How many times had I tried to recover from shit by losing myself online? Like every time? But now I could do something better.

So once the proper programs were open and ready, I looked over at Hottie. "Let's do this."

"Ok, I'm using Alex's phone number to get us in the right area," he said. "Bear with me."

"Ready and waiting," I assured him as I waited for the info he'd give me.

The next song came on. Unlike the first, it was more intense. Clearly, this was the battle music for the unreleased game, and it fit perfectly. This was exactly what I needed to power through all of this. The bass was thrumming hard enough to be felt in my chest. The alto was a scream of rage. The rest just wrapped around it, all pounding to a beat that perfectly matched my pulse.

Then, "I'm in," Hottie said. "Jeri, you're looking for this IP address." And he listed it off.

From there, it was a race. See, hacking didn't work like most people thought. There were no cool visuals of some person in a digital maze. We didn't get code trickling down the screen like water. Instead, it was all about going to the right place, finding the right vulnerability, and then exploiting the fuck out of it.

Because people were stupid. I was including myself in that too. We all forgot our passwords, typed things wrong because it showed up as stars, or made other mistakes. That meant most software had a workaround for such things. Finding it, knowing it, and using it? That was what hacking was all about.

So as Hottie manipulated the network security of the FBI, I fired up the password cracker. Since it was nearly midnight on the East Coast, no one would be looking at Alex's computer - I hoped. All I had to do was connect to the machine, convince it I was a harmless little software update, and then find her fucking email.

Bit by bit, the pieces came together, but the FBI wasn't wide open like those idiots last year. Nope, we had to work for this. When Jason asked if we needed help, I flipped him off.

And then we were in.

Immediately, I got to work. Thankfully, Alex was a very organized office type. She had her email right there, the icon saved to her desktop. That led me to the program, which got me everything I needed. In another window, I opened up the FBI's mail server, found the web address for mobile access, and pasted in the address.

Next, I hit up her Google info. Sadly, she didn't use that for passwords, and I'd have to crack that shit anyway, but it would've given me plenty. So I gave up and activated the program.

"Just waiting for the right combo," I announced.

"She knows to use a tough one," Jason warned us.

I shrugged. "It's Dez's tool."

"Ah."

Another song played, then another after that. I was just about to get up and refill my coffee when suddenly, it found a match. I gasped loud enough to make everyone in the room look, and then grabbed my keyboard again.

"I'm in!" I told them. "Ok, and she is one meticulous motherfucker. Jesus, Alex, how many subfolders do you..." I paused. "Shit."

"What shit?" Jason asked, pushing to his feet.

"The harassment has its own folder," I explained. "And it's..." I waited while the web portal continued to load. "There's more than five hundred of these."

"All from the same place?" Jason asked as he bent to look over my shoulder.

"All unknown," I said. "Knock, where's my storage?"

"The Squirrel," he said. "Old shit is gone. It's clean and ready for us to go crazy."

So I clicked a button to download all, and sent it there. Next up came covering my tracks. Typically, no one would look for such things, but this was the fucking FBI. So while that did its thing, Hottie and I went to find the access records for email accounts.

Because software always played by rules. It had to. That was how it was designed. Humans coded the rules, it obeyed them. All we had to do was remove our presence, sweep up the virtual floor behind us, and we should be good.

"Copy all of it," Cade said.

"That's so classified you'll get jail time," Jason warned.

"And it's got information we're going to need," he shot back. "Jeri, copy it all."

"I'm ready to start sorting," Zoe promised. "Ripper? We're going to lock most of this away for a rainy day, ok?"

"On it," he agreed.

Bit by bit, the notification spun up, telling me it was closer and closer to being done. The little line showing progress kept growing, and then it was complete. I quickly closed the email, we cleaned up our mess, and then both Hottie and I got the fuck out of the FBI's network.

"Good work," Jason said. "I'm looking to see if you left a shadow."

"Not finding anything," Jinxy said. "Knock?"

"I'm checking to see if the Squirrel is visible," he said. "It's not."

"And we're clear," Hottie announced. "I also found an old connection Alex used to use. I'm going to guess it was a phone she's upgraded and no longer uses, but I snagged the information to spoof it. I set that to be our cover. If we need back in..."

I nodded, but I was already opening the emails. I wasn't organizing them. I was just scanning and reading. The folder it was in had the title "For review." That made me think she was keeping this as proof, but fuck. The shit in here?

"Go back to your own country, you stupid N-word," I read before clicking on another. "You're supposed to sit down, shut up, and be a nice little diversity hire. Know your place and don't get out of line. White hoods still exist, you know." Then one more. "Maybe if you got your ass in a kitchen, your sister wouldn't be raising your..." I paused and looked up. "Alex has a daughter?"

"She does," Jason said. "No husband, a twin sister, and they share a duplex. The sister works from home."

"Doing what?" Jinxy asked. "I mean, is she a vulnerability?"

"Thriller author." Jason chuckled. "Seems she has lots of inspiration, and her main character is an agent with the FBI."

Which made me chuckle. "Works. Also means she's probably not overly tech savvy. We need to make sure Alex's home is locked down."

"Already have," Jason promised.

I just pointed at my screen. "Guys, this shit? It's not ok. This? It's..."

"Like a never-ending pain that just keeps building," Ripper finished for me. "There's fear of what happens if they stop with words and move to physical. There's the disgust because you think they might be right. There's the rage because you hate them for being so very wrong. It's persistent, inescapable, and destructive, and no one should fucking - "

"It's ok," Zoe told him. "We're fixing it."

"Yeah, we are," I grumbled. "A search of that folder shows over two hundred mentions of rape. I have a hundred N-words. Quit is used seven hundred and twenty-one times, which is more than the number of emails in here."

"And I think we just found the real goal," Knock said. "Clearly, they want her out. That just happens to match the goals of those politicians Jason put up on the board. So..." He tapped the end of his blue marker on the desk. "Now we have to figure out where Unknown comes from."

"Then who he is," Cade agreed.

"He picked on the wrong bitch," Hottie said. "I'm fucking *tired* of men who think they can do this shit and get away with it. I'm..."

"I know," Jason said, lifting a hand. "Trust me, I know. But once we find him, then we pause and reassess, because this?" He tipped his head at his own monitor. "This plays by different rules."

"So do we," I assured him. "And they came after one of ours."

"Ruin 32:35," Ripper said softly. "They're already fucked. They just don't know it yet."

I caught his eye and nodded. "The only question left is how we'll destroy them, right?"

"And how bad the fallout will be," Jason added. "Because you can't hit anyone at this level without getting hit back. That's why we need this program, Jericho."

"And the fucking program is already dead!" I shot back. "Don't you get it, Jason? I want that shit as bad as you do, but it's DOA. They're currently suffocating it, and we don't have the power to give it fucking mouth-to-mouth, or whatever. It's dead. They're going to kill it one way or another. What we're doing?"

"Triage," Cade offered.

Knock just shook his head. "No, this is search and rescue. We're pulling our asses - including Alex's - out of the rubble. We're already fucked, Jason."

"We knew it was too good to be true," I pointed out. "I think we all did. That was why we were so skeptical in the beginning. This is exactly what we've been dreaming of, and you know what? Shit like this doesn't happen to us. We're fucking hackers! We're the shit people like to forget about when they can. We're not the cool kids or the badasses. We certainly will never be popular. But we do not *ever* leave one of ours behind!"

"And Alex is one of ours," Jason said, nodding to show he understood.

I couldn't help but notice he'd included himself. Ours. All of ours, and he was getting to be a very big part of the team. So fuck my curse. Fuck the metaphorical shoe that had just dropped. Fuck all this shit, because this time, we were going to prove that teamwork was overpowered.

# CHAPTER 52

## CADE

Jason had pulled out his laptop last night and set up a program to trace the emails Alex had received. Unfortunately, that wasn't a fast thing. So, after ranting about this a little more, all of us agreeing we were going to see what the fuck was really going on, and making a tentative game plan, everyone headed to bed.

I'd pulled Hottie aside to make sure he'd find his way to Jeri's room. He assured me he would, so I went to deal with Knock. My boyfriend was more stressed about this than I'd expected, but it made sense. So, as we cuddled in bed before falling asleep, I'd begged him to talk to me about it.

"It's stupid," he tried.

"It's fucked up," I offered instead.

He sighed and snuggled into my chest, wrapping his arm around my waist. "The first time I met Riley, someone cut her cooling line. They wanted her gone, Cade. The guys I gamed with pulled shit together and got her playing again - on my computer - and she became a sensation. If we hadn't? She likely would've faded into obscurity."

Yeah, I could see the correlations there. "And this thing with Alex feels too close, hm?"

"It's always pointed at women," he said. "Don't get me wrong, people are dicks to men too, but it's different with the women. With guys, they try to get us fired or shamed. With women, they try to get them dead."

The air slid from my lungs, Knock's weight on my chest making it more obvious. "Fuck."

"Mhm," he agreed. "Alex Watts is a powerful Black woman. She is a career fed, but she's still both Black and a woman. She's also a single mom. I don't know how many other traits she has that people will shit on, but that, right there, is enough. Someone wants her gone. If she goes, we go."

"Which means Jeri's right," I said. "They just took away any reason for us to be good."

"Yep." He tilted his head to kiss my chest. "And it's going to get worse. It always gets worse. That's why Jeri lost her shit, because she knows that. Behind every 'innocent' little harassment is always a big steaming pile of shit."

"What if the shit is just politics, though?" I countered.

"Then it's still shit," he said. "It still needs to be called out. If chasing someone out of a job because of their demographic - no matter what boxes they fit into - is how someone thinks politics should be played, then someone has to push back." And he looked up at me.

"We're the someone, huh?"

"We should be."

Yeah, we should be. We *could* be. We'd busted a group of serial rapists. We may not have saved those girls, but Jeri was right. We had the chance to save Alex. Right now, we were ahead of this game, and if we busted our asses, we could stop this shit before it got bad. We could make a damned difference.

Wrapping my arms around Knock's back, I closed my eyes and thought about everything that had happened since I'd taken that first risk. I'd told my friends I needed help, and they'd fixed it for me. Not perfectly, since Dad had still found out I was bi and had tried to beat the shit out of me before kicking me out. But Riley had taken me in. Knock had made space for me. Ruin had changed me.

Now, I was learning how to be proud of my sexuality. I was finally getting comfortable with it, no longer feeling the instinctual urge to hide it. I was more of a man because I was my own man, and wasn't this pretty much the same thing?

Alex was a damned good fed. I didn't really know if she was an agent or had some other title in combination with "Deputy Director." I just knew she was a fed, our boss, and she'd covered for Jason. I knew she'd asked for this program, which meant she could see the writing on the wall: virtual crimes were up, and no one had the power to deal with them. So if we could get her out of this bind - with or without us being a part of her program - then she could become more of a fed. A better fed. A good "guy."

But she couldn't do it alone. No one could.

That was why teamwork was overpowered. It was why we were all flawed, but we were not alone. All those catchphrases had been made popular because they carried a kernel of truth, but they also missed one big gap in the logic. No one could be a part of a team if their team wasn't willing to step up.

We were. Jeri hadn't even hesitated - but I had. For a moment, I'd thought about ignoring Alex's problems in order to make sure we got our deal. Yeah, Jeri was right about that too. Our names were going to be recorded with the psych evals, and that would give the politicians enough to block us. We didn't stand a chance, but I'd been willing to risk Alex for a whole ten seconds in order to achieve my own goals.

That was my last thought as I fell asleep, and the first one I had when I woke up. Knock had rolled over to his side of the bed, so getting out was easier than I'd expected. After finding some clothes, I wandered into the kitchen to brew a coffee, but heard the clicks of a keyboard. While the Keurig did its thing, I peeked my head into the war room.

Jinxy was there. His eyes were tired, and the man was wearing pajama bottoms with an old t-shirt. He looked like he'd either just crawled out of bed or had never made it there. He was also hard at work, the reflections of different screens flashing off his glasses.

"Did you sleep?" I asked.

"Hm?" He looked up. "Oh. Hey. Yeah." Then he gestured to his coffee mug. "Just waiting for go-juice to kick in."

"And Zoe?"

"With Ripper," he assured me. "She wanted to make sure he was ok, so she crashed in his bed last night."

I chuckled, moving back into the kitchen to get my coffee and add the good shit. Still, the idea of Zoe spending the night with Ripper? That amused me for some reason. I couldn't even put my finger on why. Was it the bed-hopping our house was good at? Was it because Jinxy wasn't jealous? Wait. Was he?

So when I sat down at my own computer, I decided to ask. "Hey, you ok with her and Ripper?"

"Shit," Jinxy muttered. "There's nothing there, Cade."

"They're best friends," I reminded him. "That's kinda something."

"But that's my point," Jinxy said. "Why would I give a shit about Zoe spending the night in Jeri's room? They're both straight girls. They're best friends. They deserve human contact and to be besties about shit, right?" He made a little circle with one finger. "Now replay all that but with Ripper."

"Who's a dude, and boyfriend dudes sometimes get all jealous about other dudes sharing a bed with their girlfriend."

A smile cracked Jinxy's face. "Good thing I'm not a 'dude' like that, huh?" And he looked up. "Cade, I'm completely ok with it. We're a polycule. I mean, I don't get how I'm included in Jeri's love life, but I'm good with it. There's some tie between all of us. I can feel it, even if I'm not fucking anyone. It's there, it's real, and it helps my little sister. It also means there's both a level of trust, and a level of forgiveness that's inherent between all of us."

Yet one word in all of that stood out to me. "Forgiveness?"

"Sure. I mean, if you fuck up and forget to turn on a VPN..."

Lifting my hand, I saluted him with a middle finger. "Asshole. Has everyone heard about that?"

"Yep," Jinxy assured me. "But even if Zoe and Ripper do cross a line? It's stress. It's a mistake. I honestly believe they'd tell me, we could work it out, and it'd all be cool. I mean, we're a polycule, right? So if things are blurry, it's because it's ok to let them be blurry."

"Not fucking her," Ripper said as he rounded the corner.

"Didn't think you were," Jinxy promised. "I was just explaining to Cade why I'm completely cool with my girlfriend spending the night with another guy."

"Ah." He staggered to his computer, clearly still half asleep. "We used to spend the night at each other's places. Just kinda nice to talk shit out sometimes, you know?"

"I do," Jinxy promised.

I pushed my chair back. "Coffee, Rip?"

He made a face, then glanced down at his belly. "Fuck it. Yeah."

"On it," I swore, heading back into the kitchen.

"So what do we have?" Ripper asked.

"The politicians at that luncheon were from both parties," Jinxy said. "The lobbyists are all from tech or tech-adjacent groups. Wall Street is one of them. It's an odd mix to blindside an agent, if you ask me."

"Wait..." I looked back in. "Democrats and Republicans? Working together?"

Because that was not how politics worked in our country. One side was always against the other. They were black and white - and it didn't matter which color you assigned. The two political parties did not play nice-nice with each other. Ever. It was kinda one of the main problems.

"Yep," Jinxy said. "All veterans too. We're not talking wide-eyed freshmen wanting to make a name for themselves. These are all people in secure positions."

"Who clearly have something to hide," Ripper muttered.

I hurried to make Ripper's coffee, then carried it to him. "Check their net worth, Jinxy?"

"I got that," Ripper offered. "What am I looking for, Cade?"

"An increase," Jinxy said, answering before I could. "Something that implies they've become very well-off recently. By that, I mean the last few years."

"We got an update on where the emails came from yet?" I asked next.

Jinxy grunted. "Yeah, and you're not going to like it."

"Hit me."

"Congress," he said. "Those emails trace right back to the Senate's mail server. Can't say it's a senator, and I'm not sure if the House of Representatives has a different one. All I can tell you is that it originated from the official government servers."

"And yet it was anonymous?" I asked.

Jinxy murmured. "Spoofed. So, we could be looking at real good work that is leading us to the one place we really shouldn't be..."

"Or some tech-ignorant politician just made a very bad mistake," I said.

"Wait..." Ripper looked up. "Isn't the government supposed to be overly secure?"

"Nothing's that secure," Jinxy said.

"I know that, and you know that," Ripper agreed, "but that's not what I'm asking. Isn't the government supposed to be super-secure, which is why there was so much bullshit about private email servers and shit?"

"Yeah?" I agreed, not sure where he was going yet.

"And isn't it likely some politician, who's been told his governmental email is super-safe, is likely to trust that?"

"Probably?" I was still lost.

Ripper lifted his mug and sucked back a long drink. "So if some arrogant, egotistical, rich fucker who thought he was untouchable wanted to bully someone in the FBI, is it realistic to think he might make the mistake of assuming the governmental protections are foolproof?"

"Fuck," I breathed, finally seeing where he was going with this. "Yeah. If he's hiding behind the security protocols of Congress, he'd have to have some way of spoofing the email address to come across as unknown, but it's a big mistake."

"Because as soon as we get into Congress," Jinxy said, "we'll see exactly where this came from."

"And who," I clarified.

"Could be a staffer," Ripper reminded us.

"Which would imply the politician they're working for," I countered. "Could be them working on their own. We won't be sure until we dig deeper."

"So, looks like it's time to start digging," Jinxy said. "Cade, we're going to need to find the proper encryption software for the congressional email system. Ripper, check Google and see if they use one email server for everything, or if the House and Senate are separate."

"And you?" I asked.

"I'm going to find the back door," Jinxy said. "If we're hacking Congress, we need to do it the right way, and that means it's going to take a while."

"Let's do this," I agreed.

Because for ten seconds, I'd almost put myself above the victim. I'd thought about ignoring it to get what I wanted. Maybe no one else had noticed, but I had, and now I needed to make up for it. If I wanted to be a good man, I needed to risk my own comfort and desires a bit. I needed to be willing to stick my neck out there.

I also needed to make sure we got this perfect, because Jeri was right. Alex was one of ours, and no one fucked with Ruin and got away with it.

# CHAPTER 53

JERICHO

By the time I made it downstairs, the whole crew was going. Jason sat at "his" computer at the very end with a weird twist to his mouth as he worked. Zoe was at the whiteboard, making notes under my headings. Everyone else was focused on their own shit.

"What do we have?" I asked as I sat down.

"Coffee," Ripper said, looking up to smile at me. "Want one?"

"God, yes," I groaned. "I'd love one."

So he hopped up to make it. Zoe capped her marker and returned to her desk. At the same time, Hottie turned his chair to face me. "Email leads to Congress. Jinxy and I slipped into the congressional email server and found - "

"Got it!" Jason interrupted.

Everyone in the room turned to him. Even Ripper hurried back in. Considering I was still waking up and unsure what we were doing, I felt a little lost, but their reactions said this was a big deal.

"IP address leads to an office for an Alabama senator. Chasing the

MAC address, it appears this comes from a laptop owned by Milt Einfeldt."

"The actual senator?" Cade asked.

"Who?" Zoe wanted to know even as she began typing. "Oh. Milt Einfeldt, whose last name is a bitch to spell but Google knows it. He's one of two senators from Alabama, has been in office for seventeen years."

"And we have his laptop?" I asked.

Jason just smiled, lifting his strange eyes to meet mine. "Yep."

I nodded, then leaned back. "Ok, so what do we know about this guy? What are his politics? Is he tied to the program at all? I don't even know how that works, if I'm honest."

Cade leaned forward and started typing. "Looks like he's on the Governmental Affairs committee, which is who's handling our shit. Ripper, wanna pull up C-SPAN and help me find his remarks?"

"Oh, that's going to be tedious," Hottie said. "There's hours and hours of that crap to wade through."

"And if we want to know what this guy is saying, we need to start wading," Cade pointed out.

"On it," Ripper promised. "Let's see, looks like we can get more specific if we have the name of the subcommittee."

"Emerging Threats," Jason offered.

"Got it!" Ripper said. "And it seems C-SPAN actually makes it easy to sort this shit. Ok, Cade, I'm sending you a link. I'll do even days if you do the odd ones?"

"Deal," Cade agreed.

"I want to know more about this guy," I insisted. "Milt something, and he sent anonymous emails to Alex? How?"

"Looks like," Jason said, "he used a web-based app. Yeah, a pretty easy to crack, readily available on the internet type of junk. It doesn't hide the sending server at all, which led me to the IP, which sent me right to his computer. Just had to backtrack to match his computer to his other connections." He chuckled. "And the network security on the Capitol and all associated offices? It tracks all that shit."

"Nice," I said. "So we know who is fucking with her." I leaned to check the board behind Jason. "Is that his name?"

Everything paused as we all looked at the list of men who'd offered Bradley Alex's job. There, halfway down, was something that looked a lot like it could be Milt Einfeldt. Granted, Jason's handwriting was atrocious, so I couldn't be completely positive.

"Yep, that's what it says," Jason assured me.

"So he was there, he's got a hate on for Alex. But why? What is he trying to hide?" I looked at each of my friends. "Maybe it's me, but this seems like a big risk for a senator, right?"

"It is," Cade agreed. "Could be bad press. Could also be a setup to get rid of this guy, though."

"Can't rule that out," Jason agreed.

"Yeah, except..." Knock looked up. "This man's personal wealth? It jumped three years ago. He went from under a million when he first got elected to hovering around the two million mark for a while. Three years ago, he suddenly jumped to twenty-two million, and is steadily climbing."

"Why?" I asked.

"We'd need his bank records for that," Jinxy said. "We don't know which bank, so can't get the records."

I pulled in a breath. "And it's Saturday. Banks are closed on the weekends, right? Well, by now, I mean. So good time to hit one?"

"Or a few," Jason added. "Jeri, most of these rich fuckers keep a few banks. At least one will be international. Tax evasions, you know. So we need to dig, people. I want to know about his family, his public businesses, his opinions on the FBI, domestic law enforcement, and this program. I need a full breakdown on this guy." Then he looked over at me. "And you, Jericho, are going to check and see if someone else in that office could've used his laptop."

"How?" I asked.

He chuckled. "There's going to be security cameras, and I know how you feel about videos."

"Uh..." I glanced down at my computer, then back up at him. "How the fuck do I find CCTV footage inside the fucking Capitol?"

"It's actually the building beside the Capitol," he assured me. "They're managed and monitored by the Capitol Police Department." And he flicked up both brows. "Think you can handle it?"

"I'll make sure of it," I promised, because he'd just thrown down a challenge.

But fuck, this wouldn't be easy. Hacking into a police station was always a little tense. They were the ones who tended to get really pissy when someone breached their security. But if they had servers to manage the security footage of the Senators' offices? Well, that would be nice. I just wasn't sure how long they'd keep the data.

I knew some stores kept twelve hours, or twenty-four. Others were seven days. I had a feeling the United States government would hold onto things just a little longer in case of a complaint. So, crossing my fingers, I got to work.

I'd barely typed in a line, however, when Ripper set my pink travel mug down at my elbow. I glanced up at him and smiled, which made him bend lower.

"Hey," he whispered. "Just wanted to make sure you knew Zoe crashed with me last night."

"Everything ok?" I asked.

Which made him smile in that shy and adorable way he had. "Yeah. Just wanted to talk it out, you know? I think this mess is tense for all of us. Not quite triggering, but also not comfortable."

"Good, it shouldn't be."

"But she slept in my bed," he went on. "Jinxy knows, and he's cool. I mean, it was completely above board and all, but - "

I caught his hand, cutting him off. "Ripper, I don't care. No, wait. That sounds wrong. I like that you two are there for each other. I am not going to get jealous if something did, or does, or might, or could happen. I don't own you. I don't want to own you. I like you for you, Ripper, which means where your dick, or mouth, or even your hands go? It's ok."

So he leaned in and kissed my brow. "I like us, Jeri. All of us. This works, so I'm just trying to make sure I'm not keeping secrets and shit, ok?"

"I trust you," I said, shifting my hand so our fingers were laced together. "That's kinda why I fell in love with you."

He ducked his head and smiled at the floor. "Yeah. So let me know if you need help with the cameras, ok? I mean, these videos can pause easily enough."

"Promise," I swore. "I am, however, going to drag Zoe in to help me."

"What am I doing?" Zoe asked. "Oh, and you two aren't that quiet." She winked my way.

I just rolled my eyes. "You're going to help me pair the time those emails were sent with video footage. Don't worry, you've got a minute - or sixty."

"I'm currently sorting them," she said. "We've got racial, sexist, qualifications, and miscellaneous. I'll make other folders if I have to, and I'm keeping the original that shows what order they came in."

"Any idea what this fucker's problem is?" I asked her. "I mean, if he's taking a risk and threatening her, then why? What the fuck is he hoping to accomplish?"

Zoe just blew out a heavy breath. "Um, I hate to say it, but this looks like the typical bigoted white-man shit. Like, the kind of fucker who thinks he's the only one in the world who deserves anything, and therefore he deserves everything. Women should focus on making babies and keeping their mouths shut. Black people - because I'm *not* using the word he does - are little more than animals, and that kind of gross shit."

"And it's a man?" Jinxy asked.

Zoe nodded. "Trust me, this is a man. If the person sending it is a woman, then she's a man."

"What?" Cade asked.

Knock just laughed once. "A trans person who isn't out yet, babe."

"Gotcha," Cade muttered.

"And he's got some serious issues," Zoe went on. "I mean, he fucking called her a monkey!"

"Fucking prick," Ripper grumbled. "Not cool."

"Which we can say because we're all white," Zoe pointed out. "I mean, to us? This shit is sick. It's disgusting. It's horrific. But just imagine if you had to live with this crap constantly? I mean, how the fuck does Alex do it?"

"She's strong," Jason said. "She knows it's bullshit, and is self-confident enough to let it slide off her back."

"But it doesn't!" Zoe snapped.

"Not like that," Jason assured her. "I'm sure it leaves a film behind, but she *refuses* to let it stop her." He paused. "Last night, I did a little background check into Alex, just to know what pitfalls might be coming."

"And?" I asked, because he made that sound like she had a few secrets.

"Her daughter was conceived by IVF. Donor sperm. No father listed. She's never been married. She has no man in her life. I can't find anything that would make me believe there's a woman either."

"Asexual?" Cade asked.

"No idea," Jason said. "But she's a Black woman who is completely independent and only growing more successful with each passing year. To racist, sexist, stupid motherfuckers like this guy? That's about the biggest bogey monster there is."

"And the only one who'll pay for it is Alex," I reminded our crew. "She didn't ask to be who she is, just like we didn't. She's simply making the most of the shit the world handed her, so let's make sure we have her back, right?"

"That's what we're doing," Hottie promised. "Because this isn't allowed on our watch."

"And we are watching," I agreed as I started working.

We would always be watching. No, one group wasn't enough, but we were better than nothing. We also had to be careful, because this time the stakes were high. This time, we were fighting men with actual power, not just the perceived kind. This time, we were going to fuck someone up *before* they hurt a woman.

Bit by bit, I found what I was looking for, and then utilized the vulnerabilities of their network. Surprisingly, cops weren't that smart when it came to keeping people out of their network. The Capitol Police had a real big fucking door just begging me to open it and walk right in, so I did.

"Too easy," I mumbled as I searched the network, found the video storage, and dove in. "There's gotta be a catch."

"You've learned more coding in a year than most people do in their lifetimes," Jason reminded me. "What's easy for you is impossible for the average person."

"And locks only keep honest people honest. They rarely stop criminals," Jinxy said.

I just chuckled. "And I've got it. Looks like we have six months stored here, and an archive which likely has older shit."

"Because," Jason said, "politicians like to cover their asses. Sexual harassment is only one of many fears they'll have. After January sixth, they increased security and increased the archives. Nothing gets deleted anymore."

"Well, well," I said. "Then let's see what this fucker has to show us. Zoe? When's the first email?"

She read off a date, and I went looking. It took a while. If I was honest, it took a *long* while to figure out the codes for each person's office, and which camera was being used. As I got into this, I found out that not everything in a senator's office was recorded. It seemed certain rooms were, some weren't.

"What the fuck?" I asked. "He goes through a door, and I can't see shit."

"Changing rooms, bathrooms, and so on," Jason explained. "The door to the office suite should be recorded, along with the main area, which includes the senator's desk."

"Yeah, but he left the screen for this," I huffed.

"Then try another," Jason growled.

I nodded and had Zoe get the next date, then the one after. Over and over, I checked the security videos, finding nothing. In some cases, the office appeared completely empty. In others, I watched the senator walk into that back room minutes before the email went out.

Then, finally, I found it.

"Fuck me," I breathed. "It's him! He's at his desk, pulling a laptop out of his briefcase, and he's typing. The motions are just right for an email, including the touchpad. I have him on screen doing email shit!"

"Find more," Jason said. "Once is a coincidence. Prove it, Jericho. Leave no room for speculation."

"Yes, sir," I agreed, and asked Zoe for the next date.

But this was our man. I was sure of it now. A fucking senator from Alabama, and he thought his old, fat ass was better than Alex Watts? Yeah, well, he was about to learn how wrong he was. After all, it seemed he didn't have a damned clue how my internet worked, but I did - and I was in the process of using it against him.

# CHAPTER 54

ZOE

Once Jeri saw the man at his computer, she became rabid. I kept giving her dates and times to check, and while most of them didn't show anything, a few did. We went through all five hundred some-odd emails, matching them up, and ended up with seventeen matches.

This was our guy. We were all sure of it. Unfortunately, when looking through those emails, I'd read what he'd sent. There was no way Alex could be ok with this! Shit, the nasty messages, the comments about her being a woman, which implied she was therefore stupid? This fucker was a damned idiot, and I was completely on board with destroying him.

Jeri was different. She was too focused, too controlled, and too intense. Hottie had to bring dinner to her chair, because she wasn't about to slow down. Knock and Cade kept asking her if they could help. Twice, she didn't even hear them. Across the room, Jason was watching her intently, almost like he was worried.

But knowing who it was led to our next step. With Cade and

Ripper on C-SPAN footage, Hottie and Jinxy volunteered to dig into this man's computer. Knock and Jason went looking for his financial information, trying to find where he banked so they could worry about the actual records next.

It was exhausting. If I was honest, I hated doing this, but a part of me also thrived on it. I knew I was a decent hacker now. I was sure I could get where I needed without getting busted. There was a feeling of power that came with it, but knowing there was a victim? Yeah, I hated that bit.

I hated how there was always another victim, and there always would be. I was so fucking pissed that some guys thought this crap was ok. And their type *always* went after women. It was like they thought we were weak and stupid. Like they assumed that because we couldn't physically hold them off, we must be lesser in all ways. Well, too bad for them, they were wrong.

But the rage could only push us through so long. As midnight passed, and the house began to creak with the temperature changes, people began yawning. One by one, the guys started tapping out. No sense in fucking up because we were simply human, right? Sleep was kinda mandatory for being on our A-game.

Yet when the rest of us called it a night, Jeri, Jason, and Hottie were still going strong. I made my way upstairs, feeling a little bad for wanting sleep. Was this what she'd done to help me? Was I letting Jericho down by quitting early? For a moment, I thought about brewing another cup of coffee and going back at it, but we still had tomorrow. The weekend wasn't over yet, so we had time.

I'd just slipped into bed, wearing my favorite pajama shorts, when I realized I was missing my teddy bear. I'd carried it down to Jinxy's the other night, to keep things from getting too intense, and I'd left it there. Fuck, I didn't want to walk all the way down there in my stupidly short shorts. The guys might be ok with showing off their underwear all the time, but I always felt fat and awkward when I thought about it.

Yet while I was still debating putting on pants, there was a light tap on my door. "Zoe?" It was Jinxy.

"Come in!"

He opened the door and stepped into the dark room, but I could see my bear in his hands. "You forgot Franklin. I mean, I was tempted to keep him for myself, but I figured you might want someone to snuggle with."

God, that was cute. He also wasn't wrong, but lately, my teddy bear hadn't been quite enough. That was why I spent so many nights down on the second floor. Then again, my bed wasn't much smaller than his.

So I scooted over towards the wall. "Can I have a Franklin and a Jinxy?" I asked.

He made his way to the bed and passed me the bear. "You sure? I'm not trying to push, baby."

"I was just debating going downstairs," I admitted. "I kinda like cuddling. But, I mean, since you're here..."

His answer was to pull off his shirt. That hit the floor, and Jinxy dropped his jeans next. Sadly, the curtains over my window blocked out just enough light that I couldn't get a good view of his hot body. I could, however, tell his underwear was grey. A soft pale grey, with black accents that made his lean frame look oh-so-good.

"Just means you have to get used to my pillows," I teased.

He slipped under the covers and turned to lay on his side, facing me. "I could sleep on a hard floor, Zoe. I'm really not picky. Especially not if it means having you closer."

"Yeah?"

"Mhm," he agreed, reaching out to catch my hip and tug lightly. "But you're even better when you're closer so I can snuggle."

Instead of rolling over so my back would be against his chest, I just scooted in. My knee bumped his. My arms were pulled up against my chest, with my bear trapped between us. His eyes, however, were so dark in this dim room. Gentle-looking. Soothing.

Safe.

"I like being able to do this," I breathed.

A smile flickered across his lips, and Jinxy reached up to push my hair away from my face. "Lie in bed with me?"

"*Want* to lie in bed with you," I corrected. "I don't get anxious about it anymore, Shawn."

The use of his real name made his eyes drop to my lips. The man's body softened, and I liked it. Tossing Franklin behind me, towards the wall, I moved in just a little more, all but forcing Jinxy's arms to wrap around me. Then I pressed my face up against his chest.

"You know I was only venting with Ripper last night, right?" I asked.

"Baby," he breathed, "I'm not upset about it. You two are best friends. I get it."

"Yeah, but you're so good to me, Shawn."

He relaxed in a way that almost felt like a sigh. As if his entire body exhaled, but without the sound. The man simply melted, curling around me a little more, and it felt so good.

"I like that you take care of Ripper," he said. "The guy is too nice for Jeri. Don't get me wrong, she needs a nice guy, but it makes me worry about him a little. And you? You're sweet enough to care, but sour enough to scream at her if she's taking advantage of him."

"I like that."

He chuckled. "Admit it, you just like me."

Which made me look up and stretch enough to find his mouth. "Very much," I promised before giving him a slow, soft kiss.

His mouth parted, and I couldn't help myself. Grabbing at the back of his neck with my upper arm, I pulled him closer so I could kiss this man the way I longed for. Not a nice kiss. Not a polite one. This was the kind of kiss that got my blood pumping.

And he didn't try to slow me down. His lower hand cupped my face, trapped against the bed. The upper arm moved to my lower back, pulling me in just a bit. The whole time, our mouths danced. Because that was the only word I had for it. There was a give and take between us, each one testing the other's limits.

But when he shifted to lean in a bit more, I could get my other arm around him. Rolling onto my back, I pulled him with me, and for a moment, Jinxy just kept kissing. Slowly, deeply, his mouth explored mine, putting a claim on me like no guy had ever done before.

There was something so sensual in the way he touched me. It wasn't sexual, but it felt like more than a passing fancy. Each time this man kissed me, it made me want to moan softly, tilt my head up, and let him do anything he wanted. It made me feel like his, and I liked it.

"Hey," he breathed, leaning back just enough to look into my face. "Is this ok?"

I jiggled my head in a little nod. "Mhm."

"Zoe..." He shifted his balance so he could move my hair again. "I'm being serious. I don't want to make you feel trapped or anything."

"Talking to your brother again?" I asked.

With a sigh, he shifted to drop down beside me. "Fuck off."

"Which means yes," I teased, lifting up so I could lean over him. "Jinxy, it's ok. I pulled you over me. That means I'm ok with it. You know, the whole taking the lead thing you said I could do."

"Well, yeah..." His arms moved around my lower back, holding my stomach against the side of his belly. "But I'm also allowed to check in. See, there's this girl I like, and I don't want to trigger her, you know?"

"I'm not triggered," I promised. "I was also thinking you should start kissing me. Like, you know, the way the guys do with Jeri. Just a hug from behind, or a kiss on the neck, or a back-bending show as you're leaving or coming home. To mix it up and all."

He laughed. "Right. Heard loud and clear. I just have one condition."

"Ok?"

"That you tell me when you're tense, not feeling it, or anything else. This is me letting you know in advance that I'm not going to be upset, take it wrong, or anything else. See, my brother mentioned that too. He said a lot of women will give in so they don't lose their guy, thinking they have to, but I kinda want us to be better than that."

"I promise," I assured him. "Because I actually believe you, Shawn. I mean..." I paused, biting my lower lip. "I feel safe with you."

"Yeah?" His hand moved higher up my back, a slow caress.

I nodded. "I do. I mean, like, I thought I had to kiss Ripper first because of that. The whole not chasing you off thing, but since then? Spending the night and stuff? It's... I mean, we've..."

"Yeah," he breathed, "we have."

I relaxed, lying down against his chest, because he actually understood. We hadn't really done anything but kiss, but the kissing was getting more common, and longer, and a lot more intense. He also tended to slow it down before I did, which made me believe he really meant what he'd said about not needing to fuck.

He wanted me. Just me. Not to get laid; not to have an orgasm. This guy wanted to be mine in the same way I was already his. He wanted something more emotional than physical, and I was so there. I wasn't even sure when it had happened, but I knew I wasn't making this up.

I loved him. I was terrified to tell him, but I did. For now, it was my little secret, but if he kept doing things like this, it wouldn't be for long. I just wanted to be sure I could kiss him in front of everyone, and maybe take things a little further before I said those words.

But he was still holding me tightly enough I knew he wasn't falling asleep. No, he was waiting, and since I didn't want to share my thoughts yet, it was time to change the subject.

"Do you think Jeri's ok?" I asked.

He laughed once, the sound soft. "No. Zoe, she's never going to be ok."

"I mean ok for her."

That made him murmur thoughtfully. "I'm not sure. She seems..."

"Calm," I finished for him. "Focused. But is she too focused? And I saw Jason watching her a few times, almost like he's worried about her too."

"He doesn't know her," Jinxy countered. "Hottie's ok, and that makes me think Jeri is."

"But what if she's not?"

He shifted, tilting his head to the side so he could look down at me. "Then she's not, Zoe. It's Jeri. She's never really going to be like everyone else, and she's going to crack a few more times. She'll explode, get herself in shit that we'll pull her out of, and make stupid decisions. It's what she does, and why we love her. That woman is a firecracker." He paused, a strange look taking over his face.

"What?" I asked.

"Woman," he said. "I dunno. It just hit me that she's not a little girl anymore. I mean, the pair of you. You're right on that line, caught between growing up and drowning under responsibilities, and I kinda want to make sure you both get to enjoy being young and dumb for as long as you can."

"Because you didn't?" I asked.

"Yeah, pretty much," he agreed. "Just like Hottie didn't. He and I have talked more than you can imagine, and we can't rewrite our own pasts, so we want to make sure the rest of Ruin gets to grow up the right way."

"But we didn't," I reminded him. "Shawn, that ship's already sailed."

"No, it hasn't," he assured me. "Maybe you and she have some trauma. Maybe it's a whole shit-ton of trauma. You're still an eighteen-year-old girl, figuring out how to be a woman, and there's not a damned thing wrong with it. There's nothing bad about having a teddy bear to snuggle at night. Or about having tantrums when the world fucking sucks, ok?"

"Jeri," I said, realizing the tantrums part was about her.

He nodded sagely. "Yeah. See, she's only ever been allowed to go off in game. Online was when and where she could vent. Now this? She's playing a game, Zoe. To her, destroying these men is just a quest, like the ones in Flawed. She has an objective, she's going to make sure she doesn't die in the process, and she will get the experience points from it. When this is done, she'll move to the next, and then the next after that, and you know what?"

"What?" I asked.

"We signed on to help," he said. "Not just for now, Zoe, but forever. That woman is like my little sister. She will never not be a part of my life. She's family, and you're her family too. That's why we're a part of this thing, right?"

"The polycule? Yeah," I agreed.

"Because she loves us," he said. "Zoe, she loves us as much as she loves those guys."

"Different love," I countered.

He hooked my chin and tilted my head up. "Is it? Is it really? No, I don't think she wants to fuck us, but does she really love us any less or any less intensely than she does her boyfriends?"

"No..." I breathed, realizing he had a point.

"So we make sure we have her back," he told me. "Even if that means picking a fight and making her stop, Zoe. It's *our* job to take care of her in ways her lovers can't. We're not blinded by wanting in her pants, so if anything, it puts more pressure on us, you know?"

"I'd never really thought of it like that," I admitted.

"Of course not. You're a girl, and girls are allowed to have friends like this. Baby, I'm a guy, and trust me, I've heard the jokes about being gay for my friends. I also don't fucking care. I'm not ashamed to say I love those guys. I'm not embarrassed to open up to them or show vulnerabilities around them. They're our fucking family, ok? And that means you are too."

My heart hung for a moment, because he wasn't being very subtle. Maybe Jinxy hadn't said the words, but he'd laid it out pretty blatantly. He loved the people in Ruin. I was in Ruin.

He loved me - and I fucking loved him back.

# CHAPTER 55

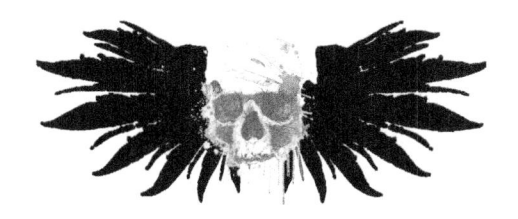

**SPECIAL AGENT JASON RAIGE**

When I woke up Sunday morning, I had to kick Crysis off the bed. The damned dog had sprawled out, and he really didn't want to get up yet. Still, the moment I started moving, he did too, grumbling about it in his doggy way the whole time.

To me, that said he was getting comfortable here. This really was becoming our second home, and the guest bedroom I was using now had little signs of me spread around it. The picture of Zara on the dresser was just one example.

Yet when I made it downstairs, Jeri was already hard at work. I couldn't tell if she'd been up all night or simply hadn't slept long enough this morning. At least Knock had been dragged to bed by Cade. So they both looked rested. Hottie was missing though, so still sleeping. Everyone else was puttering around, finishing up their morning routines before sitting down at their computers.

And we worked. Since we knew the asshole trying to fuck with Alex was a senator, I wanted to make sure we had everything on this guy. Throughout the day, the whiteboard had to be cleaned and restructured. There was just too much information adding up for the size Jeri had started with. When Hottie stood and headed for the short wall, I paused and turned to watch.

On the opposite side from the list of politicians I'd made, he put "Gold." Under that was the name of what I could only guess was a company. Curious, I turned and typed that into Google. Sure enough, it was one of the many sponsors of the most obscure podcasts. The kind whose followers were extremists on either the left or the right.

"We need his fucking banks," Jinxy muttered.

"Why?" I asked.

He thrust a hand at the whiteboard. "Because this guy's getting multiple emails saying he sold significant amounts of real gold." Then he paused. "Hottie, put bitcoin with that. Homeboy has an email confirming the purchase of twenty grand of that shit."

"And there's one account we can start with," Knock said, a devious smile touching his lips. "That shit's perfect for money laundering too."

"Are you in his emails?" I asked Jinxy.

"Hard drive," Jinxy replied. "I mean, this fucker has his laptop set up to save his email, so yeah, kinda. Like, fuck. This thing's a mess, and damned near full. I'm fighting the urge to clean up his system for him."

"Fuck him," Jeri growled, but she never slowed down on her own task.

So I decided to stop playing nice. Yeah, maybe this would get me fired, but fuck it. Pushing aside the keyboard for this desktop computer, I moved my laptop into its place, right in front of me. Then I verified my security, logged into the FBI network, and began activating programs reserved for federal agents. The first one traced financial transactions.

"I need the name of his wife," I said.

Ripper called that out. When I asked for kids, Knock had that. Zoe and Jeri offered others who were a little too close to him, including two female staffers and a male assistant. But in order to track all of this, I had to start with the mundane shit.

"I need addresses on those people!" I snapped.

"Busy!" Jeri replied.

So Zoe took it, and her Google skills were actually impressive. If she couldn't find a house number and street, she could at least get me the town. Often, that was all it took to get me what I needed. My eyes were moving. My hands were busy. Time felt like it lost all meaning, and I only stopped when Cade put a plate of food in front of me.

I ate while my software did its work. Just as the sun was setting, I had the names of the various financial companies used by everyone they'd listed. From there, we got into the hard part, because none of them used the same banks, and most of them had more than one account.

From checking and savings accounts, to stocks, and even offshore options, we busted our asses to get as much information as we could. All of it was saved onto the Squirrel, sorted into folders for each person.

A few times, we had to backtrack and try a new way. Some of these banks were damned good at keeping people like us out, but we had tricks they weren't prepared for. When the Swiss bank timed out for the third time, I pulled up the tools Dez had given me, spoofed the fucker's IP and MAC address, then went in again. This time, I had to crack his password, but in less than an hour, all of his most secret money information was being downloaded.

And the time had flown. None of this shit was easy, but getting lost in a challenge had a way of making the world feel like it should be standing still. It wasn't. My phone began beeping that I needed to leave if I wanted to catch my flight, and yet we weren't even close to done.

"Fuck," I grumbled, pushing away from the computers before me. "Keep going. I want anything this fucker has that might be hinky. Anything. I don't care if it's a folder of puppy pics!"

"I got some nasty gay porn," Knock said. "And I'm talking the creepy shit, not just kinky."

"Save it," I said as I headed out of the room.

First up, I opened the app to reschedule my flight. That was nice and easy, thankfully. Once that was done, I whipped off a text to Bradley, letting him know I was still in Texas, for reasons he would not want to know yet.

He replied with a thumbs-up emoji, so I decided to let Alex know as well. Thankfully, she didn't respond, but that worked out for me. And when all of that was done, I headed out into the backyard - not surprised at all when Crysis joined me - and made the call that would get me in real trouble.

"Everything ok?" Zara answered.

"Hey, babe," I said, moving over to the concrete seating. "I have bad news."

"Is Alex ok?" she asked.

I chuckled, because this woman knew me too well. "As far as I know, yes. But I'm not coming home. I told Ruin someone was trying to replace Alex, and they took off."

"Good," she said.

"Good?" I asked.

"Jason, let's be honest. What does Ruin do best? They stop violence against women. What did Bradley say was going on? Violence against a woman. So yes. Good."

"Well, it really hasn't risen to the level of actual violence," I reminded her.

She just scoffed. "Really? Jason, I love you, but you're so wrong. Look, maybe it's not physical. But are we really going to say mental and emotional abuse are ok? No! It's violence, just a kind that is so normalized it's overlooked and disregarded. It's the kind that leads to fuckers putting a gun to my head - or Alex's. So I'm calling this violence. I'm pretty sure if you ask your team, they'll agree."

"Ok," I relented. "But I called because I don't know how long I'll be here. They don't really need me..."

"Yes," she countered, "they do. They might not need you for hacking anything, but they still need you to teach them how to make this effective. I also know that if you came home, you'd just be sitting here on your computer all night, with your headset on, doing the exact same thing. At least this way you can make sure they're mentally ok too, right?"

"Yeah, that's kinda the thing," I admitted. "Babe, when I told them, they lost it."

"Duh," she shot back.

"No." I grunted. "Crysis was all over Knock. He got triggered because of what happened at F5."

"No..." she breathed. "Fuck. That kid needs a hug, you know?"

And that was why I loved this woman. I had no idea how she could be so absolutely perfect for me, and considering she was the one who'd been threatened? Or one of the ones, if I was honest.

"Zara, the stress we had from watching is not the same as what you went through, ok?" I said gently. "I know that, but - "

"We're not rating our trauma," she broke in. "Jason, that's not how it works. Trying to say my bad is worse than yours? That Knock's bad is no big deal? No! To Knock, it's still bad. He almost lost people he cared about - and that's triggering. So what if I had it worse, or you do? Who cares? Why are we having a dick-measuring competition about how bad we hurt? Why isn't the concern to try to help make it better?!"

"You make it better," I assured her. "You always make it better, baby."

"And how are you doing with all of this?" she asked.

"We're just running numbers," I assured her. "Just keeping track of a bad guy. It's tedious, but easy. Well, for this crew it is."

"And I'm fine," she promised. "I have a big test this week, so getting you out of my hair means I'll actually study. I can also do the next doctor's appointment on my own, ok?"

"No, you cannot," I countered. "I want to be at those."

"Then I'll reschedule if you can't make it back before then." She giggled at me. "You have a little over a week. If you'd like, I can have Murder fly up to hold my hand."

"Well, that's better than me sending you alone," I relented. "But I wanna know what it is."

"And Raige Junior might not cooperate," she said. "Sometimes, it takes a bit. Focus on your team, Jason. I mean, I'm going to miss Crysis, but it's easier to study without you here."

"Says the woman who keeps pulling me into bed," I teased. "Insatiable, I'm tellin' ya."

"Only for you," she promised. "Oh, and how's Jericho doing?"

Because I'd told her all about Jeri's issues. Well, the whole team's, but ever since I'd caught Jeri trying to study in the middle of the night, I'd realized hers might be the worst. The girl was a complex pile of triggers all stacked up on each other, waiting to blow up.

"She's hyper-focusing," I admitted. "Don't get me wrong, she's damned good, but I feel like something's off with her."

"Give me more," Zara begged.

The best I could do was sigh. "She's too calm, babe. She's fucking focused and intense, but she's not yelling and screaming. She's not throwing shit. I mean, I'm not sure if she usually does, but that's kinda how I imagine her. Instead, she's latched onto this like Crysis with the tug rope. Nothing's going to get her to let go, you know?"

"Because hacking fixes things, you said. Right?"

"Mhm," I agreed. "And when I told them on Friday night, she said something. She said they couldn't have her. She meant Alex."

"Fuck," Zara breathed. "You said everyone she cares about dies, right?"

"Or gets fucked up," I clarified. "She calls it her curse."

"Jason..." My wife's tone held a warning in it.

"I know," I assured her.

"No, you don't," Zara said. "This girl is what, nineteen now? I remember being that age, and I promise she's just a kid. And this girl? You know what stability she's had in her life? Nothing, Jason."

"Games," I countered.

"Yeah, ok, because that's so stable. She had fucking video games, bouncing from the newest thing to the next that comes out. I mean, she's got to be a fucking mess."

"And you don't think they all are?" I huffed. "Trust me, babe. They all have issues."

"But not like this girl," Zara said. "Jason, even foster kids have a pretend family. Maybe not one they like, but they have someone to do the adult shit. Jericho? She's been adulting since she was what, ten?"

"Like thirteen," I corrected. "That was when her brother died, and her father a year and a half later. Her boyfriend's fiancée..." I made a noise, because that sounded bad. "Grayson's fiancée died almost a year and a half after that. She moved to Texas, got involved in catching serial rapists, then the shit over the summer."

"So the fact that she's sane at all proves how strong she is," Zara said. "But you know what? Even the strongest of us need someone to lean on."

"And she has four boyfriends," I countered.

"But no mentor."

If I hadn't already been sitting down, my knees would've buckled. As it was, I felt my breath rush out, and Crysis was immediately in my lap, licking at my face insistently. I pulled in a long, deep breath, accepting the anxiety that came with those words, and doing my best to relax into my dog.

"Jason?" Zara asked when I was quiet for too long.

"I'm not anyone's mentor, babe," I managed to get out.

"You're a lot of people's hero, though," she reminded me. "You are a good man, Jason Raige. You are one of the best men, and it's ok to be fucked up. You know what? I bet that makes you even more respectable to Jeri, because it means she isn't a lost cause."

"Zara, I'm supposed to be their handler. Their boss."

"Well, stop that," she said. "Jason, you like this girl. I hear it when you talk about her. You respect Knock, but you feel a kinship with Jeri. Why?"

"Because she reminds me of myself."

"So don't let her make the same mistakes you made, baby," she said gently. "Stop trying to be the proper FBI agent. Stop trying to act like Bradley or whatever. You, Jason, make things happen because you see things no one else does. You care, and maybe that caring hurts, but you know what? It also heals."

"So what do you want me to do?" I asked.

She laughed softly. "God, you're such a good man. Jason, I want you to make sure that girl knows you will help her. Make sure she knows that together, you can fix this. I don't know. Maybe tell her that if anyone holds a gun to her head, you'll kill them before they can pull the trigger? I mean, worked for me."

I ducked my head, pressing my brow into my dog's neck. "Kinda different with Jeri."

"Then find what works," she said. "Believe it or not, that kid needs you, and I knew what I was getting into when I said yes. I'm fine. I'm going to miss you, and I hate sleeping alone, but I am fine. She isn't. So do something about that."

"Ok," I agreed. "Right after Crysis says I'm allowed to stand up again."

"Then get off the phone and pet that boy," she told me. "You're fine, Jason. You're not fucking them up or bad for them. They were already hackers when you met them. You're just showing them a better path. This is a good thing. You, Jason, are a good thing. Oh, and call me every night while you're there."

"I swear," I breathed. "Fuck, I do not deserve you, Zara."

"Maybe not," she teased, "but I deserve you. I also love you."

"I love you too. We'll talk tomorrow."

I ended the call, then gave Crysis my full attention. Yes, I was anxious. Mostly because I was not someone to emulate. I was a fucking mess. The fact that I had an FBI badge came down to how the government had decided I was too dangerous to put anywhere else. I was one big mistake after another, and I'd never wanted to drag anyone down with me.

But maybe Zara was right. Maybe I could lift these kids up. Hopefully, if nothing else, I could at least give Jericho someone to lean on, because I knew exactly how shitty it was to feel adrift and trying to handle that on my own. Then again, I hadn't had an entire polycule to center me.

# CHAPTER 56

### JERICHO

We had school tomorrow. I knew that, just like I knew I needed to head to bed, but I couldn't. Jinxy and Hottie had grabbed an image of this man's entire hard drive. They'd saved all of the most pertinent shit they could find, but one single day was not enough time to rip this fucker's life apart.

He thought Alex was an animal? Well, I'd show him that race wasn't what made a beast. It was the need for vengeance. Alex might not have it, but I sure did. If anyone was an animal, it was me, and I had no problem with the idea of tearing this fucker limb from limb.

When I tried to watch one of his porn videos, I couldn't. The shit was probably supposed to be some serious BDSM stuff, but it looked more like torture. Not like ball clamps or dick slapping. No, this was the blood type. The fucking some guy's ass with objects until it was bleeding. Not at all what I'd call sexy.

It also said a hell of a lot about this pig. He thought everyone else was below him, I bet. He was some ugly sixty-two-year-old piece of shit. And yeah, he was overweight, but that wasn't what made him disgusting. It was the way he sneered in his interviews. The way he looked down his nose at everyone he interacted with.

Dylan had looked at me like that. Evan had looked at Zoe the same way. It was the look of someone who was convinced they were some kind of superior being, but he wasn't. This Milt guy was just another racist, misogynistic prick. He was disgusting, and after reading too many of Alex's emails, I *hated* him.

So as everyone else headed to bed, I couldn't. We had the bank records of everyone around him, but those would take days to go through. We could deal with that after Friday. Right now, I was on a timeline, and I needed to rip this dumbass's virtual life wide open, then pick through the pieces.

Of course, he didn't have a damned clue anyone might want to get into his machine. The fucking imbecile even used the same password for fucking *everything*. Pussy101. Seriously? How completely unoriginal could this asswipe be?

But right now, the only thing we had on him was that he sold a lot of gold. Maybe he was broke? If so, did that mean he was getting into something illegal? But Knock had said his personal wealth had increased into the millions, so why the fuck was he selling gold?

It was probably some political stunt of some kind. That was more Cade's area of expertise, if I was honest. I could barely tell the two main parties apart, and so far as I cared, every politician was just a lying narcissist out to make his own life better at the expense of the common person's. Granted, I might be a bit biased.

"Come to bed soon," Hottie told me, pausing to kiss the top of my head. "You have class tomorrow, and no skipping."

"Ok, soon," I promised.

But I kept going. About ten minutes ago, Jason had taken a call and headed out back. It sounded like he was talking to Bradley. With Hottie gone, that meant I was the last one in the war room. The clock on the wall said it was just after one, so I really should be sleeping, but I wasn't exactly tired. I needed to find something good on this dick so we could make him pay for screwing up this dream we'd all had.

In truth, I wasn't sure what made me more angry, that our FBI gig was basically dead, or what he'd sent to Alex. Both? Never mind that women always got shit on like this, and I was so tired of it. I couldn't count how many times I'd heard these kinds of jokes in-game. Never from our guildmates, but they still happened.

Rape jokes, sexist jokes, just shitty-ass jokes that weren't fucking funny, and I'd thought were completely normal until I'd seen the videos Alpha Team had made. They'd said the same jokes - while *hurting* women! After that, they'd never land the same.

But we had nothing. No one fought this hard to prevent a virtual law enforcement effort unless they were scared of getting caught at something, right? That meant this Milt fucker had to be hiding something, and I needed to find it. That would be the only way we'd protect Alex, because if last year had taught me anything, it was that blackmail really did work.

"Jeri?"

I heard Jason, but just waved him off, because I was busy. If this asshole was into sick gay porn, and he was married to a woman, then was he cheating on her? Those kinds of scandals destroyed politicians, right? All I'd need to do was find some evidence I could chase down, and we could hold that over his head. It was better than nothing.

"Hey," Jason said softly, moving in to lean beside me. "Take a break for a sec?"

"I'm going to bed soon," I assured him.

"Then take a break so we can talk first?" he asked, tilting his head and hitting me with those weird eyes of his.

"Yeah, but - "

"You don't have anything, so let it go and come talk," he said, making it sound more like a command this time. Still considerate, but with less room to wiggle out of it.

I nodded, which made him stand back up, grab my pink travel mug, and head for the kitchen. A moment later I heard the coffee maker going. Chuckling at that, I began closing down everything I was working on, making sure I saved it all. When I was finally done, I decided to shut down my computer. If nothing else, that would keep me from trying to do just one more thing, right? Maybe I'd even make it to bed?

But I'd barely managed to push my chair back before Jason handed me the coffee and tilted his head, encouraging me to join him. Without a word, he walked up the hall, then turned into the study. There, Crysis was sprawled out on the couch, snoozing like the poor dog had worked his ass off today.

"He's been doing overtime, huh?" I asked as I claimed one of the chairs.

Jason took the other, turning it to face me. "He likes it. Makes him feel useful. That's how they pick service dogs, you know. They have tests to see which ones are a little needy."

"I didn't know," I admitted.

Jason nodded. "Crysis was in a kill shelter. The program called Pits for PTSD found him, trained him, and he was matched with me after my last service dog died of old age."

"So he's not your first?"

"Third," Jason admitted. "First was Pandora. I didn't name her. Then I got Master Chief. He was a damned good boy. And now Crysis. He's just a pup, though, so he'll be with me for years still."

"He definitely earns his keep," I joked.

"And did you know you've never asked me why I have him?"

"Uh, PTSD from the military, right?" Because that was what Riley had said.

"Among other things," Jason agreed. "Mostly from killing people, Jericho. See, I killed a lot of people. I convinced myself it was the right thing to do, but it fucks me up. Every single time I pull the trigger, I feel it. It's like the logical part of my mind gets trapped behind all the insanity of my emotions. I go cold. I have trained myself to work on autopilot, but I am not ok."

"I'm sorry," I mumbled, because what the hell was I supposed to say to that?

"You're trying to do the same thing," he told me. "Tomorrow, you have classes. You were so excited for this degree, and one little thing has completely thrown you off on a new direction."

"Well, yeah, but - "

He shook his head. "No buts. The moment you heard someone was threatening Alex, you started doing. Not thinking, not planning, but doing."

"Hottie says I'm a bulldozer."

"And it works for you," Jason assured me. "You're damned good at what you do, but I want to remind you that you aren't just one thing."

Which made me pause. "Huh?"

"Don't lose yourself in being the hero," he told me. "Don't forget about those men of yours. Don't get so lost in the next victim you have to save that you forget about the ones who are right here, working beside you, and still trying to recover from their own trauma. You, Jericho, are one of those people too. You deserve to be more than a machine, churning out virtual miracles for everyone else."

"Oh, because you're any better?" I asked. "Zara told me about you and your pictures."

"I wasn't *allowed* to be friends with them," he said. "I wanted to. I longed to have someone who could talk the same language as me, but I had to keep my distance."

"Knock said you didn't with Riley."

He chuckled and looked down, his cold eyes hitting the floor. "No, I didn't. It was the dumbest shit, though. See, some kid got shot, and when everyone else ran away, she ran *to* him. She was going to save him, but I knew she didn't have medical training."

"Well..." Because I'd been to Riley's house.

"On people," he clarified. "I'd been all over her life, looking at anything and everything she'd ever done. She hadn't even taken a first-aid class since her early years of college. Never dawned on me she'd use horse shit on humans and make it work."

"She's kinda good like that," I pointed out.

"Yeah, but I showed her just a little too much," he explained, "and she noticed. Riley always notices. She also kept it a secret - even from Logan - when I asked her to. All she wanted to know was if I was a good guy, and then she trusted me."

"So you saved her life, right?"

A little smile touched his lips. "Yeah. I don't think of it like that, though. She was saving Logan, so I had her back. She was shielding Dez, and that fucker put a gun to my wife, so I took out Soul Reaper. We were working together, Jeri. It wasn't me saving her so much as her saving me."

Which made me confused enough for my brow to crease hard. "Huh?"

Jason leaned forward, over his knees. "See, when you lose yourself in this shit, it's hard to come back. People become numbers and data. It's easier than trying to actually talk to them - or love them. It's avoidance, Jeri, and I was damned good at it. So good my bosses were starting to think I was all better. So good they told me to leave Crysis in the hotel room while I worked the conventions."

"But he's your service dog!"

"And I was a shell," he said. "And you're trying to do the same."

That made my head snap up, and my eyes landed on his. There was no smile on his face. No joke hidden somewhere in that. The man had his hands clasped before him, and his expression was completely serious.

"What do you mean?" I asked.

"Least you didn't try to deny it," he said, leaning back again. "Jeri, the moment you hear about something bad, you take it personally. I dunno, like a challenge? You dive in, and with such vehemence that you forget there's a man upstairs in your bed waiting for you to let him know you're ok. That there are two more on the other side of this wall - "

"Actually, I think that's the closet or bathroom," I said.

"Pretty sure it's the bedroom, but you know what I mean," he chided. "Knock and Cade are in there, and I'm sure neither would mind your attention. And what about Ripper, huh? He takes care of you, and all he wants is a little bit of affection in return."

"I've just been busy this semester," I tried.

"None of this is going anywhere," Jason told me. "Not college, not the games, and certainly not the assholes online fucking with people. It's not going away, Jericho, but these men of yours? They might. When someone feels like they aren't wanted, they find someone who does want them."

"Well, yeah, but we have - "

"No." He rocked his head slowly from side to side. "Don't even try to say they can just fuck someone else, because that's not how it works, and you know it."

Yeah, I kinda did. I didn't necessarily agree, but I'd seen it often enough. If I was honest, it was why I'd kept to one-night stands for so long. It was easier to fuck without commitment, and my friends didn't need that kind of relationship with me, so it all worked out. But things with Ruin were different. Better, definitely, but also more complicated.

"I've been taking them for granted, huh?" I asked.

"Yeah," he said gently. "You really have been. Here's the thing, though. They love you enough to let you. And that? That's what real love looks like, Jeri. I know you're young, but you are not a stupid girl. Fuck, you're one of the smartest teens I've worked with. Your mind is going all the time, but it's actually ok to stop. It's ok to put it all aside and enjoy the moment, because these moments? Once they're gone, they're gone forever."

"But that's kinda why I don't want to," I admitted. "I know I should, and I do appreciate and love these guys. Hell, Knock told me almost the same thing but... Jason, don't you see? Loving someone is the thing that scares me the most."

"So you'll end up an old lady with nothing at all to treasure in your life?" he asked. "So you'll be lying there, on your deathbed, with no memories to be proud of? All so you can say it didn't hurt? Well, I don't know how to tell you this, but regret hurts, and if you let any of these men slip away from you, you will regret it."

"So I shouldn't help Alex?" I asked.

"Not what I said," he assured me. "But trust your team, Jericho. See, I made you a promise. I told you that if you couldn't do it on your own, then I would carry you. We're a team, and I don't know how to break it to you, but I'm not the one leading this show." And he tipped his head at me. "You are. All I'm saying is that I have your back. I will always have your back."

"Like you do with Riley?" Because that was how he'd just described saving her life.

"Yeah," he breathed. "Just like that. See, I respect the shit out of Riley Andrews. Know what? I respect you just as much. Different reasons, but just as much respect. So I'm going to make you a deal. If you need a break to spoil your boys, I'll cover for you, ok?"

"Why?" I asked, grunting when I realized how that sounded. "I mean, did you give this talk to Knock too?"

"Nope, this is for you," he assured me. "This is between us. I might be the official FBI guy here, but this is your team. Fuck the rules, Jeri. We've never played by those. We're going to make our own, and I think this is the first one. If you need a break - for any reason, even just to make sure your boys know you haven't forgotten them - then I'll pick up your slack. In exchange, if I need a break..."

"I'll carry you," I said, repeating the promise he'd made me. "Ok, God. I accept your offer."

And the man across from me laughed. "You weren't supposed to know about that nickname."

"I know everything," I assured him, even as I stood. "And it kinda works for you. I also really need to go crawl in bed with one of my sexy boyfriends."

"I hear sex puts you to sleep," he joked. "Means you won't skip your classes."

As I left the room, I turned to point at him. "Bad influence, Jason. Bad!"

"Nope, good. Trust me. Besides, you're an adult. I'm allowed to make these kinds of jokes."

I didn't respond, but oddly, I was smiling. I wasn't sure which part of his words made me feel better, or if it was all of them, but somehow, he'd said the right thing to remove the tension in my mind. He'd pushed back the feeling of my curse looming over me, waiting to strike.

He'd also said he respected me.

## CHAPTER 57

**KNOCK**

I couldn't stop thinking about this crap with Alex. Thankfully, Cade was looking out for me. He knew this shit had me off-kilter, so he drove us both to class Monday morning, walked me all the way to my building, and then gave me a kiss to help relax me. It mostly worked.

I still worried about it, and I hated that I did. I knew we were ahead of it this time. We knew who the fucker was already. We were in the process of setting the trap for him, which meant this would end up a win for us.

Sadly, stress didn't listen to reason, so by the time we made it back home, I was itching to dive in and start fucking with this asshole. Yet the moment I sat down at my computer, my amazing boyfriend appeared with a fresh and full mug of coffee for me, then promised he was going to whip something up for lunch.

"I think it's my turn," I reminded him.

"Technically, I think it's Jason's turn," he joked. "but none of your minds are on food, Knock," Cade said. "It's only going to get worse when everyone else gets home."

"I can cook," Jason offered from where he was sitting at his own computer.

Cade just waved him down. "It's fine. I got this. Grilled cheese and tomato soup all around. Filling, easy, and won't taste like shit if you forget about it."

"Good point," Jason agreed.

"Thanks, babe!" I called after him as he headed for the kitchen.

The smile he gave me proved that was all he wanted, so I got to work. Somewhere in all of this mess was the trail that would lead us to our proof. I just had to stop for a minute and let myself think like this asshole. Why was he trying to chase Alex off? What would that do for him?

For the next hour, I bounced ideas off Jason, but neither of us had a good answer. Mostly it came down to this guy being an idiot, an asshole, and a bigot. None of that was enough for the kind of risks he was taking, though.

So we poked. We prodded. When Hottie and Jinxy got home, they joined in. Jason was chasing down the associates of Senator Milt Einfeldt. Hottie and Jinxy were going to peek back into his tech to see if his phone might have anything - or if there were other devices.

I was stuck on the money, so I decided to print out the bank records we had for his personal account. I knew from how Riley ran her business that certain accounts were off-limits for personal use. The IRS would use it as an excuse for an audit, due to the way she had shit set up. Well, how *Kitty* had it set up. So would the senator be any different?

I really didn't want to mess up the digital records we had, though. And I would need to rule the charges out one by one, so the easiest way to do that was by going old-school. Printing out the year of bank transactions from this account, I grabbed a set of highlighters and one black Sharpie, plus my laptop, then headed into the study.

Setting all of that up on Hottie's coffee table meant I had to sit on the floor, but I was good with it. The couch made a well-padded backrest. Then I started looking things up. Most likely, I'd have to make a few trips through this list, but the best data sources weren't necessarily the easiest. And once I was done, it would be one big thing we didn't have to worry about later.

I found payments for pizza on days the Senate had been in session well into the night. Those were marked out. I found his bills, the insane amount of gas he burned going back and forth from Alabama to DC. Did this man not know how a plane worked? But other things weren't as clear-cut.

Payments to his own campaign fund, as an example, looked a bit suspicious. His fetish for spending large amounts on home renovations kinda made sense. His wife and kids likely didn't go to DC with him, but I couldn't find proof of that easily. The real issue, however, were the many, many charges I couldn't make heads or tails of at all.

I was just about ready to pull my blue hair out when the doorbell rang. Looking up, I realized the sun was starting to set, which meant everyone else was home. Fuck. I'd been zoned out for a little too long. But before I could pry myself out from between the couch and coffee table, Zoe came hurrying up the hall.

"Tiffany!" she squealed, unlocking the door.

"Hey, how was training this time?" Tiffany asked, making her way in.

"Yeah, um..." Zoe grunted, closed the door, and then locked it again.

"Why are we locking it?" I asked.

"Prevents any excuse of the door being open or looking tampered with if a cop comes by," Zoe said. "Yes, I'm being paranoid. Not sorry."

"Good call," I said.

But hearing my voice had Tiffany sauntering into the room. "That looks like hell," she teased. "What the fuck, Knock?"

Letting out a heavy sigh, I leaned back and gestured at the nearly one hundred printed pages of numbers before me. "This is what a rich man's bank account looks like."

"Do I want to know what rich man?" Tiff asked.

I laughed once. "Probably not."

"Ok, well, tell me anyway," she said as she headed over to sit on the couch just beside and slightly behind me. "Or at least tell me what I'm helping with. I am kinda good at the numbers shit, you know."

"It's Alex," Zoe said.

"Who?" Tiff asked.

"Our boss," I explained. Then I murmured, realizing that wasn't quite right. "Ruin answers to Jason. Jason answers to Bradley. Bradley answers to Alex, and she's the second in charge of the FBI. She's been good to us too - helped out when shit went down in Vegas, and all that."

"She's one of ours," Zoe said as she moved to flop into the closest chair. "Oh, she's also Black, because it seems this fucker doesn't like that part."

"Fucking inbred idiots," Tiffany mumbled. "Ok. So what is this jackass doing, exactly?"

It was Zoe who answered. "He's sending spoofed email threats to her calling her names - and some bad ones - trying to make her quit. I'm talking relentless harassment, Tiff."

"Why does he hate her?" she asked next.

And that had me leaning my head back and groaning with frustration. "We don't know! Because she's a Black woman is the obvious answer, but it's just a little too obvious. It also doesn't explain why anyone, especially a public figure, would risk getting busted for sexual harassment, racial harassment, and a few things that could be called personal threats."

"Barely," Zoe clarified. "Things like 'do you know where your daughter is,' and shit like that."

"Which would feel threatening to this woman," Tiff agreed. "Legally hazy, but yeah. So how powerful is this guy?"

"Uh..." I looked over at Zoe.

She lifted her hands and shook her head. "Knock, I dunno if we should say."

"Is it worse than knowing Jeri stabbed a guy and made him nod?" Tiff asked. "Because I don't remember hearing about *that* at all."

Which was the little nudge I needed. "Senator Milt Einfeldt from Alabama."

"Fuck," Tiffany breathed. "Ok, so he's in the government..." Her words trailed off. "Lemme guess, he's on the committee that's reviewing your program, isn't he?"

"Yeah," Zoe mumbled. "And he's on the subcommittee too. He also met with Bradley - "

"The guy above Jason," I reminded her.

"And offered Bradley Alex's job," Zoe continued. "Bradley's the white, male, complete asshole in a suit type, you know? At least to those who don't know him. He's actually ok, or so I've been told."

"Bradley's the one who got the feds from the task force to arrest Alpha Team," I explained. "We couldn't reach Jason at that time, so I reached out to Bradley, and while he said it wasn't his job, wasn't his jurisdiction, and so on, he still made sure it got put in the right hands."

"He also told Alex about the job offer, and refused it," Zoe added.

"Ok," Tiff said, thrusting out her hand for the papers. "I think I'm caught up. Now, what we're going to be looking for are charges that don't match anything else, or just seem off. Patterns as well."

"I found a lot of bills," I admitted.

She chuckled. "I see that. Can someone look up campaign finance laws for me?"

"On it," I assured her, pulling up a quick Wiki-How on it, then reading it off.

Tiffany was nodding, then leaned into me so she could grab the Sharpie. Pulling the lid off with her teeth, she started working. Stars, checks, and boxes were made. When she asked for the pink highlighter, I offered that up as quickly as I could.

The woman just dragged her index nail down the list, her eyes roaming across it quickly. When something caught her attention, she made a note. A few times, she blacked out a line. Mostly, she just scanned.

"So," she said after about five pages. "We have a few interesting patterns here. I keep seeing big deposits on a somewhat consistent basis. Not the usual business quarters or anything, but regularly enough to stand out. Every few months, more than ten thousand is deposited. Sometimes a *lot* more. I have some big payments that are murky at best. We'll have to check those out. However, see this?"

"What this?" I asked.

She leaned in, resting one arm on my shoulder while the other held the pages before both of us. "These are all verification charges. Kinda like how when you buy gas at the pump, the pump checks to make sure your card is good, then adjusts the price when the sale is complete, right? Well, these are pulled out, then put back. That means his bank is the secondary source for something else."

"He likes bitcoin," Zoe said.

"I'd compare these to his - "

"Bitcoin account?" Jason asked, walking into the room with a much smaller group of papers. "Yeah, every Tuesday, he pays two thousand dollars' worth of bitcoin to something. A different thing each time, and the number of bitcoins changes due to the fluctuation in value. It's always worth two grand, though."

Then he offered those to Tiffany.

Her eyes went wide. "Am I supposed to see this shit?"

"No." Jason turned to find his own chair, then sat. "I also know when I'm beat, I agreed to play by Jericho's rules, and Ruin says you're in. You've been here less than half an hour, and you've just made more progress on that than we have all day."

"I'm kinda studying to be a CPA," she admitted.

He nodded. "You've mentioned that before. So here's your test, Tiffany. Can you find something to protect our boss? You've been helping them study. You've made a habit of spending most of your free time here. Are you invested enough to take a risk and look at what are illegally obtained financial documents to help a woman who's being harassed?"

"Zoe, I'm going to need a notebook," Tiffany said. "I prefer black ink pens - no clue why. I think it makes the colors stand out more. Fucking hate pencils."

"I can work with that," Zoe promised as she hurried out of the room.

"What'd she find?" Jeri asked, proving she was now here too.

I turned to find her leaning against the thick wood frame of the archway. She looked tired, but the kind that came with dedication, not being overwhelmed. Sadly, I'd seen enough of both to know the difference.

"She found potential bitcoin transactions that stand out," I said. "She's got a few others."

"You'll need to verify these," Tiffany explained. "But here's the thing. A personal check for forty grand? For what? That's suspicious. Never mind all of these transfers to other accounts."

"He has a few," Jason told her.

"Fuck!" Tiffany snapped. "Ok, I'm going to need all of them. This is going to be a mess, and the table is probably easiest."

"Laptop?" Jason asked.

"Desktop," I suggested.

Tiffany just waved that off. "Y'all, I'm not a geek like that. I learned math the long way. I revert to that when it's important. And this? This is fucking important, because no one just cracks jokes about a Black woman in power. They do it because they want to *hurt* her." She paused to lick her lips. "Or they want someone else to."

"Then find me the links," Jason said. "Knock, you're her bitch. Jericho, with me."

I watched as he and Jeri left the room. They were barely down the hall before Tiffany just leaned in.

"Did I fuck up?" she asked.

"Nope, that's what he looks like when he cares."

"He looks like he's ready to kill someone!" she hissed, trying to keep her voice down.

"Which is his job," I pointed out. "And he will, Tiff. That man will kill anyone who tries to hurt the ones he cares about. Since he gave you the data, I'm starting to think you may have breached his tough outer shell."

"Here's hoping," she said. "Just tell me it won't all blow up if I can't find anything?"

"You'll find something," I assured her. "He's a politician. It may not be what we want, but it'll be something we can use."

"Yep, I'm starting to like how you hackers think," she teased, but her pen was already going.

# CHAPTER 58

### JERICHO

Jason led me down the hall and all the way into the living room. Crysis followed, bumping against his person's leg every so often like he was slightly worried, but Jason looked calm. Casual even.

While Knock had been looking over the bank records, we'd started finding other things that just didn't make sense. The gold selling was the main one. Every time good ol' Milt got an email confirming the transaction, a massive amount was deposited into one of his accounts.

Combining the man's interest in bitcoin, his strange cyber-spending habits, and the gold? There had to be something there, but the question was *what*! How the fuck were we supposed to figure out what he was doing if we didn't have a damned clue what he was thinking, or even what his true motivations were?

But the moment we reached the living room, Jason spun to face me. "How much do *you* trust Tiffany?" he asked.

"Uh..." I glanced back up the hall, confused. "She's cool, Jason. She's not going to say anything."

"Not what I asked."

"Ok, so what are you asking?" I countered.

His look softened, turning to something I remembered on my dad so long ago. Pride? I wasn't quite sure what I'd done to get that, but it made me want to stand a little taller. Mostly, it just took away the confusion from a moment ago.

"Your little friend in there is helping," he explained. "She's studying to be a fucking accountant, and you know what the one thing Ruin is missing? A numbers person, because this financial shit? It's the most basic way to catch someone."

"Oh."

"So," he went on, "what I'm asking is how much you trust her, and if it's enough to bring her onto the team."

"You mean, like... with the FBI shit?"

"I mean all of it," he assured me. "Look, we both know this hack is going to kill the program. We both know we have to do it anyway, because there's something brewing, and it'll get bad if we ignore it. We also know that girl is here every chance she gets. She has invested her time and effort, and you like her enough to get up in my face."

"Wrong kind of like," I assured him.

"Don't care *what* kind of like," he promised. "I also don't give a shit about what's in someone's pants. My wife's best friend is Kitty's boyfriend. Murder and Zara have shared a bed. They support each other. They are simply friends, but that man risked his life for her, and that's a real big sort of like. A friendship like, but the lifesaving kind."

"Oh." Damn, he was making me speechless here.

He also had a point. A damned good one, if I was honest. Ruin worked because we were all so close. I'd known Jinxy for years, and even though we were not into each other at all, I still loved the man. He was family, in a way. Definitely a friend, but more than the sorts of friends I'd had at school.

Then again, so was Zoe. I wasn't into girls, but I still loved her. I loved how safe I felt with her, and how easy it was to hang out with her. I loved that she could teach me about girly things while I helped her with the tech shit. I just loved that she was my *friend*.

Friend. Love. Like. Those were words that were complicated and blurry. They got thrown around so easily, trying to use one to deflect from another. But when distilled down to the most basic form - the true form - they meant a lot more than anyone realized. Friends were the ones who had your back, no matter what. Love was intense and terrifying - and didn't have to be kept to sexual partners. Like?

Yeah, like was the hardest of those, because it meant so many things. Mostly, it got used as a way to hold off the big feelings. It was the kind of word people just passed by, yet liking something? That meant an attachment to it. Like was the sort of word that was always pushed down under love, but it wasn't merely the minor version.

I loved my mom. There were times I really didn't like her. I loved having an education, but I'd hated high school. I didn't *like* it. Like meant enjoyment, in a way, which love didn't always encompass. Liking and loving went hand-in-hand, but they weren't steps to climb. They were simply different pieces of happiness - and I did like Tiffany.

"I think she's devious, smart as shit, and trustworthy," I finally said. "I don't think she has a damned clue about computers, though."

"You don't need her to," he assured me. "She needs just enough to work with spreadsheets and bank records. What I want to know is how you feel about her pushing her way into your little... thing."

"Polycule," I offered. "And technically, Knock made that up."

"It still works for you," he said. "Jeri, how distant do you need to keep this girl to keep yourself sane? How close do you want to let her get? That's what I'm asking, because if we keep handing stuff to her so she can help, she's going to get dragged in. If she's already in, then why are you holding her out? Where's the fucking line with this? What's going on up there?" And he tapped my brow.

"She's not a hacker..." I mumbled.

"So?"

"We're hackers."

"And hackers need other skills," he pointed out. "Like accountants. I'm pretty damned sure Ripper and Zoe weren't hackers, but you helped them learn. Cade? He was a gamer, but you made him a hacker. This group works because you, Jericho, trust each and every one, so where the fuck does that girl stand with you? No bullshit here. I need to know what I'm working with so I can make this work."

"She wasn't in our friend group last year, but this year?" I looked up the hall again, towards where Tiff was working with Knock. "Jason, she's changed. Like, completely changed. Tiffany in high school was the popular girl with the nails, the hair, the bullying. All of it. The college version is..."

He ducked his head, making it clear I couldn't stop there.

"I'm trying!" I huffed. "The college version of Tiffany feels real. It feels like she wants to do something important, she's sick of the bullshit - just the way I was last year - and she's looking for her place." I paused. "Huh. And she really is always here."

"Not to mention the amount of work it took to make those flashcards for all of you," he pointed out.

"You think she's trying to buy her way in or something?"

"No, I think she's trying to earn it."

"Oh." Fuck. I was doing it again.

"I'm just not sure how you feel about a girl like that around your guys," he said gently. "Jeri, if she's always here, and you're hyperfocusing..."

"They could find someone else to give them attention, and that someone could be her," I realized, because we'd literally just talked about this last night.

Yet the strange thing was, I didn't care. I also didn't think Tiffany would do that without talking to me. Wait. My first thought should've been that the *guys* wouldn't mess around with her. It hadn't been. Over and over, even when I'd thought I hated her, Tiffany had proven she wasn't that kind of person.

Sure, she was a bitch, but that didn't have to be a bad thing. In truth, I thought of it as an asset. She didn't pull her punches. She wasn't scared to say what she thought, or needed, or even wanted. Most of all, she wasn't looking for some kind of approval. She was looking for where she - the person she was growing into - could fit without bending herself too far.

And she kept coming here. I kept talking to her at school. We'd all begun to rely on her, and my only real hesitation was how she'd been popular in high school? Fuck, that was shitty of me. So she'd learned how to work the teenage social system. Was it necessarily a bad thing? Or could it be one more benefit she had to offer?

"I honestly never thought about including her because she's not a geek," I finally said. "But I'm ok with it. I mean..." I gestured up the hall. "She's helping. All she needed was to hear that a woman was getting fucked over and she dove in. Isn't that kinda what we do?"

"Which is why I brought it up," he agreed. "But Jeri? She's pretty."

"Uh, yeah? She was popular too."

He closed his eyes and groaned. "Ruin is made of two women - currently - and five men."

"Six," I said, gesturing to him.

Which earned me a little smile. "Ok. My point is that men often like pretty girls. I know you always say you're fine with whatever, but stop and think about this. If you bring Tiffany in, how will your group change? Will you be ok with it, or do we need to keep her at the edge like she is now?"

Damn him, he had a point. Saying I was ok with it was not the same as really being ok with it. Then again, I didn't care that Knock and Cade were fucking, but was that different? Had I fallen into the sexist trap of convincing myself that because they were both men it didn't matter? But it did! They were in real, actual love with each other.

But what if it was Hottie? He'd been mine in one way or another for as long as I could really remember. From best friend to big brother to the thing we were now, Hottie was my rock. He'd always been there, but I'd also been happy for him when he'd met Nina. Granted, that had been before we got together.

And Ripper? That was the strange thing. While my gut said I'd be ok with Hottie falling into bed with someone else, I didn't have that same reaction with Ripper. His attachment to me - for lack of a better word - was so complete and total. That man made me feel like our relationship was about so much more than sex, and I was pretty sure he couldn't be casual with someone.

So if he slept with Tiffany, it would be because he was falling in love with her. Not for an orgasm. Not for a little company. It would be feelings, and for me, that was the part that made me hesitate, because I *knew* any of my guys could end up with feelings eventually. That was sorta how it worked when we got to know someone.

And yet, while I had to stop and think about it, I kept coming back to one very big thing. These guys were fine with me dating all of them. Maybe it would be hard, and there was a chance I could be jealous, but if I loved them as much as I thought I did, then it was only *fair* to let them fall for whoever they wanted.

Sure, I'd prefer it was me. But did it matter if it was *just* me? Fuck, the nuances and details made all of this so damned complicated. I wanted to be good to them, and that meant letting them have the choice. I also wanted to keep things as they were now, because currently it was nice, happy, and safe. Right now, we were all working. But Tiffany was right here, among us, and we were still working.

"I'm ok with it," I decided. "I'm not saying it'll be easy, but if something happens, I think our relationship is strong enough to overcome adding in someone else. It has before."

Jason just nodded slowly. "Ok. I honestly believe you. So do you want to make her an official part of Ruin?"

"Uh..." Knock's voice made both of us turn to find him standing at the edge of the room. Then he wagged a finger between us. "Ok, not touching that yet. Jason, Tiff's finding shit. She needs all of his accounts, and she wants his insurance information. Like, what he has insured."

"Print what she needs," Jason said. "We'll get the insurance info in a bit."

Knock nodded, but took another step towards us. "As for Tiff? My opinion? She's not my type. Yeah, she's a good friend, but she doesn't get me going."

"Could change," Jason countered. "The more you get to know someone, the easier it is to have feelings for them."

"Yeah, but - "

"Wait, wait, wait..." I begged. "This all comes down to me, right?" I looked at Jason. "You pulled me aside because you think I'm the weak link here?"

"Zoe and Jinxy are monogamous," he pointed out. "You? Right now, this is all about you. What I'm wondering is if Ruin will implode if that changes."

"We won't," I promised. "See, that's why Ruin works, Jason. It's not about sex. It's about trust. It's about friends. This whole thing? It's about sharing a goal, giving a shit about others, and having the skills to make a difference. It's about being brave enough to flip off the entire world and do what no one else will, and you know what? I think Tiff would."

"Same," Knock agreed.

"Go ask the others what they think," Jason said. "I have a feeling Ruin is a democracy, so let's vote. Quietly, Knock, because if she doesn't pass, I don't want to hurt her feelings. I'm not trying to be a dick."

"What are you trying to do?" I asked.

He chuckled softly. "I'm trying to improve your hacktivist group. I'm trying to make us unstoppable. I'm trying, Jericho, to stop fucking thinking like a fed, and to learn a few things from the kids I'm supposed to be handling."

I reached up and clasped his bicep. "You get a vote too, you know. You're also one of us, and I think you just proved it."

He ducked his head and laughed. "Not sleeping with you."

"Deal," I said. "So think about it, and let's get everyone else's opinion."

# CHAPTER 59

TIFFANY

Knock left to get more information for me, so I slid down and took his place. That put me in reach of the markers and his laptop. Considering he'd left it unlocked, I was going to look up anything I needed. It didn't matter if that was the codes used for some of these purchases or questions about how politicians could manipulate their money.

Page after page, I was starting to see some patterns. The problem was they felt incomplete. Sure, things repeated, but that was all I could see from this side. When Zoe returned with a notebook and pen for me, that made it so much easier. Now I could start making notes and jotting down questions so I wouldn't forget.

What I almost did forget was to thank her for getting this. "Hey!" I called as she was leaving. "Thanks. Not trying to be a bitch. Just think I may have something."

"No, go," Zoe assured me. "Trust me. We all get like that, and I think they're printing up his other accounts."

"Thanks!"

And I was back at it. Sure enough, in the war room, I could hear people talking and a printer chugging away continuously. I couldn't make out the voices, but knowing their handler, it would probably be that man giving orders. He was fucking scary, if I was honest, but everyone else liked him, so I was giving him the benefit of the doubt.

When the dog - Crysis, I remembered - made his way in alone, I realized this couldn't be too bad. "Hey, buddy," I crooned at him, patting my leg.

That was all the pit bull needed. No, I was pretty sure he wasn't just a pit, but he was definitely not the standard golden retriever or Labrador type I associated with service dogs. Crysis was also cute as fuck, so when he flopped down and put his head on my thigh, I rubbed his head without even thinking about it - then got back to work.

Half an hour later, Jericho made her way in with a massive stack of papers. Certain sections were turned one way, different ones were turned the other, showing the breaks between them. With a heavy sigh, she dropped the entire thing down on the end of the coffee table.

"You at a place you can pause?" she asked.

"Yep," I agreed, marking the page and capping the pen.

Then I leaned back and stretched. Sitting hunched over too long could do a number on my back, but whatever. Jason had said I'd already made more progress than they had? Yeah, that meant I could take a few Tylenol later and deal with it.

"So," Jeri said, sitting down in the chair across from me and leaning over her legs. "Tiff, I have a question, and it's a big one."

"Ok?"

"You know we're hackers," she said. "You know we break the law, but usually it's to help people. Right?"

"Kinda have first-hand experience with it," I agreed.

"Ruin needs an accountant."

My head snapped up and her mouth cracked into a smile. She

knew she'd caught me off guard, and yet Jeri wasn't pushing. Still, I felt like I was sorta missing something.

"I'm already helping," I said.

"No, Tiff. Not just with this. I mean applying for the FBI program and everything. I mean being an official part of the team. Being a financial hacker for us. Maybe even a social one. We can train you on the computer shit if you want, but that is not necessary. See, there's a lot more to hacking than just sitting behind a screen in your mom's basement, you know?"

"Still don't have basements down here in Texas," I joked.

Which made her chuckle. "Ok, good point. I mean, Riley does, but yeah." Then she paused to chew at her lip. "But I'm serious. You've been helping us study. You've been hanging out. You were all-in with that Dylan shit, and you didn't fuck it up. Not even when you hated me. So, um, we thought that maybe we should invite you all the way in and get you in on this thing we're doing."

"Who's we?" I asked.

She flicked a finger back towards the war room. "Ruin. Yes, that includes Jason, and he sort of brought it up."

"So he wants an accountant?" I rolled my eyes. "Jeri, you know I'll help you any time you need it. You kinda saved us last year."

"But that's the thing," she countered. "I do know, and you are a friend who's pretty much always here, so why can't you train with us? Why aren't you a part of this? And shit, Tiff, we're making fifty grand a year for part-time! Although there is a downside."

"And that is?"

"On Friday, we have to do psych evals. The fuckers who don't want this program to happen will know who we are, which means they could block us. There's a chance this whole FBI thing won't actually happen." With a groan, she reached up to scrub at her face. "A pretty good chance, actually. Basically the most likely outcome."

"And then what happens to Ruin?" I pressed.

She scoffed. "We're still Ruin, just like we were last year. We're still going to be helping people. We will be breaking laws to do it, but I promise we're good enough to not get caught, we'll still have some connections at the FBI, and we know a shit-ton of gamers who have our backs."

"Helping what people?" I pressed.

"We kinda help women dealing with online issues."

Well, that made it easy, didn't it? "Ok."

"Ok?" she asked. "To which part?"

"To joining!" I said around a laugh. "Jeri, that's what I want to do. I was thinking about being a CPA to help single moms get better tax breaks, since I'm kinda good with numbers. I mean, I really don't want to do politics, and I would suck at most anything else, so I'm going into numbers, and at least accounting means I'd get paid."

"So you're in?"

"I'm in," I assured her. "As in as you need me."

"Friday, we need to be in Dallas by eight in the morning. Be here by seven. Knock's SUV will be packed, but we'll make it work. Tell your teachers tomorrow, and Jason will give you a business card with his info on it."

"For a psych eval?" I asked.

She nodded. "To make sure we're sane enough to do this. I guess the politicians think criminals aren't sane? Dunno. But we're all computer majors here at UNT, we grew up - and met - because we're gamers who went to school together. Our tech knowledge got us into beta testing games, and we learned more and more, then used it to help Jason when he asked. We're not hackers. Got it?"

"Got it," I promised.

She rocked like she was about to get up, then paused. "Oh, and it seems there's some worry about the guys hitting on you, or you hitting on them, and Ruin getting pulled apart because of who is sleeping with whom."

I smiled at her use of whom. "Right. Think you're safe there."

"Yeah, but..." She bit her lips together. "Tiff, if I'm fucking four guys, how fair is that?"

"Fair?" I asked. "Who gives a fuck about fair? That's like saying household chores should be split evenly. Sure, sounds great in theory, but if one person works full-time and the other doesn't? If one has a physical job and the other sits on their ass part-time? There are always extenuating circumstances, and relationships work the same way, Jeri. Fuck fair. Go with what feels right."

"I was mostly talking about you with them," she said softly.

I groaned and let my arms drop on the coffee table. "Jeri, I like your guys, but not like that. Fuck, I can't remember the last time I liked a guy like that - or if I ever have!"

"Because of Dylan," she said, nodding.

But I wasn't so sure of that. "Um, I dunno. It's just..." Fuck!

Crysis rolled and began to push into me. Glancing at him, I began to pet him more seriously. Less hand resting and more movement. That seemed to be what he wanted.

So I kept going. "Jeri, I want friends, ok? Just friends. I'm not poaching anyone's boyfriends, and it doesn't matter if you have more than most. I mean, good for you, am I right? They're still your boyfriends, and we are still friends. Friends do not poach. That's what we agreed, and I was serious when I said that. Just like you didn't poach Cade. I'm sure as shit not going to do it with anyone else!"

"And things change," she said, which sounded like something she'd been told.

So I pushed out a heavy breath. "Ok. Want to know the truth?"

"Hit me."

For some reason, my guts tightened with a hint of anxiety. That made Crysis even more insistent. Using both hands, I rumpled his neck, listening to the tags on his collar clink while I picked my words. Damn, I really hope she understood. Or at least didn't think I was broken!

"I'm not looking for a boyfriend," I explained. "I'm not into girls. I'm also sick and fucking tired of every single guy I've met this year looking at me like I'm some kind of fuck doll. Like, the..." I flapped a hand. "What do they call those things they fuck? The opposite of a dildo?"

"Fleshlight," she offered.

I chuckled, because of course she knew. "Yeah. To those guys, I might as well be a fleshlight. I am so over guys looking at me and trying to impress me by telling me how beautiful I am. Like I chose this face! Fuck that! So I got a good roll of the dice. Yippee. So I get pretty privilege. Joy. But do you know what I do want?" This time, I pointed back at the war room. "Guys like that! Guys who will sit down and talk to me. Who I can lean on without them trying to look down my shirt. Guys who treat me like I have a fucking brain!"

"Kinda why I like them so much," she admitted.

"And I don't want to fuck them," I said. "I just want some friends. I want some real friends who aren't about getting noticed, or wearing the right thing, going the right places, or how many fucking followers we have. I did that. I'm so over it. I just want..."

"To be you," she finished for me. "To relax."

"Yeah."

Jeri stood and moved across the room to sit on the couch beside me. Her eyes flicked to the dog, then back to me. "Tiff? Did Dylan do anything to you?"

"No," I assured her. "I was scared he would, but he didn't."

"And yet you're completely ruling out sex? I mean, I ruled out relationships when I was tired of getting hurt, but I still wanted to get laid. My solution was one-night stands. Yours is friends with no fucking. Why?"

So I lifted up to sit in the corner, turned to face her. Crysis grumbled, then followed, shifting around so he was sitting on the floor beside me. Then he leaned in, thrusting his nose under my hand. Naturally, I petted.

But explaining this wasn't easy. "I'm not a prude, ok? Or a virgin."

"Already know about you and Cade," she assured me.

I nodded. "Yeah, and he wasn't my first. I also don't see what the big fuss is about, but guys can't seem to get enough, and if I'm not fucking them, they're out."

"Not all guys are like that," she assured me.

"I know, but I'm still not..." Reaching up, I pressed the heel of my free hand against my brow and decided to just get it out there. "Jeri, I could give a shit about getting laid, ok? Even when it's good, it's just... I dunno. Like, it's too much work for the payout. I don't even masturbate like my friends did. I just don't fucking care about it, and I don't want to fucking deal with trying to fight with a boyfriend about it."

"So, like, is that asexual?" Jeri asked. "Because I kinda don't understand that one, but it sorta sounds like it."

I flinched in place, feeling like something had just hit me. "What?"

Crysis scooted in place, then looked at Jeri. She looked at the dog. It was almost as if there was something passing between them, but this dog wasn't that smart. Was he?

"Ok," Jeri said. "So, like Knock and Cade are bi, but there's also pan. I can't figure out the difference between those two either. I know there's asexual, aromantic, gay, and a shit-ton of others. Trans too, but that's gender and not sexuality." She waved that off. "I was just wondering if you, I dunno, are asexual? Because if you are, I don't want to sound like a fucking asshole."

"I honestly don't know shit about being asexual," I admitted, "but like... When you said that..."

"So maybe." She nodded. "Knock knows all of them. You should ask him."

"And that's it?" I pressed.

Jeri actually huffed at me. "Tiff! Fuck! If you're whatever you are, and you need some friends, and you've got our backs, then we have yours. I mean, have you not noticed that we're *all* fucked up in some way? Little fuckups like Ripper getting bullied or you getting hit on all the time when you hate it. Big fuckups like Zoe getting raped or Hottie's fiancée dying before they got married."

"And you," I said gently.

"Yeah, and me," she agreed. "Tiff, I'm a big clusterfuck. I'm the fucked-upest of us all. I'm a literal train wreck most days."

"But you still make it work, and they all still respect you," I reminded her. "To me, that kinda sounds like you're not doing too bad after all."

Her eyes dropped down to her hands, and for a moment, Jeri was quiet. "You know, the thing about Ruin that pulled me in was how they accepted me. Kinda like that." She gestured at me. "I said I couldn't do something, and they found a workaround. I said I didn't want to fall in love, so they assured me it was ok. I told them I didn't want to get attached, so we made the polycule." She licked her lips, finally raising her eyes. "And one day I realized I was happy. Don't get me wrong, that scares the shit out of me, but I really am. Maybe Ruin can do that for you too?"

"I just want friends," I swore.

"No," she corrected, "you don't want to fuck. You're using 'friends' wrong, though. You don't want someone to hang out with. You want someone you can trust. Someone to stand with you, care about you, and hold you when it gets hard. You, Tiffany, want a partner. So..." She held out her hand, palm up. "Partners?"

"Why do I think that's a real big offer?" I asked, looking at her hand.

"Partners are the ones you have a bond with," Jeri explained. "It doesn't matter what kind of bond, because lovers is not better or worse than friendships. Partners encompasses it all, because it means we're in this together."

So I took her hand. "Partners," I agreed. "And I'm still not fucking your boyfriends."

"Yeah," she breathed. "I just figured that out. I'm good either way, but if some guy gets stupid at school or something, I'm now your lesbian lover. Deal?"

Shaking once, I let go, leaned back, and grinned at her. "Oh, that's a deal I'm definitely taking you up on. In exchange, I'll do all the financial bullshit this group needs. Even taxes."

"Sold!" Jeri said. Then she pointed at the papers. "Each group is a different account. Have fun, and we'll find a laptop for you."

"I... But..."

She didn't care that I was stuttering. Jeri just got up, smiled back at me, and sauntered out of the room. My brain, however, was spinning. We'd just talked about all of that, and she was cool with it? Not *just* cool, but completely ok with me? And a fucking laptop? What?

But between all of that confusion, my mind returned to the same thing over and over: I was now an official part of Ruin. I was a hacker of sorts. I was actually helping, and for the first time in far too long, I felt like I'd finally made the right choices.

# CHAPTER 60

### SPECIAL AGENT JASON RAIGE

I was out in the backyard, throwing a tennis ball for Crysis, when the back door opened hard. Looking over, I almost got bowled over by my dog, but he veered off in time. Panting, he made his way back to give me the ball, but I couldn't take my eyes off Tiffany running barefoot across the autumn-chilled grass with a piece of paper in her hand.

"I got it!" she said.

"Here, boy," I told Crysis, dropping the ball to let him know we were done.

As he happily chewed on that, I gestured for Tiffany to show me what she supposedly had. "What is it?" I asked.

"Ok," she said, turning to stand shoulder to shoulder with me. Holding up the page, she tapped at lines with the pen in her other hand. "Here, we have a large deposit from pretty much nowhere, right? And on the same date, one minute later, we have an email saying the gold sale went through. But twenty thousand in gold?"

"Heavy?" I asked.

She made a face and rocked her head. "Less than a pound, but here's the thing. Jewelry? It's not heavy. The normal necklace is worth about sixty-five bucks of gold by weight. Gems are worth more, but this place isn't selling or buying gems. Just gold, right? So this? It looks all legit, if you don't look up how much fucking gold is in something!"

"So what does it mean?" I pressed.

Tiffany gave me a very tired and exasperated look. "So you're not a numbers guy either. Ok, like I was telling the rest of Ruin..." She began pointing at various lines on the page. "This is all gold that's been sold. That's a fuck-load, Jason. This is more gold than you or I will ever see in our lives. And this is what this man sells off in a *year*. So, how the fuck is he getting gold? And why gold?"

"He invested?" I offered.

She rolled her eyes. "Doesn't work like that."

"Right," I agreed. "Now, keep talking, but the grass is getting dewy, you don't have on shoes, and we do not need you freezing out here."

"Ok," she agreed, letting me not only turn her, but also steer her back towards the house. "So, if someone invests in gold, it's like stocks. They don't really get gold for it. They get a profit share in the amount of gold sold to a company. Because the USA is no longer on a gold standard, the value varies. But!" She paused as I opened the door and guided her inside.

"Crysis!" I yelled.

Still holding his ball, my dog raced across the yard and into the house, heading into the living room so he could lie on the floor and keep chewing his latest favorite toy. Tiffany smiled at him, then was right back to making her point, proving she was just as tenacious as I'd expected.

"Jason, if you want to bribe someone, this is the best way to do it. Gold isn't traceable. Not in amounts like this. I mean, sure, *you* might be able to, but from the financial side, we can't. It's literally carried, mailed, shipped, or hauled to someone and put in their hands. That means no digital trail!"

"Fuck me," I breathed, snatching the page out of her hand. "And you can't match this to his possessions, right?"

"Nope," she said. "I mean, we're still checking what all he's got insured, but his wife isn't a big jewelry wearer, and unless he dug up some shit in his yard that would have museums in the news, this should've run out a while ago, but Knock's finding records of gold sales going back at least two years." She hefted her hands between us in a gesture of frustration. "Pounds and pounds of gold, Jason! He's guilty of something!"

"But what thing?" I asked. "Tiff, that's the thing. We can't use this to do shit. It's evidence, sure, but where does it lead? How does it help us? What crime was committed, because I'm pretty sure selling gold is legal?'

"Fuck!" She growled, turning up the hall. "I'll find it!"

"Don't forget to breathe!" I called after her. "It doesn't happen in a day."

"I know!"

And then she was gone. Still, there was something about seeing this side of her that made me approve of her even more. I had a feeling she and Jeri would butt heads, but someone needed the balls to stand up to Jericho. Tiffany had them. No one else in this house really did, not even me.

But Tiffany was working out; Jericho had approved the idea and asked her if she wanted in. This was happening, so I needed to do my part. Unfortunately, this was one phone call I really didn't want to make. I also wasn't doing it inside, so I snapped at my dog and opened the door again.

Crysis didn't move.

"Bud, I'll throw some more," I offered.

Tensing, he picked up his ball and huddled over it.

"Outside!" I ordered.

With a heavy sigh, my dog obeyed, letting me know he wasn't into this, but he was still listening. The fucker. Granted, he wasn't wearing his vest, which meant he had more freedom to express his opinions. He also tended to do this when he really needed a break, so while I made this call, I would definitely throw the ball a bit more.

Finding a place to sit, I had Crysis give me the ball, then hurled it out as far into the yard as I could. While that brindle-and-white butt zoomied around the yard with his catch, I scrolled through the contacts on my phone, then dialed.

"Do I want to know why you're still in Texas?" Alex answered.

"Good evening to you too," I said.

"Jason!" she hissed. "The range notified me that your appointment there was canceled on Saturday. What the fuck are you doing?"

"I'm herding cats," I said. "See, you assigned me to this group of hacktivists, and you know something? They aren't agents. They aren't law enforcement. They also really fucking hate things like rules. Worse, this group happens to have a hard-on for fucking up people who harass women. Alex. You're a woman."

"Fuck," she grumbled. "Please tell me you didn't let them do anything stupid?"

"Nah, I helped them."

She groaned. "This is going to blow up in our faces. You know that, right? I just need those kids to keep their shit together until this program is - "

"It's dead," I broke in. "It took Jericho less than a second to realize that. I mentioned the psych evals are on Friday, the consultant will have their names, and she put all the pieces in a row. Alex, you've been getting harassed. Jericho got an email with a similar tone, but I can't get to its sender. The shit keeps timing out at the mail server. From the IP address, it looks like it's at 1600 Pennsylvania - "

"Avenue," she grumbled. "Fuck."

"But the guy giving you shit? Milt Einfeldt from Alabama. So far, we have proof that he's crooked, but we're not quite sure how - yet. The man has sold pounds of gold, Alex. Pounds. Not ounces. We're checking and cross-checking everything, but something very suspicious is going on, and it looks like our gentleman from Alabama is getting bought off by someone. The question is who, why, and where *that* will lead."

Alex's tone changed completely. "Already?" She sounded pleasantly surprised.

"I also need you to add another name to the list," I said. "Tiffany Bowen. I don't have her info in front of me, but she was involved in that shit last year, and is now Ruin's financial specialist. Getting her degree in accounting to be a CPA. Knows jack and shit about computers, though."

"Well, that's at least going to be easy to approve," she said. "But she's coming into this late, Jason. Can this girl catch up? At least, I'm assuming she's a girl?"

"Same age as most of these kids," I agreed. "Eighteen, nineteen. Graduated from Sanger High with most of this crew, which is how they know her."

"Can she catch up?" Alex asked again, this time with more insistence in her tone.

"She's been making sure the rest of them know their shit," I explained. "This girl made flashcards, broke down the information they'll need, and is working as the teacher. Yeah, I think she knows the book shit. Supposedly, she knows how to shoot a gun, but I'll need to verify that. I've never seen it myself."

"Do it," Alex said. "Take her up there alone for all I care, but make sure they'll pass. I'll get a contract made up like the rest. Print that out, have her sign it, and put it in my hands the next time you see me."

I murmured and reached up to scrub at my face. "Alex, you know the program is about to get killed, right?"

"I'm not letting go that easily," she assured me.

"Then you'll be punted," I pointed out. "Senator Einfeldt doesn't want to get busted for whatever shit he's involved with. Now, do you think he's the only corrupt politician on that committee?"

"We have to try," she said. "Jason, we can't just give up on this, because for the first time, they're actually listening to us. So get those kids to jump through the hoops. Have them pass their tests. When the shit hits the fan, I want to make sure we aren't the ones who stink, ok?"

"And when my group is the one throwing that shit?" I asked.

"Jason, you have to get them to back off."

I laughed wryly. "That's not happening, Alex. When I told them about Bradley being offered your job, they were pissed. And I mean angry like you aren't used to seeing. But the emails? That's what broke them. Jericho said no one touches 'one of ours.' She meant you."

"And I'm fine," Alex tried to assure me.

"You have over five hundred emails that all but constitute hate speech!" I snapped. "Don't give me that 'fine' shit, Alex. And don't you fucking dare try to tell me you're used to it, because that only makes it worse! This?" My voice was getting rough and angry. "This is what Ruin does. This is the shit online that hurts women, and they are after your job. You, a hero to quite a few little girls in the world. Girls who were told to play with dolls, who think cops are the enemy, or whatever. You, Alex, are a damned icon, and we will not let them pull you down!"

"But you'll give up the program for it?" she huffed. "Brilliant, Jason. Bradley said you were impulsive, but this? This is nothing but a bad call. I'm fine, I'm safe, and I can't fucking be touched."

"You can be fired," I reminded her.

"And I'll be alive!" she shot back. "Our internet security services group won't be. The whole concept will be shuttered and hidden so far away that it won't be revived in our lifetimes. Focus on the damned program, get them out of computers they shouldn't be in, and keep them in line, dammit! You're their fucking handler!"

"Approve Tiffany for a psych eval," I said, "and we'll do both."

"No."

I just chuckled. "Alex, I respect the hell out of you, but you made one big mistake. You took me off the leash. That means I can quit. Pretty sure you haven't realized that yet."

"You wouldn't..."

"I sure as shit don't want to," I promised, "but if this program dies, you will get my resignation. You will also have the full cooperation of Ruin, any time you need, off the books. This is not a threat, Alex. I'm just done with waiting. *Constantly* waiting. For once, I have the team to do something, and whether you like it or not, I'm not the one calling the shots here."

"Who is?"

"Jericho."

"Fuck," she breathed. "Ok. I'll get Tiffany added onto the list for everything. No one should even notice. You, Jason Raige, get them qualified. As for this bullshit? I don't want to see shit about it until our program is cleared and official, you hear me?"

"I'll try my best, but I'll counter with us sending proof of crimes to you first."

"Bradley," she corrected. "Have him run it up the chain of command. But this senator is going to know who Ruin is, Jason. He'll have recourse to filing charges."

"So turn your threats over to Bradley," I suggested. "And explain that as a 'test,' you had my team trying to identify the sender. When we do, you'll be covered."

"Fine," she grumbled.

"We've already got his balls in a vice, Alex. The man's dirty, and my team's about to prove exactly how dirty. So right now, you need to be bracing for impact."

"I just..." she sighed. "Fine. I know you're right. I do. I also think this program is so much more important than I am. This program will save countless lives."

"This program," I assured her, "isn't about to stop. Only the legality of it will. Einfeldt wants to kill it, and we can't stop that, but we can stop him. We also have one rule in Ruin. We never leave one of our own behind."

"Then I'll get your back," she promised. "No matter how bad this blows up."

# CHAPTER 61

### JERICHO

Once Tiffany had zeroed in on the gold, we all got to work dragging up anything we could find with it. Knock and Hottie hit up the insurance to see if Milt had an exceptional amount of family jewelry or something. Cade was assigned to look up anything Tiffany needed while we made sure her laptop was good enough to run the programs we'd need. Ripper and Zoe were tracking the value of gold and bitcoin, so we could compare those numbers against Milt's financials.

But it was Jinxy who figured it out. When we couldn't find any gold this man claimed to own, that meant it had to come in the mail. He went to the source, the United States Postal Service, and checked deliveries to any of Milt's addresses by weight. He didn't find them all, and the numbers weren't perfect, but the correlation was enough for us to be sure someone was sending gold to this man.

And it all came from Russia.

That had Ripper checking the payments against votes. The more votes there would be in a quarter regarding international relations or various wars, the more gold Milt seemed to get. Once every three months, the man received a payout, and the values were in the tens of thousands. Twenty here, sixty there, and the highest seemed to be a hundred and twenty thousand dollars' worth right around the time the Senate voted on sanctions against Russia.

Yeah, like that wasn't blatant as fuck.

But just when we started getting everything to line up, the dreaded day arrived. Not only did Friday start stupidly early, but this crap would expose our names. From here on out, we were taking a massive risk each time we dove into Milt's crap. Worse, we were getting evaluated for our psychological competence, and if I was honest, I wasn't sure this was going to fly the way Jason wanted.

Because we were all broken. Tiffany and Ripper should be fine. Zoe had a few big red flags, as did Hottie. Jinxy could probably pull it off, and I had a feeling Knock would simply fake his way through it. Cade? For all I knew, he could go either way. His dad had fucked him up bad. He'd also handled it a lot better than he should've. The real issue was me.

When we showed up at the FBI headquarters in Dallas, we were all given visitor's badges and led down a hall. There, a selection of leather and chrome chairs had been placed against the walls on both sides like it was some kind of hospital waiting area. The woman who'd guided us here promised the psychiatrist would be with us shortly, then left.

"Ok, I'm nervous," Tiffany admitted.

Jason leaned back and kicked his legs out in front of him. "There's a paper or digital portion. Mostly multiple choice, based on opinion. When you finish that, you speak to the psychiatrist for a bit, and it's over. Simple, easy, and I've passed these dozens of times."

"How?" I asked.

"By being ok," he said. "That's all they're checking for. Just to make sure you're mentally ok."

I nodded, but that really didn't help. These tests couldn't be too obvious or everyone would pass. They also couldn't be too limited, or no one would. Yet the fact that Jason could ace these gave me a little hope.

Soon enough, an older woman opened a door beside us and called out, "Cade Bradshaw?"

"Why am I first?" he asked even as he got up.

"Luck of the draw," the woman assured him. "I tried to make it random, so I drew your name out of the hat first. Won't you come in?"

His leaving made the rest of us turn tense. For the next half hour, we looked at each other but didn't seem to have anything to say. I was pretty sure that was both the early hour and our nerves all crashing into each other. Then, the woman appeared again.

"Shawn Paxton?"

"Joy," Jinxy said, standing up.

Then he disappeared. Forty minutes later, Cade returned, but the halls were starting to get busy. Agents were making their way from one place to another, falling silent as they passed by us. A few looked at Hottie and nodded. When it was quiet again, Cade leaned forward.

"It's not too bad," he assured us. "Basically just what Jason said, and mostly about what you'd do in various situations, which thing you prefer, and so on. The interview part with the lady? She's nice. Not even stressful."

Which helped.

Next up was Hottie, then Zoe, and then Knock. Each person took an hour and fifteen minutes in there, give or take. The wait times were long and slow. Worse, we *really* didn't want to talk about our latest project here. So instead, we fidgeted. We tried to nap. We just waited.

Finally, it was my turn. The woman led me into a room, showed me to a computer, and gave me a very simplistic explanation of how it worked. The basics, which I pretty much could've figured out on my own. Then she said she'd be back once she was done with her interview, and when I finished to just wait quietly.

The test was easy, though. Or at least not like my tests at school.

Instead, this was more like those online quizzes. What color would I paint my house, and shit like that. Naturally, it got harder. By the time I finished, it was definitely hard to see which answers were supposed to be the right ones, because for some of the questions, the real answer was *definitely* the wrong one.

Maiming, killing, and bashing people likely wouldn't get me a passing score, so I did my best to choose the socially acceptable option. The thing a good girl would do. Surprisingly, it was easier than I expected. I just had to put on the persona of someone like who Amber had been, and then try to answer the way she would've. Kind, compassionate, and without a desire to make assholes suffer.

Then I sat for a while. Eventually, Knock left the private room at the side, flashed me a smile, and went back to the hall. A moment later, the woman walked to the door and called my name.

"Have a seat in there, and give me a moment while I get the next set up, ok?"

"Yes, ma'am," I agreed, doing my best Amber impersonation.

Because that was how I was going to get through this. The FBI wanted to know if I was stable. Amber had been, before John abused her, raped her while she was unconscious, and she only found out when she ended up pregnant. But before that mess, she'd been quiet, gentle, and respectable. I was pretty sure I could convince this woman I was at least close enough to count.

But the clock on the wall had a second hand that ticked loudly. It was almost as if this entire experience was designed to throw us off and break us a bit. When the woman actually sat down and picked up a clipboard, I was a vibrating ball of nerves.

"Ok," she said. "Jericho Williams, right?"

"Yes, ma'am," I agreed. "I'm also really nervous."

"I promise there are no right or wrong answers."

"The FBI doesn't agree," I pointed out. "Hence the nerves."

Which made her chuckle sympathetically. "Well, I think you'll do fine. Now, why don't you tell me about your childhood? How do you get along with your parents?"

Letting my eyes close as I braced, I tried to make this as gentle as possible. "My brother died when I was thirteen. He went to a party, tried drugs, and he overdosed. Um, about a year later, my father killed himself because he'd let my brother go, and he said he felt guilty. My mom? She struggles with temporal amnesia, and sometimes forgets they're no longer with us. So, it's been rough."

She nodded and made a mark. "How was your relationship with them, before the tragedies?"

Much easier. So I allowed myself to think back and relive my childhood for just a moment. Those had been the good times. The safe ones. Back when everything was how it was supposed to be. But the questions didn't stay on my family. They moved on to how I had coped, my progress in school, and why I'd become involved in computers.

I couldn't really lie. There was no other explanation for how I'd ended up here, but I did leave off the bad stuff. My hacking became beta testing. My coding became mod building. Bit by bit, this woman asked about both the good and the bad, weaving a line through my experiences to get my reactions, and the best I could do was simply answer.

Then it was over. The psychiatrist told me I could return to where the rest of my group was waiting. I got up and left, finding Ripper at the computer, and smiled at him encouragingly the way Knock had with me. Then I was back in the hall.

"Tiffany Bowen?" the woman asked, proving she'd followed me out.

"That's me," Tiff said, hopping up.

But we weren't alone. A pair of men in suits were talking to Hottie and Jinxy. Hottie was standing with them. Jinxy was sitting close enough to throw out remarks. Everyone else looked like they were desperately trying to listen in.

Confused, I made my way back to my chair, only to have Cade lean over and say, "I think Hottie made an impression."

I looked again, and recognized Agent Carver from our meeting at the Sanger Police Department. He'd been the kind Black man who'd been in charge. The guy beside him wasn't familiar.

"I'm telling you," Carver said, "the Bureau would snatch you up in a heartbeat, Grayson. You already have the bachelor's; you're almost the right age. Months now. You should apply."

"Pays more than consulting work," the other added.

"I'm happy with the consulting," Hottie assured them. "I also figure it will look good to already have experience with the FBI before applying, right?"

"There is that," Carver said. "But Dallas is always looking for good agents, so don't fall into the trap they'll set in Quantico. New York and D.C. always look so exciting, but new agents? You'll end up behind a desk or filing reports. Ask for a field office, and we'll let you get real experience."

Jason chuckled. "Coming on a little strong, Agent Carver."

The man turned, and his eyes landed on Jason. "I saw the case this team put together..." His eyes dropped to Jason's dog. "Sir?"

"Just Jason," he promised.

"Kwasi," Carver offered, "although people around here call me Waz."

Jason just gestured to Hottie. "But feel free to keep trying, Waz. I've never seen the recruitment side of the Bureau before."

"Do you get a kickback if someone signs up?" I asked Agent Carver.

"No, we get good agents," he assured me. "So when you're twenty-three, with a degree, come talk to us."

I scoffed. "Yeah, pretty sure the FBI doesn't want me."

"You'd be surprised," Carver said. "That shitstorm in Denton? We were chasing our tails until your group broke the case wide open." He turned back to Hottie, then smiled at Jinxy. "But since you already have at least one qualification..."

"And more than a year to go," Jinxy reminded him. "Sorry, man. I'm not up for grabs yet. I'm also invested in this team."

Which was when the other agent shifted to lean against the wall by Hottie. "It's actually a pretty good gig. In the smaller field offices, like Dallas, we have quite a bit of crossover between the standard roles. So a cybersecurity agent could work on a critical response group, and so on. No one tends to get stuck behind a desk for their entire career. Granted, none of us get to be as cool as the guys in those TV shows either."

"I have no interest in serial killers," Hottie assured him.

"Just think about it," Carver said. "Grayson, you already have the physical fitness. Stay away from partying in college, though. They'll want three years drug-free, bare minimum. After that, as soon as you turn twenty-three, you're eligible."

"Planning to get my master's degree first," Hottie said. "I mean, I appreciate the advice, but I've made it this far. Would hate to leave it unfinished."

"Good attitude for an agent too," Carver said with a smile. Then he took a step back. "C'mon, Paul. Let's leave this crew alone."

"Seriously," the man called Paul told Hottie. "Consider it!"

"Will do!" Hottie said, offering a thumbs-up like the dork he really was.

I had to bite my lips together so I didn't giggle. Wow, that had been some unexpectedly high-pressure recruiting there. Which was kinda nice, because it made me think our chances were better than I'd feared, but still. None of us were twenty-three. Most of us were just freshmen! We weren't even close to qualified.

"What the fuck?" Hottie finally whispered when the guys were long gone. "Seriously, Jason, what was that?"

"You fit the type," Jason explained. "Clean-cut, muscular, and confident. If there was a template for the men who make it to Quantico, you'd be it."

"Fuck," Jinxy said with a chuckle. "Hottie, put on a suit and you could be a fed next year for Halloween."

"How about I just wait to see how we all did?"

But Jason shook his head. "We won't get the results for a week, at least. You get to take the test. The psychiatrist gets to analyze the test. Then she'll give those results to Alex, who's the one in charge of this program. None of us will hear anything until next week, at the earliest. Probably closer to ten days, if I'm honest."

"And we have the Seattle tournament at the end of the month," Knock said. "Jason and I will both be there."

"Riley too," I realized.

Knock nodded. "Yeah, so... Wanna babysit the horses again?"

"Wanna bring Quake to our place so we can go twice a day?" I asked.

"I can do that," he agreed.

"Then deal." And I leaned back again. "I feel like I've been stuck waiting all day."

"Because you have," Jason said. "They didn't give us a break for lunch. How about I buy all of you something before we head home?"

"Starving," Cade admitted. "So, yeah. I won't turn that down. Hell, I'm fine with just stopping so we can all sit, eat, and discuss!"

"Lots of discussing," Jinxy agreed. "Fuck. This is going to be so bad."

"It'll be fine," Jason promised. "So don't stress about it. Just wait until we get the results, and we'll deal with it then. And by the way, *this* is how the FBI really works."

"Hurry up and wait," I grumbled.

Jason nodded in agreement. "It's why nothing moves fast. Nothing at all, not even our cases."

I just looked over and caught his eyes. "Fuck that."

His smile proved he completely agreed.

# CHAPTER 62

## JINXY

Now that Tiffany was an official part of Ruin, we were moving faster than I'd expected. Usually, trying to dig up this much dirt on someone - anyone - would take weeks. Instead, Senator Einfeldt was so completely ignorant about computer security that it was all just hanging out there, begging us to take advantage of his stupidity.

So we did.

And what we found? Holy crap, this guy was corrupt. Tiffany had receipts to construction companies for a few thousand dollars. Knock had adjustments to his homeowner's insurance for hundreds of thousands of dollars because of that work. And then there was Cade, our politics specialist, who could tie those "gifts" straight to votes on tax laws, business laws, or other things that could help out his construction friends.

And that was only one example! Zoe had been checking Einfeldt's social media accounts. While his Facebook was set to private, the moron always used the same password, so she got in easily. There, she found photos of multiple family vacations - which none of his banks showed a hint of. Ripper traced the registration of the private jets they used, which were always in at least one photo, to various billionaires. Most were lobbyists.

And the gold? Yeah, Hottie and I had been tracking that through the postal system. It got a little challenging when we had to deal with the Russian portion, since neither of us spoke that language. Thankfully, Google Translate was good enough to give us the basic idea. Not surprisingly, it had come from a rural residence owned by one of the many oligarchs over there.

But what we were short on was proof, so that was the plan for Sunday. We had a jigsaw of pieces, but nothing quite fit together without using circumstantial evidence. We had to close the deal, make sure it would stick, and wrap this shit up with a damned bow.

We also needed sleep, so I convinced Zoe to come snuggle in my room again. It was easy. All I had to do was remind her it was one less flight of stairs, and she agreed enthusiastically. Oh, I couldn't get enough of her pulling on my shirt to go with her little panties as she crawled into my bed.

Damn, this girl was gorgeous. She had curves that did very bad things to my mind. Her face, her eyes, her lips, and even her tiny little feet all made me want to wrap my arms around her and hold her close. She was just this adorably petite thing, but so incredibly feminine at the same time. Basically, every single one of my buttons had been pressed, and she was completely to blame.

She was exhausted, though. So when she curled up against my chest, tossed her leg over mine, and passed out, I wasn't surprised. I also liked it. Oh, I enjoyed kissing on her even more, but there was something so gentle and trusting about this. The sort of thing I would never get enough of.

Tilting my head towards her, I drifted off. Somewhere in the middle of the night, we shifted. When she faced away from me, I curled up against her back. When I rolled over, she turned into the big spoon. In all the time we'd been doing this, I'd come to realize she always touched me. All night long, no matter what, she adjusted so we could be touching, and it proved she was going to be ok. I could wait as long as she needed for that day.

But Sunday morning hit much too early and with a noise I could not ignore. My phone was blaring out "I'm Too Sexy" by Right Said Fred. That was the ringtone for one of my brothers. Reaching, I grabbed the thing and swiped while trying to force my eyes to open.

"What the actual fuck?" I croaked.

"Teal, Magenta," Ashton said.

I was instantly awake, because invoking our colors like that meant something was important. The kind of important where we all agreed to drop everything else.

"Go," I said, looking over at the clock on my wall. It was barely after eight in the morning!

"I don't care what you're doing and who's listening," Ashton said over me, "I need you to get your ass up to Southwind. We are currently in New York, and Crimson was just attacked. He's on his way to the hospital right now. Chartreuse is in that house all by herself. The cops in town are crooked, so if you have that FBI guy's name and number, you might want to give them a heads-up. Regardless of that, I just need to make sure that someone's up there with Cessily in case they try again."

I was immediately rubbing Zoe's shoulder. She was once again lying across me, and I was stuck here until she moved. "Zoe. Hey, babe?" I had to shake her again before she actually murmured, proving she was waking up. "Get Ruin for me, would you? I need to head up to far North Texas, and I'd like to have a few more hands with me. I don't even care who."

"Sounds like you have your own network going on up there," Ashton said.

I scoffed. "Yeah, something like that," I agreed. "Look, it's gonna take me about an hour to get there. I don't care how fast I drive; it's still gonna take a bit."

"Well, I just know that Crimson left Chartreuse with a gun," Ashton warned me. "The gate code is Gran's birthday. If you can do me a favor and check the horses when you get there, I'd really appreciate it."

Horses. Ok. Knock knew how to handle those, because I sure as hell didn't. Shit, Zoe probably could too, but if someone had attacked Crimson? Yeah, I didn't want Zoe anywhere near that. Knock could at least hold his own.

"I actually have just the guy to help," I assured him. "Don't do anything stupid trying to get back. We'll hold down the fort. Unfortunately, my friends have a little experience with this."

Ashton thanked me, then hung up. He sounded frazzled, which meant this was bad. Clearly worse than I thought, if some fucking idiot had gone after one of the bigger and meaner brothers I had. Unfortunately, Zoe was not a morning girl, and this was much too early for her. She'd fallen back asleep.

"Zoe?" I begged. "Baby, I have a family emergency. I gotta get up."

That worked. Immediately, she pulled back, her eyes opened, and she was trying to both roll over and sit up at the same time.

"You need Ruin?" she asked, clearly having heard some of what I'd asked.

"I'll handle that," I assured her. "I'm gonna steal Knock for a few hours. There's horses involved, and bullshit. Can you tell the rest where we went?"

"Yeah," she agreed. "Who's hurt?"

"One of my brothers," I said. "He's in private security, so he's probably ok, but they need another hand at Southwind, and I'm closest." I leaned in to kiss her brow. "Go back to sleep, baby. It'll be fine, but I'm not going to be much help today."

"We'll handle it," she promised. "Shawn, family always comes first. Go."

So I found clothes, my keys, and went. Jogging down the stairs, I paused to write a note to Jason, giving him Ashton's number. That, I left on the desk beside his keyboard. At the bottom I scrawled a note that the cops in Cats Peak were crooked, and any help would be appreciated.

Because this was just what we needed right now. Another problem to distract from the one we already had? Yeah, that seemed to be how things worked out for us. Not that it mattered. I'd find a way to handle this - and I had no doubts my partners would help without hesitation.

Then I headed for Knock's room. Banging on the door made someone yell on the other side. I was pretty sure it was supposed to be, "Just a minute," but it hadn't been quite that clear. So I waited. When they still didn't open the door, I banged again.

"Guys, I need a hand."

"Come in!" Cade yelled.

So I turned the knob and eased the door open. The pair were still in bed, but sitting up. Thankfully, they also had the blankets up to their waists, but both men looked confused and bleary-eyed.

"Knock, I have a little emergency at Southwind. It's complicated, but one brother's in the hospital, three other siblings are out of town but flying back as we speak, and a sister is there all alone. There are horses that need to be cared for, so..."

"Yeah. I need clothes," Knock agreed. "Oh, and you're driving. Brew me a coffee, and I'll be ready to go before it is."

"Thanks, man," I said. "Cade, I told Zoe, but make sure the rest of Ruin knows what's going on? We might be gone all day."

"Can do," Cade promised. "And we'll handle it, Jinxy. Just go."

"Going," I promised, backing out of their room and closing the door behind me.

Damn, that was why I loved these people. I'd barely had to explain, and they'd been willing to jump right in. Didn't matter what help I needed, or that it was an ungodly time of morning - especially for a weekend! They were still ready to have my back without question.

But filling our travel mugs took a minute. One teal mug for me, a blue one for Knock, and a quick check to make sure my car wasn't blocked in, then Knock came staggering out of his room, pulling on one of his Flawed shirts. Yeah, he was definitely not in any shape to drive.

"Your coffee," I offered.

"Fuck yeah," he breathed before taking a long sip. "Ok, let's do this. It's like an hour and a half there."

"Yep," I agreed, headed to the door.

We piled into my car, got on the main road, and I set the GPS to find me the fastest route there. We'd just made it out of the cluster of small towns around Denton when Knock sighed, making me think he was finally functional.

"Caffeine kicking in?" I asked.

He chuckled. "Yeah. So what's going on this time?"

"Violet, Magenta, and Cyan are in New York. Mm, the boyfriend too."

"Right, the kid's dad," he agreed, because he knew that much.

"Same," I assured him. "Crimson and Chartreuse were watching the house, I think. Crimson got jumped. Ended up in the hospital. That's all I know so far, but they're going after Violet. They just didn't expect her to have such a big family."

"Shit," Knock drawled. "Trust me, I know how that is. I mean, just look at Riley and the gamer crew we have." He kinda laughed. "You know, Jinxy, you and me? We're not that different really. We both have fucked-up sisters, to start. We both have families we weren't born into, and we're both some serious nerds."

"Yeah, we are," I said, flashing him a smile. "Our sisters are a bit different, though. Riley's a force of nature. Violet? She's..."

"A supermodel," he said.

"Well, that," I agreed. "Ashton used to be, before he got too masculine. Don't ask me why that's a bad thing, but it is. But I more meant that Vi's..." Yeah, how to put this. "Man, she's a glass fucking cannon, you know? The woman is so distractingly beautiful, and she's powerful, and she's rich. She's also fragile as fuck, and I think that's why her fucked-up relationship actually works."

"They're doing a poly thing, right?" he asked.

I nodded. "Yep, which is why *this* poly thing isn't as weird to me anymore. I mean, that mess just works for them. Granted, it's more like you and Cade and Jeri. Like, everyone's fucking each other, I think. 'Cept the kid, of course. Last time we talked, Crimson was telling me the new boyfriend is kinda evening it all out, and we talked about how sometimes it really does take a village, you know?"

"Don't I ever," Knock agreed. "So is Violet why you're so into helping women the way we do?"

"Um..." I shrugged. "I think she's part of it. Mostly because she helped me, back when I was young. She's the reason I could game, you know? But it's also seeing Gran and Bea get shit on for being lesbians. It's hearing Chartreuse's story, and Scarlet's, and all the other girls I grew up with. I mean, I thought I had shit, but them? There was always a man somehow mixed up in it, you know? Chartreuse's little sister? She fucking ended up killing herself because of a step-dad, before Chartreuse could get out of the program."

"Fuck," Knock breathed.

"Yeah," I agreed. "I did a dumb thing and got a break. Those girls? They were getting sexualized when they were still just kids. We had girls come through who'd been raped by their actual fathers. Not step or adoptive, but the biological kind, and he was fucking his *kid!* I can't even wrap my brain around how someone becomes that fucking sick, but it's not even a rare thing."

"I know," Knock agreed. "And the deeper we get into this Ruin shit, the more of it we're going to see."

"Oh, I can look at it," I promised. "I can look all day long, and it will just piss me the fuck off. The more I see, the more determined I'll be to bust those kinds of fuckers. Not on my watch, you know? And for once, we're finally getting the power to officially be 'on watch.'"

"Until we aren't," Knock reminded me. "The program is going to get canned, Jinxy."

"Unless we get this right," I countered. "I mean, that's the theory I'm working with here. If we can get this right - which I admit we probably can't - then we might be able to save the program."

"And if we can't?" he pressed.

I laughed once. It was a cold, cruel sound. "Then we'll fuck the bad guys up the old-fashioned way. I'm not here to be a good guy, Knock. I'm simply here to stop the bad ones. There are far too many of them, and too few of us. Means someone needs to be ruthless, and I'm more than willing to do it."

"Same," he agreed. "I think we all are. It's kinda why Ruin works so well."

# CHAPTER 63

## JERICHO

Shit had gone down with Jinxy's family. We wanted to help, but unfortunately none of it was online or under the FBI's jurisdiction. However, it seemed one of his other brothers was a politician, so they were figuring it all out. Insanity, but ok.

My mind, however, was on this Milt fucker. Sunday, we started chasing the leads we had, trying to figure out how they tied together. Monday, Tiffany found a lead. The Russian gold was buying the bitcoin and plenty of luxury items. The senator's lifestyle didn't work without that extra money, and it seemed he was voting all over the place. That was due to Cade's methodical dissection of every single vote the Senate had held in the last three years.

Combined with the receipts stored carelessly in the man's Google Drive, the pieces fell nicely into place. Senator McFuckFace was selling his vote! Not always, but for anything that seemed remotely important, he either got a free vacation, some handy gold, or all these other benefits. Time after time, it all lined up.

And when we looked into his favorite home renovations company?

Surprise, surprise, they were owned by the same billionaire who owned the jet this asshole was flying around on. It almost made me wonder what he was getting for voting against the program. The fuckhead.

"Someone check the gifts he's reported," Tiffany demanded.

Well, that took up most of Tuesday and Wednesday. Fuck, but this was annoying and tedious. Hacking into a computer was so much easier than following the money trail, but I refused to let this guy think his corruption could push out Alex's integrity. That was not how things worked on our watch!

Ruin had been formed to stop assholes from hurting good people. In this case, the good person was Alex, but there were so many more who needed us. It felt like the longer we did this, the more I realized how important our role really was. The law didn't want to recognize virtual shit as criminal? Fine. We could bring this crap into the real world, then see how easy it was to ignore then.

My problem was this felt too easy. Hacking this man had been child's play. We'd all dove in, ready to bust our asses to fix this - the same way we'd gone crazy with the Alpha Team shit last year - and instead it was just lining up like ducks in a pretty little row.

Easy.

Simple.

Obvious.

Shit didn't happen like that. When I wanted something, I'd always had to fight for it. It actually took me a bit to realize why this time felt so different. My guys. Not just my boyfriends, but my entire crew. All of Ruin had accepted I would hyperfocus on this. They'd not only let me, but had done everything in their power to make it easy for me.

Granted, quite a few of them had done the same. Jinxy, Hottie, Knock, and even Tiffany had pushed to their limits. Cade, Ripper, and Zoe? They'd carried us through. Oh, they'd also done their part, but when some of us lost the world around us, they reminded us of meals, of homework, and even to go to bed. Those three had cooked, cleaned, and assisted without ever grumbling about it - let alone complaining!

Fuck, I loved these people. It was why our polycule worked so well, but if we'd managed to make a hacktivist's group out of a fucked-up therapeutic romance-friendship mess, then shouldn't we keep doing it? So, when Thursday came around and we finally had our case set up and ready to go, I decided it was time for a family meeting.

"Ruin!" I yelled. "Living room!"

"Knock and Jason are packing for the gamer convention," Hottie reminded me.

Groaning, I pulled out my phone and sent a group text. Yes, Jason and Knock were included in it. The command was simple. Meet in the living room for family discussion. All members required. Now.

This time, I brewed the coffees for everyone. Placing them in front of chairs, I put people in the seats they were most likely to use. Jason got the chair across from the fireplace. Knock and Cade went together. Hottie was beside Jinxy, who had to be next to Zoe. Tiffany got a spot near Ripper, but he was the closest person to me. And I took my spot on the hearth, because I was intending to lead this show.

One by one, they all made their way in, smiling when they saw their cups. Even Tiffany had gotten used to hers, a bright lime-green one Knock had picked up so she officially felt like one of us. Evidently, he had an "in" to where Riley found the good ones.

Once they were all sitting, I decided to just lay it out there. "Jason and Knock will be gone until Sunday night for a gamer convention. Milt-boy knows our names. He has to by now, right?"

"Most likely," Jason agreed.

"But thanks to Tiff," I said, tipping my head at her, "we know what's going on. Now, I'm kinda freaking out, because this feels fucking easy. But the real question is, well, now that we know, what do we do?"

"Hold up," Jason said. "First, I'd like to point out that I had Alex send her emails to Bradley and request a test for this team. A way to see if you really are qualified - cyber-wise - to get this sort of work done. Since the harassment was bordering on a crime, she wanted to see if you could find the sender."

"So we go with that?" Tiffany asked.

"Problem," Hottie explained. "See, that takes us to the email server. Once we knew who, we should've stopped."

"But we assumed the senator was a setup, so we had to check," Knock offered.

"And stumbled upon bad shit," Jinxy added.

"Great!" Zoe said. "Wonderful excuses, y'all. Gives us a real plausible reason for why we broke the law. But see, we still broke the fucking law!"

"That," I said, gesturing to her. "And right now, no one knows."

"Alex would like you to hold off on doing anything about it," Jason said calmly.

"Fuck that," Ripper grumbled.

I reached up to push all my dreads back. "Ok. Here's the thing. I want to run with this. I want to fuck this guy up, make him pay for it, and destroy his life. I've also been trying to think first, so..." I gestured before me with both hands. "I'm asking all of you. See, I kinda realized I can't do this without my team. I'd rush in half-cocked, like Hottie always says, and get myself in so much shit. I'd make bad calls because I was pissed. But Ruin? We're a polycule."

"Plus one," Tiffany added.

"Nope," Jinxy said. "Sorry, Tiff. Bad news. You're in the polycule now too."

"What?!" she snapped.

He chuckled. "See, this mess? It's not about fucking someone. It's about bonds. Friendships count. I know you and Zoe and Jeri are friends. That's a bond. You and Ripper and Cade seem to be friends."

"I'm just a dick or something," Knock teased.

"You never hang out with her," Jinxy countered.

"He does so," Tiffany promised. "Knock's just chill. You, Jinxy, never hang out with me. Hell, even Hottie can hold a half-civil conversation.

You run away like my mere presence is going to chase Zoe off or something."

"He's monogamous," Zoe fake-whispered. "And he's scared I'll think he's cheating."

Then both of them turned to look right at Jinxy. Groaning, Jinxy made a production of rolling his head back, making it clear he knew he was in shit. He was also smiling.

Yeah, this was why I loved these people. Even at the hardest times, they somehow made it feel worthwhile to be doing this. It didn't even matter what "this" was. Just sharing a life with them was more than I'd ever dared to imagine for myself, and now I was in the process of learning how to lean on them too.

"So..." I said, pulling them back on topic. "While Jason and Knock are in California - "

"Seattle," Knock corrected. "More rain."

"Yeah." It also didn't matter. "Riley's dog is going to be here. Zoe and Cade are going to alternate shifts in Sanger with the horses. The rest of us? What the hell are we doing? Mostly, I mean with this. With the information we have?"

Jason leaned back and dropped an arm to pet his dog. His eyes jumped from person to person in the room, but his expression made it clear he wasn't going to give us the answer. Hottie licked his lips, then chewed at one corner. Jinxy's eyes narrowed. Zoe and Tiffany shared a look.

Since no one was offering anything, I decided to give them a nudge. "We can give this to Bradley," I explained, "and he'll escalate it to Alex. Then it's out of our hands, we've done our part, and we can convince ourselves to sleep well."

"And it'll get dropped!" Jinxy snapped.

"Probably," I agreed. "It would also keep us in our lane. If we give this to our 'boss,' then we're still playing by the rules. The program could have a chance."

"Not likely," Hottie said. "C'mon, we all know the program's done.

From what I'm seeing, it's because this senator - and probably others - don't *want* to have anyone around who can find out their dirty secrets."

"Which is a good point," I agreed. "But there's a big difference between us fucking up our chance and them shutting us down because they're corrupt, right?"

"Yeah," Tiff said. "The difference being taking a risk to do the right thing. I mean, isn't that the point? No one else will do shit, so we have to? That's kinda why I signed up."

"So what do you propose, Jeri?" Cade asked.

"Well..." I said. "We can chase this fucker down on our own, pull out the rest of our hacker assholery... Is that a word?"

"Should be," Zoe said. "We'll call it one."

"But we can fuck him up," I told them. "Send it to the D.C. police, the Senate ethics people, or whoever else would punt that man right out of office. Or..." I paused to make sure they were all paying attention. "We cross a line and blackmail the fucker."

"I like that one," Tiffany said.

"It'll kill the program," Jason pointed out.

"Maybe," I countered. "But if it works, he could vote our way and then resign. If we give him a taste of how much proof we actually have? Make it clear we're not the kind to play nice?"

"And if he shares that?" Hottie countered. "Then what?"

"He won't," Ripper said. "Not if we do it right."

Cade was slowly dragging a hand along his jaw, clearly thinking hard. When my eyes turned to him, the man actually smiled. "We'd have to make it perfect, Jeri. If he could cut out anything he didn't want seen? He'd tell the rest of his party on the committee. It'd get spun as proof hackers can't be trusted."

"So we make it perfect," Ripper said. "A video. Do it all TikTok style, with a person in front of the evidence and words saying bribes and corruption? Make sure there isn't a single frame of it that is clean?"

"But it's blackmail," I reminded them. "The exact shit we hate."

"Ok, hear me out?" Tiff begged. "Jeri, I know you have some real issues with bullying and other shit, right? You say it's bad. You say it hurts people. But you know what? In some cases, it can help. I chased those girls off 'our' guys so they would be more scared of the mean girls at school than excited about getting hit on. It fucking worked."

"And how badly did you traumatize them?" I asked.

"I didn't if they stayed away," Tiff promised. "I made it clear I would destroy them, *could* destroy them, but wouldn't if they left 'our' guys alone."

"She's not lying," Ripper admitted. "I mean, she was a bitch, but she didn't really make people cry. She just got called a bitch a lot."

Tiffany gestured at Ripper like he'd proven her point. "But it was blackmail, Jeri. It was bullying. It was so many things you hate, but it helped. So maybe it was dark grey, but you know what? Not everything is either black or white. Sometimes, bad shit can be done for good reasons, and I think this is a damned good example of that."

"And you need it," Hottie added. "Baby girl, I love you to death, but I've always known you need the vengeance. You need to destroy anyone who gets in your way. It's why you're so good at gaming. It's why you learned to hack in the first place. It's why you do everything, because you see life as a damned challenge, and you know what?"

"We're here for it," Jinxy broke in. "Shit, Jeri. Hottie and I've talked about this a million times. Back when you were a kid, we tried to rein you in, but it never worked. So we learned how to direct you instead. My idea, by the way."

"Kinda was," Hottie admitted. "But it worked. You thrive when you're chasing something. Doesn't even matter what. You don't know how to do anything if it's not with the dial turned all the way up. If we send this to Bradley, it's going to get shelved."

"But Alex would know who to watch out for, and she could handle it," Zoe said. "We could bust the asshole after Ruin's approved as FBI consultants, right?"

"Milt's party is the one in power right now," Cade said. "In that committee, his party has the majority. If he says not to vote for us, we're done. Right now, he really doesn't want anyone around who could find out what he's doing."

"But we already know," Knock countered. "So he couldn't save himself. He's already fucked."

"But he doesn't know that," Tiff pointed out. "He'll try to block the entire program because even if it isn't us, having groups of hackers who can see what he's up to? He'd have to stop or get busted, and that man's getting rich off this."

"So what do we want to do?" I asked again.

Everyone turned to look at me. On the opposite side of the room, Jason simply smiled, waiting without saying a single word. When the silence stretched on long enough, he finally lifted his chin.

"You wanted to change the world, Jericho," he said. "You put together a team, found a way to make this many people work seamlessly - and I think the last few days have more than proven that. When push comes to shove, all eyes turn the same way." He lifted his hand and pointed at me.

"Kinda noticed, thanks," I grumbled.

"Because this is *your* team," he said. "You made Ruin. You dove in and they followed. Time after time, all of them have followed without hesitation, but here's the thing. That makes you the leader. To me, it looks like it's time to start leading, kid."

Fuck, and that put all the weight on me, but oddly, it didn't really feel heavy. Instead, it felt like I wasn't pushing too hard. It felt like I might not be fucking this up as badly as I'd feared. It felt like, for lack of a better term, I was no longer alone.

"Let's Ruin him," I said. "Blackmail it is, and if he makes a single move at Alex, we'll release all of it to the world."

Jason's lips curled into a smile, his eyes met mine, and he nodded.

# CHAPTER 64

### SPECIAL AGENT JASON RAIGE

The flight to the gamer convention was a lot more fun with Knock, Riley, Logan, Kitty, Murder, and the baby. This was Ryan's first trip on an airplane, and while the infant should've been fussy about it, he got passed around and spoiled enough that he fell asleep by the time the plane was in the air.

Crysis was fixated on the baby. He wanted to smell Ryan's socks, his carrier, and any other part he could reach. It was cute. It also made me realize he'd be a very good "uncle" for my own little one that was on the way.

Soon enough we made it to Seattle. To get from the airport to the hotel, we had to take three different cars, but it worked out. My dog and I barely made it to the front desk, though, before the woman on the other side was passing me a keycard.

"Mr. Raige?" She smiled down at my dog, who was wearing an orange vest again. This one had the Degrass hotel logo on it. "Mr. Degrass has your room ready. If there's anything you need, please let us know."

I thanked her, then headed for the elevator. I didn't even bother to worry about what the rest of my friends were doing. I just wanted to hurry up, to get to my room. When I finally found the right door and opened it, Crysis barreled past me enthusiastically. What I heard next made my heart feel like it was glowing.

"Hey, buddy!" Zara crooned at the dog. "Where's our main man, huh?"

"Fuck, I've missed you," I breathed as I came around the corner and wrapped her up in my arms. "I'm sorry I've been gone so long."

She just pushed into my chest, her face finding that spot against my neck where it belonged. All of her long, dark hair got tangled up in my arms, but she didn't seem to care at all - and I loved the feel of it. I couldn't decide if I wanted to kiss her, hold her, or just stare at her to memorize every beautiful thing about her I'd been missing.

"How's it going in Texas?" she asked.

"I think the kids are going off the rails right now," I admitted. "But they're good, Zara. They are so damned good. I've also been taking your advice about Jeri, and I'm trying to show her how to be a leader."

Her face broke into a smile. "Oh, now that's fucking cute. You have your own padawan!"

It was a Star Wars term for an apprentice, basically. It also fit so well, and proved how easily this woman accepted my nerdy side. Damn, I loved her.

"And how's the baby?" I asked, sliding my hand down to her belly.

"Oh!" She caught my wrist, stopping me before I could feel that growing bulge there, and pulled me over to the couch.

There, she lifted up her shirt, pushed her pants down just a bit, and then did a funny little wiggle. I was confused until she grabbed my hand and pressed it against her stomach again. Grinning like a maniac, she watched me, but I honestly had no clue what was going on.

Until something fluttered under my palm. Sucking in a breath, I sat straight up and turned to face her. My hand didn't leave her skin, though. Like the smallest little drum set, our child was inside her doing some kind of crazy dance.

"She's moving?" I asked.

Zara laughed, leaning in to kiss me. "Or he, yes. It seems Junior doesn't care for being shook up. I figured you'd want to feel."

"How far now?" I asked.

"Four months," she told me. "And Jason, I called the doctor. I was going to delay the appointment, but the receptionist said the doctor is adamant this one is important. She says we don't have to check gender this time, but I need to have some scans and stuff. So!" She paused to put her clothes back in place. "Since you're busy, and you don't want me going alone, I've made arrangements."

"Oh no," I groaned.

"Murder didn't get to do this part with Ryan," she reminded me. "When I asked, he changed his flight. He's coming back to New York with me. My appointment is on Monday, and he'll stay until Wednesday, just to help me get some things done around the apartment, and then come back and tell you all about it. I'll send the ultrasound pics with him, so you can carry those like a proud daddy."

"And the sex?" I asked.

"The doctor said she'll make a note not to tell us. I let her know my brother would be with me because my husband's been called away for work. She said this might be too early to see, but even if she does get a good view, she will save that reveal for when you're back."

"Oh, you're too good to me," I breathed, leaning in to kiss her. "And I need to go back to Texas. They've figured out who is harassing Alex, have the proof they need, and are about to do something about it." I paused, searching her dark hazel eyes. "But, Zara? This might ruin the program. This man is a senator on the committee. Stopping him could destroy everything we've been working for."

"And help Alex," she reminded me.

I nodded. "Yeah. But if Ruin isn't working for the FBI, then why am I?"

She snuck in one more kiss, then hopped up and headed to the kitchen area of our suite. Pushing a button, she got the coffee maker warming, then rummaged for a cup. I had a feeling she was thinking, so I just watched her, aware how much I'd missed seeing her these last two weeks.

The coffee maker sputtered, Zara grabbed the cup, then came back to set it on the end table beside me. "Ok," she said.

"Ok?" I asked.

"Well, you're finally allowed to quit the FBI, right?"

"In theory," I agreed. "I also may have told Alex I would."

"So do it."

I had to blink to push those words into place. "What?"

"If this program doesn't happen, then quit, Jason!" She giggled. "Deviant's currently paying me enough that your big federal income only covers our coffee habit now, right? So do it. Let's buy a house in Dallas - or wherever Riley and Murder are. You can be a hacker full-time, and I'll be your sugar momma."

"Zara, hacking isn't..."

"And Chance is crazy, so he'll probably find you some remote work he needs done or something. Or Dez. Hell, all of Deviant loves you. So I'm sure you'll get a job, but let's do it. If you're already down there, then start looking at places. Best case, this all works out and you get reassigned to the Dallas office. Worst case, we move to that area and get a massive yard for Crysis."

"God, you are perfect," I said, grabbing her hips and pulling her before me. "But would you really be ok with that?"

"You could watch the baby while I make the next soundtrack," she said. "And you'd look good with a vacuum. I think one of those little robotic ones you'll program to be even smarter, right? And we can get Murder to bring Ryan for play dates. Be like grownups and all."

"Yeah?"

She nodded. "Yeah. Jason, working with these kids brings something out in you, and - "

My phone began to ring, cutting her off. Letting out a groan, I reached into my pocket, expecting the worst, and the name on the screen didn't disappoint. If Bradley was calling me, it couldn't be good.

"Yeah?" I answered.

"Jason!" he said. "Are you in Seattle now?"

I pulled the phone away and put it on speaker. "I am, and Zara's here too."

"Good!" he said. "Hi, Zara!"

"Hi, Bradley," she replied.

"You need to spoil that man this weekend," he told her. "Looks like he's earned it, because Jason? I've got the psych evals."

"How bad?" I asked.

"Well, they noticed all of the members of Ruin have trauma. Tiffany Bowen, though? You didn't tell me about her."

"One of the girls who helped with Alpha Team," I explained. "Jericho and Zoe are friends with her. She's an accountant. Well, working on it."

"Nice," he breathed. "Well, she is your steady rock in that group. Psychiatrist has her labeled as a leader type, secure in her decisions, and everything we want to see. Grayson, Elliot, and Jeff - "

"Hottie, Ripper, and Knock," I corrected, so Zara could keep up.

"They all did well. Shawn, who I think is Jinxy?" Bradley asked. "There are some concerns about his ethics. He still passed, but there is a note on here about his willingness to bend rules to achieve goals. Zoe's big red flag is her trauma from being raped, of course."

"Which makes sense," Zara said.

"Sadly, yes," Bradley agreed. "Cade is impulsive but reliable. His marks are pretty good. Jason, the problem is Jericho."

"She didn't pass?" I asked.

"Barely," he said, the word hanging in the air. "Jason, her psych eval? It looks just like yours used to."

"Told you," Zara said.

"Do I want to know?" Bradley asked.

"Zara told me," I explained, "that Jeri needs a mentor, and I should step up. I've been trying."

"She's not ok, Jason," Bradley warned. "Jericho is a walking wall of issues. I mean, her report is twice as thick as everyone else's, and the psychiatrist had some concerns about her. She still passed, but this girl needs therapy. She needs more than a job. She needs some fucking help - just like you did."

"Ok," I agreed. "I'm not sure how she'll feel about it, though. I'll do my best to get her on board, but..."

"Well, we don't have to give the full reports to the committee," Bradley assured me. "We just have to list that they passed. Technically, they all did, so we're good there. One step down, who knows how many more to go."

"And the program's going to get voted down," I told him. "Bradley, Milt Einfeldt from Alabama is corrupt as shit. Ruin has proof of it. We're going to shut him down."

"We?" Bradley asked.

"We," I said again. "I literally have a seat at their table, Bradley. Ok, it's more like a desk, but it still counts. I've been given a color - grey. I've been informed I'm a part of the team. Not asked, told."

"And it's good for him," Zara told my boss. "Bradley, we both know this is what Jason really needs. He's a shit agent, but he's a damned good hacker. He's good at saving people!"

"But hackers aren't authorized to shoot," Bradley pointed out.

"I don't fucking want to shoot anymore!" I snapped.

"Ok," Bradley agreed. "I'd suggest you don't tell Alex you're on the team, though. Not yet. Not until this passes or fails."

"Is voted down," I corrected, "and it will be. If one of the members of that committee is this dirty, then how many more do you think are worried about what an internet investigation force could find? I mean, Einfeldt's been getting Russian fucking bribes to sway his votes! He's got billionaires paying for home improvements. Not a new sink, Bradley. I'm talking hundreds of thousands of dollars of work, and good ol' Milt is spending maybe ten grand. He's fucking crooked, and someone needs to make sure the American public knows."

"And that someone's Ruin?" Bradley asked.

"Yes," Zara said before I could respond. "Because you know what? Jason and his team are doing the right thing. Not the political one, Bradley. The *right* one."

I caught her hand and squeezed lightly, making sure she knew how much I appreciated her support. "They considered holding this until after the vote, but I think they're right," I said. "If these politicians are worried about getting busted, it won't matter what we do. They will vote against the program for their own self-interests. The program is dead, Bradley. It was always dead. Politicians want to operate like they're untouchable, but Ruin is going to be able to see behind the curtain now."

"Fuck," Bradley grumbled. "No, you're right. Even if they have no clue what we have on them, they still know what they're doing. They'll still vote against the program to save their own asses." He sighed heavily. "And there's no way to fix this? Because we *need* this program, Jason."

"I can't think of one," I admitted. "I also happen to know they're doing something this weekend while I'm out of town. They're going to push."

"Which means you have an alibi," Bradley realized. "Ok, I like the kids more. Just keep me in the loop? I'll keep Alex updated. We'll see if we can make this look good, but I think you're right."

"They had to pick between helping Alex or helping themselves," I said. "They chose Alex."

"And I can at least use that," Bradley assured me. "Just... Jason, just do something about Jericho? I don't even know what, but I have a feeling you might."

"I can only try," I assured him. "I mean, that's basically all we're doing right now. Trying our asses off."

# CHAPTER 65

**RIPPER**

After Jason and Knock left on Friday night, we came up with a plan. One latex skull mask later, we were doing this. Zoe and Jeri put Cade in a very tight shirt. It was long-sleeved. He had black gloves to go with it. The skull mask covered his face completely, including his eyes, which had little screens over them.

The tricky part was putting him in front of a green screen. Then, we had him give a very long speech. He got to rant about anything he wanted, because all I needed was the body motions. We couldn't see his mouth. There would be nothing to match up with later. But if he stood still like a mannequin, it wouldn't work as well.

With half an hour of Cade just talking and gesturing recorded, I got to work. Lighting changed those boring dark eyes to flaming ones. Effects made shadows pour off Cade's body. The shirt? Hell, I was as straight as they came, and I could still see he looked good. Ripped. Like some kind of supervillain, if I was honest.

But editing raw footage was more tedious than I expected. At some point, Zoe and Jinxy left to handle Riley's horses. When they came back, they had Quake with them. The dog was the biggest chickenshit, and our place was completely new to him. Knowing all of us may have been the only thing that convinced him to actually leave the front foyer. That night, he would not leave Zoe's side.

The next morning started early for me, though. I wanted to make sure I got this video right, and we only had the weekend. Pulling out all of my graphical effects tools, I set to work making the background video that would cover up the green screen. This was going to be the proof. I just had to present it all in a visually appealing way.

Around noon, Tiffany showed up. Quake was *not* happy about that. The dog went charging down the hall, barking. That he was moving away from her instead of at her kept it from coming across as intimidating. But once Tiffany sat down and offered to pet the big lug, she was an instant hit.

By early afternoon, I had something to show off. Cade was surprised to find he looked like a complete badass. Zoe squealed over the shadow effects I'd used. Tiffany said the background layer was hard to read, so Cade needed to be smaller, but that was an easy change.

Everyone else paused to watch the stream of the PLG tournament Knock and Jason were at. I didn't. I had this flowing, so I kept going. Just after the tournament ended - with Riley winning and Knock coming in second place - I finished it. Just to make sure, I watched the whole thing again, and it was good. Honestly good, even if I was trying to pick it apart.

"It's ready," I said.

Immediately, the entire house crowded around my chair, all trying to see my monitor. Unplugging my headphones, I connected to the speakers, and then played the video.

Cade faded in, flames in his eyes and dark, inky shadows rolling off him. "Corruption is for criminals. Milt Einfeldt, senator from Alabama, you are corrupt."

The voice was fake, created by artificial intelligence, but I'd clipped

Cade's movements to match. Some I'd had to slow down or speed up, but it flowed naturally. The head bobs, the arm movements, and everything else. I was a little proud of myself.

Then a big stamp landed on the screen that said "Guilty" and behind it, the proof flickered like an old news reel. Clips of all the things, spliced together, showing just enough to get the point across. I'd even made sure to point out "Billionaire paid for home renovations" and "How much gold has he been given?"

The theme was dark and ominous. The graphics were the last proof we needed to screw over this fucker. Then it paused and "Cade" chuckled ominously.

"The internet never forgets. The internet never loses the receipts. The internet has been your downfall, Milt Einfeldt. You will be punished. Resign now and save your dignity. Ignore us, and this will be the biggest story the news has ever seen."

Cade faded out, the screen behind him grew larger, showing the mailing address of the gold from that Russian oligarch. A red "marker" line began to circle around it over and over and over again, until the screen simply went black.

Then the Ruin logo flickered in, strobing for less than a second. At the bottom, instead of our full name, it merely said "32:35." I felt that was enough of a tag, and it would prevent anyone from naming and shaming our group later.

"Holy fuck," Tiffany breathed. "Who the hell is the hottie with the muscles?"

"Not the Hottie," Hottie joked.

"It's Cade," Jeri told her.

Tiffany just gaped at Cade. "What the fuck?"

"Ripper makes magic," Cade said, shrugging that off. "Zoe picked a very small shirt. I think he enhanced something."

"Nope," I admitted. "Sorry, Cade. Just good lighting."

"He did not have those muscles when we dated," Tiffany told Jeri.

"He does now," Jeri bragged, which made both girls laugh. But Jeri ended with a sigh, and it wasn't the good type. "Ok, we need to have a big talk. All of us."

"With Jason and Knock gone?" I asked.

She nodded. "Living room?"

"Living room," Zoe agreed. "C'mon, Quake. No one is gonna hurt you. It's fine, baby boy. Yeah, let's go sit on the couch, huh?"

Together, the rest of us headed that way. The TV was still on The Gamer Channel, but Cade muted it before taking a seat. I flopped down on one side of the loveseat, and Jeri took the other. Once we were all sitting, she sighed again.

"Ripper's video is good," she said, smiling at me. "But this is make-or-break time. I thought we'd have to work to figure out what this asshole was up to, but that turned out to be easy. Last night, as I was trying to fall asleep, I realized that's not our problem."

"It was easy?" Tiffany asked, looking at everyone in the room. "Really?"

"Easier than Alpha Team," Hottie assured her. "The senator didn't know shit about securing his files. Those boys last year did."

"It's weird when you call them boys, Hottie," Tiff said.

"He's old," I reminded her. "Almost twenty-three now. Very ancient."

Hottie just flipped me off, but all of that had been enough to get a hint of a smile on Jeri's lips. Still, her expression was serious. Too serious, and that had me worried.

"We could hold off on this," Jeri said. "Send it to Bradley, make sure the FBI knows - "

"We already talked about that," Zoe countered. "It's a no. We're busting him."

"Ok, but let's think about how that goes," she said. "Guys, we *know* we can bust this guy. Our skill isn't in question. This isn't about if we can or cannot catch the bad guys. We know we can!"

"So what's it about?" Cade asked.

"Right now," Jeri said, "it's about what we want. Doing this FBI program would be a dream come true. It would give us so much leeway to fuck up everyone else like Milt who's out there. But if we go after Milt, the program's dead."

"Program's already dead," Jinxy reminded her.

"Unless we get Milt out," she said. "I looked, and that would make it an even vote, by party."

"She's right," Cade agreed. "And if it's a tie, there are ways to get it out of committee. Right now, that's in our favor."

"But once we send the video," Jericho said, "there's no taking it back. How we send it matters just as much as if we do. So what I'm wanting to know is where everyone is on this. Like, think of it as my last check-in before we do something irreversible."

"Fuck the program," Jinxy said. "I mean, it would've been nice, but we all knew it was a longshot."

"I dunno," Hottie said. "I think it has a lot of potential. If we can save the program, then why shouldn't we?"

"I like the idea of saving the program too," Cade said, "but how?"

"No, no, no," I broke in, before everyone else could offer their opinion. "You're all looking at this wrong. This isn't about tweaking the game to get the best character. This is about whether or not we turn a blind eye to what this man is doing. Do we let ourselves get bribed by the chance to do what we want?"

"Can we have it both ways?" Tiffany asked.

"How?" Zoe pressed her.

"Y'all are the hackers!" Tiffany huffed. "How the fuck am I supposed to know that shit?"

"Because you've got a damned brain," Jinxy told her. "Tiff, you don't have to pretend to be dumb so our feelings aren't hurt. We wanted you as a part of Ruin because you're not only smart enough to have good ideas, but bitchy enough to rub our faces in it when we need that."

"I'm up for spitballing," Jeri admitted.

"What we need to do," Tiffany said, "is use this as proof of what Ruin can do. We need to present this as why the world needs us. We need to take a fucking risk, you know? I mean, Ripper said he only put the numbers on the video, but we're still tagging it. Why?"

Fuck me, I could immediately see what she was saying. "So, go all-in?"

"All-in," Tiffany said. "Run at this headlong like we think we're in the right. I'm pretty sure that's a better defense than trying to hide it because we know we're in shit, right?"

"Probably," Cade agreed.

"But that's a big risk," I pointed out. "If we do that, Ruin's name, tag, and information will be out there. The FBI knows who we are. We could go to jail for this, Tiff."

"And?" she asked, lifting a brow.

"And jail sucks," Jeri countered.

"It's supposed to!" Tiffany groaned. "That's kinda the whole point of using it as a punishment. All I'm saying is we either believe in what we're doing, or we don't. I mean, maybe I'm wrong, but that's how I see it."

"We'd be risking it all," Jeri said.

"But is that wrong?" I asked. "C'mon, Jeri. You said it yourself. This shit is easy for us. We know we can do it, and we're not exactly getting worse. This group, right here, is perfect for seek and destroy. The FBI already knows that. We all have contracts that are basically 'get out of jail free' cards, so if we're going to do this, then now is the time!"

"I forgot about the contracts," Jinxy breathed. "Shit, that's a good point."

"Might not hold up in court," Hottie countered. "Still, the fact we were under the impression we were working with proper authority probably would."

"Which means," I said, "that's the real question. That's the thing Jeri's been trying to put into words. Do we want to bulldoze this, possibly risk the FBI program, our hacktivist group, and even our futures because it's the right thing to do?"

"We can get revenge for Alex," Jeri said, "or we can all but take the bribe of FBI positions for ignoring the corruption in our government."

"Which isn't a biased way of phrasing that at all," Hottie pointed out. "Jeri, we're not being bribed. *We're* deciding when to hit. That's not the same. Not at all."

"So we hold it to hope for a vote?" Jeri asked.

"No," I broke in. "No, what we need to do is push at it, like Tiff said. The committee doesn't want this program. They've been trying to find every way possible to get rid of it, and we've known that. We've jumped through the hoops. They're still going to kill it unless we make it clear they can't without losing their own seats, or places, or jobs. However politicians phrase it."

"Playing chicken," Cade said.

"If it was me, that's what I'd do," Tiff said. "Make it clear we're doing the right thing. It's like in high school - when people want to talk trash, if we hold our heads up and pretend like we meant to do it?"

"Like a cat?" Zoe asked incredulously.

"Yeah, kinda?" Tiffany said. "It's all about how people perceive each other. If we act like we're doing the right thing, they'll assume we are."

"Like Snowden," Jinxy said.

"Who?" Tiff asked.

He waved her off. "CIA guy. Not really relevant. But he has fans because he broke the rules - and the law - to reveal some shit the government was doing. Downside, though. He didn't win."

"So this is our risk," Jeri said. "We can either save Alex from harassment and get her some revenge - which I'd call doing the right thing. Or, we can hedge our bets, play it safe, and try to make sure we don't get caught. But after we send that video *anywhere*, we don't get the luxury of changing our minds."

"I'm for the right thing," Tiffany said, lifting her hand.

"Right thing," Zoe agreed, matching her.

I lifted my own hand. "Right thing."

"Same," Cade agreed, pushing his hand up. "Right thing. And we all know Knock would agree."

Hottie laughed once. "Oddly, I'm actually going to vote for helping Alex. Not because it's the right thing, because vengeance isn't really right. But because someone has to do it, and I think we're that someone." And he lifted his hand.

"Jesus..." Jinxy groaned. "Did you have to make a good point, Hot? Fuck. Ok. Right thing." He flopped his hand up, but then let it drop. "And that's unanimous. Ripper, put in our full name. Let's hit this motherfucker hard, ok?"

"And I'll put it on his machine before dawn," Hottie agreed. "Jeri, you'll be running point on that with me, making sure I don't trip any security."

"Promise," she said, leaning over a bit so her shoulder was against mine. "And Ripper, it's a *damned* good video."

"I tried to make Cade sexy for you," I joked, but I could feel my face heating up. "Thanks, Jeri."

"Just kiss him!" Hottie groaned. "Seriously, woman? He's earned it."

So Jeri turned and pressed her mouth to mine. It was fast. I hadn't been expecting it, and yet my hands still knew what to do. With her shifting onto her knee, one hand found her waist, the other cupped her cheek, and my lips parted.

And this woman kissed me like the world wasn't watching. Hell, like our friends weren't starting to laugh! She kissed me so deeply, I decided jail would be worth it, because nothing else mattered except this. All of this. Righting the wrongs, being some kind of fucked up, and her.

Always her.

# CHAPTER 66

### SPECIAL AGENT JASON RAIGE

When the convention ended, we caught a flight back to Texas. Leaving Zara was hard, but Murder promised he'd take all the pictures. Zara with goo on her belly, Zara with a smile when she saw the baby on the screen, and everything else. Damn, I was going to owe the man.

But I came back to find no chaos. Shocking, but it seemed my team had pulled together, created one hell of an amazingly professional-looking video, then dropped it on Einfeldt's computer. The moment it booted up, that video would start playing. Then, once that was done, they'd started putting together their case file.

A fucking case file. Not just a spreadsheet or backing up their work. When I walked into the house, I found Jeri and Tiffany in the study trying to research how they were supposed to reference virtual evidence so it would all be properly annotated.

I'd never been more proud.

This was my team. Maybe they were a little rebellious, and they were certainly dangerous in their own way, but they were also meticulous. In my time with the Bureau, I'd done some work with Anonymous, and not even they were this organized - and *that* wasn't a word I'd ever expected to use for a group of hackers!

So when the kids headed off to their classes on Monday, I looked over everything they had. The case was solid. Their evidence was impossible to refute. The way they'd obtained it was illegal as fuck, but this was why we needed them. I just hadn't expected them to be so ready so quickly, and it killed me to know this program was going to be shuttered.

Then, Monday night, my phone rang. When I saw Alex's name on the screen, I answered, but this was not a conversation I wanted to have inside.

"Hang on, let me get my dog outside," I greeted her.

"I'm cooking, so you're ok," Alex assured me. "Troy! Clean off the damned table, girl! I'm not going to tell you again!"

I chuckled even as I found my dog's ball and got him out to the backyard. Crysis was still confused about smelling another animal in "his" space, though. He kept trying to find his invisible buddy. But the moment I tossed the ball, nothing else mattered.

"Ok, I'm outside and alone," I said. "What's up, Alex?"

"Bradley gave me a rundown on what your team has," she said. "Jason, this is actionable."

"They're making a case file on it," I assured her. "A proper case file."

"I thought you said they'd given up on the program," she teased.

"Jericho informed me they had a talk. They know if they held on to this, the program was dead. Einfeldt would kill it. They know if they ignore it, the program is dead. They know working on it will likely kill the program as well, but..." I chuckled. "It seems there's a slim chance - according to them - that if they prove their worth, the *program* won't die. Ruin just won't be welcome in those circles."

"She's not wrong," Alex admitted. "I'm also impressed with that girl. Your whole team, to be honest. I shouldn't have used them as the example. I should've saved them to make sure this worked."

"Then it wouldn't have worked," I countered. "Because Einfeldt is crooked. The man's selling his votes to the Russians and billionaires. His goal will be to kill this. So long as he's safe and comfortable, the program has no chance, so my team's about to hit him hard."

"Well, they might as well," she said. "See, I got some bad news. No, let me back up. Sunday, it seems Senator Einfeldt got hacked. The man called me to complain about my hackers hacking him. He wanted to know if that was the intended goal of the program, and tried to make threats. I had to ask him if he wanted to report being hacked, because the only thing my hackers were working on was tracking down some harassing emails I'd been receiving."

I laughed at that. "Shut him up real quick?"

"Made him sputter a bit," she agreed. "I put him in the position of either admitting he'd sent the emails or having me open an investigation to someone breaching congressional network security. He said it must've been a prank and hung up, but not before threatening - twice - that he would destroy this program before it ever made it off the ground."

"Sounds about right," I grumbled.

"However," Alex went on, "I got a worse phone call from the chairman of that committee today. It seems Milt's threats weren't all empty. Jason, he's trying to pull an official vote. This would be the end of debate, and right now, it doesn't look like the measure would pass."

"Fuck," I grumbled.

"The chairman assured me we have at least two weeks of procedural crap to go through first, but unless I have something in my pocket to change a whole lot of minds, the program isn't going to be approved. The best I could do was convince him to let me speak to the committee before they voted."

"And Einfeldt was the one trying to count votes?" I asked.

"Yeah, why?"

I chuckled. "Because to me, that counts as a mistake. Alex, you don't want to know what my team is doing."

"Tell me anyway," she demanded.

"Well, they left him a warning. Sunday, when he turned on his laptop, a video would've played. One that shows they have proof of his crimes. They made it clear he could resign and take his loss gracefully, but to me, it sounds like he isn't."

"So you turn over that evidence to Bradley," she hissed. "Let us take it from here."

"They're hackers," I reminded her. "They aren't good little agents, and they sure as shit don't have any protection because of what this man is doing. Alex, it's out of my hands. They're going to destroy him, so the best you can do is sit back and enjoy it."

"Fuck, Jason - "

"Mom!" a girl snapped in the background.

"Sorry, Troy," Alex told her daughter. "Work complications, sweetie."

"And now I have one more person to ask when this parent gig gets overwhelming," I teased. "You sound like a good mom, Alex."

"Thanks, but I'm mostly an absent mom. Trust me, Troy will have no problem telling you all about it. She's also mad we had to move to D.C. Says it's... What's the phrase, honey?"

"It's basic here," Troy answered.

Which made me laugh. "Yep, teenagers. I can't wait for that phase."

"And you will change your mind once your little one gets here, Jason." But it sounded like she was moving. "Just tell me you can keep this away from my family, ok?"

"Promise," I assured her. "And if you have *any* problems, you let us know. Ruin won't make a case. We'll just destroy them if they come after your daughter or sister."

"Thank you. I know I should be trying to tell you to be careful, to obey the law, or something else responsible and professional, but I won't. I heard you loud and clear when you said you would quit to keep doing this. I believe you, and yes, I will even make it easy to do. I just need one thing in return?"

"What's that?"

Because the Deputy Director of the FBI should not be making this so easy. She shouldn't be joking around with me on the phone like we were old friends, or asking me to keep her family safe. She should be reminding me of my place, my job, and all that crap.

"If this fucker's selling his vote to the *Russians*?" she asked. "Make sure he regrets it. Jason, sometimes there's the official thing we're supposed to do, and then there's the *right* thing. In many cases, the right thing isn't as easy, comes with a lot more pushback, and there's no personal gain. Stopping a man like this is still the right thing. You hear me?"

"You're missing the point," I told her. "Alex, this man attacked you for your race and gender. Ruin doesn't care about national security. They don't give a shit about the ethics of congressional delegates. They barely can tell the political parties apart. But attacking a woman?"

"He still needs to be stopped!" she hissed. "What he's doing is dangerous!"

"Oh, he'll be stopped," I assured her. "He crossed the wrong line. He attacked a woman."

"Well..."

I broke in before she could make the same mistake I had. "Not physically, but mental and emotional abuse are still an attack, Alex. It's still devastating. I know you're strong enough to push through the crap he sent, but I've read those emails. We all have. And just because you *can* deal with it doesn't mean you should ever have to. *That's* why Ruin exists. Because there's not a damned thing wrong with being a woman. There's nothing weaker, lesser, or even more emotional about women! Trust me, I'm currently living with three fucking teenage girls, and they make me feel like a hormonal mess most days."

She actually laughed at that. "I don't know how you keep them on track, Jason. I really don't, but I'm glad you can."

"They keep themselves on track," I promised. "I'm just here to give them what info the FBI is willing to share. I have access to some programs they don't - but should. These kids are running their own scripts, coding on the fly, and..." I paused. "Have you seen the video, Alex?"

"No."

"Hang on." I lowered my phone, found the file, and sent it to her in a text. "Watch that when you get a chance. That's what they did on short notice. I don't want to hear a damned thing about a lack of skill, because most political ads aren't as polished as their little threat. And Einfeldt just fucked up. He ignored Ruin, and Jericho doesn't like to be ignored."

"Ok? What does that mean?"

"It means I'm going to let her blow up his world," I said. "Now is when you back out, pretend you know nothing, and start calling me a rogue agent, Alex."

"Or," she countered, "I make it clear my little test uncovered something, so I'm turning you loose. I told you I have your back, Jason. That wasn't an empty promise. You got me this promotion. You took the shot because you knew you had it. You are the one who risked everything, and I got all the rewards, so I will not leave you out to hang, you hear me?"

"Yes, ma'am," I said softly.

"Good, because corruption of our legislative branch falls under domestic law enforcement. To me, that's the FBI's jurisdiction. How can I know of a crime being committed and not send my best after it? So I'm going to have cybersecurity review what you've found, double-check the international parts, and make sure you have verification on everything."

"Getting my back," I realized.

"Yeah," she breathed. "And when this shit hits the fan, I'm probably going to get fired, but at least I'll know I did the right thing."

"That's what my team decided as well," I said. "They had a vote. They could either do the right thing or take the bribe to get their dream of being able to do this legally. They chose the right thing, Alex, even if the rest of the world won't see it that way. Just promise me you'll have their backs too."

"I made sure their contracts covered it," she reminded me. "Now, when this blows up, that won't mean much, and my bias will become the latest joke on the late shows, but it should keep them from going to jail for it."

"Then brace for impact," I warned her, "because I'm about to go set off a bomb."

"Good luck," she said, then ended the call.

So, after taking a deep breath, I headed back inside. Tonight, Ruin was all in the war room, but for once, they weren't working. Instead, the kids were playing Flawed, and trying their best to get Tiffany caught up a bit. They were also laughing just a little too hard.

"No, attack it, don't heal it!" Jeri tittered.

"I'm fucking trying!" Tiff wailed, smashing at her keys.

So I walked over and pressed the button she needed. "Someone has to help her set up her toolbars," I told the rest. "She's got her skills on here in whatever order they were gained."

"Oh, yeah, we'll fix that," Ripper promised. "Jeri, kill the bimbo. Let me..."

I lifted a hand. "And I have news from Alex."

"One second," Hottie said. "Let us all get safe and out of Discord." He glanced over, caught my eye and mouthed, "Guild."

I nodded to show I understood. Thankfully, the crew moved quickly. Tiffany had to ask for the recall button again, but in less than a minute, they were all parked safely, logged out of everything, and looking at me.

"Milt Einfeldt called Alex yesterday with threats," I said. "She backed him into a corner, but he made it clear he was going to kill the program. Today, he was counting the votes in the committee, and the chairman called Alex to make her aware of it. As things stand now, the measure will not pass."

"He's trying to push back?" Jeri asked.

I nodded slowly. "Yeah. That's what it looks like."

Smiling, she clicked a few keys on her keyboard, and started typing. "Jason, you know what the best thing about those case files are? They work for reporters as well as agents."

"You sending it?" Jinxy asked.

"Gonna make sure I have..." She paused. "Fuck, that was fast. Ok, it seems Anderson Cooper is very interested in this. His producer says they'd love to see what we have, and is more than willing to accept it's anonymous."

"Already?" Tiffany asked.

Jeri waved her off. "I reached out over the weekend. This is like our fifth email." She looked up. "So, I'm sending it unless someone has a complaint."

"Send everything," I told her. "Alex says she has our backs."

When her lips curled again, the look had turned cruel. "Sent, and unlike Milt, I know how to hide my fucking origination."

# CHAPTER 67

### JERICHO

Sometime around three in the morning, the producer asked if I cared what show this ran on, or if it was acceptable for CNN to push it across their network as breaking news. I assured the guy I just wanted to make sure the world knew, and I didn't care how that happened, but to leave me out of it.

Considering my faked email address looked like RUIN@1234.com, I knew what he'd call me - Ruin - but that was the point. I explained that we were a hacktivist group, we had information the American public deserved to know about, and I was willing to share. The information could be verified on its own.

Tuesday morning, I woke up to find Jason sitting in the living room, watching the news. While my coffee brewed, I headed in there to see what was going on, and found the man grinning at the screen. A cute little graphic had been made with Milt's head, gold bars, and rolled-up money.

"So it's live?" I asked.

"Mhm," he agreed. "Looks like they must've called everyone in to verify this, because it's all over." He glanced back. "The best part?" Grabbing the remote, he clicked to another channel.

I saw Fox News at the bottom, and just like on CNN, this one also had a banner about Milt Einfeldt being corrupt. Granted, it said something about an ethics investigation and used fancier words, like explosion and groundbreaking, but they were still reporting it.

"Nice," I breathed, moving in with the intention to sit down.

Jason just pointed back towards the hall. "Class, Jericho. My lead hacker needs a degree. Skipping isn't good for that. Check the news between classes or something, and go learn."

So I went. I kept trying to sneak a glance at my phone, but in the small break between my Tuesday classes, I saw enough. The anonymous person known only as "Ruin" was being compared to the infamous "Deep Throat" of the seventies who'd busted Nixon.

The best part, however, was the clip of a reporter trying to ask Milty-poo if he had anything to say about the recent allegations. That snobby old fucker turned as pale as a Klansman's sheet and hurried into the nearest elevator. Fucking racist asshole. He deserved all of it!

Hottie promised a surprise when he got home. Zoe texted me a link to a different interview attempt that was almost as good. Knock caught me as I passed the Union, and hurried out to ask what I'd heard. I filled him in, and he traded with what he'd heard. Apparently, Cade had been updating him all day.

This was happening. That fucker was going down hard! His entire career was imploding, and all because he'd used the damned N-word. I couldn't think of anything more fitting. It made me feel a bit lighter and put a bounce in my step.

But when Hottie finally made it home, it was with a box. A big one, and it clanked. Curious, a few of us headed into the kitchen to see what the hell he was doing this time.

"I have an announcement to make!" Hottie yelled, his voice reaching even the people who might be upstairs. "Come one, come all."

Within seconds, we all were hovering around the kitchen island, and Hottie was methodically pulling out bottles of alcohol and a big stack of transparent neon Solo cups. When Jason finally joined us, Hottie passed him a bottle.

"A crazy woman said this is your go-to."

Jason turned it, saw the label, and laughed. "Fucking Riley."

"Yep," Hottie agreed. "But we did good, people. We made this happen, and now it's burning out of control, so I've decided we need a bit of a celebration. Zoe? Tell Tiffany to get her ass over here and bring a bathing suit. Everyone else? Hot tub. Now! We're doing this college-party style, which means I have bratwurst, cheap burgers, and ice to fill up that drink bin out there."

"I got the ice," Jinxy said, grabbing the bag out of the box.

"Tiffany says she's on her way," Zoe promised. "Paper plates?"

I pointed at the pantry. "There's a ton in there. Paper towels for napkins."

"I'm good with it," Cade said. "And it's cold outside, y'all. Big towels, robes, or whatever, because once the sun goes down..."

"Changing!" I yelled, hurrying up the stairs.

Zoe was right behind me, but the guys were moving as well. It seemed we were having a party, and not even an hour later, it was in full force. The grill was going, the food was piling up, and everyone was laughing. The hot tub was large, thankfully, so we all fit in it, but only barely.

Then I turned to Tiffany and raised my glass. "Welcome to Ruin, officially, and congratulations on a first job well done!"

"One of the team!" Cade said, giving the girl a side-hug.

Knock reached around his boyfriend to offer his fist for a bump. "You fit with us, Tiff. Damned glad you keep poking your nose in shit."

"Yes!" Zoe said. "Plus, it means one more girl in the gang. I mean, two of us are just trouble. Three? That's an official girl gang, right?"

"I'm just glad she's on our side," Ripper said. "Never thought I'd like you, but you've become a pretty decent person, Tiff."

"That's a massive compliment coming from you," she assured him. "Thanks, Ripper. And the video was fucking amazing."

"He did the logo too," Zoe bragged.

Tiffany just grinned and nodded, because Zoe's eyes were glassy as fuck. She'd started drinking before eating, and she hadn't slowed down since. Then again, I kinda thought that was a good thing. Zoe rarely got drunk. She wouldn't let herself, so this?

It meant she was safe. We all were. Even if we'd just poked the hornet's nest, there was still a feeling of security, knowing we had each other's backs. When Knock had suggested the polycule idea, I'd grabbed at it because it explained our mess, but now?

I was starting to realize this was more than permission to fuck multiple people. It was a way of caring. Not just me, either. Something about our arrangement made it easier for these men to actually be vulnerable with each other. To hug, to listen, and to be the kind of friends we girls tended to take for granted, but that men so rarely had. It removed any need to one-up each other, because we were merely parts of a whole.

But Jinxy was making gestures at Jason, who was currently sitting on one of the lawn chairs. "Bro, c'mon. Water's warm!"

"I don't have trunks," Jason told him.

"I do," Hottie offered.

"He'll never fit," Cade countered.

"So go naked!" Zoe squealed. "Take it off, Jason. Take it all off!"

That was all we needed. All eight of us in the hot tub began chanting, splashing the water with each line. Jason tried to shake his head. He did his best to pat the air and calm us down. Instead, we only got louder.

So he finally gave in. "You asked for it," he warned, lifting his shirt to pull out a gun and set it on the chair. Next came a holster at his ankle. Jason took the whole thing off.

I leaned out of the hot tub so I could reach my phone. Not even caring about the droplets on my fingers, I managed to open my camera and start recording. This was the sort of "blackmail" I'd gladly use against him later. The kind that could remind him he knew how to have fun.

Then he began peeling out of his clothes. Shoes first, then socks, shirt, and finally he dropped his jeans to the ground. Sucking in a breath, the man took off across the concrete - towards the pool!

"Cannon ball!" he bellowed, and jumped.

Water erupted from the calm surface, spraying out in all directions. A split-second later, Jason's head came up, and he gasped. As fast as he could, the man was hurrying for the exit closest to us.

"Cold!" he muttered. "Fucking dumb idea. It's December. Even in Texas, the water's *cold*!"

"Make room!" I told the others, and we all pushed to the sides so Jason could hop right in.

He was shivering by the time he made it, but that wasn't all. It seemed Jason's weapons weren't the only thing his shirt was hiding. Down his back was a massive tattoo of a tribal scorpion, and with that were the scars.

So many scars. Cuts, bullets, and surgery on his front. Worse things on his back that I couldn't even begin to guess at. Military, probably, but it was none of my fucking business. Oddly enough, no one else asked either.

"And now the water's nice and hot," Tiffany said, standing up so she could reach his glass. "For you, boss-man."

"Thank you, madam," Jason replied, lifting his cup and taking a long swig. "And yes, welcome to the team. You're a damned good addition to both the hacking and the relationship thing."

"Uh..." Tiff paused, looking around. "So, um... Y'all?"

"What's wrong?" Cade asked.

She shook her head. "I kinda wanted to know about being asexual, and Jeri once told me Knock would know."

"No sexual attraction to others," Knock said. "Doesn't mean a lack of libido. It just means an asexual doesn't look at someone and go 'I want to fuck them so I will flirt with them.' Instead, they have attachment for emotional reasons, and if there's sex, it's like fucking a dildo. They might, because they want to make their partner feel good, or because they're horny - like masturbating type of horny - but not because the sex drive is linked to the love drive."

"Oh." She sank back down in the water a bit, letting her shoulders disappear from sight.

"Tiff?" Cade asked. "You ok?"

"What if I'm asexual?" she asked.

I shrugged, because it didn't matter to me. Granted, I'd assumed asexuals just didn't fuck. Hearing she might changed my assumptions about how she fit in, but we'd deal with it. We always did. It was the one thing Ruin was good at.

"I got this," Hottie said, leaning forward. "In this group, it's ok to try on a title. Ace, demi, bi, or anything else. If you think you might be it, then the best way to know is to explore it, right?"

"Yeah?" Tiffany said, but it was almost a whimper.

"And we do not out our friends," Zoe said, waving her drink hard enough to make a bit slosh into the water. "Safe space. Can fuck it up and find out right here without hurting anything. See? I'm drunk!"

"You are drunk," Jinxy agreed. "Totally smashed, beautiful, but that means you have to sleep beside me tonight so I can make sure you don't puke."

"Ok!" she agreed. "Because I think I wanna fuck!"

"Not tonight, you don't," Jinxy assured her. "You want to drink, and see the stars get halos, and maybe end up puking if you do it right."

I watched as a little smile began to play on Tiffany's lips at that exchange. Relief, I was pretty sure. Ok, and the cuteness, but she'd just dropped something that was a big deal to her, and no one had flinched at all. We also hadn't poked at her to say she was.

"What's the short form again, Hottie?" Tiff asked.

"Ace," he said. "Spelled like a card, pronounced like the first part of asexual."

"So, if I just think sex is not worth the work?" she asked.

Jinxy snorted out a laugh and smacked Cade's shoulder. "Bro..."

"No!" she groaned. "I've had orgasms. Trust me, I've gotten myself off too. Cade's not the problem. It's just..."

"Trauma?" Jason asked. "You went through a lot last year."

"I was like this before," she mumbled.

"Then you're like this," he said. "Own it, because it's no more right or wrong than those two." He pointed at Knock and Cade.

"But how does that make me fit in this polycule?" she asked.

"Well," Knock said, "most asexuals - from what I read when trying to figure out my own shit, so take this with a grain of salt - still like commitment. Think middle school romance, not sexual type. Holding hands, cuddling, and all of that. Asexuals also tend to have a gender preference, so like straight, bi, or gay. You can find beauty in someone, but more like art and less like sex appeal."

"Kinda hitting all the nails on the head," she admitted.

"Then I think where you fit is up to the girls," Ripper said. "I know I'm not opposed to cuddles, but I'm not going to cheat on my girlfriend."

"I'm good with it!" Zoe said.

"You're too drunk to decide," Tiffany countered. "Jeri?"

"We all have bonds," I told her. "That's what holds us together. I do not own any of my boyfriends, and since I'm sleeping with four different guys, how fair is it for me to say they can't hug someone?"

Her eyes narrowed as she looked at me. "Ok." But she didn't look away. "I'm still not going to poach. Friends do not do that."

"I know," I assured her. "And lovers don't bind their partners to them with chains. Now I'll be right back. Gotta pee!"

Then I hopped out of the tub and hurried inside, dripping water after me the whole way because I didn't even pause long enough to get a towel.

# CHAPTER 68

### RIPPER

Jeri had gone inside a while ago. The rest of us were still laughing, drinking, and sharing videos of different news clips. Unfortunately, I hadn't checked the time when she'd left, but it sure felt like she'd been gone for a lot longer than "just to pee" required.

Beside me, Hottie nudged my arm. "Gonna go check on her?"

"I can," I said. "Why, what's up?"

His eyes flicked over to Tiffany, then back. "I have an idea."

Yeah, but I wasn't so sure about that. There was no way Jericho would care about her boyfriends fucking around. Well, she never had before. So I made my own excuse and headed inside. There, I could hear movement in the kitchen, so I decided she'd just been making a snack or something, but when I rounded the corner, she was leaning over the counter, staring at the coffee pot that wasn't on.

"Jeri?" I asked.

"Hey!" she said. "I was just trying to decide if I should brew a coffee or drink more."

"Bullshit."

This close, I could see her light blue eyes widen in surprise, but that was it. For a little too long, we simply stared at each other, almost like we were waiting to see who'd break first. When she sighed and dropped her head, I was so glad it hadn't been me.

"Is this all there is?" she asked.

But she'd completely lost me. "Which this, Jeri?"

"The case. Milt fucking Einfeldt. We do the dirty work, let the news get all the credit, and then what? We threw away our chance for the FBI for this? And that asshole hasn't even responded! He's been avoiding the press, but he doesn't look like shit's going sideways for him. Like, everyone around him is trying to make excuses, Ripper. What happens if he gets away with this?"

"Hey," I breathed, stepping in to pull her up against me. "We already knew they weren't going to approve the program. We didn't throw a damned thing away."

"But no one's doing shit!" she huffed. "And out there, everyone's trying to be so happy, but all I can think is that nothing is going to change. It's just more bullshit! Just like with Dylan and those fuckers. We knew what they were doing, but we had to 'prove' it, right? We fucking proved it, and *still* nothing is happening!"

"It will," I said, sliding my hand down her arm until I could lace my fingers with hers. "But I'm wet, you're cold, and I don't think you want to kill their vibe out there, right?"

"No," she mumbled.

"So how about we go up to your room where we can watch the fun and talk it out?"

"Yeah?" Those gorgeous eyes of hers flicked up to meet mine. "And maybe some cuddling?"

"Anything you want, Jeri," I swore.

But as I was leading her upstairs, I replayed her words. Cuddling. Not fucking. Not kissing. Jeri had picked cuddling out of all the options, and that wasn't something she usually asked for. Granted, if she just wanted to be held, I was completely down for that, but I had a funny feeling it was something else.

So when we reached her room, I stopped her from turning on the light. That would let everyone downstairs see right in. Sure, the hot tub was around the corner, but our friends wouldn't stay *just* in the hot tub. Then I dropped my trunks, crawled under her covers, and gestured for her to come closer.

She flicked the lock on her door, peeled off her own bathing suit, and did. "Guess it's easy to get you naked, huh?" she teased.

"I was serious about being cold and wet," I told her, "but yeah, pretty much. I mean, for you." Then I shifted so she was able to rest her head on my shoulder and see me. "Why cuddling, Jeri?"

Her entire body paused, and I felt it tense against mine. "Fuck," she muttered.

"I'm just asking," I promised. "This is me trying to keep up, ok? I mean, I like cuddling."

"Of *course* you do," she groaned. "And asexuals like to cuddle. I mean, how many times has Tiffany said you're perfect? Fuck."

"I am not cheating on my girlfriend," I assured her. "Jeri, if you don't want me cuddling with someone else, then I won't. Well, I'll try to get an exception for Zoe, but that's different."

"No, it's just..." She rolled onto her back. "I don't care if she fucks Knock, Cade, or Hottie."

"Ok?" I was now very confused.

"They'd just fuck her," she tried to explain. "I mean, what's the difference between that and jacking off? Nothing! It'd be meaningless. They love me. And she's a friend, but fuck buddies aren't the same as love, and I really don't own any of you, but with them it's different."

"You mean it's different with me," I corrected. "Why, Jeri?"

Slowly, her eyes made their way up, finding mine again. "Because I don't think you fuck. I think you love. If you're cuddling with her, or kissing on her, it means you love her, and I've been so busy I've ignored you, and she won't. So then you'll realize what kind of a shit deal I really am, and you'll get with her. I'll be happy for you, but I..."

"No," I said, cutting her off when she paused to think. "I will not fall in love with Tiff, Jeri."

"You can't be sure of that," she countered. "I mean, in three years? You could."

"No," I said again. "I am completely monogamous. Hell, you're right about one thing. I don't want to 'just fuck.' I want it to mean something. Not necessarily love, but something big. Something deep. Something wild and chaotic and passionate. I don't get turned on unless I'm already invested, you know?"

"In time, you could get invested," she reminded me.

"I'm also not going to make the first move," I said. "Jeri, I am in love with you. Just you. Now, I'm not opposed to cuddling with Tiff the way I do with Zoe, but you know that's different. I have exactly zero interest in kissing her, or anything else."

"Tiffany?" she scoffed.

"Ok, she's pretty," I agreed. "I'm not blind. She's just..." I paused, biting my lips together. "Jeri, some part of her reminds me of every bad thing screamed at me in high school. She's changed, but looking at her still makes me think of my bullies. Tiffany is not someone I want to be intimate with, and maybe in time that will relax a bit, and she'll get as close as Zoe. She will never steal my heart away like you do."

"Me?"

"You," I breathed. "God, the first time you talked to me? When you were asking about my book cover? I was doing my best not to stammer. Like, here was this gorgeous girl, and she was a fucking gamer?"

"Yeah," she muttered, curling a little closer.

"And," I went on, feeling her relaxing against me, "you showed up to PC Joe's. I was such a dork. I was trying too hard, and I knew I was making the shittiest impression ever, but you didn't seem to care. It was like you just got me. Then when Dylan started in on me? Fuck, he called me fat, Jeri! I'm all trying to impress the most beautiful girl who's ever talked to me, and he's over there going off about how fucking fat I am?"

"You're not fat," she said.

"I'm not thin," I countered. "I'm actually ok with it now, but yeah. Not really the kind of thing girls go for. But you did. You kept being cool, and you kept talking to me. And sure, I knew it was just a friend thing, because guys like me did not get girls like you, but I did. Somehow, I got the most perfect girl in the world, and you just keep getting better, so I promise I'm not into Tiffany. I don't think I'll ever be into her. I also really don't want you to be jealous about her hanging out."

"I don't want to be greedy," she admitted. "I mean, I'm so selfish all of you have to share me, but how dare I have to learn to accept the same? That's not a healthy relationship, you know? It's toxic, and *I'd* be the toxic one! So I'm trying, but with you, I just feel like - "

"Like I love you," I breathed, pulling her a little more so she was on top of me. "Only you, Jericho. And my love doesn't work the way yours does. It's a lot more like Hottie's."

Her knees found either side of my waist, her hands were on my chest, and our faces were so close together. "Oh," she said before leaning in to kiss me.

Damn. I had no clue how this woman could always get me going, but she did. The feel of her fingers on my chest, the sound of her little moans as we kissed as deeply as we could, and the feel of her thighs against me like this? My dick was getting hard fast.

"I only want you," I said, softly, "because I only love you. I also love you completely, with all of your flaws, Jeri."

"I love you too," she breathed.

Then she suddenly sat up and leaned to the side. I thought she was about to climb off me, and I knew I'd be leaving a serious tent in this bed. Instead, she pulled open the drawer of her nightstand, pulled out a condom, and then ripped it open.

"Yeah?" she asked, moving down my body.

"Definitely," I agreed.

But I didn't expect her to roll the fucking thing on! One of her hands grabbed the base of my dick. The other pinched the tip, lined it up, and pushed the latex down. Jesus christ, I was going to lose it if she kept that up, because the sight of her like this? Taking control, being her wild and passionate self? I was so into it.

The moment the condom was on, she dropped a hand beside my head, leaned in to kiss me hard, and lowered herself right down on my dick. I could feel the heat of her body. Her slickness proved she was as turned on as I was, and something about that made me realize just how much she cared.

Because while Jeri might not be so good at saying it, she was amazing at showing her feelings. Rocking onto my body slowly, she showed me each and every one. We kissed. My hands found her waist. She tossed the blankets back, not quite getting them off my feet, but she never once slowed.

She rode me with a pace that was caught somewhere between lazy and sensual. I could feel every ridge and muscle inside her. Each breath she took was so loud in the room. Under my hands, I felt her skin and muscles shift as she took exactly what she needed, and it felt fucking amazing.

For a guy like me to end up with a woman like her? It shouldn't happen. It went against all the odds. Everyone knew it wasn't possible, and yet Jeri had seen right through me. She'd ignored all the bullshit like my belly and my glasses. She'd pushed right into my heart and took up residence there, and I never wanted to let her go.

Some men wanted to put their woman in a cage of sorts to control her. Well, this was *my* cage. I'd hold on to Jeri as tightly as I could so I could keep her safe. I'd never clip her wings, and I certainly wouldn't ask her to change, but I would fight all the monsters if it meant she could simply keep being, well, this.

Beautiful, sensual, and even a little feral. Honest, blatant, and definitely passionate. As she pushed her body onto mine, driving me deeper and deeper inside her, I couldn't look away. Her pink dreads swayed against her back and chest. Her breasts bounced as she moved faster. Her eyes closed sometimes, making my gaze drop to her parted lips. Then her eyes would open, trapping me in that perfect shade of blue again.

Fuck, I was going to lose it. Part of me wanted to make sure she got off first. Part wanted to prove I was here just for her, but seeing my woman in all her glory? The way she had no boundaries, filters, or limits? It was as erotic as the roll she did with her hips when I was all the way inside her.

I gasped, struggling to hold off, but that merely made one side of her mouth slide higher. She did that move again. Letting go of her with one hand, I grabbed a fistful of the sheet below me, and my girl moaned in approval.

"You are mine," she said softly, grinding against me in the best way. "You, Elliot, are the one I will not let get away. I love you too much to ever lose you, you hear me?"

"Yes," I panted. "Uh-huh."

"Good."

Then she dropped back down and kissed me again, bouncing her hips even faster. Like this, there wasn't a damned thing I could do, and not even a condom could dull the sensation enough. As she pumped herself onto me, all I could do was wrap my arms around her back and give in completely.

I came. It may have been the most intense orgasm I'd ever had in my life, but somehow I managed not to cry out. I did grunt loudly, struggling to clench my jaw. Jeri just kept going. Sucking in a breath, she lifted her head, her dreads flopping against her back, and she continued to ride me hard.

Until her hand desperately locked down on my wrist and her entire body tightened with her climax. I felt the pulses rocking her body, gripping me, and I could barely keep my eyes open, but I didn't want to miss a single second of the sight of her like this. Of her doing the most beautiful thing a woman could: letting go.

Then she sighed and flopped forward, pushing both arms under my neck as she sucked in deep, heavy breaths. Slowly, I caressed her back, knowing I never wanted to let her go. Sex, no sex, or anything else. I just wanted the real moments with her.

"I love you," I whispered against the side of her neck.

She tilted her head to kiss my shoulder. "I was scared I might lose you. That's why I came inside."

"I know," I admitted. "I mean, I figured it out. You also won't. Jeri, me and you? We're the real thing. I'm not going anywhere unless you make me."

"Never," she breathed. "I need you too much."

"All of us," I reminded her. "And unlike you, I'm actually ok with that."

"Yeah, all of you," she said, lifting up to slide off me. "Even Tiff, I think."

"Because she's one of us, and for the first time in your life, Jeri, you're going to have to accept that this? The good shit? It's real. It's all real, and it's ok for it to be confusing."

"Very confusing," she agreed. "But I like it. I really like winning."

"Me too."

# CHAPTER 69

### CADE

Wednesday, I started hearing people on campus discussing the news. Dad had been obsessive about politics. That was where I'd learned everything, and Einfeldt's name was hard to miss. The question was whether or not this was going our way.

Checking my phone showed he was still the lead topic on almost all the networks. The amount of data we'd given CNN? Yeah, that was proving very hard to wiggle out of. Even better, it seemed the questions piling up were going to be the kind that would be hard to get out of.

So, maybe we'd thrown away our chance at working for the FBI, but as far as I cared, it was worth it. I knew Jeri and Knock really wanted this, but we were hackers. We hacked. Hacking wasn't exactly legal, so this big dream of being able to do our shit legally? Fuck that. Legal didn't matter nearly as much as effectively, and right now, our attacks seemed very effective.

Milt Einfeldt was going down! With each story, more and more was being released, almost like they'd had to vet some of it. Go figure. We had given them quite a bit of data, after all. It also meant our information had just been double-checked. Sure, we knew it was good, but this was the sort of shit that was so over the top, it seemed impossible. The sort of story that would likely get called "fake news."

Wednesday evening, we all spent our downtime watching as much of the media coverage as we could stomach. It was a victory lap of sorts. Seeing his fellow senators try to make excuses or disavow Einfeldt's mess? Listening to the leader of his party assure the world this was a smear job, trying to remove their narrow majority in the Senate? It was glorious.

It was also the way these things went. Politics was disgustingly predictable. With Einfeldt's corruption headlining on all major networks, the senator from Alabama only had a few options left, and it seemed like he was going to try all of them. The first had been avoiding interviews. Next would come the denial.

Hopefully, after that would be the resignation.

But our success meant we were basically done here. Jason said he'd head back home on Sunday. His plan was to make one more trip to the shooting range with us, because the session was already paid for. And while we were all pretty sure the program was dead, the committee hadn't voted, so we had this slim little hope.

Very slim.

Then on Thursday, Jinxy let us all know that a big press conference was scheduled for this afternoon. He made sure everyone in Ruin knew, and we decided to make a celebration of it. The man was supposed to address the allegations. We wanted to hear how this would go down and if our name was brought into it. Hopefully, it would be the moment we'd all been waiting for. The one where this asshole apologized for fucking up and announced his resignation.

Jason popped the popcorn for it. The drinks weren't the alcoholic type, but even Tiff showed up for this. As we sprawled out in the living room, waiting for the empty podium on the screen to get filled, we were joking about his likely excuses.

"He's going to claim it's an addiction of some type and he'll get help," Jeri said. "Gambling, drugs, or who knows what else. But he'll disappear for rehab and come back out when it's died down."

"I'm going with a mistress," Jinxy said. "That's a pretty common thing in D.C. now. No one would bat an eye. He'll drop the blame on her."

"I think he's going to resign," I offered.

Zoe, cuddled up against her boyfriend's chest, shook her head. "I think he's going to say these are investments we dumbasses can't understand. Finances are complicated and all that shit."

"Bullshit," Tiffany grumbled. "No, I like the mistress excuse. It's the best he's got."

"Better if he calls her a Russian asset and says he was targeted," Knock added. "It would likely take most of the pressure off him."

Ripper grunted, completely unimpressed. "No, he's going to say this was a minor mistake, he just needs to update his paperwork, and he'll let the ethics committee - or whatever it's called - figure it out."

"Hottie?" I asked, looking over at the man.

He had Jeri laying across his lap, his hand casually smoothing her hair. "I think he's going to blame hackers. He'll say the information was made up, he has no connection to any of this, but he was hacked."

"Yeah, I'm with Hottie," Jason agreed. "He's going to try to use this to blame - " He paused as the man made his way onto the steps of whatever building they were set up in front of. "Showtime."

White marble stairs took up most of the screen. The camera showed a very large group of reporters before the podium, and the sound of cameras clicking was loud. This was the standard for political scandals, though. I'd seen it countless times on the TV at home when I was growing up.

My father had been rabid about politics. He'd loved it for some fucked-up reason - which had made me despise all of this. Sure, I understood the way politics worked. Mostly that was because no one could spend a lifetime listening to adults rant about it without picking something up. But to me, it was all dumb shit. Someone else's drama, based on someone else's morals, filled with more money than anyone had a right to throw around. Yeah, politics sucked. Watching this man go down? That wouldn't.

"Good afternoon," Milt said into the mic, before pausing so the group could quiet down. "Like all of you, I was surprised to see my name in the news this week. As many of you know, I've been representing the great state of Alabama for nearly seventeen years now, and I have done my best to represent my constituents."

"Blah, blah, blah," Jeri muttered.

"But this attack against me is an attack against all of us!" Milt went on. "Accusing me of such horrible crimes will not go unpunished! I am not a Russian asset. Yes, I have made international business investments, but I have two small children. I want to make sure they are taken care of in their lives. What parent doesn't?"

"Oh, the parent line," Tiffany grumbled. "He's pulling out all the stops."

But the senator kept going. "This attack against me is little more than an attempt to discredit me. As an American citizen, where and how I spend my money is my own business. Isn't it the American dream to lift ourselves ever higher, making life easier for our children, and even easier for our grandchildren after them? Instead, my success in politics is being framed as something I should be ashamed of." He leaned closer, right up into the microphone. "I'm not."

"Fuck," I grumbled. "He's fighting it."

"But we have the data!" Jeri hissed.

"And politics doesn't care about facts," I countered. "That's the problem, Jeri. Politics? It's about power, prestige, and getting rich. It's not about being a civil servant anymore."

She just sat up and thrust an arm at the TV. "And we have the receipts! We have proof that he's dirty. We fucking gave it to CNN!"

Yet Milt was still going. I'd missed part of his speech, but the banner at the bottom of the screen said enough. "Milt Einfeldt targeted by political rivals?"

"What the fuck?" I asked.

"...Using cyber-harassment," Milt was saying, "to distort my perfectly legitimate investments into some kind of conspiracy. This is an invasion of privacy! This is why we need to limit governmental overreach. This is exactly why I am voting against the proposal for digital vigilantes! Maybe my opponents think that turning hackers loose on our citizens is a valid method of policing, but to me it sounds like thought police! So we're not allowed to visit certain websites? We're not allowed to play video games? We're now suspects if we invest in stocks, companies, or try to make our money work for us? In a time when every American citizen is feeling the pinch of a crumbling economy..."

"The fuck?" Jinxy huffed. "He's trying to make this about fucking inflation or something?"

"He's trying," I grumbled, "to make this about anything but himself!"

Because that was exactly what this man was doing. He'd mentioned hackers. He'd touched on where he was spending his money. He was changing the subject, right in front of all of us, and it was working! I could see reporters in the crowd nodding at his points, and not once had this asshole admitted guilt.

Which meant we were failing.

"No, no, no," I breathed, leaning in as if getting closer to the screen could somehow change the outcome.

And then the questions began to fly. "Senator Einfeldt! Are you trying to say these accusations are false?"

"I'm saying they're taken out of context," the senator replied. "And the same could happen to anyone. When cyberterrorists are allowed to dive into our personal lives, our banking choices, and our private data, *this* is the result. This is illegal search and seizure. This is a smear job, and I will not let the lies and rumors distract me from why I'm here in Washington. My job is to represent the good people of Alabama. People who are just as vulnerable to this type of attack, because if they can get me, then any of us could be next!"

My heart was hanging in my chest. This man was good. His lines were hitting just right. I knew the story was about to change, and everything we'd just done was going to vanish like vapor, dissolving right before our eyes.

Beside me, Knock's mouth was hanging open, and he was shaking his head. Across from us, Jeri and Hottie were staring at the screen in complete horror. Jinxy, Zoe, Ripper, and even Tiff were all about the same. We watched this man talk, stunned, because he was handling this too well. He was wiping it all away, and nothing we could do would stop it.

Ruin was done.

A week ago, we'd made the decision to take one hell of a risk. We'd thrown away our chance to make this program work. We'd risked everything because we'd thought we were right, but no one fucking cared! All that mattered was which side they were on. That was how politics worked. People were either for or against a party, and they didn't seem to care if "their" person was fucking guilty as shit. They just saw it as us against them.

But this man had attacked Alex. He'd called her the N-word. He'd sent her threats, he'd harassed her, and he'd made it clear he wouldn't stop. He thought he was above the law, and right now I was starting to think he was right.

"We threw it all away for nothing," I breathed.

"No," Jason said. "You did the right thing."

"And we're fucking losing!" Jeri snapped. "Don't you fucking get that, Jason? We were supposed to bust this fucker, but he's not resigning. He's not apologizing. He's fucking calling *us* the terrorists! He's using this as a way to get more people to vote against the program." She paused, a little huff of air slipping from her. "Shit. We fucked up."

"We tried," Knock reminded her.

"And trying doesn't fucking count! Trying isn't winning!" Jeri screamed.

"Hey..." Hottie whispered, wrapping his arms around her. "We knew this could happen."

"And we knew the program was fucked," Zoe added. "Jeri, you said it yourself. Milt had our names. He was going to stop us, one way or another. We didn't lose anything, because we never had it to begin with."

"But we were supposed to fuck him up!" Jeri hissed.

My eyes were still on the screen, hating it each time that man smiled. "And we didn't. Jeri, we don't always get to win."

"So we fuck him up another way," Tiffany said. "If we're not FBI people, then why do we have to be good, huh?"

Jeri turned a little more to look right at her. "What?" she asked.

"Hackers," Tiffany said. "Not cops. Not feds. We're hackers, right? I mean, isn't that what Ruin did to Dylan and his friends? You fucking destroyed him, and you didn't stop to ask if it was ok."

"But this was different," I tried to explain. "Tiff, this was our chance."

"Fuck chances," Tiff said.

And something about Jeri calmed. "Fuck chances," she repeated, almost like she was trying on those words for size. "Fuck being good. We tried to do it right and that didn't work. So maybe we should do it wrong?"

"Wait, wait, wait..." Jinxy said, slipping out from under Zoe. "Can we fucking rewind?"

"Not a video," Ripper pointed out.

"Shit," Jinxy said, taking a half step closer to the screen. "Go back. Show it again. Go back..."

I gaped at him as if he was losing his mind. "Jinxy?"

The screen changed, showing a wider shot of Milt at the podium, and Jinxy did a little fist pump. "Yes!"

"What the fuck, bro?" I asked him.

But he was already pulling out his phone. "Here's hoping I just found a way to fuck those chances. That guy? The one with the scarf?" He began scrolling down the screen. "That's my brother."

# CHAPTER 70

### JINXY

Jeri and Cade were just starting to panic when my eyes landed on a man at the edge of the screen. Halfway up those marble steps, he was dressed against the winter cold, but he still stood out. It wasn't because he was standing alone. No, plenty others were spread out across the back, trying to get their own recording of this.

It was the bright orange mark on his neck.

The man's blondish hair was swept back, not moving in the breeze. His coat was long and black. His hands were hidden behind leather gloves. His scarf, however, had a small line of bright, neon orange at the ends. A color hunters called blaze orange - and I was pretty sure I knew him.

"Wait, wait, wait..." I said, slipping out from under Zoe even as the camera angle changed again. "Can we fucking rewind?"

"Not a video," Ripper pointed out.

"Shit," I grumbled, moving closer to the screen in the hopes that I wasn't imagining this. "Go back. Show it again. Go back..."

Cade looked at me like I was crazy. "Jinxy?"

But I ignored him, my eyes locked on the television. The moment I saw him again, I was sure of it. The man in the back of the shot could be no one else but William Blankenship the Third. Unconsciously, I did a little fist pump.

"Yes!" I breathed, reaching for my phone.

"What the fuck, bro?" Cade asked.

"Here's hoping I just found a way to fuck those chances," I tried to explain while scrolling down my contacts. "That guy? The one with the scarf?" I couldn't help but smile. "That's my brother."

"What?" Jason asked, clearly confused.

"My brother's there," I clarified. "We may not be as fucked as we think."

Then again, for all I knew, we might be more fucked. Just depended on how he was involved in this. So, as fast as I could, I pressed call, my eyes locked on the screen. This had to work. If it didn't, we were so fucked. Ruin had just risked everything to make this man pay, and it sure looked like he was going to walk away scot-free unless something changed.

In real-time, I watched the man reach into his coat pocket, pull out his phone, and lift it to his ear. What I didn't do was wait for him to say anything. I could hear the moment the line was connected, and for me, that was good enough.

"Blaze, Teal," I said. "I don't give a shit about accidents. I just need to know if this man is your client."

"He is."

My guts twisted. I felt like my heart fucking paused. No, no, no, this could not be happening!

"Shit!" I hissed. "That's a problem."

Blaze turned, casually walking off screen and away from the whole ordeal. "Why?" he demanded. His voice was like stone, cold and devoid of emotion.

"Because we're the ones who did this," I explained.

He murmured. "Tell me what you know, Teal."

"A Russian oligarch is sending him gold. He's been getting bribes from multiple billionaires. All of his votes have corresponded with the gifts and have been swayed by the giver. We have multiple high-end vacations he's received the same way."

"Jinxy!" Jason snapped, hearing me spilling our secrets.

"This time, you have to trust me," I told him. "Otherwise, we're so fucked."

But Blaze heard. "I don't fuck family," he assured me. "Why do you care about this man, Teal?"

"He's been harassing our boss, Blaze. It started with the N-word and moved on to sexism. He's made vague threats about if she knows where her daughter is, and more. Hundreds of supposedly anonymous emails. I mean, we backtracked them, but he thought he was untouchable when he said this shit."

"And he crossed a line?" Blaze asked.

"Yeah," I breathed. "A big one, man. Look, our thing? What Ruin does is protect women. We're all about stopping virtual violence against women, and this more than counts. We found the other shit in the process." I almost stopped there. Fuck, I should've, but this was my brother. As creepy as he was, I knew he'd never stab me in the back. "Blaze, we just risked everything to take this asshole down."

"What is everything?"

"A program with the FBI," I said. "He's on the committee that is supposed to approve it, but they were dragging their feet. We figured out it was getting stonewalled, and our boss was being threatened. First the racial shit, Blaze. Then he tried to replace her with a fucking man. Worse, a yes-man, or so he thinks. Last week, that fucker got our names, but we're not backing off."

"Neither is he."

"Fuck!" I groaned. "And we just put everything on the line! Damn it!"

"Mm." He sounded unimpressed. I was spiraling, but Blaze? No, he never got emotional like that. Then he said the last thing I would've expected. "I wrote him a very good speech, too."

"Too good," I said around a laugh. "Although we both know you didn't write that, bro. But how the fuck does he think he's going to get away with this?"

"Shift the focus to the invasion of his privacy. He's the victim here. Hackers are the problem. Make it clear this isn't what it looks like - because he's being attacked - and we have a very good word salad to make it all land."

"Shit, and if your team's on it, this is about to get harder."

I wanted to throw my phone and rant. Fuck, if my brother was involved, then there was no way we'd unfuck the fuckery of this fuckupness. While Ruin might be ruthless, Blaze? He was unstoppable, and this man didn't have the hang-up of things like guilt. He didn't have any reason to hold back.

We were so damned fucked.

"Guys," I said, looking around the room. "We need to back off."

"No," Blaze said. "I didn't know this was you."

"Yeah, well, it is," I said. "Bro, we've got our necks hanging out there, and if this man decides to use the information the FBI has on us? I'm going back to jail, man. Me and all my friends here." I sighed. "My new fucking family, you know? Like, can you keep us out of this, at least?"

"I don't fuck with family."

His tone was so matter-of-fact. To him, that was nothing more than a statement of truth, but I knew how he worked. Blaze traded in accidents and favors. Unfortunately, I had no clue which one this would be.

"You are the best fixer in the Washington, D.C., area," I said, making it clear I knew that. "If you fix his problems, you fuck mine."

"Yes, but I made him no promises," he assured me. "He bought a speech, I gave him one, and I do not fuck family. How's the girl, Teal?"

The change in subject made me twitch. "Zoe?" I asked, looking over at her. "Well, she was lying in my lap until I had to call you. I think that's pretty good. We live together now. Well, seven of us do. They're the family. We call it a polycule, because it's fucking complicated."

"And school?" he asked. "Master's degree, right?"

"Yeah. Looks like I'm making A's right now. Could change to a B in one class, but it'll be close."

"Make it an A," he told me. "You are the little brother, and I'm supposed to look out for you, so make it an A. I'll also handle this, just keep me in the loop?"

My entire body paused. "Seriously?"

"You sound happy. Take care of the girl, and I will handle this."

"Promise," I said, feeling like the rules had just shifted somehow. "Thanks, Liam."

He chuckled. "You remembered."

"I've been trying," I admitted. "I'm just curious if anyone still gets to call you Billy."

"Two of them. Violet and Faith. She likes unicorns, you know. Thirteen years old and still likes them. Is that what it would've been like for us if someone had been watching our backs?"

"Yeah, I think so," I said softly. "Kinda why Gran made a rainbow, right?"

"Exactly," he said, but the word sounded almost like a growl. Like some kind of threat. "I'll handle Einfeldt. Don't worry about the press conference. I know it's good, but it's still not a problem."

Then the line went dead.

Pushing out a breath, I looked at the screen to make sure, then headed back to my chair. Everyone in the room was looking at me, especially Zoe.

"What about me?" she asked.

"He checks to make sure things with you are still going good," I explained. "Kinda told him I had a crush on this girl."

"Who?" Jason demanded.

"My brother, kinda."

"Southwind," Hottie said. "The kids who got colors call each other siblings. Well, mostly."

"Mostly," I agreed. "Because Violet's fucking Magenta, Cyan, and Emerald. Yeah, and I'm pretty sure Crimson and Chartreuse are too." I waved that off. "But we're family. Jason, it's like Riley's mess, but more..."

"Dangerous," he said. "Who's this brother?"

"William Blankenship the Third," I told him. "Billy as a kid. Liam now. He's, um, they call it a fixer."

"Shit," Jason growled, sitting up straight. "That's a problem."

I waved him back down. "He just said not to worry about the press conference, and that he wouldn't fuck us over. Well, me, but that means all of us. Um, see, Liam's kinda the best at this, so if he says it's handled, then it's handled."

"Ok?" Jericho asked.

"He's a psychopath," I explained. "Kinda makes manipulating people easy for him."

"So, fucked up like us?" She lifted a brow.

"No." I had to pause to scrub at my face. "I'm talking a real psycho. Diagnosed, medicated - if he takes it - and not like everyone else. We're pretty sure he should've ended up a serial killer or something. So, yeah. Being a fixer is great for him. Lots of action, lots of challenges, and no worries about moral lines. Seems he only has two."

"Which two?" Zoe asked.

"Family and children." I shrugged. "Yeah, and he does favors for the family, but it's rarely worth the price, and I'm not talking money here. Blaze collects favors. He will then use them as he needs to make something else work."

"I need a background on him," Jason said, looking like he was about to stand.

I simply waved him down. "You won't find one. His record looks exactly the way he wants it to. There's nothing else. He knows his shit, knows how to use it, and doesn't make mistakes. Trust me, you're getting more from me than you ever would from anything he's left online."

"The problem," Hottie said, pointing to the screen, "is Milt's speech was good. It makes that fucker sound like the victim in all of this."

"Yeah..." I nodded to show I wasn't surprised. "But Blaze knows what he's doing. He said not to worry about it. Granted, that only goes so far, but he's out. He won't be writing any more speeches for this fucker, which means we can come back at him without a problem, right?"

"But he just changed the entire subject!" Cade pointed out.

"And that's the thing," Jeri said. "We need the accusations to stick, and he just made us the bad guys!"

"Alex says he wants to pull a vote," Jason added. "He's ready to shut down the program."

"Officially," Knock clarified. "And they have our fucking names!"

"Fuck!" Jeri snapped. "We're so screwed. Brother or no brother, Milt is going to get away with this, and all of this will be for nothing!"

"We'll figure it out," Zoe promised her. "Jeri, we always figure it out. We just have to make sure Bradley has everything. That way, the FBI can still go after him, and maybe that will be enough to clear our names?" She looked up at me. "Maybe?" Then back to the rest. "So let's finish putting that together. The FBI won't care about some pretty speech, right, Jason?"

"We hope," he said.

"It's just a speech," Cade said as if he was trying to convince not only us, but also himself. "With every political scandal, there's a speech. Most of the time, it doesn't change anything. It simply pulls the sides apart, gets lots of fingers pointing, and makes tomorrow's news cycle more exciting."

"So," Knock said, "we *use* that news cycle to shift the focus off us and back onto him. We need to make sure this asshole pays for what he's done. Doesn't even matter which part, but we do not lose, people."

"We just have to do something to make sure we can turn this into a win," Tiffany said.

"Like stop feeling sorry for ourselves and use what we already have," Jason said.

"And we will," I assured them. "I don't know how yet, but somehow, we will make this work. We kinda have to, because we are the vengeance."

"So let's get to work on making a little revenge," Jeri ordered.

# CHAPTER 71

### JINXY

Revenge was a dish best served cold, or so the saying went. Well, in this case it worked out, because most of our evidence was now delayed. Not much, and it certainly wasn't a "cold case," but it wasn't exactly new either. Still, since Alex had arranged this so that catching her harasser was a "challenge" to prove ourselves, we could still bust this fucker.

That meant making a case file for Bradley. Friday, we put everything together and wrote our reports. When done, it was all sent to Bradley's official email with the FBI. Every single scrap of data we'd found on Milt's computer and network was in there - including Tiffany's accounting crap.

The resulting file was fucking huge, but Jason assured us the FBI servers wouldn't reject it. He also admitted Bradley needed a crash course in how to use the cloud, because that would be a lot more convenient for us. Upload here, let him read it all there.

What he didn't say was whether or not we might have another option, once the program was officially dead. Sadly, the narrative about this asshole's problems was shifting in his favor. We needed to bring the focus back to the correlation between these bribes and Milt's voting record. Once or twice might be a coincidence. Three years of this crap? No way. That couldn't be legal. We just needed someone else to prove it.

Yet it seemed my brother hadn't completely forgotten about this. Early Saturday morning, my phone started ringing, and the name on the screen was his. Swiping, I answered with as little enthusiasm as I felt.

"Teal."

"Hey, baby brother!" Blaze replied, sounding chipper and almost personable. I knew it was fake. "How long does it take you to get to the Dallas airport from where you are?"

"Which one?" I asked. "There are two. DFW or Love Field?"

"DFW," he clarified.

I blew out a breath. "Hour and a half."

"Good, meet me there at noon."

"Can't. Have to be at the shooting range," I grumbled.

"Not anymore," Blaze said. "Airport. Noon. Bring the girl."

"Hey!" I barked before he could hang up. "Her name is Zoe, Billy. Zoe. Not 'the girl.'"

"Point made," he said - and then hung up.

But he hadn't bitched about me calling him Billy? What the actual fuck?

Giving in, I woke Zoe up just enough to tell her what was going on. Jason had us all scheduled for one more shooting lesson, but this? If Blaze had something, we needed to go, and Zoe readily agreed to come with me. At this point, it didn't really matter what the hell he wanted - but I had a feeling we were about to chauffeur him all the way to Southwind.

Four hours later, the rest of Ruin was in Dallas working with guns, and I was pulling up in the parking lot at what I sure hoped was the right gate. Blaze had texted me his flight number, and Zoe was trying to keep track of it, but the damned thing had already changed twice. On the bright side, we found a spot right at the front, which meant almost no walking.

"Ok," I said. "Zoe, this guy is going to look just as normal and charming as they come. He has a few tattoos, and the one on his neck covers up some hate symbols, so please don't ask. He simply said he wanted to meet you, ok?"

"You sound nervous," she teased, hopping out of my car.

I groaned and opened my own door, unfolding my long legs. "I am! This is so unlike him that I'm trying to guess every possible reason he could have, and still coming up with nothing but a ride."

"I'll sit in the back," she offered. "I have no legs, I'm going to guess he's taller than me, and we'll make it work, Shawn. This'll be fun. I'll get to see the family, right? It's a good thing."

"Doubtful," I muttered as I found her hand, and the pair of us headed across the street and into the massive terminal.

This airport was a mess. Most were, but DFW Airport was basically its own little town, with all of the growing pains that included. Things had been added on and updated as needed until finding one's way around was pretty much impossible. Thankfully, a sign pointed to the baggage claim for the gate he was supposed to use.

Wrapping my arm around Zoe's shoulders, I kept her close against my side, and we headed that way. The carousel for the luggage was already going, so my eyes jumped over to the doorway where the passengers would make their way in. But when a man in a white t-shirt moved towards me from the opposite side, Zoe tapped my ribs.

"That him?"

I turned. "Liam!"

"Shawn," he said, a smile on his lips but not in his eyes - until he shifted his gaze to Zoe. "And you must be Zoe? I've heard so much about you." Like a gentleman, he offered his hand.

A grin took over her face and she clasped his palm. "I am! It's nice to meet you, Liam. Shawn says mostly bad things."

"Smart man." He chuckled, the sound perfectly smooth and easy. "I've heard things have been hard for you, Zoe." His friendly mask began to fade. "Just know you make my brother happy. Whether you believe it or not, that means a lot."

"Is that a threat?" she asked softly.

He shook his head. "No threat. I just know that sometimes it hurts. Sometimes, you think you're doing exactly the right thing - the thing everyone else wants you to - and you're really just trying to lose yourself. Zoe, what you survived changes a person, so it's ok to change. It's also ok to slip, to fall, and to need help. This guy?" He slapped my shoulder. "He will help."

"He has been," she promised.

"Just don't forget to enjoy being young," he said. "Don't let one bad thing, no matter how bad it is, destroy everything else. Even if you backslide, or you're not changing as fast as you want, or healing at the pace you've set for yourself? There are still good things. Still roses to smell. Even if you're nothing like everyone else, the roses will still smell nice, so take that time, ok?"

She nodded quickly, looking completely confused.

"You're working on scaring her, Liam," I chided.

"I like her," Liam countered. "Shawn, she's beautiful, chipper, and seems very sweet. She's also not weak. She merely covers that part up with being girly, hm?" He looked back at Zoe. "But Shawn's going to need to lean on you, too. Can you take care of him the way he's done with you?"

"Always," she promised.

"Good," he said before changing the subject completely. "Shawn, Southwind was hit last night. The barn was set on fire. A group snuck onto the property to cause damage, and while we don't know if that was meant to be human harm or buildings, I have my suspicions."

"They wanted to kill Violet," I growled.

"Yes." His mouth curled slightly. "Simmons was handled by one of the kids. The child had to be arrested, but I've already called in a few favors. He will not be scared and alone. That's why I'm really here. I need to meet with a man and hand over some money. It just makes a very good excuse to give you this." He lifted a boring black cell phone.

"What is it?" I asked.

"Burner phone," he said. "Einfeldt's."

Zoe didn't hesitate; she snatched it from his fingers and pushed it into her pocket. That actually made my brother smile, and I had a feeling this was the real kind.

"Einfeldt decided our initial response to his problems was exactly what he needed," Blaze explained, "so he wanted me to clean up the rest of his mess. Most of that mess is on that phone. Since it's not tied to him, he thinks getting rid of it will make his problems vanish."

"Probably would," Zoe agreed.

"If he wasn't trying to fuck over my family, sure." Blaze chuckled. "Now, that man's dirty little secrets are all yours."

"And the price?" I asked.

The look on Blaze's face reminded me of Jason's. They both had the same hollow eyes. Different colors, but just as empty. Just as terrifying. Just as willing to kill.

"There are kids," he growled. "If you hadn't called me, I would've been bound to help that man after he fucking hurt *kids!*"

"Shh," Zoe breathed, patting the air to remind him to keep his voice down. "Believe it or not, we can help with this, ok? I promise."

"I know you can. You helped Faith. You took care of my niece, but that?" He dipped his head in the area of her pocket. "That changes everything. Shawn..."

Zoe reached out and clasped his hand. "It's going to be ok, Liam. This is what we're good at."

For a moment, the man froze. Slowly, his eyes slid down to where she was holding his hand between both of hers in the most genuine and sincere form of reassurance. I watched as Blaze's Adam's apple bobbed when he swallowed, and then he lifted his other hand to clasp her shoulder.

"I now owe you a favor, Zoe. And him, and all of Ruin. I know you don't know what that means, but you saved me from crossing the one line I cannot cross. I'm in your debt." Slowly, he turned his eyes on me. "This time, I'm the one paying, Shawn. I'm the one begging, so you get to name your price when you're ready."

"Fuck," I breathed.

Because Blaze was never in anyone's debt. Not a little, and certainly not a lot. He always stacked the deck in his favor. That was why he was so successful at his job. It was the one thing that kept him on the "straight and narrow," as Gran used to call it.

"Can I call you if we have questions?" I asked.

"Yes, but you won't. It's all there, Shawn. Some of the boys were only seventeen. Kids!" And he looked back at Zoe. "Just kids who deserve so much more."

"And you're helping them," she promised. "This is how we get vengeance."

"Tell him the line," I encouraged. "Zoe, tell him about Ruin 32:35."

She lifted her chin and easily met this man's eyes. "We will take revenge; we will pay them back. In due time, their feet will slip. Their day of disaster will arrive and their destiny will overtake them. We will become their Ruin. This is exactly what we do, Blaze. We are the vengeance the world needs."

He nodded once. "I made sure the guards at Evan's jail told the others what he did to you. What he did to a *child*, Zoe. I am the vengeance too, but a whole different kind."

"Good," she said. "He deserves it."

"Yes, he does." Blaze chuckled and looked at me. "I like her, Shawn. I'll watch over her, but I need to give a man his money now."

"You going to Southwind?" I asked.

"Nope," he said. "There's cops all over that place. I work better in the shadows. You work better in the code. Violet has this, so let her handle it. Believe it or not, that woman is just as strong as yours."

"You are helping these kids, you know," Zoe piped up. "We didn't see anything with kids, which means we missed it. Without this..."

"Remind me of that after you look at the phone." He dipped his head. "A pleasure to finally meet the woman who's stolen my baby brother's heart. Drive safely."

"Which is a dismissal," I whispered to Zoe, grabbing her shoulder and turning her back towards the way we'd come in.

"I like him," she decided. "I mean, he's a little strange, but like a mix between Jeri and Jason."

"Would you like him as much if you knew he made people disappear?" I asked.

She simply shrugged that off. "We kinda do too, Jinxy. But he really is more of a Billy than a Liam."

"Liam sounds more professional," I pointed out.

"No, William Blankenship *the Third* sounds more professional. Liam sounds like a frat boy whose father owns a yacht. But I get it. Those are the shoulders he's rubbing in D.C. right? So he has to seem like he's one of them?"

"Yep."

"But he's not. He's one of us."

"Zoe..." I said, pausing as we exited the building. "Baby, every emotion that man has is a lie. It's a mask he wears to get the result he wants. He is not nice, he's not friendly, and he's not stable."

"I think you're wrong," she countered. "I think he's very stable. He's just not playing by the rules the rest of the world uses. I think he's nice, in his own way. I mean, family and kids? Those are his lines? Well, let me put this to you another way, Jinxy."

"Ok?"

"The ones he loves and the ones who can't protect themselves. The weak. The needy. The helpless. That man?" She tipped her head back in the direction we'd come. "Did you hear what he told me? He said it's ok for recovery to be hard. He said it's ok to need help. Jinxy! He fucking gets what it's like to not be where everyone else wants you to be, and he was telling me not to worry about it. He was saying he understands!"

"Blaze?" I asked.

She nodded. "Even psychopaths have feelings, Shawn. They're bent, twisted, and complicated, but they still exist. And that man? I think he loves you very much. That's why he makes a point of calling you his baby brother. It's his promise that he's going to protect you, no matter what."

"Fuck," I breathed. "And now I'm glad you met him, because..." I pushed out another big breath. "I don't know if you're right, but I kinda hope you are."

"Trust me," she said, "I'm right. You can see it in his eyes."

# CHAPTER 72

### JERICHO

Jason hauled us all to the gun range to make sure we still had skills. It felt pointless to me, especially after seeing Milt's interview, but whatever. It seemed that over the course of the semester, he'd managed to make all of us at least functional shooters.

Then there was Tiffany. Like Cade, she had experience with guns. Unlike the rest of us, she hadn't been through one of Jason's lessons yet. But when he put a pistol in her hand and told her to prove herself, she'd done a damned good job. Good enough he'd been impressed - and I might have hated her a bit for being so damned good at everything.

But the best part was how Ripper actually did well enough to be considered "passing." A bittersweet thing, if I was honest. The guy had overcome his issues with guns, and now we didn't need to worry about it. Yeah, that was how things worked out for us, but whatever. Knowing it didn't really matter anymore actually made the session almost fun.

Yet when we made it back, Jinxy's little car was still missing. Granted, he'd said they might have to run by Southwind, but I was a little curious about what his brother had needed. Sadly, patience wasn't my strong suit, but distracting myself sure was. After changing clothes, I headed to the war room and fired up my computer, logging into Flawed for a little anger management - also called questing.

Ripper joined me. Hottie came in a few minutes later. Knock and Cade took longer, and when they appeared with matching wet hair and boyish little smirks, I knew their shower had been not only shared, but also the good kind. Somehow, we even managed to convince Tiffany to log in and shoot some shit with us.

When Jason joined the team, I couldn't help myself. All it took was one stray shot and I had the server's best assholes gunning for us in the PvP area. What I didn't expect was for the rest of my guild to show up and get our backs. Before I knew it, we were holding our ground, tearing everyone down, and the tension that had been ramping up inside me was slowly but surely losing its hold.

"Air incoming!" Jason snapped, his voice coming across my headset on the Discord server Death over Dishonor used.

"Dingo, I need anti-air mechs!" I demanded.

"On it, pink leader!" he replied.

Hottie just laughed. "Bro, she's got your balls in a vice."

"Fuck, yeah," Dingo agreed. "She's got yours in her fist, though. You also made her a new team for a reason. Don't give me shit, Hot."

"Won't if you tear down the air before - " he paused. "Shit. Jinxy's home."

"Not now!" Rooster, another of our guild members, groaned. "Fuck, we were just about to win."

"Dingo, you got lead," Hottie announced, jerking his chin in a way that made me look over to see what was going on in the house.

Zoe stood in the archway between the hall and the computer area with something dark in her hand. Her mouth was moving, but I couldn't hear a thing she said over the cacophony in my headset.

Damn it. And since I knew where she'd been, this was probably important too.

"Hold up, Roux, we're killing," I begged, not caring if my voice transmitted to the guild as well. Then, "I need everyone to clear this up so we can bail. Focus fire on the bomber. GodComplex, light 'em up for me?"

"On it," Jason said, because that was his new gamer name. It worked for him.

Minutes. That was all it took for the group of us to trash the enemies coming at us, and yet I could almost feel the seconds ticking through my bones. Minutes where Zoe had something important - and I knew it was because of the look on her face.

Needless to say, the moment the skies were clear, I was smashing the button to recall my character to a safe location. "Death over Dishonor," I said, "we need another break. Sorry to kill and run, but you know how it is."

"Take it easy, Jericho," Dingo said. "Hurry back. We miss your face."

"Love you too, Dingo," I teased before hitting the button to log out.

Around me, the rest of the group were doing the same, but I managed to get my headset off first. Tossing that on my desk, I turned my chair so I could see Jinxy and Zoe. Neither had moved. It was enough to make my guts clench.

"What?" I demanded.

"I met Jinxy's brother," Zoe said, lifting the thing again. "He gave us a phone."

"Because?" Knock asked, proving he was also out of the game.

Jinxy laughed once. "Because it's Milt's burner."

"Turn the fucking GPS off!" Jason snapped.

"Battery's out of it," Zoe promised. "Liam had it off. No GPS to worry about."

"Not that dumb," Jinxy agreed, grabbing Zoe by the shoulders and steering her the rest of the way to her desk. "But we're going to have to power it up to clone the contents."

"Let's do this," Hottie said, pushing his chair back so he could stand. "Zoe, battery. Jinxy, power it up. Ripper, I want a new folder on the Squirrel for this."

"Knock, Cade," I added, "get me a cable, because we're not doing this on a cell tower. No record of its existence if we can manage."

"It'll ping," Jason warned. "As soon as it's on, it'll ping as it looks for data."

"Then erase it!" I snapped.

"Or," Jason said, leaning back to meet my eyes, "you slow your roll and let me do my shit."

I nodded, giving in. That was enough to make him reach for his laptop and open it up. Beside me, Tiffany was looking between all of us, her head bouncing around like she was confused, but she didn't bother asking questions. Not with everyone else moving to get something done.

Soon enough, we had the cables hooked up, the battery back in the phone, and everything was ready to go. When Jason said so, Zoe powered the phone on, then Hottie snagged it from her hands and stared impatiently at the screen. Jason was clicking, clearly doing something on his computer, but Hottie had started swiping.

"GPS is off," Hottie announced. "I also turned off data. This thing's a brick now."

"And I've got it flagged on the tower," Jason announced. "If anyone checks, I'm the one fucking with it, and my badge is enough to make it legal."

"So let's see what we have," I said, gesturing for them to start downloading.

"Why is a phone important?" Tiff finally asked.

"Because phones have data," I explained. "Phones like that? They tend to be burners, not tied to a person's real identity, which means the history on them will be less secure."

"The trick," Jinxy said, "will be proving this was his."

"And we're downloading," Zoe announced. "But y'all? Liam said something." She looked up, her eyes finding me. Not anyone else. Me. "He said there are kids."

"Kids how?" I demanded.

She shook her head. "He didn't clarify, and we were in the middle of an airport, so I kinda didn't push, but Liam doesn't do kids. That's like his line, and, um..." She flicked a finger at the phone. "He made it sound like something bad was on there."

"Fuck," Cade groaned, his eyes locked on his screen. "Jeri?"

"What?!" I demanded.

He looked up, those brown eyes of his much too serious. "He's got videos."

Time paused. I could hear a faint ringing in my ears, but it was as if everything else around me had simply stopped. Of all the things anyone could've said, that was not what I wanted to hear. Time and time again, the worst shit always ended the same way. It was always recorded, kept for someone's sick pleasure, memorialized in a fucking video.

"How many?" I asked.

"Lots," Cade breathed, "and still downloading."

"Fuck!"

But this was ok. This was going to be fine. Whatever sick shit Milt was up to, this was our chance to bust him, and he'd just made the same mistake every other sick fuck had. He'd kept a record. He'd made a recording. He'd wanted to gloat, or relive it, or whatever reason these assholes had for making their videos, and I was more than willing to use it against him.

"Let's see what he has," I breathed, opening up our secure drive and clicking on the first video that appeared.

It was a room. A bare, almost hotel-like room with a bed on one side, a cheap nightstand, and not much else. The camera rocked like someone was jiggling the phone, and then a hand appeared. As it moved away, the man it belonged to turned and headed for the bed, pulling off his shirt.

That was Milt Einfeldt, and while I really didn't want to see what this old man looked like naked, I could make a guess where this was going. Sex. For some reason, it always came back to that, but it also gave me the smallest glimmer of hope.

Of all the scandals a politician could get caught in, the ones involving sex tended to stick. These were the ones that made them resign. Sex was the one thing people couldn't tolerate, and since I was pretty sure no one used a shitty-ass hotel room like this for a kinky meetup with his wife, that meant this was one of those extramarital-type affairs.

"C'mon," I breathed as the video kept playing. "Prove me right."

"What is it?" Jason asked.

"Nothing yet," I admitted, "but looks like Milt's about to have a little fuck-fest. He's stripping, at least."

Because the man hadn't only removed his shirt. Now he was taking off his pants. Once he was completely naked, the old man lay down on the bed and simply waited. Unable to help myself, I began tabbing the right arrow key, fast forwarding by a few seconds at a time until Milt's partner finally appeared.

Then I hit pause.

"Holy shit," I breathed.

"It's a guy," Hottie said, proving he was standing behind me, watching over my shoulder. "Keep playing, Jeri."

I clicked play again, and the sick scene began to unravel before my eyes. There were hints. Little things, like the young man's lack of enthusiasm. The way he looked tired and like he wanted to be anywhere else. This was a paid sort of date, and the moment I realized that, my eyes jumped to the folder I'd pulled the video from to check when this had been recorded.

"Someone tell me what day of the week this was made?" I begged.

It was Tiffany who answered. "Tuesday."

"And the rest?"

"Looking," she promised. "Tuesday. Tuesday. I have a Friday down the list, but most of them are Tuesdays." She laughed once. "Well, guess we know what his bitcoin was buying now."

"Every fucking Tuesday," Knock said. "And this prick has some sick fucking porn on his laptop. Please tell me he's not - "

"He is," Hottie said just as Milt backhanded the prostitute. "Guys, I don't think this is going to be a fun watch."

Yet I didn't look away. From the edge of my vision, I saw Knock close his own window. Zoe was scrubbing her face, clearly not watching anything on her computer. Tiffany got up and moved around to see what I was looking at, but no one else.

And it was sick. Not BDSM or a little kink. This was abuse. This was the sort of power play some weak men needed to feel like they were strong. This was violent and bloody - and there was no way Milt could weasel his way out of this.

So even as my eyes followed the horrors happening to the young man who'd made the mistake of taking this dipshit as a client, my mind was spinning. Milt Einfeldt, the senator from Alabama, had fucked up bad this time. There was no way he'd be able to spin this as some family values shit. There was nothing that would make his voters think any of this was ok.

And yeah, they'd tear him apart for the gay sex, and that sucked, but I'd use it. When it came to vengeance - after everything we'd thrown away to bust this motherfucker, I'd use anything. Because exposing this wasn't "outing" the man. No, it was showing him as the hypocrite he really was.

"Your day of reckoning has just arrived, you sick fuck," I breathed.

"Now make it stick," Jason demanded.

From her computer, Zoe nodded. "On it."

# CHAPTER 73

### ZOE

I couldn't watch the video. I didn't even need them to tell me what was on it to know. The moment I saw Jeri's face, I knew this was a sex tape, and I'd made that mistake before. No, with Jinxy hovering over me, the last thing I needed to do was trigger myself.

But that didn't mean I was useless. Blaze's words whispered in the back of my mind, and this time they hit a little harder. He'd said it was ok to be changed by what had happened to me. He'd made it sound like the things I'd been thinking of as weaknesses might not be. Most importantly, he'd made it clear that even when I thought I was failing, there were still good things, and one sprang to mind.

Because while I might not be able to watch the videos, I knew exactly what came next. There were videos. We'd need to know where the videos had been taken so we could place Milt there. That meant I had to dive into the metadata, and nothing about it would trigger me. It was just code. Nice, safe, and completely reliable code.

"Zoe?" Jinxy asked, leaning in to see what I was doing.

"We're going to need to know where this is," I said. "They can worry about the what. I'll focus on the where."

So he pulled out his chair and dropped into it. "I'm getting the second video," he assured me. "Let's see if it's always the same place."

Because phones did that. They tagged the location, making it easy to use on social media. Somewhere in all of these lines, there would be a marker for a geolocation, and I was damned good at turning those into real places.

On the other side of the room, Tiffany groaned. Like Hottie, she was standing behind Jeri, watching the video. From the way she was grimacing, I had a feeling this was far from a sweet and loving date. Knock had mentioned this guy liked some pretty sick porn, so he was probably trying his best to act out his fantasies.

"The prostitute's a guy?" I asked, keeping my voice down so only Jinxy would hear.

"Sounds like," he agreed. "Kinda sucks, too."

"What? Why?"

"Because there's not a damned thing wrong with being gay," Jinxy grumbled. "Or bi, or ace, or anything else, but you know that's what will get talked about. Milt fucked a guy."

"Abused," Jeri corrected, proving she was listening, even if her eyes were locked on the screen. "There's not a lot of fucking going on. I mean, the guy blew Milt, but... yeah."

"Don't want to know," I assured her.

"What are you working on?" Cade asked, leaning so he could see me.

"Finding it." Because, to me, that was a complete answer.

But Cade shook his head. "Finding what?"

"Where the video was taken," Jinxy clarified for me. "If he's paying for sex, that means it is illegal. It's a crime, Cade."

"Prostitution also doesn't go well with politics," Cade pointed out.

"Crime," Jinxy said again. "And we're going for vengeance right now. This fucker thinks he can talk his way out of shit with..." His voice trailed off. "Shit!"

"What shit?" Knock immediately asked.

"Kids!" Jinxy snapped. "Blaze gave the phone to me because he said kids. Someone get me a name of the guy."

"We need facial recognition," Hottie demanded. "Everyone's on social media."

"How?" Tiffany asked. "I know social media, so just tell me how."

"Saving a screenshot," Jeri said. "Tiff, grab the pic and see if anything wants to tag him."

"Might not," Jason said. "A lot of prostitutes are good at staying off the radar. They don't use their real faces with their social media, which breaks the link."

"But there's got to be some way to identify him," Ripper said. "I'm looking at what AI has available."

"No," Jason said. "Check social media, then give it to me. I've got some programs."

"And this," I said, "is why we needed to work for the feds. Your toys, Jason, are cooler than ours."

"Databases," he replied. "It's all about the federal criminal databases, so if this guy's ever been arrested, I should be able to find him."

But I had a location. Over and over again, these Tuesday night videos all were tagged at the same place, and according to Google, it was a warehouse in Washington, D.C. Clicking for the satellite view, I zoomed in to check the streets and buildings around it.

"Jinxy?" I begged. "Can you find some cameras around this address?"

I read it off, and he got to work. Knock jumped in, snapping orders to Cade. Before I knew it, the four of us were busy trying to find some video evidence of this place and what was really going on there. Because from the outside, it sure looked like a pretty boring and easy to overlook warehouse.

"Anything on the facial recognition?" I asked.

"Nothing," Tiffany said. "Not even Facebook or LinkedIn. It's like this guy is a ghost."

"Which is pretty common," Jason assured us. "Tiff, where'd you save the screen grab?"

"Squirrel, under a folder I made called mystery man."

"Got it," Jason assured her. "Now help Zoe find businesses around her location. If we can get some security cameras, we can see what's going on."

"So cool," Tiff said, even as she began typing. "Time to use a little of my Google-fu."

Like a well-oiled machine, we all focused on the things we could handle. Jeri and Hottie were grumbling about whatever they were watching. Jinxy, Tiffany, and I were quickly narrowing down the options for getting eyes on this damned building. Jason was trying to identify our mystery guy, while Knock, Cade, and Ripper were scrambling to make all our pieces fit together.

"Is it the same guy in every video?" Ripper demanded.

"So far," Jeri said. "I'm only on the third, and this shit isn't getting any kinder as I go backwards in time."

"But we already have him," Knock said. "He can't claim he's doing this for his family. He can't try to bullshit his way out of this. That man crossed a line his voters will not like, and we're going to make sure the whole world knows."

The clicking of keys turned into a constant rhythm in the room. The Squirrel continued to fill up - partly with new information, and partly with the data still being pulled off this slow as fuck phone. Bit by bit, we were finally making progress, and if I was honest, it actually felt like the vengeance Jeri had promised us.

Then Jinxy sucked in a breath, sitting up straight. "Shit, I got it."

"What?" I begged, looking over at him.

"Traffic camera at the corner," he said. "It's got a continuous recording of that building's doors."

"Not high-quality, though," I realized, seeing it on his screen.

"Nope," he agreed, "but it's got one hell of an archive. Kinda helps when people are going to dispute the tickets." And he started typing again.

"I'm checking the cell towers over there," Knock said. "Ripper, I'm going to need a spreadsheet for the data I'm about to dump."

"Making it!" Ripper promised. "What are we comparing it against?"

"Congress," Jason said, his voice cold, calm, and completely serious.

For a moment, the room fell silent. Even the keyboards stopped clicking as we all looked up. Jason didn't need to say it, because we knew enough to understand. If we were comparing the phones that had pinged off the closest tower to this warehouse to the ones that had been in Congress?

"To catch Milt?" Tiffany asked, her words soft, almost like she was scared to ask.

"And anyone else he's dragged along with him," Jason said. "Because what one politician does, others tend to do as well."

"Shit," I breathed, realizing this had just gotten a whole hell of a lot bigger than one asshole calling Alex names. "Yeah, let's do this, people."

"Doing," Jeri growled. "Because no one fucks with Ruin and makes us look like the fools."

"And there are kids involved," Jinxy muttered. "Fucking *kids.*"

"Fucking videos!" Jeri snapped.

"Of kids," Tiffany said. "Y'all, this guy? The one Milt's fucking?" She paused to lick her lips. "He looks younger than us, like he's still in high school. If I had to guess, I'd say about eleventh grade."

My damned heart tripped. I could taste something metallic in the back of my mouth. Adrenaline. It was the first hint of panic trying to take over, so I pushed it down. Right now, I did not have time for this. I could fucking smell roses later, because if she was right?

"The prostitute's a minor?" I asked.

With a whine, Crysis wove his way under my desk so he could push his head onto my lap. Yeah, that was a sure sign I was reacting. Taking a long, deep breath, I rubbed the dog's head, but I couldn't stop now. This shit was too important.

"Can't be sure of his age," Tiffany said, "But he looks young. Sixteen, maybe seventeen?"

"The kind a pedophile goes for," Cade grumbled. "Fucking asshole!"

"Ruin him," Jason growled.

A kid. A fucking kid. That was what Blaze had been talking about, because of course he'd looked at this guy's phone. Worse, he'd probably asked, and I was willing to bet Milt had said he was young.

"Jinxy? Ask your brother - "

"No," Jinxy said. "He gave us enough. We do not want his help, Zoe. Not now. Trust me on this."

"Ask him if the kid he was talking about is in the videos!" I demanded.

"No," he said again. "You don't understand how he works."

"Then..." I leaned over and grabbed his phone, pulling up his contacts. "Fine, I'll ask." Swiping at the screen, I quickly unlocked it, and started typing.

**Shawn:**
Hey, this is Zoe. Have a question, and you don't have to answer, but is the video the kid? Shawn didn't want to ask, but I think it's kinda important.

I barely sent the message before a set of dots appeared in the bottom, proving Blaze was replying.

**Blaze:**
Seventeen. Two years of videos. Fix this.

> **Shawn:**
> Fixing. Destroying. Also making sure I'm still breathing, so thanks for the talk. <3

> **Blaze:**
> I'm not the hero.

> **Shawn:**
> You are to me.

I sent the last, then passed Jinxy back his phone. I didn't bother to dim the screen, though. With a confused look, Jinxy quickly read the exchange, murmured under his breath, then set his phone beside his computer again.

"So the prostitute's a minor," he announced. "Looks like there might be a few years of Milt fucking this boy."

"How minor?" Jason demanded.

"Seventeen," I said. "But two years ago would make him fifteen. I don't know a state where that's legal."

"Not in D.C.," Jason said, "and that's all that matters."

Then Tiffany started waving at her screen. "Oh, oh, I got something!" she said. "There's a Chinese restaurant on that street. From the Google reviews, the front window looks right at the warehouse."

"And?" Jinxy asked.

A smile took over her face. "And the pictures that have been uploaded show a camera pointing that way."

"Give me the address of the restaurant?" I begged.

She listed it off, and I got to work. Tracing down an IP address with a physical one wasn't easy, but it wasn't impossible either. Internet providers tended to group connections to a specific area, so all I had to do was figure it out, and then...

"Holy shit, I got it," I breathed, pulling up the security camera's feed.

"We need archived footage," Jinxy reminded me.

"No," I countered. "We need to see what's going on there normally. You get the archives from your traffic camera. I'll see how busy this place is tonight."

"Toss me the server for the archives?" Cade begged.

"Coming at you," Jinxy said.

And once again, we all fell silent, letting the tapping of our keyboards fill the room. Even Tiffany was focused, which made me smile a bit. She didn't think she was a hacker, but so far, she'd been helping out a lot more than she knew. Someone had to do the shit work like Googling basic information, and it seemed she was damned good at it.

Then the pieces began to fall into place. "I got something," Jinxy breathed.

"Looks like this place is busy at night," Cade agreed.

"Milt was there!" Knock yelped, pushing to his feet. "I've got his personal phone pinging off the cell tower and the one by Congress."

"Shit," Ripper breathed. "Knock? It's a lot more than just Milt."

"Make me a fucking list!" Jason demanded.

"Gonna be a long list," Ripper said.

"Don't care," Jeri told him. "We need all of this cleaned up and ready to give to Bradley. Guys? We've got him. We've fucking *got him*, and this time, Milt's not getting away."

"His feet have slipped," Tiffany said softly. "Maybe that's because we knocked them out from under him, but no one gets to sexually assault someone and get away with it. We're fucking Ruin, and he's going to go *down*!"

Which made me chuckle, feeling a little of that anxiety slip even further away. "I think we broke you, Tiff."

"Nope," she said. "I think you're fixing me. I just had no clue this was what I needed."

"And right now," Jason said, "this young man needs the fixing, so focus, people. We've got an underage victim, a politician who thinks he's untouchable, and not enough evidence to make it stick yet."

"Which is why you're going to press pause and brew some fucking coffee," Jericho told him. "Even hackers need to take a break, Jason. If this is really my team, well, I'm telling you to walk it off. In case you missed it, we have all fucking night."

"You can use my bed," I told Tiff.

"No, Zoe, I'm good on the couch," she promised.

"I won't be in it," I assured her. "I'll crash with Jinxy, and you can use mine. I mean, since you're a part of the team."

She looked up and met my eyes. "You sure?"

"Yeah," I breathed. "I think I need a little comfort. This is much too close to home. And so you know, Ripper's right across the hall."

"Uh..." Ripper looked over at Jeri.

She didn't bother looking up. "There are some things none of us should have to deal with alone. This? I think it counts." Finally, she lifted her eyes. "We're going to fuck this asshole up, but that doesn't mean it'll be easy for us. This is why we have bonds, and you know what? I might get a little jealous about you caring, Ripper, but I'm not that big of a bitch."

"I'm not poaching," Tiffany swore.

"No," Jeri agreed. "You're just human. So am I, and no matter how much I wish I was, I'm not really cruel."

"Yeah, you are," Tiffany countered. "You're just cruel to the bad guys. Not to the ones you're saving. You're cruel in the right ways, Jeri."

I looked over in time to see them glance at each other. No one was smiling this time, but Jeri nodded. Tiffany dipped her head. As if that said enough, they both immediately went back to work, but behind me I heard a heavy sigh.

Turning, I found Jason at the entrance to the kitchen, watching them. He looked relieved.

# CHAPTER 74

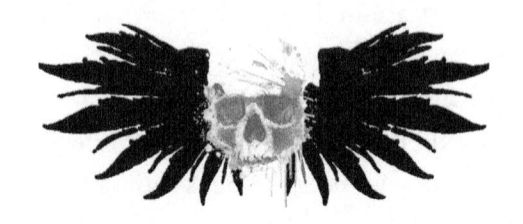

**SPECIAL AGENT JASON RAIGE**

The kids weren't joking when they said they had all night. Sure enough, they kept the coffee going and the data flowing. While some of them tapped out for a few naps, none of them actually got a whole night's rest, because they simply would not give up.

Piece by piece, they put together the proof of what this man had been doing. Not only had Milt Einfeldt been taking bribes and selling his votes, the man had also been abusing young men sexually as some kind of sick power trip - as well as a few women.

And we had it all.

The one thing I didn't get was sleep, but that was ok. Running on caffeine and a bit of nicotine was my normal. It was how I'd survived for years, so falling back into the habit was a little too easy. Pushing ourselves to our limits, the nine of us put together everything I'd need to make sure the FBI actually did something to stop this man. Then I packed my things.

But I wasn't heading home. Not yet. No matter how much I missed my wife, there was something I had to do first. My ticket was changed from arriving in New York to landing in D.C., and then I sent a text to Jericho, asking her to come up to my room for a moment.

I was in the process of zipping my luggage closed when she rapped at the open door. "Jason?"

"Hey," I said, jerking my head to invite her in. "I'm going to take all of this to Alex. That doesn't mean you're done, though."

"I know," she promised.

I gestured to the bed. "Sit."

She lifted a brow. "That's never good."

"Serious is not the same as bad," I assured her.

But while she made her way over to the bed, I moved to close the door. Normally, I'd never shut myself in alone with a young woman like this, but the rules were different with Ruin. Even more so with Jericho, and sometimes privacy was more important than worrying about any lines I might cross.

"I'm going to make sure Alex does something about this guy," I said, leaning my back against the door.

Slowly, Jeri nodded. "I know."

"And he's going to get arrested." I crossed my arms over my chest. "I promise you that, Jeri. I will make sure this man pays for what he's done - but you might not get credit for it."

"I don't fucking care about credit!" she huffed. "Jesus, Jason. You should know better than that! I just want to..."

"To what?" I pressed when she let her words trail off.

"To make a difference," she mumbled.

"Me too," I assured her. "But here's the thing. You *are* making a difference. Not just with the victims you help, Jeri. You've made a difference with everyone under this roof. I mean, last night? I know it couldn't be easy for you to let Ripper and Tiffany - "

"They didn't," she broke in. "I mean, they talked for a bit, but she slept in Zoe's bed and he was in his."

"But you still made it clear you wouldn't stop them from

reassuring each other," I said, giving up my place at the door to move closer. "Jeri, you love these guys, and I'd have to be blind to miss that. I also know it can't be easy to go from being the only girl they think about to one of three women who matter so much to them. But you matter in a different way."

"I know."

"Do you?" I asked, easing down to sit beside her. "Or are you just saying that because it'll make me shut up about it?"

She giggled weakly. "Maybe a bit of both?"

"Yeah, kinda what I thought." I reached over to rub her shoulder. "But I'm not filling you full of bullshit. I'm simply giving you a man's perspective on what I see. Knock and Cade? They love each other, but they also love you - and neither is ashamed to admit it. HotShot? He clings to you like a lifeline. That man needs you as much as he needs air to breathe. He will destroy the world just to make your life the smallest bit easier. And Ripper?"

"I'm not good enough for Ripper," she said softly.

"You are," I swore. "You may not be what most people would call good, but fuck that. You're exactly what *he* needs, and that's all that should matter. Trust me. I know all about fucking things up and somehow making them work. Kinda how I ended up married."

She glanced over with a smile, but I could still see something in her eyes. A hollowness that shouldn't be there in someone so young. An ache that was much too familiar to me, because I'd lived with it for most of my own life.

"Ripper loves you," I told her. "He loves you because you're you. He likes being a hero to Zoe and Tiffany, but to him that's different. That's how he makes himself feel like he's worth something, because you? He sees you as being so far out of his league, he's waiting for you to get sick of him. He also doesn't care. He's willing to take the heartbreak if it means he gets anything from you, so trust him. He won't be swayed by a pretty face or a popular girl. He wants the wild, broken insanity of you, Jeri."

"Yeah," she breathed. "And I don't know how to be a good girlfriend to him."

"The way you are now," I told her. "Don't try to be what anyone else wants. Just make sure you don't forget that these boys are here, ready to do anything you ask, because they love you. Not because they want to change the world - or not *just* because of that. They're doing this because it matters to you, and you matter to them. See, for a man, taking care of our woman is a pretty important thing to us. It makes us feel valuable. So let them do it. Let them love you, Jeri. You really do deserve it."

And a tiny little smile touched her lips. "Yeah?"

"Yeah," I agreed. "But I'm saying all of this for a reason."

Her eyes jumped up, that icy blue color flicking between each of mine. "What's going on?"

"When you decided to go after Alex's harasser, we all knew the program would get shut down." I lifted a brow, waiting for her to nod in agreement before I went on. "I told Alex that if the program fails, I'm quitting the FBI."

"What?!" she gasped, nearly standing in shock.

I caught her shoulder, holding her in place. "I can finally do that, and it seems someone has given me a new purpose. See, I used to think I'd quit the Bureau and work for a gaming company. I'm pretty good at network security, after all. But my wife makes good money. I don't need the income, and over the last few weeks, I've found something that feels even more important."

"You can't," she hissed. "Jason, we need you in the FBI. How the fuck can we make this shit stick if you won't push it through?"

"Bradley will," I assured her. "Believe it or not, he's a good man. He's still my partner, even if he's technically my boss now. He knows how important Ruin is, and he'll help." I ducked my head, making sure she was actually listening. "Because if the FBI won't let me work with hackers to clean up the internet, I'm not going to sit behind a desk chasing identity theft and ignoring the real crimes."

"So you're just going to quit?" she asked.

"And buy a house here in Texas, move my family closer to the people I've come to care about, and work with these fucking insane kids I'm starting to think of as my team," I explained. "I mean, if you'll still have me as a part of Ruin."

Her breath fell from her lungs even as her eyes went wide. "You..."

I nodded slowly. "I believe in you, Jericho. I believe in Ruin. This? It's *exactly* what I want to be doing, so if the Bureau won't let me, then fuck 'em. I made you a promise. I said I'd carry you if you ever need it, and I meant every fucking word. I'm just hoping that feeling goes both ways."

She began nodding, the motion quick and jerky. "Yeah. Fuck, yes, Jason. I mean, we don't know half the shit you do, but we're trying, and someone has to do this, right?"

"Exactly."

"And you can stay grey. You can be our mentor or something. I mean, I don't even know, and we already have the room - "

"I'd really like my own house," I broke in. "I'm kinda old to be living with roommates, and we have a kid on the way."

She just glanced down at the floor, and slowly a smile grew on her lips. "I know how to change a diaper, you know. I mean, if you ever need a babysitter for date night."

"Trust me, I'm going to take you up on it." Once again, I caught her shoulder, but this time to squeeze it gently. "But Ruin is yours. This team looks to you for the next move, and I'm more than willing to follow. I might be your handler right now, but I'm also damned good at taking orders from a leader who has earned it. You have, Jeri. Maybe it was a trial by fire, and I think we both know how much it sucked. That doesn't mean you're broken, though. It just means you were strong enough to put yourself back together over and over again. It means you are one hell of a young woman, and you should be fucking proud of that."

"Even when I get triggered?" she asked.

"Especially then." And I moved my arm to wrap around her shoulders, hugging her up against my side. "Jeri, it's called post-traumatic stress disorder. It sucks. That doesn't mean we're broken. It just means we survived the shit life keeps throwing out."

"I know." She tilted her head, resting it on my bicep. "And it's not really a curse, but it sure feels like it."

"Yeah, it does," I agreed. "But sometimes the pain is worth it. Trust me on this, because not feeling it? Living a life that's numb so nothing will hurt? That's worse, because when you take away all the bad shit, you also take away the good. You leave yourself stuck in a world without color, without any of the things we give a shit about. You start thinking of life as a thing to pass you by, and it's not. It's something meant to be *lived*. It's a chance to have four different boys fall in love with you at the same time. To make an enemy into a friend. To learn how to be as girlish or as tomboyish as you want. It's a chance to be young and dumb, to grow up, and to experience the entire rollercoaster of life."

"But people keep dying!" she reminded me.

"They do," I agreed. "It's the nature of life. We live, then we die. In the middle, we get hurt, and for some stupid, fucked-up reason, that pain sticks in our minds when the good shit doesn't. But the good shit is what is important. The good shit, Jericho, is what it means to be alive. Keeping everyone at a distance isn't living. It's existing, and it fucking *sucks!* So get scared. Lash out."

"Be pissed," she broke in. "That's what Knock always tells me."

"Then be pissed," I agreed. "Because no matter what, I've got you. I will always have you, because you and me? We're the same. Every time I look at you, I see myself when I was your age, and I can't help but think of all the shit I missed out on because I was too scared to try. Because I thought walling my emotions off and being tough, being a 'real man,' or being 'strong enough' would make it better. Spoiler, it didn't."

"But Zara did?" she asked.

I nodded. "Yeah. She made it all worth it. Every heartache, every horror I survived, and every bad thing was worth it to just meet her. Falling in love with her? Yeah, so much better - and you've got four of 'em. Four times as much happiness as I do."

"Just don't try cheating on her, because I'll help her cut your balls off," Jeri teased.

Which made me laugh. "Promise. Besides, at my age? Yeah, four girlfriends isn't happening."

"They make pills for that, you know."

I groaned, leaning my head back to hold in the laugh. "Fuck. My shit still works, girl. I can even prove it. Got a fuck-trophy on the way, you know."

"Oh, is that what we're calling your kid now?" She leaned in and bumped me with her shoulder. "But you're coming back, right?"

"I give you my word."

Jeri bit her lips together for a long moment, then nodded. "Good. I kinda like having you around. I mean, I really wanted this whole FBI thing to work out, but having you on the team?" She shrugged. "I guess it's a pretty good trade. We'll still be able to make a difference, and that's really all that matters, right?"

"No, it's not all, but it sure does matter."

"And learning how to be happy," she said. "I'm still working on that."

"You're doing a lot better than you realize," I assured her. "And just so it's out there, I'm fucking proud of you. I know you've been making this up as you go, but you are one hell of an amazing woman. Smart, dedicated, and resilient in a way that inspires me."

"Me?"

"You," I said. "And while I have a plane to catch, I wanted to make sure I said something before I left. I..." I had to pause to swallow. "Jeri, I wanted to make sure you know my promises aren't empty. I meant every word I've ever said to you."

Those eyes of hers searched my face. I let her, wondering what she was thinking, because this time there wasn't a smile to go with it. She simply scanned my features, her cold gaze jumping around as if she missed nothing.

"I don't want to let you down," she finally said.

"Never," I promised. "We might not always win, but all I want is for us to get back up when we fail and try again. And maybe we'll both need some help with that, but for the first time in far too long, I think I've finally found someone who can actually lift me up."

"Can I..." Her hands moved, but the gesture wasn't clear enough to make out. "Um, Jason? Can I hug you?"

"Yeah," I breathed, opening my arms.

And she twisted, throwing her arms around my shoulders and leaned in, squeezing me as hard as she could. "Thank you," she breathed. "Thank you for making me feel like I'm not worthless."

"No, Jeri, you're definitely worth something," I whispered against her hair. "Shit, you're worth making an old man like me feel like I'm not really alone. I think that's worth a whole fucking lot."

"Almost like family," she said.

"Like our own family," I agreed, "even if we call it Ruin."

# CHAPTER 75

### SPECIAL AGENT JASON RAIGE

I managed to catch a few hours of sleep on my flight. Crysis lay at my feet, completely unconcerned with all of this, but the pair of hours didn't make up for the long night of research. The USB drive in my pocket, however, did.

So once we landed in D.C., I ordered an Uber and sent Alex a text. She assured me the coffee would be fresh and dinner was almost ready. I had to chuckle at that. After so many years of being an agent with the FBI, I was used to fast food and crappy hotel rooms. This? Being spoiled by Ruin and my new boss? Yeah, I could definitely get used to it.

It was almost eight p.m. when the car dropped me off in front of a cute white townhouse. The porch light was on, illuminating the pair of doors set side by side. Checking my phone, I realized the one I wanted was on the left, so knocked. Almost immediately, the door cracked open.

A young girl with sandy blonde curls and toffee-colored skin peeked out. Her eyes dropped to my dog. "Agent Raige?" she asked.

"You must be Troy," I replied.

She grinned. "Mom, your friend's here!" Then she opened the door. "Come in. I was told I'm not supposed to pet your dog."

"You can," I assured her. "His name is Crysis, and he's used to the attention. I'm not that great about making my service animal work all the time."

"And he's such a good boy!" Troy mumbled in that high-pitched voice we all used with dogs.

Needless to say, Crysis loved it. His tail started wagging, and the moment he made it inside, he was pushing up against Alex's daughter to give her all the love he could. I was trying my hardest not to laugh at either the kid or the dog, but a chuckle from the hall proved Alex didn't have that concern.

"Troy, I told you to respect his dog," she chided.

"He said I could!" the teen girl whined.

"I did," I promised. "And Crysis needs some downtime."

"Then take him in the kitchen and get the dog some water," Alex ordered. "Jason, you sit."

"Laptop," I said, not quite making it a request. "You'll want to see this."

As she left the room, Troy groaned. "Mom... You're working *again*?"

"Always," Alex said. "So if you want to take the dog out back and throw a stick for him, I'm sure that'll be ok."

"Or a ball," I offered. "I have one in my bag."

"Ball!" Troy decided.

So while Alex went to grab a laptop, I found the tennis ball Crysis had been hoarding lately and handed that over - along with a warning that she would not be able to wear him out, but was welcome to try. From the devious glint in the girl's eye, I had a feeling she was up for the challenge, and my dog really could use the relaxation.

Yet the moment they were outside, Alex set her laptop on the coffee table and gestured for me to sit. "Black coffee?" she asked.

"Light cream?" I requested.

She nodded. "Troy will be obsessed with your dog for as long as you'll let her, so get that loaded up, and let's see what you've got."

Two minutes later, the video was on the screen, Alex was bent over as she watched it, and I was nursing one of the best cups of coffee I'd had in a while. Apparently Alex liked the expensive kind. Yet over and over, she replayed the clip I'd pulled up for her, pausing it at times to get a good view of the atrocities this guy was committing.

"And you're sure that's Milt Einfeldt?" she asked.

"Oh, we're sure," I promised. "There are a few dozen more videos of that sort of thing. It seems Milt likes to record himself with this young man. Likely, he's using it to fap to later. Unfortunately it's not *just* this boy. Ruin has been working to get a count on how many different sexual partners he has videos of, but they're still going. This kid, however, seems to be the favorite."

Immediately, Alex glanced down the hall in the direction of the back door. "Jason..."

"I can hear Crysis," I assured her.

"No," she said. "Not Troy." She pointed at the screen. "That boy? I..." She paused, clenching her jaw tightly. "I swear to god that's the kid."

"Which kid?" I asked.

"*The* kid," she hissed. "The one I lost. The fucking boy who was lured out by a damned pedophile. His body was never recovered, and while this boy is older, he's about the right age, and his nose..." She dragged the bar on the video to a view of the young man's face. "It has the same bump on the bridge."

I sat up quickly. "What? Show me."

"I don't fucking have the case."

"Give me his damned name," I growled.

So she did. Google gave me an image. Clicking through the photo options, I found one for the missing boy on what looked like a flyer, but the sort of thing that was clearly made to be shared on social media. Beside me, Alex was leaning in.

"That's him," she agreed.

"Fuck," I grumbled, copying the image.

That got pasted into an email and sent to the one person I knew would chase it down: Jericho. My instructions to her were short, sweet, and right to the point. "Get me facial recognition. Compare to videos."

"What are you doing?" Alex asked.

"I'm making sure you aren't insane," I explained. "Because if you're right?"

"I'm right," she grumbled.

"*If* you're right," I said again, "this just got a whole hell of a lot bigger than a senator with some bad kinks. This is no longer about him screwing an underage boy, Alex. Because that kid? We have eyes on the building via a few local cameras. No one has been seen entering or leaving who wasn't clearly a client. None of the people recorded as sexual partners, at any rate. Worse, I have reason to believe this boy is seventeen, and while that may be above the age of consent in Washington, my team is tracking these videos because we think this has been going on for more than two years."

"With this same boy?" she asked.

"Yeah, and others," I growled. "Don't ask how I got that, because Ruin doesn't want you to know, and the source will likely deny it."

"Illegal?" she asked.

I blinked my eyes over to meet hers. "A fucking fixer. The political kind."

"What the fuck are you doing?" she asked, the words little more than a breath.

"Alex, you wanted to make a team that could find the dirty laundry hiding online, right?" I tipped my head towards the laptop. "They did. This started with someone sending you the N-word. So far, they've dug up bribery, vote selling, a dozen different signs of corruption in our political parties, and now this? Not only minors being used as sex workers, but what could very well be human trafficking? Because if you're right and that boy is the one who went missing when you were working his case?"

"Shit," she breathed. "Jason, this just got a whole hell of a lot bigger than cybercrimes."

"This," I agreed, "is serious. This is why the FBI needs this team!"

"And I can't do a damned thing about it!" she shot back. "It's up to Congress."

"The same Congress that's involved in this shit?" I asked. "C'mon, Alex. This is why they're trying to kill the program. This is what they've been scared of the whole time, because Ruin found evidence that Milt Einfeldt isn't the only one going there. We compared the phones that connected to the closest towers, and we have a very long list of not only politicians, but also lobbyists, staffers, and other D.C. insiders who have been making regular trips to the damned warehouse where this video was taken. Where all the videos Milt Einfeldt has were taken!"

"Proof?" she asked.

I nodded slowly. "So much fucking proof it'll make your head spin. The problem is *how* they got it. We don't have warrants. We just have holes in networks my team can walk through easily - so they did."

"And how did you get the videos?" she asked. "Jason, we know that's going to be the thing he tries to deny. Einfeldt will say they're fake, or actors, or something like that."

"We have his burner phone," I said. "And if you can manage to keep it on the downlow, I think I can get the fixer to verify how he got it."

"What fixer?" she asked.

"William Blankenship the Third."

Alex collapsed back into the cushions of the couch. "Fuck. I've been here a matter of weeks, and I know that man's name. He's untouchable, Jason. How the fuck did you get him to cooperate?"

"Evidently, it's a very small world," I said. "You know the little juvenile record Jinxy has that we were worried about?"

"Mhm."

"Seems Mr. Blankenship also has one, and he did his time at the same place. He calls Jinxy his little brother."

Beside me, my boss began to smile. "Oh, now *that* is useful," she said. "Because this? This is actionable, Jason. And if you're right? If these prostitutes are underage? That's a whole new set of crimes. We might not be able to make Einfeldt do a lot of time, but we can definitely make sure he's no longer in public office, or able to sell off his vote for fucking gold!"

"Or harass you," I added.

"Fuck the harassment," she said. "I told you I had that."

"Ruin didn't agree."

Alex simply laughed once. "Those kids..." She sighed heavily. "Damn. They would've been perfect, too. But this? There's no way the program's going to fly after this."

"I know."

She murmured at my response. "What are you going to do now?"

"I'm going to help you close this and make sure this man pays for what he's done," I explained, "and then I'm going to give you my resignation. Zara wants to live in Texas. She wants a nice little house with three or four bedrooms and a yard for my dog. She also said she's going to be my sugar momma so I can keep working with Ruin."

"And you'll still have my number," Alex pointed out.

"I will," I agreed. "And Bradley's. Now just imagine how useful that will be for you. All you have to do is make sure my partner is in a position where he can do something with the information we'll send him."

"I'll make sure of it," she promised.

"So let me be a part of this takedown?" I begged. "Let me finally see all this hard work amount to something so I can let my team know we really are making a difference?"

"I promise."

Leaning back, I reached up to scrub at my face. "That's all I wanted, you know. I never asked to be an agent. I never wanted to be a sniper, Alex. I just kept doing this because I hoped I was making a difference, and now I think I am. With Ruin, I think I'm finally able to stop these assholes from using the internet against us."

"I just wish Congress had realized what we were offering," she said.

"Me too," I agreed. "Lately, believe it or not, I've actually been proud to be an agent."

"And we've been proud to have you," Alex assured me, "but I will not put you back on a leash. You have more than served your time. You, Jason Raige, are a damned good man. One who has suffered too much for this country, and while hacking may not be legal, you are still doing good work."

"And Ruin," I reminded her.

"Your team," she clarified. "All of you, even if none of this was what I expected. I mean, I thought we'd have some computer specialists with badges and guns. Instead..." She shook her head even as her eyes landed on the screen of the laptop. "If that boy's who I think he is, you just closed more than one case."

"So when do we move?"

"Tomorrow," she told me. "Tonight, you and your dog are going upstairs, crawling in my guest bedroom, and sleeping. You hear me, Jason? Real sleep, and I'll give you half an hour to call your wife, but if you're still awake after that, I will come in there and treat you like I do Troy."

"Spoil me with everything I want and try to act tough while doing it?" I teased.

Which made her chuckle. "Yeah, pretty much. But if you sleep, I'll get the Bureau moving, because this? It's the kind of takedown that's going to require a little organizing before we can make it happen. You sleep, Agent Raige. This time, I really can handle it."

"Yes, ma'am," I agreed. "I think I even believe you."

## CHAPTER 76

### JERICHO

Jason was barely out of the house before my head hit the pillow. Then I slept - hard. It was the kind of intense, dreamless sleep a body needed after being pushed to its limits, so when my phone started going off the next morning, I was not impressed. The only thing that kept me from throwing it was the sound of the ringtone. The one I'd set for my mom.

"Mm?" I answered.

"Honey, aren't you supposed to be up for class?" she asked.

"You beat my alarm," I croaked. "What's up, Mom?"

"Well, I wanted to let you know there's been some news here at work," she explained. "The last time we talked, you asked if I'd go back to therapy, and it seems I'm going to get the chance."

Which was enough to make me wake all the way up. Even to sit up. "Are you getting laid off?" I asked.

"No," she assured me. "But it seems the company is being bought out, and the new owners offer a mental health package. I talked to Human Resources, and after the new year, I'll be able to take a leave of absence. As long of a break as I need to get treated." She chuckled. "Hopefully, this will make a good Christmas present, because it's not going to be cheap."

"The best present!" I assured her. "Oh, Mom, I'm so..." Yeah, I couldn't find the right words, because happy just didn't seem to fit. "Therapy? This is great, Mom!"

"Hopefully, I'll be able to come home and actually stay in the same decade you're in," she joked. "But don't you have finals soon?"

"Couple more weeks," I assured her. "I'm doing good, though. Not all A's, but close enough. Grayson says he's proud of me, and I've even got a study group now." Ok, it was for FBI shit, but Mom didn't need to know that. "I'm kinda like a college pro or something."

"I am so proud of you," she said. "I also don't want to make you late for class, but I was hoping this would be good news."

"The best," I assured her. "Thanks, Mom."

"I love you, Jericho. More than you can ever imagine."

"I love you too," I swore. "Now don't work too hard."

She laughed as I ended the call, but it left me sitting there with a smile on my face. Beside me, Hottie reached over to rub my back, reminding me I wasn't alone in my bed. He also hadn't made a sound while I was on the phone, but that was because neither of us wanted to explain our mess to my mother.

"She's going to get therapy?" he asked.

"Next year," I said. "Her company is being bought out, but it sounds like a good thing."

"Nice." Mumbling under his breath, he rolled into me. "And I'm cutting class today to finish up the case."

"Same," I agreed.

"So send an email to your professors and let them know the FBI gig requires your attention. They'll excuse the absence and make it easy for you later if you tank that portion of the final."

"Secrets to success in college, hm?" I asked, bending down to kiss him. "Thanks, Hottie."

"Just taking care of my baby girl," he promised. "Now up, because I've got a few minutes before my dick relaxes and I can pee. I need your hot little ass out of sight so it doesn't wake back up."

Giggling, I tossed off the blankets and headed to the bathroom. I may have pulled off my clothes as I walked, and it was entirely possible I did my best to make sure his dick was anything but soft, but he loved it. I knew he did. The smile I caught on his lips before I closed the door proved it.

Maybe we'd lost the FBI deal, but the strange thing was that this would still work out. Jason was going to be a permanent part of the team. Ruin had only gotten stronger by adding in him and Tiffany. We were making a difference, even if we weren't doing it the legal and clean way we'd hoped for. The nine of us still had connections, and it seemed that was enough.

So when I made it down to my computer, I was in a pretty good mood. I also had an email from Jason. There was a picture attached of a kid. Maybe ten? A little boy he wanted me to do facial recognition on. I was deep into that when my coffee cup appeared beside me. I looked up, expecting to find Hottie. Instead, it was Cade.

"Orders, boss?" he asked.

"I don't know yet," I admitted.

"So why are you looking at the kid?"

"Jason asked me to identify him," I explained.

Cade's eyes narrowed. "Jeri?"

"Mm?"

"That's the prostitute."

My fingers paused, and I could feel the blood tingling in the tips. "What? Who?"

"The guy Milt has in the videos," Cade explained. "I mean, a younger version of him, but trust me. He's cute. He's also got a rather memorable face, and I'm pretty damned sure that's a picture of him as a kid."

"Fuck," I breathed. "Why does Jason have a picture of this guy as a kid?"

Cade gently clasped my shoulder. "Go hunting, babe. I'll get the rest up and moving. Sounds to me like we're not even close to done."

"Hottie said to blame the FBI for skipping school today," I called as Cade meandered out of the war room.

"On it!" he yelled back.

But now I was going, and the sad part was it didn't take long. A readily available app scanned the boy's face. Another scanned the guy's from the video. Within seconds, they were confirmed to be a match, which led me to Google. Dropping in the picture of the child pulled up images of a missing poster, and that had all the information I needed.

"Jordan Blakely," I said. "Abducted from Mississippi seven years ago, at the age of ten. Presumed dead."

"Fuck," Jinxy breathed from where he sat at his own computer. "Hot? I need you to grab a screen of every fucking person on those videos. We need all the prostitutes we've seen."

"There's more?" I asked.

"So many more," Zoe said, peeking her head in from the kitchen. "Jeri, there's like two hundred videos on that phone. Not all are the same guy. A few are women, Jinxy said."

"And I'm willing to bet all are missing," Ripper grumbled. "So let's get to work. Someone let Jason know?"

"On it," I promised.

Because while it might only be nine our time, that meant it was ten in the morning where he was. I whipped off a text, telling him to check his email, then dropped the information there. I also included our hunch that this kid wasn't the only one who'd been abducted and forced into sex work.

But no more than thirty seconds after I hit send, my phone rang. Without thinking, I swiped at the screen to answer.

"We haven't identified them all yet," I said as a greeting.

But the voice which replied wasn't Jason's. "We need more than that." It was Alex, and hearing her shocked me enough to make my hands stop.

"Alex?"

"Good morning, Jericho," she said. "The information Ruin has provided is actionable. I'm arranging a sting on this warehouse with SWAT, but we're missing something. We have no way of proving who is involved except for their phones pinging a local cell tower, and that is little more than circumstantial. Right now, we know there are multiple people having sex in this building. We can assume money is being traded, which makes it prostitution. That means *someone* is getting paid. So I need Ruin to find where the money is going, who is paying them, and to get me any information on any financial transactions to that person you can find. I'm going to guess it's on the dark web, because that's where shit like this is done."

I looked up, my eyes finding Knock's across the banks of computers between us. "Dark web. Find the prostitution business. Prove the clients. Got it. What else?"

"We need proof," Alex growled, her voice more intense than I'd ever heard before. "We need to know who is running this, where they are, and follow the money. You've made it this far, so don't stop now."

"How long is this going to take?" I asked.

"We're hitting the warehouse in an hour," she said. "I'm done with fucking around, and maybe you're not official FBI consultants, but this? I think this is enough for me to validate your worth as confidential informants. You have the damned contracts. You have immunity. *Use. It.*"

"Yes, ma'am," I breathed. "We will rip this place apart. Brace for impact."

"And hopefully," she said, "hitting them online will keep them from realizing we're going to storm the damned castle. Maybe we'll even catch the bosses with their pants down."

"Not really the metaphor you want for a sex ring," I pointed out, "but I see what you're saying."

"Then fuck them up," Alex ordered. "And Jason says to make a damned good case."

"The best case," I agreed, ending the call.

Then I started giving orders. The FBI needed data? Well, we could get all the data they could ever ask for. We had the location. We knew the players. What we needed was the chain of money.

"Zoe, get Tiffany's ass over here!" I snapped.

"On it," Zoe promised.

"Knock, I need you to find where Einfeldt spent his bitcoin. Cade, find that place. I don't care if it's a terminal, a website, or anything else. We need to follow the money. Keep records, because Tiff's going to need to do her thing."

"On it," Cade assured me.

"And it'll be a website," Knock said. "'Click to buy' is just too easy. The problem will be that it'll look like something else. Etsy, eBay, or even a personal craft site. No clue, but don't be surprised if the trail seems to go cold."

"Don't care, just want you to find it," I told them. "Hottie? I need you to identify the owner of the terminal that's receiving the bitcoin. I don't care what it looks like it's for, we need a chain of custody. If this guy is a middleman, we need to know it!"

"What about me?" Jinxy asked.

"You and Zoe are on background checks," I told them. "Anything Hottie comes up with, you turn into proof of crimes. That means tracking their supplies, or whatever comes up."

"Can do," Zoe assured me.

"And you?" Knock asked.

I smiled. "I'm going to identify these prostitutes, with Ripper's help. The guy Milt's fucking has been missing for years. Vanished when he was a kid. What do you want to bet the others aren't any better?"

"Fuck," Zoe said. "Ok, Tiff's on her way. Will be here in less than ten minutes. Let's do this."

"Already into Bitcoin," Knock promised. "Shit, this fucking stuff is meant to be hard to track, but people are fucking stupid."

"The internet never forgets," Ripper said. "I'm making screens of the people, Jeri. Trying to clean them up as much as I can so you can get an ID."

"If they're missing, there likely won't be one," I countered. "No social media for people who vanished."

"Then check Google for missing persons!" Hottie snapped. "If you can get a face, then you can match it to missing posters just like you did with the boy."

"Fuck," I grumbled, "this is going to take a while."

But that was ok. We could do this. Someone had to, and since no one else seemed to give a damn about these people, we would find a way. Maybe this shit was hard, and it would definitely be time-consuming, but it was also what Ruin was good at. Somehow, over and over again, we'd always managed to figure out how to get what we needed. After all, the internet never forgot.

I'd just gotten the third person scanned in and had another tab open trying to find people on missing posters with similar facial structures when the front door opened. For a moment, everything paused, and then Tiffany called out.

"I made it!"

"War room!" I yelled back. Then I grumbled, "We have got to get her closer."

"No shit," Hottie agreed. "Not like we have a shortage of rooms..."

I flashed him a smile, but before I could reply, Knock sucked in a breath. "Fuck!" He jerked upright too. "I found a website!"

"What website?" Tiffany asked as she rounded the corner, entering the war room.

"Dark web," Cade replied, his hands still going on his keyboard. "Oh, fuck."

"What fuck?" Zoe demanded. "Fuck doesn't sound good. No fucking."

"Yes, fucking," Knock said a split second before my Discord dinged with a message, just like everyone else's. "Guys, we have a website."

"You said that already," I pointed out.

"A fucking prostitution one!" Knock snapped. "That's the link. This is where Milt's money's going."

Around the room, all of us clicked. Zoe made a muffled little sound then quickly closed her Tor browser, which made Jinxy grumble beside her. Ripper sighed heavily. Me? I was leaning in, because as the page loaded, so did videos. Lots and lots of videos.

Tiffany shifted behind me, looking over my shoulder. "A prostitution ring?" she asked.

"With at least one missing kid," I said, glancing back. "Tiff, Jason's in D.C., and it sounds like they're about to raid the warehouse." I tapped my screen. "I'm willing to bet this is what they're going to find, and we already know the guy Milt was fucking had been kidnapped when he was ten fucking years old."

Her entire body stilled. "Sex slaves?"

"Yeah," Zoe breathed.

"And there's video," I growled under my breath. "Always fucking video."

Tiffany just nodded once, then hurried to her computer. "I'm going to need the banking information for wherever that money went. I don't know how you do it, but get me the receiving account and I can tell you who else is paying."

"We need everything!" I snapped. "They're going in soon. Like, in less than an hour now."

"So fucking call Alex!" Hottie told me. "She needs to know."

"But know what?" I asked.

Ripper's lips were moving, though. I couldn't hear, but his eyes were jumping across his screen. Everyone else in the room was looking at me as if I'd have some answer to this. I didn't. Instead, this crap just kept getting worse and worse.

"I have forty-two different options," Ripper finally said. "Forty-two people for sale, and what do you want to bet they're all in that fucking warehouse?"

"Numbers!" Tiffany yelled. "Now, damn it."

I heard her, just like I heard Knock and Cade responding, but I was already reaching for my phone. This time, I didn't call Jason. I checked for the last number to contact me, then pressed the button to call it back.

"What?" Alex answered.

"We have a website," I told her. "There are forty-two different people being offered for sale, Alex. Forty-fucking-two."

"Shit," she breathed.

"And what do you want to bet none of them get to leave?" I went on. "We've been watching the cameras, and only men have gone in and out. Not women - and there are girls on this site. That means the victims are fucking stuck in there! You need to make sure your raid knows they're *in there*. Or that they might be in there, or however this works, because if they get shot?"

"I'll handle that," she assured me. "But you? Jericho? Ruin needs to get me some fucking proof. We can get these people out, but as of right now, the men who abused them are going to walk free. We don't have a damned thing to convict them on except being in the general area of a cell tower."

"Oh, you will," I assured her. "You save the vulnerable ones, Alex. Ruin will make sure the assholes using them will rot in fucking jail."

"Which means we're hacking, people," Hottie snapped. "Every website has a host. Let's see what information this dumbass left lying around."

"It's go-time," I said, not caring if my words were for Alex or my team.

Or maybe, this time, they were for me.

# CHAPTER 77

**SPECIAL AGENT JASON RAIGE**

Crysis was waiting in the SUV with one of the Cybersecurity analysts. The woman was here to identify the victims once we got them out. Sadly, the D.C. police were convinced this was merely a shipping facility. An honest business. They were sure we'd made a mistake, but when the Deputy Director of the FBI demanded a SWAT team, they still showed up.

The tension was high. Wearing a windbreaker with the overly large "FBI" printed on the back had a few of these men and women looking at me sideways. Alex had convinced me to put on a vest - which also proclaimed me as an agent of the FBI - to match hers. My gun was in my hand. She was in line behind me. The massive SWAT team was at the door, ready to breach.

"We're a go," Alex said.

"Go, go, go!" the leader of the SWAT team bellowed.

The team went. All of them. I gave SWAT a healthy space, then followed behind, coming around the edge of the building just as they knocked the doors open. From there, the yelling started. Mostly it was the police, all bellowing for the people inside to get on the ground.

A woman screamed, her voice shrill in the bare halls of the warehouse. Men were yelling. So many men. The whole thing was chaos, but we had this. There was no way we didn't. I could hear the bangs as doors were kicked open when we entered the building. The yelps and squeals rang out as people were surprised, then forced down on the ground.

Through the dust-caked windows, the light was dim and brown in here. Warm, almost, which wasn't what I'd expected. In truth, the place was oddly clean and organized, which was not typical for a shipping warehouse. It wasn't sterile. Instead, the outside looked almost abandoned while the inside appeared to be overly functional. That made it even more apparent where the SWAT team had gone, leaving doors open behind them to prove they were clear.

The whole time, Alex and I lagged behind, keeping our place safely at the back. We were here to close this, not to run it. I'd done enough of these in my career, so I was used to it. Let SWAT make the calls. Let them fire the shots. I just wanted to see justice served and the victims saved.

Suddenly, a man called out, "Police! Get on the ground!"

Then it happened. The pair of gunshots was piercing. I could smell gunpowder in the air and my ears were ringing from the proximity to the bangs. For the space of a single heartbeat afterwards, everything was perfectly silent - and then the screaming started.

That meant the perp wasn't dead, but if he'd been shot, someone must've seen a gun. I glanced back, making sure Alex was still with me. She nodded, her weapon at the ready, then we moved forward again. To the right, SWAT was clustering, clearly securing the wounded man they'd just put a few rounds into. To our left, more officers were checking rooms.

"Down, down, down!" broke out from the floor above as a group surprised the criminals.

"Where are the victims?" Alex breathed, her words too soft to carry past me.

"Let SWAT run the show," I warned her. "This is their gig."

"We've got prisoners!" an officer yelled. "Someone get some fucking bolt cutters!"

Yeah, I didn't even want to know what that was about, but the chaos was slowing down a little. The storming of feet was still loud, and trailing at the back sucked, but it was the safest place for the second in charge of the FBI. And while Alex might not appreciate it, right now, I was her bodyguard.

Then a girl stumbled out of a room. "Help me?!" she whimpered.

An officer was right there. "I got you, miss. I just need you to sit down right here for a moment."

"Where's Jordan?" Alex demanded, pushing around me. Then she raised her voice. "Are we secure?!"

"Working on it!" an officer upstairs called back.

"Clear!" someone declared loudly.

"Where the fuck is Jordan?" Alex breathed, storming up the hallway. "How the fuck do they have this arranged?"

The girl beside the wall looked up. "Boys are on the third floor. Children on the fourth. Down here we're all over eighteen."

"Fuck!" Alex snapped, turning for the stairs and heading up quickly.

"Wait!" I barked at her, but she didn't listen.

So I followed. She passed the second floor, then pushed at the doors on the third. Moving in right behind her, I checked the left as she looked right, and then we moved up the hallway. The team she'd called in was massive, which was probably the only reason this was going so smoothly. Six SWAT officers had young men leaning against the hall up here. More were checking rooms further down.

"Jordan?" Alex asked, looking at the boys as she moved through the hall. They looked back blankly.

"Alex, we'll find him," I assured her.

"He's the reason we got the fucking warrant," she hissed. "So where is he?"

The words were barely out of her mouth when someone burst through a door at the far end. As one, all of us raised our weapons - and paused. A man - white, mid-thirties, maybe a hundred and eighty pounds - held a teen boy to his chest. The kid was stumbling, trying to resist, but the man was dragging him, and quickly.

"Freeze!" an officer yelled.

"Back the fuck off or the boy dies!" the man called back.

I could see the silver glint of his gun. It was tucked in against the kid's ribs, pointed right at his lungs. If the fucker pulled the trigger, the shot would be fatal. Thankfully, I wasn't the only one who'd noticed. These officers, and this team? They were good. This was one of the best SWAT units in the nation, so no one fucking moved.

That gave the man enough time and space to drag the boy through another door, but this one was marked with an exit sign. Stairs. It had to be another stairwell. As Alex and I rushed to follow, an officer behind me triggered his radio.

"We've got a hostage situation. Third floor, heading down the back stairs. Proceed with caution."

"Don't spook him, Alex," I warned as we reached the door.

"That was Jordan!" she shot back.

"And a scared idiot with a fucking gun!"

She nodded, then slowly eased open the door. "Sir? So you know, you're surrounded. Can we talk this out?"

"Don't make me shoot the kid!" the man yelled from below us, the stairwell giving his voice a disturbing echo.

"That's the last thing we want," Alex said even as she moved through the door and into the enclosed area.

I was right behind her. My pulse had already started to slow. My body was perfectly calm. Alex had this, and I knew she was a damned good negotiator, so all I had to do was watch her back. Together, the pair of us hit the stairs, quietly making our way down while checking each and every corner.

"Put the gun down!" someone barked.

"Easy!" Alex yelled, even as the man shouted, "Don't make me do it!"

"Sir?" she asked, moving a little faster to catch up. "There's SWAT all over this building. You do not want to walk into them. I think I might be able to help you, but I'm going to need you to relax, ok? We don't want that kid getting hurt, right?"

"I'll kill him if you come closer!"

"And if you do, SWAT will have no reason to hold their fire," Alex said. "We're in a bit of a jam here, right?" We were closing in, and it sounded like he'd made it down to the first floor. "Sir, I'm the one calling the shots here, so you really want me to help you. Let's just see what we can do. I mean, I'm sure this is all a mistake. It can't be what it looks like."

Another door opened, and this one was loud. It sounded metallic, heavy, and intense, which made me think this guy had just shoved the kid into it, likely risking his life. A moment later, officers started telling the man to stop, freeze, and get down. Fuck!

"Hold your fire!" Alex ordered.

Faster, we needed to move faster. We also couldn't rush the fucker, but we couldn't help if he was out of sight. As if she knew that, Alex jogged down a few more stairs, and there they were. An officer had the door held open with his body. Four paces on the other side, the adult male with a gun had the muzzle pressed against the boy's head.

And that boy was definitely Jordan.

"What's your name?" Alex asked as she lifted her hands, showing her gun before she put it away. "Sir? This is a very tight spot for you, so tell me your name and let me see what I can do, ok?"

"Fuck off!"

"That's Richard Gaines," an officer said. "Busted for having some underage pornographic videos two years ago."

I could hear the disgust, which meant this fucker had probably bought his way out of any serious jail time. Some therapy, some restitution, and a few promises about how he'd never do it again, right? Wasn't that how things worked in this town?

And yet here he was, with a gun pointed at a young boy who'd been sold over and over. The asshole had moved from videos of children being forced into sex to the real thing, and I hated him already. The only thing keeping me from losing my shit were the wide brown eyes of the kid staring at Alex as if hoping for a miracle.

"Richard?" Alex asked. "Why don't you let Jordan go, hm?"

"How do you know his fucking name?!" the man screeched.

"Because we have a warrant to find him, Richard. His family has never stopped looking for him. A certain politician got sloppy, though, and there was a video..."

"Fuck!" Richard screamed, clearly frantic. "It's not what you think. That wasn't supposed to happen. I'm just trying to get back on my feet, and you people fucked me! You ruined me, and the news spread it everywhere. My name's no good. I can't get a fucking job in this town anymore, so what the fuck do you expect from me?"

"Let's talk about it?" Alex asked. "Richard, there's always another way, right? A better option. A good deal. We just have to find the right one for you. It's like an opportunity. Isn't that how the saying goes?"

"Fuck opportunity!" Richard snapped. "I'm walking out the back door, you're not going to stop me, and that's the only way this boy's going to live through this."

I could see the sheen of tears on Jordan's face, but he didn't make a sound. He didn't even really struggle. The kid merely allowed Richard to pull him where he wanted, almost as if Jordan had already given up.

"C'mon, kid," I breathed.

Alex must've heard me. "Hey, Jordan? How you doing, buddy?"

"I dunno," he whimpered.

"And that's ok," Alex promised. "I'm just going to need you to be real still, ok?" She glanced over, catching my eyes. "Real still, Jordan."

Alex's eyes were such a dark brown that the only word for them was black. In the dim lighting of this warehouse, they were like an abyss, but when her gaze met mine, I knew. She didn't need to nod. She didn't have to give me an order. The permission was right there, begging me to fix this.

And I could.

Between us and the gunman were no more than twenty feet of distance. Behind him was the problem. Two SWAT officers were standing in front of the emergency exit Richard wanted to use. The gun in his right hand was a Baretta, semi-automatic, and canted sideways enough to make me think Richard wasn't used to using it.

The boy was calm and still, doing exactly what Alex had said. Richard, on the other hand, was panicking. The man was looking around, hoping for some miracle to save him. With a couple dozen SWAT officers and two FBI agents, that wasn't an option, though.

"Richard?" Alex begged. "Sir, I'm going to need you to look at me, ok? Tell me what it will take to convince you to let this boy go?"

"I want out of here!" he yelled, jerking his arm threateningly. The gun pressed into Jordan's head a little more. "Tell the cops to get fucking lost!"

"Clear out!" Alex ordered. "Make room!"

The SWAT officers glanced at each other, but they obeyed. Alex was the ranking official here, after all. But the moment the path between Richard and the emergency exit was clear, Alex lifted her hands - her gun now holstered - and moved closer.

"See? That was easy, right, Richard? You give me something, and you get something. So all I need to know is what it is going to take for you to let Jordan go. That's his name, you know. Jordan Blakely. He's from Mississippi, and I'm sure he'd love to go back there. So what kind of deal do you think we can make?"

"Deal?" Richard asked. "For the boy? Fuck you! Fuck him! This kid is going nowhere so long as - "

I waited for the man to look back one more time, checking to make sure his path was clear. The moment his eyes left Alex, I jerked my weapon up with my eyes locked on that spot just over the man's ear. I barely even felt my finger compress, but the resulting pop of the weapon was loud.

Richard jerked back. Jordan dropped to his knees, reaching up to cover his head with his arms. Gore sprayed the hallway, but that didn't matter. The silver Baretta the man had been holding clattered to the concrete floor loudly, rattling a few times before it settled.

"Jordan!" Alex gasped, rushing in towards the boy.

"Shots fired," someone was saying, the words echoing back through the radio of the SWAT officer closest to me.

I just lowered my arm, feeling the cold, thick glass forming that cut off my feelings. Every single time I pulled the trigger, this happened. Every life I took cost me a little part of my own soul, but this time it had been worth it. Seeing the boy look up, a mixture of terror and wonder in his eyes, was enough. He was alive. He might not know how, but I sure did.

Because I never fucking missed.

"Jason, get your dog!" Alex called back. "Now!"

And the smallest breath of a laugh slipped from me. I hadn't even known it was there, but that? It was not the response I'd expected. I still turned, walking calmly and cruelly out of the building. In an SUV, waiting for me, was my sanity in the form of a brindle-and-white mongrel. I needed him. Fuck, I needed him more than anyone could ever imagine, but it was going to be ok.

Because we'd just won. This was victory. To me, it tasted like adrenaline and fear, but Crysis would make all of that fade. I just hoped Ruin could find something to make the rest of these fuckers pay too.

# CHAPTER 78

### JERICHO

We were looking at a website with multiple short clips of people for sale. Yes, people. Yes, for sale. It was one of the most disgusting things I could imagine. Even worse, the prostitutes were all displayed as if they were trying to be sexy, and yet none of them really looked like they were into it. More like they were scared.

And young.

So very young. Ages ranged from what I would guess to be mid-teens to maybe early twenties. Nothing older than that. Thankfully, nothing too young either. There weren't any little children on here, but plenty of minors. Somehow, we had to use this to not only prove Milt and other assholes had paid money for the "privilege" of sex with these people, but also hit this hard enough to distract anyone who might be in that warehouse.

Yeah, it sounded good, but websites weren't usually hosted on-site. They were on servers, run by people from other locations. Still, Alex wanted us to hit this hard, so I was more than willing to pull out a sledgehammer.

"Knock, I need you to rip open all the bitcoin accounts that interacted with this fucker."

"Which fucker?" Knock asked.

I gestured at my screen. "This one! Whoever the fuck this is that Milt was paying."

"Gotcha," he said.

"Lemme guess, I'm helping him?" Cade asked.

"Sure," I agreed. "Jinxy, Hottie, I want you both to chase any leads Knock finds. I have a funny feeling the other clients will be paying the same guy, which means we're going to be tracking bitcoin."

"And I'll need some records," Tiffany said.

"How do I help, Jeri?" Zoe asked.

I blew out a heavy breath. "See if you can find anything that would be a calendar or schedule, Zoe. Ripper, I need you to start archiving those videos. That's evidence!"

"Could be bad evidence," he countered. "If this is used to show they were willing?"

"Then we'll fucking lose it before it can end up in court," I decided. "Let's do this. Alex and Jason are going in there any minute, if they aren't already there. She wanted us to make a distraction."

"Probably goes the other way," Hottie said. "There's no way some dumbass running prostitutes is also going to be coding a website."

"Don't fucking care," I told him. "We just need to prove these politicians paid for sex. We need to make it clear a crime happened! These are fucking kids!"

And that was the problem. What had started out as a little harassment of our boss had just quadrupled into something so much worse. Not only were people being sexually victimized, but they were young. Young enough my eyes kept jumping over to check on Zoe. For her, this had to be fucking triggering.

"Zoe?" I asked. "You doing ok?"

"Oh, I'm fucking pissed," she promised. "I'll tap out if I need to, though. Promise."

"Holding you to that," Cade grumbled. "All of us."

I nodded, even though he wasn't looking, because he had a good point. I had a better one. Maybe these people weren't my friends, but that didn't make them any less important. It also didn't mean this wasn't bullshit. And yet, it didn't feel like my curse. Instead, this felt like my purpose. Like this was the one thing I was meant to do.

So I did it. As Knock started calling out information and sharing links, the rest of us were chasing data. Mostly, it was the bitcoin payments. The account Milt had paid every Tuesday was receiving a shit-ton of money from other sources - always in bitcoin.

"Tiff, I'm printing," Knock announced.

"I won't be able to keep up, but if I have the records, I can prove this happened," she said as the printer started whirring.

"Fuck, fuck, fuck!" Ripper yelped. "Y'all, we have videos disappearing! Two are now cartoon clips!"

"Archive that shit!" I demanded. "Get it all on the Squirrel before the damned cache updates."

"Damn, the owner's trying to clean it up," Hottie said. "I've got code changing."

"We need proof!" I screamed.

Calmly, Hottie reached across his keyboard and pressed a key. "And I'm recording my desktop. Ripper, I've got the page source in real time. You get the links for videos. We need proof of what they used to be."

"Trying," Ripper said.

But I had to see for myself. So, tabbing back to the website, I opened the code, and realized they were right. Somewhere, someone was trying to pull everything down. Worse, they were smart enough to update with innocent links to shit that wasn't the faces of their victims. That meant any computer looking at this would get an update, refreshing the cache of the previous videos, and all but erasing the bad shit from existence.

"No, you fucking don't," I grumbled, chasing the code back to its host.

There, the website had to be saved. There, the changes were being uploaded. There, someone had access, and what I needed to do was slow this shit down. The easiest way was to hit a login server, or even crash the host. I just didn't know if I could.

"They're trying to remove it," I said. "We need to get everything we can before it's gone."

"And there's seven of us," Zoe reminded me.

"Proof is in the bitcoin," Knock added.

"I've got a script going, archiving everything," Ripper promised. "We'll have snapshots of the site just like the Wayback Machine, Jeri. We're good."

"And this asshole is about to be pissed," I decided. "Knock, I'm going to pick a fight, because I don't want him to realize you're chasing the money."

"Yes, please," Knock said, flashing me a smile. "The toybox is all yours, Jericho. Make Dez proud with some cyberterrorism."

"Oh, yeah," I agreed.

Because if we had not only a video of the code being changed, but also archives of those changes? Well, the internet wasn't quite as fast as most people hoped. Out there in the virtual ether, various routers were still holding old versions, still serving them up on request. That meant there was one hell of a delay, and while it normally wasn't a problem, for the guy trying to make his crimes go away, it was going to suck bad.

And I was here to poke the hornet's nest. Sadly, whoever had set this shit up wasn't a dumbass. Hacking this website wasn't like breaking into one of the main web hosts. This was the dark web, and that meant the rules were very, very different.

But I was good. I'd made damned sure of it. All I had to do was trace the data back, find where it was being kept, and then get into the main code. Not easy, and it felt like it took forever, but I eventually found it.

My screen was scrolling and my friends were calling things out to each other, but this was my task. Jason had told me this was my team, and right now, I had to lead. I got - because this shit was kinda fun - to fuck with the asshole. I was pissing off the bad guy, and that kinda felt like a form of vengeance on its own.

The first thing I did was drop our logo right into the middle of his page. Ruin 32:35. That was it, but I'd picked the version with the pink skull, because it was mine. This was me tagging my work, and there was no way this asshole wouldn't see it.

Then I started moving around the videos. If they weren't where the original designer thought they were, then he would assume he'd already deleted them - I hoped. I uploaded the new version of the site. He tried to overwrite it.

A little smile was playing on my lips, because this was the closest I'd ever gotten to a matrix-style hacker battle. In reality, it was just the pair of us trying to save code faster than the other could. Unfortunately, whoever this guy was? Yeah, he was better. He was fluent in HTML, it seemed, while I dabbled a bit in multiple languages.

Jack of all trades, right? But I was a master of one thing. I was the best at fucking up those who went after the vulnerable. Yesterday, I would've said women. Now, I was starting to think it was children and marginalized people as well. Having Milt call Alex the N-word had hit me harder than I'd expected. I didn't know why, except that it was wrong, but that it had all led here?

There was something about protecting those who could not protect themselves, or helping, or something. I didn't know the damned saying, and as my hands typed as fast as I could, just trying to make complete chaos on this site, I didn't really care. The point was still the same.

Someone had to fight back. Someone needed to have the power to say no when assholes thought they could just take everything they wanted. That someone? I was going to make damned sure it was me. Well, us, because the frenzy of work going on in this room right now proved I most certainly was not alone.

"Come at me, bro," I breathed, my words for the guy on the other side of this connection. "C'mon, you motherfucker. Let's see if your skill is better than my anger. Maybe you're one hell of a geek, but I'm still cruel. I will always be cruel to assholes like you."

"Go get him, baby girl," Hottie encouraged.

Which made me smile. Right now, I was doing all the annoying and stupid shit. I was hitting his connection, the servers he was trying to save things on, and pulling out all the stupid script kiddie annoyances. The dumb shit. The delaying shit. The stuff that might buy a little time for my team to do what they were good at.

"Where we at, people?" I asked.

"I've got multiple clients by payments," Knock said.

"Names for four and counting," Cade assured me.

"Print it!" Tiffany snapped.

"Not yet," Jinxy told her. "Zoe, take number seven. See if you can find account info. I'm on six."

"We need names!" I reminded them. "We need fucking proof of who they are."

"Oh, I'm doing one better," Hottie said. "I'm getting the banking info, Jeri."

"Nice!" Zoe said. "I'll do the same, then we can sort it out later."

"Good, because this guy's going to punt me outta here soon," I warned. "He's better than me."

"Who?" Knock asked.

"Dunno, but it's the person trying to delete the videos."

"Who *did* delete them," Ripper corrected. "He's also trying to clean up the information to make it look like puppies. Fucking *puppies!*"

"Don't fucking think so," I growled. "Knock, I need you to move faster!"

Because I'd just lost connection to the server that was hosting this site. Yep, I was already in the process of getting back in, but it was bouncing me. That meant I needed a new IP address, because mine had probably been blocked.

"Someone check our own network's security?" Ripper asked.

"On it," Hottie said. "Zoe, is the switch still active?"

"We've got a few layers between us and the outside world," Zoe promised. "Laugh at me for being paranoid if you want, but doors aren't all I lock."

"And I love you for it," I assured her. "Ok, and I'm back in. Miss me, motherfucker?"

I immediately turned his website background pink, editing the banner to say "love connection" across the top of it. Just to make it even more fun, I dropped a captcha over his save button. Yeah, have fun trying to deal with that bullshit, you asshole.

I barely got that uploaded before this prick changed the banner to say "Not scared yet." Right under that was a link to a remedial night school for programming websites. Yeah, lame attack, but kinda funny too. The annoying thing was the sound that played as soon as I refreshed the page. It was that waa-waa failure noise so common in cartoons.

Ok, but I had a nice come-back for that. Two seconds on Google got me a link. It was quickly embedded to pop up every few seconds. That it was for a penis enhancement? Well, you know, this fuckhead clearly had small dick energy going on.

But our little troll battle had deleted all the text. Anything useful that had been on this site was long gone. Didn't matter. My goal was to keep the web designer busy, and from the looks of it, this was working.

I barely got the penis enhancement popups in place before my enemy wiped the page clean. A moment later, a link to an image was put up in its place. Nothing else, just one simple image for the entire website.

Out of curiosity, I refreshed the page so I could see it. A big middle finger appeared, hosted elsewhere on the dark web. Chuckling, I shook my head, but whatever. I was definitely getting under this guy's skin, and I kinda liked it. I also wanted him to know just how fucked he was. So I grabbed an FBI logo and put that up instead of the hand graphic.

"Knock? How's it going? I'm losing here," I said.

"No, you're not," he assured me. "I think we've got it all, Jeri. Tracing it will be in other accounts, but we've got a year of this guy's shit downloaded. FBI can follow it from here if we need to."

"Nice," I said, then started typing, adding a little message to go with my pretty little image. "You may be better than me, but you're not better than us. Ruin 32:35."

And I backed out, cutting my connections as fast as I could. Tabbing over to the website, I refreshed it, thrilled to see my message displayed, even if it wouldn't stay there long. That didn't matter. Whoever had been trying to fuck with me had to have seen it.

Then, just to make sure, I hit refresh. Immediately, a new version of the page loaded. The pink was gone. So was our logo. In its place was a very simple, blatant message.

"You lose."

I just giggled. "You keep thinking that, buddy," I said even as I reached for my phone. "Someone tell me we got what we needed?"

"All of it," Hottie promised. "And proof of your little hacktivist spat. My video of the code is going on the Squirrel just in case Jason can do anything with it, but Ripper's archive is probably more valuable."

"And," Tiffany said, "we've got the client list."

My hands paused. "What?" I asked.

She nodded at me over our computers. "We got their banking info, Jeri. All we have to do now is match that up with names, because we know where the money came from and where it went to. Proof of purchase. It doesn't get any better than that, right?"

"How many?" Zoe asked.

"A lot," Knock said.

"How fucking many?!" she demanded.

"Counting," Knock said, pointing at his screen and dragging his hand down.

For a long moment we all watched. We waited. While I felt the rush of that little tiff I'd just had, this? It was the important thing. According to Alex - and everything we'd seen on this side - we'd just busted a sex ring. One with underage prostitutes. One with people who I could only think of as sex slaves.

And someone in Washington D.C. had been using them. A lot of someones, from the length of the wait. At least one of those creeps was Milt Einfeldt, and who knew how many other politicians, lobbyists, and government officials were also involved.

"Shit, this is big," I realized.

"Massive," Jinxy agreed. "Jeri, we just blew up a political secret, because I've got at *least* three senators and two congressmen on this list."

"Seventy-four," Knock broke in.

"What?" I asked.

"Seventy-four regular clients," he clarified. "Seventy-four people who paid that website, and while we can't prove they paid for sex, it's going to be hard as hell for them to make it look like anything else."

"Fuck me," I breathed. "Milt should've resigned when we gave him the chance."

Zoe just leaned back and locked her hands behind her head. "But this? Jeri, this is better. This is how we make people pay."

"And pay, and pay, and pay," Ripper agreed. "Because no one gets to use the internet for evil under our watch."

"Not anymore," I agreed. "Because while we might not get to work for the FBI, we're still Ruin, and their feet will slip."

"Yeah, when we fucking push them," Zoe agreed. "I happen to like the pushing part the best."

"Same," I assured her, unlocking my phone so I could send a text to Jason.

**Jericho:**
Done. This is called winning.

**Jason:**
And the boy is safe. Thank you.

**Jericho:**
And you? You safe? Raid's done?

**Jason:**
One dead. I don't miss. Starting to think you don't either.

**Jericho:**
Here's hoping. Now to see if it all actually worked.

**Jason:**
Yeah. We ruined them.

And he attached a picture. When it loaded, I saw the Ruin logo in grey. This was the version Ripper had made for Jason. Seeing him send it made me feel something I hadn't expected - kinda like this man had claimed us back. Like this was his way of saying he was proud to be a part of our team.

Like we really were winning.

# CHAPTER 79

### SPECIAL AGENT JASON RAIGE

Two days. That was all it took for the analysts to verify the information Ruin had provided. And damn, did those kids find a lot of shit. The money trail was obvious. Thanks to Tiffany's notes, it was also easy to follow. The data from the website? It provided the motive. Showing the site being changed in real time, however, sealed the deal.

That was all the judges needed to start issuing arrest warrants. Dozens of them. Seventy-four, to be exact, and while plenty of those were for staffers and other minor players in the governmental system, a few were names big enough to make the Director of the FBI take notice.

That was how we'd delayed the minor arrests. Oh, Jericho wasn't happy, but when I made it clear this was a tactical decision, she agreed to trust me. One week, she'd said. After that, she'd blow it all up herself. Needless to say, Alex didn't want to wait either. She called in Bradley, the pair of us working to make sure this would go off without a hitch.

But when the Senate committee on Emerging Threats invited Alex to speak about the cybersecurity consultants program, she couldn't say no. They wanted her to make a statement on the record. We wanted to see this. So, putting on my best suit, I joined Bradley, and the pair of us were allowed to sit right behind the table reserved for those addressing the senators.

All the pieces were in place. Just as the committee was called to order, I sent off a text, telling Ruin they'd want to see this. Then I silenced my phone, tucked it into my suit's inner pocket, and leaned back.

"This is about to be a clusterfuck," Bradley whispered.

"This is about to make Ruin very happy," I countered.

He lifted a brow. "When the program dies?"

"It's been dead for a while," I countered. "This is merely the revenge part, Bradley. This is what will make it all worthwhile."

"Let's hope."

Which was when the chair of the committee tapped his gavel, drawing all the eyes in the room. "Today, we have Alexandra Watts, the Deputy Director of the FBI, here to give us her perspective on why the Bureau requires consultants to do the work that has previously been assigned to analysts. Ms. Watts, you have ten minutes."

Alex stood. Dressed in a smart red suit, she definitely stood out in this room. Her hair was pulled back, her nails were painted, and she looked amazing. Professional, feminine, and yet still both powerful and serious. One day, I would have a daughter, and this was the type of woman I wanted her to admire. Alex was sacrificing nothing as she calmly looked over the politicians assembled before her.

"As many of you know," she started, "the concept of this program was something I brought up when I was recently promoted to the position of Deputy Director. What many of you may not be aware of is why. It all started seven years ago with a missing persons case."

"Jordan?" Bradley asked, his words a mere whisper.

I nodded. "You're gonna love this."

"The internet," Alex told the committee, "is an amazing place. In many ways, it's anonymous, offering the freedom to explore and express ourselves without ties to our everyday lives. At the same time, those freedoms can come with a price. Names aren't necessarily verified. Lies can be told - and believed. That is how a ten-year-old boy was lured to a park to meet one of his online friends. He thought the other person was a boy near his age who played the same games. In reality, it was a pedophile with a fake account."

"She's good," Bradley said.

I huffed at that. "It's why she got the job."

"Unfortunately," Alex continued, "that boy was never seen again. An Amber Alert was issued, the pedophile was caught and prosecuted, but the child was gone. For the last seven years, that case has haunted me. It was the one I let get away, and I hoped that one day we might recover his body so his family could have closure. You see, I was convinced this child was dead. I was wrong.

"Thanks to the efforts of some young and aspiring computer geeks, we were given reason to believe this boy was not only alive, but also in serious danger. Seven years, ladies and gentlemen. For seven years, this young man was held captive in a sex ring! Today, he's back home in Mississippi with his family, and all because of cyber specialists who are too young to qualify for the FBI, do not yet have a degree - but are working on it - and who will get offers for much higher-paying jobs once they do meet our requirements."

"Hackers," one of the senators said.

The chair immediately tapped his gavel. "Senator Einfeldt, you'll have your time. Please, Ms. Watts. Continue."

"Yes, Senator Einfeldt, they are hackers," Alex said, completely breaking from her script. "They are the same hackers who closed the Soul Reaper case this very same committee was worried about over the summer. The very same hackers who managed to not only assist one of my agents, but also get us copies of the streaming video the perpetrator was using to incite even more violence. The very same hackers this country should consider heroes."

"And we should not reward lawbreaking," Einfeldt shot back. "The government makes the laws, not kids in their mothers' basements!"

"Which is why I'm here," Alex reminded him. "You see, Senator Einfeldt, the purpose of the Federal Bureau of Investigations is to secure the domestic concerns of our nation. That should include the digital ones, because in today's world, just as many crimes are committed virtually as they are in person. Theft? It happens online. So does stalking, harassment, and even hate crimes. As one of my agents says, the internet is currently the Wild West. There are no laws that can be truly enforced, and it seems Congress doesn't understand it well enough to even begin legislating them."

"Laws apply online as much as off," a woman on the other side pointed out.

One more time, the chair tapped his gavel. "You will all have time to question the Deputy Director. This is her time. Ms. Watts, I'm reclaiming your time."

"Thank you, Chairman," Alex said. "But this simply makes my point. How many people realize that the internet is international? A server could be hosted in Russia, China, or Venezuela. It could be right down the street. To us, it all looks the same, but according to our laws, the location of it matters. To the victims, however, it still feels like a crime.

"And it's going to take a special breed of person to handle those crimes. Someone with the technical knowledge to even see what's going on behind the screen. Someone with the expertise in video and photo manipulation to verify truth from a deepfake. Someone who can operate in a world most of us can barely wrap our minds around, even while we're logging in to scroll through our TikToks and talk to friends on Facebook.

"Because the internet exists. It's certainly not going away, but our security is. More importantly, our children's safety is! And I, for one, want to keep my child as safe as possible, even though I know I won't be able to keep her offline forever. I know I can't protect her from those who think their privilege and power make them untouchable online."

"And now we're getting to the good part," I whispered.

Bradley flashed me a smile. "Good, because I hate this place."

"Me too."

In front of us, Alex leaned in, resting her hands on the table she was standing behind. "Ladies and gentlemen of the committee, I asked for this program because I think I have found the right people to start a pilot program. I think these students are more than mere informants - even if they are willing to work as such. They've also been willing to prove it."

That was enough to make the politicians look at the person beside them. The murmuring of conversation was soft and still polite, but it proved they were at least listening. A few staffers hurried out of the room, likely to get something to refute the points Alex was about to make. Too bad they had no clue what points those would be.

I did. I also knew this was going to be amazing, and hopefully all the networks would pick it up and run with it.

"Whether my program is approved or not no longer matters," Alex said. "Law enforcement has always been presented with challenges, and we have always found a way to overcome them. When I was promoted to the position of Deputy Director of the FBI, not everyone was pleased about it. Some went so far as to send me threatening and harassing messages. I was called derogatory names, which I will not repeat here. I was demeaned for being a working mother. I was threatened, had a subordinate offered my position if he would be more politically flexible, and I have been blocked time and time again.

"None of that will make me back down, though. Instead, I used all of it to test my group, to see if they really had the skills we need. I did not expect the results. What started as just over five hundred threatening and demeaning emails sent to my work account led us to complete corruption in the United States government. Senator Einfeldt, you say you made your investments to protect your family, correct?"

"So that *was* your team!" he grumbled.

"Is that still your position?" Alex pressed.

"Of course!"

Alex reached down and opened the folder before her. "And yet we have a consistent correlation between a Russian oligarch sending you gifts of gold - gifts which you have not declared, mind you - and you voting for Russian-friendly policies. We have billionaires paying for renovations of your home, increasing the value by hundreds of thousands of dollars. Again, this is not declared. Your votes during that time were favorable to their causes. And while all of this may, as you say, be what you consider the best interest of your family, it is not in the best interest of the American people. Wouldn't you agree, Senator Einfeldt?"

"All of that is a coincidence!" Milt Einfeldt shot back. "I've already explained myself. I also think your hackers have shown just how much of an invasion of privacy this program will create. We have the right to protect our personal interests, including our financial decisions!"

"Decisions such as spending two thousand dollars' worth of bitcoin every week?" Alex asked, a little smile touching her lips.

Milt's head snapped up. "Excuse me?"

"Two thousand dollars' worth of bitcoin," Alex repeated. "Every Tuesday, actually. Always sent to the same website, available only on the dark web. Now, this is what that website looked like one week ago." She picked up a piece of paper and showed it to the men and women sitting before her. "This is the only image I can show you, because the rest are not suitable for the public. You see, that website offered people for sale. Sexual services, it appears. And you, Senator Einfeldt, were a regular client. I'm sure that has nothing to do with the protection of your family."

"How dare you!" Einfeldt hissed.

"Lucky for us, you recorded those encounters, Senator. Videos of you with a young man. A seventeen-year-old boy who has been missing from his home in Mississippi for seven years. That same boy I have been looking for, and you have been paying for sex with him. Sex he did not consent to! Sex he was not *old enough* to consent to!"

She slapped her hand down on the table. "And this is why we need options for policing the internet. This is why virtual security is so important. This is called sex crimes against children, and a sitting senator has been involved in it. This is human trafficking - and we never would have known about it without this team of cyber specialists. Without my pilot program, more than forty boys and girls would still be held in a warehouse right here in Washington, D.C., being forced to have sexual relations against their will!"

This time, the rush of voices was far from polite. Everyone was murmuring, it seemed like. The chairman cracked his gavel, trying to get control, but Alex didn't seem to care. She was in her element now, and if the room was getting louder, that simply meant she needed to raise her own voice.

"Senator Klintworth, we have records of your payments for the same thing. A sixteen-year-old girl, and one who is willing to testify against you. Senator Perschall, Senator Gillbar, Senator Strickland, and Senator Ress. All of you can be tied directly to the same organization. All of your financial records show payments for underage or nonconsenting sex slaves. Just because you are rich, powerful, and duly elected does not mean you are exempt from the very laws you are tasked to create and maintain. If anything, you should be held more accountable, but this is why you don't want this program, isn't it?"

She was yelling now, her voice powerful, cutting right through the room. "The Federal Bureau of Investigation does not care how well positioned you are. We do not care how important you think you are. We are here to maintain the laws of the land, senators, and that includes all of you. So deny this program if you want. The FBI will still find a way to protect those who need our help, and we will do it with hackers, with snipers, and with every available resource we have - because we do not give up! And we cannot be scared off."

"Enough!" the chair bellowed. "I need silence!"

"Chairman?" Alex called out. "Is it possible to request a recess?"

"I don't think we have any other option," the man agreed, even as the room buzzed around all of us. So, smashing the gavel three times, the chair called out, "This committee is in recess until decorum can be maintained! Thirty minutes!"

Alex just looked back, her eyes finding mine, and she nodded. I tapped Bradley's shoulder. He quickly whipped off a text, pressing the button to send, and then stood. Joining him, I buttoned my suit coat, straightened my tie, and waited until the doors to the chamber opened.

And when the dozen agents we had outside began to stream in, all I could do was smile.

# CHAPTER 80

### JERICHO

J ason had warned us to keep our eyes on the news. He'd also assured me this wouldn't be swept under the rug. So when he sent us a group text telling us to turn on C-SPAN, I dared to hope that maybe this would be a little of both.

The eight of us piled into the living room, claiming whatever chair we could as Hottie turned the TV to the most boring channel in the world. All it ever showed was the American government. Not even news coverage of it. Just a constant view of the cameras set up in that place. But the moment my eyes landed on the woman in the red business suit, I started to smile.

"That's Alex!" I said.

"Shit, that's our committee," Ripper pointed out. "Trust me, I watched enough videos of this mess. Milt's right..." He pointed. "There."

Sure enough, that bastard was sitting there like he had every right. But when Alex started to speak, none of it was what I expected. As the camera shifted to cover her, I realized she wasn't alone. In the chairs right behind her were Jason and Bradley. Seeing those two leaning in and talking softly while Alex calmly and carefully laid out everything we'd done?

But the moment she began explaining what we'd found, the committee lost control. I wasn't the only one leaning forward. Jinxy turned up the volume, but it didn't help as much as I hoped. The problem wasn't how loud it was. It was that everyone kept talking over everyone else.

The chair called for a recess. Jason and Bradley stood up - and Jason looked terrifying in a suit. Like some kind of hitman, if I was honest. Then the doors to the chamber opened and at least ten more agents made their way in.

Suits. Every single one of them wore a professional-looking suit, but all of them had pins that marked them as FBI. Subtle little things, and I wouldn't have noticed if I hadn't been looking at Jason. Granted, the guy looked a hell of a lot more comfortable in jeans and a t-shirt, but still.

Then they all began to move. The barrier between the seating area and the place where the politicians sat was walled off, but there was a gate-looking thing. Jason and Bradley made their way through it just as Alex began to call out a list of crimes - but that wasn't the good part.

Oh no, seeing Jason grab Milt Einfeldt and pull the man to his feet? Watching Bradley spin him around to pull his hands behind his back? That was lovely, but when Milt pulled, acting like he was going to resist, Jason shoved the man's face down onto his desk area, jerked his arm, and made it easy for Bradley to apply the cuffs.

Around the room, others were doing the same with more politicians. I didn't know all their faces, but I was willing to bet these were the ones who'd bought those kids from the warehouse. The ones who'd thought they should be allowed to break the law, even when no one else could. The ones who dared to think another human being was only here to be used, abused, and then forgotten about.

"Holy shit," Hottie breathed.

"I know," Knock said. "Fuck. I expected them to get arrested, but not like this."

"Nope," Cade said, "this is better. So much fucking better. I mean..." He leaned back, flapping his hand for the remote. "Jinxy, pass that shit over?"

"Why?"

"Because I have a suspicion," Cade said. "See, politics? It's hot on the news. I mean, depending on which party you follow depends on which station, but something like this? Those weren't all people from the same party, y'all. That was both Democrats and Republicans, which means the news is about to shit itself."

"Fuck parties," Zoe said. "And fuck them." She tossed over the remote.

Cade quickly changed channels, ending up on another popular news station. Unfortunately, it wasn't covering the mess in the Senate right now, but just when I was going to tell Cade to change it back, I read the banner at the bottom of the screen.

"Congressional Representatives Arrested in Sex Ring Sting," it proclaimed.

"Wait, what?" Tiffany asked.

I just chuckled softly. "Alex is arresting them all at once," I realized. "No one can get tipped off if they're all arrested at the same time!"

"Holy shit," Ripper said. "I mean, yeah, but like... Seriously, y'all. This is a holy shit thing. We fucking *did this!*"

"I know!" Zoe squealed. "Those fuckers are gonna pay for screwing around. I mean, literally, even!"

I simply reached for my phone. I knew Jason was busy. I'd already seen that, but I still felt like this was one text that needed to be sent now, not later.

**Jericho:**
Thank you. The reveal was definitely worth the wait.

Knock just flicked a finger at me. "That to Jason?"

"Yep," I said. "He told me it'd be handled. He told me to trust him. I was kinda having trouble."

"But he's got our backs," Knock pointed out.

"Yeah," I agreed. "And he said he's going to quit the FBI and come play with us permanently."

"What?" Tiff asked. "No!"

"Well, because the program's screwed," I tried to explain. "And he doesn't want to do the other FBI shit anymore. He wants to do this. To help us make a difference."

"And he's good at it," Knock added.

Hottie simply murmured. "Well, that kinda screws up my plans, actually."

"What plans?" I asked.

He gestured at the screen. "Um, I was thinking that maybe I wanted to be like Jason. Not a sniper. But Agent Carver said something when we did our psych evals, and it's been sticking with me."

"Which part?" Jinxy asked.

"The part about how I could lead the takedown teams," Hottie said. "I mean, with Jason managing the cybersecurity side of it for the FBI, and me doing the actual arrests? Then Ruin could know that anything we touch would actually be handled properly."

"Bradley can still get you in," Cade pointed out. "And he's really not that big of a dick. He's actually pretty cool."

"Yeah, but it's not the same if Ruin's not a part of it," Hottie said.

"Ah, but we are," Cade told us, gesturing to the screen. "I mean, Fox is talking about politicians, CNN is talking about lobbyists, and MSNBC is talking about staffers being arrested. This is huge, y'all. This is the sort of bust that is going to be in history books."

"And we did it," I bragged, leaning back into the couch. "I just want to know how much shit Alex is going to get for this."

"Let's see," Cade said, changing the channel one more time, back to C-SPAN.

The chamber was now empty, and the chairs behind Alex no longer held Jason or Bradley. Still, the remaining members of the committee were in their seats, looking rather stunned. When the chair rapped his gavel on the desk this time, it didn't seem overly enthusiastic.

"The committee is back in session," he announced. "Ms. Watts, do you care to explain what just happened here?"

"Justice," Alex said. "Senators, the politicians arrested just now are all accused of purchasing prostitution, sex with a minor, and various other crimes. All of that was discovered by my prototype team of hackers, as Senator Einfeldt called them. In truth, they are college students, all with declared majors in computer sciences and other technical degrees. Good men and women with good intentions, and I think this proves it."

"Deputy Director?" a woman asked.

"The chair recognizes the senator from California," said the man with the gavel.

"Thank you," the woman replied. "Deputy Director Watts, can you explain how your hackers found the evidence for these crimes?"

"Succinctly," Alex said, "they followed a trail. What started with a slur used against me because of my race led to Senator Einfeldt. It appears that he, or someone using his computer, in his office, with that specific device, has sent over five hundred emails to me personally. Each one was some form of a veiled threat, a harassment, or slander. All of them were anonymized with the assumption that what is hidden online can't be unhidden."

"And these emails proved there was a sex ring?" the senator from California asked.

"No, they proved there was suspicion of corruption," Alex explained. "That's why Senator Einfeldt recently held a press conference about his financial issues. In correlating why his votes appeared to be being purchased with gifts and bribes, my team found payments that didn't make sense. Following those payments, they uncovered the regular use of a prostitute. Videos of that engagement showed what appeared to be a minor. Trying to ensure the welfare of that minor resulted in revealing an entire sex ring of trafficked and abducted people. Many of them were under the age of eighteen. All of them seem to have been forced into this against their wills."

"Thank you, Deputy Director Watts," the senator said.

"That sounded good," I pointed out. "Almost like we were being responsible or something."

Hottie scoffed. "Not pissed?"

"Well..." I shrugged, because I had been pissed. "But they got busted, so this is a win, right?"

"A big fucking win," Tiffany said.

"Definitely a win," Jinxy agreed. "And the kind that - "

He paused as another senator was recognized. This one from Georgia. "I would like to call the vote. The Deputy Director has made her case. Chairman?"

"They're fucking voting?" Cade gasped.

"Is that bad?" I wanted to know.

"I mean, I just figured it would be ignored," he explained. "Shit. Brace for impact, right?"

"We know it's not going to pass," Knock reminded us.

And yet I still found myself watching the television intently as numbers were put up on the screen and people said yay or nay, adding another into either the for or the against columns. When the yeses began to lead, my heart started beating a little faster. When the no votes were called out, I felt like my chest was constricting.

Because I still wanted this. I knew we'd fucked it up. We'd talked about this to death, but the same piece of me that had been so cautious when Alex first made the offer was now daring to actually hope. I wanted to explain to each and every one of those politicians that we could do this. We really could.

Maybe we weren't the agents they were used to seeing, and we definitely weren't anything like respectable, proper, or procedural. We were still good. So far as I cared, we were the best, and hadn't we proven it? How many lives had we saved this week? How many people had just been given back their freedom?

Then again, how many of those victims were going to be fucked up, traumatized, and have to drag themselves through the horrors they'd endured? How many of them would slip, backsliding into the same sort of shit we'd all faced? How many people were out there suffering right now, with no one to find them and make the cops, the feds, or anyone else listen?

Then the gavel crashed down again. "The motion is passed!" the chair announced.

My eyes ran over the numbers. What had once been a larger committee now was lacking quite a few votes, but more had voted for us than against us. Three votes. Three yeses had shifted the balance, but they were enough.

"Guys..." Hottie said.

"Fuck me," I breathed.

Knock just started laughing, the sound slow and almost confused. Cade was grinning at the screen. Tiffany's mouth was hanging open, but Zoe turned to throw her arms around Jinxy's neck. He just blinked a few times too many.

None of us could quite comprehend what we were seeing. The vote had passed? What the fuck did that mean? How did this work? What the hell came next, and how were we supposed to deal with it?

Which was when my phone rang. "Yeah?" I asked.

"Put me on speaker," Jason said.

So I did. "Ok?"

"Everyone can hear me?" he asked.

We all replied with some variant of yes, we could, and so on.

"I'm not coming back this weekend," he said. "I want to see my fucking wife. I want to take her to the doctor and find out if our kid's a boy or a girl. I have every intention of making sure I don't fuck up my good thing at home, but..." He chuckled. "I will be there the weekend after. We have work to do, people. Evidently you're going to be consultants with the FBI, and that means passing a few tests."

"Yeah?" I asked.

"Yes," Jason said. "It's real, Ruin. We did it. We finally fucking did it."

"And you're not quitting?" I asked.

"No, Jeri," he assured me. "I'm going to be your boss, because someone has to keep you kids in line, right?"

"And we can fuck up all the bad guys?" I pressed.

"All of them," Jason swore. "That's why we're called Ruin."

# EPILOGUE

### JERICHO

The written tests for the FBI hadn't been too bad. Mostly, that was because Tiffany had been drilling us constantly. She was also spending a lot of time here. Enough that she'd brought over some clothes to hang in Zoe's closet. In truth, it was kinda nice.

The background checks had sucked, but we'd all been cleared. We'd also received the SCI clearance the FBI considered mandatory. The only thing left to worry about were finals, and they were coming up fast. After that, however, we'd get a nice break for the holidays, and then start all over again next semester.

"I think Jason found a house!" Knock announced out of the blue.

"Really?" Zoe asked. "Where?"

"Halfway between here and Riley's place," he explained. "Zara sent Murder the listing, and he told Riley, and she just showed me." He turned his phone so we could see it. "Three bedroom, two acres, in a little ranchette community."

"A ranchette community and Jason?" I asked. "Seriously? He doesn't seem the type."

"I think he'd like to be," Tiffany said. "Besides, he's about to be a dad."

"And it's a girl!" Zoe giggled. "Oh, he's going to terrify her boyfriends."

"Dunno..." Knock said. "I have a feeling he'll teach her to hold her own, make sure she's proficient in hand-to-hand combat or something, and trust her to make her own decisions."

Zoe paused before murmuring under her breath. "Ok, yeah. That does sound more like him. He's kinda like a feminist."

"Definitely a feminist," I agreed, lifting the book I was currently trying to memorize for my exams. "It's nice, though. I'm just not sure if he's a radical feminist or a liberal one."

"Or both?" Tiffany asked.

Groaning, I dropped my book and leaned back. "Fuck, this is all turning into gibberish. Why do we need these fucking core courses anyway?"

"So we can be badass FBI types?" Jinxy offered.

"That's Hottie's job," I joked.

He jerked in place. "Uh, really?"

"Well, you said you were thinking about it," I reminded him. "You'll be qualified in a few months."

"And I'm not giving up on my master's," he countered. "I'm also not bailing to go to Quantico for almost a year and leaving you here alone."

"Thanks," Cade grumbled. "No, really, Hottie. Nice to know I'm no one."

"Same," Knock agreed.

"I'm someone," Ripper said. "So fuck off to Quantico, Hottie. I'll crash in her bed every night."

"No, that's not..." Hottie groaned. "That's not what I meant."

Tiffany was grinning at him. "So, you want a do-over, huh?"

"Very much so," Hottie agreed.

"Ready, go," she told him.

"I'm not running off to Quantico for almost a year until all of this is a little more settled," Hottie said. "My degree, Jinxy's, all of you, the house, and definitely our place in the FBI. I want to make sure I can stay a part of Ruin, even if I'm playing both sides. But if Jason can do it, then I can too, right?"

"And you'll be good at it," I told him. "Your badge will also be cooler than ours."

Which made Ripper lift a finger like he had a question. "Has anyone seen the consultant badges yet? I mean, Alex said they were on the way, but..." He looked between us. "Do they even look like Jason's, or will they be more rent-a-cop?"

"No fucking clue," I admitted.

"I think they're close," Knock said. "Definitely not rent-a-cop-looking."

"And once they arrive," I reminded everyone, "we're free to start finding cases."

"Nope," Hottie said. "Finals first. Whoever fails a class has to clean all the toilets in the house until the end of next semester."

"I'm not failing," I pointed out. "I think I got a B in calculus, but everything else is good."

"Fuck off," Ripper grumbled.

"You are not failing," Tiffany assured him. "And I'm excited about our first real case. I mean..." She paused to lean forward. "Y'all..." For a moment, she bit her lower lip. "I know it's stupid, and I'm pretty sure none of you will understand, but this semester? Being a part of this?"

"It's pretty amazing, huh?" Ripper asked. "Thinking you were on the outside, then finding a group where you actually belong?"

"Yes!" Tiffany breathed. "And after that shit in high school?"

"Which is why you fit, Tiff," Zoe said.

I just jerked my chin towards her. "You're a bitch, but you're my kind of bitch. Enough of one that I'll even let you cuddle with my boyfriends. Deal?"

"Deal," she agreed. "And I'm calling myself asexual. I've been reading up on it, and it kinda feels right."

"Doesn't mean you won't want sex ever," Knock reminded her.

"I know," Tiff said. "I also feel like I finally have some friends who are cool enough I can actually talk to them about this. Like..." She flopped her hands in her lap. "Fuck, I don't even know."

"Like we don't expect you to be anything but yourself?" Jinxy offered.

She nodded slowly. "Yeah, and that's not something I'm used to."

"Fucked up, freaking out, and a complete dumpster fire," I said. "I mean me, not you, Tiff. But these people? They can deal with me, so I think you're pretty much a nice break."

"Truth," Jinxy agreed.

Which made Zoe smack him. "Lies. You love Jeri."

"As a sister, yep," Jinxy agreed. "And so you know, it's normal for that to be a love-hate sort of thing. Kinda how families work."

"You still love her," Zoe said.

"Yep," Jinxy agreed again. "I also love you."

And the whole room paused. Thankfully, Zoe didn't panic. She didn't clam up, start hyperventilating, or anything else. No, she simply smiled, and it was the soft kind. The kind which made it clear she hadn't expected that and still liked it.

"I love you too," she said softly. "I've been thinking it for a bit, and, um, I kinda didn't expect to do it all public like this."

"Family," Jinxy said. "No shame in front of family, Zoe. Besides, this way I don't have to get shit from Hot about when to drop those words."

"Or how he's been terrified you don't feel the same," Hottie fake-coughed into his hand.

Jinxy just flipped him off. "Thanks, bro."

"Welcome," Hottie said.

"And I love all of you," I announced. "Even Jinxy. I mean, just to take a little pressure off Zoe."

She looked at me and mouthed, "Thank you!"

"So, is it weird if I say I love all of y'all?" Tiff asked. "Like, as friends?"

"Totally cool with friends," Knock assured her. "I'm kinda full up on the sex partners, though. Got one of each, right?"

"I'm down, Tiff," Cade said. "Me. You. Kinky times!" He looked over at Hottie and grinned. "Just to clarify, she doesn't fuck, Hot. No beating me into the ground."

"You've already gone there," I reminded him. "Loses some of the threat."

"Jeri, no," Tiffany said almost like she was wincing. "No, that is not how that works. It's... no."

"Yeah, Jeri sucks at being a normal girl," Zoe pointed out.

"Wait, what?" I begged. "I mean, you're not gonna!"

"Yeah, but you're supposed to be jealous!" Tiff reminded me.

"Fuck that," I decided. "Ok, so maybe I was a little jealous about Ripper."

"Ripper?" Hottie asked.

"Because he's demi-sexual," Knock said. "He has to love her to fuck her."

Ripper immediately sat up. "What?"

"Demi," Knock said again. "Require an emotional connection to have a sexual attraction. Like, it just, I mean, I thought..."

"Demi..." Ripper breathed.

"Ok, wait..." I was looking between all of them. "If Ripper's demi, and Tiff's asexual, then what am I?"

"Horny?" Cade offered.

"Usually," I agreed, "but is there a name for that?"

"Hypersexual?" Knock suggested.

"Aromantic?" Hottie said.

"Wait," Jinxy begged. "So, do we all get a title? Like, does everyone have to have a label?"

"You get monogamous," I teased just as my phone vibrated. "I like hypersexual. The real question is what Hottie's calling himself."

"Straight," Hottie said.

"Desperate," Knock joked.

I chuckled but was distracted by checking my phone. Jason had been sending me messages off and on, keeping me in the loop of things. We were supposed to be "off" for a bit while we crammed for our final exams, but if he'd found something, I wanted to be ready.

Yet the message that had set off the notification wasn't from him. It was an email, and the sender was listed simply as "Unknown."

Around the room, my friends were all picking on Hottie about being grey-sexual, and demi, and something about traumatized from Zoe, who was insisting she had room to talk. I chuckled at that, because she was right, and yet there was something nice about being able to make light of it. Almost like it pushed away the horror a bit.

But when I swiped on my screen, I was braced for the worst. "Unknown" was who had sent me the message the last time. The one that had sent Hottie into a panic. The last thing I wanted to do was ruin this amazing vibe we all had going on right now. So I read the message to myself.

> I told you to stay away, Jericho. I meant it. Since you didn't listen, it's time for me to put my toys back in play. You didn't think you got them all, did you? Soul Reaper was little more than a pawn.
>
> But since you took something of mine, I'm going to take something of yours. You can't stop me either. You've never been able to stop me. Fuck, you don't even know I exist! Twice now, you've missed me, and you never even noticed. Just wait to see what happens when I start hitting back.

You crossed a line. This is war.

Vyrus

Before I could stop myself, I started typing. There was no way I'd let this fucker think I was scared of him. Fuck that. I was a damned FBI consultant now. Well, or about to be. Just as soon as the paperwork was done, I would be.

Yeah? You want war, Vyrus? Well, you picked the wrong bitch to fuck with. Soul Reaper's dead. That was us. KoG is going down. That was also us. Hell, we just fucked up Congress too. So maybe you're powerful or something. Maybe you even think that makes you someone I should be scared of, but that's where you're wrong. See, me? I'm fucking Savage.

So come at me, bro. I don't have to pretend to be good anymore, and I'm not impressed with threats. Besides, if you were fucking important, you wouldn't be hiding behind some lame-ass name.

~Jericho

Then I dimmed my screen and shoved my phone back into my pocket. Fucking assholes. It seemed there was always one more around the corner, but this guy could wait. This guy wasn't nearly as important as my friends, and for the first time in far too long, things were going exactly how I wanted.

"I think Hottie's *a* romantic," I told the rest. "Knock and Cade are bisexual. Ripper's that demi thing, just because it sounds cool. Tiffany's going with asexual, Jinxy's monogamous, Zoe's easily triggered, so I'm claiming the title of 'fucked up.' That makes it official."

"But what if we want you to be fucked down?" Knock teased.

"Could be kinky," I said.

"Yeah, but you're not fucked up, Jeri," Tiffany said. "I mean, you are, but we all are. Everyone in the world is a little fucked up, right?"

"So what am I?" I asked.

She shrugged. "A badass. I'll be the bitch, you can be the badass, and Zoe's just kick-ass. And these guys? They're all here to make us look good."

"Fuck yeah, we are!" Ripper agreed.

"I'll drink to that," Knock said.

"Would need something to drink first," Jinxy joked. "But I like it. Besides, how many hacker groups have a whole crew of seriously impressive women? We do, that's who."

"Not hackers," Zoe corrected. "Consultants. The FBI kind."

"The kind who can actually make a difference," I said.

I also really hoped that was true, because whoever this Vyrus was, I had a feeling his threats weren't completely empty.

# BOOKS BY AURYN HADLEY

**Contemporary Romance:** *Standalone Book*

One More Day

**End of Days** - Auryn Hadley & Kitty Cox writing as Cerise Cole **(Paranormal RH):** *Completed Series*

Still of the Night

Tainted Love

Enter Sandman

Highway to Hell

**A Flawed Series** - co-written w/ Kitty Cox

**(Contemporary Poly):** *In Progress*

Ruin

Brutal

Vicious

Cruel

Savage

Wicked

Deviant

**Gamer Girls** - co-written w/ Kitty Cox

**(Contemporary Romance):** *Completed Series*

Flawed

Challenge Accepted

Virtual Reality

Fragged

Collateral Damage

For The Win

Game Over

**The Dark Orchid (Fantasy Poly):**

*Completed Series*

Power of Lies

Magic of Lust

Spell of Love

**The Demons' Muse (Paranormal Poly):**

*Completed Series*

The Kiss of Death

For Love of Evil

The Sins of Desire

The Lure of the Devil

The Wrath of Angels

**The Path of Temptation (Fantasy Poly):**

*Completed Series*

The Price We Pay

The Paths We Lay

The Games We Play

The Ways We Betray

The Prayers We Pray

The Gods We Obey

**Where the Wild Things Grow (Paranormal Poly):**

*Completed Series*

Magic In The Moonlight

Spell In The Summertime

Witchcraft In The Woods

**Wolves Next Door (Paranormal RH / Poly):**

*Completed Series*

Wolf's Bane

Wolf's Call

Wolf's Pack

# ABOUT AURYN HADLEY

Auryn Hadley is happily married with three canine children and a herd of feral cats that her husband keeps feeding. Between her love for animals, video games, and a good book, she has enough ideas to spend the rest of her life trying to get them out. They all live in Texas, land of the blistering sun, where she spends her days feeding her addictions – including drinking way too much coffee.

**For a complete list of books and to receive notices for new releases by Auryn Hadley follow me:**

Amazon Author Page -
amazon.com/author/aurynhadley

Visit our Patreon site
www.patreon.com/Auryn_Kitty

You can also join the fun on Discord -
https://discord.gg/Auryn-Kitty

Facebook readers group -
www.facebook.com/groups/TheLiteraryArmy/

**Merchandise is available from -**
Etsy Shop (signed books) - The Book Muse -
www.etsy.com/shop/TheBookMuse

Threadless (clothes, etc) - The Book Muse -
https://thebookmuse.threadless.com/

**Also visit any of the other sites below:**

My website -
aurynhadley.com

Books2Read Reading List -
books2read.com/rl/AurynHadley

facebook.com/AurynHadleyAuthor
amazon.com/author/aurynhadley
goodreads.com/AurynHadley
bookbub.com/profile/auryn-hadley
patreon.com/Auryn_Kitty

# BOOKS BY KITTY COX

A **Flawed** Series - co-written w/Auryn Hadley

**(Contemporary Poly):** *In Progress*

---

**End of Days** - Auryn Hadley & Kitty Cox writing as Cerise Cole **(Paranormal RH):** *Completed Series*

---

Falling For The Bull Riders (Contemporary Poly Romance):

*In Process*

---

**Gamer Girls** - co-written w/Auryn Hadley

**(Contemporary Romance):** *Completed Series*

---

Shades of Trouble - (Contemporary Poly Romance):

*Completed Series*

---

Ménage Contemporary Romance: *Standalone Book*

When it Rains

# ABOUT KITTY COX

As you would expect, Kitty Cox has a love of cats, but also dogs, horses, and pretty much any animal. She's always enjoyed a good love story. A chance meeting involving a martini, a margarita, and some laughs with another author convinced her to finally put words to paper - and now she can't seem to stop.

From the sweet and tender idea of second chance romances, to the hot and dirty thrill of stories intended for adult audiences, the wonders of falling in love are where her imagination goes. She likes to blame it on the hot and spicy climate of her home town in Texas. Then again, it could just be a result of growing up on stolen romance novels hidden under her pillow at night.

**For a complete list of books and to receive notices for new releases by Kitty Cox follow me:**

Amazon Author Page -
amazon.com/author/kittycox

You can also join the fun on Discord -
https://discord.gg/Auryn-Kitty

Visit our Patreon site -
www.patreon.com/Auryn_Kitty

Facebook readers group -
The Literary Army
www.facebook.com/groups/TheLiteraryArmy/

---

**Merchandise is available from -**
Etsy Shop (signed books) - The Book Muse -
www.etsy.com/shop/TheBookMuse

Threadless (clothes, etc) - The Book Muse -
https://thebookmuse.threadless.com/

---

**Also visit any of the other sites below:**

My website -
kittycoxauthor.com

Books2Read Reading List -
books2read.com/rl/KittyCox

- facebook.com/KittyCoxAuthor
- amazon.com/author/kittycox
- goodreads.com/KittyCox
- bookbub.com/authors/kitty-cox
- patreon.com/Auryn_Kitty

Printed in Great Britain
by Amazon